I0761878

THE KEEPER ORIGINS BOOK 3

PHOENIX RISING

J.A. ANDREWS

Phoenix Rising, The Keeper Origins Book 3

Paperback ISBN: 979-8-8197772-1-3

Hard cover ISBN: 978-1-7362326-1-3

Website: www.jaandrews.com

AUTHOR'S NOTE

HELLO, Dear Reader!

Welcome to the final installment of Sable's story.

If you haven't yet read the story of the ***Ghost of the White Wood*** (that has such huge repercussions in Sable's story), you can **download it for free from my website**.

It's short, only a few chapters, but I'm rather fond of it.

You can find it at jaandrews.com/ghost

And now, without further ado: the final chapter of Sable's story…

For Jason,
The last, quick (240,000) words
of the story you helped create.

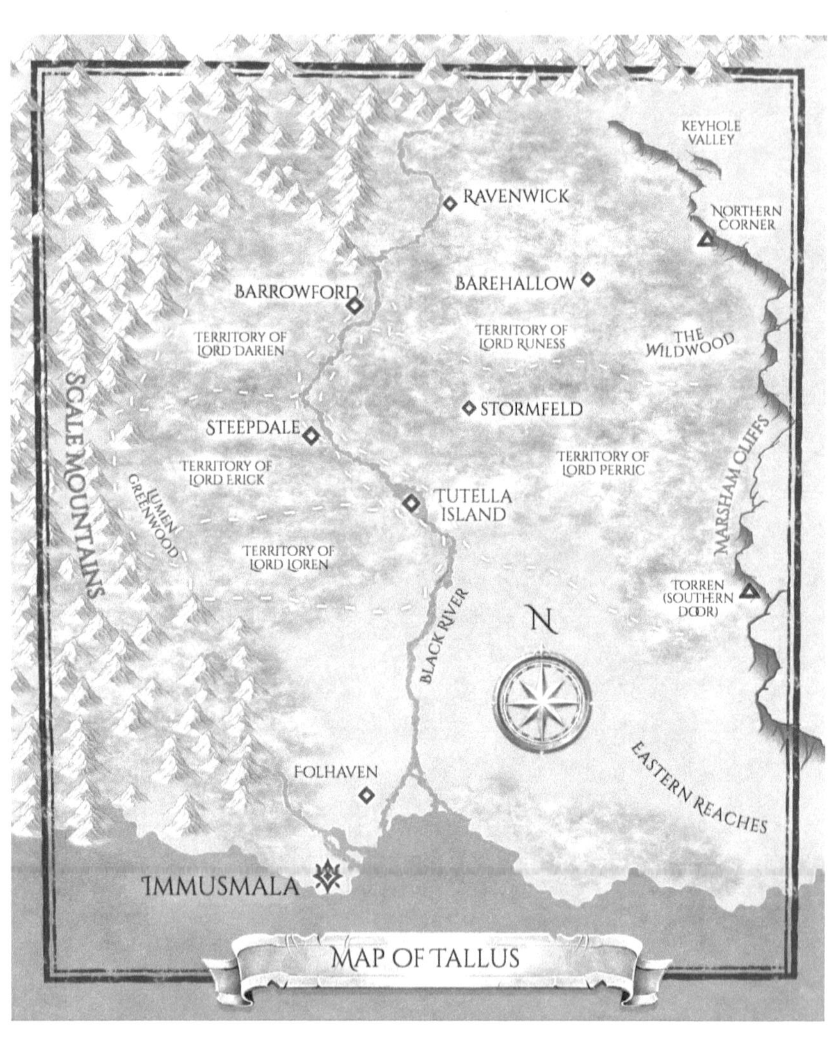
KEYHOLE VALLEY
RAVENWICK
NORTHERN CORNER
BAREHALLOW
BARROWFORD
TERRITORY OF LORD RUNESS
TERRITORY OF LORD DARIEN
THE WILDWOOD
SCALE MOUNTAINS
STORMFELD
STEEPDALE
TERRITORY OF LORD PERRIC
TERRITORY OF LORD ERICK
LUMEN GREENWOOD
TUTELLA ISLAND
MARSHAM CLIFFS
TERRITORY OF LORD LOREN
TORREN (SOUTHERN DOOR)
BLACK RIVER
N
EASTERN REACHES
FOLHAVEN
IMMUSMALA
MAP OF TALLUS

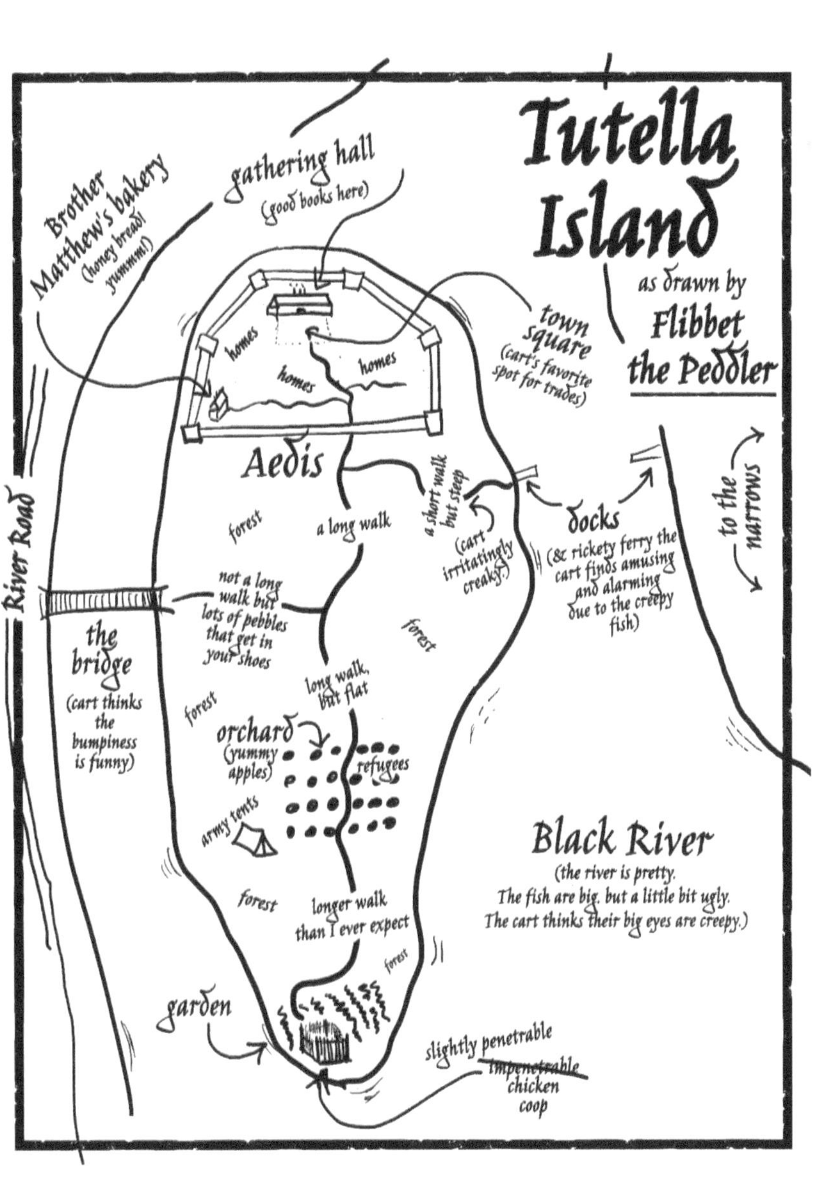
Tutella Island
as drawn by
Flibbet the Peddler
gathering hall
(good books here)
Brother Matthew's bakery
(honey bread! yummm!)
town square
(cart's favorite spot for trades)
homes
homes
homes
Aedis
a short walk but steep
(cart irritatingly creaky.)
docks
(& rickety ferry the cart finds amusing and alarming due to the creepy fish)
to the narrows
River Road
forest
a long walk
not a long walk but lots of pebbles that get in your shoes
forest
the bridge
(cart thinks the bumpiness is funny)
long walk, but flat
forest
orchard
(yummy apples)
refugees
army tents
Black River
(the river is pretty.
The fish are big, but a little bit ugly.
The cart thinks their big eyes are creepy.)
forest
longer walk than I ever expect
forest
garden
slightly penetrable
impenetrable
chicken coop

NUDGES OF FLAME

—an excerpt from Chapter 2
of *Interesting Beginnings*
by Flibbet the Peddler

I WISH MORE of the nudges that shaped history were the gentle kind—the signing of a treaty, the commitment to protect the weak, the spreading of a story that will enlighten minds.

Alas, humans are more prone to stagnate than to change willingly, and so most nudges are affected with force and terror and blood.

Most nudges come at the slicing of a blade or the searing of a flame.

The final chapters of Sable's beginning certainly did.

More blades than I hope to see again, and the fire…

Who could ever forget the fire?

The further history moves from those early days, the more it would have me call her Issable, but when I met her, she insisted on Sable.

She'd been a year in the service of the Prioress Narine when I encountered her again, but it was the Prioress Vivaine who controlled her, using the skill Sable had for recognizing truth and lies to further negotiations with the Kalesh Empire.

For years I had harbored a distrust of Vivaine, but it wasn't until the summit on Tutella Island that I let that distrust grow.

Ah, I have shifted to talk about myself as I'm wont to do when I think of this time. I so rarely get to be a part of these things.

But you are here to read of Sable.

That summit was pivotal. It was where Sable took back the voice Vivaine had stolen from her and stood against the Kalesh. Had she been allowed to really speak, perhaps the rest of history would be different.

But there was the fire.

I have recorded many horrible, haunting things in my time, but the fire that killed my dear friend Narine is one I cannot bring myself to touch on.

Something about the flames burned Vivaine as well. If I had to guess, I would say Vivaine loved Narine, in whatever way her cold, twisted heart could love. Narine may have been the only truly good person left in Vivaine's life, and with that loss, Vivaine made the final turn toward darkness.

Whatever the reason, the control she'd held over her own lust for power cracked that night, and something far more dangerous and deadly bubbled out.

But worse, something about that fire nudged her dragon. Something about that act shifted the relationship between the prioress and the creature. That was the moment when the dragon stopped being merely a prop for Vivaine's posturing, and became a force in his own right.

When I ran across Sable in the rebel camp with Andreese and Tanis, it was the first time she was in the right place. In Immusmala she'd been a prisoner, with Atticus she had been finding her family, but with the northern rebels, she was finally home. She didn't know it yet, maybe the home wasn't even created yet, but the shift that day was so foundational I could barely string words together.

That was the day I gave her Ghost of the White Wood. It was the story of the zabat Melia, the rebel leader who had fought the Empire with her elven friend Evay. It felt right, of course, to give Sable the story of the woman the Empire had failed to crush, but I couldn't have known how pivotal the story would be.

When I gave Sable the book, she was broken. Her dreams of the rebels had been shattered by a connection with her old gang boss Kiva, and she was ready to leave.

I admit I stepped in.

I try so hard not to. The disaster I caused at Pyrrenford haunts me, and so I do try. But this…this was too much.

She belonged there, she was needed there, and she was going to leave.

If I hadn't, would she have gone? Would the rest of it have happened if I had just stayed in the background like I should?

But I didn't stop, because I knew, with a clarity that I rarely attain, that she should stay. These were the rebels and she was the zabat. So I told her that exhausting, impossible thing the old man told me so long ago when he gave me my cart. The day he told me the true price of it.

You can escape, or you can take the world as you find it, broken and jagged and weak, and you can step right into the midst of it. Take what it is and spend yourself making it what it should be.

Even as I said it, everything inside of me wanted to weep for what it would mean to her.

Because I knew she would listen.

And she did.

The world moved toward war, and she rallied the troops of three Northern Lords, managing to unite them in a way no one ever had.

It might have been a great victory, until Vivaine.

Immusmala had never been in danger. Vivaine had merely tricked Sable into bringing the army south, and then punished the north by sending Kalesh troops to attack their unprotected homes. The prioress sold out countless innocent people to the brutal Empire in a bid to keep her own city safe.

It wasn't just about the city, of course, there was so much more to it than that. But at the time, we still thought it was merely about one small city on one small peninsula jutting into the Southern Sea.

What we did know was that swords had been drawn, and the first battle had been waged.

Sable had almost ensured it would be the last, but there were too many swords, and too much blood.

The nudge had been given at the edge of a blade.

But it was nothing compared to the fire that was to come.

PART I

The stage, at the beginning must be dark, for it was a dark and troubling time.

It cannot be too dark, because things got worse.

But lanterns should be shuttered, costumes muted. Like the stage is covered with shadows from the storm you thought was past…

-Stage notes from the opening scene of ***The Phoenix Rising*** by Atticus the Playwright.

CHAPTER ONE

SHADOWS SPREAD LONG GRASPING fingers over the shore of the Black River, and the bloody, exhausted line of soldiers waiting to board the riverboats. Those already on board shuffled supplies into place, their shoulders set in a quiet, grim determination.

Sable sat in the bow of one of the larger boats, ripping another strip of cloth from the pile of fabric, rolling another bandage and adding it to her growing pile. She let her hand rest on the pile for a moment.

Reese lay beside her, his skin grey and waxy. She reached out and brushed a lock of blood-crusted hair off his brow. His forehead was cool, and she pressed her palm to his cheek, pushing a little more *vitalle* into him.

"Watch him," Serene had said when Sable had first found Reese lying bandaged and unconscious on Kiva's merchant ship in the docks of Immusmala. "Give him a little *vitalle* if you can spare it."

But after hours of offering him what little energy she had while they sailed to the mouth of the Black River, the flow was down to a trickle. Now that they were finally settled on a much smaller riverboat, ready to head back to the north, the *vitalle* she pushed into him barely warmed his skin before it dribbled to a stop. Underneath her hand, he grew cold again.

A spray of fire shot over the trees along the riverbank, leaving a trail of glittering sparks as Innov circled the shore choked with soldiers. Hundreds of weary eyes turned up toward the phoenix, bathed in her golden light until she skimmed over the side of the boat and alighted on the rail above Sable's head. A shower of embers rolled and bounced harmlessly down the wood like tiny fires, settling on Sable's shoulders and lap, burning for a breath on Reese's cold skin before winking out.

Atticus's voice came from the gangplank, convincing the soldiers that fitting his wagon onto the riverboat was a perfectly logical thing to do. From where Sable sat, she could just see the roof, a bit of bright, cheery blue, like some fluttering decoration from a distant festival that had been caught up and blown here to land among the muted sea of uniforms.

Serene crossed the deck toward Sable. Her black robe was streaked with dirt and wet in spots with something that glistened more darkly than water. Her eyes were shadowed with smudges, her nearly black hair was pulled back in a tight knot, and her face was drawn.

Jae came with her, carrying another pile of fabric and a lantern. His normally quick smile was weighed down with exhaustion as he dropped the cloth onto Sable's pile.

"Has he woken?" Serene asked, handing Sable a waterskin.

Sable shook her head. Serene knelt on the other side of Reese, setting her hand on his forehead.

"How bad is it?" Sable asked quietly.

Serene cast out. Both she and Sable lit up in Sable's senses like bonfires of *vitalle,* blazing with life, but between them, Reese's body held only a hint of warmth, no stronger than a bed of dying coals.

Serene's wave rolled farther across the boat, and first Jae, then the soldiers flared into towers of heat. The small sensation of warmth from Reese faded until Sable was left gripping his cold hand.

Serene sank back against the side of the boat, meeting Sable's eyes with a grave expression. "His ribs aren't broken, but the cut was deep. He lost so much blood I'm surprised he's still alive. I cleaned the wound and closed it as well as I could, but…" She looked back down at Reese. "If it doesn't get infected, and if he gets a lot of rest, he may recover."

Sable looked between Serene and Jae. Neither of them looked hopeful. "May?"

Serene watched Reese take slow, shallow breaths. "Or he may not. If he lives, it will be a long time before he's strong enough to fight. He needs time and rest and a good dose of luck."

"And *vitalle*?" Sable asked.

"It helps. It gives his body the strength to heal." Her hand moved to her own stomach.

Sable sat forward. "Does it hurt the baby when you heal people?"

Serene shook her head. "Not if I'm careful."

"We hope." Jae's eyes, lined with worry, lingered on Serene before he moved over and knelt next to Sable. "Teaching you how to manipulate *vitalle* is long overdue. We've had too much to worry about since we met you. But we have time on our hands now, so I thought we'd remedy that. Luckily for us, and unluckily for Reese, he is the perfect exercise for practicing control."

"Jae is a thousand times better at teaching than I am," Serene said, pushing herself to her feet. "So I'll leave him to it. Whenever Reese is awake, get him to drink." She motioned to the waterskin. "There's wartroot in here. It'll help with his pain. When we get to Tutella Island, we'll have someone who knows what they're doing look at him."

"Be careful," Jae said to his wife as she started across the deck.

She gave him a weary smile over her shoulder.

With a sigh, he turned back to look at Reese. "His most pressing problem is that he lost a lot of blood. His body will make more, but it is a slow process, and until then, he'll be incredibly weak. We can help that to a limited extent. All our *vitalle* does is give his body the energy to do what it's already doing. He's not strong enough to use a flood of it. He needs slow trickles, just enough to help the healing. As he gets stronger, he'll be able to use more."

Sable set her finger on the cool skin of Reese's arm. "And if he gets weaker?"

"Then there will come a point when no matter what we do, his body won't be able to use it." He looked up at her with a small smile. "We're not at that point, and we won't worry about it unless we get there."

"I feel like I don't have much left to give."

Jae nodded thoughtfully. "Your body is flooded with *vitalle*, but only a little is available to use. The rest is busy keeping you alive. You can access that with a lot of effort, but you can also kill yourself in the process."

He turned his hand over and showed the old scars on his palm. "There are limits. When we move too much *vitalle*, we burn ourselves, then if we continue, we deplete the energy we need to live. How much we have to use varies. Serene has ten times more than I do. Maybe more. She can move tremendous amounts of *vitalle* at a speed that would kill me." His words were warm. "And probably kill you, no matter how much you train, but that's her strength. She is not as good at things that require a low level of steady control."

Jae held his hand out, and Sable got the impression of heat flowing out from it in a thin sheet. He waved his fingers toward her, and a swirl of wind blew past. "For instance, she's horrible at moving air, which requires creating a stable boundary layer that you can push. It's why she dislikes healing. Directing a thin line of *vitalle* delicately enough to help a body close a wound takes a lot of energy and a lot of control. Lucky for us, she's done the hard part in closing Reese's wound. All we need to do is offer his body more *vitalle* to help it continue healing." He looked at her hand. "Show me how you do it."

Sable focused on her palm and pushed *vitalle* into Reese's skin. Like before, it was only a small trickle.

"Pushing is the least effective method." He set his hand on the back of hers. "It's the natural instinct we have, but we end up wasting energy in the pushing part. Reese is so much weaker than you are, you don't need to push. Just open a channel, and the energy will flow into him."

Vitalle moved from Jae's hand, through hers, and into Reese. Instead of a shove, it slid like water.

"It's like you're full to bursting, and he's hollow," Jae said. "The energy will try to fill him." He cut off the *vitalle* and pulled his hand away.

Sable focused again on her hand, imagining an opening filling her palm. Imagining the *vitalle* flowing through—

A rush of energy gushed out of her and into Reese. His arm suddenly flamed with heat, and she yanked her hand back, her palm red and hot.

"Well done," Jae said with a smile. "Maybe a smaller channel this time."

Sable tried twice more, discovering that it took only a very thin connection before *vitalle* began to move.

"If we need more energy than we have available," Jae said, "we draw *vitalle* from things around us. There are obvious ethical questions about pulling *vitalle* out of other humans or animals, but most people are comfortable drawing it out of plants or fire." He opened the lantern glass. "See if you can follow the heat."

They set their hands back on Reese's arm. Jae opened his other palm toward the flame, and a trickle of heat pulled out toward him. She could almost trace the path it took up one arm, across his shoulders, and down the other arm. A gentle warmth passed from his hand, through hers, into Reese.

"Fire is a great source of energy, but it can grow powerful very quickly. Stick with something small like a candle or a lantern for now. And, in general, don't drive *vitalle* across your chest. You have important things in there like lungs and a heart. If you're going from one hand to the other, bring the energy up high across your shoulders."

He set the lantern next to her, and she put one hand toward it. Once she could feel the warmth of the flame on her palm, she opened up a channel. The heat slipped into her hand, making her feel a bit like she was filling with hot water. It pooled inside her palm until she pulled it higher up her arm. The warmth seeped through her like a mist, and she directed it across the top of her back and down her other arm. Her palm near the flame was painfully hot, but her palm on Reese let out barely a trickle.

Still, Jae nodded encouragingly. "Good. As you practice, you'll get better at not letting it disperse inside you. Some people think of a tube that the energy moves down." His mouth quirked up in a smile. "Serene says it's not her energy, so why would it go into her body unless she told it to? But for most of us, it's not quite that simple."

Sable tried again to pull warmth from the flame, and this time a bit more of it made its way into Reese.

"Good. Any questions?" Jae asked.

Sable shook her head.

"The more tired you are, the more you'll waste, and the less will go into Reese, so take your time." He picked up the pile of bandages she'd rolled earlier. "Besides, if you exhaust yourself, Serene's going to be mad at both of us." His gaze dropped to Reese, and he sighed. "Just do what you can." With a smile that wasn't particularly reassuring, he headed across the deck toward Serene.

Sable set her hand on Reese's chest, but his heartbeat was weak. Innov shifted on the rail above them, but even the sparks of her fire didn't take away the greyness of his skin.

"Can you help him too?" Sable looked up at the phoenix and patted her hand on Reese's chest. "You helped Narine when she was weak."

Innov twitched her head, then launched off the rail, tucked into a tight circle, and spiraled down to land in a flurry of fire in the center of Reese's bandage. Tiny tongues of flame flickered along her feathers as she settled her wings. Her warmth pressed against Sable's cheeks like she was sitting by a glowing hearth. But more than that, a gentle current of hope seeped into the air, smoothing the jagged edges of worry and fear inside Sable and the aching emptiness left by all the things lost in the battle at Immusmala.

Sable ran her finger down Innov's chest. "Thank you."

Reese didn't move.

What if he never did? What if he never sat up next to her, solid and protective and…alive?

She swallowed and took his hand again. "I need you to live," she whispered, the truth of the words warming the air around them. "I thought you were dead once already, when I saw you fall in the battle." The heat swirled through the air between them, pooling around Reese. She focused on it, willing it to sink into him. "Actually, when you hear what I did after that, you're going to be really mad."

An officer approached and saluted, the motion including Sable as well. "Preparations are almost finished. We'll be pushing off soon, leading the fleet north up the river."

The word "fleet" was too sophisticated for a haphazard cluster of borrowed merchant boats and would have been amusing if everyone boarding them hadn't been exhausted, wounded, and filthy.

The officer was looking at Reese, who didn't move.

"How much of the army is here?" Sable asked.

The officer shifted his attention to her. "Everyone well enough to march from Immusmala."

"Any news on the Kalesh forces who already went north?"

"From what we've gathered, they have a four-day head start. With the boats, we should shave at least a day off their lead."

"Only a day?" Sable asked.

"We'll be rowing against the current," the officer said, his eyes straying to Innov perched on Reese's chest. "We'll be moving no faster than someone could walk along the shore, but we'll row in shifts so we can continue moving through the night. If all goes well, we'll gain on the cowards a little."

"Thank you," Sable said.

The man saluted and, with one last glance at Reese, started back across the deck. Atticus's wagon finally rolled on board, and there were a few moments of commotion as some crates were moved to fit it into the back of the boat.

Next to Sable, Reese groaned, and she leaned closer, grabbing his hand. His eyes cracked open.

"Reese?" she whispered.

He focused on her face. His fingers twitched, trying to squeeze her hand, but she could barely feel the pressure. "Are you hurt?" His voice was whisper quiet and strained.

"Me?" A breath escaped her, sounding more like a sob than a laugh. "I thought you were dead."

His eyes closed. "I hope being dead isn't going to hurt this much."

"Serene says you need to drink. There's wartroot in it for the pain." She lifted his head, and Innov flapped her wings, fluttering up to the rail of the boat, dousing them in a shower of sparks.

Reese took a few swallows before his head lolled to the side. "Where are we?"

"Back on the river." Sable gave a quick explanation of how they'd taken a merchant boat from Immusmala to the river, and how they were now readying to row north on the smaller riverboats.

He squinted up at her. "How did we get merchant boats?"

Sable shook her head, remembering how Kiva had escorted her to his ships. "I'll save the details for when you're feeling better and have the energy to be properly angry with me."

When he looked like he might object, she continued. "We won the battle, though." In broad strokes, leaving out her own involvement, she explained the end of the fighting. As she talked, though, his eyes began to glaze over.

Innov shifted on the railing, and embers cascaded around Sable's shoulders.

Reese blinked and focused on her. "You look magical."

She let out a short laugh. "I'm too dirty to look mag—"

"And plain," he declared.

She tilted her head. "Plain?"

His eye slid shut and he nodded weakly. "Plain." His voice was warm with truth.

"Thanks, Reese." She patted his shoulder. "That's very sweet."

He didn't answer for so long, she thought he had fallen back asleep. Finally, his hand tightened on hers. "Don't," he whispered.

"Don't what?"

"Don't..." The word was slurred. "...leave..."

She set her hand on his cold cheek. "I'll stay while you sleep."

He shook his head slightly. "Not...enough," he mumbled. "Not..."

"Reese?"

He didn't answer.

She slid her fingers down to his neck. His pulse was weak and thready and his skin so cold she reached out toward the lantern and funneled more *vitalle* into him. The merest hint of warmth flowed between them.

Dropping her hand, she leaned back, her arms and head heavy. She closed her own eyes, and the world spun slightly. The groan of some wounded soldier floated across the deck, and she forced her eyes open. There were more bandages to make. She picked up a new piece of cloth.

As she tore it into strips, the events of the day replayed yet again in her head.

Ending, like it always did, with the thought of the raven racing toward the Empire. The Kalesh would be returning soon. It was inevitable. When they did…

Her hands closed around the cloth.

There was an obvious solution.

A painful one, but an obvious one.

She pointedly refocused on the fabric, starting a tear and ripping off a strip. Rolling it neatly in her pile.

Atticus's voice rang across the deck again as he climbed on board. His wavy white hair and beard came into view with several familiar faces following him.

Sable breathed out a long, slow breath.

As soon as they were all gathered, she'd tell them what had happened.

They'd see the solution too. They might argue a little at first, but they'd agree in the end.

CHAPTER TWO

SABLE HAD ALMOST FINISHED ROLLING the makeshift bandages she'd been given when Atticus's footsteps stormed toward her on the deck. The sky had darkened to a deep blue, and a handful of bright stars were struggling to shine in the east.

Jae and Serene came with him, both dropping down gratefully on the deck. Jae's curly hair was damp with sweat, his robes and hands as dirty as Serene's and his face almost as exhausted.

Atticus stayed standing, his arms crossed. "Sable, what is this I hear about Bastian capturing you?"

Sable shook her head. "He didn't capture me."

Leonis stepped past Atticus, sitting next to Sable and stretching out his legs. "Letting yourself be captured is poor form, Sneaks."

Thulan thunked down on the far side of Reese, the evening light picking up strands of red in her short-trimmed beard. "You look terrible," the dwarf said, nudging his foot with her own. When Reese gave no response, her brow creased.

"He hasn't woken yet?" Leonis asked, reaching past Sable to set his fingers on Reese's wrist.

"He did for a few minutes," Sable answered.

Leonis exchanged a look with Thulan that was so brief Sable almost didn't catch it before he pulled his hand off Reese's wrist and sat back.

Atticus still stood with his arms crossed. His troubled gaze rested on

Reese for a moment before he refocused on Sable, his voice more subdued. "What is this I hear," he repeated, "about Ambassador Bastian capturing you and taking you to General Goll?"

"He didn't capture me," Sable said again. "I..." She glanced around at the people around her. "I asked him to take me to Goll."

This was met with a moment of silence before Atticus burst out with, "Goll? Of all people, you went to *Goll*? When the battle was already won?"

Flibbet pushed his little handcart up the ramp onto the boat and tucked it against the stern. Sable waved him over, ignoring Leonis's comments about stupid decisions and badly formed plans. "Have a seat," she said to the peddler. "You're going to enjoy this story."

Atticus was still glaring down at her.

"Atticus," she said, "are you going to make me speak to an audience who's looming and scowling? You might like this story too. It has some unexpected twists."

He frowned at her. "The only reason I'm sitting is because it obviously has a happy ending." He shooed Leonis's legs out of the way and sat directly in front of her.

She watched him get situated. "I'm not sure it does."

An officer called out a command, and the wood behind Sable vibrated as the oars clunked into place.

She looked at the familiar faces around her, a surge of relief rising in her that she was sitting here, with them, on a boat about to start north up the Black River, instead of sitting imprisoned on a Kalesh ship, sailing toward the Empire. She glanced down at Reese, watching his shallow breaths, the relief fading.

"I suppose Bastian did capture me," Sable began, turning back to Atticus, "but not the way you might think. At dawn this morning, I was headed to find Rabbit and get out of Immusmala when Bastian met me near the Fallen Gate and invited me to the top of the city wall."

"Invited?" Atticus asked.

The soldiers heaved on the boat, pushing it deeper into the water, making it rock sharply. Innov let out an irritated cry before launching herself into the air. They slid slowly down the sand, the ground rasping under the hull, until they broke free and swung out into the river. The order was given to row, and the boat heaved slowly upstream.

"There were several Kalesh guards encouraging me to take up his invitation," Sable admitted, "but it felt more invitation-like than capture-like."

Atticus gave an annoyed noise.

"What did Bastian want?" Leonis asked.

"To help," Sable answered with a small smile. Almost every look turned skeptical. Serene merely nodded in agreement. Flibbet's expression was thoughtful, as though he was fitting together pieces of a puzzle.

Atticus narrowed his eyes. "Why?"

Sable's smile faded. "He said he owed me more than he owed the Empire."

Flibbet sighed, as though something unpleasant had been confirmed, but the others merely exchanged confused looks.

Until Atticus drew in a sharp breath. "Melia," he breathed.

Sable nodded. "I told you you'd like the twist."

"What does the Ghost of the White Wood have to do with you?" Leonis asked.

"A bit more than I expected," Sable said. "It turns out that when Melia left the Empire, she headed this direction and settled on the Eastern Reaches, where she married and had three daughters."

Sable waited as the shocked expressions came over them.

"Melia was your mother?" Thulan asked.

Flibbet let out a breath that was more of a grimace than a laugh. "Your mother is the fabled Ghost who killed the Imperial prince?" He glanced at the others. "Prince Turrn was the current Emperor's brother."

"No wonder they never stopped looking for her," Thulan said.

"I look like my mother," Sable said, "and Bastian recognized me the first time we met." Bastian's expression as they'd stood on the city wall together came back to her. The earnestness. The plea to let him help her. "At the very least, he'd harbored a lifelong admiration of her. He claimed knowing her had changed him. Changed how he thought of the Empire and the people they conquered. He said she'd convinced him to mitigate some of the violence the Empire spread."

"He was always a voice of peace in Vivaine's meetings," Serene agreed.

"He betrayed the Empire to help you, Sable," Leonis said, "based only on the memory of your mother. I'd say that signifies more than admiration."

Sable nodded. "He tried to find her before the Empire did, to warn her. He said her exploits are still famous. Rebellions rally around her name. Kalesh parents tell their children the Ghost will come visit them if they're naughty."

"More than that." Flibbet leaned forward. "There's a town on the far eastern side of the Reaches where a lot of refugees have fled from the Empire and settled here. That's where I got the book about the Ghost of the White Wood in the first place. They told me stories about her. After Melia killed Prince Turrn, any time the Empire caught even a rumor of her location, they sent hundreds of troops after her. They slaughtered entire villages because they heard she might be there. They burned down a whole forest when they thought she was passing through it." He glanced at Sable. "I'm not surprised they burned down your town to get your mother. I'm surprised they didn't burn the entirety of the Eastern Reaches."

Sable shifted against the wood behind her. "That was the sense I got from Bastian as well. And Goll."

"Then it's a very good thing," Atticus said, "that the Empire doesn't know her three daughters exist. And that one of them is currently with the rebellion."

Sable's gaze shifted among the nods around her.

Atticus grew apprehensive. "What did you do, Sable?"

"The story must be told in order, Atticus. If we skip to the end, you'll miss Serene's big moment where she almost destroyed the Sanctuary."

Jae turned to look at his wife. "What's this?"

"Sable's exaggerating," Serene told him. "It wasn't that dramatic."

"Actually, it was," Flibbet said. "I was there."

Sable nodded. "Serene and I found out Vivaine had all the merchants in the Sanctuary, turning them against the north. But when we got there to convince the merchants to come help the army—"

"They were burning my books!" Serene broke in.

"What?" Atticus looked at her sharply. "Vivaine loves books."

"Clearly," Serene said to him. "Which is why she was burning a huge pile in a show of solidarity with the Kalesh."

"How many?"

"Hundreds."

"What did you do?" Jae asked, somewhat cautiously.

"She took the fire from the books," Sable said, "and she lit all the bushes and trees across the front of the Dragon Priory."

Flibbet nodded. "The flames grew higher and higher until the heat broke the windows and lit drapes and who knows what else inside." He looked at Serene nervously. "I thought the stones themselves might catch fire."

Jae reached over and turned one of Serene's hands over so he could see her palm. It was perfectly normal looking. "How…?"

Serene turned the other palm over, which was equally unharmed. "You know how you've always said the stones of the priories have something magical in them? You were right. Not all of them, but some. When I started to move the *vitalle,* there were…paths. A lot of paths through the stones." She glanced at her feet. "I felt it across the bottoms of my feet, but it didn't hurt. Or if it did, I didn't notice." She gave Jae a rueful look. "I was angry."

"What did Vivaine do when you set her priory on fire?" Atticus asked.

"She came outside," Sable answered. "Her Mira got the fire under control, and since everyone's attention was focused so nicely, I took that opportunity to climb the steps and tell the merchants what Vivaine had done. How she'd been manipulating everyone and made secret deals with the Kalesh."

"She mentioned how Vivaine wraps light around herself to make herself appear more holy," Flibbet added. "Which was…unsettling."

Atticus looked impressed. "And they believed you?"

"It's Sable," Serene said. "They believed her…And that's when Argyros tried to burn her alive."

"What?" Atticus demanded.

Sable nodded. "And we're still not to the part you're going to be really mad about." She pointed to where Innov flew over the forests next to the river. "Innov saved me. She intercepted the flames, and when Argyros stopped, Innov attacked him. She gouged out one of his eyes, and he retreated."

"She attacked the dragon?" Thulan asked.

Leonis nodded approvingly. "I knew I liked that bird."

Atticus looked between Innov and Sable. "At some point, you are going to sit with me and give a very detailed account of all of this. This will be the greatest play ever written." He glanced at Thulan. "How will we ever show dragon fire and a phoenix?"

"Where does that leave Vivaine?" Jae asked before Thulan could answer.

"Weakened," Serene answered. "Severely. The Merchant Guild distrusts her, Argyros is wounded, and the city on the whole has turned against her."

"But," Sable said, "she did have one more important thing to say. Before we left the Sanctuary, Vivaine argued that the Kalesh still wanted our gold, and even if we drove them away, they'd be back." She paused. "Unless we had something more valuable to offer them."

Atticus's gaze flattened. "Issable." His voice held a sharply disapproving tone.

Sable raised an eyebrow at her full name. "If you can see where this is going, you can't deny that it made sense."

"Sable was going to offer them the daughter of the Ghost," Thulan said, shaking her head, "in exchange for the Empire not coming back."

"I did offer. And Goll accepted."

There was a moment of silence, and in that breath, the full weight of that offer fell on Sable again. The hopelessness it had ended in.

"Bastian agreed to this?" Atticus asked.

"Bastian did not agree, but he took me to the general anyway and verified my story." Sable closed her eyes, seeing Bastian crumpled on the ground, unmoving. The horrible stain spreading across his back. "Goll killed him."

When she opened her eyes, the others were looking at her with a mixture of horror and shock.

"Goll took me prisoner, and we were headed to a Kalesh ship. Until Kiva stopped us from actually leaving."

Now every face stared at her in shock.

"Kiva?" said Atticus faintly.

Sable nodded. "He claimed the north wouldn't stand for me being taken." Her fury at the man rose again. "He killed Goll to 'save' me."

"Wait," Serene said. "Kiva killed both Goll and Tanis? That doesn't make sense. Why kill both the general of the Kalesh army and the general of the northern army?"

"Kiva didn't kill Tanis," Sable said.

"It was venom from his snake," Atticus pointed out.

"But Kiva swears it wasn't him, and he was telling the truth. He thinks it was Vivaine, and she used the vayakadyn venom to put the blame on Kiva. In one move, she weakened the northern army and made sure they would hate the Merchant Guild."

Atticus took in these words with a slow, pained nod. "There's a logic to that."

Jae turned to Sable. "The fact that Kiva brought you to the boats explains why the soldiers keep talking about the southerner who protected the Flame of the North. I was having a hard time puzzling that out."

Sable glared in the general direction of Kiva, back in Immusmala, all the fear and frustration and defeat of the last day funneling into how much she hated his smug, horrible face. "He was trying to solidify a relationship with the north and thinks they owe him now. He plans to leverage that as much as he can. I would imagine with Vivaine weakened, we'll be seeing more of Kiva in our negotiations with the south."

"Kiva is an unpleasant man to owe a favor to," Atticus said.

"We don't," Sable said firmly. "All he did was destroy the one chance we had to deter the Kalesh from coming back."

Leonis shook his head. "The north will think they owe him. At least the parts of the north that are enamored with you. Which is not an insignificant portion of it."

"And the south as well," Jae added. "I heard more talk of the Flame of the North in Immusmala than almost anything else. Because you have Innov, you're thought of as...not a prioress, but maybe as something similar. Or even something more."

Flibbet was nodding slowly, watching Sable with a wondering expression.

A new sort of fury rose in her at their reactions. "That's ridiculous."

"Hardly," Atticus said. "You unified an army and led it down to defend a city that isn't even their own, you wrested the power of Immusmala away from Vivaine, and you turned the Kalesh ambassador to your cause." His shoulders drooped. "I'm utterly superfluous. I could never, ever have orchestrated all of that."

"It wasn't orchestrated!" Sable shifted her frustration toward the old man. "It was one failed, desperate attempt after another to not be destroyed by the Kalesh!"

"I know!" Atticus stared at her almost helplessly. "And..." He flung one hand toward Innov flying over the river. "You have a phoenix—who defeats dragons! How would anyone have ever thought to include a phoenix?"

"I'm sure Purnicious played a role," Thulan said.

"Of course I did," came Purnicious's voice from up near the rail of the boat.

"Who's Purnicious?" Flibbet asked, looking warily at the empty air.

"And she has a kobold!" Atticus added, raising his eyes to the sky. "Because why wouldn't she also have a kobold?"

Flibbet's eyes widened. "A kobold!"

"You're all missing the point!" Sable snapped, loud enough that several nearby soldiers glanced over. "I can't be the Flame of the North anymore," she continued, trying to keep the words quieter. "The fact is that Goll sent a raven before he died. The Emperor himself—who hates Melia with a passion—knows I'm here." The air around her grew warm with the truth of it all, and she clenched her fists so tightly her nails dug into her palms. "Not only are they coming back for the gold, but they're coming for me, just like they came for my mother. And at some point, they are going to learn about my sisters. Anyone who stands against them is going to die, and everything we were trying to save is going to be overrun. Every single thing I did made this mess worse. It doesn't matter that Innov is still here for reasons I don't understand. Or that Purnicious thinks I'm more than I am." She ignored Purn's huff of indignation. "None of it matters!" she flung at them. "Because I—" She bit back the next words.

Reese lay cold and still in the heat of her words, as dim as Narine had been in her last moments. A grasping, desperate fear rose. The others around Sable were blazing towers of life, but when the Kalesh returned, how many of their lives would be snuffed out, left broken and cold?

Her friends would fall, one by one, and it ripped something out of her.

Her voice came out as merely a whisper, but she shoved the truth into it. "I destroyed everything."

The heat of her words flared through the bow of the boat with the heat of a bonfire. Jae and Serene tensed at the strength of it.

Atticus shook his head. "No, the Kalesh destroyed everything."

"And Vivaine," Serene added.

Sable held up a hand to stop them, her arm shaking with fury. "But they know I'm Melia's daughter because I told them. That changes everything for me, and I'm the one who changed it. When they come back…"

The threat of it all hung palpably in the air. The conversations farther down the boat droned on, the oars clunking rhythmically against the oarlocks, the beat shoving them inexorably forward.

"I can't stay," she finished.

"Leaving won't stop the Kalesh," Thulan said. "They'll just track you down."

Sable took a deep breath and nodded. "That was my mother's mistake. She ran, and they chased her, killing hundreds of innocent people in the process. They didn't stop searching for her until she was dead."

She paused, looking at the familiar faces around her. "There is one solution to this. The Empire needs to believe the Flame of the North is dead."

Atticus glared at her but said nothing. She could see his mind ripping the idea apart, looking for the argument against it.

"You can't spin this into a happy story, Atticus," she said. "In the real tragedies, everyone knows the terrible end is coming, even from the beginning. This ends one of two ways: The Empire kills me for real, or we make them think they did."

There was a moment of silence.

"Pretending Sable is dead…" Leonis said thoughtfully.

"Could be fun," Thulan agreed.

Atticus narrowed his eyes. "No," he said firmly. "You're the Flame of the North."

"Atticus!" Sable said, the word sharp with exhaustion and frustration. "I need to die."

"No." He ran his fingers through his beard thoughtfully. "The Flame needs to be martyred."

CHAPTER THREE

THE WOODEN DECK of the ship creaked and groaned beneath Sable in time with the rhythm of the oars. Soldiers' boots shuffled and scraped against the deck in the darkness, but Sable sat in silence in the bow of the boat, turning over the idea of a martyrdom in her mind. There was something distasteful about the whole idea of faking her death, but it felt necessary.

Reese still lay beside her, sleeping restlessly. The others had spread out to find places to sleep, and Innov had come to perch on Sable's arm. The glow between the phoenix's feathers shifted like a living, breathing bed of coals.

A glimmer of green light appeared near the back of the boat where Atticus's wagon was parked. Leonis must have opened the panel in the wagon's walls, revealing his small *sede* tree.

From the ground, the tree itself only stood as tall as Sable's elbow, but its trunk was twisted and ropey, and its faintly glowing leaves spread out in a thick arching canopy.

The tree shone with the same sort of serenity that a forest held. That sense that life was long and storms were fleeting. That things as gentle as sunlight, rain, and fresh air were the true powers in the world, slowly and steadily breathing life into everything.

The presence of the tree was more subtle than Innov's flames, but it was good of Leonis to share it with the boat—and a little surprising, seeing as he usually kept it protectively tucked away.

The leaves of the tree shuddered, then moved.

Sable peered through the darkness at it.

It was definitely moving. Quivering and jolting.

And getting closer.

It was halfway across the dark deck before she could see Leonis and Thulan illuminated in dim green on either side of it, carrying its heavy pot.

If Leonis was going to set it in the middle of the deck and risk some soldier hurting it, he really was feeling generous.

But he and Thulan continued closer until they reached the bow of the boat.

"Careful," Leonis warned as they lowered it on the far side of Reese. "Watch the branches."

"I know how to carry the tree," Thulan muttered, but she set her side of the pot down gently and backed away so Leonis could adjust it to his liking.

"What are you doing?" Sable asked.

"He's worried about Reese," Thulan answered. "Thinks somehow a tree can help."

"Thulan is worried," Leonis said easily, running his fingers gently over the leaves. He glanced down at Reese. "And I admit to being concerned."

The tree felt…maybe it felt like nothing. Maybe it was just the glitter of the green light that was nestled into the base of each leaf. But maybe there was more, something like the impression of *vitalle* floating slowly into the air. Like the tree was giving off a faint scent of hope.

"Thank you," Sable said.

Leonis pulled his eyes away from Reese, clearing the worry off his face. "Besides, if the tree's here, there's more room to spread out in the wagon. Since the entire crew is too intimidated by you and Reese to come mess with it, it's perfectly safe here." He pointed at her. "But don't let anything happen to it."

"It'll be fine," Thulan said, taking a step back to look at the bow. "Between the phoenix and the tree, you look rather otherworldly, Sable."

Leonis nodded. "As nice of a stage as we've ever put together, I'd say."

"I hope you're not expecting me to put on some sort of show," Sable said.

"I'm not saying that if you don't, it's a missed opportunity," Leonis said with a small smile, "but it's a missed opportunity."

"Ignore him," Thulan said. "Serene told us to ask if Reese has a fever."

Sable shook her head. "Still cold."

Leonis's smile faded. "Apparently, that's good, and a fever is *really* bad."

"Shut up," Thulan said, smacking his arm. "You're making her nervous."

"Me?" Leonis objected. "I brought her my tree! It's Serene who's scared of the fever."

Thulan gave Sable an exasperated look. "I apologize for Leonis's presence. And existence." She started back toward the wagon. "I call the tree's corner and the three blue pillows."

Leonis spun and hurried after her. "No! My tree, my space. You sleep by the window."

Sable watched them go, then looked up into the leaves of the tree. Each individual leaf had a tiny light, and the breeze running over the boat made them shiver, blinking out from between each other like little fairies playing some elaborate game.

It lit the bow with a calm green light, but Reese's skin looked sicklier.

Sable ran her finger down the feathers on Innov's neck, listening to the chirp of frogs from the riverbank and the repetitive, quiet splashes of the oars. Reese's still form felt like an anchor drawing back all the horror of the day. The battle, the losses, the death.

Innov leaned into her hand, and Sable desperately tried to draw some of the phoenix's hope into herself.

All she felt was the old, familiar longing surfacing again. The air of the river had a wild freshness. The untamed breeze of the forests and the open hills. With every moment, the ship drew farther from Immusmala and closer to someplace better. Someplace free.

"Will you come with me?" The whispered question slipped out before she could catch it.

Reese didn't answer.

She reached over and took his cold hand. "I have nothing left to offer, and I can't have more people dying because of me." She kept her words quiet but pushed the warmth of the words toward him. "I know you'll say it wasn't my fault or that many more are going to die no matter what I do. But it will be worse if I'm with them.

"If I had any way to help, I would stay, but…" She kept her eyes fixed on his hand. "I want to live somewhere quiet, Reese. It can be in a tiny cottage—I don't care."

The idea bloomed in her mind. A small home. Quiet, peaceful. Free.

She looked at his sleeping face. "You offered that to me once. On the wall on Tutella Island. Do you remember? You said you'd take me away from all of this."

His chest rose in such shallow breaths, she could barely see it moving.

"I swore to Narine I'd leave. That I'd try to find a place to live out from under the thumb of people like Vivaine and Kiva and the Kalesh. But every step I take puts me more under their control. I fight to drive them back, but I fail and end up trapped again. Always trapped. Even now, I'm not getting away." The thought of Goll's raven racing toward the Empire dragged cold fingers across her skin. Her voice dropped to a whisper. "They're going to come for me."

She glanced at his bandage. "I know you'd try to stop them. You'd die trying. So many people would die trying."

The boat rocked under them, the oars slowly pushing them up the river. She leaned her head back against the side.

There were already so many who had died. Bastian, killed for his loyalty. Reese's friend Tylar burned alive by Vivaine when the prioress couldn't reach Sable. The soldiers Sable had convinced to go to Immusmala. Their families left unprotected at home, even now being attacked by the Kalesh army who had snuck north…

The idea of a small cottage lingered in her imagination, and she focused on it. A snug timber-framed home like the buildings on Tutella Island. Not in a town. Just in a bright patch of woods.

A garden along the sunny side, like her mother had always tended. Sable rubbed the fingers of her free hand together, remembering the feel of the damp earth in that tiny plot. The subtle smell of the climbing beans when they were ready to be picked. The way they'd snap when you bit them.

The air would be fresh and wild. No fish stench lingering around the docks, no stale air trapped in a huge stone priory. A small home in the wide forests of the north.

Just trees and sky and freedom.

Off to the side of the cottage, a small trail led off into the pines, and—she looked at Reese, who was pale and exhausted. If things were perfect, she admitted, that little trail would wind off toward Reese, wherever he'd gone that morning to hunt.

Except, the truth was that if he recovered, the Kalesh invasion would keep him with the army for…who knew how long. Her anger at the

Empire smoldered like an ash-covered heap of coals, and she closed her eyes again.

A line of stepping stones wound up to the door through a yard that was cleared but not tamed.

On the path, two chubby little legs hopped toward the door, dirty bare feet jumping happily from one stone to the next. Long auburn hair ruffled in a breeze Sable couldn't feel, fluttering across the back of the girl's smock.

The child paused and squatted down, reaching out her hand to pluck a violet wildflower as she sang a little snip of song.

Sable strained to hear it, but there was nothing but the hums and clunks of the boat. The idea began to fade, and she scrambled to keep hold of it. Willing the little girl to stop. Turn around.

But the trees frayed and drifted away, the cottage paled, and the path disintegrated, taking the garden and the wildflowers and the bare little feet with it. The dim green light of Leonis's tree surrounded by the dark deck of the boat replaced it, and Sable let out a ragged breath.

"Is it too much to want a home?" she whispered.

Reese breathed slow and shallow. The bandage around his chest shifted as the fabric grew thicker and softer, each thread plumping up a little. An edge that had been pressing into his skin loosened.

"Thank you, Purn," Sable said quietly.

With all the soldiers nearby, the little kobold stayed invisible but patted Sable's hand.

"I'd make it even more comfortable," Purnicious said quietly, "but he did call you plain earlier."

Sable smiled. "I'm plainer than everyone thinks, Purn."

"No, you're stunning and perfect, which he knows. He's just a little dense sometimes." The blanket Sable had folded under Reese's head thickened a bit.

"Be careful, Purnicious. Someone might think you're starting to like him."

The little kobold snorted. "If I liked him," she said from the thin air, "I wouldn't have bellished the cuffs of his favorite pants with a sparkly gold silk he's going to hate."

Sable smiled.

"When he wakes up," Purn added.

Sable took in Reese's pale face, tinged green in the light of the tree. Her smile faded. "When he wakes up," she agreed quietly.

"It's not wrong to want a home," Purnicious said.

"I don't want to leave, Purn, but Melia's daughter leading a rebellion is just a target for the Kalesh to aim for. A goal they'll carve a path to no matter how many bodies they leave in their wake."

Purn set an invisible hand on Sable's shoulder. "Atticus will figure out a way to convince the Kalesh you're gone," she said confidently. "Then we'll sneak away and find the perfect home. We'll make it everything you want it to be."

Sable ignored the ache growing in her at the thought of leaving. She pressed her hand over Purn's bony fingers. "Everything *we* want it to be, Purn."

"All right, then." Purn's voice came from the darkness. "Everything you want it to be, plus a lot of fabric."

CHAPTER FOUR

THE CLEAR WATER of the Black River split around the bow of the boat, gliding smoothly down the wooden hull, flowing single-mindedly toward the Southern Sea. Sable leaned over the rail and looked into the water, watching the glints of midmorning sunlight flash off the surface. Smooth sections slid past unexpectedly, like windows into the clear depths, revealing the stones covering the bottom, colored in greys and browns and surprising purples, and thin smooth fish that slipped past almost faster than she could see them.

It was the third morning of the long row north, and they wouldn't even pass Tutella Island for three more days. It would be at least a day past there before the soldiers began to disembark and chase down the Kalesh ravaging the north.

Atticus and Jae had taken turns telling tales to the boat to keep the soldiers' spirits up, and Leonis had pulled a lute out of their wagon and wandered the deck singing lively songs, many of which featured a cowardly female dwarf who ran from danger at every turn. Judging from how impressed Atticus looked at the especially clever lines, Leonis was making them up as he went. Thulan retaliated by sharing countless embarrassing stories of Leonis's past with the soldiers, many of which blatantly contradicted each other, but all of which were uproariously funny.

But for the moment, the boat was quiet, and even if they were moving faster than an army could march, their progress was still achingly slow.

She let her eyes roam over the hills that piled up behind each other as far as she could see on both sides of the river. The dark green of the pine needles mixing with the brighter green leaves called to her. In a way that didn't make sense, moving north felt like coming home.

Her idea of the cottage fit perfectly here.

Except she still had a gaping problem she couldn't find a way to fix. She mulled over it again as the shore on the eastern side of the river dipped down. The wide path the Kalesh troops had trampled on their way north became visible, cutting through the grass like a scar.

"The wastrel looks a little better today." Purn's voice from the air next to Sable interrupted her thoughts.

Sable turned away from the ugly evidence that the Kalesh were far ahead of them. Reese lay in his usual spot, tucked in the bow near her feet.

Purn's words had been warm with truth, but he was still pale. He'd spent most of the last three days sleeping. Even when he did wake, he usually barely stirred. Only a handful of times had he managed to sit up for a few minutes' conversation.

Even in the bright daylight, the light of Leonis's tree lent a greenish tinge to the bow, and while the tree was soothing, it didn't help the color of Reese's skin.

"I'm not sure he does, Purn."

"I'll show you." There was a little pop, like the bursting of a bubble, then silence.

"Purn?" Sable asked quietly.

Another pop sounded, and a dingy bit of fabric fluttered down onto Reese.

"See?" Purn's voice came from the air. "Yesterday he looked like that." Invisible hands smoothed the fabric onto Reese's arm. "Today he clearly has more color."

The snip of cloth was decidedly paler than Reese. His skin looked a bit reddish next to it.

"It's a little odd that you have this," Sable said, smiling as she knelt down and picked up the scrap.

"No, I just remember colors well. This is from a soldier's shirt. When I saw it, I thought, 'That is wastrel-colored.' But today, I'll need to find a different shade." She gave a little giggle. "Maybe when he's better, I'll give him a new shirt made of all the colors of his recovery. He has some lovely purple and blue bruising on his side."

Sable held out the fabric toward Purn's voice. "As long as I'm there when you give it to him."

"He'll love it." The fabric was pulled from Sable's hand and disappeared.

Sable looked down at Reese. There were several flaws in her plan of creating a home, and Reese was only one of them. She needed a more complex solution than she'd thought of yet.

Turning to look over the boat, she searched for Atticus's white hair. This was the largest boat in the fleet rowing up the wide river, but not so big that she couldn't immediately pick out the playwright standing at the edge of the officers.

Sable approached him. "Will you help me sort out a problem?" she asked quietly.

Atticus pushed himself off the rail and motioned for her to lead the way back toward the bow. "I don't have a plan for your staged death yet," he said quietly when they'd moved far enough from the soldiers. "To make it have the most impact, it needs to be witnessed by an assortment of people."

She ignored the nagging discomfort that had begun to accompany the idea of faking her own death. "Let's make it as soon as possible. I have a second problem we need to solve before the Kalesh get here." She stepped up to the rail. "The first play I ever performed with you was Terrelus's tale, and in that story, long before the middle, we know that Terrelus is destined for a tragic ending."

Atticus frowned at the direction of the conversation, but she continued before he could object.

"Everyone knows he's going to die. Even Lady Argent knows. Her speeches go from reasoned and calm to desperate and pleading. The only person who doesn't recognize that his own destruction is sure is Terrelus himself."

Atticus sank back against the rail. "You are not Terrelus."

Sable smiled at his exasperated tone. "I hope I am smarter and less stubborn than he was."

"You are a thousand times more stubborn."

Her smile widened. "I'll settle for smarter, then. The real tragedy of the rest of the play is that all of Terrelus's loved ones also suffer for his mistakes."

Atticus's eyes narrowed. "What are you asking?"

Sable took a deep breath. "The Kalesh are coming back to get Melia's daughter—but Melia had three daughters."

"Not many people know that."

"True, but the ones who do aren't trustworthy. At some point, everyone will learn I'm Melia's daughter. At that point, I need Talia out of Kiva's reach and Ryah away from Eugessa."

Atticus crossed his arms. "True."

"Purnicious can find them whenever we want. She can't feel Ryah when she's inside the priory, but we still know where she is. My problem is that I have no idea how to get them safe. If I could talk to Ryah, alone, I might be able to convince her to leave the priory or at least get away from Eugessa. Talia, though..." Sable sighed. "It's been a long time since Talia listened to any warning I gave her."

"She doesn't trust Kiva, does she?"

"I don't think so. Not completely, anyway."

"Does she understand the kind of person he is?"

Sable paused. "I hope so. But I think he's careful with her. I think he keeps his more disreputable qualities hidden when she's around. She's in the world of the merchants, where he portrays himself as an upstanding member of the Guild. She knows he's conniving and sneaky, but I don't know if she realizes how brutal he is."

Atticus looked south along the river. "They're both in Immusmala," he mused. "We need to get them out and safely with us in the north."

"Neither Eugessa nor Kiva will just let them go, but stealing them away would bring down the wrath of the priories and Kiva on us, which we don't need."

Atticus scratched at his beard. "Let me think about this for a bit. And talk things over with Serene and Jae. And maybe Flibbet. He's good at puzzles." He turned back to Sable with a slight crease in his brow. "In any case, you're right—they shouldn't be left where they are. Not with what's coming."

Sable nodded. "Thank you."

He set his hand on her shoulder. "Don't thank me yet. I don't have the ghost of a plan for rescuing one of them, never mind both."

There was a commotion at the side of the boat, and a smaller boat pulled up alongside. Soldiers reached over the rail and helped the small, wiry form of Lord Loren climb on board.

Atticus frowned as the larger Lord Darien and the nondescript Lord Erick followed, along with several of their highest-ranking officers.

The three Northern Lords had stayed back from the fighting in Immusmala, leaving Tanis, and eventually Reese, to lead their forces as they'd agreed. Sable had seen them each commandeering their own ships for the trip north but hadn't seen them since.

The lords caught sight of Reese and started toward him.

"I believe General Andreese has some guests," Atticus said.

Sable glanced down at his unmoving form. "If they're here for a conversation, they're going to be disappointed."

"I would guess they're here to take their armies back," Atticus said, not bothering to lower his voice.

Sable turned to look at him. "Are you serious?"

"It's hardly *taking*," Lord Darien said, planting his large frame in front of them. "Tanis was given temporary leadership of our joined forces. The time for that is over."

Lord Erick kept his gaze firmly fixed on Reese. Lord Loren studied the tree, as though trying to decide if it was really glowing.

"We are here to formally relieve General Andreese of duty," Lord Darien said, glancing at Reese. "Clearly that was unnecessary."

"You're honestly here to split up the army?" she asked. "After it finally is unified?"

"Our troops will return to our own territories," Lord Loren said, "to root out the Kalesh invaders."

"Who've been attacking our unprotected homes since you convinced us to bring all our troops south to support that lying, backstabbing prioress," Lord Darien added.

"That's foolish," Sable said. "Don't divide the army. Deploy them in the units they trained in. The men from your territories have learned to fight alongside each other and—"

"The men from our territories," Lord Darien interrupted, "want to defend their own homes. We don't need strangers navigating lands we know by heart."

Sable glared at the men but kept her mouth shut. She was leaving. Whatever happened to the army was out of her hands—*should be* out of the hands of Melia's daughter.

Lord Darien's gaze flicked to her. "No impassioned speech to stop us? No plea to take us off in a direction that will ultimately backfire and lead to massive destruction?"

Leonis stuck his head over Lord Darien's shoulder. "I want to hear an impassioned speech," the half-elf said.

"I don't think you'll get to," Thulan said, walking around the lords and leaning against the boat rail. "This is just squabbling, whiny lords declaring they're taking their toys and going home."

Leonis shouldered his way between Lord Darien and Lord Erick, receiving irritated looks from both, and moved next to Thulan. "That's too bad. Odd that they all came to announce something we already assumed, isn't it?"

Thulan nodded sagely. "If this were a play, the only reason Atticus would have three such esteemed persons appear to say something so predictable and so firmly within their given rights would be if they needed a show of force. If they did not believe the decision truly *was* firmly within their given rights."

Lord Darien and Lord Erick glared at the dwarf, but Lord Loren shifted uncomfortably.

Leonis studied the lords with a mock interest. "By your ancestors' shaggy beards, Thulan," he said, "I believe you're right. Do these men look nervous to you?"

Sable took in the lords' increasingly hostile expressions. "I don't think 'nervous' is the right word."

"Not regular-person-nervous," Leonis answered easily. "Actor-nervous. They don't know if they're acting well enough."

Thulan hummed in agreement. "Makes their anger look a little sickly."

"But what," Leonis said theatrically, without the slightest note of question in his voice, "could three powerful lords possibly be nervous about? Certainly not their plans for their own soldiers."

"Unless," Thulan said, "they're worried the soldiers now belong to the Flame of the North." He nudged Reese's foot with her own. "Or the good general here."

"If you're quite done," Lord Darien said icily, "we didn't come to speak with actors."

"Splitting up the army is a mistake," Sable said flatly. "This is the time to bind the north together, not splinter it—"

"That's not your concern," Lord Darien interrupted. He motioned toward their waiting boat, and the two other lords headed toward it. Lord Darien looked down at Reese before he met Sable's eyes again. "I've seen too many men look like that," he said bluntly. "Don't hope for much. War isn't known for happy endings." He followed the others back toward their boat.

"I didn't think it was possible to dislike that man more than I already did," Sable said, glaring after him.

Atticus turned a tired look at Thulan and Leonis. "There's a reason we don't invite you two to important discussions."

"There's a reason we often don't come," Leonis said. "That was boring, except for our contribution, of course."

Sable looked down the long line of boats rowing laboriously up the river behind them. "They're not really afraid their troops would follow us instead of them, are they?"

"They're very afraid of it," Atticus answered.

"What sort of idiot do they think would attempt a coup right now?" Sable asked, sinking back against the rail.

"Obviously, they think you two are that sort of idiot." Leonis gestured toward Sable and Reese.

Sable glared at the retreating lords.

"Maybe you should be that sort of idiot," Atticus said thoughtfully. "A coup that unifies the troops might be the best possible thing for the north."

"I don't think Reese is up for a coup," Leonis said.

Atticus turned to Sable. "Are you?"

She stared at him. "You think Melia's daughter should not only stand against the Kalesh, but first lead a rebellion against all the lords of the north?"

He shrugged. "I've heard worse ideas."

"I haven't. Your flair for the dramatic is getting the better of you."

The playwright shook his head. "I think we're missing an opportunity here."

Sable sank down and sat next to Reese. "I have no desire to take over the north."

Atticus ran his fingers through his beard, an argumentative set to his shoulders.

"Let it go, Atticus," she said tiredly.

"Fine. Then I'm going to go plan your death." He spun on his heel and stalked away.

"Not words I ever thought I'd hear him tell Sable," Leonis said, heading after Atticus.

"No," Thulan said, following him. "I've always assumed the one he'd kill would be you."

Sable's gaze drifted over to where the Northern Lords had been. The deck was empty of everything but the normal soldiers rowing steadily upstream.

"It was probably better to sleep through that visit," Sable said quietly to Reese. "The Northern Lords are irritating even when you're not wounded and they're not unraveling everything you've worked for." She glanced down at him and paused.

It was hard to tell in the green-tinged light from Leonis's tree, but his cheeks didn't look completely pale.

"Reese?" The word came out tentatively. There was definite color in his face.

She touched his cheek.

His skin was hot.

She pressed her hand to his forehead, then the side of his neck. Every bit of his skin was burning up.

"Purn," she whispered. "Get Serene."

CHAPTER FIVE

Sable's shoulder shifted against the hard wood of the deck, and a cold drop of water rolled onto her neck. She pushed the damp blanket away from her face, shaking the edge of it and spraying tiny drops around the dark bow of the boat.

The oars thunked and splashed rhythmically, as they had for days. The summer weather had been mostly clear for their laborious trip upriver, but each night had been cool, and a thick fog rose off the water before dawn each morning, surrounding the boat with darkness and beading every surface with water.

Sable reached a tentative hand toward Reese. In the hazy light from Leonis's tree, she could barely make out his shape, but she could imagine the feverish flush on his cheeks and the shadows under his eyes.

His skin still burned. Over the past two days, his fever had stayed high. He'd woken fitfully, if at all, speaking little and barely drinking. Serene, Jae, and Sable had taken turns giving his body whatever *vitalle* they could to strengthen him, but he slowly, inexorably, grew weaker.

By all accounts, they should reach Tutella Island near dawn. The Northern Lords had ordered the boat to continue north with the others, but when Reese had grown sick, Sable hadn't even needed to ask before one of the officers informed her they'd stop at the island to let him off, and anyone else who was staying with him.

"The monks will help," she whispered, trying to wrap Reese with the warmth of the words, but she'd repeated them too often, and they came out cold and hollow.

Sable wrapped her blanket around her shoulders and stood, looking over the bow. The light from Leonis's tree barely reached past the bow, and beyond it, the world was a thick, depthless grey. Lanterns along the outside of the hull cast golden light into the nearby fog.

Sable leaned on the rail, peering ahead and willing the island to appear. People stirred on the deck, and Serene joined her, stopping to kneel by Reese.

"Any sign of the island yet?" Serene asked, rising.

Sable shook her head.

They stood in silence until the sun rose and the fog thinned. The shadows solidified into tall pine trees, and Tutella Island emerged in the middle of the river.

"Finally," Serene said, her voice flooded with relief. "I thought we'd never get—"

Distant voices echoed across the water from the island.

"That sounds like women," Sable said. "Are there usually families on the island?"

"I have no idea."

A distinctly feminine voice called something out sharply, and a child's voice answered.

Sable felt Serene cast out. A wave rolled across the cool water and into the trees, turning them into towering pillars of warmth.

Sable closed her eyes to concentrate as the wave rolled farther away. Suddenly, it swept over a cluster of blazing hot shapes. Dozens of them.

Sable opened her eyes. "There are a lot of people on the island."

Serene cast out again, her brow pinched in concentration. This time, the wave rolled out in a single focused path, and when it hit the people, Sable could almost pick out individuals clustered together. Most seemed to be sleeping.

"Wounded," Serene said, without opening her eyes. "Some of them are wounded or very weak."

Sable focused on the end of the wave and realized Serene was right. The bodies on the ground weren't just sleeping. They were dim.

"Wounded soldiers?" Sable asked.

"If there are women and children," Serene answered, "it's more likely refugees."

A dock emerged from the fog, and their boat veered toward it, while the rest of the army continued slowly north.

Sam stood on the pier with several other warrior monks from the island, all dressed in their usual leather armor. "You're a welcome sight," he called. His gaze followed the other boats moving slowly north. "You're all a very welcome sight."

"Reese needs help," Serene said before the boat had reached the dock. "He was wounded in the battle, and a fever started two days ago."

Sam glanced behind him. "Rob?"

An older monk with grey streaks running through his dark hair was already moving forward. "Wounded how?"

"Stabbed by a sword along his side," Serene said. "I cleaned it and closed it, but…he's getting worse."

Despite his age, Rob reached for the boat before it was settled against the dock and swung his legs over the side. He hurried to kneel next to Reese, taking in his sunken eyes and dry, cracked lips and pulling his shirt up to see the wound. Around the puckered line Serene had closed, Reese's skin was red and swollen.

"Get me a stretcher," Rob called. He turned to Serene. "You can't close deep wounds. If an infection starts, it'll have nowhere to go but deeper in." He backed up as two monks loaded Reese onto one of the army's stretchers. "He's had the fever for two days?"

Serene nodded, her own face pale.

Sable stepped closer. "Can you help him?"

Rob glanced at her, then back at Reese. "We'll do what we can," he said and strode after the stretcher.

Sable and Serene followed him, but Sam stopped them on the dock. "Rob won't let anyone but monks into the infirmary while he's working." He frowned. "Not that you'd want to be there. If he cuts Reese open and finds an infection, the smell will be horrific. Best to let monks with strong stomachs deal with this part."

Sable looked after the monks moving quickly up the road. "Will they be able to help?"

Sam was quiet for a moment. "A fever that has run this long is not good. He's weak and dehydrated, and who knows how far the infection has spread. But if it was hopeless, Rob would have told you flat out. He's not one to raise hopes unnecessarily."

"He hardly raised my hopes."

Sam set his hand on Sable's shoulder. "Reese has spent enough time on this island over the past year, he's practically one of us. They'll do everything they can."

"I made it worse…" Serene whispered.

"If it weren't for you, Reese would have died on the battlefield," Sable said.

Serene didn't answer.

Sam nodded. "Battlefield wounds are different from the usual sicknesses or accidents people have. Unless you'd trained as a healer, you wouldn't know the risks." He glanced back toward the river, where the last of the boats were still rowing past. "I think we're going to need all the healers we can get. If anyone wants to learn how to help, Rob can teach you the basics."

Behind them, Atticus maneuvered his wagon toward the gangplank, and Serene and Sam both headed over to offer help.

Sable took a step after Reese. "Purn?" she whispered. "Keep your eye on him. Let me know what's happening."

Purnicious's invisible hand squeezed Sable's, then there was a tiny pop.

Atticus finally rolled the wagon onto the dock, and Flibbet followed with his little handcart. The soldiers pulled the gangplank back on board, and the boat pushed out into the river, continuing north.

Sam started up the path from the river as the last of the fog burned away. They wound uphill until the town of Aedis came into view, its stone wall grey and imposing. A few monks patrolled the top and guarded the single arch leading inside.

From the gate, Sable could see up the winding road into the timber-framed town. The cobblestone street ran between the buildings, little paths branching off toward each front door. She could almost see Narine's bright yellow wagon rolling up it.

Sam paused by the gate. "We have a house you all can stay in while we take care of Reese, but…" He glanced at Atticus's wagon. "If you don't have anything pressing, our orchard is full of refugees and wounded soldiers. They've been through a lot, and a famous theater troupe could do wonders for their morale."

"Serene and I would like to talk to them too," Jae said. "See if we can record what's happened here."

Sable paused, looking into the town, as though she could see where Reese had been taken.

"Someone will come find us the moment they have any news about

Reese," Sam said to her. "I promise."

Purnicious would find her first, but that didn't make the waiting any easier. With a sigh, she started with the others toward the orchard.

Morning shadows lingered in the thicker parts of the forest, and layers of old pine needles, still damp from the fog, crunched with a muted rustling under Sable's feet. The creaks of the wagon were echoed in the fluttery bird calls as Sam led the group deeper into the island toward the orchard.

"What have the Kalesh been doing?" Atticus asked Sam.

"The troops marched by our island on the eastern bank. They hit the town of Brookfield in force, razing it to the ground and slaughtering nearly everyone. Then took every boat from the docks and crossed the river a day south of Steepdale. We sent warnings as soon as we realized what was happening. We went to the cities first and sent out more men from those places to warn the smaller towns.

"But instead of hitting the cities, the Kalesh split into small raiding parties and struck deep into the territories, razing villages and homesteads to the ground, burning fields and slaughtering livestock. The cities themselves are flooded with refugees and quickly running out of supplies.

"The raiding parties are small, and when the local people have had time to prepare, they've stood against them and had some victories, but the Kalesh are fast, and the lack of trained soldiers to defend us has been devastating. The Kalesh played their game well."

"It was Vivaine," Sable said quietly. "She lied to us about Immusmala being in danger. She'd made a deal with General Goll to clear the north of soldiers so he could sweep in with a small force."

Sam gave her a shocked look. "The High Prioress?"

"I don't think she's the High Prioress anymore," Flibbet said from behind them. "Not after Sable and Serene got through with her."

Sam glanced at the two women. "Good."

With the help of Serene and Jae, and despite the added commentary by Leonis and Thulan, Atticus told Sam of the battle in the south.

When they'd finished and the group had fallen into silence again, Sam turned to Sable. "I owe you an apology," the monk said. "I have no good news about our search for the dwarf who started the fire in Narine's house. We tracked him along the river to Revel, a small town on the eastern bank, where he disembarked. It's not terribly far from here, but then we lost his trail. We assume he headed east to Torren, but I have no idea why someone from the dwarven city would kill a prioress."

"There are no dwarves in Torren," Sable said. "Last year, Thulan tried to take us there, but the southern door to the city was blocked by a cave-in. It looked like no dwarves had been there for years."

"Really?" Flibbet asked. "I saw a dwarf near Torren, must have been..." He paused. "Never mind, that was years ago." He sighed. "Why are years so hard to keep track of?"

"I wish I knew," Sam said. "One of our monks who delivers food near the Marsham Cliffs has commented that he hasn't seen any dwarves in a couple of years. The rest of us assumed that was because...they're dwarves, and you don't see many ever." His gaze trailed off into the distance. "I suppose the dwarf from Narine's fire could have gone farther south. We assumed since he headed for the eastern bank of the river that he wasn't going down to Folhaven or Immusmala, but we'll expand our search in that direction."

"Are you sure it was a dwarf?" Sable asked.

"Three witnesses saw him. Stocky, even for a dwarf, with a thick black beard."

"What?" Sable stopped, and Atticus pulled the wagon to a halt.

"The dwarf had a black beard?" Sable asked. Memories of every time she'd stepped in Kiva's office flooded into her mind. Kiva's cunning, vicious face, and the ever-present dark form of Pete in the corner. The burley dwarf with the perpetual scowl and the bushy black beard. "Did he travel with a human?"

Sam nodded. "The innkeeper in Revel saw him leave with a fellow so huge and unsavory that the innkeeper busied himself elsewhere."

Fury at Kiva rushed into Sable, and she turned to Atticus and the others.

"Pete and Boone—a dwarf with a black beard and an enormous man—are Kiva's favorite henchmen." She stared at Atticus. "He was scared to talk to me when I went to see him in Immusmala. He claimed it was because I'd come back at the head of an army, but it felt like more than that. The little scab was afraid I'd found out about Narine!"

"But why would Kiva kill Narine?" Atticus asked.

"Because Eugessa wanted him to," Sable answered. "Or because he's the sort of monster who kills old women." She pointed a finger at the playwright. "Once I'm supposedly dead, the first thing we're doing is getting my sister away from that man."

Atticus nodded grimly. "Agreed."

CHAPTER SIX

SABLE STARTED WALKING FORWARD AGAIN, and Sam fell in beside her.

"You're going to be supposedly dead?" he asked.

Sable winced. "I shouldn't have said that."

"When we failed to protect Narine on our island," Sam said with a small smile, "I swore to you that you have a home here if you ever want it and that we will offer you any help we can provide. That oath is good until your real death. Whatever you have planned, just know that the monks will help you in whatever way we can."

She considered the monk, but it didn't take much to admit that she trusted Sam, and, more than that, Reese knew him well and trusted him. "Have you heard the Kalesh story of the Ghost of the White Wood?"

When Sam shook his head, she told him of A'Melia and the elf Evay, about how Bastian had met them years ago, and how, now that the Empire knew Sable was Melia's daughter and was helping lead a rebellion, they'd track her down no matter where she went.

"Faking your death should stop them," Sam agreed, "but I confess I'm a little sad to see the end of the Flame of the North. I can't remember the last time there was a person who could unify even small parts of the north."

"So am I," Atticus said from behind them.

"But I'm not really that person," Sable pointed out. "I am a figure propped up by Atticus's stories and made impressive by Innov's fire."

"In Immusmala, you negotiated with both Vivaine and the Kalesh general," Atticus said. "Neither of which I was involved in."

Leonis nodded. "And you turned the Kalesh ambassador to our side."

"Inadvertently," Sable said, exasperated. "We've been over this."

"No," Atticus said. "You did all that *naturally*, because you actually are what a rebel leader should be. As is Reese, who took over when Tanis was killed and led the army to defeat the Kalesh."

"Enough, Atticus. I don't want to leave. I'd stay, I'd even play the role of the Flame of the North again if I thought it would help—"

"It has never been a role," Atticus interrupted. "It was just you. All I did was help your voice reach a little further."

"And fix your hair because it usually looks messy," Thulan added. "Like right now."

"Regardless," Sable said loudly, "if the Flame is visible, the Empire will kill everyone who stands between them and me."

Atticus tugged on the end of his beard the way he did during rehearsals when he was trying to figure out what was going wrong in one of his plays. "Maybe there's something we're missing. What we have is a layered audience. That means that there is more than one group of people watching, and they each need a story created for them. The first, most obvious layer is the north, and they already see you as the Flame, and it inspires and unifies them. But the second layer is the Kalesh, who see you as someone to be eradicated before you cause them more harm."

"You make all of this sound so fake, Atticus," Sable said.

"It's not fake. Every day, everything we do, we are telling the world the story of who we are. It may be the only thing we really have control over in our own lives. What story we live. Yes, people can lie. Kiva clearly excels at making people believe he's something he is not. But you are different. All the things you have done have been you being you. I have merely tried to give you enough of a stage that people see it." His brow creased. "But you're right. The north and the Kalesh will perceive your story very differently."

"Since the second layer is the one who's going to come kill me, it feels like I should focus on that one."

Atticus's gaze strayed to the trees around him. "Layered audiences are my favorite kind, and I don't think I've ever had two more adamantly opposed to each other." He looked pointedly at Sable. "Yes, the Kalesh want to kill you, so you should disappear, but staying as the Flame would give the north hope."

"What if I have no hope left to give them?" Sable asked. "Melia died. The Empire tracked her down and killed her. Right in front of me. They killed every single person in our town to get to her. What good is being a rebel leader if the Empire always wins?" The old fears of fire and smoke and death were there at the edges of her mind, no less smothering than they'd always been. "I am out of hope, old man."

Atticus didn't answer immediately. The horse's hoofs clopped dully on the dirt road, the wagon creaking in its familiar way. "Hope isn't something you have," he said finally. "It's something you choose."

She let out an annoyed breath.

"And," he continued, raising one finger, "it's contagious. Just like despair."

Walking next to the wagon, Leonis tilted his head to the side. Thulan shook her head.

"Those two don't work together," Sable said, not bothering to hide her irritation. "You can't both choose it and catch it."

"That doesn't mean they're not both true," Atticus said, undeterred.

Sable sighed. "I know you think you're doing the right thing here, Atticus, but I'm *not* the leader you need."

A murmur of voices came through the trees, and by the time the road wound out of the forest and into the wide, neat rows of an orchard, the air was tinged with a soiled, damp smell that reminded Sable of the poorest alleys in Dockside.

Underneath branches holding small green apples, countless refugees sat or lay, their clothes dirty, their faces weary. Sam greeted them quietly as he walked. Parents with their children and elderly grandparents clustered together, sharing small loaves of bread that Tutella monks handed out and watching the bright blue wagon pass with dull eyes.

Even Leonis and Thulan grew quiet.

Flibbet took one look around the orchard and wheeled his cart into the trees, greeting the people around him with a kind smile.

The rest of them stayed on the road and rolled past a family. A small girl took a step toward a filthy doll lying at the edge of the road, but the wagon moved closer, and she scampered back, shrinking down with terrified eyes.

Leonis squatted and picked up the doll, brushing off some of the dirt and holding it out to her. It took several moments for her to work up the courage to reach out and snatch it away before scrambling back and clutching it to her chest, her eyes still wide with fear.

"How long will all these people have to stay here?" Sable asked Sam.

"Most of them have nothing to go back to. Their homes were burned, their crops, their animals." Sam looked over the orchard. "We don't have the means to support them here, but I'm not sure anywhere else does either."

They started forward again, moving deeper into the large orchard.

"Find a place we can set up," Atticus said to Leonis.

The half-elf climbed up on the wagon bench, then up onto the roof. He stood easily, despite the jolting of the wagon, waving to anyone who would look and peering ahead down the road.

On one side of the road, between the first two rows of apple trees, a line of soldiers was laid out, some with thin blankets beneath them, some with nothing but the ground. Their uniforms were stained with blood and dirt. Monks moved among them, checking bandages or washing wounds. Sable almost choked on the scent of sweat and blood and unwashed bodies.

"Tanis left two units of men at Steepdale," Sam said in a low voice, "when the rest of the north went down to Immusmala. They deployed as soon as we knew we were under attack, but they were vastly outnumbered." He looked along the line of men. "We think only a quarter of them survived."

Sable walked along the line. They were bandaged and bloody, their uniforms torn. Dirt was caked on their shoes and in their hair.

"Issable!"

She looked ahead to see a vaguely familiar man dressed in the grey of Lord Loren's troops. His head was heavily bandaged, but he pushed himself up to sit.

He elbowed the soldier next to him dressed in Lord Darien's dark blue. "Wake up, Tor!"

Tor, whose arm was wrapped tightly across his chest, groaned and opened his eyes, and Sable tried to place his face as well.

"How about we set up here, Leonis?" Atticus said, stopping the wagon before Leonis could answer. "Right where the soldiers will be able to see."

"We heard the news about General Tanis," the first soldier said. "And we heard General Andreese was wounded too." He searched the people around the wagon, looking troubled when he saw that Andreese wasn't among them.

"We heard he was dead, Quem," Tor corrected him.

Quem winced. "Don't say that to *her*."

"Well, you just lied to the Flame of the North," Tor said.

"I'm sorry I woke you," Quem grumbled. "Shut up and go back to sleep."

Their bickering voices brought back a memory of the army camp at Steepdale on a foggy morning.

Sable snapped her fingers. "I remember you two. You were fighting over the bread."

Quem smacked Tor on the shoulder, eliciting a groan of pain. "I told you she'd remember us."

"She remembers how stupid you were," Tor said.

"You were both being fairly stupid, if I remember right," Sable said with a smile. "But, yes, Andreese was wounded. The monks are caring for him." She glanced along the line of soldiers but didn't recognize any of the other people listening. "I didn't expect to meet soldiers I knew here."

"Astonishing coincidence," Atticus agreed cheerfully. "Thulan, Leonis, let's get a small stage set up here." He climbed down off the wagon and took a seat at the edge of the road, near Quem's feet, before glancing up at Sable. "This meeting feels…hopeful, does it not?"

Sable sat also, pointedly ignoring him. "How did you both get here?" she asked the soldiers.

"We weren't sent south with the army," Quem said. "Which we were bitter at for a bit, thinking we'd miss all the fighting. Until the black-masked cowards showed up and started killing women and children."

Tor's expression grew bleak. "Burrowed into the land like worms."

"We tracked 'em down and drove 'em out, though." Quem looked at Sable. "Where do we fight next?"

She shrugged. "The Northern Lords broke up the army and pulled all their troops back to their own territories. I imagine you'll all be sent back to your own lands soon."

"It's a bit late for all that," Quem said. "Flame of the North told us it was time the northern brothers grew up. And we did. Now that we know how strong we are together, they can't pull us back apart."

Tor nodded. "They won't. The Flame is here."

His voice was confident, but Atticus glanced at Sable. "Is she?"

She frowned at the playwright. "I'm done playing roles."

"No roles," he said. "Just be honest with them."

The soldiers to each side of Quem and Tor were awake, listening to the conversation, and Sable took them all in. Despite their curiosity, they were bloody and broken. Most looked like they couldn't stand up, and one past Quem had skin so pale she was surprised he was still breathing.

Their enthusiasm almost kindled a little hope in her, but she focused on their wounds. On the horrible pain they were suffering and the scars they would carry their whole lives.

And this was just from the first skirmish with the Kalesh.

"I recently learned," she said, pouring the truth into her words, pushing it forward so they would hear and believe her, "that my mother was a famous rebel in the Empire. Years ago, she killed the Emperor's brother. A man who, by all accounts, was corrupt and brutal."

Low mutters of approval rippled across the soldiers.

"Excellent job, Issable's mother," Quem said.

"It's just Sable," she said. "My mother's name was Melia. She escaped the Empire and built a life for herself on the Eastern Reaches. Until the Kalesh tracked her down and killed her."

The mutters turned angry.

"Now the Emperor knows I exist and that I helped the north." Sable paused. "They're coming back for me."

"They can't have you," Quem said bluntly.

Sable gave him a weak smile.

"So what are you going to do?" Tor asked.

"I..." She paused. "I think it would be best if the Flame of the North disappeared. You're all risking so much already. I can't have you risk more for me."

Quem's eyes widened, and he held his hands up toward Tor. "Don't start! Not to her!"

But Tor was shaking his head adamantly. "People in charge always think they have this choice."

Quem groaned and gave Sable a defeated look. "I can't believe you said that."

"Said what?"

"I apologize for my friend," Quem said desperately. "He has this thing about—"

"The only thing," Tor interrupted him loudly, "that we all truly have a right to risk is ourselves. People in power always think they have the right to sacrifice the people under them. They think they can send them to do their fighting, or take their crops, or tax their money because it's the leader's right. But none of it is!" He pounded his uninjured fist on his leg along with each word. "It is not about the leader!"

"Tor," Quem said, a note of pleading in his voice.

"The only person"—Tor pointed directly at Sable—"who has the right to risk my life is me."

His words were warm with the truth.

"I decide if I'll join an army," he continued. "I decide if I'll fight in a battle. I decide if I'll send money or crops to some lord who may or may not need them. Yes, there might be consequences if I choose not to, but *I* decide, not you." He held her gaze without any apology in his expression. "So I'm afraid it's not your choice whether we risk ourselves or not, Issable."

"Sable," she said quietly.

He shook his head. "It's not your choice, Sable. I will fight the Kalesh to keep my home safe. You're part of the north, so I'll fight to keep you safe too." He shrugged. "Even the Flame of the North doesn't get to decide this for me."

There was a moment of silence.

Atticus grinned at Tor. "I like you."

"We're not stupid," Quem said. "We know the Empire could wipe us out, and if an enemy capable of that merely gives us a hard shove, like they did, they weren't trying to beat us. They were trying to feel us out, see what sort of fight we have in us. See who'd shove back." He gave Sable a pointed look. "And who'd run."

Sable crossed her arms. "I'm not running."

He raised a hand. "You got your reasons. If the Empire was coming for me specifically, I might run too. But you can ask any soldier of the north whether they'd rather you left or stayed. Even knowing what staying means, everyone will tell you the same thing *you* told *us*. We're stronger together. Even the Flame of the North is stronger if she's with the rest of us."

"I can't fight, though," Sable said. "I don't know anything about military strategy, and I've given you the only speech I really know."

Tor shrugged. "If every soldier decided he didn't have enough to offer and left, we wouldn't have much of an army. You just gotta decide whether what we're doing is important enough for you to risk what you have to fight with us."

Sable looked between the two soldiers. "If I'd known you would team up this effectively against me, I'd have let you keep arguing over that loaf of muddy bread."

"So?" Atticus said to her. "Is the Flame of the North going to stay here? Or do I still have…plans to make?"

Sable kept her eyes on the soldiers. "You know I'm not from the north. I was born on the Reaches, and I spent more years in Immusmala than I'd like to think about. But that city never felt like home." Her gaze strayed to the pine trees and the deep blue sky. The breeze moved past her, wild and free, even though it was tainted with the bloody scent of wounded men. "I haven't even seen the north in a time of peace. Every day I've spent here has been contaminated with war, but it still feels like home." She looked back at Tor. "You're right. I do think what you're doing is worth risking everything I have for."

Atticus gave a smug chuckle.

"Shut up, old man," Sable said.

He just grinned at her.

Tor lifted his face and called out, "Sable, Flame of the North!"

The soldiers around him echoed with cheers.

"Issable sounds better," Atticus said. "It was excellent to meet you, Quem and Tor." He stood and gave the men a bow. "I'm indebted to you."

"You can repay us with shows," Quem said. "We're bored out of our minds."

"The best shows you've ever seen," Atticus promised. "I had been tasked with writing a new play"—he gave Sable a pointed look—"but that seems to be unnecessary now, so I am at your disposal."

Sable climbed to her feet and looked at the two men. "I haven't seen a lot that's given me hope lately, but the fact that you two got over your bread quarrels and turned into this"—she gestured at the two of them—"feels very hopeful. Please take care of yourselves and each other. The north needs men like you."

Quem set his fist to his chest in a salute and grinned up at her. "It'll take more than a couple dings to stop the north, Sable."

She smiled at the name. "Good."

This will be the greatest play ever written." Atticus glanced at Thulan. "How will we ever show dragon fire and a phoenix?"

CHAPTER SEVEN

THE MAIN ROOM of the house Sam had given them lay mostly in darkness, held back only by a single candle and Innov's glow. Sable sat at the table, jotting down the entire story of what she'd done in Immusmala. Everyone else was still in the orchard, the troupe entertaining refugees and soldiers with plays or songs, Serene gathering the stories of what the north had been through over the past few weeks, Jae entertaining them all with tales.

The room was gloriously quiet, only occasionally broken by the sounds of people passing outside. This house sat far from the main square of the town, blocks away from the home Narine had stayed in, but it had the same homey feel to it. Almost homey enough to let Sable relax.

She glanced at the front door for the hundredth time, but it stayed quiet and closed.

Purn had brought her several quick updates, but Rob had found her near lunchtime to report that they'd opened Reese's wound and cleaned out the infection but that he was keeping Reese in the infirmary for the rest of the day.

"Is he going to recover?" Sable had asked.

Rob had met her gaze, said, "He hasn't died yet. That's not nothing," and walked away.

Purnicious hadn't been much more help, but she came whenever Sable called to report things like "He's still sleeping and still feverish," or "The wound doesn't smell like something crawled inside him and died anymore."

It felt like "the rest of the day" should be over by now, but there was still no sign of Reese.

Sable tapped her quill on the table, then refocused on her notes. According to Atticus, the way to make the Flame of the North useful again was to spread the story of what had happened in Immusmala. From his expression every time he talked to her, he was already composing the stories in his head.

"Do you think writing all this out will keep Atticus from taking liberties?" Sable asked, underlining the detail of how when Argyros's fire had shot at her, Sable had done nothing but stand there and wait to die.

Innov gave no indication she was listening.

"I don't either."

Sable was halfway through writing out the entire series of events when a small pop next to her chair made her jump. Purnicious appeared out of thin air, and Sable dropped the quill.

"They're bringing him." The kobold's voice wasn't cheerful, and her forehead crinkled in a frown. "Don't expect him to look any better. If anything, he looks worse."

"But they helped?"

Purn's brow creased further. "I don't know. The healers sound...not hopeful, exactly. But not as grim as they first did. They were getting him situated on a stretcher when I left."

Sable set the quill and papers aside and rose, lighting more candles around the room. She paced from the window to the door and back enough times to wear a groove in the floor before they finally brought him.

Rob and another healer carried the stretcher, and Sable led them to a small room in the back of the house with a bed and a comfortable chair.

Reese did look worse than before. The healers had removed his shirt, and a new bandage was wrapped around his ribs, although not particularly tight. His skin was ghostly white, but worse than that, he looked thin. His neck was thin, his shoulders, his arms. Along the bottom of the bandage, she could see each rib.

The monks settled him in the bed, and Sable set her hand on his forehead. "He's still so hot."

"He will be for at least another day," Rob answered, standing next to her.

A strange scent wafted up. Sweet but tinged with something sharper.

Sable leaned closer to the bandage. "Why does he smell like spicy honey?"

"Because his wound is still open and packed with some cloths soaked in a number of things, including herbs and honey. I'll send someone every morning to change the cloths and check on the wound."

"For how long?"

Rob paused. "As long as the wound needs to heal, which might be a long time. If you'd brought him here even half a day later, I'd have said he'd have no chance, but we may have caught it in time. Hopefully his body will fight off the last of the infection over the next day or two and the fever will drop. If so, he'll be on the way to improving. But it will be slow."

"And if not?"

Rob shook his head. "Let's not worry about that unless we have to. What he needs is rest and water. More rest than he's going to want and more water than you can probably get him to drink, but if you want him to improve, focus on those two things."

Sable nodded.

Rob pulled the chair over next to the bed so she could sit near Reese's head. "I've always liked Reese," he said, "and respect him enough that I'm not going to lie to you. He is the sickest soldier I have on this island, and I have done all I can. Now we have nothing to do but wait, which feels like the worst part to live through, but I assure you it is not. If we are waiting, there is still room for hope." He glanced into the front room, where Innov perched on the back of a chair. "But from what I've heard of you, hope is something you are good at."

Sable let out a breath that was too defeated to be a laugh. "I'm better at offering that to other people than to myself."

"It's terrifying to hope for something that could be torn away at any moment." His words moved warmly through the room. "All the more terrifying because things are torn away. Every day. For no discernible reason. All we are really left with is the choice to hope or to despair. But despair feels like surrendering to death before the fight has been fought." He looked up at Sable. There were streaks of grey through his eyebrows and his short-cropped beard, and the crease between his brow was deeply carved, as though it often sat in this troubled expression. But his eyes held a fierceness and a stubbornness that she recognized. "I don't like to surrender."

Sable gave him a small smile. "Neither do I."

"Good." He set a hand on her shoulder as he turned to leave. "Then we will hope while we can."

Sable's hope almost ran out before the fever broke two days later. Even then, the only real change she could see was that Reese slept with cool skin instead of hot.

The following day, Sable sat in the chair next to his bed, her feet propped up on the edge of his mattress, reading over an account Serene had written about the burning of the books in the Sanctuary. A small stack of paper sat on the table near the door, waiting for her to look through it and tell Atticus if there were any errors from her point of view.

"Sable?" Reese's voice rasped.

Sable dropped her feet and tossed the paper on the table, grabbing his arm. "Reese! How are you? How do you feel?"

He shifted and groaned. "I…hurt." His eyes traveled around the room. "Are we in Aedis?"

"Yes." Sable pulled a cup off the table. "Drink this. They put wartroot in the water, and it should help with the pain." She helped him lift his head, and he took a long drink.

His head dropped back onto the bed. "How long have we been here?"

"Today's our fourth day."

His brow clouded slightly. "The last thing I remember was…a boat." He thought for a moment, then squinted at her. "Did I call you plain?"

His voice was low and scratchy, his eyes blinked slowly, and his skin was still far too pale, but each word felt like water dripping onto some part of her that had grown dry and parched. She grinned at him. "With a great deal of warmth."

He smiled back. It was a thin shadow of his real smile, but the sight loosened something inside her.

"You weren't plain," he said slowly. "Innov was just fiery behind you, and you were…"

She still held the cup, but she wrapped her other hand around his. "Plain?"

He let out a breath that could almost have been a laugh. "Something like that." His eyes slid closed, and his fingers twitched against her hand.

"For a while there," she said, "I thought those were going to be the last words you ever said."

He opened his mouth but seemed to lose energy to talk before any words came out.

"See if you can drink a little more." She shimmied her hand under his head, but when she lifted it, it lolled to the side. "Reese?"

His only answer was a long, shallow breath. She let his head down slowly and set the cup back on the table. Leaning over him, she slid her fingers into his beard, feeling the rough hairs and the smoothness of his cheek. She set her forehead against his, the warmth of his breath brushing against her lips. "You can call me plain any time you want, Reese," she whispered quietly. "Just keep waking up to say it."

Later that afternoon, as Sable and Atticus rehashed the parts of the battle Sable had seen from the walls of Immusmala while Serene took detailed notes, Sam came to their door.

"A delegation from Lord Perric and Lord Runess arrived," he said, addressing Atticus and Sable. "I'd love Reese to brief them on what happened in the south, but I'm guessing he isn't up for talking. Could you two come?"

Atticus stood. "Are those two lords finally going to join the rest of the north?"

"They seem to at least be joining forces with each other," Sam said. "This is a step in the right direction."

Sable glanced into the back room, where Thulan sat near Reese, her feet propped up on the edge of his bed and her head tilted back as though she were napping.

"He's still sleeping," the dwarf said without opening her eyes. "Still boring. Go get some fresh air. I can force water into him if he wakes as well as you can."

"Probably better," Leonis said from where he lounged on a long padded bench. "You're not nearly as nice as Sable."

"True," Thulan admitted.

Sable and Atticus followed Sam outside and back down to the orchard, where a few army tents had been set up in the far corner.

"Perric and Runess have combined their forces," Sam said. "Which, if the other three lords are still unified, would mean we've moved from five separate factions to two."

"That's a surprisingly positive move," Sable said.

"As soon as Kalesh troops came north and started to attack the other three lords, Perric and Runess sent troops out of their own territories to help defend the north." He moved toward one tent and ducked inside.

The tent held a half-dozen soldiers and several tables covered with papers and maps.

"So if we can convince Darien, Loren, and Erick to reunite," Sable said, "and if we get some help from the south, maybe we can mount an actual defense against the Kalesh when they come back."

"The north can take care of itself," a man said. "We're hardly new to the idea of war."

The speaker was a man with close-cropped dark hair and a square, severe jaw. His uniform was charcoal colored, and he leaned on a table. A touch of grey dusted his temples.

"This is General Braddick of Ravenwick," Sam said. "He's one of several men leading Lord Perric's and Lord Runess's troops."

Sable looked at the man with more interest. "Reese is from Ravenwick."

"He was," Braddick said lightly. "Until he deserted."

Sable crossed her arms, and Atticus's expression lost its polite edge.

"He didn't desert," Sable said. "He left Lord Runess's army because he got tired of killing his neighbors just so Runess could get more power and land."

Braddick studied Atticus and Sable, clearly unimpressed. "The famed playwright I recognize, which means you must be Issable, Flame of the North." He made the name sound cheap and theatrical.

"Just Sable," she told him, trying to keep the irritation out of her voice.

"At some point, you're going to get tired of correcting that." Rabbit's voice came from the corner of the tent. "Although...no, you'll still probably feel the need to for a while."

Sable turned to find the man sitting against the tent wall, a pile of tiny rolled papers stacked in front of him. "Hello, Rabbit. What are you talking about?"

"Your new title."

Sable glanced at Atticus, who looked as lost as she did.

"It's so nice to be back somewhere we can get information." Rabbit picked up three little rolls. "Especially when it contains interesting tidbits like the fact that people are now calling you Issable, Queen of the North."

Any soldiers in the tent who hadn't been obviously listening stopped now and faced Rabbit.

"That's…ridiculous." Sable glanced at the people around her, seeing emotions varying from amusement to shock. Braddick gave her a flat look laced with a healthy dose of contempt. She turned back to Rabbit, several objections vying for the right to be said first, so she started with the most obvious. "There is no 'North.'"

"True," Rabbit said, "and yet the title has spread among the soldiers who know you. And I'd imagine they're spreading it among the refugees and everywhere else they're headed. Cities, villages, homes." He gave a small smile. "There is a bit of restlessness going on in the troops now that you're not with them anymore. I'm not saying they'd rather have you than their own lords, but…"

Sable spun toward Atticus. "Are you responsible for this?"

The playwright grinned at her. "No, but I love it."

"Flame is one thing," Sable said, "but I'm not a queen."

"No," Braddick said. "You are not."

"And yet"—Rabbit held up the scrolls—"the name is spreading."

Sable shook her head. "That makes no sense."

Rabbit shrugged. "People love a symbol."

Braddick's eyes shifted among them, as though trying to gauge if they were serious. "It doesn't matter who the commoners are infatuated with. The Northern Lords are not impressed with any of you."

"Well, if the *Northern Lords* aren't impressed," Atticus said blandly, "then we must not have done anything impressive."

Sable smiled.

"I was hoping to speak to someone with even a hint of military background," Braddick said. "Lords Perric and Runess would like to know how it is that three of the north's armies were drawn south, leaving half the north vulnerable to an attack. I understand it was General Tanis's decision, but I always thought the man was too shrewd to fall for such a ploy."

"The south had called for help," Sable said, "and we answered."

"The south sent out a false call for help," Braddick said, "and you fell for it."

"The city of Immusmala was threatened," Sable said. "As a general, you can't see the strategic military value of the only port city on the southern coast? You think that's something that won't affect the north if it falls into the hands of the Kalesh? Are you so small-minded you can't see past the tiny borders of your own land?"

Atticus set his hand on her arm. "You've had a tiring few days. Why don't you let me give our report, Your Highness."

Sable yanked her arm away, giving him an incredulous look.

He merely smiled at her. "Insulting the general might not be the best route forward."

"You are more than welcome to talk to him," Sable said. "If anyone can get a blind audience to actually see the truth, it's you."

"Actually, on most days, it's you," he said. "But even queens have off days."

"That's not funny, Atticus."

He grinned, but she turned and strode out of the tent.

Rabbit's voice came from inside. "I thought it was funny."

CHAPTER EIGHT

WARM AIR SWIRLED in the open door, fluttering the paper in Sable's hand.

The edges of a small stack on the table lifted, and Serene moved her inkwell on top of it before it could blow away. "How did Innov get out of the Phoenix Priory when the dragon tried to kill you?" she asked.

Sable looked over from the recounting of how the army had originally been formed in Steepdale. "Pixy, I think. I saw her standing at a broken window afterwards. I didn't see Innov until she was flying in front of me, though."

"I'll ask Flibbet if he saw it," Atticus said from where he sat at a different table with papers spread across it.

Mid-morning sunlight streamed in the door and reflected off the smooth wooden planks of the floor, painting the room in a homey light. Serene no longer looked exhausted, nor did Jae. Thulan and Leonis sat on a bench along one wall, leaning over the outline of a play, discussing staging ideas.

In the five days since they'd reached the island, the group had split their time between entertaining the refugees and wounded soldiers, and recording and organizing written records of recent events. Reese had spent his time sleeping, waking barely long enough to sit up and eat something before falling asleep again.

At whatever point Reese was able to travel, Atticus wanted to be ready with new stories and hopefully a new play featuring the Flame of the

North and the brave exploits of the northern army. His plan for how to unify the north again with these tales was sketchy at best. But since Sable didn't have any better idea of how to go about it, she turned her attention back to reviewing the facts in this latest story.

A shadow fell across the sunlight, and Sam stopped in the open door. He glanced around at the room. "Reese isn't up and about yet, is he?"

Sable shook her head. "He sat up a few times, but that's it."

Sam gave a disappointed hum. "Some soldiers from Lord Loren's territory arrived this morning, and they have six Kalesh prisoners. I was hoping Reese could question them. As far as we can tell, they only speak Kalesh."

"Serene and Jae speak it, too," Atticus offered. "They could question the prisoners."

Sam glance at them. "Would you?"

"We could try," Jae began.

"Kalesh prisoners won't talk," Reese said quietly from the back of the room.

Sable spun in her chair to find him standing in the doorway, holding on to the doorframe for support. She pushed herself up and crossed the room.

"You're standing!" Leonis said. "I was beginning to think things like moving yourself around were firmly in your past."

Sable set her hand on his arm, which felt thinner than before. His face looked thinner too, and his neck. He wavered slightly on his feet, and she ducked under one of his arms. "Come sit," she said, leading him toward the bench and waving Leonis's legs out of the way.

The half-elf made room for them both.

"Serene can probably convince the prisoners to talk," Thulan said.

Reese shook his head. "They have strict training on what to do if they're captured. If they're questioned, they'll lie." He looked at Sam. "What are they like?"

"Wearing the usual black uniforms. Most of them appear to be common soldiers. The last one is…different. He killed three men before he was captured. He's definitely more dangerous." Sam leaned back against the wall by the door and crossed his arms. "How sure are you we won't get anything out of them?"

"Very sure. With Sable's help, we might be able to piece together some of what's true, but mostly they'll just tell us lies. They already have their stories ready in case they're captured."

"It's too bad Gwen isn't here," Sable said.

"Vivaine's Mira?" Sam asked.

"She left Vivaine," Sable said, "and she can read your mind if she touches you."

Sam's eyebrows shot up. "That's...impressive."

Gwen and Terrane and a good number of the other people who had originally been in Tanis's rebellion had been on other boats moving up the river and were, by now, spread out across the north.

Sable glanced at Reese. There was another person who could talk to the soldiers, someone who might convince them to talk freely. He was pale enough, though, that she dismissed the idea.

He caught her eye. "I have an idea."

"If you're talking about the same idea I just had," she said, "it's a bad one. You could barely walk across the room with my help."

"I wouldn't have to walk anywhere," Reese pointed out.

"What are you talking about?" Sam asked.

"Reese wants to be dressed like a Kalesh soldier and be put in the same cell as them," Sable said. "Which is out of the question."

Sam considered the idea. "You're right—you wouldn't have to walk anywhere. It's hardly unusual to transport wounded prisoners on a wagon."

Atticus's face lit up. "This is a brilliant idea. They'll talk to you if they think you're one of them."

"You've perfected the exhausted, wounded, beaten-down soldier look," Thulan said.

"They *may* talk to me," Reese said, ignoring Thulan, "if I have a Kalesh uniform. The bigger problem is that if I were a Kalesh soldier, I'd already know the information they know. I can't ask a stupid question like 'What are we planning to attack next?'"

"But," Atticus said with a mischievous gleam in his eye, "if they were encouraged to talk, they might let good information slip. If, perhaps, someone else was there with you. Someone people are generally inclined to talk to anyway..."

"You want to be there too?" Reese asked. "Why would we capture an old playwright?"

Atticus shrugged. "Say I'm a Kalesh sympathizer. Say I was caught harboring you, trying to keep you safe from these wild heathens who don't understand the greatness of the Empire. Tell them whatever you want. If I'm there, they'll be more likely to talk. It doesn't even matter that I won't understand them. They'll just want to talk."

Sam looked speculatively at Atticus. "So it's not just me who tells you more than I mean to?"

Atticus gave him a bright smile.

"No, it's not just you," Reese said. "Atticus is magical." He glanced around the room. "Half the people in here are. Sometimes it's useful. Usually it's just mildly unsettling."

"Usually," Serene said, "it's not a topic we discuss with people."

"It's Sam." Reese waved off her words. "He needs to know what sort of weapons he has to work with."

"I'm a weapon?" Atticus asked mildly.

"In a war, everyone's a weapon. Some people are just more dangerous than others. I've trained to fight for most of my life, but among this group, I'm mediocre at best. You, Atticus, are..." Reese shook his head. "Give you the right people and the right stage, and you could take down an entire city yourself."

Atticus smiled proudly. "That's because there's more power in stories than swords. All you warrior folk try to run in and stab people right away, but a few well-placed stories could change everything if you just gave them a little time."

"I'd take Serene over Atticus," Thulan said to Leonis. "If we're picking weapons."

"Absolutely," the half-elf agreed. "Enormous fires beat either stories or swords."

"We don't need to destroy a city at the moment," Sam said, "but it's painfully clear we're unaware of what the Empire is planning, and I'd like to find out what they know sooner rather than later."

Reese nodded. "I have no magic, but I'm up for a little talking."

"Excellent," Atticus said.

"This is a terrible idea," Sable said. "Rob made it very clear that Reese is supposed to rest. This is the opposite of resting."

"You think it's a good idea," Reese said, nudging his shoulder against hers. "You're just worried about me."

"Yes, I'm worried! You were practically dead for days, and now you want to go into a cell with men who will make you actually dead if they figure out you're not one of them."

"They won't figure it out," Atticus assured them.

"It wouldn't be hard to get Reese and Atticus looking suitably captured," Thulan said. "Where are the prisoners kept?"

"In the chicken coop," Sam answered.

A roomful of confused looks turned to him.

"They have foxes on the island," Reese said. "Very persistent and resourceful foxes. This isn't your average chicken coop."

Sable walked next to the wagon carrying Reese as it rolled into the orchard. It was a small mule-drawn cart that looked like it was used to carrying vegetables from the garden instead of wounded soldiers. Reese lay on his back, his feet dangling off the end.

"Stop looking so worried," he said, grimacing when the wagon hit a bump in the road.

"I've been convinced you were dying for days. I reserve the right to worry as much as I want." Sable looked up at Sam, sitting in the small driver's bench. "You won't leave him in the coop long, right?"

"No. And we'll have plenty of people close by." Sam led them to the little group of tents they'd met Braddick in. A slowly growing group of northern officers was gathering and comparing notes on what had happened in the area as wounded soldiers continued to trickle onto the island.

An officer Sable recognized vaguely from Steepdale came out of the largest tent.

"We're in need of a Kalesh uniform," Sam said. "One that will fit Andreese."

"None of them are in good shape," the officer said.

"Good," Sam said, climbing down from the wagon. "Give him a worn one and make a big rip across the chest. Let's get him looking like a wounded, captured Kalesh prisoner." He ducked into the tent.

One of the soldiers motioned toward a smaller tent. "This way, General."

Reese climbed slowly down from the wagon. "It's not General anymore." He stood with one hand balancing on the back of the cart for a moment before following the soldier toward a nearby tent.

Leonis pulled his worried look away from Reese and focused on the officer helping them. "Can you make Atticus look like he's been captured and had a rough time of it?"

The officer paused at the odd request but nodded. "He's too clean." He motioned to another soldier. "Take him back to the creek and muddy him up a bit."

Reese returned dressed in the black uniform of a Kalesh soldier and scowling. His tunic was black and torn across the front, showing what looked like the edge of a dingy white bandage. He wore black pants, and Sable's eyes lingered on the boots that were wrapped up to near his knees with leather straps.

He sank down on the back of the cart. "I hate this uniform."

His collar was twisted, and she reached up to fix it, but her fingers hesitated just a breath before touching it. "Just a costume," she said, though the words didn't sound particularly reassuring.

He nodded, but his expression didn't clear.

Serene came up next to them. "I agree with Sable that this is a bad idea. You should be resting, but since you seem to be stubbornly determined…" She set her hand on his shoulder, and Sable felt some warmth move from Serene into Reese.

Reese let out an appreciative breath. "Thank you."

Moments later, Atticus came back, so dirty Sable almost didn't recognize him. His tunic, which had been a light cream color, was mottled with several different browns, and one sleeve was torn. His blue pants were frayed at the knee and the hems covered in mud. His normally wavy white hair was clumped with dirt on one side, his beard smeared with a little more.

He rubbed his hands together, grinning. "It's been ages since I played anyone this filthy. Let's go trick some Kalesh soldiers."

Sam came back outside along with two other monks. Behind him, Braddick stopped in the open flap of the tent, his arms crossed.

"You don't look like you could carry a coherent conversation in your own language," Braddick said to Reese, "never mind a foreign one."

Reese looked up with an irritated expression, but when he saw who it was, he tensed.

"I thought this was a bad idea when Sam brought it up," the general continued, "but now that I see you, I'm putting a stop to it. I don't need the prisoners killing another man from the north."

"It's been a lot of years since I answered to you, Braddick. I don't need your permission to do this or anything."

"No, but you're stupid not to listen to me." The general turned to go back into the tent but paused and glanced at Reese over his shoulder.

"Best not get into a fight in there. You're easy to take down when you're *not* mostly dead."

Reese glared after the man as he disappeared into the tent.

Serene dropped her hand from Reese's shoulder, and he straightened, his face holding a little more color.

Sam stood looking at Reese. "Are you sure you want to—"

"Let's go, Sam," Reese said.

The monk paused, then nodded. "The coop is in the garden. It isn't far." He motioned for one of the other monks to climb into the driver's seat.

Sable sat next to Reese on the back of the wagon as it started off again. She took his hand and began to funnel *vitalle* into him.

He leaned his shoulder against hers. "Thank you. Between you and Serene, I'm starting to feel almost human."

"'Almost human' isn't the same thing as 'up for facing Kalesh soldiers,'" she said. "So please be careful."

He squeezed her hand, but the motion was weak.

"So," Thulan said from the side of the wagon. "You and Braddick seem fond of each other."

Reese looked back at the tent. "Braddick's one of Lord Runess's captains. Everything he does is to gain Lord Runess, and himself, more power."

"He seems well respected," Jae said.

"The north respects ruthless men who help their territory grow." The wagon rolled into the trees, and the tent was lost from sight. Reese leaned against the side of the cart. "It doesn't hurt that he's also been the Harvest Moon champion for as long as I can remember."

"What does that mean?" Sable asked.

"The Harvest Moon," Thulan said, "is the biggest festival in the north. The territories gather each fall and bludgeon each other in civilized, controlled combat instead of in endless real skirmishes."

"Essentially," Reese agreed. "It's along the Black River at Barrowford. Each territory brings their best fighters, archers, horsemen. There are all sorts of competitions, but the sword fighting is what people come for, and Braddick wins every time."

"We've seen him fight more than once," Leonis said. "No one's come close to beating him. Takes a bit of the fun out of the contest, really. Most of the betting is over who'll take second."

"Did you ever fight him?" Thulan asked Reese.

"Twice. Once we were matched in an early round during the Harvest Moon. We already didn't get along, and he didn't even bother to use his sword. Just swept my feet out from under me and pinned me within a few seconds of starting."

"So you decided to fight him again?" Leonis asked.

"The second time was under more personal circumstances," Reese said grimly. "Which is when I learned that I still didn't know how to block his leg sweep."

"Plan on fighting him a third time?" Leonis asked. "Because it sounds fun to watch you get knocked down."

"I'd planned on never seeing him again," Reese said.

Sam held up his hand to stop the wagon when glimpses of a wide clearing became visible between the trees. A thick row of bushes sat between them and the garden, and Sable hopped down and moved closer to it until she could see through the branches to neatly planted rows of greenery. Several monks worked among them like Narine's abbesses had in the priory garden.

Unlike the wounded soldiers and the refugees, whose pain had made her want to run, the garden called to her. She wanted to go kneel by a monk the way she'd knelt by her mother when she was young. Do simple, straightforward work. Push aside the leaves to find ripe melons, search out the weeds that always found their way in, uproot them and toss them aside.

"That's a chicken coop?" Thulan asked, and Sable pulled her eyes away from the garden.

At the far side of the clearing stood a wooden enclosure twice her height. The walls were made of thick wooden posts set a few finger-widths apart. The tops of the beams bent outward and were sharpened like the battlement of a great fort. Bits of glass were set into the wood, broken edges glittering in the morning light. The ground around the base of the wall was covered with large rocks, and the door was barred with a heavy wooden beam.

Four monks stood guard at the corners of the coop.

"Those must be some foxes," Leonis said.

Sam shook his head ruefully. "They're the smartest animals I've ever seen. We're in a constant war with them."

Sable caught sight of black figures between the posts.

"Where are the chickens if the Kalesh are in the coop?" Thulan asked.

"Running amuck in Aedis," Sam said. "We've already seen two foxes scoping out the wall to the town."

Atticus climbed up on the wagon next to Reese.

Sam tied their hands. "I don't think any of the prisoners speak our language, but be careful what you say no matter which language you're speaking."

Atticus looked indignant. "We'd hardly cast off our roles so easily. Do you think we're amateurs?" He looked at Reese. "You're an amateur. No coming out of character. We are on stage as of this moment. And on stage, we do not break character."

"It has nothing to do with breaking character," Reese said. "I'm not stupid enough to give myself away when I'm trapped, unarmed and weak, with Kalesh soldiers."

Atticus rolled his neck and let out a breath. His shoulders slumped, and his face slackened into an expression of defeat.

Reese gave her a nod and a tight smile. "Let's get this over with."

CHAPTER NINE

SABLE WATCHED from the trees as the two monks drove Reese and Atticus to the coop, then pulled them out of the wagon and toward the door.

"Let's find somewhere closer," Serene said. "If the Kalesh figure out what is happening, Atticus cannot protect himself, and Reese can barely walk."

"I'm coming, and you can interpret what they're saying." Sable nodded toward the garden. "That row of crops closest to the coop looks like it needs some attention, don't you think?"

"I do," Serene answered.

"Dwarves are not cut out to be gardeners," Thulan said. "Let's find somewhere in the trees to watch from," she said to Leonis.

"Elves garden," the half-elf protested. "Plants like me."

"I'll show you where," Sam said. "We'll circle around and listen from the tree line behind the coop." He glanced at Jae. "Care to come interpret for us?"

Jae gave Serene a worried look. "Be careful. Don't do anything…dangerous."

She patted his arm. "Wouldn't dream of it, dear."

Sam headed into the woods, followed by Thulan, Leonis, and Jae.

Sable moved around the bushes and walked into the clearing, pausing to pick up a wide basket. She walked down the row of vegetables that ended a half-dozen paces from the left side of the coop and knelt by the last plant, facing the prisoners. There were enough slats between the posts that the Kalesh were easily visible.

Serene knelt next to her as the monks finished untying the hands of Atticus and Reese and left them in the coop, barring the door behind them.

The Kalesh soldiers were still dressed in their black uniforms, but their masks were gone. They sat with their backs to the walls of the coop. One of them, though, was separated from the others, as though they were giving him a wide berth.

One of the other soldiers muttered something.

"The barbarians are imprisoning old men now?" Serene interpreted, keeping her voice low and her eyes turned toward the plants.

Reese nodded and leaned against the wall nearest Sable. Kalesh words rolled off his tongue.

"He said 'Only those who have the decency to help us,'" Serene said quietly. She ducked her head to hide a smile. "Reese introduced Atticus as Atty."

Sable grinned at her. "I think we should make that stick."

"What are you telling them, boy?" Atticus asked loudly, sitting along the front wall so Sable could see his side.

"Just your name, Atty," Reese said.

Atticus frowned but didn't answer.

"They are surprised such a frail old man was captured," Reese continued.

"Frail?" Atticus asked.

A series of dark, suspicious mutters came from the Kalesh.

Serene's brow creased. "They're wondering how Reese speaks our language," she said quietly.

Reese sank down heavily until he sat propped up against the wall with his back to Sable. He tossed off some words in Kalesh.

Serene looked vaguely amused. "He told them he's been here for over a year, stationed on the Eastern Reaches. He met a woman in the town they seized. Dark-haired. Had an interesting pet bird." She listened for a moment. "One agreed that a woman was the only reason to learn such an ugly language."

As Reese talked, his voice grew angry again.

"He's telling them that Atty was protecting him," Serene said, "and caring for his wounds when the men from the north found him. They took Atticus prisoner, declaring him a Kalesh sympathizer."

There was a general murmur of disgust.

A blond Kalesh man spoke again.

"The rest of the men are newly arrived." She summarized the conversation of the Kalesh as they discussed travels and their forced march north.

Sable focused on the plants in front of her. She pushed aside the wide green leaves to find finger-length dark green squash growing. The earth under the plants was soft and dark but dotted with a jagged, skinny-leafed weed. She pulled one, and the leaves came off in her hand, but the stem stayed anchored in the ground.

She grabbed for the stalk and found it surprisingly hard to pull. When it finally slid out, there was a long, thick root dangling below it.

She tossed it into the basket and moved to the next as she listened to Serene tell her the soldiers' words. They spoke of nothing momentous. How long and cramped the journey had been from the Empire, crowded into ships. How bad food was on the march north.

Sable grabbed the next weed tightly, a growing irritation making her pull it hard. For such a tiny plant, it was unreasonably difficult to uproot. The leaves tore again, but the root stayed lodged in the dirt. She tossed the leaves into the basket with a huff of irritation, and Serene glanced at her.

"We don't really have to weed," Serene said quietly.

Sable sank back on her heels, keeping her eyes fixed on the weed. Inside the monks' prison, the Kalesh soldiers talked in low voices. Even without understanding their words, their tone was familiar. "They sound like our troops."

Serene nodded. "Except that one."

The quiet soldier sat in the far corner of the coop, his arms folded across his chest. He watched Reese and Atticus with an emotionless expression.

"The rest sound guarded," Serene said. "They don't trust Reese."

"Are all these men from the Empire?" Atticus asked, his voice awed. "Ask them if they've ever met the Emperor."

Reese glanced at him. "None of these men have met the Emperor, Atty."

Atticus nudged Reese's foot with barely contained enthusiasm. "Maybe they have. Ask them!" The playwright turned to the Kalesh, raising his voice and enunciating each word. "Have you met the Emperor?"

The soldiers looked at him curiously, and Reese said far too many words in Kalesh to be merely repeating the question. Several of the soldiers laughed.

Serene listened for a moment. "They're asking how much of the language Reese knows." She shook her head. "They don't trust him—" She paused. "This should be interesting. Reese says he started by learning how to impress a woman."

Sable raised an eyebrow. "Not a skill he's ever shown."

Serene grinned, but Reese used the wooden posts to pull himself to his feet and scanned the clearing until he focused on Sable and Serene. His hand gripped one of the posts, and he wasn't entirely steady on his feet, but when he called them, his voice came out stronger than Sable expected.

"Hey!" He let out a little whistle.

"Did he just...whistle at us?" Sable asked quietly. "Like we're dogs?"

"Hey, woman!" he called again.

Serene fixed Reese with an annoyed look.

One of the Kalesh soldiers called out something.

Serene's mouth twitched like she wanted to smile. "That man," she said quietly, "said very colorfully that Reese doesn't know what he's talking about."

Reese waved the man's words off and said something in Kalesh.

"He's not trying to impress the angry one, but he bets he can make the other one smile with only three words." Serene bit her lip and looked down to hide a smile. "They pointed out we both look angry."

"If he whistles at me again," Sable said, picking up a clod of dirt, "I'm throwing this at him."

Reese motioned for the soldiers to be quiet and turned his back on them. He faced Sable through a gap in the wall. His eyes locked on hers, and, after a pause, his expression softened to one much too personal for the fact that he was in a prison and she was digging in the dirt.

"What's he doing?" Sable whispered.

"What are you doing, boy?" Atticus asked, a note of caution in his voice.

"Teaching these good men three words that will make a woman smile," Reese answered, not looking away from Sable.

A bit of a smile curled up the edge of his mouth, and he leaned against the wooden posts. His eyes were warm, and for a moment she forgot the dirt and the weeds and the other soldiers. Her hand tightened, and the clod crumbled between her fingers.

When he spoke, the words were surprisingly gentle and heartfelt. "You're very plain."

A laugh burst out of her, and she pressed the back of her hand to her mouth to stifle it.

Reese grinned at her. The soldiers behind him laughed and applauded, calling out questions to him. All except the quiet one. Reese gave one last smug smile before turning and sliding down the wall to sit next to a chuckling Atticus.

Even the monks stationed around the coop looked amused.

"He's very sweet," Serene said with a smile.

"He's something." Sable brushed off her hands.

The soldiers in the coop all talked over each other, and Serene refocused on the plants, her head tilted as she listened. "They're talking more freely," she said quietly.

Sable glanced at the one in the far corner, who was still quiet. "Most of them."

They settled, and one soldier started speaking.

Serene frowned. "He's mad they never went into the city."

"Immusmala?" Sable asked quietly.

"I think so. He came all this way and expected to see the dragon lady."

Sable glanced at her. "Vivaine?"

Serene shrugged. "The others agree."

Another man launched into a long string of words.

Reese turned to Atticus. "That man says he saw the Emperor speak at a festival in the capital. The summer when the unrest grew."

The man talked again, and Reese interpreted for Atticus. "It was the first time the Emperor had spoken of the Zenivah dreams."

"Zenivah?" Atticus asked curiously.

"A mythological woman," Reese said, but the Kalesh man waved his hand toward the sky and launched into a long story.

"Zenivah was a woman who had a black dragon. In the beginning of the great Empire," Reese explained as the man spoke, "there were greedy factions who wanted to kill the Emperor and seize power for themselves. They were corrupt and harsh to the people in their territories. They didn't like the goodness and generosity of the Emperor, and they sowed discontent and violence wherever they could.

"Until a woman came out of the north with a black dragon. She found the fortresses of three of the *Sarvoton*—the leaders of the rebellion—and took their...*zel*, their scepters. She destroyed the *Sarvoton*, their families, their troops. Then she walked into the Emperor's throne room and bowed before him, offering him the three *zel*.

"Her name was Zenivah, and the great Emperor brought her up to stand at the side of his throne. With her help, he quelled the rest of the rebellion and ushered in what turned out to be hundreds of years of peace and prosperity. The Emperor tried to make Zenivah his wife, but once the Empire was safe, the woman and her dragon left, promising to return if ever she was needed."

Atticus looked at the Kalesh soldiers with rapt attention. "There is a woman here, in the south, who has a dragon, but it's silver."

Reese repeated Atticus's words in Kalesh.

The man nodded. "Zenivah." He launched into his story again.

"She left the Empire," Reese said, "and started a family in the west, but the Emperor's enemies followed her. She was too strong for them to kill, but while she was away, they killed her family and drew her and her dragon into a trap. They tricked them into going deep into a rift and then collapsed a mountain on top of them."

"An entire mountain?" Atticus asked, but the man kept talking, leaning closer.

"He says they left her for dead," Reese said, "but not long after, the shepherds on the nearby hills said the earth groaned, and they heard words on the wind."

"Deliciously creepy," Atticus said.

The Kalesh man lowered his voice and began a sort of chant.

"She is coming closer, rising from the flames of the setting sun. The ground will tremble, the seas will rise, the swords of her enemies will turn to dust in her hands. The unfaithful will drown in their fear, and she will cleanse the land of their wickedness."

Another man jumped in and began speaking.

"A year ago," Reese explained to Atticus, "Emperor Prenn proclaimed that he'd been visited by Zenivah in his dreams. She had decried the division growing in the Empire and promised to return."

"That's..." Atticus paused. "An interesting story."

The first man spoke again.

"Many in the Empire believe Zenivah will return soon," Reese said. "There is unrest in the territories, and for the last generation, Zenivah's story has been a favorite among the people. At every festival, people tell stories of her great victories."

The men inside the coop nodded and chimed in with their own stories.

Sable looked at Serene. "The Kalesh Empire thinks Vivaine is some mythological savior?"

Serene dropped a weed into the basket. "That is not good for us."

CHAPTER TEN

THE WARM WEIGHT of the morning sunlight landed on Sable's back as she knelt next to the plants, mechanically pulling out the stubborn weeds while Serene continued to quietly interpret the conversation among the Kalesh. Their talk turned to complaints about military life again, but they had only vague ideas of being tasked with ravaging the north rather than any clear idea of what else the Kalesh were planning.

Sable glanced up at the quiet soldier occasionally, but the man didn't move or speak. Reese had shifted slightly against the wall. He talked comfortably with the other soldiers, but she noticed he never fully turned away from the man.

Sam strode into the garden flanked by two monks. They unbarred the coop door and entered with drawn swords.

"Get up, old man," Sam said. "We have questions for you." He grabbed Atticus's arm and pulled him up. One of the monks pushed him toward the door.

Reese stood. "Leave him alone."

Sam stepped up close to Reese, not bothering to draw a weapon. "Oh, you're coming too." Sam took him roughly by the arm and dragged him out of the coop.

The last monk backed out and barred the door again, and they started back across the garden. Reese stumbled and fell to his knees, his head sagging forward, and Sable tensed. Another monk grabbed Reese's other arm, helping to drag Reese out of the garden.

The Kalesh soldiers muttered among themselves, all watching Reese and Atticus disappear into the trees. The silent one kept his eyes fixed on Reese's back.

Sable watched them leave. "How obvious will it be if we stand up and follow them?"

"Obvious." Serene kept her attention on the weeds.

A moment later, though, Sam came back into the garden, looking over the people working in the garden. His gaze fell on Serene and Sable, who were the only women kneeling among the plants. He snapped at them, "You two! I have work for you." With that, he turned and left.

"Next time we pretend to be something," Sable said quietly, brushing off her hands and picking up the basket, "let's make a rule we can't be whistled at or snapped at."

"Agreed," Serene said.

Without looking back at the prisoners, they walked quickly out of the garden. They caught up to the others around the first turn in the path.

The wagon was parked under a tree, and Reese lay in the back with his eyes closed.

"Reese?" Sable asked, reaching over the side and taking his hand.

He cracked an eye. "That was exhausting." His brow creased. "That quiet soldier is troubling."

"Maybe if I sit closer to him, it will help," Atticus said.

"I don't think that's a good idea." Reese looked at Sam. "Does he have any tattoos?"

Sam shrugged. "What do tattoos mean?"

"A lot, depending on what they are and where they are."

"That Kalesh who was tracking Purnicious when we first met you had tattoos on his forearms," Sable said to Reese.

Serene nodded. "His was something about a snake."

"Probably the motto of his battalion," Reese said. "Words or symbols on their arms usually are. But there are some elite units with distinctive tattoos, usually on their chest. The *Mija,* which means vipers, have snake tattoos, usually very elaborate. The *Tien Sark,* the Emperor's elite assassins, tattoo dragon scales across their chest. The higher they rank, the higher the scales go." His brow creased. "I wouldn't expect the Kalesh to be wasting any of their elite troops here, but he was more dangerous than the average soldier."

"Especially if there's unrest in the Empire," Atticus agreed. "We can't be the most important thing the Emperor is dealing with right now."

"Until he found out about Sable," Serene said.

"The Emperor only learned about Sable a few days ago," Reese said. "He couldn't send elite soldiers here that fast. It would take at least two months."

"Can we talk about something besides the Emperor sending his people to kill me?" Sable asked. "Like that myth about Vivaine."

Atticus brushed the dirt out of his hair. "If the common people of the Empire know the story, and the Emperor himself is using it as propaganda in his speeches, it already has a lot of power."

Sam climbed up onto the wagon and started it moving. The others fell in behind it.

Sable glanced at Atticus. "Doesn't it all seem a little too coincidental? A woman with a dragon? Coming from the *flames of the setting sun.* How many people have a dragon and live west of the Empire?"

"I've never heard of any real person who has a dragon aside from Vivaine," Atticus said.

"You think the Emperor made it up when he heard of Vivaine?" Jae asked. "She is the first Dragon Prioress to have an actual dragon, after all."

Reese lifted his head. "She is?"

Sable nodded. "The priory always had only a dragon egg. A lot of people didn't even think it was real."

"Until Vivaine hatched it," Jae said. "It's how she became Dragon Prioress at the unheard of early age of twenty-five."

"Huh," Reese said, dropping his head again as the wagon trundled down the road. "I thought all three animals had been around…forever. Still, the story of Zenivah is hundreds of years old. There's an entire city near the capital named after her."

"Had you heard the myth before?" Sable asked.

"Yes. Never would have connected it to Vivaine, though. Zenivah's dragon was black. And huge. It destroyed buildings with its claws. And Zenivah is just one of many dragon myths."

"It has the feel of an old story," Jae said thoughtfully. "Bits and pieces remind me of other myths. Being buried in a rift is familiar from somewhere. And the foreboding prophecy on the wind is always a good touch."

"It explains some things, too," Serene said. "Like why ambassadors and generals from the Empire are willing to work so closely with Vivaine.

In Immusmala, she's important, but to the Empire, she should be nothing but the religious leader of some small city."

Sable looked over at her. "I'd never really thought of it like that."

"Hmmm," Atticus said slowly. "I always assumed that when the Kalesh came, she just did what she usually does and drew them in, so they began to work with her." He glanced at the others. "If they came seeking her out, that's..."

"This is not something Vivaine is going to shy away from exploiting," Sable said.

The path opened up into the orchard, and the wagon rolled toward the army tents.

"I'll report to Braddick what we learned." Sam glanced at Reese lying in the back of the wagon. "Want to come?"

Reese didn't answer.

"I think he's asleep," Sable said.

"You're welcome to use the wagon to take him back to your house, then." Sam pointed to some wide baskets piled with bread sitting to the side of the road. "Help yourself to those if you're hungry," he said, unharnessing the horse from the wagon. "Brother Matthew's honey bread is delicious."

Sam headed toward Braddick's tent, and Sable went to the baskets of bread with the others. The dark loaves were small, and she picked up a few of them. Leaving the others to discuss the Zenivah myth, she went back to Reese and set one loaf on his stomach. She sat next to him, dangling her feet off the end, mulling over the depressing idea that Vivaine was revered in the Empire.

Sable bit into the bread, and every thought of Vivaine disappeared. The crust was thin and almost crispy. The inside let out a puff of steam as her teeth sank into the warm, buttery sweetness.

"Reese!" She smacked the side of his leg. He started, and his eyes flew open. "Eat the bread!"

He obediently picked up the loaf, and his eyebrows rose. "Is this Matthew's honey bread?" He took a big bite and groaned. "I love this stuff."

Flibbet pushed his handcart slowly through the trees. When he caught sight of them, he wheeled over his cart, which creaked over the rough ground. When he parked it alongside the wagon, he rubbed one of his palms. "None of you have anything that will sand a rough spot of my handle, do you?"

"Thulan's personality is abrasive," Leonis offered, coming back from the basket with an armful of little loaves. "You could rub her across it."

"If Leonis's wit wasn't so dull," Thulan said, "it could be useful for…something."

"Have you finished your book, Flibbet?" Atticus interrupted before Leonis could answer.

"I have!" Flibbet lifted the cover of his cart. The entire top hinged open until it stood upright along the back, revealing an open space in the center. He folded open some smaller pieces of wood along the edges until they sat like little shelves along the sides.

Atticus's eyes lit up. "May I read it?"

"A book about what?" Sable asked.

Flibbet reached into the cart. "An accounting of the last time we were all in the Sanctuary."

"Didn't Serene already write that?" Sable asked.

"Mine is more…narrowly focused than hers." Flibbet pulled items out and set them on the shelves. "In the Sanctuary, after the fire, I nearly stepped on a very small flower that was growing up between two of the broad stones in the plaza." He paused, and his eyes grew unfocused, his expression tinged with wonder. "The petals were white, just like the stone, so I wouldn't have seen it, except it had managed to grow tall enough that the tiniest bits of green leaves were reaching out."

He held a small bowl absently. "Beauty…from sheer tenacity." He turned back to Sable, his expression earnest. "Remarkable, don't you think? One stunningly beautiful flower, so bright white I swear it glowed."

Sable glanced at the others, who were listening with varying levels of bemusement. "A flower?"

"In the Sanctuary," he clarified, pulling a small silver cylinder out of the cart and pointing it at Sable. "They don't let things grow between those stones."

"That's true," she admitted. "I'm sure it's some abbess's job to root them up and keep the plaza clean."

He looked at her curiously. "Do you think they tear up all the glowing flowers?"

"It was really glowing?" Thulan asked. "What would make it do that?"

Flibbet shrugged. "I was hoping Serene would tell me that."

Serene frowned. "I thought you were just exaggerating for poetic effect. If you really think it was glowing…" She glanced at Jae.

"There's some sort of magic in those rocks," he said. "If it's enough to make weeds grow with magical properties, I would guess they're harvesting them, not throwing them away."

"I agree," Flibbet said, as though they'd just proved his point. "Which is why it needed to be recorded." He set the cylinder down and peered back into the cart, then pulled out a very thin book. The cover had several words written on it, each too small for Sable to make out, each in a different color.

He handed it to Atticus, who opened it with obvious pleasure, flipping through several pages of colorful, disorganized writing.

Flibbet began to tuck things back into his cart.

A scrap of bright yellow fabric caught Sable's eye, and she picked it up. "Purnicious would love this."

Flibbet's eyebrows rose. "The kobold?"

Sable nodded. "She loves fabric. She can make amazing things from the smallest scraps."

He lowered his voice. "Is she nearby? Can I meet her?

Sable glanced around. "Purn, would you like to meet Flibbet?"

There was a little pop, and Purnicious appeared, tucked into the shadows between the wagon and the handcart, smiling shyly up at the peddler.

Flibbet beamed at her. "You're blue! Like the sky when the first stars appear."

Purnicious's smile widened. "It's nice to meet you, Flibbet."

"You are only the second kobold I have ever met." He squatted to look at her closely. "The other was a dusky red color and not dressed nearly as lovely as you. That is a magnificent cloak."

Purn straightened, shifting her purple cloak on her shoulders. "Thank you. It is one of my very favorite things."

"Because it came from me," Reese said from where he lay.

"It was the only time the wastrel has shown good taste when it comes to clothing," Purn answered primly. She took a step forward and peered at Flibbet's cart handle. "I can fix that rough spot." She reached her blue fingers up and ran them lightly over the surface of the wood. "It's easy to shrink off the burrs." She glanced at the other handle, then smoothed that one as well.

Flibbet rubbed his hand over the spot she'd fixed. "That was amazing!" He motioned to the yellow scrap of fabric in Sable's hand. "Let me repay you with that. It's the only fabric I have at the moment."

Purnicious took the cloth and clasped it to her chest. "Thank you!"

"I'll find you if I get any other interesting fabric," Flibbet said with a smile and resumed putting his things away.

Reese pulled himself up to a sitting position. "If you give her stuff, make her promise she won't somehow work it into my clothes."

"Start wearing better clothes," Purn said, "and I won't have to."

"Purn," Sable said quietly, "you have to try this bread." She held out one of the small loaves and the kobold grabbed it before pulling back into the shadows.

Reese leaned toward Flibbet's cart. "Is that a spyglass?"

Flibbet paused in the act of putting the metal cylinder back into the cart. He turned to look at Reese, bumping the cart with his hip and eliciting a sharp creak from the wood. The peddler's expression sharpened, and he held it out. "It is."

Reese took it, and Flibbet settled against the creaky cart, watching him closely.

The cylinder was dull silver, and Reese pulled on the ends, extending it until it was almost as long as his forearm. He held it up to his eye and pointed it toward the trees at the far side of the orchard. "Where'd you get it? I haven't seen one like this since I left the Empire."

"I traded a young man for it in the south," Flibbet said.

"I didn't realize you traded human beings," Leonis said lightly. "Would you take Thulan in exchange for something?"

"I meant I traded *with* a young man," Flibbet said with a grin. "I don't trade people."

"But Thulan's not a people. She's a dwarf. How much do you think she's worth?"

Thulan peered into the cart. "You have anything in there that would make Leonis actually funny? I'd pay a lot for that."

Reese had lowered the spyglass and was studying the peddler. "You must have traded with a Kalesh man for this."

Flibbet looked at the spyglass. "I traded with a dying man," he said quietly.

The cylinder was a bit tarnished, but Sable could almost make out a design etched on the outside of it. Reese offered it to her, and she ran her finger over the pattern of leaves winding around it. She held it up to her eye. The pines across the orchard jumped closer, double their normal size.

The memory of Vivaine drawing images closer flooded into her mind, how the prioress bent the light until Sable could see things clearly even though they were far away. She lowered the spyglass and refocused on the trees. "Just like Vivaine."

Reese nodded. "The only skill of hers I envy. Do you know how nice it would be to see this far when I'm hunting?"

Thulan took her turn with it. "What does a dying man trade a spyglass for?"

"A song." Flibbet took a deep breath and looked at Reese. "In all the times I've seen you, we've never traded. Would you like the spyglass?"

Reese watched it as it passed to Leonis. "Yes, but I have nothing to trade for it."

"Would you accept a propensity for throwing himself into harm's way?" Leonis asked. "He has plenty of that."

Reese gave him an unamused look, holding out his hand for the glass. "Don't you have anything else to do right now?"

"Yes," Atticus said, his attention still on Flibbet's tiny book. "I want to talk to the wounded soldiers. I don't have a good idea of how deeply the Kalesh made it into Lord Erick's land before they were caught." He started across the orchard.

"Reese also has an overdeveloped need to protect people," Thulan pointed out to Leonis as they followed Atticus. "He could trade away a bit of that and probably be safer for it."

Flibbet watched them go with a smile. "I like those two."

"You could offer Flibbet your regular shirt in exchange for the spy glass," Purn offered, still nibbling at the bread. "It's boring and plain, but he traded Sable *Ghost of the White Wood* for a worn servant's dress."

"Then what would I wear?" Reese asked.

"Trade him this black one too. It's as boring as your regular one. I'll make you a new one," Purn said. "A yellow one!"

"He'd be foolish to trade a spyglass for dirty shirts," Reese said.

The kobold's brow creased indignantly, and she tugged a thread out of her purple cloak. She reached up and grabbed his arm resting on the side of the wagon, and, with her long nose nearly touching it, she set the thread on the fabric and traced a shape with her finger. When she backed away, a beautiful violet flower was embroidered onto it, so skillfully shaded and highlighted that it looked almost like each petal was lifting out of the cloth.

"Purn!" Sable said. "That's beautiful!"

"Impressive!" Flibbet leaned closer to see it.

Purnicious gave Reese a triumphant look.

"It's now a dirty black shirt with a pretty flower," Reese said.

"True," Flibbet rested back against his cart again, and it groaned quietly. The peddler kept his eyes on the flower. "How long did you serve under Tanis?"

Reese paused at the question. "A year with the rebels, but I'd known him for almost ten years before that."

Flibbet shifted, and the cart squeaked again. "And you were close?"

Reese nodded. "He was like a second father."

The peddler finally lifted his eyes to meet Reese's, his own expression vaguely apologetic. "I will trade you the spyglass for this kobold-ed shirt plus the story of how Tanis died."

Reese tensed, and Purn clutched the end of her bread to her chest and looked up at him with wide eyes.

His hand tightened around the spyglass before he held it back out to Flibbet. "Thanks anyway."

The peddler took it, and Reese lay back in the cart, closing his eyes.

Flibbet tucked the glass back into his cart with a sigh.

"That was a high price to ask," Sable said quietly.

"It was too high." Flibbet's voice was annoyed, and he dropped the lid of his cart closed with more force than necessary.

Purnicious popped out of view at the noise.

Sable watched the odd little man glare at his cart. "Then why did you ask for it?"

"What choice do I have?" he asked, exasperated, lifting up his cart handles and shoving the cart into motion. "*Apparently* that's what it was worth."

CHAPTER ELEVEN

FLIBBET ROLLED his cart back in among the refugees, stopping to talk to a family.

Sable sat on the end of the small wagon, Reese's legs next to hers. She glanced back at him, lying down. His chest rose in long, slow breaths. Deeper breaths than he'd had for days.

"Did you really fall asleep this fast," Sable said quietly to Reese, "or were you just trying to get rid of Flibbet? Because he's gone."

He didn't answer, and she set her hand on his knee. The dark fabric of the Kalesh uniform was warm in the sunlight. "We should have gotten you out of this uniform."

He still didn't answer, and she turned her attention to where Atticus spoke with some of the wounded soldiers. Sable couldn't hear his words from where she sat next to Reese, but the men around him nodded and answered his questions. Leonis and Thulan moved easily among the soldiers, stopping to exchange words with them. Even from this distance, Sable could see the mood lifting visibly wherever they paused.

"I forget sometimes how good they are at that," she said, more to herself than Reese.

Nearby whispers caught her attention, and she turned to find a knot of children gathered under the closest tree, watching her. When she smiled at them, they pushed one girl forward.

"Are you the Flame of the North?" she asked.

Sable took in all their eager expressions. "It's one of my names, yes."

"Do you really own a phoenix?" a boy asked.

"Of course she does," the first girl said. "That's how she got the name."

"The phoenix's name is Innov," Sable said, "and I don't own her, but she's a friend of mine. A very independent friend who disappears and reappears whenever she pleases."

"And a kobold?" a red-haired boy asked, his eyes wide with interest. The rest of their faces were equally curious.

"Where did you hear that?"

The girl next to him sniffed. "I told you it wasn't true."

"She didn't say it wasn't true," the boy said. "We heard it from Atticus himself, and he'd know."

"Atticus is telling a lot of stories, isn't he?" Sable looked around at all the nods. "I do have a kobold who is a friend also, but not many people have seen her."

"Kobolds can be invisible," the red-haired boy explained in a scholarly tone. "They can move magically over long distances, and if you save one, it will bind itself to you."

Sable nodded. "Those things are all true."

"Did you save yours?" he asked.

"We saved each other," Sable said.

"Does she always know where you are?" the boy asked.

Sable nodded. "She can always hear me, and always see what's around me, unless it's pitch dark."

The children looked around as though Purnicious might appear at any moment.

"Would you tell us about when you were attacked by the dragon?" the girl who'd first spoken asked.

Every child turned quickly back to Sable.

"Did Atticus tell you that story too?"

"He did." The red-headed boy gestured at the first girl. "Gilly thinks you were scared, and I think the Flame of the North doesn't get scared. So we want to hear you tell it."

Sable looked at Gilly. "The Flame of the North is scared more often than not. But sometimes you have to do something, even if you're scared, because there are things that need to be said and people who need to hear it." She had their rapt attention, so she settled more comfortably onto the cart. "I wasn't actually scared at the beginning. At first, I was only angry."

She began the story of finding the merchants gathered in the Sanctuary when they were so desperately needed on the battlefield.

The wagon was a tiny stage, and her audience even smaller, but the story spun out effortlessly, and Sable fed warmth into her words as the tale began to take shape. They reacted with enthusiastic gasps and questions, and for the first time in well over a year, Sable remembered the way it felt to share a story with people. To somehow, through just words, come together and share an experience. Feel the same hopes and fears. Feel, just for a few moments, that they were actually united.

At some point, Reese woke and worked up the energy to walk to go find his own clothes. When he returned, he sat next to Sable, giving his own input and asking the children questions about what they'd been through over the past few weeks.

The late-summer sun was high overhead and their young audience had grown three times larger when shouts drifted out of the end of the orchard. The children all turned to look in that direction, and a minute later, a monk ran out of the trees toward the command tent. Somewhere toward the end of the island, a plume of smoke appeared, rising slowly into the air.

Sable pointed at the smoke. "That's not the direction of the coop, is it?"

Reese shook his head. "There's nothing that way but forest."

Braddick and Sam emerged from the tents, along with a handful of other soldiers, and met the monk not far from the wagon where Sable sat.

"What's burning, Edwyn?" Sam asked the monk.

"Only one stand of trees. We're building a break to keep it from coming farther into the island, but I don't know that we can stop it from spreading toward the shore. The brush there is too dry. It'll look big, but I don't think it will damage anything important. We need more men to build the break, though."

Sam called out some orders to the nearby monks, and they headed in the direction of the fire. Braddick motioned for a half-dozen of his men to follow.

Sam glanced at the sky. "At least it's not windy."

Atticus, Leonis, and Thulan came over, Jae and Serene not far behind.

"It was started on purpose," Edwyn said, lowering his voice.

"This is the problem with taking in people like this," Braddick said. "Some ignorant ones decide they want some privacy and start a cookout in the woods."

"If so," Edwyn said, "they wanted a big cookout. In the center of the fire are two dead pines, and it looks like a pile of brush was stacked under them."

"Someone wanted to start a forest fire?" Sam asked.

Reese straightened, looking back at the smoke. "How far is that from the coop?"

"Is that close to the Kalesh prisoners?" Braddick asked at the same time.

"The fire is too far into the woods to even see the garden," Edwyn answered. "The prisoners aren't in danger."

"But it'll draw all your monks away," Reese said.

"Men!" Braddick snapped at the few soldiers still around him. "On me!"

"Get more brothers to the garden," Sam ordered Edwyn.

Leonis, Thulan, Serene, and Jae joined the rest running toward the garden.

Over the trees, the tower of smoke reached high into the clear sky.

Reese moved to climb out of the cart, but Sable stopped him. "It's a long walk."

"I can make it," he said.

"Here," Atticus said, leading the horse back to the wagon. "I'll harness her up. Just hold on."

Reese pushed himself off the back of the wagon. "Hurry up. The fight will be done before we get there." He started toward the road, but his steps were slow.

"Reese," Sable said, following him. "You won't even make it that far."

"I could hook up six horses to six wagons and still make it there before someone walking your speed," Atticus said, tightening the last of the straps. "Get back in the wagon. But we're only going close enough to see what's happening. This is a situation best left to those who can actually fight."

Reese kept walking but hadn't even made it out of the orchard by the time Atticus pulled past him with the wagon. He climbed into the back, and Atticus set off at a hurried trot. Sable walked alongside it as the little cart bounced down the road. Atticus pulled over when they neared the garden, parking along a row of bushes blocking the clearing from view.

A cry rang out, and Sable moved closer to the thicket until she could see the garden through a gap in the branches.

A section of the chicken coop wall was twisted, the top of it leaning in, the bottom jutting out, leaving a hole large enough for a man to crawl through. The bodies of two monks and two Kalesh soldiers lay unmoving on the ground beside it.

Leonis's and Thulan's voices came from the forest past the coop, shouting things Sable couldn't quite understand.

Along the outside of the coop, Jae wrestled a prisoner up against the wall. Serene reached for the prisoner's head, but the Kalesh man fought his arm free and drove his fist into Jae's cheek. Jae stumbled back, but Serene, livid, slapped her hand onto the man's forehead, and he collapsed onto the ground.

Scuffling sounds came from near the bushes, and Sable caught a glimpse of movement close to the branches. Reese edged around to the side, and she followed until she could see Braddick wrestling with the Kalesh soldier, the one who'd watched them all silently in the coop. Braddick's sword lay on the ground far out of his reach, and in a single smooth movement, the Kalesh soldier flipped Braddick onto his back, crushing the nearest plants and wrapping his hands around the general's throat.

The Kalesh man's back was to the bushes, and Sable couldn't see Braddick's face, but his legs kicked, and he punched at the soldier's head in a futile attempt to break the stranglehold.

Reese ducked around the edge of the bushes and ran straight at the Kalesh soldier's back.

It was only a half-dozen paces, and he managed to stay running until he wrapped his arms around the Kalesh soldier and bowled him over. They crashed to the ground, and the man twisted, trying to break Reese's grip.

"Braddick!" Reese yelled. "Get your—" The soldier slammed his elbow into the side of Reese's head. "Sword!" he groaned as the soldier scrambled away. Reese grabbed for him but only caught a handful of his shirt, tearing a huge rip across it.

Braddick sat up, coughing and gasping for air. His sword lay half hidden by a crushed row of leaves not far from Sable, and she saw the Kalesh man's eyes light on it.

She ran out from the bushes, picking up the sword, her only thought to keep it from him. The Kalesh man yanked his shirt out of Reese's grip and rushed at her.

She took a step back, lifting the heavy blade and knowing her only defense was in keeping him back, but Braddick kicked out at the man's feet and sent him crashing to his knees. The general drew a knife from his belt and ran up behind the prisoner, wrapping an arm around his neck.

A huge flap of the soldier's black shirt hung open, revealing his stomach covered in tattoos.

Braddick brought his knife to the man's throat.

"No!" Reese gasped, reaching out a hand from where he still lay on the ground. "Don't kill him!"

Braddick's knife hesitated but didn't drop.

"Look at the tattoos!" Reese pushed himself to his knees. "He's Tien Sark."

Braddick's expression was vicious. He coughed between heaving breaths. Sable's eyes stayed locked on the knife as she waited to see it stab into the soldier's neck.

Braddick didn't relax, but when the blade didn't move, Reese sank back, letting out a groan.

Serene and Jae came closer, taking in the man's tattoos and Reese lying on the ground.

"Serene," Reese said, "put him to sleep."

Braddick started to protest, but Serene set her hand on the tattooed soldier's head. He snarled something and twitched toward her, but Braddick's knife tip jabbed into his neck and he stopped.

"What did he say?" Sable asked Jae.

"'I welcome death,'" Jae said.

Serene leaned down and said something equally harsh in Kalesh.

Jae stiffened.

The Kalesh man glared at her, then his eyes glassed over and a frantic look crossed his face before his eyes slid closed and he sagged against Braddick.

Braddick slowly let the man down. He felt the soldier's neck, then backed up and stood, his eyes on Serene.

"Do we want to know what she said to him?" Atticus asked quietly, coming up behind Sable.

Jae paused. "She said, 'And death welcomes you.'"

"Did she kill him?" Atticus whispered.

"Did you kill him?" Reese asked, still lying tiredly on the ground. "I said don't kill him."

Jae cast out toward Serene. His wave rolled over the group of people, and the warmth of all of them, including the Tien Sark, washed over Sable. Even Reese's warmth was noticeable.

"Not dead," Sable whispered to Atticus.

Serene turned to Jae. "You checked? You really had to check?"

He shrugged. "Lately, you've been a little..."

"Don't say it," Atticus warned under his breath.

Serene stood, giving Jae a mild look that seemed somehow more dangerous than a scowl. "I've been what, dear?"

"Efficient and powerful," Jae said.

"So is he dead or not?" Reese asked.

"Of course he's not dead," Serene snapped. "Why would I bother to come over and kill a man who had a knife against his throat? Do you think I just walk around all day moving *vitalle* like it's nothing? Like it's as easy as you waving your knife around?"

"I have no idea." Reese gave her a tired look. "You said, 'Death welcomes you.'"

Serene paused, then a smile turned up one corner of her mouth. "I thought it'd be funny to make him think he was dying when he was just going to sleep."

Reese stared at her. "Funny for who?"

She grinned. "Me, mostly."

Sable moved over to Reese, holding out a hand and helping him to sit. She caught some movement in the woods across the garden as the northern soldiers came into view with Thulan and Leonis.

Braddick motioned them over. "Where are the other Kalesh?"

"We killed them. Their bodies are in the woods," one of the soldiers answered.

"Go find some rope for this one." Braddick retrieved his sword and took in Serene and the others around her. "Who are you people?"

"We're the ones who did nothing impressive in the south," Leonis said.

Braddick's posture didn't relax. "Andreese," he snapped, "you'd better start explaining what's happening."

Reese nodded toward the Kalesh soldier. "That man is Tien Sark, part of an elite battalion of soldiers who work directly for the Emperor. Most often they're used as assassins."

The man's shirt was torn open across his stomach, and every inch of visible skin was covered with tattooed scales.

"How high up his chest does it go?" Reese asked.

Leonis bent over and shifted the torn shirt up, revealing scales as far up as they could see. Thulan grabbed a fistful of the fabric and yanked, tearing it up through the collar.

"To the bottom of his neck," she reported.

Reese's brow knit. "What's he doing here?"

"Explain the scales," Braddick ordered.

"When a soldier joins the Tien Sark, they get three rows of scales around their stomach. The higher they move in the ranks, the more scales are added."

"What do the highest ones look like?" Leonis asked. "Are their whole heads covered?"

Reese nodded. "If the scales are visible on their neck, they're very high ranking. The highest shaves his head and the scales cover his scalp. Everything but his face."

"Wouldn't that make him a sort of obvious assassin?" Thulan asked.

"At that level, he would get his underlings to kill for him. This one is a midlevel officer. But the fact that any Tien are here is...odd."

"We're at war with the Empire," Braddick observed. "It's not odd that they've sent soldiers here."

"It's odd that they sent this kind of soldier. It's like if Lord Runess sent his personal bodyguard to settle some trivial border dispute. The Empire is huge, and if what the other soldiers were saying is true, there's a lot of unrest going on. Compared to all that, we're merely a distant land that may have some gold. That's hardly the level of fighting that calls for the Emperor's personal assassins."

"We have Sable," Leonis said.

Reese pointed at the Tien's boots. The soles were worn near the toe, and the black was scuffed off. The cuff of his shirt was frayed as well. "This man has been traveling for a long time. Long before anyone knew about Sable."

"What does Sable have to do with anything?" Braddick asked.

"She does more unimpressive things than the rest of us," Leonis answered.

The northern soldier returned with rope and tied the Kalesh soldier's arms and legs.

"We need to get the Tien somewhere secure and wake him up." Reese said. "We need to know why the Emperor sent him and who he's here to kill."

CHAPTER TWELVE

INSIDE THE CROWDED CHICKEN COOP, Sable leaned against the wall next to Reese, watching three monks repair the damaged section of wall. She turned a piece of glass over in her hands, catching the afternoon light on its broken surfaces. The lashing the Kalesh had cut through hung limply as the monks hammered in several wooden beams across the outside of the wall.

The Tien Sark lay slumped in one corner, his feet bound and his hands tied behind his back. He was the only surviving prisoner, and three northern soldiers stood watch over him. Jae and Serene filed in, followed by the troupe.

Reese studied the unconscious man.

"What does Tien Sark mean?" Sable asked him.

"Shadow of the dragon."

"Please don't say they have a dragon," Leonis said, nudging the Kalesh man's foot with his own.

Reese shook his head. "There are no dragons in the Empire. But the Tien Sark are..." His brow creased. "They're almost a religious faction. The Empire as a whole is enamored with dragons, but the Tien Sark almost worship them. They consider the dragon to be the pinnacle of aggression and power. Their training grounds are called temples, and they fight like men with a religious fervor."

"So they'll worship Vivaine's dragon?" Thulan asked.

Reese nodded slowly. "That's what's so troubling about them being here. If they're here, and there's a dragon here…It's not a good combination for us."

"The wall's almost fixed," Sam said, walking into the coop.

The enclosure was crowded with northern soldiers and Tutella monks. Another ring of monks stood guard outside the coop. A monk came into the garden from the woods to the east, running up to the enclosure, saluting Sam.

"We found and killed two Kalesh in the woods, neither of whom were from our prisoners," he said. "One was carrying a tinderbox. Close as we can tell, those two started the fire, then attacked the coop when it only had two guards."

Sam nodded. "Any sign that there are more of them?"

The monk shook his head. "We found tracks from the fire to the garden. Definitely only two men."

"Any of the other Kalesh have tattoos?" Reese asked.

"Only a few symbols on their forearms. Nothing on their chests."

"The wall is ready, General," another monk reported.

Sam glanced around at the armed men inside and outside the coop. "If this isn't enough men to contain one tied-up Kalesh soldier, then we're all doomed and might as well die today." He motioned for a monk to close and bar the door.

The wood slid into place, closing them in, and Sable shifted.

Serene approached the Tien Sark. "Are we ready?"

"If he's as highly trained as you say," Braddick said, "he's not going to tell you anything."

Reese pushed himself off the wall and stood at the Kalesh soldier's feet. "He wouldn't talk to you, but these people can get what they need out of him."

Atticus moved up next to Reese.

"What are you going to torture him with, old man?" Braddick asked. "Your beard?"

"Torture isn't effective," Atticus said, kneeling down. "All you need to do is listen. Everyone has a story to tell. They're dying to tell it. They just think no one wants to hear." He set his hand on the Tien Sark's foot. "All you have to do is listen." He nodded to Serene.

She stepped forward. "Don't be surprised if he flails a bit," she said. "Sometimes angry people don't wake up peacefully." Serene leaned down and set her hands on the Tien Sark's temples.

The man's eyes fluttered, then flew open, and he snapped his head to the side, a momentary terror crossing his features before he saw Serene. His eyes narrowed and bored into her with loathing.

"Doesn't look like he thought the 'death welcomes you' thing was funny," Thulan observed.

The man snarled something at Serene in Kalesh.

She patted his cheek. "That would be unwise."

"I will make it slow," the man said, his accent as rough as his tone, "and painful." The words swirled through the air warmly, as though being imprisoned, surrounded by guards, and tied up were inconsequential.

"I'm sure you'd try." Serene stood and stepped away from the man. "He's all yours, Reese."

"Well, that was easy," Reese said, looking down at the man. "I thought it might take some effort to get a Tien Sark to admit you speak our language."

"You are wasting your time," he said. "The Tien do not answer to the weak."

"Perhaps we're not as weak as you think we are," Reese said. "Let's start with something simple. Why are you here?"

The Tien merely stared at him.

"Or how long have you been here?" Reese continued. "You can tell us your name, or your rank, or how many other Tien are here. Who you are targeting. What part of the Empire you are from. Really, you can start anywhere."

The man opened his mouth, then pressed it shut again.

"This is going well," Braddick said.

Atticus leaned toward the prisoner, still touching his foot. "How do you feel about the fact that we have a dragon and you don't?"

The man gave a derisive snort. "You have nothing. Zenivah has a dragon."

"Ah," Atticus said. "Zenivah."

The Tien Sark's attention fixed on the playwright, but he clamped his mouth shut.

Sable stepped up next to Reese. "She's not the mythological goddess you're hoping for—I can assure you of that."

The Tien Sark's gaze slid to Sable, and she tried not to shift under the savage hatred she saw there.

"You're not here for gold, are you?" Atticus said. "You're here for Zenivah."

"What are you talking about?" Braddick asked. "The Kalesh are here for the gold."

Atticus studied the prisoner. "Not this one, I think."

"You realize you're in the wrong part of the world," Sable said. "Your fake mythological savior is south of here."

"It is not my place to go to her," the Tien said calmly. "I merely make a path for her to ride her dragon into the north." His words swirled tendrils of warmth through the air.

Leonis shook his head. "That dragon isn't big enough to ride."

"And," Thulan added, "there's already a nice wide road that leads up here. No new path needed."

The man ignored them.

"How many Tien are here?" Reese asked.

The man glanced around at the number of armed men surrounding him. "Even one seems too much for you. It makes no difference how many are here. If you defy Zenivah, you will fall."

"I've defied her a good number of times," Sable said, "and I'm still standing. In fact, your Zenivah recently had a major setback, and I don't think she has the power you think she does."

He barely looked at Sable before turning back to Reese. "Prepare your people to surrender, or you will be destroyed. The Tien Sark have always served the dragon. The time foretold long ago is at hand. Your land is nothing. We are here to serve Zenivah and usher her into her rightful place."

The air grew hot at the words, pressing against Sable with an uncomfortable intensity. The man's eyes took on a touch of fanaticism.

"He believes that strongly," she said.

"Fantastic," Thulan muttered. "Just what we need. Highly trained, brainwashed zealots serving Vivaine."

The Tien Sark gave the dwarf a contemptuous look. "The dwarves are not safe in their caverns. We will root them out, take their treasures, and leave their bodies to rot in the darkness."

Thulan faced Leonis. "That felt like too much. Too dramatic."

Leonis leaned toward the Tien Sark. "You're overacting, friend. Subtle threats are more intimidating. Try something like, 'We will creep in through the darkness and pluck out your beards.'"

"He will not touch our beards," Thulan said.

Reese let out an annoyed breath. "If this man gets free, he will kill both of you. Stop mocking him."

The dwarf and half-elf exchanged looks.

"Then what will we talk about?" Thulan whispered.

"How are you going to help Zenivah?" Sable asked the prisoner.

The man gave her a dismissive look, but next to her, Atticus's fingers made a small circle, the gesture he used when they rehearsed a play, the one that meant he wanted her to draw out a scene and put more emotion into it.

"She'll need a lot of help," Sable continued, wondering what Atticus wanted. She caught the hint of a nod from him. "First, you'll have to see if her dragon is healthy, since he was recently attacked by a phoenix. I believe he's blind in at least one eye."

The man's smug look flickered slightly.

"Do you like phoenixes as much as dragons?" Sable asked. "Because after seeing the two of them fight, I think the phoenix is the stronger of the two." She pushed some warmth into her words, and a definite hint of irritation crossed the man's face. From the corner of her eye, she saw Atticus circle his fingers again.

"Of course," she continued, "her dragon is silver and very small. Maybe he's weak. As far as dragons go, he's less impressive than the ones in old stories, anyway." She leaned a little closer. "Maybe all stories of dragons are exaggerated, and dragons are actually like this one. Just oversized lizards."

"The dragon could kill you with a breath," the man snapped. "And with the battalion of Tien Sark behind him, nothing will stop him. Or Zenivah." The words were warm.

"A whole battalion? Is that true?" Reese asked, directing the question to Sable instead of the Tien. When she nodded, his expression darkened.

The man hesitated at his misstep, then shrugged. "A whole battalion. How will your little land stand against that?"

Reese studied the man. "When?"

The Tien Sark let out a low laugh, then looked into the distance and began to chant in Kalesh.

"I hate when they start chanting," Thulan said.

Reese listened to the man chant for a moment, then glanced to Serene. "I doubt he'll tell us more right now."

The man twitched toward Serene, and his chanting took on a more stubborn tone.

"What's he saying?" Sable asked.

"'…may the wings of the great dragon shelter us, dress us in blood and terror.'" Reese made a distasteful face. "'May the wrath of the dragon flow from us, deal death to the chattel who stand against us. Raze their crops, burn their homes.'" The man's voice rose and Reese scowled. "'Cut their children from their arms and tear their sons and daughters apart.'"

Serene growled and crouched down next to the man. His eyes flicked to her, then he pointedly looked forward again, keeping his chanting steady.

When she reached toward his head, he flinched.

"You have it backwards," she said softly, her voice cold. "I can call down the wrath of the dragon, and you are the chattel."

She shoved her palm into his forehead, slamming his head back against the wall, and his eyes widened. A look of terror came over him, and he screamed.

It cut off abruptly, and he collapsed to the side.

Serene stood and brushed off her hands, her expression cold. "I don't like this one."

The northern soldiers and the monks all shifted their attention to Serene, watching her warily.

"Don't they usually fall asleep more…peacefully than that?" Leonis asked in a low voice.

Thulan nodded. "Is he breathing?"

"For now." Jae's voice was as hard as Serene's.

Serene turned away from the prisoner and walked toward the door. Thulan and Leonis stepped out of her way. She gave them a pointed look. "He shouldn't have threatened the children."

"Noted," Leonis said quickly.

She strode past them and stopped at the still closed door. "Open it."

The monks outside glanced toward Sam, who nodded. They pulled off the bars, and the door swung open. Serene stalked out.

Reese looked after Serene, then glanced at the slumped Tien Sark. "Assuming he wakes up at some point, Sam, we'll need to decide what to do with him."

"That won't be your decision," Braddick pointed out.

Reese ignored him. "Until then, keep him tied up, and keep as many monks as you can spare guarding him. Assume he's much more dangerous than you think he is." He glanced at the group around him. "An entire battalion of Tien Sark…"

"What does that mean?" Sable asked. "They're sending a battalion of assassins?"

Reese shook his head. "There is one more thing the Tien Sark are trained to do. If this many are coming, they're coming at the head of a lot more Kalesh forces. This won't be like facing General Goll and his battalions. The Empire will send a true army, and they will be efficient and brutal. Unless their goal is to keep things like local agriculture in place, they'll raze the land before they take whatever they're after. Since they're after our gold, I can't imagine they'll do anything but kill everyone who stands against them." He shook his head again. "Whatever chance we had against the Kalesh just disappeared."

CHAPTER THIRTEEN

SABLE STOOD in the corner of the command tent next to Thulan and Leonis, watching soldiers and monks file in. Flibbet wandered in, spent a moment taking in all of the people gathered, then ambled over next to Sable with a cheerful smile.

Outside, the late afternoon was hot, and inside, the still air was stifling. Low, murmured conversations filled the space.

Leonis looked around the tent. "It's awful in here. Do you think they'd mind if we cut a slit in the tent?"

"Who cares if they'd mind?" Thulan answered. "It's hot. With a second opening, maybe we can get a breeze moving."

"I have a knife outside in my cart," Flibbet offered.

Sam called for everyone's attention, and a monk closed the tent flap.

Leonis groaned. "So much for the breeze."

The sunlight shining through the beige canvas filled the space with a bland light as the assembled soldiers quieted.

"We've learned some troubling news from the Kalesh." Sam motioned to Reese. "Andreese, who has spent time in the Empire, is here to explain the significance of it."

Reese stood next to Braddick and Sam along one side of the table that took up the center of the tent. A few large maps covered its surface. "One of the Kalesh prisoners is a Tien Sark, a highly trained assassin who works for the Kalesh Emperor. Usually, these men are sent out in very small teams to assassinate a rival of the Emperor or to take out the heart of a rebellion somewhere. But occasionally, when there is a war the Emperor must win, he sends an entire battalion. Then they're sent to lead a large military force, and they'll do it brutally. They'll infiltrate strongholds you'd think were impenetrable and assassinate the leadership. Unless the Empire is after some natural resource, the Tien will turn the land against their enemies. They'll poison water sources and livestock. They'll burn forests and fields."

He paused to look at the gathered faces. "If the Empire has really sent a battalion of Tien Sark, then he is no longer mildly interested in our gold. He is determined to destroy us. By now he knows the strength of our forces, and he will send more than we can fight off."

There was a moment of silence.

"Then what do we do?" someone asked. "Surrender?"

"The north does not surrender," Braddick said.

The attention of the room shifted to him for a moment, then back to Reese.

"If we surrender," Reese said, "the Empire will come and take over every aspect of your lives. Your villages will be redirected to serve some need the Empire has. If they need wool, you'll find yourselves in charge of more sheep than you can count. You'll have quotas of how much wool you are to ship out annually. They'll take every young man and conscript him into the army. Maybe a local force, maybe sent to the Empire to fight in some land you've never heard of. If he's killed there, you will never know it. Your children will be educated at a school run by the Empire. They will be taught to serve the Emperor and to disdain whatever life you had before the Kalesh came."

Braddick's frown darkened the longer Reese spoke. "You paint a bleak picture. If the force coming is as strong as you say, then we stand no chance."

Reese looked around the tent. "They think we are splintered and weak. So first, we unify the north, then we gather more allies until we grow stronger."

"The north is unlikely to unify," Braddick declared. "Even Perric and Runess aren't unified as much as working toward a mutual goal. And the three western lords are currently reeling from the Kalesh attacks." He leaned forward and looked over a map of the north. He tapped one area and opened his mouth.

Rabbit spoke first from the side of the tent. "I can get word to the south. The troops stationed in Immusmala and the mouth of the Black River will be ready to help. The merchants will be on our side too. They're livid that the Kalesh attacked their city. It'll take me a couple of days to get whatever message you want to them."

Braddick's brow creased in annoyance. "We don't need—"

"Through Kiva?" Sable asked Rabbit. Everyone in the tent looked at her curiously. "Because we can't trust him."

"Kiva is not my only contact," Rabbit said, "and he's useless when it comes to military matters. I have other contacts in the Merchant Guild, some among the Sanctus guards, and more among the military you left down there. I think we can gather most of the fighting men of the south to our cause."

"Does anyone have contacts on the Eastern Reaches?" Sam asked. "The monks visit some of the closer towns occasionally, but not past that."

"There are barely any people on the Reaches," Braddick said.

"But there are some," Atticus noted. "We've traveled there often. It'll take time to get word to all the larger towns, but I think we can get some help. The Reaches have been dealing with raiders attacking their villages for generations. When they discover some of those raiders were Kalesh in disguise, they'll be willing to fight back."

"And the Kalesh may send their troops over the Reaches again," Sable said. "We need someone watching out for that."

"You do realize none of you have any say in the north, right?" Braddick asked, standing with his arms crossed. "Not to mention that even if you could get help from the south and the Reaches, that's hardly a substantial number of people."

"The dwarves could watch the Reaches," Leonis said, as though Braddick hadn't spoken. "You can see most of the plains from the watchtowers on the Marsham Cliffs."

Thulan shot him a scowl. "There are no dwarves."

"That we've found," Leonis corrected her.

"The tunnels were collapsed with no sign of even attempted repairs!" Thulan said, exasperated.

"Maybe it's time we solved that little riddle," Atticus said, nodding slowly. "We should send someone to find the dwarves."

"Who better than a dwarf?" Leonis asked.

Thulan glared at him.

The room broke out in arguments again, and Atticus started shouting over them.

Flibbet leaned closer to Sable. "I thought Thulan might be happy to go home."

"She left Torren years ago," Sable said quietly, "after a cave-in killed her husband and two sons."

The peddler looked at Thulan. "Oh," he said quietly.

"We also need to talk to the elves," Atticus yelled, finally gaining the attention of the room.

Sable nodded.

Leonis shook his head. "That's a waste of time."

"Both sets of elves," Atticus continued, ignoring him. "We need to visit your people in the Wildwood, Leonis, and also someone needs to go to Ayda's people in the Greenwood. I don't know how many elves live in the Greenwood, but if we could get them on our side, they'd be powerful allies."

"The elves?" Braddick asked. "How? Wander their woods and call out to them? You won't find them."

"Leonis is a half-elf," Atticus said.

Leonis turned a scathing look on the old man.

Atticus waved him off. "It's hardly a secret." He turned back to Braddick. "If Leonis goes to the Wildwood, they'll talk to him."

Leonis crossed his arms and scowled at the playwright. "They'll never join us."

"I don't know," Sable said. "I distinctly remember elves being unhappy with people who burn trees. I think the elves will fight to keep that from happening."

"We'll find a way to convince them," Atticus said. "Because we need their help."

Atticus's words were warm, and Sable nodded.

"Nothing is going to convince the dwarves to help," Thulan said loudly. "Even if we can find them."

Sable looked at the map on the table, thinking of everything they'd discussed—the strategy, the training, the fighting. All that she was useless at, but this she could do.

The elven woods and dwarven tunnels were marked out on the map, far from Tutella and isolated from the human world. Even getting to them would be a challenge, but…

All we are really left with is the choice to hope, Rob had said.

Sable leaned forward. "They can be convinced," she said, pushing warmth into her words. They spread out like a strong wind, and the argument paused. She waited until the entire tent was looking at her. "Everyone can be convinced if you just ask the right way."

"You haven't dealt much with dwarves, have you?" Thulan asked.

"She's dealt with you plenty," Leonis said.

"They can be convinced," Sable said, fueling her words with confidence. "They live in this land, so they have a stake in this problem."

Atticus looked pleased but curious. "I agree. Are you volunteering?"

Braddick gave a derisive snort. His jaw and brow were squared off in the contemptuous look they'd kept since she'd met him, and something about it reminded her of Eugessa.

She held the general's gaze. "Yes. I'll go."

"That is an excellent idea," Rabbit spoke up from his corner of the tent. "We send the Queen of the North."

"There is no Queen of the North," Braddick said, not looking away from her.

Sable nodded. "That's our problem. There is no real Queen of the North. Nor King of the North. We need their help, but who do I ask them to ally with? There is no North to join. Shall I say, 'You can come fight alongside five bickering lords who mostly just want to expand their own land and refuse to work together and will probably splinter at the first sign of trouble'? Because that's not a very tempting offer."

"You're not saying anything. Whichever messenger goes to the dwarves and elves needs to be sanctioned by the Northern Lords—" Braddick began with an imperious tone.

"How long will that take?" Reese interrupted. "Because if the Emperor is already organizing the Tien Sark, I'd say our time to gather troops is limited to a couple of months at the most, and you know how quickly the lords agree on anything."

"What's your suggestion?" Braddick asked. "Send actors throughout the land to gather an army together?"

"These actors are good at motivating people," Reese said, "and I think sending the Queen of the North is a good idea."

"That's not funny," Braddick said.

Atticus stepped forward. "It's not meant to be. You need an emissary to ask for help. We have one."

"She is not a queen," Braddick growled.

"Of course she has no real power," Atticus said, as though that was the least important aspect of an ambassador. "She's a symbol, but some of the north follow her, and trust me, more will join if she asks. She's right—the north is nothing but five squabbling lords. You are outmatched by the Kalesh and need help. Neither the elves nor the dwarves are going to commit to joining a cause that is so divided at its core."

"She is nothing!" Braddick slammed his hand down on the table. "And you can't make her something merely by pasting an imaginary title on her."

"It doesn't matter what she actually is," Atticus said, exasperated. "The only important thing is that the people believe in her!"

"Enough!" Braddick snapped. "We hardly need the advice of an old man who earns his living parading before the masses for applause." He turned to Reese with a withering look. "You used to be a good leader, Andreese. A man the troops respected because you led them rationally. You've clearly lost that. Feel free to leave. The north has no use for a man who has forgotten his roots."

Voices shouted something unintelligible outside the tent, and Sam gestured for a monk to investigate.

For the brief moment the flap was open, a jumble of voices flowed in.

"I agree that we need to find allies," Sam said, speaking louder to be heard over the noise, "and I don't think we have the time to wait for the Northern Lords to meet to discuss this. Here on the island, we have officers from every northern territory. We can agree on a set of temporary ambassadors and send them out, and as they're searching for allies, we'll speak with the Northern Lords about formalizing—"

The tent flap opened again, bringing with it the noise, and the monk stepped back inside. He let the flap drop, looking uncomfortable. "A unit of wounded soldiers just arrived from Lord Erick's territory."

"We'll take their report soon," Sam said. "Find them a place to rest."

The monk hesitated. "They didn't come to report, sir. They heard the Flame of the North is here in the tent."

Sable straightened. Braddick looked at the man incredulously, but most of the other eyes in the tent turned toward Sable.

"You should go say hello," Atticus prompted her.

"After we're done here," she said. "This is important."

"More important than offering some happiness to men who were wounded fighting for our cause?"

She turned to argue with him, but he was looking at her with an intensity that brought her up short. As though this decision was of huge importance.

"You should go," Braddick said, "because you have absolutely nothing to add to this discussion."

Sable ignored him. "Why?" she asked Atticus bluntly.

"Because the Flame of the North has never been about convincing generals of anything," he said. "Just go say hello to the men. I can't imagine what they've been through. If it can give them a little joy to see the Flame," he said, leaning toward her, "it's worth it." His last words swirled with warmth.

She stared at him for a moment, searching for a reason for his sudden interest in the men outside.

His beard twitched with the slightest smile, and one eyebrow rose like an entreaty. "Don't you think?"

"Yes," she said finally, "but they're going to be disappointed that I don't have Innov." She pointed at the playwright. "Make sure the people here make good decisions."

"I'm working on it," he said with a small smile.

She felt every eye on her as she walked over to the tent flap, pausing to glance down at her plain clothes. Her shirt was dingy, and the knees of her pants were muddy from kneeling in the garden. It was a far cry from the dresses she'd worn in Steepdale when Thulan and Leonis had taken it upon themselves to "keep the Flame of the North looking bright and shiny."

Well, it was about time the northern soldiers saw that without Innov, she was just a regular woman.

She straightened her shoulders and pushed the tent flap aside. The bright sunlight nearly blinded her as she stepped forward, letting the rough canvas drop closed behind her. Two dozen soldiers dressed in blues and greys stood outside the tent. When they saw her, a cheer went up.

Sable smiled at them, the motion feeling uncomfortably fake while she struggled to let go of her irritation with Braddick.

"Hello," she greeted them, trying to think of something appropriate to say.

The men were bandaged and so filthy she immediately forgot about her own dirt. Several were supported by their comrades, and others used rough crutches to help bear their weight. She searched their faces but didn't recognize any of them.

The ones who had use of their right arms pressed their fists to their chests in salutes, and she waved the motion off, but her gaze caught on one of the nearest soldiers. He was tall, but he couldn't have been older than sixteen. His round cheeks were covered with the lightest dusting of patchy stubble. He wobbled on his crutches, trying to keep his salute. He held his left foot off the ground, the entire leg of his grey uniform dyed red with blood.

Whatever words she had drained away.

The young soldier straightened as much as his crutches would let him under her gaze. "We cleared the Kalesh out of Lord Erick's southern hills, Issable," he reported. "A bunch of cowards, attacking women and children and undefended farms."

There were nods of agreement.

"What's your name?" Sable asked him.

"Tom," he answered.

"Baby Henry," someone called from behind him, and a ripple of laughter ran through the men.

"Nice to meet you, Tom," Sable said. "Please call me Sable."

She looked around at the others. Every one of them looked weary and several looked ready to collapse.

"Sit down," Sable said. "Please, there's no reason to be standing like this."

They stared at her, unmoving, so she sat down in the dirt. "Sit, please."

Tom glanced at the tent. "That's the command tent…"

"It's hardly hallowed ground," she said. "None of the officers in there would have anything to whine and argue about if it weren't for you men doing the real fighting. Now sit before you all fall down."

An older man near the back with a close-cropped greying beard sank to the ground with a groan. "Sit down, boys. When a woman tells you to sit, you sit. Where are your manners?"

The others exchanged looks, then, slowly and with a lot of suppressed groans, they sat. Sable looked over the crowd of dirty soldiers against the backdrop of the orchard trees.

"Where are you all from?" she asked. "I see greys of Lord Loren's troops and a few blues from Lord Darien. Are there none of Lord Erick's men, even though you were fighting in his land?"

There was an awkward silence.

"Nat and Pool were both from Lord Erick's land," Tom said. "We made it to Pool's town, but not before the Kalesh." His eyes dropped to the dirt. "He'd have liked to know we cleared them all out."

Several heads nodded in agreement, and Sable suddenly saw that wrapped up in the weariness of their faces were deep streaks of loss.

"Thank you," she said quietly, the words barely audible. She pushed some truth into them, trying to help the men feel how deeply she meant it. "Thank you for fighting. Thank you for stopping them from destroying more towns."

The air around them warmed, and a few of the men managed small smiles.

"Have you heard reports from Lord Loren's lands?" a grey-clad soldier asked. His expression was half hope, half dread.

"I know we defeated the Kalesh there," she said. "With the farmsteads more spread out, the Empire wasn't able to destroy as much. I don't have information on specific towns, but I'll find someone who does." She glanced at the blue uniforms in the group. "In Lord Darien's lands, the Kalesh struck mostly in the southwest."

Several heads turned toward the older man in the back, who kept his eyes fixed on the ground.

"Grey's family is there," Tom said. "In a town called Pinebur. He built a house there, just off the town square. His son had a baby girl last winter. Grey talks about her all the time."

A Tutella monk Sable vaguely recognized came up behind the seated soldiers, looking curiously at them before skirting the group and heading for the command tent.

"Excuse me," Sable said to him.

He paused. "Good afternoon, Issable."

"Embarrassingly enough, I don't remember your name."

"Durnek," he answered.

"Well, Durnek, these men would like to know which towns were attacked by the Kalesh."

The monk nodded. "We can make a list of the towns they're interested in if they send an officer to request that information."

"Our captain died yesterday morning," Tom said.

"Then who's in charge?" the monk asked.

The soldiers glanced at each other, several looking back at Grey, who showed no interest in acknowledging the role.

Sable motioned at the tent. "I saw the map with the information right inside on the table in front of General Braddick," she said mildly. "We only need it for a few minutes."

Durnek hesitated. "It's the only map we have, so there's a procedure in place for this. If you send a commanding officer to bring a list of the areas they are interested in, I will personally check them."

"But they don't have a commanding officer," Sable pointed out. "And neither do I. What I do have is the assurance from Sam that the Tutella monks will help me with anything I need. Right now, I need the map."

Durnek gave her a conflicted look.

"These men just want to know if their families are safe," she said.

The monk nodded. "I'll ask Sam."

"Excellent. We'll wait here."

CHAPTER FOURTEEN

Sable looked at the soldiers sitting in front of her. They were exhausted, and there was a desperation lurking at the edge of every expression. She wanted to draw back from whatever stories they were holding so tightly, but her gaze fell to Tom's leg, the blood-soaked pants. The things these men had done deserved more than a change of subject.

Everyone has a story to tell, she heard Atticus say. *They're dying to tell it. They just think no one wants to hear it.*

She took a deep breath and met their eyes, facing the pain they were trying not to show.

"Aside from Nat and Pool," Sable made herself say, "how many men did you lose?"

No one spoke for a moment, and she forced herself not to shift. Atticus never shifted when he waited for people to speak. He did nothing but wait, patiently.

"Cooper," Grey said from the back. The others nodded.

"What was he like?" Sable asked.

"Obnoxious," someone said to a spattering of laughter.

"He loved carrots," another added.

"Who loves carrots?" Sable asked.

"No one but Cooper."

"Every time we camped near a farm, he snuck through the fields and dug up carrots," Tom said.

"Those stupid carrots," someone muttered.

"We lost the boy," Grey said.

"The boy?" Sable asked.

"His name was Robbin," Tom said. "He was fifteen and no taller than you."

"The boy could shoot a bow like no other," someone said.

"But dreadful with a sword," another answered.

There was another moment of silence.

"Captain nearly made it back here," one soldier said quietly.

The others nodded.

"What were Nat and Pool like?" Sable asked.

Several heads turned toward a man on the left side of the group, and he gave a small smile. "They were cousins, and you've never met two men who bickered more." He launched into a story about Nat and Pool arguing over the right way to trap frogs, and soon the whole unit was grinning and nodding along.

Sable caught sight of Grey in the back, tears rolling down his cheeks into his beard.

The tent flap opened behind her, and Durnek reappeared, holding the rolled map. Sable stood and took it from him, blinking back her own tears.

"If there are no notes by the town," he said, "it's unharmed, as far as we know."

"Thank you." She walked around the seated men and handed the map to Grey.

He held it for a moment before unrolling it, his eyes searching until they froze on one point. He read the note scrawled beside it. The map began to shake in his hands.

"Grey?" someone asked quietly.

The older man started to roll up the map, but his hands shook so badly that he dropped it. The man next to him picked it up but didn't open it.

"You can all use it," Sable said quietly.

The man held the map out to Sable. "None of the rest of us can read."

Grey dropped his head into his hands, his whole body trembling. The men around him put their hands on his shoulders, their faces bleak.

Sable unrolled the map, searching for Pinebur. It was a small dot in Lord Darien's land, not far from the border. Next to it was the note: *Attacked in first wave. Town burned. No known survivors.*

"Pinebur?" Tom asked, his voice barely audible.

Sable opened her mouth, but Grey let out a sob, and she just shook her head.

"Is Hillock on there?" Tom asked, his voice frightened. "A day's walk southwest of Barrowford?"

Sable searched the map. "Hillock looks unharmed."

Tom let out a breath of relief, then his expression turned guilty, and he glanced at Grey.

"Rowntree?" another asked. "A half day west of Barrowford."

Sable found the town. "Some of the outlying farms to the south were attacked, but the city fought off the Kalesh."

Durnek waited as soldier after soldier called out names of their homes and Sable searched the map. Three more towns were marked destroyed with limited survivors. The rest were either unharmed or too small to be marked.

When every man was done, she rolled the map back up and handed it to Durnek. "Thank you."

The monk looked over the men. "You fought in Lord Erick's territory?" To the answering nods, he pressed his fist to his chest in a salute. "We heard multiple reports from refugees of your bravery and the sacrifices made by some of your brothers-in-arms. Many of the families here are alive today because of you."

He turned and went back into the command tent. Voices drifted out while the flap was open, and Sable thought she heard Reese, but she couldn't make out the words.

She walked back to the front of the soldiers, at a loss of what to say. She almost sat again, but this moment deserved...something. So she stayed standing, feeling like she was on a stage. Except no one had given her a script.

Ryah would know what to say, she realized, thinking back to the funeral her sister had dressed up like an abbess for.

Sable looked at Grey, the fact that he would never again hold his granddaughter tightening her throat.

"My sister," she said, the words coming out ragged as she looked over men, "has a prayer for those who've been lost." She waited, but when none of the men objected, she thought back to how Ryah had prayed with Thulan, back in the dwarven cave where her family had died. She tried to recall the first words.

"For those who no longer walk with us, but still move within our hearts—" The final words caught in her throat. She closed her eyes, seeing

Narine laughing with Flibbet. Seeing Bastian's face as he walked steadfastly beside her toward his own death.

She kept her eyes closed and pushed all that pain into her words, forcing the next ones out, even if her voice broke. Trying to make them a gift to these men whom she had nothing else to offer.

"For those whose hands are out of reach but whose touch we still feel." Her voice dropped to barely above a whisper, but the soldiers were silent. The warmth of her words stretched toward them, wrapped around them.

"For those who can never be untangled from our past, or our hopes, or our souls." She heard a sob from the back.

"May their names be spoken by our lips and heard in our ears. Bless us with the strength to carry the loss, and may we remember them well."

She stopped, and the heat from her words dissipated into the normal warmth of the afternoon. When she opened her eyes, most of the soldiers' heads were bowed, the faces she could see weary and tear streaked.

Squeals came from past the men, jarring and loud, and two children raced out of the orchard. A girl, no older than ten, held a piece of bread out in front of her, grinning and looking back over her shoulder at a younger boy chasing her, his face lit with laughter. The girl turned and skidded to a stop, almost running into the man next to Grey.

Every soldier turned to her, and she took in the group with wide, surprised eyes, then flashed them a bright smile. "Sorry!" she called as she whipped around and ran back toward the trees, the boy scrambling after her.

Sable watched them run in among the trees. Behind her, voices rose in the command tent, still arguing, and she let out a sigh.

"Are the Kalesh coming back?" Tom asked, his eyes still fixed on the children disappearing among the refugees under the trees. "Grey's been telling us they're coming back." He looked at Sable. "These people aren't safe yet, are they?"

Sable looked at the soldiers again, wishing there were someone else standing in front of them to give them this news. These men should all be home, living their lives, not here, wounded and broken.

Every one of them looked back at her, waiting for her answer, their expressions varying from hope to numbness to anger. From the back, Grey lifted his head, and she forced herself to meet his gaze.

"They're coming back." She wanted to come up with something that would be comforting, something that would give this man some sort of hope.

It is better to tell the truth, she heard Narine's voice quietly in her mind, *or say nothing at all.*

Sable kept her eyes on Grey. "You have lost more than anyone should ever have to lose, and all I want is to undo it all and send you back home whole, back to your safe, living families." She poured the truth and fear of it all into her words. "I hate," she said, her voice breaking, "that we have to ask more of you."

The tent flap rustled behind her, but she kept her eyes fixed on Grey.

"The Kalesh are coming back, and in greater numbers. We fought them off in the south, but…they're coming back. Angrier than before."

The grief in Grey's expression shifted to anger. Around him, shoulders slumped and heads dropped forward.

"We are faced with an enemy who vastly overpowers us," she continued, "and wants nothing more than to destroy everything we are. No one should have to give what you've already given, but the north still needs you. The south needs you. We need thousands of more men like you, and I don't know where we're going to find them. The Northern Lords will command you to fight, but a soldier reminded me recently that the only person who has a right to risk your life is you." She forced herself to finish, hating every word. "We need you. Will you still fight for us?"

Grey stared at her, anger and grief warring in his expression.

"Did you really kill the Kalesh general?" Tom asked.

Sable looked at him, uncertain how to answer such an odd question.

The soldiers perked up with interest.

"And the Kalesh ambassador?" the man next to him asked.

"And that Dragon Prioress?" another called out.

A breath, caught somewhere between a laugh and a sob, escaped her. She shook her head. "No. The Dragon Prioress is alive, although Innov, the phoenix, did blind her dragon in one eye."

Mutters of approval rolled through them.

"The Kalesh ambassador was killed, but not by me," Sable continued, quietly. "He turned out to be a good man and betrayed the Empire in an attempt to help us. He was killed by the Kalesh general Goll for it."

Raised eyebrows met this claim.

"I didn't kill the general either," she said. "But I was there when he died. A man from the south killed him."

"That's enough to anger an Empire?" Grey asked. "The death of two of their men during a battle?"

Sable paused. "That's not what they're angry about. They discovered that I'm the daughter of a notorious rebel. My mother took part in a rebellion years ago and assassinated the Emperor's brother."

A low mutter of approval came from the men, and she gave them a weak smile. "She sparked other rebellions and caused the Empire endless problems. So they tracked her down, all the way to the Eastern Reaches, and killed her."

The soldiers quieted.

"But now they know I'm alive, and in their eyes, I helped fight them off in the south." She shrugged. "They're very angry."

Grey gave her a grim smile. "Good."

She opened her mouth to point out it wasn't good, but Tom let out a whooping cheer.

"Issable!" he shouted. "Flame of the North!"

"It's Sable," Grey corrected him.

Tom grinned. "Sable! Flame of the North! Bane of the Kalesh!"

She let out a laugh. "Hardly a bane."

But her voice was drowned out by the other soldiers taking up the cheer.

Behind her, she heard Atticus ask, "Still think she's nothing?"

Sable glanced back to see him next to Braddick, who was watching her, his arms crossed. He took in the soldiers and the cheering, then turned calculating eyes back on Sable.

"You put her anywhere," Atticus continued, "and it is the same."

She looked back at the soldiers. "Thank you, again, for everything you've done. We are indebted to you."

A few of them nodded back awkwardly.

"Captain." She looked at Grey. "Please take care of these men."

Grey's eyes narrowed at the title, but a murmur of approval rose from the other soldiers, and he didn't object.

Braddick stepped up next to Sable, and she stiffened. He raised his hands, and the men quieted. "I'm Braddick of Ravenwood."

A ripple of recognition moved through the seated soldiers.

"I'm the general of Lord Perric's and Lord Runess's troops." Several men started to push themselves to their feet, but he held up his hand. "Stay seated. You've earned the rest."

They sank back down, but their postures straightened.

"I'd like to hear your report from Lord Erick's land, Captain."

Grey stood and saluted Braddick before beginning his report. Sable watched the older man talk. The dirt on his cheeks was rubbed clean in places from his tears, but his voice was steady as he reported on the fighting the men had seen. He held his arms tight against his side like every soldier she'd ever seen give a report to their superior officer. But all she could think about was his granddaughter and the fact those arms would never reach down and pick her up again.

The image shifted to her own dream cottage in the woods, the little girl squatting down to pick a flower.

The anger that had been held at bay by these men's loss swelled up in her again. So many cottages destroyed. Families, homes, dreams. And all for what? Some gold mines?

Grey recounted the losses they'd taken, and somehow his voice held firm, but Sable felt her own breathing growing faster, more ragged. Grey met her gaze and held it. She saw her own anger mirrored in his face.

Next to her, Braddick shifted, the motion irritated. Grey turned his attention back to the general, but it didn't stay there. Every few sentences, the newly made captain's attention would shift between Sable and Braddick. And what she'd first taken as an appreciation of her emotional support, she soon recognized as something else.

Grey was reporting to both of them. As equals.

The few seconds of doubt she had about the idea were put to rest by Braddick's increasing tension every time Grey addressed her.

Atticus had moved a little off to the side, and Sable caught him watching the interaction shrewdly. As Grey's report drew to a close, the playwright fixed Sable with the intense, expectant look he always gave her on stage, demanding she play her role passionately.

She turned her attention back to Grey, and, as the man finished, she stepped forward a step, smoothly pulling everyone's attention to herself. Out of the corner of her eye, she saw Atticus smile.

"Thank you, Captain," she said. "As we spoke about earlier, the Kalesh are coming back, and in greater numbers. We have been attempting to convince General Braddick that the Northern Lords are in desperate need of allies from the south, but also from the elves and the dwarves."

Several of the soldiers nodded in support of this, and Sable could feel Braddick's eyes on her.

"That's exactly what we need." Grey turned to Braddick. "There aren't enough men in the north to fight. We need allies."

"The Flame of the North is right," someone said. "She's been with us from the beginning—she knows."

"Some are calling you the Queen of the North," Tom said with a little grin. "You could send some ambassadors yourself. Get us some help if the lords won't."

Braddick stepped forward at this. "If there really were a queen in the north," he said dismissively, "she could certainly do that. As it is, I have considered the reports from the troops who have fought here and those who faced the Kalesh in the south. While I don't believe the north is as weak as Issable believes"—she straightened at the accusation—"I agree that there is no harm in meeting with our dwarven and elven neighbors. Their lands are in danger from the Kalesh as well, and it is right that we both warn them and offer them a chance to fight alongside us if they wish."

Sable caught sight of a frown on Atticus's face.

"So," Braddick continued before she could speak. "I have named Issable ambassador to the elven and dwarven people on behalf of the north." Braddick turned to her. "Your orders are to bring news of the Kalesh to our neighbors and invite them to join in our defense of the land."

The soldiers let out a cheer.

"Orders?" Sable murmured.

Braddick set his hand on her shoulder and gave her a condescending smile, waiting until the soldiers quieted. "You leave at dawn. You are to report to me and the rest of the northern leadership in Barrowford as soon as possible."

Without waiting for her to answer, Braddick dropped his hand and turned back to the soldiers. "Space has been prepared for you to rest and recover," he said, in the tone of a general giving a dismissal.

The men rose quickly.

Durnek stepped forward. "If you will follow me, we'll find you a hot meal and see to your injuries."

With a few parting salutes that included both Sable and Braddick, the soldiers followed Durnek toward an open part of the orchard.

Sable crossed her arms and frowned up at Braddick. "You named me ambassador?"

"That's what you wanted, isn't it?" the general said. "To prance around and get attention? Well, now you can do it with the north's blessing. Just do it far away from here. Neither the dwarves nor the elves will have any interest in assisting our cause. But by all means, go ask them. It should take you a few weeks, and that's a few weeks we don't need to see you."

The ideas of Grey's granddaughter and the little cottage in the woods and the lost soldiers were still too fresh in her mind for Braddick's insults to be anything more than an irritation.

"I will go," Sable said firmly, "and I will convince them to help, because we desperately need them, as you very well know."

Braddick's expression remained bland.

Sable stepped closer to him, lifting her chin to look up at him. "But not because you're sending me. I'd go talk to them even if you tried to forbid it, because I am not your pawn." She shoved the truth into her words. "I'm not your soldier, and I'm not a tool for you to use to gain more power."

The air around them warmed, but Braddick gave her an unconcerned shrug and leaned forward. "It doesn't matter whether I truly have the power to order you around, right? It only matters that the people believe I do." Without another word, he turned and reentered the tent.

Atticus walked up next to her, smiling widely. "I'm starting to enjoy watching people boss you around. It makes you fiery." He nudged her shoulder with his. "Come back inside the miserably hot tent, Your Majesty. We'll map out exactly how we're going to get all these allies."

CHAPTER FIFTEEN

SABLE LEANED her hip on the side of a desk near the flap of the tent, her irritation with everything growing by the hour. She fanned herself with a piece of paper holding a long list of supplies for the army.

Braddick still stood along the center of a wide table, dominating the discussion. On either side of him, officers from the northern armies gathered. Every situation that rose, no matter how many territories of the north were represented, somehow Braddick ended up controlling the conversation. Even now, when they'd managed to find someone from each territory who had some degree of authority, Braddick still took the role of general.

Reese sat with Sam at one end of the table, the two of them talking more often to each other than the whole group. A handful of the officers who'd gone south clustered around them.

"So," Reese interrupted another longwinded argument, "we've named delegates to send to each Northern Lord and tell them what we're attempting. Atticus will lead an effort to find allies on the Eastern Reaches. Jae and Serene will be sent to the Greenwood to meet with the elf Ayda and the elvish king. Rabbit can get word south and organize both the northern troops who are still there defending the city and any forces the merchants are willing to supply."

When no one objected, he continued. "Then, we have Sable, Thulan, and Leonis, who will head east. They will visit the Wildwood, where Leonis has family—"

Leonis sighed heavily at the words.

"—and Thulan will lead them to the northern entrance of the dwarves, where hopefully we will find some dwarven allies as well."

Sable glanced at the people gathered in the tent. Her satisfaction at getting to be the ambassador was shadowed with a strange loneliness. Traveling with Thulan and Leonis would be entertaining, and it would be harder to worry over the future amidst all their banter. But it would be strange to not have Atticus along. Or Serene and Jae.

Sable's eyes strayed to Reese. He'd started out the afternoon standing but had found a chair at some point and now sat at the table, leaning on his crossed arms. He certainly wasn't up for a journey. Rob had said he needed at least two weeks of rest. It would take longer than that to talk to the elves and the dwarves.

A contingent of monks and the soldiers on the island would leave for Barrowford soon to join up with the rest of the north. Based on the number of conversations between Reese and Sam about how to keep Braddick from taking over there as well, Reese would make sure he was healthy enough to travel with them.

At least by the time Sable reached Barrowford, Reese should be back to full health.

As though he felt her eyes, he glanced over and offered her the ghost of a smile, then Sam said something and drew his attention back to the larger discussion.

"Andreese," Braddick commanded. "You'll go with them to the elves and dwarves."

Sable straightened.

Reese raised an eyebrow at the tone and opened his mouth.

But several of the officers near him bristled. "You don't have the authority to give General Andreese orders," one of them said.

"He's not a general," Braddick said dismissively. "It was a temporary field promotion in an army that no longer exists—"

Voices erupted again as the officers who'd gone south objected.

Sable studied Braddick, trying to figure out his motivation.

"You can't send him away," one of the officers near Reese shouted, "just because you're threatened by him."

If she hadn't been watching Braddick so closely, she would have missed the flicker of anger that challenge caused before he smoothed his expression.

"This delegation is supposed to be representatives of the north," Braddick said. "There should be at least one northerner among them."

"Didn't he accuse Reese of forgetting his northern roots earlier?" Leonis asked loud enough for the question to carry. Thulan grinned and nodded.

The rest of the tent dissolved into arguments.

Sable watched Reese rub his hands over his face in exhaustion. "I am going with them." His words were lost in the tumult of the tent.

Sable stared at him, torn between disapproval and relief.

She gathered herself to speak, ready to infuse some *vitalle* into the words and get the tent's attention. Reese's expression was annoyed, though, and she paused at a new idea.

Focusing on Reese, she pushed her words toward only him. "Try again," she said quietly, threading the words through the chaos of the room.

He turned toward her, looking mildly surprised.

"Say it again," she said, sending the words to him.

He opened his mouth, and she focused on him, weaving her desire for his words to fill the tent into the path she'd already created, hoping he wasn't too far away for it to work.

"I'm going with them," he declared again, and Sable infused the sound with *vitalle*.

His words blasted out into the sweltering tent, deafeningly loud.

Thulan jumped so violently she fell off the table. Leonis slapped his hands over his ears.

Throughout the tent, soldiers flinched or ducked, many of them grabbing for their weapons.

Atticus stared at Sable, his mouth open in shock.

Sable pressed her hand to her mouth to stifle a laugh in the utter silence. Reese glanced at her with a raised eyebrow, then turned back to the tent, which was now completely focused on him.

"I'm going with them," he repeated in a measured tone, "because I think that finding allies is essential in surviving what's coming. The Tutella monks have a relationship with both the elves and the dwarves, but with the number of refugees and soldiers here, they do not have a single man to spare. Sam has asked me to go as an ambassador from the Island, and I've accepted."

Next to him, Sam nodded. "Andreese has worked closely with the monks. We're confident he will represent us well."

Braddick shrugged. "Then it's settled."

His words were offhanded, but the general seemed pleased. Relieved almost.

The soldiers around Reese who'd fought at Immusmala still muttered amongst themselves. He shifted his back to Braddick to face them. "The unity you found needs to expand to the rest of the north. You're the ones who know it can be done." He gestured behind him. "Men like this haven't seen it yet. They still think the old divisions matter. Show them they're wrong."

The officers around him nodded, if somewhat reluctantly.

Braddick kept his expression unimpressed. "We'll expect a report in Barrowford as soon as you can finish your task."

Reese met his gaze. "Try to do something useful while we're gone. Power plays won't help the north survive what's coming."

"Worry about your own task," Braddick said with a dismissive wave. "Try not to let us all down."

People started to leave the tent, and Sable followed Thulan and Leonis out of the stifling space. They moved to the shade of the nearest tree, and Sable lifted her hair and let the gloriously cool breeze blow across her neck.

Reese came out and moved over to stand beside her. "I think Purnicious is rubbing off on you," he said with a small smile. "I appreciate the help in there, but it was...more exuberant than I had expected."

She laughed. "I wasn't sure it would actually make your words louder, so I poured a lot into it." She paused. "If I'd been thinking, I would have muted Braddick the whole time."

He shifted until his shoulder was leaning against the tree. "Let's try that next time he talks."

Atticus exited the tent, rubbing his hands together and coming to join them. "That could have gone worse," he said cheerfully, all signs of his recent frustration gone.

"It could have gone better," Sable said.

Atticus shook his head. "Despite all the blustering and fighting, they all know it's time to unite. They'll angle for more influence when it happens, but we're on the path now. The armies are all headed to Barrowford, which is the obvious place to solidify the north into one land. And it's in Lord Darien's territory," he finished, as though this was fantastic.

"The Lord Darien who is constantly derisive and rude to us?" Sable asked.

"Exactly the one," Atticus said. "He is also *not* one of the two most powerful lords. So neither Lord Perric, whose army is the largest, nor Lord Runess, whose is nearly as big, will have the advantage of gathering the north in their own territory, and Darien knows he's only powerful enough to compete with those two if he stays unified with Loren and Erick. It's not full unity, but it's headed in that direction."

"That doesn't help us convince the dwarves and elves to help," Sable said. "Any brilliant ideas for that?"

Atticus's gaze drifted to the nearby trees. "In a story, characters are never driven by only one thing. They often appear to be, but if you can find the secondary things that drive them, you'll find the way their hearts and paths can be changed." He refocused on Thulan and Leonis and set his hands on their shoulders. "The elves and dwarves are as driven by relationships as the rest of us are. If anyone can gain their help, it's you two. Just lean into your connections there."

Neither of them looked pleased at the idea.

"I know it won't be easy, but the point of all this is that we can break down the walls that have kept people separated for so long," Atticus said with a smile. "Even the individual walls we put up around ourselves."

When Thulan and Leonis did not return his smile, he sighed and patted their shoulders. "Just…don't start any fights."

He dropped his hands and stepped back but kept his eyes on his two actors. "Do your best to reach Barrowford quickly. If you get there before me, start the stories again among the troops. Anything you can think of that puts Sable in a good light. Remind them of who the Flame is, and make sure that the troops who don't know find out. It doesn't matter if the Northern Lords like her—we need the people to know who she is. They'll need a symbol to rally behind. And tell the exploits of the troops in the south, how much they did once they unified. Let's make sure the northern soldiers are excited to become one force."

He turned to Sable. "Here in the north, they need a symbol of hope, and you've given them that, but the elves and the dwarves will be different. They'll need to know they are needed and be convinced they are already involved in this just by living here. Pay attention to your audience, and help them see whatever they're missing."

She raised an eyebrow. "You really think I wouldn't?"

"He's having a hard time with the fact he's not going to be with us," Leonis explained.

"I am," Atticus agreed. "You are all far too lackadaisical about planning." He looked at Reese, sighed, and shook his head.

"No advice for me?" Reese asked.

Atticus looked pointedly at where Reese was leaning his shoulder against the tree. "How are you possibly going to walk all day across country?"

"Sam offered me a horse."

"Can you stay awake long enough to ride it?"

Reese smiled. "I should be fine."

"You *should* stay here and rest until they're back, but since I know I'll never convince you of that, just...be careful. And..." He glanced at Thulan and Leonis, then back at Reese. "Please try not to get in any fights."

"We're a diplomatic delegation," Reese said. "If we're getting in fights, things will have gone very wrong."

Atticus sighed again. "That's what I'm afraid of."

PART II

The backdrops are key.

The elven wood must breathe with life. (Ahh, to capture those woods…a feat worthy of fame in itself.)

The dwarven tunnels of stone must feel weighty. Impenetrable. Dark, but not *dark. Protected, but intrinsically dangerous.*

These backdrops shape everything. Confine everything. Form the limits of what she can accomplish, like the bars of a cage.

The backdrops are key.

-Stage notes from act two, scene one of ***The Phoenix Rising*** by Atticus the Playwright.

CHAPTER SIXTEEN

As the sun rose the next morning, Sable walked next to Reese, who led his horse across the narrow grassy plain east of Tutella Island. Storm-scented wind blustered against her back, driving strands of black hair into her face.

She shifted the pack a monk had given her as thunder rolled in the distance.

"You took too long getting up, Leonis," Thulan said, trudging ahead of them with the half-elf, a large, heavy pack on her back. "The rain is going to catch up with us."

"Sable didn't want to get up at the stupid time you and Reese picked either." Leonis's own pack was surprisingly large and carried with surprisingly little complaint.

"That's true," Sable said to Reese. "It was too early."

His pack was loaded on the horse with several other sacks of supplies. "I seem to remember a few times that you were happy to wake up early with me."

She glanced over at him and caught a faint smile. "There were a couple of times that were worth it."

Leonis and Thulan's banter fell into a familiar, habitual flow.

"I didn't expect you to come with us," Sable said, keeping her voice low. "I thought you'd stay with the army and try to keep Braddick from taking over."

He let out an annoyed breath. "Braddick has positioned himself well. Really well. From where he is now, I don't see anyone unseating him. When the north unites, he'll lead the army." He squinted into the distance. "I'd have only gotten myself in trouble if I was around while that was happening."

"Is it really bad for the north that he'll be in charge?"

"He's a good strategist, so he won't make stupid mistakes with the army, but he's far too ruthless."

"That might not be a bad thing against the Kalesh," Sable said.

"Maybe," Reese answered.

They walked quietly for a few minutes while Thulan and Leonis squabbled about whether they'd reach the distant trees before the rain hit.

"So, avoiding Braddick..." Sable said thoughtfully. "Is that the only reason you came?"

Reese kept his eyes facing forward, but the corner of his mouth quirked up. "No."

When he didn't continue, she looked over at him. "What exactly was your other reason?"

He glanced at her, and his smile widened a little. "I didn't want Purnicious to miss me."

Sable raised an eyebrow. "Ah."

He stopped walking and flipped the cuff of his sleeve over to reveal thin pink threads embroidered into a row of flowers. "What would she do with her time?"

Sable took his arm and pulled it closer. The stitches were tiny and perfect, and she brushed her fingers over the back of his hand. "I would imagine there will be sunrises every day on this trip, unless we're inside dwarven tunnels."

"I'll be awake for them," he said.

She looked at him. "I will be too. If you wake me up." He smiled, but his shoulders were sagging. "If you're tired, you should ride," she said. "Rob made me swear I would tell you to take it easy."

He shook his head. "I'm tired of sitting and resting. I can walk a little longer."

Another rumble of thunder sounded, louder this time, and Sable glanced back at the pile of clouds rolling closer, their tops brilliantly white in the morning sun, their undersides dark and heavy.

An arc of golden light, trailing shimmering embers, shot across the nearest cloud.

Sable shook her head. "I had no idea Innov loved thunderstorms so much."

They watched the phoenix dive into the clouds, disappearing from sight, then started walking again.

"It's a good thing she's here," Reese said. "I think our negotiations are going to need all the help they can get. You remember last time Leonis came close to the elves, right?"

Sable nodded. To say the commander of the elven guard, Victis, had been displeased was an understatement. He'd forbidden Leonis from being even along the edge of the Wildwood and ordered them away with so much authority in his voice that the words had felt like they might crush her.

"Nothing has changed," Reese continued. "His elven father still doesn't want him there. Nor do any of the elves who had to fight to avenge the death of his human mother." He shook his head. "I'm not sure what family ties Atticus thought would be helpful here."

"True, but the elves wouldn't show themselves to anyone else."

"The only one who's going to show himself is Victis, and he'll be very commander of the guard-ish and tell us to go away."

"Cintis might show up too," Sable said.

"Some low-ranking elf friend isn't enough to make me feel more hopeful. And it's bad enough that Leonis is going to bring two humans with him, but Thulan too? There's a reason we all think elves and dwarves don't get along."

"I'm less worried about Thulan with the elves than I am with her returning to the tunnels." Sable looked up at the dwarf who was nearing the top of the hill. "If we were heading back to where my family was killed, I'd be a mess."

Reese sighed. "There's a good chance this is not going to go well."

The forest ahead was hidden by a small rise, and Sable's thoughts shifted to the elves and dwarves. Convincing them to join the fight couldn't be any harder than convincing the three factions of the north to unite before they'd gone to Immusmala. It was a matter of seeing their shared humanity—or shared whatever it was with dwarves and elves.

"Thulan," Sable called. "Talk to me about how the dwarves make decisions."

"It's simple," Thulan answered. "The High Dwarf invites his council to a dinner and tells them what he wants done. If it's not incredibly stupid, and the food is good enough, they agree. If it is stupid, they'll argue and usually fight it out, but by the time the second round of ale is poured, all business is done."

"So the strongest dwarf gets their way?" Sable asked.

Thulan shrugged. "With humans, the person with the most political strength gets their way."

"That's unfortunately true." Sable walked for a few moments in silence. "So I either need to convince the High Dwarf or some other dwarf strong enough to convince the others."

"To fight the others," Thulan corrected her.

She looked at Leonis. "How about the elves?"

"If there's a decision to be made," Leonis said, "the king presents it to a gathering of all the elves, anyone can speak up who wants to, and whichever decision has the most support wins. There's no arguing."

"Even if the king disagrees?" she asked.

"The king is just another elf," Leonis replied. "His opinion counts no more than any other."

"But he has authority, right?" Sable asked.

Leonis nodded. "The king's words hold more authority than any elf's, but he won't use that to change anyone's mind."

"Then what's the point of having it?" Thulan asked.

"He commands the forest," Leonis said.

Thulan snorted. "To do what? Uproot themselves and march somewhere?

Leonis looked thoughtfully at the sky. "I don't think they could do that, although I've seen the king command a tree to change its shape. Mostly he uses it to talk to the trees, and sometimes the animals."

"Sounds like a waste," Thulan said.

A huge crash of thunder rolled across the sky.

"Time to move quicker," Thulan said. "Up on the horse, Reese!"

A spatter of rain hit Sable's arm, then her shoulder. Behind them, the hills past Tutella Island were already hazy with rain. Thulan broke into a run, and Leonis and Sable followed. Reese mounted the horse and trotted behind them. In moments, rain pelted down on them, drenching Sable's shoulders and hair, dripping into her face.

By the time they reached the first trees, she was soaked. Leonis led them in farther until the canopy thickened enough to catch most of the rain in a loud, rushing patter. Sable sank down next to Thulan.

"Is rain a sign of good luck or bad?" Sable asked.

"Good," Leonis said.

Thulan shook her head. "Bad."

Sable pushed her wet hair back. "Leonis, what if I told the elves that my mother was friends with an elf? I could tell them that there was some blood oath between Evay and Melia."

"That is a terrible idea. She was an elf from"—Leonis waved toward the east—"somewhere in the Kalesh Empire. They won't care about her. Elves are territorial. They are fiercely protective of the elves they live with. It's why Victis would avenge my mother's death. Not for my human mother, but because they'd killed the wife of one of the Wildwood elves."

He shook his head. "It's why they don't really like me. I'm not truly a Wildwood elf. I'm too contaminated by the not-Wildwood world. They wouldn't even be swayed if you had a blood oath with Ayda or some elf from the Greenwood, and that's only a fortnight's journey away from them."

"They don't care about other elves?" Sable asked.

"Maybe slightly more than they'd care about humans, but in general, no. Don't bring it up."

"Well, what is going to convince them to help us?"

Leonis shrugged. "Nothing, which is why I never thought it was worth asking. You're the one who said they could be convinced."

"How many days is it going to take to reach the Wildwood?" Thulan asked, pushing herself back up to her feet.

Leonis looked up, as though he could judge from the trees around them. "Probably six days. We could shave that down to five if Reese stays on the horse so we can move faster."

"We'll have at least that many days to reach the northern door of the dwarves," Thulan said, "which is going to be another useless stop. Then nearly a week to get back to Barrowford, where, if we're going to spread stories about Sable, we need all the time we can get. Let's shave off as many days from this pointless trip as we can."

"If you two think we're doomed to fail," Sable asked, standing up and shaking her arms more out of irritation than because it would actually make them any drier, "why did you two agree to come?"

"Atticus asked us to," Leonis said, as though it was the most obvious thing in the world.

"And you needed our help," Thulan added. "No one was going to talk to the two of you by yourselves. But it's still not going to work."

"Atticus should have asked you both to be encouraging," Sable said.

"He's not dumb enough to do that," Thulan answered with a grin.

On the fifth morning, the sun crept over the horizon with dazzling rays of light chasing fleeting strokes of color across the clouds.

Just like it had the other four days.

It would have been a fine sunrise to sit and watch.

Instead, just like the other days, Sable yawned through the dim light, climbing up a long hill as they hurried toward the elves.

They reached the top and paused. This crest was the highest point in any direction, and with a break in the trees, the world spread out around her with breathtaking views.

Ahead of her, the dark green of the Nidel Woods rolled over low hills like motionless waves in a wide lake of trees, running east until it butted up to the base of the Marsham Cliffs.

To the north, the forest and the cliffs continued as far as she could see, and behind her, the hills stretched away into the distance where Tutella Island must lie. Unlike the blazingly bright sun shining in the clear sky to the east, the clouds above and behind her were dark and brooding. A line of grey rain marched toward them from the northwest, obscuring everything past it.

She followed the others down the hill toward the forest.

When they reached the trees, well ahead of the rain, Leonis peered around. "We should head that way," he said, pointing in a direction that looked no different from any other. "It'll take the rest of the day to get to the edge of the Wildwood." He moved to the closest tree and set his hand on the bark, closing his eyes. He stood silent for a moment, then shook his head. "These trees aren't awake enough to send any sort of message. When we get closer, I'll see if I can get Cintis to come to us."

"The trees will talk to Cintis specifically?" Sable asked.

"No, they'll chatter to any elf who'll listen, but Cintis is with the guard, and they're always listening. They'll get the message to him." He sighed. "Let's get this over with so we can move on to making Thulan go somewhere she doesn't want to be."

The rain reached them sometime in the morning, but the canopy was thick enough to keep them relatively dry. By midafternoon, it wore itself out, and the sun shot through the thick forest, with occasional beams of light breaking into the hazy green. They followed a path that bordered a small stream moving deeper into the woods. The forest was beautiful, but Leonis's mood soured as the day dragged on, and Sable found herself staring most of the time at the dark leather of Thulan's back. Behind her, Reese's horse kept up a steady pattern of hoofbeats.

"Are you sure we're getting closer?" Thulan asked from a few paces behind Leonis. "Or are we just wandering?"

"We're getting closer," Leonis said, irritated. "Not that it matters. None of this is going to work. I'm the last person who should be on this diplomatic mission. I'm not even supposed to come back here."

"Cintis said you should," Sable pointed out.

Leonis shook his head. "Victis disagrees."

"Does that matter, though?" Sable asked seriously. "Victis is the commander of the guard, but does he have the power to say you can't come back?"

"No," Leonis answered, "but Victis is a very old friend of my father. And if my father doesn't want me back, then I really don't want to be here."

"Do you look like your father?" Sable asked. "I didn't think you looked elven until we saw Cintis and the others last time."

Leonis shrugged. "There's a slight resemblance." He sighed. "At this point, I probably look older than him. He won't look old for hundreds of years."

"How close are he and Victis?"

"They were very close until my father married a human."

"Then Victis is stupid," Thulan said. "If your father wanted to marry her, Victis should have been happy for them."

"Human lifespans are so short," Leonis said. "Victis thought it could only end in tragedy, and he was right."

"So we shouldn't love people just because they might die before us?" Thulan asked. "The fact that someone dies doesn't make the time you loved them worthless. Or wrong." Her words grew warm. "Or bad in *any* way."

Sable nodded, and when Leonis glanced back at Thulan, he took in both Sable and Reese as well, his irritation softening. "I know," he said. "Of course it doesn't. It's just..." He closed his mouth and refocused on the forest again.

"He's your father, Leonis," Thulan said. "Do you have *any* idea how much a father wants to see a son he lost?"

Leonis stopped but stayed facing forward. Thulan pulled to a stop too, and Sable paused. Reese's horse stepped up next to her. Sable couldn't see Thulan's face, but her arms were crossed.

"What if…" Leonis fell silent. Slowly, he turned back to Thulan, his expression torn.

Sable leaned back slightly, as though it was possible to stop intruding on the raw pain in Leonis's eyes. She bumped into Reese's leg, and he set his hand on her shoulder.

Leonis shook his head slowly. "*You* want to see your sons, Thulan, but what if he…" His voice caught, and he started again. "What if everything left him too broken?"

"You, of all people," Thulan said, her voice so low that Sable strained to hear, despite herself, "know that losing Brunn and the boys broke me." Her words filled the woods around them with heat.

Reese's hand tightened.

Leonis nodded. "I know. But you…" He gestured to her, the motion almost hopeless. "You survived. You took the pieces, and you…"

"I ran away." Thulan flung one arm toward the unseen Marsham Cliffs. "I left the pieces there, in that rubble, and I ran away. If it weren't for this bloody Empire and their bloody greed, I'd still be running!"

Leonis shook his head stubbornly. "I wish he'd run away. I wish he'd done anything. He…" He raked his hand through his hair, the motion desperate and almost lost. "He stopped *living*, Thulan."

She took a single step toward Leonis, her hands curling into fists. "So did I," she hissed.

He opened his mouth, but she pushed past him, storming down the trail, leaving blistering warmth behind her.

CHAPTER SEVENTEEN

THE FOREST HAD GROWN BRIGHTER and more vivid as they moved farther north into the Nidel Woods, but now that they'd reached the Wildwood, the leaves were such a vibrant green the air seemed to glow. Fingers of breeze moved along the forest paths with a wild freshness that dusted off the weariness from the day's travel. Reese even climbed down off his horse and walked for the afternoon.

Rain had come in spurts throughout the day, but rarely hard enough to make it through the branches above them. Innov soared over the trees, only coming down to Sable occasionally with water sizzling and steaming on her back. Despite the vibrant forest, neither Leonis nor Thulan had spoken much since their argument earlier.

Without Atticus to write her speeches, Sable found herself rehearsing in her mind what she could say to the elves. The farther into the woods she walked, though, the less convincing her arguments felt. This forest felt like its own separate world, and it was very easy to believe the elves would not care what happened outside its borders.

She peppered Leonis with questions about other times the elves had fought in battles, but he had very few answers.

By the time he led them into a clearing with a stream where they could set up camp, she was thoroughly frustrated.

"If their home is in danger," she said to Leonis for the tenth time, "they'll fight."

He didn't bother to answer her again but looked glumly at the trees around them. "I need to find a talkative tree." Without another word, he wandered into the woods.

"I agree about their home," Reese said, pulling the saddle off the horse so he could graze. "Convincing them the wood is actually in danger will be the hard part." His eye caught on something in the forest, but when Sable looked, there was nothing but trees.

"I'll see if I can find us something to eat." Reese pulled a knife out of his belt and moved into the trees.

Sable dug through the saddle packs for a flint and a pot and brought them to Thulan. The dwarf hunched down near the stream, stacking sticks for their cook fire.

Squatting down next to Thulan, Sable set down the flint. The dwarf grunted something sounding vaguely like thanks and returned to her sticks. Her face was set in a scowl, and there were shadows under her eyes. Sable thought of the map she'd seen on the island. If they'd entered the Wildwood, then even though she hadn't caught a glimpse of the Marsham Cliffs through the trees, they must have passed near the southern entrance to Torren sometime today. Any frustration Sable had evaporated at the thought of how close they must be to the place where Thulan's husband and sons had been killed.

Sable put her hand on Thulan's shoulder. "If Ryah were here," she said quietly, "she'd have something comforting to say."

Thulan kept her eyes on the pile of sticks. "About time we broke that girl free of the priories, don't you think?"

"I do," Sable said.

Thulan looked into the woods. "I'm tired of her being stuck there, and I'm tired of missing her."

"Me too."

Thulan dropped her head and sighed. "See if you can find any tinder dry enough to burn in this stupid, wet elf-land."

Sable nodded and stood, heading for the base of the largest trees, looking for any dry moss or old leaves. The forest glowed in the evening light, the ferns beneath the trees feathery soft, the canopy above them filtering the setting sun until the entire forest was a lush, vibrant green. A pine was tucked in among the leafy trees, and Sable knelt next to it, brushing aside the top needles still damp from rain.

"You might have better luck on the other side of the trunk," Reese said quietly.

She spun to find him standing next to a nearby tree.

"You," she said, pointing a finger at him, "are very quiet when you want to be."

He lifted the two rabbits he was holding. "Hard to sneak up on something in the woods if you aren't."

"Were you trying to sneak up on me?"

He smiled. "I came around the tree, and there you were." He gestured up at the trunk of the pine above her. "All the rain came from the west today, and you're kneeling on the wet side. You'll have better luck finding dry needles on the dry side."

The trunk above her was dark with moisture.

"Well, obviously." She stood and dusted off her hands. "But where's the challenge in looking on the dry side?" She rounded the tree and knelt again, brushing off the damp top needles to find a thick layer of dry ones beneath.

He knelt next to her, bumping his shoulder into hers. "No challenge at all." He scooped up his own big handful with his free hand.

Sable leaned against him. "You look better."

"I feel better. Let's stay in these woods forever."

She smiled. "I'm sure the elves would love that." The thought sobered her. She ran her thumb over the sharp end of a pine needle. "I need them to help. And the dwarves." He looked over at her, but she kept her eyes on the tangle of needles in her hands. "Not just for the rest of the world. I need us to somehow drive off the Kalesh for…me."

Putting her cottage into words felt precarious. As though trying to share it would cut all the tiny threads that connected her to it, and it would drift away like the dream it was.

He sat next to her, solid and steady, just waiting for her to find the words. She looked up into the treetops. "It feels foolish to even talk about it right now, but I want a cottage in the woods. A home somewhere in the north. Maybe near a town, but not in it. Surrounded by trees, with a garden and peace and quiet. Where no one wants me to be more than I am or less than I am."

Even that much detail felt vulnerable.

"This cottage," he said slowly, "are you going to live in it all by yourself?"

A bit of smile pulled up the edge of her mouth. "Well, I don't know how to hunt. Or fish. Or garden, really. I don't have the money to buy a house or the skills to build one, so I was thinking…" She glanced at him, her smile widening. "Maybe you could come work for me. Hunt. Build things. Find edible plants. Stuff like that. You could be my huntsman."

He nodded slowly. "Huntsman to the Queen of the North. It has a nice ring."

"Well, since my queen-ness…Queenhood? Queenessence?"

His eyebrows rose.

"Since my *title*," she said, "isn't real, I won't have any real money to pay you. Will that be a problem?"

"Hmm," he said, the sound thoughtful.

Putting down his pine needles, he moved until his face was close to hers. He brought up his hand and lifted her chin. His first kiss was gentle and quick. The second stronger and longer, and Sable lost track of the forest and the pine needles and the elves. When he pulled back, she opened her eyes to find him looking at her, the barest hint of a smile on his lips. "Shouldn't be a problem, Your Highness. I never needed much money anyway."

She realized she was clutching his arm and let go. "It's settled, then," she said, her breath coming a little faster than usual. "As soon as the Kalesh are gone, we'll find a place, and you can be my huntsman."

His smile faded a little, but he nodded. "As soon as the Kalesh are gone."

A throat cleared behind them, and they turned to see Cintis standing a little way off. He gave them an embarrassed smile. "I didn't mean to intrude, but there is not much time until other elves arrive. They allowed me the courtesy of coming first, since Leonis asked, but I'm not sure how long Victis will wait." The elf's long hair had more green in the brown than she remembered, and it looked almost light against the dark, earthy color of his tunic.

"We're over by the stream." Sable waved her big clump of pine needles in the general direction. Through the trees, she could see Thulan lying on her back next to the still unlit fire, her head propped against her pack and her eyes closed.

Sable and Reese stood, and they started back toward the clearing. "I'm glad you're here," Sable said to Cintis. "Leonis is…"

"A mess," Reese finished.

Cintis grinned at them. "He always has been a mess." He raised his voice. "I blame his human blood."

"You've missed my mess," Leonis said from where he sat, leaning against a tree. "You're bored with only elves, and you know it. Which is why you get so excited when I bring humans into the woods." He didn't get up, but he greeted the elf with the first real smile Sable had seen him give all day.

"And the dwarf is back!" Cintis exclaimed.

Thulan sat up. "We bring joy wherever we go." She waved Sable and her pine needles over to the fire. "Finally. I thought you'd been eaten by a bear."

Sable added Reese's to her own and tucked them into the hollow Thulan had left in the stack of wood. "And you were so concerned you took a nap?"

Thulan shrugged and grabbed the flint. "Reese was out there too. He's the one we expect to throw himself at a bear."

In moments, a tiny flame lit the edges of the pine needles, and Thulan blew on it gently. Sable glanced back to see Leonis rise and clasp Cintis's forearms before Leonis pulled him into a hug.

"Ah," Cintis winced, "it's getting worse, you know. Your human tendencies." He did return the embrace, though, patting Leonis on the back.

"That's true," Thulan agreed. "Gets worse every year."

"You need to stay here and see if you can end all of this hugging." Cintis stepped back from Leonis, and his gaze caught on Innov, who was perched on a branch above them, her head tucked down near her wing. "A phoenix?" His voice was awed. "Where did you find a phoenix?"

"It's Sable's," Leonis said. "I'm hazy on the details of how she got it, but I think she stole it from a dying old woman."

"That's Innov," Sable said, ignoring Leonis, "and she exhausted herself flying around in the rain all day."

"Well, she's beautiful," Cintis said. He turned back to Leonis, growing sober. "Tell me why you're here before Victis comes and starts commanding everybody."

The two of them sat, and Leonis began to explain the situation while Reese skinned the rabbits and Thulan constructed a small spit to cook them on.

Sable settled down, leaning against her pack, her eyes scanning the woods for any sign of Victis's copper hair and painfully strong voice. Reese came and sank down next to her.

"Do you see him?" Sable asked quietly.

Reese shook his head. "No, but it's impossible to see elves unless they want to be seen."

"This is not going to work," Cintis said bluntly. "You know that, right?" He looked at the others. "The last time the elves fought the Kalesh, it was because Leonis's mother had been killed. And that wasn't really for her." He looked apologetically at Leonis. "They wouldn't have gone for a human. Victis convinced them that the Kalesh had stolen something of value from your father, and so they went."

"Victis?" Leonis said slowly. "He hated the fact that my father married her."

Cintis nodded. "But he loved your father. He led the hunting party himself, and they cleared a lot of Kalesh out of the Eastern Reaches. But four elves were wounded, and the dissension among the guard over whether they should have been involved was...deep. There are times I still don't think we've recovered."

"Victis?" Leonis repeated faintly.

"It was not for your sake," a voice spoke from the edge of the woods.

Sable tensed as the pressure of Victis's voice shoved against her.

The tall elf stood straight-backed below a thin young oak. His face was cold enough that it could have been chiseled from stone. In the dying light, his hair shone with a rich copper hue.

"You are not welcome here," Victis continued. "Your journey here has been in vain. The elves will not take part of the squabbles that eternally rage among humans. Kill yourselves off with your stupid greed. It matters not to us."

His words filled the clearing with a vague warmth, but with so much force that Sable couldn't breathe until he stopped.

Leonis sank back, but Sable rose to her feet.

"Is that your decision to make?" she asked. "I was under the impression you are the commander of the guard. Not the whole of the elves."

Cintis winced.

"He does not have the right to make the decision," Leonis said. "But it is a common sentiment we'll find from most of the Wildwood."

"And what of when the Kalesh come and burn your woods?" Reese asked, sitting forward. "Because when they come, their goal is to destroy the land in order to cow the people into submission."

"If they try to hurt our forests," Victis said, the words shoving against Sable with so much weight she took a half step back, "they will regret it."

"I told you this was a waste of time," Leonis said

Sable crossed her arms as a barrier against Victis's words. "We are an official envoy from the Northern Lords and the Tutella monks, and we were sent with a message for the elven king." She pushed the truth into those words and shoved them across the clearing.

The warmth reached Victis, and his entire body stiffened.

Her own words decreased the pressure of Victis's, though, and she infused the next ones with even more *vitalle*. "We were not sent to speak to the commander of the guard," she continued. "No matter how *common* his opinions may be."

Victis's eyes flashed, and even though he was across the clearing, Sable had to force herself not to back away from him.

Cintis grimaced.

Reese stood, moving to stand at Sable's shoulder, his attention fixed on Victis. The copper-haired elf gave Reese a condescending look.

"So, will you escort us to the king?" Sable asked, shoving her frustration into the question. "Or must we wander in your woods until we stumble upon him?"

Victis studied her as though she were a puzzle. "I will bring your request for an audience to the king," Victis said. "He will decide if any of you are permitted to enter the wood."

"Excellent," she said, "When can we expect his answer?"

"I will return at dawn." He didn't move, though. Instead, he watched her, his gaze probing.

Sable glanced around at the others. Thulan looked amused, Reese looked angry, and both Leonis and Cintis looked apprehensive.

No one else spoke, and when Victis still made no move to leave, Sable shifted her weight. "Then we'll bid you good evening."

Judging from the twitch in Victis's jaw, she hadn't kept the note of dismissal out of her voice.

"Unless," she said dryly, "you'd like to join us for dinner."

Cintis's attention snapped up. Leonis closed his eyes and covered his face with his hands.

Victis's mouth dropped open for a moment before he snapped it closed. His eyes flickered toward the two skinned rabbits, then he returned his glare to Sable with a ferocity that made her draw back.

With obvious effort, he gave a sharp nod. "I would be honored," he managed, the words sounding strangled. "Allow me to gather some of the bounty from the forest to—" His gaze touched on the rabbits again. "Complement the meal."

Sable stared at him, but he spun quickly, stepped behind the nearest tree, and disappeared.

CHAPTER EIGHTEEN

SABLE STARED into the empty stretch of woods.

"What were you thinking?" Leonis demanded, his voice quiet.

"I..." She blinked at the others. "I wasn't serious! Why did he accept?"

"You invited an elf to a meal," Cintis groaned. "He had to accept."

"Refusal would be an insult," Leonis agreed. "More than an insult. A declaration of enmity."

"A what?" Sable asked. "He knew I wasn't serious!"

"You invited him, Sneaks," Leonis said, as though that explained everything.

"Not only did you invite him," Cintis said to Sable, "you first declared you are an official envoy of the north and he is the representative of the king. So a refusal of the invitation could be seen as the elven kingdom insulting the Northern Lords."

Sable stared at them. "Seen by who? There's no one here! Cintis, go tell him I was joking. Blame it on some bad form of human humor."

Leonis shook his head. "It's done."

"Two rabbits were already going to be a lean dinner," Reese said. "We'll need more."

Leonis waved away the words. "Doesn't matter now."

"Victis doesn't eat meat," Cintis said.

"More for us, then," Thulan muttered, sliding the rabbits onto a spit.

"We can't eat those," Leonis said. "Just put them aside. We'll figure out something to do with them later."

"*I* can eat these," Thulan said.

"Unless you want me to offer your dwarves a nice fruity bottle of leeswine every chance I get," Leonis snapped, "you will sit there politely and try not to anger one of the most powerful elves in the forest."

Thulan frowned at him. "You wouldn't. With the wine."

"That all depends on how well behaved you are tonight."

Thulan grumbled something under her breath but yanked the rabbits back off the spit.

"Well," Sable said, "the purpose of this whole thing is to find allies. A dinner isn't the worst way to begin."

"I saw some ruffle mushrooms nearby," Reese said. "Cooked, they taste vaguely like meat." He set his hand on Sable's shoulder as he walked past her. "This should be interesting."

"This is your fault, Sable," Thulan said, pointing the spit at her, "so you get to cut up the rabbit. Slice it thin, and we'll smoke it overnight. We'll need extra food tomorrow anyway, after a dinner of mushrooms."

Reese brought Thulan a pile of frilly white mushrooms, and Cintis dug up and cleaned some yellow roots.

Sable knelt next to Thulan, breaking the mushrooms into small pieces. "Maybe we can get Victis on our side."

Thulan snorted. "You've met him, right?"

Sable glanced around the woods. "If the northern territories can come to see they have more in common than they thought," she said, pouring truth into her words, "then the same can happen with the elves." The wave of warmth rolled out around them, flaring Thulan into a densely burning form, catching Reese, Leonis, and Cintis as it spread across the clearing and flowed into the towers of trunks.

A brighter, hotter shape moved near the edge of the trees.

"I hope," she added quietly, turning to see Victis striding stiff-backed toward her, holding six snugly wrapped leaf packets.

The elf dipped each into the stream, then set them, sizzling and spitting, at the edge of the fire. He then stood and faced Sable, looking as though he was exerting great effort to appear polite.

He said nothing, merely looked down at her.

Sable stood, realizing they'd never been formally introduced. "I'm Sable," she said. "That's Andreese, and this is Thulan."

Victis gave them each a cold nod. "Victis, son of Turris, commander of the king's guard." He finished this with an expectant look.

Sable glanced behind Victis to where Leonis sat, and the half-elf pantomimed offering the stern elf a seat.

"Oh, yes," Sable glanced around at the complete lack of seats in the clearing. "Have a seat, Victis. We're…" She couldn't manage to get "pleased you're here" out.

The clearing fell into awkward silence as Victis stiffly sat right where he'd been standing.

Sable brushed the last bits of mushrooms off her hands while he stared at her with the focus of a hawk watching a mouse. The cold, distant feel of the entire situation reminded her far too much of Vivaine's peace councils.

She paused. What was the least Vivaine-like thing she could do?

With more determination than friendliness, she moved over and lowered herself next to Victis, facing the fire. He didn't move.

Reese rubbed his hand over his mouth, hiding a smile, but he came and sat next to her.

"It seems to me," Sable said, "that we can either treat this meal as some dull, formal affair, which I have never been fond of, or we can sit together and enjoy a meal as…" She stopped at Victis's cold look. "Perhaps not as friends, but maybe as people who might someday call each other friends."

One of Victis's eyebrows rose in a twitch that conveyed a surprising amount of incredulity.

Sable worked her lips into something she hoped looked like a smile. "In the distant future."

Thulan let out a snort. "Even for a human, that's a bit optimistic, Sable."

"Hardly." Sable took in each face in the clearing, having to turn to see Cintis and Leonis, who still sat behind them. "This group is the most optimistic group I've ever met when it comes to making unusual friendships. We have Reese, a soldier of the north who's been fighting for unity there, despite generations of enmity between the territories. Thulan, a dwarf who considers humans and a half-elf to be her family—"

Thulan started to object, but Sable raised a finger. "What was that you were saying about Ryah earlier?"

Thulan snapped her mouth shut.

Sable motioned impatiently for Cintis and Leonis to join the rest of them closer to the fire. "Cintis was thrilled at the chance to talk to humans and a dwarf tonight." She ignored the elf's guilty glance at Victis as he sat next to Thulan.

"And Leonis…" She paused, and Victis's posture grew even stiffer as

Leonis took the seat between him and Cintis. "Whatever the history is between you and Leonis," Sable said to Victis, "he is living proof that elves and humans can love each other deeply."

The commander pulled his gaze away from Leonis and focused on the fire.

"I'm not saying," Sable continued, trying to keep her voice light, "that you and I will ever wed each other, Victis."

The elf jerked his gaze back to her. Past him, Cintis's jaw dropped open and Leonis closed his eyes with a despairing expression.

Sable grinned at Victis. "But I think there's a chance we could end up as at least amiable acquaintances, don't you?"

Victis opened his mouth, but no words came out.

"I mean, it's just the six of us in a beautiful clearing in a beautiful wood," she said. "Why can't this be a dinner among fellow travelers?"

"There are eight more elves in the trees around us," Cintis noted.

Sable scanned the trees in irritation. There was no sign of anyone. She raised her voice slightly. "Well, invisible lurkers at the edge of a friendly dinner don't count."

"Do *not* invite them too," Thulan warned.

Sable ignored her and turned back to Victis. "Are you amenable to a relaxed dinner?" she asked, not fully banishing the irritation in her voice. "Or must we keep up this stiff formality?"

He studied her for a moment, as though searching for the trick in her words. Then gave a curt nod without relaxing his posture at all.

"Great," Sable said, forcing a smile. "Thulan, how long until the food is cooked?"

"It's mushrooms," Thulan muttered. "Does it matter?"

"The packets you brought smell delicious," Reese said to Victis, making an effort to sound casual, and Sable gave him a grateful look.

"These," Cintis said, his voice brighter than his expression, "are *gaz'lim*. It means 'little treasure.' Commander Victis is known throughout the Wildwood for his exceptional *gaz'lim*."

Victis acknowledged Cintis with a nod, and the clearing fell silent again.

"So," Sable said, searching for something to say. She thought of and discarded a dozen questions.

"Cintis is the only elf I've ever had the pleasure of sharing a meal with," she said finally. "Have you eaten many times with humans?" She glanced at Thulan. "Or dwarves?"

Leonis grimaced.

Victis folded his hands, even his fingers managing to look stern. "I have not."

The words pushed against her, and she regretted trying to make the elf talk.

Although, if the pressure in his words was from some sense of authority, maybe, if they could talk about pleasant things, he'd be less disagreeable.

When the conversation evaporated again, the last of Sable's patience disappeared with it. This was the problem, right here. Elves, dwarves, and humans were sitting within arm's reach of each other, but none of them could manage to bridge that tiny distance.

Thulan stirred the mushrooms and poked at the roots impatiently.

Sable blew out a breath. How was it she could find absolutely no common ground with this elf? She ran over what she knew about him. He was grumpy. His words were painful. He was the commander of the guard who hated Leonis because Victis had had to lead elves to avenge Leonis's mother's death—

Sable straightened and turned to Victis. "I believe," she said, quietly, "that I owe you a great deal. I believe I owe you my life."

The elf twitched, then faced toward her.

"When you led elvish warriors onto the Eastern Reaches," she said, "after the Kalesh had killed Leonis's mother, I'm told you found several other raiding parties of Kalesh and killed them all."

Victis's eyes pierced into her, and she knew she was treading on ground she shouldn't, but she held his gaze. "I've heard that you, or at least some elves, did not want to fight for the sake of humans, but I'm one of those humans. Kalesh raiders had burned my town and murdered my parents by the time your warriors arrived. A Kalesh soldier had a sword raised to kill me when an elvish arrow took his life."

He stared at her for a moment. "What town?" he asked stiffly.

"Pelrock. A small village, a half day's journey from the sea."

Victis nodded again.

"You saved my life," Sable said, pushing the truth into her words, trying to warm the space around them. "And the lives of my two sisters. We owe you a great debt."

Victis studied her again, as though he was looking for a trick.

Sable held out her hand. "I know I have very little to offer, but you should know that I am in your debt, and if you ever need anything that I can provide, it is yours."

The silence in the clearing had a different feel now. Thulan had stopped, her spoon halfway out of the pot. Reese watched Victis closely, looking tense. Cintis and Leonis both leaned forward with shocked expressions.

Victis looked down at her extended hand, then met her gaze again. "The saving of your life was not intentional," he said slowly. "The Kalesh had taken something—" His eyes flickered to Leonis and back. "They had taken the life of one who had been bound to our people. For that, they had to pay."

Sable felt a small smile grow at Victis's discomfort. "Whether you intended it or not, the fact is that I am alive today because of your choice. And my two sisters are as well. We owe you our lives."

Victis still didn't move. Past him, Cintis stared at her, his jaw hanging open.

"Sneaks," Leonis said quietly. "Do you realize you're offering a blood debt—tying your life to his? That's not taken lightly."

"I don't mean it lightly." Sable let her hand drop to her lap, searching for a way to get Victis to understand. "My sister Ryah is the sweetest person I've ever met." Sable infused the words with all the love she held for her sister, the longing to get her away from the priories and somewhere safe. "She's kind and generous and *good.* But not in a way that's cloying or fake. Somehow, being around her makes me think that it's possible to be a better person. That we could all be better people." The clearing warmed.

"Talia, my other sister, is smart and stubborn, and she drives me crazy because she never does what I think she should. But she's trapped in an ugly situation, and she's somehow managed to transform it into something good. She's taken the plans of a loathsome man and...redeemed them. She's managed to help a lot of people in the process."

Victis's posture had shifted, and he leaned ever so slightly toward her, his eyes piercing, as though trying to pull something out of her.

"And we're all alive because you brought the elves." She stretched her hand out again. "Will you allow me to thank you?"

Victis opened his mouth, and for a breath, Sable thought he would agree.

Then he very carefully folded his hands in his lap.

Sable stared at his long fingers, tightly wrapped together, and slowly dropped her hand.

"I cannot accept your pledge," he said, his voice merely nudging her. "I did not save you that night. I was not even near that town." She started to object, but he shook his head. "But I received the reports from every elf who was, and I know the warrior who saw some children and left them safely in a small cellar."

Sable leaned forward. "The root cellar."

"His name is Artis." Victis paused, his face conflicted. He struggled for a moment, then nodded sharply. "Tomorrow, even if the king refuses a formal audience, I will take you into the Wildwood and introduce you to Artis."

Leonis and Cintis exchanged stunned looks.

"Thank you," Sable said fervently.

Victis gave a slight bow of his head, then turned toward Thulan. "The *gaz'lim* should be hot enough, Mistress Dwarf."

Thulan raised an eyebrow at the address but lifted the now slightly blackened leaf packets out of the fire with two sticks, setting one before each person along with a small bowl of mushrooms and yellow roots.

"If you unfold the top leaf," Cintis said, opening his own packet, "it folds out like a bowl."

Sable pulled the hot leaf up, and a rich, buttery smell wafted out. The leaf pack was filled with little chunks of roots, tiny mushrooms, and something that looked like cubes of green apple.

"That smells delicious!" Thulan said, leaning forward over her own and breathing in deeply. She picked up a piece of something potato-like and took a bite. Her eyes widened. "This *is* delicious!"

Victis gave her a polite nod of acknowledgment.

Sable took a bite of apple and got a burst of flavor both tart and rich.

"What's in this?" Thulan asked, picking up a chunk and eating it.

Victis stiffened.

"It's impolite to ask," Leonis said, giving Thulan a quelling look.

"Impolite?" she said. "It's a compliment. This is better than anything we have eaten on the road. Ever. And better than most things we've eaten when we're not on the road. I would make this for us every day if I knew what it was." She pushed the pieces around with her finger. "Are you sure there's no meat in here? It tastes very meaty."

"We're sure," Leonis said between clenched teeth.

The dwarf looked up and blinked at Victis's stony look. "But—"

"Thulan." Reese shook his head with a pointed look.

She shifted her attention to Reese. "You're woodsy. Do you know what's in it?"

Reese gave an exasperated huff and the smallest nod.

"Excellent!" Thulan beamed at Victis. "This is excellent. Thank you."

Leonis let out a long-suffering breath, and Victis, without any of Thulan's enthusiasm, went back to eating.

Sable sat next to the commander of the guard and worked her way through the *gaz'lim*, as well as the mushrooms and roots Thulan had cooked. The entire meal was delicious.

The clearing descended into silence again, but the edge of hostility seemed to have worn down slightly.

A light flashed from deep inside a thickly leafed tree, and Innov flew out, circling the clearing once, then swooping down to land in the coals of the fire.

Victis stared at her, his mouth open slightly.

"That's Innov." The flames licked up around the phoenix's feathers, and the subtle bit of hope Innov always brought with her rolled out from the fire.

Victis glanced between Sable and the phoenix. "A remarkable companion."

"She is," Sable agreed.

Victis kept his eyes on the phoenix as he finished his food and folded the leaves into a neat little packet. He turned his head a bit toward Sable. "Your sister Talia sounds very much like my daughter Arseya."

Cintis almost dropped his bowl of mushrooms, and Leonis froze, a bite of apple halfway to his mouth.

Sable paused in the act of folding up her own leaves. Victis's words held a bit of warmth, but none of his usual forcefulness.

"She is strong-willed and persistent," he continued, "and is aging me beyond my years." A hint of a smile crossed his perfectly smooth and ageless face. "She almost never does what I want her to, but I cannot deny that everything she does makes our woods better."

Sable let out a rueful laugh. "That is very much like my sister."

"I suppose the world needs people like them," Victis said with a note of resignation.

"It does." Sable finished folding the leaves and set them aside. "I just wish they could help it in a way that caused us less anxiety."

This time, Victis's face relaxed into something that definitely qualified as a smile. "Something we can agree on."

CHAPTER NINETEEN

From the dusky shadows of the forest, Victis gave Sable a stiff, formal bow of his head and a nearly gracious-sounding thanks before he walked into the trees. She blinked, and he was gone.

When she turned back to the clearing, Thulan and Reese were cleaning the cook pot and bowls in the stream, and Leonis and Cintis were watching Sable, both of them grinning.

She crossed her arms. "What is so funny, and why couldn't you two have been at least vaguely helpful during that entire dinner?"

"Helpful?" Leonis said, letting out a laugh. "I wouldn't have changed how this evening went for all the leeswine in the world."

Sable frowned at him. "What are you talking about?"

Leonis scanned the woods, then gave Cintis a questioning look.

The elf shook his head. "They all left with Victis. Or pulled back far enough to give us privacy."

Leonis laughed again. "She invited Victis to a dinner of rabbits!"

"I have never seen him that discomposed," Cintis said, leaning back against a tree with a wide smile.

"Don't elves ever eat together?" she asked.

"All the time. They just don't make a formal invitation out of it."

"It's a stupid rule," Sable said.

"I don't think so," Thulan said. "That leaf thing was delicious. Reese, what was in it?"

Cintis rubbed his hand over his face. "She asked him what he puts in his *gaz'lim*!"

Both of them fell into gales of laughter.

Reese nodded to Thulan. "They were mostly roots and mushrooms. I'll show you how to find them."

"I know of less than a dozen elves who've ever been treated to Victis's *gaz'lim*," Cintis said, still chuckling.

"Really, Sneaks, the night would have been worth it just to watch Victis have to accept your invitation, but then you tried…" Leonis started to laugh again, this time hard enough that he could barely speak. "A blood oath!" he managed, dropping his head into his hands, his shoulders shaking.

"He saved us," Sable said. "And what does it matter to him? I was the one giving the oath. He didn't have to do anything but accept it."

"And be bound in a blood oath with a human!" Cintis grinned. "Victis!"

Reese looked amused. "It all seemed reasonable to me."

"Thank you," Sable said.

Cintis shook his head. "Victis is deeply opposed to any sort of interaction with humans. Or dwarves. He believes the other races are barely more sophisticated than animals and that elves shouldn't waste their time on them. It's why he's so hostile toward Leonis."

"Except," Leonis said, wiping his eyes. "He told Sable about Arseya."

"His daughter?" Sable asked.

"Victis's daughter is…" Cintis trailed away.

"Arseya is beautiful," Leonis said. "The sort of beautiful that Atticus would turn into a play. He'd pit kingdoms against each other, fighting over her. She's vibrant and wild and impulsive. She's everything Victis is not."

"She's perfect," Cintis added.

"And Cintis is a bit taken with her," Leonis said. "But the point is, Victis talked to you about her. He never talks about her."

"He never talks about anything personal," Cintis agreed.

"Well, whatever happened," Sable said, "I hope it helps our chances with getting an audience with the king."

"Oh, it did," Leonis said. "That's not a problem anymore."

"Not a problem? Victis said he didn't know if the king would see us."

Cintis shrugged. "He's introducing you to Artis."

Sable blinked at him. "Is Artis the king?"

Leonis let out another peal of laughter. "No, Artis is a mid-level guard who is entirely too relaxed for Victis's tastes, but elves only introduce their friends to each other."

"The surly elf commander is calling Sable his friend?" Thulan asked.

Leonis grinned. "Apparently. And there is no way the king will refuse an audience to the very special friend of the commander of his guard." He shook his head. "I don't know how you pull these things off, Sable, but I hope you're ready to talk to the elvish king tomorrow, because you're the one he's going to talk to."

Something nudged Sable's shoulder, and she opened her eyes to find the sky lit with the palest hint of morning.

"Your buddy Victis will be here soon," Reese said, squatting down next to where she lay. "Since you tend to wake up with hair that would terrify most mortals, I thought you might want a little warning. Best not to start a day of negotiations with the elves on such a frightening note."

Sable squinted up at him. "It's abnormal to be awake and talkative this early."

"It's almost sunrise." He smiled down at her brightly.

"You look like you're feeling better."

"I feel great." He looked up at the trees. "If I'm ever wounded again, I'm coming here to recover."

"No more being wounded." Sable closed her eyes again. It had been late before Leonis and Cintis had finished entertaining them with old stories of themselves and Victis.

"Thulan mentioned something about washing your hair," Reese said. "And said if you want to have time to heat up the water, you'd better get moving, or she's just going to dunk your head in the cold stream."

"I'm up." The morning was misty and slightly cool. Sable wrapped her blanket around her shoulders and went to heat up some water, running over in her mind what she wanted to say to the elves.

The sky had lightened and a few wispy clouds to the west had turned pink before Thulan was done washing, brushing, and braiding Sable's hair.

"You should wear something better than dirty traveling clothes." Thulan pinned two small braids into a knot at the back of Sable's hair.

"I picked out a dress from Atticus's stash." Sable pulled a roll of light blue fabric out of her bag.

Thulan held up the blanket in front of a thicket, offering Sable a little privacy to change. The air was chilly on her wet hair, and the blue dress, which was simple enough to be almost elegant, was thin.

Sable stepped out from behind the blanket, shifting her shoulders under the fabric. "Honestly, it'd be more comforting if this were a costume I could hide behind and just say whatever lines Atticus gave me."

"Atticus can't write lines as well as you can speak," Reese said from where he packed the saddlebags. "You're the best person in the north to do this."

Even from a dozen paces away, she could feel the warmth in his words, and she straightened her shoulders.

"You're the delegate from the monks," Sable pointed out. "You are supposed to help me talk."

"No," Cintis said quickly. "Don't speak to the king unless he addresses you."

Reese shrugged. "Sable's the one good at speaking anyway."

Thulan looked critically at the dress. "Purnicious?"

Purn popped into view, her brow crinkled. "It's a little big." She moved around Sable, running her fingers over the hems and the seams, adjusting it until it fit.

"Leonis," the dwarf called. "Are there enough flowers around to make one of those chains?"

"As though I hadn't already thought of it," Leonis said, stepping up to Sable and holding a string of braided grass woven with light purple flowers. "Necklace or belt?"

"Necklace," Thulan said.

"Belt it is." Leonis stepped up behind Sable and wrapped the chain around her waist, fiddling with the back of it for a few moments. Purn hummed in approval and made some adjustment Sable couldn't see.

The three of them stood back, examining Sable. The dress felt better, and Sable took a deep breath.

"You look lovely," Purn said.

"Not too bad," Thulan agreed.

"She's looked better," Leonis said, "but elves aren't usually swayed by human beauty anyway, so she should be fine—what is this?" He reached forward and pulled the leather cord around her neck, drawing the crooked sword necklace out of the front of her dress. "You're still wearing this ugly thing?"

Reese glanced over, and his gaze caught on the necklace. He raised an eyebrow.

"Take it off," Leonis said. "You can't wear a sword to a peace treaty,"

"That's barely recognizable as a sword," Thulan argued.

Sable lifted it out of Leonis's fingers and tucked it inside her dress. "It stays."

Reese smiled and went back to packing the saddlebags.

"But…" Leonis stared at the cord around her neck. "It's so ugly."

"So are you," Thulan said, patting him on the shoulder, "and she keeps you around."

Leonis frowned. "Just don't let anyone see it. Victis will take you to the king, but you need to remember that it's not him you're convincing. There will be plenty of other elves there. They know you're coming, they know what you'll be asking for, and it's probable you won't even be questioned by the king. Normally, in a situation like this, you'd be questioned by Victis in the king's presence, but since he's introducing you, the task will have been given to one or two other elves." His brow creased in worry. "Be prepared for the fact that no one here wants to help us. The best we can hope for is polite refusal. We may encounter something stronger than that."

"If there are elves who might be more inclined to listen, tell me," Sable said.

Leonis shifted. "I lived on the very outskirts of the forest, and…we didn't spend a lot of time in the main woods. There are plenty of elves I don't even know. Plenty felt like Victis did about my mother." He looked at her apologetically. "Being friends with me is not going to help your cause."

Sable shook her head. "The fact that I'm friends with you is the whole point of being here." The words came out fervent and hopeful and warm. "People don't have to come from the same place to care about each other."

The warmth spread, and Sable felt Victis at the edge of the trees. Purnicious popped out of view.

Victis wore a long dark blue tunic that had an air of formality to it. He inclined his head toward her in a gesture that was slightly more respectful than anything he'd done last night. "If you'll come with me, Sable, I would be honored to introduce you to Artis." He glanced at the others. "And then the king has agreed to meet with your entire delegation."

Sable felt a wave of relief, and she gave Victis a smile. "Wonderful. Thank you."

She caught sight of Leonis, who was paler than usual, but he merely motioned for her to lead the way.

The others fell in behind them, and Sable searched for something to talk about. "A beautiful morning," she said, the words sounding a bit stiff.

Innov soared down from where she'd perched in a tree, and Sable stretched out her arm. The phoenix landed in a shower of sparks, and Sable ran her finger down the phoenix's chest, trying to draw in whatever peace she could.

"It is." Victis watched the flames run over the red and orange feathers. He gestured for Sable to walk with him into the woods. "I hope you found the night restful."

She fell in beside him. "Cintis and Leonis kept us up too late entertaining us with tales of their youth," she said lightly, "but I enjoy Cintis's company so much, it was worth it."

Victis brow creased the slightest bit.

"And," she continued, lowering her voice until Victis leaned toward her, "I have traveled with Leonis for a while now. I never see him as happy as when he is here with his old friend." Victis straightened, but Sable continued, "I have heard that all elves are connected to their woods in ways I can't quite understand, but I do understand the idea of a home, and Leonis, for all the pain these woods have held for him, still feels like this is home. A feeling I'm sure you can relate to."

Victis kept his eyes facing forward, and for a very long minute, they walked in silence. "It is always good to return to the woods," he said finally.

Sable began to catch glimpses of figures moving through the trees with them. Perhaps a dozen elves, almost always out of sight, ringed the procession like an escort.

"What is your title?" Victis asked her.

She shook her head. "I don't—"

"Issable, Flame of the North," Reese offered from behind them.

"Sable," she corrected him.

"Right," Reese said. "Sable, Flame of the North."

Sable waited for Victis to ask her what sort of title that was, but he took in the phoenix on her arm and nodded. He glanced at the others.

"Andreese led the northern troops during the battle of Immusmala,"

Sable said, not certain that Reese would accept the title of general anymore.

"You are young for a general," Victis said, and Sable winced.

"An unplanned field promotion," Reese said, keeping his voice neutral.

"Ahh." Victis kept the word short, and whether it represented understanding or dismissal, Sable couldn't tell. "We heard of the battle near the city on the sea, but none of the details. Did you outnumber your enemy?"

Reese told Victis how the battle had gone. Victis wasn't pleasant, exactly, but he listened with interest and asked enough questions that Reese had described most of the battle before Victis was satisfied. He turned to Thulan. "Do you have a title, Mistress Dwarf?"

She shook her head. "Just Thulan."

Victis nodded, and they walked mostly in silence as the sun climbed in the sky and the tops of the trees shone bright green in its light. Long slanting rays cut through the canopy and reached the ground before they passed the first house.

Or Sable assumed it was a house.

The bottom branches of a tree were pointed down until their tips brushed the ground, forming a cone-shaped shelter. The branches and leaves made a thick, soft roof.

They passed and Sable saw, though a door-like gap in the branches, a tidy home with a small fire burning in a stone hearth. She glanced back at Leonis, who was looking at the house with a pained expression. Cintis set his hand on the half-elf's shoulder for a moment, then let it drop.

Another house came into view ahead of them, then a handful more. Elves moved between them, stopping to watch the unusual procession. Music came from somewhere, although Sable couldn't quite pinpoint where. A flute, or maybe a single voice.

Victis halted outside the doorway of a leafy house, and Sable stopped next to him, peering into the green-tinged home. Someone moved inside, and a tall elf stepped up to the door, meeting her gaze with a solemn expression.

Memories of the night her parents died flooded in. The smoke and the terror and the elves felling the Kalesh one by one. This elf striding across the yard, meeting Sable's frightened look with a terrible grimness.

"It's you," she whispered.

CHAPTER TWENTY

"Artis," Victis said, his voice formal, "it is my pleasure to introduce you to Sable, though you have encountered each other before."

Artis pulled his eyes away from the phoenix, and the same sympathy she'd seen in him that night long ago colored his expression now. "I am pleased that you survived, Sable," he said, "I had feared you were too young."

Sable reached toward him, and his eyes flickered down to the motion. "I…" She swallowed. "I cannot thank you enough for your actions that night. My sisters and I…" Her heart pounded at the memories she couldn't quite push away. "Thank you."

He inclined his head. "I am grieved we did not arrive sooner. There was great loss that night."

Sable opened her mouth, but he held up his hand.

"Before you say more," Artis said, his voice kind. "You owe me no debt. I was following orders, and while I am gratified that lives were saved because of our actions, it was not my arrow who felled the man who held you. It was one of my brothers, but I do not know which, and I will not seek out the answer. That was a night of death and vengeance. It was ugly, and there is much to mourn. The fact that three lives were spared is a good thing, and we rejoice in it with you."

Sable nodded slowly. "When you speak to the other elves who were there that night, will you convey my thanks to them as well?"

Artis reached out his hand, and Sable took it, wrapping her hand around his forearm as Leonis and Cintis always did with each other. His long fingers clasped her arm. Without looking at Victis, Artis leaned forward slightly. "It is a pleasure to meet you again, Sable. May your time in the Wildwood be filled with the success you seek."

Victis stiffened slightly at the sentiment, but Sable gave Artis a wide smile. "That would be nice."

Artis straightened and released her arm, giving Victis a nod that looked like a salute.

Victis returned it, in a much smaller measure. Sable walked with him deeper into the town of tree houses, the cloud of her parents' deaths still lingering over her.

They entered a wide clearing ringed with houses and scattered with dozens of elves, and the commander glanced at her out of the corner of his eye. "Welcome to Aelosia," he said. "You are the first ambassadors from the humans to set foot here in a hundred years."

"Really?"

"Have I given you the impression this happens regularly?"

She grinned at him. "No, you have not. Thank you for bringing us here."

He raised his face toward the treetops as though searching for patience. "Do all humans give thanks this often?"

Sable laughed. "Only when offered once-in-a-century favors."

"Not true," Thulan said from behind them. "Some of them do it all the time. Isn't it annoying?"

Victis almost smiled as he headed toward one of the houses on the far side of the clearing. There was nothing unusual about the tree or the home. Nothing that set it apart from any others.

"Many of these elves fought on the grasslands," Victis said quietly. "Do not let your hopes run unchecked."

Sable glanced up at him, but he was looking sternly at the house ahead of them.

"I wish my hopes were running unchecked," she murmured back, wiping one of her sweaty palms on her dress. "Right now, I'm dragging them along by my fingernails."

"No one would fault you for letting them go."

She ran her finger down Innov's chest. "And admit defeat before it's begun?"

"Acknowledging the truth of the situation is not a defeat."

Sable stopped walking and turned to him. The attention of the entire clearing was on them, but she ignored their eyes and waited until Victis stopped as well. "Can you tell me there is no hope at all?" she asked quietly.

He surveyed the gathered elves, his eyes lingering on a few of them, before facing Sable. "No. But I do not believe there is much."

"Then I shall keep dragging it along by my fingernails, no matter how difficult that is."

His mouth twitched in what might have been the start of a smile. "May we continue?"

She nodded, and he started forward again. Despite her words, her grip on any sort of hope was growing more slippery. They arrived in front of the unassuming house, and Reese stepped up close behind her.

Sable glanced behind her to see Leonis's eyes moving from face to face, his expression pinched. Cintis remained next to him, his shoulders set in a stubborn stiffness. Thulan kept her gaze on the house in front of them, as though they weren't surrounded by dozens of elves.

Innov shifted on Sable's arm, spreading her wings for a moment and letting out a shower of sparks. A ripple went through the surrounding elves.

There was motion inside the house, and an elf stepped out of the door. He was tall and thin, like the rest of them, but his light brown hair was streaked with strands of silvery white. His tunic was long, like the one Victis wore, but in a rich, deep green. It had the same sort of formality that Sable couldn't quite pinpoint. There was nothing about him that looked old, but he seemed to carry the weight of centuries.

Victis bowed from the waist. "I present Sable, Flame of the North, emissary from the northern territories of the humans."

Sable braced against the pressure in his voice.

"Sable, may I introduce Corelis, Elder of Aelosia, Heart of the Forest, King of the Wildwood."

Sable bowed to the king, who gave her a gracious nod. Several elves fanned out behind the king, considering the delegation. Off to the left, Sable caught sight of Artis watching with a solemn expression.

She cleared her throat. "Thank you for meeting with us," she began. She heard Victis breathe out a very quiet huff at yet another word of thanks, and she smiled before infusing her next words with warmth and pressing them out toward the listening elves. "We come to you with news of a grave threat, and while we come to ask for aid, we believe that your woods are in danger as well."

As the heat of her words reached them, each elf focused on her a little more intently, and she let her fear and longing and pain fill the clearing as she explained the Kalesh invasion and the betrayal of the Dragon Prioress in the south.

If there was one thing Atticus had taught her, it was how to read an audience. But even if she accounted for the general stoicism of the elves, this audience was not a receptive one.

A few heads nodded at her description of the danger. The majority, including Artis, stayed carefully neutral. A small but highly visible number of elves looked actively hostile.

King Corelis himself watched her with an unreadable expression.

Two elves drew closer to the king as she spoke, one male, one female. The male was dressed in a rich red tunic with the crisp-uniform feel of the clothes Victis usually wore. His face was stern, and he definitely fell into the "actively hostile" group.

The female was dressed in a tunic of dark, earthy brown, and her expression was even harsher.

Both of their postures grew more unbending the longer she spoke.

"The Kalesh are relentless," Sable said, desperation rising in her. She met their eyes, pushing her words toward them. "They will not stop. They have more soldiers than we can imagine, and they are determined to come. When they do, they will burn your forests without a thought—"

"We know of the Kalesh," the female elf said. Unlike the others, whose hair hung down freely, adorned with small braids, her russet locks were pulled into one thick braid that lay over her shoulder. There was something about her that looked old. Not old like the king, but more aged than the other elves in the clearing. Her gaze dug into Sable with open hostility. "What do they want?"

Sable paused. "The gold, as I told you."

Scorn edged the elf's expression. "And?"

"They believe the Dragon Prioress is a woman out of their myths," Sable said, trying to keep her voice even, "and they are also after me."

"Why?" the male elf behind the king demanded.

"Because my mother was a rebel in the Empire who assassinated the Emperor's brother." Her shoulders had grown tense, and she forced them to relax. "And they found out I'm involved with the north."

"How will you protect yourself from such a threat?" the russet-haired elf asked, her voice cold. "Or do you expect us to protect you?"

Sable turned her attention to the elf, whose face was icy. "I..."

"Can you wield a blade?" she pressed.

"Not well."

"At least you carry a bow?" The words were laced with so much contempt that Sable drew back slightly.

Sable shook her head. "I don't know how to shoot."

The elf's nostrils flared in fury or derision. "Then you are already dead. You were dead the moment they wanted you to be."

The words scraped across the space between them, rough and jarring.

Sable pointedly looked away from her and back at the king. "If you know about the Empire, you know what they're like." He didn't deny it. "And you're still unwilling to fight to keep them from taking over our land—*your* land?"

"They will not touch our land," the king said, as though it were an undisputed fact.

"What if they burn every bit of land around it and swarm it with Kalesh who will slowly, inevitably, chip away at the sides of your forest for lumber?"

The king's expression didn't change, but the male elf behind him shook his head. "We know how to protect our own land. It is not worth the effort to try to protect the humans. You will all kill each other in the end anyway."

"I'm not asking you to protect me or any other human." Sable filled her words with warmth. "I was hoping that the elves had enough value for life—and love of the land outside their own border—to want to keep it from being destroyed."

Many more faces hardened at the accusation, but Sable took a step forward. "I know you like to stay in your forest, barely even showing your faces to travelers who pass because...actually, I have no idea why you do that.

"My mother grew up in the Kalesh Empire fighting against them along with her friend—an elf." From behind her, she heard Leonis let out a small groan. "I know, you don't even care about *elves* who aren't from your woods, but this elf and my mother had a bond, a blood bond, so somewhere in the world there are elves who are willing to step outside their own small bubble and do something that matters to more than..." She waved her hand around the small clearing.

She stopped at the winces she saw on Leonis and Cintis.

"So you'll be fighting on the frontline against the Kalesh, then?" the female elf asked. "With all your skill in battle?"

Sable turned back, but before she could answer, Reese stepped up to her side. "Sable has been doing more than her part to stop the Kalesh for well over a year. When any of you have done the same, you can question her."

"Not helping," Leonis said very quietly.

Sable took a deep breath, trying to get her irritation under control. Everything about this conversation was wrong. The elves were a cold audience, already inclined to disagree with everything she said. The king himself was quiet and emotionless, and the two who were speaking were openly hostile.

"We need your help," Sable said, trying to keep her voice level. "You know we do. But this fight is yours too, and if you know about the Empire, you already know that."

Another elf shuffled into view around the side of the king's house.

This elf was ancient, his back bent forward, his long ash-colored hair hanging limp, his skin creased with wrinkles.

Victis tensed.

Behind Sable, someone drew in a sharp breath.

"Humans are not worth protecting," the russet-haired elf said loudly, her chin raised as she took in the entire clearing. "They die too easily—" She froze when she caught sight of the elderly elf, her mouth still open. A mortified look crossed her face. She gathered herself and bowed in his direction. "*Feliserae*," she said, the apology clear and wrenching. "*Feliserae*."

The older elf did not appear to notice her. His gaze landed on Sable but pushed past her, his eyes searching with a terrified, haunted look.

"Father?" Leonis's voice came from behind her, the word strangled into a whisper.

"Leonis?" The elf took a step forward, his eyes widening in wonder, his old, withered hands shaking as they reached forward. "*Lialis*? Have you finally returned?"

CHAPTER TWENTY-ONE

Leonis stepped forward, brushing past Sable, his face pale. He bumped Innov, who let out an annoyed squawk and launched herself into the air in an explosion of sparks.

The phoenix rose, drawing almost every eye up toward the open sky.

Leonis didn't look away from the elderly elf. "Father?"

"*Lialis,*" his father whispered, shuffling forward.

Leonis closed the distance between them, taking his father's hands, his gaze running over the hunched old man. "What…what happened?"

The elf's body trembled, and he curled forward until his head rested on Leonis's chest. "You returned, *lialis,*" he whispered.

Cintis stepped forward too, stopping at Sable's shoulder. His face was lined with pity. "What is *lialis*?" Sable whispered to him.

"Beloved," he said quietly.

"I…" Sable paused. "I thought he didn't want to see Leonis."

"So did I," Cintis answered, watching the two with a puzzled look.

"He is older than I expected," Sable whispered.

Cintis shook his head. "No older than Victis. It's his grief. It aged him."

Victis watched the reunion with an impassive face, but his hands were balled into fists at his side.

The entire clearing was silent as Leonis drew his father over toward the king's house and helped him sit on a bench. Innov soared in a leisurely circle near the treetops, showering down glittering bits of fire.

Many of the elves kept their eyes turned up toward her, whether because they were fascinated by her fire or reluctant to intrude on Leonis and his father, Sable wasn't sure. Either way, she felt a spark of hope that Innov's fire could somehow warm the tension that filled the glade.

The male and female elf spoke with the king before stepping back.

"We have heard your petition," King Corelis said to Sable, drawing everyone's attention back to himself. The words were calm, but the weight of them rolled out, pressing against her with an oppressive force. He surveyed the clearing slowly, and Sable saw a few slight nods, but many more subtle shaking of heads from the elves around them.

She looked at Artis but caught no response from him at all.

The king finally turned to the two elves at his shoulders. The male elf shook his head. "This fight does not belong to the elves."

The female kept her eyes on Sable. "It is not worth—" She glanced toward where Leonis sat with his father. "Human lives are short and violent." She pulled her gaze away from the frail elf. "There is enough to grieve in the world without binding ourselves to those who will be dead in a few seasons."

The king nodded and faced Sable again. "The woods have spoken." The words swept around her, crushing her until she couldn't breathe. "This fight belongs to you, not the elves."

The pressure of the words evaporated, and Sable drank in a deep breath, staring at him, waiting for something more. "It will be your fight when they come and burn your forest."

"Perhaps," the king acknowledged, the words only brushing past her, as though they didn't see her any longer. "But for now, the day is still young, and we will not keep you from your travels. To reach the dwarves, you have a long journey ahead. Victis will provide you with sustenance and escort you through the woods. We wish you peace."

Sable opened her mouth to object, but Cintis set his hand on her shoulder. "It's done."

Elves around the clearing dispersed or gathered in small clusters, watching the phoenix.

The king gave Sable one last nod, which seemed to hold sympathy but nothing else, and returned to his home.

Sable pulled her shoulder away from Cintis. "That's it?" she demanded.

"The woods have spoken," Victis said.

Sable turned, taking in the departing elves. "What else can we do? Who else can we talk to?"

The two elves who'd stood at the king's shoulders moved away through the forest, their backs stiff.

"There is no one else." Victis watched them go with a grim expression. "Human struggles have overflowed into our lives before."

Leonis rose and came over to them.

His expression was so ragged, it cut into Sable's anger. He gave them an unsteady smile. "May I introduce you to my father?"

Thulan set her hand on his arm. "We'd be honored."

He looked down at her. "He's so weak." The words came out with a hint of question, as though Thulan held some answer he didn't understand.

Her fingers tightened. "Aren't we all?"

Leonis stared at her for a breath, then started back toward his father with Thulan next to him. Sable, Reese, and Cintis followed. The older elf looked up at them, the same expression of wonder he'd had since he'd set eyes on Leonis encompassing them all.

"This is my father, Parseis," Leonis began. "Father, may I introduce you to Sable and Reese. Don't let their unassuming appearance deceive you—they've been causing a commotion in the human lands."

"Unassuming?" Parseis said, his eyes bright. "They came in with a phoenix, did they not?"

"Sable is good at accessorizing," Leonis said. "This…" He set his hand on Thulan's shoulder. "Is Thulan."

"The dwarf," Parseis said, looking at Thulan warmly. "Cintis tells me Leonis is very fond of you."

"Fond is an exaggeration," Leonis said, leaving his hand on Thulan's shoulder. "But I've grown accustomed to her presence."

"I've met very few dwarves in my life," Parseis said thoughtfully, "and I do not believe any of them have been female. You have a very nice beard."

Thulan smiled at him. "Thank you. Leonis, why didn't you inherit any of your father's charm?"

"He's lying," Leonis said easily. "It's customary for elves to greet strangers with what they believe will be a compliment, even if it's untrue."

Parseis chuckled. "It is not a lie." He held out his hand to Thulan, and she took it without hesitation. The elf's long pale fingers were almost lost in her thick hand. "Thank you for keeping my son company all these years."

Thulan squeezed the old elf's hands gently. "He's kept me company as well." Sable waited for some snide remark, but Thulan just gave the elf an earnest look. "He's wanted to return for as long as I've known him. He is just afraid."

"Thulan," Leonis said. "Shut up."

"I've never seen him as frightened as he's been this morning," Thulan continued.

Leonis made an aggravated noise, but his father kept his eyes locked on Thulan, clinging to her like a drowning man.

"Afraid of what?" Parseis whispered.

"That you don't want him," Thulan said simply.

Parseis blinked up at her, his eyes suddenly wet. "I've wanted him every day since he left."

Thulan nodded. "Of course you have." She took Leonis's hand and put it in his father's. "He's just too dense to realize it," she said gently.

Parseis squeezed Leonis's hand. "Sit with me for a moment before you leave again."

Leonis sat, still holding on to his father's hand. "Maybe…" He glanced at Thulan, his expression conflicted. "Maybe I don't have to leave. I could stay here. Getting us an introduction to the elves was my only role in this little expedition."

Thulan stood perfectly still for a moment before she managed a smile. "Yes, this was the part you were needed for, and Sable did most of the work anyway."

Parseis patted Leonis's hand. "I would love that." He paused. "I'm sorry the wood refused your request for aid. There are many elves who have been grieved by their interactions with the human world. Such things leave scars that are difficult to overcome."

"Do you know of anything that would change their minds?" Sable asked.

He shook his head. "I would vote to assist you, but it will take an elf with more authority than me taking your side if any hearts are to be swayed." He turned back to Leonis. "Do you believe in this cause?"

Leonis glanced at Thulan, Sable, and Reese. "The Kalesh will destroy many places and people I love."

Parseis patted his hand again. "Then you must go and help your friends, *lialis*. But when you are done, perhaps you can return with Thulan and tell me of all your adventures."

Thulan raised her eyebrow. "Maybe I'll come for a visit without him."

Parseis smiled widely. "I'll tell Victis you are to be admitted whenever you appear."

"Sounds good to me," Thulan said, grinning at the approaching Victis.

The commander of the guard stopped next to Sable. "Any friend of Parseis is always welcome," he said in an emotionless voice. "And right now there is a warm breakfast awaiting you all, if you will follow me."

"Did you help make it?" Thulan asked with unfeigned interest.

Victis almost smiled. "I did not, but my daughter had a hand in it, and I assure you her skills at everything surpass my own."

Leonis didn't rise. "Come get me when you're finished," he said to Thulan.

She gave him a quick grin. "I'll eat your portion. I'm sure leaving it uneaten would be rude."

Sable walked next to Victis as he led them north out of the Wildwood, frustration wrapped around her like a scratchy blanket. The late morning sun shone weakly through the forest, veiled by a thin layer of clouds, and she looked back several times, still searching for a way to make the Wildwood listen.

The elves who had served them breakfast had been polite but distant, and Victis had returned to a stony silence.

Reese walked next to her, his bearing equally frustrated.

"Have you seen any trace of the dwarves near the door to Torren?" Thulan asked Victis.

"You're the only dwarf who's been seen in the woods for more than three years," he answered. "The trees speak of them far to the north occasionally. But the herds they kept in the edges of the forest have wandered away, and the orchards they'd been cultivating have gone wild."

Thulan frowned. "They never collected the herds?'

"Not in this part of the wood."

The dwarf looked through the trees, puzzled. "What are they eating if they don't have the herds and the orchards?"

Sable pulled her mind away from where it still churned over the events with the elves, trying to focus on their next obstacle. "We went to the southern door over a year ago and found the tunnel collapsed. Do you know what happened?"

Victis considered the question. "Over three years ago, in the spring, the earth trembled. It was not severe, but it happened several times over the course of a few days. It did no harm to the wood, but I remember because several of the younger elves believed the great cliff was falling and would crush the forest. There was a great deal of foolish talk about such a catastrophe destroying the Wildwood."

Thulan shrugged. "A rock doesn't have to be particularly big to destroy trees."

"A rock would not destroy our trees," he said bluntly.

"If more than one collapse happened," Sable said, heading off the argument she could see forming, "maybe more of Torren was harmed than just the southern door."

Thulan shook her head. "The tunnels wouldn't collapse. Not any of the major ones. They were solid."

"An earthquake?" Reese asked. "They can destroy entire cities."

"I know what an earthquake can do," Thulan said. "You don't live under millions of tons of rocks and not know how often they shift. The tunnels are designed to accommodate that. The dwarves have had all the fault lines in Torren mapped out for a hundred years and know exactly what can be disturbed and what can't. Rocks move all the time. The tunnels would have held."

"Except..." Leonis said slowly from where he walked behind them with Cintis, "sometimes they collapse."

"That's different," Thulan said. "Small individual caves can collapse because of a weakness in the rocks, but an earthquake strong enough to collapse entire tunnels would have made the trees of this forest shake like grass in a windstorm. You'd have felt it at the Black River."

"Then what happened?" Leonis asked.

"If I knew that," Thulan said, exasperated, "I wouldn't be trying to figure it out with a bunch of elves and humans who know nothing about the earth."

They walked in silence for a while before Leonis's voice came quietly from behind them. "I had no idea my father...He's aged so much."

Cintis sighed. "I thought you knew, and I didn't want to speak of it unless you mentioned it."

"Is he dying?" Leonis asked.

Sable glanced back to see Cintis shake his head. "The toll your mother's death took on him just aged him."

Leonis looked behind them through the trees, as though he could see his father still. "Have I made it worse?"

"It is always this way when a lifelong mate dies," Victis said. "Elves lose something when one they are close to dies. Years. Centuries sometimes."

"You told me he didn't want to see me," Leonis said, his words sharp. "You told me he wanted me away from the wood."

"He did," Victis said. "You know he did when you left. Your presence reminded him of your mother."

Leonis stopped walking, and the commander paused too, turning slowly to face him.

The half-elf's hands were clenched at his side, and his words came out through clenched teeth. "Last time I was here, you said he wanted me gone. I *believed* you. But that was a lie."

Victis didn't answer immediately. "Last time I saw you, I had not spoken to Parseis for many years about you. I believed he still felt too much pain to want to see you." His posture softened almost imperceptibly before he continued. "When he found out you had been near, he seemed... sorrowful. But until this morning, I did not know that he wanted you to come back."

Thulan looked up at the tall commander. "You never asked him?"

Victis didn't answer.

"You have been a terrible friend to Parseis." Thulan took Leonis's arm and pulled him away.

Victis stayed still for a moment, his eyes focused on the spot where the dwarf had stood. Without a word, he followed her.

Hours later, Victis stopped at a stream. "The path ahead will lead you toward the dwarven realm."

Cintis clasped Leonis's arm, then pulled an elvish bow off his shoulder. "Every time I see you, you're carrying some weak human bow. Take this, then you won't be able to blame the weapon when you miss."

"Probably a waste of a good weapon," Thulan said from beside him.

"Probably," Cintis agreed, "but we have to help him where we can."

He set his hand on Thulan's shoulder. "Leonis told me of the loss of your husband and your sons."

Thulan stiffened at the words, but Cintis continued. "We have a saying: *The heart heals in the shade of familiar trees*. I know home for you isn't among the trees, but I hope when you are back in the tunnels that you find healing, not just pain." He held out his hand.

Thulan swallowed, then grasped his forearm with her thick fingers. "The tunnels feel more like a crypt than a home," she said quietly. "But thank you."

Victis watched the two of them, his face unreadable.

Reese patted the neck of his horse. "Dwarven tunnels are no place for a horse. He belongs to the monks on Tutella Island, but would it be possible to leave him in the Wildwood? I don't know when we'll return for him."

Victis nodded his permission, and Reese started to unbuckle the packs from the saddle.

"You sure you don't need him a bit longer?" Sable asked.

Reese shook his head. "I should have come to the Wildwood sooner." He glanced at Victis. "There's something about the woods…"

The elf gave a slight shrug. "There is healing under the trees."

"I'm beginning to understand why elves live so long," Reese said, pulling the packs off and handing one to Thulan.

"Is there any chance the elves will change their minds?" Sable asked Victis.

"If there is anything that will sway them apart from an attack on their borders, I do not know what it is."

Sable looked into the quiet woods. "Then I don't imagine I'll be seeing you again."

Victis studied her. "The elves have not given you what you needed," he pointed out. "I'm sure you will be back."

"You said they wouldn't change their minds."

He nearly smiled. "Will that stop you?"

"No, it won't," Reese said, handing Sable one of the packs. "She'll be back."

Victis gave Sable a formal nod. "Until next time, then. For your sake, I hope you find more success among the dwarves than you did here."

"Be careful," Sable said with a smile, "or I'll start thanking you again."

His mouth quirked up in the corner, and he took in the group one last time. "May your travels be safe and swift."

He turned and walked back the way they had come, and Sable watched him until he stepped past a wide tree and disappeared.

"It's unsettling that you people do that," Thulan muttered.

Cintis smiled at them all. "Good luck with the dwarves. I'll speak to the elves who wanted to support you and see if anything can be done. Don't hope for much, but I'll try."

Leonis pulled the elf into a hug.

Cintis groaned. "Go, go. Maybe the dwarves will appreciate all the hugging."

Leonis stepped back, grinning. "Maybe they will. I'll have to try that."

Thulan started down the trail. "You do that, Leonis. I'd like to see how that goes."

Sable pulled off her pack and sat gratefully against a boulder in a clearing that was already sinking into dusk. The thin layer of moss beneath her did nothing to soften the ground.

The more distance they'd put between themselves and the elves, the more the tension and disappointment of the morning had faded, leaving a deep exhaustion in its place.

Purnicious popped into view, kneeling and setting her knobby blue hand on the moss. It grew spongier, and Sable shifted against it.

"That's the most comfortable thing I've ever felt, Purn."

Purnicious beamed at her. "I doubt that is true, mistress, but it's a little better."

Thulan already had a neat stack of wood set for a fire, and Leonis appeared at her shoulder with a wad of dead pine needles. The half-elf had been unusually quiet for the entire day, and after handing Thulan the kindling, he went to lean against a wide tree trunk.

When the fire was started, Thulan pulled out four leaf-wrapped packets that the elves had given them and tucked them against the edge of the fire.

Reese stepped up to Sable and held out one of his knives, handle first.

She looked from the knife to his face. "What's that for?"

"Training."

Sable glanced over at Thulan and Leonis. "For what?"

"For the next time you're 'invited' somewhere with an enemy or meet a Kalesh general. Or get waylaid by Kiva. Again."

"Can't she kill people by touching them?" Thulan asked.

"Yes, didn't she almost kill you the first time she kissed you?" Leonis asked. "She doesn't need a knife. She can just kiss people."

Reese kept the knife held out. The handle was plain, wrapped in worn black leather. The blade itself almost fit inside Reese's hand. Memories of endless, exhausting sword practices came back to her.

"Reese..." There was a stubborn set to his shoulders that she recognized. "Can we start tomorrow? I'm tired."

"Well, in that case, of course we should put it off." He didn't lower the knife. "You'll never be put in a dangerous situation when you're tired."

She frowned at him. "Is there any way I can convince you not to do this today?"

"If you swear to me on the lives of both of your sisters that you will never again willfully put yourself in a situation where your life is in danger."

"It's not like I intend to do these things."

"And yet, they continue to happen." He leaned closer until the knife handle was right in front of her. "Take the knife and stand up."

She wrapped her fingers around the leather, and he let go. The knife was not heavy, but it felt solid.

She climbed to her feet. "Now I learn to stab things?"

He shook his head. "Now you learn to slash things. Stabbing is harder than it looks because things like ribs get in the way, unless you know what you're aiming for."

"Yes," Thulan said, adding twigs to her small fire. "Like when that Kalesh soldier tried to stab Reese in the chest, his ribs protected him."

"And he was fine," Leonis added.

"I was not fine," Reese said, undeterred, "because it turned into a deep slash." He backed away to the center of the clearing and motioned her to come closer. "We'll start with the knife, then you need to learn to grapple too. You can have that blade to carry with you, and you should know how to use it, but in reality, most fights come down to grappling."

Thulan grunted in agreement.

"If I'm grappling with someone," Sable said, "I'll be touching them, and I could just pull out their *vitalle.*" She looked down at the knife. "Besides, every time I've been captured by anyone, I've been outnumbered and outsized. Kiva's the only man who's even close to my size, and he's always surrounded by huge thugs. What good is a knife?"

He stepped close to her and wrapped his hand around hers, tilting the blade up so it wasn't pointing at him.

"Will you do it," he asked, tightening his grip on her hand, "just because I need to feel like I'm doing something to protect you?"

Her objections trailed away at the entreaty in his voice. She nodded.

He smiled. "Good, then let's start with the obvious. You're holding it wrong."

CHAPTER TWENTY-TWO

THE ELVISH FOREST had been roofed with a sunlit green canopy, but each day they traveled north, the forest shifted to darker green pines, their tops framing slices of brilliant blue sky.

Sable started rising before dawn with Reese, prodding Leonis awake, and urging Thulan to lead them to the dwarves at a quick pace. Despite the failure with the elves and the fact that Thulan assured them the dwarves would be no different even if they could find them, Sable still grilled her with questions.

"We can use their love of fighting," Sable said on the third afternoon. Innov perched on her arm, and Sable watched the glitters of light tumble out from between her feathers every time she shifted. "If the Kalesh take over the human lands, they'll at the least find the orchards and herds that the dwarves keep outside the cliffs, and they may decide that the treasures of the dwarves are worth attacking the tunnels for."

"The dwarves would be mad about the food," Thulan said, "but the Kalesh won't find the door to Torren, never mind get through it."

"Can we find any influential dwarves?" Sable asked. "Victis and Parseis both said an influential elf might have changed minds in the Wildwood. Do you know any dwarves important enough to sway others to our cause?"

Thulan scowled down the path ahead of them. "Maybe."

"Great. When we find them, you can introduce us. Maybe we can gain their support before we speak to the High Dwarf."

Thulan made a noncommittal noise.

"What's wrong?" Sable asked.

"I just don't have a lot of hope," the dwarf answered.

"Well, hope's not something you have," Sable said with a small smile. "It's something you catch. Or choose. Or something. Atticus didn't make enough sense for me to remember what he said, but the point is that we're the ones who have to make the hope. Everyone else is already hopeless. If we don't find a way to generate some, we've already lost."

Thulan kicked a rock on the path, sending it skittering into the trees. "I'm here, aren't I?"

They walked a few steps in silence before Sable shifted Innov to the arm closer to Thulan. A shower of embers shook loose and drifted to the ground.

Thulan reached out her hand and caught one. It sat glowing on her palm until it winked out. "Why don't her sparks burn anything?"

"I have no idea." Sable watched another burning speck fall and roll along Sable's sleeve. "Of course, I don't understand most things about her."

Thulan watched the firelight crawl between Innov's feathers. "I may know some dwarves who can help us."

"Then that's where we'll start."

The dwarf sighed. "If we can find them."

Later that afternoon, Sable walked next to Reese, drinking in the colors and sounds and freshness of it all. Leonis strolled along with Thulan behind them, their banter light and familiar.

"Are all the northern forests like this?" Sable asked Reese.

He nodded. "Everything north of Steepdale."

"Then I don't care if I ever go south of Steepdale again." She looked around the woods. "My mother used to go on extended hunting trips by herself. It was the only time she used her elvish bow, and she would tell us tales of the forest when she returned. She must have come to the Nidel Woods, although it would have taken her days to get there from where we lived. But I understand why she did and why she always seemed sad to get back home to the treeless hills of the Eastern Reaches."

"She probably hunted in the southern forests where the trees are better," Leonis said. "These pines are too stiff. They have no arms."

"What do they need arms for?" Sable asked. "Thulan, do the tunnels change as you move north? Or are they all the same?"

"How could there be a difference?" Leonis asked. "They're pitch-black tunnels of rock. Hard to find much variety there."

"The part we're headed for," Thulan said, ignoring him, "is the Northern Corner. It's been mostly unused for generations. These rocks are denser than the cliffs near the southern door, and they're laced with silver cab flakes, which make the walls glitter. They're completely different from the porous tunnels in the south."

"If no one's used these for generations," Sable said, "how will we find any dwarves?"

"The dwarves have been seen in the north, and this is the only door in the north with access to the forest. If they're using it, it'll be easy enough to follow the signs in the tunnels back south to Torren. It'll be several days' walk once we're inside, though."

Sable glanced up toward where the Marsham Cliffs were still hidden behind the trees. She imagined stepping into a dark tunnel, the weight of the rock above her pushing down, the dark stretching out endlessly, the roughness of stone under her hands as she dragged them blindly along the wall.

"We have to walk in the dark for days?" Leonis asked.

"It's not dark," Thulan said. "It's beautiful and peaceful and you never have to worry about rain."

Sable glanced at Reese. "Have you been in tunnels before?"

"A couple of caves, but never far enough in that I couldn't see daylight."

"You are all missing out," Thulan said. "Just wait until you see a natural cavern lit by nightmoss. Nothing out here compares." Her words were steady, but there was something about her voice that caught at Sable's attention. The words had not been entirely warm.

"Something called nightmoss does not sound very bright," Leonis said.

"Just wait," Thulan repeated. "You'll see."

"Do you think we'll face the Kalesh army at Barrowford?" Sable asked, handing Thulan the flint as the dwarf set the fire for dinner on their fifth night out from the elves.

"I hope not," Reese said, pulling out his bedroll. "It's a good central spot for armies to gather, but strategically it's not great."

"I thought the city had the strongest wall in the north." Sable moved to the packs and found the little blanket and pillow Purn liked to sleep on. "And doesn't it have a fortress?" She carried the bedding to a nice flat place by the fire and laid it out neatly. Purnicious popped into view with a grateful smile and started fluffing the pillow a bit.

"The city itself could be defended for a while," Reese said, "but it doesn't protect anything. It's surrounded by a wide plain, and there are infinite ways north around it. The Kalesh can just siege it and wait for it to surrender while taking out the rest of the north."

"That's the same problem anywhere in the north, though," Thulan said. "We may go to all this effort to unify the army, then have it split apart to fight a dozen different battles."

Reese nodded. "We need to think farther south. The narrows near Tutella Island are defensible."

"What are the narrows?" Sable asked, pulling out her own blankets and moving between Purn and Reese's.

"That grassy plain east of the river." Reese finished adjusting his bedroll on the ground. "The Black Hills block any army from coming north except along the river at the narrows. Once they're past Tutella, though, they could head in any direction and attack anything." He glanced at Thulan. "With a big enough force, we could hold the narrows."

"You should lead it again," Leonis said. "Don't let Braddick take over."

Thulan nodded. "Assuming you don't freeze up like you did last time and get stabbed."

A flicker passed over Reese's face almost too fast for Sable to catch. She'd seen it before when Leonis or Thulan had goaded him about his injury, but she'd assumed he wasn't ready to hear jokes about it. Maybe it was more. Now that she thought about it, there was something odd about him freezing in the middle of a battle.

Purn appeared at Sable's shoulder, beginning the process of plumping up Sable's pillow. Leonis dropped down next to Thulan as she worked on the fire, handing her a large wad of dried pine needles, but Reese caught Sable's eye, motioning for her to follow him. He walked through the trees to an open space a short distance away. "Tonight we grapple," he said with a smile. "There's plenty you can do even if you're small and don't have a knife. Turn around. I'm going to grab you from behind."

She turned, and he wrapped his arms around her shoulders.

"First, grab my arms," he said, "and drop your weight lower."

She set her hands on his forearms. "What happened during the battle when you were stabbed?"

His arms hardened under her hand.

"Something happened," she said, "and it's still bothering you."

When he spoke, the words were stiff. "I froze."

The words hadn't been cold, but Sable shook her head. "I know you wouldn't lie to me, but that was hardly the truth."

He didn't answer.

"It's been weeks, Reese." She paused. "Narine always insisted that your troubles lost their power when you shared them, so if you don't want to tell me, tell Leonis or Thulan. Tell someone. Not today, if you're not ready, but at some point, find someone to tell."

He still didn't speak, so she squeezed his arms one last time. "I wasn't listening before. What do I do now? Drop my weight?"

He pulled her tighter against his chest. "I didn't make friends at the Kalesh school," he said, his voice low, "except for Vann. He was from a small town at the edge of the Empire and hated being there. He could out-strategize everyone in our class and half the instructors, so he and I won a lot of the contests they'd give us. His favorite thing to plan, though, was how to steal sweets and liquor from the officers. We got away with it often enough that rumors started to circulate that a spirit haunted the school."

Reese's tone was guarded, but his words were warm with truth. Sable turned her head toward him, but he tightened his grip on her shoulders.

"He was funny and learned everything faster than me and got himself into more trouble than anyone I've ever met, but what he wanted most was to go home and see his parents. The Kalesh had overrun his people when he was twelve and conscripted all the boys into the army. He'd never been back. The Empire doesn't waste minds like his, though, and they sent him off to join some pointless, distant battle. I'd been saving money to leave for a long time by then, and that was the final straw. I left within a fortnight."

For a long moment, the only sounds in the forest were the pecking of a bird on a tree and Leonis's faint voice through the trees. "During the battle at Immusmala, we were fighting back a wave of Kalesh, just one black-clad soldier after another, when—" He broke off, and Sable closed her eyes against what was coming.

"I know it wasn't him," he said. "This soldier was young. As young as

Vann was when I knew him, but something about his face was so familiar." He swallowed. "Thulan hit him with her hammer, and all I wanted to do was stop her. Every soldier in front of me was suddenly a boy who'd been torn from his home by the Kalesh, forced to fight some pointless battle in some distant land." He shook his head. "I couldn't have kept on fighting even if he hadn't thrown his sword. I saw it coming, and I could have avoided it, but..."

His arms relaxed, sagging over her shoulders. "All of a sudden, I couldn't see the point. When that blade hit, the pain was...almost welcome."

She gripped his arms.

"It was your voice that brought me back," he said. "You'd brought more men, and the fighting moved away. I should have wanted to help them, but mostly I was just relieved that you'd kept me from having to fight again."

Reese leaned his forehead against the back of her hair. "It's the problem with fighting the Kalesh. Every Kalesh soldier we kill is Vann. A man who was taken from his home and trained to kill for the Empire. They're basically prisoners, but if we don't fight them, every young man in our land will be dragged into the same fate."

Thulan's and Leonis's voices came quietly through the trees, but the rest of the forest was quiet.

His arms were loose enough that she turned and looked up at him, wrapping her arms around his back. "What other option is there?"

"Tanis would say we should be looking for a way to make the Kalesh less interested in our land. I've been trying, but..." He gave her a defeated look. "Between the gold, and you, and the Tien Sark believing Vivaine is their mythological savior, I can't think of anything that would drive them away."

Sable leaned her cheek against his chest. "Neither can I."

The next afternoon, the trail spilled out of the forest into a bright break in the trees, and Thulan's steps faltered before she strode out into the sunlight. Leonis, Sable, and Reese squinted at the huge, bright rock face. The light grey stones of the Marsham Cliffs rose five times higher than the trees, sheer and impassable.

Sable stopped next to Leonis, craning her neck to see up the rocks, feeling small and fragile next to the massive cliffs. "Are we close to the northern door?"

"We'll reach it tonight," Thulan said over her shoulder as she continued back into the trees, "if you all stop gawking at the cliffs as though you've never seen rocks before."

"I thought the Marsham Cliffs were tall way down where we tried to get in the southern entrance to Torren," Sable said. "These look much, much taller."

"They are," Reese said. "And they just get taller the farther north you go, until they meet up with the Wolfsbane Mountains."

"I'm not coming back to find you all when you get lost!" Thulan yelled from somewhere out of sight. "I'll leave you all to rot, eaten by bears and wildcats and monsters!"

"There are no monsters in these woods," Leonis called back. He lowered his voice. "She's getting crabbier the closer we get to Torren."

"Do you think we'll find dwarves?" Sable asked quietly. "Or will it be deserted, like the southern door?"

"Thulan thinks we'll find them," Leonis said, "or she wouldn't be this nervous."

Sable looked after the dwarf, who was striding away down the path, looking like she was marching into a battle. "She's nervous?"

"The only other time I've seen her like this was when we were going up to the southern door." He watched Thulan's back disappear into the trees and started toward the path. "For her sake, I can't decide if I want to find the dwarves or not."

The sun shifted lower in the sky, leaving long trails of light angling through the trees, before Thulan turned onto a small path heading for the cliffs. It was well trodden, with no little snips of green growing in the dirt. Thulan stared down at a boot print.

She put a hand over her eyes for a moment then dragged it down her face before squaring her shoulders and starting down the path.

Leonis looked at the boot print, giving a little sigh. "We found the dwarves." He lifted his gaze to Thulan, sighed again, and followed her.

"Someday," Reese said, "we should visit somewhere one of us is actually excited to get to."

"Where would that be?" Sable asked, starting down the path.

"I don't know," he answered, "but it feels like a nice goal."

CHAPTER TWENTY-THREE

THE TRAIL REACHED the edge of the woods, and Thulan came to a stop. Ahead of her, the opening between the forest and the Marsham Cliffs was covered in rocks from a massive rockslide. Huge boulders piled against each other, mounded a third of the way up the cliff, while smaller stones filled in every cranny between them. A wide jumble of rocks spilled out across the ground, rolling into the trees.

Thulan stood looking at the rocks, her hands balled into fists. She turned to the others. "This won't be like visiting the elves."

Leonis glanced up the rock face. "Who would ever think we'd find elves in there?"

Thulan glared at him. "This won't be a peaceful little council where people listen and give imperceptible nods to show their vote. I have never been to an important meeting that didn't include some sort of fight." She stretched her fingers out and took a deep breath. "It's usually short. Honestly, it's more tradition than anything. A couple of cousins exchanging some blows. Almost a performance."

Leonis's brow creased in something that looked like disapproval.

"Cousins?" Sable asked.

"Dwarves all call each other cousin," Leonis said. "It's weird."

"It's not weird," Thulan answered. "We're all cousins if you go back far enough. Regardless, any fight will be merely a few swings to show people care about the idea. People rarely get hurt, and I know the High Dwarf.

He's a bit thickskulled but basically decent." She glanced toward the rocks. "He'll listen to me." The words sounded almost confident.

"The High Dwarf will listen to you?" Sable asked. "Why didn't you say that before?"

Thulan waved Sable's question away with an irritated motion. "This is important: None of *you* can fight. If anything happens, leave it to me. If I fight someone, that's passionate negotiation. If one of you does it, it's an act of aggression from a foreigner."

"So we're supposed to stand around and watch them pummel you?" Leonis asked.

Thulan crossed her arms and leveled a blistering look at him.

"Fine," Leonis said, "you can hold your own. It's us standing around not helping that's going to be a problem."

"Which is why you're swearing to me right now that you won't step in."

Reese shook his head. "I can't promise to just stand by while you're attacked."

"It's not a duel to the death or anything," Thulan said. "There aren't rules exactly, but usually whoever gets knocked down first loses. If I get knocked down, it's over." She pointed at Reese. "You step in, and we go from losing their vote of confidence to starting a war between dwarves and humans." Thulan's words were warm.

"That's all it takes to start a war with the dwarves?" Sable asked.

"If it happens in the throne room and involves official delegates from the north?" Thulan asked. "Yes, that's what it takes. Swear you all will stay out of it."

"You promise it won't be a serious fight?" Reese asked.

"Just a scuffle," Thulan assured them. "But not even any posturing from you. Just stand by like you're watching some entertainment."

Reese glanced questioningly at Sable, and she nodded. "She's telling the truth."

"Of course I'm telling the truth," Thulan said irritably.

"All right," Reese said. "I'll stay out of whatever dwarvish scuffle you get yourself into."

Thulan turned to Leonis, who was scowling darkly.

"Fine," he said. "Can I taunt them?"

"No." Thulan shifted to look expectantly at Sable.

Sable raised an eyebrow. "You really need the same promise from me?"

"Yes," Thulan said. "You do stupid things when people you care about are in danger."

"That's true," Reese said.

Sable raised one hand. "I solemnly swear not to join in any dwarvish fight."

Thulan studied her, as though trying to see a loophole in her words.

Sable laughed. "I promise, Thulan. I have no desire to fight a dwarf."

"Excellent," Thulan said. "Then let's get this over with." She started toward the cliffs.

"I do have a desire to speak to them, though," Sable said.

Thulan stopped. "Let me talk first. When it comes time to actually plead our case, I'll introduce you. Until then, probably best if you don't talk much." She pointed at Leonis. "You should not speak at all." She turned her face up the rockslide toward a part that looked no different from the rest of the rubble. "C'mon."

Sable paused next to Reese and Leonis. "What if she fights and loses?" she asked quietly.

Reese watched the dwarf tromp over the rock-strewn ground. "I don't think she will."

"Thulan can fight," Leonis agreed.

Sable frowned. "What if all dwarves can fight?"

Leonis shook his head. "When she left Torren after her husband and sons died, she was, in her own words, ready to tear apart the world. She joined a traveling show where she fought people for money. If she could knock them down, they paid. She played up the female thing, because that combined with her height led a lot of men to think they could beat her. But she was good. Really good."

Reese made a thoughtful noise. "That explains her fighting style. She's scrappy."

"Shut up and come on," Thulan called over her shoulder.

Leonis started forward, walking carefully among the rocks. "When we first saw her," he continued quietly, "Atticus stood and watched her for hours. Every fight was a performance, he said. She'd mastered the idea of a layered audience. She tailored her reactions and posture and motions not only for whoever she was fighting, to make them think they had a chance, but also to whoever in the crowd she thought would be next. You know Atticus—that was enough for love at first sight. By the next morning, he'd lured her away from the fighting through some bargain I've never heard the details of, and she's been with us ever since."

Sable stepped from rock to rock, keeping to the ones bigger than her foot, trying not to slip into small cracks between them. "I thought she'd been with you the whole time."

"She doesn't like to talk about the fighting," Leonis said.

"Really?" Reese asked. "She's always so confident."

"It wasn't the fighting. It was the rest of it. The playing up that she was a female, as though that were a weakness, always pointing out she was different so people thought they could take advantage of her. When I first met her, she was…not like she is now. She was distant and brusque. Never smiled." He watched Thulan's back with a worried expression.

"And now she's going back to the tunnels, which have painful memories," Sable said quietly, "and will possibly have to fight in something that is 'almost a performance.'"

Leonis sighed. "I hope the dwarves reject our request as fast as the elves did, and we can just move on."

Ahead of them, Thulan had reached the point where larger rocks had piled up against the cliff base. She clambered over a small boulder and disappeared.

Sable followed and found the beginning of a thin section of stair carved into the rock. The entire thing was hidden from the forest, tucked behind large stones. A dozen steps up, the stairs wound around a large boulder. Thulan stomped around it, muttering to herself.

Sable started after her. The stairs wandered back and forth across the rockslide from one edge to the other. Sable caught glimpses of the trees as she climbed, but mostly she could see nothing but tall rocks on either side and the clear blue sky above. Near the height of the treetops, Sable caught a glimpse of Innov soaring in the sky and paused.

"I doubt Innov will like being in caves," Reese said from behind her.

"Fire is bad in a cave," Thulan said over her shoulder. "Doesn't matter that she doesn't put off smoke. They won't like her."

Sable watched Innov dart down toward the forest. "I think we may miss her hopefulness."

Thulan grunted in agreement but trudged higher without looking back.

At the fourth switchback, Thulan stopped. The stairs wound farther up, growing more ragged and broken as they meandered higher, but Thulan stood with her arms crossed tightly, peering into a fissure between an enormous slab of rock and the cliff face.

Sable looked over her shoulder. A flat rock blocked the fissure about an arm's length in. "Is that a door?"

Thulan tossed her chin toward the scuffed dirt and boot prints near the rock.

"Did you knock?" Leonis asked from behind Reese.

"If you want to bloody your knuckles knocking on a rock, go ahead." Thulan said.

"If we don't knock, how do we let them know we're here?" he asked.

"They're using this door," Thulan said, her posture stiff. "That means they're guarding it. They've probably known where we were for most of the day."

Distant chirps of birds and squirrels came up from the forest below them, but there was no sound from the door.

"Can they hear us?" Sable asked. "You could introduce yourself."

"They can hear us." Thulan's voice grew louder and more annoyed. "And they should be smart enough to recognize a cousin when they see one."

"It's been a while since you were here," Leonis pointed out. "And you didn't live in this part, maybe they think you're some strange dwarf from—"

"Thulan?" a muffled voice came from inside. "What are you idiots doing? Open the door!"

Thulan tilted her head slightly.

There were indistinct, irritated voices from the other side of the door, but the only word Sable could pick out was "humans."

"It's Thulan, and you know it," the voice said. "Open the door, Pardrun, or I swear I will pull out your wisp of a beard and use it for kindling."

"Mari?" Thulan said.

There was more muted conversation and one loud thump, then the stone doorway hinged smoothly into the mountain, revealing a tidy room crowded with dwarves.

The dwarf nearest the door had a neatly trimmed walnut-colored beard with delicate braids threaded through it. "Thulan!" She ran out into the sunlight and wrapped her arms around Thulan's shoulders.

Past her, a half-dozen dwarves, all of whom had thick, braided beards, looked at Thulan with varying levels of hostility and curiosity.

"Where have you been?" Mari asked, pulling back and holding on to Thulan's shoulders.

"Mari?" Thulan said again. "You're…here?"

"Where else would I be? Come in!" She motioned Thulan into the entrance. "Get your fat head out of the way, Pardrun. It's Thulan!" She waved the largest of the dwarves out of her way. None of the dwarves moved, their eyes locked not on Thulan but on Sable, Reese, and Leonis.

Their expressions were decidedly unfriendly.

Reese moved in front of Sable and faced the dwarves.

"Humans." A dwarf stepped close to Reese, cleared his throat, and spat.

Reese looked down at the wet glob muddying the dust on his boot. His hands had balled into fists, and he forced his fingers to uncurl. "Thulan…" Reese said slowly.

"These are friends of mine," Thulan protested. "I will vouch for them. They're emissaries from the Northern Lords here to speak to—"

"Thulan!" Leonis called.

Two dwarves crept toward him on the stairs. One held a hammer and the other a vicious-looking axe.

"Pardrun," Thulan said, her voice growing angry, "they're not a threat—"

"Humans!" Pardrun growled. He was huge for a dwarf. Not as tall as Reese, but at least twice as wide, with wild brown hair, and his voice rolled out of the cave with a furious edge. He gave a sharp, slicing motion. "Take them."

CHAPTER TWENTY-FOUR

Pardrun pushed past Mari, grabbed Thulan's arm, and dragged her into the cave. Two more dwarves rushed out and grabbed Reese, and the ones near Leonis closed in. The half-elf backed up to Sable, slinging his bow off his back in a smooth motion.

Reese held up his hands as he was pulled toward the cave. "No fighting, Leonis."

Leonis nocked an arrow. "I won't if they'll back off."

"Do *not* shoot them," Sable said. "We're here on a diplomatic mission," she said loudly, shoving warmth in the words.

Dwarves dove at Leonis, tearing the bow from his hand and shoving him up against a rock on the side of the path.

"Diplomatic!" Mari repeated. "Leave them alone!"

"That means peaceful, you idiots!" Leonis grunted. "Thulan, you never told me dwarves were so stupid."

"Pardrun!" Thulan shouted from inside the cave, struggling against the dwarves holding her.

They yanked her arms behind her and locked manacles on her wrists.

"We're here to see High Dwarf Dirthor!" she yelled. "Get your hands off me!"

A dwarf approached Sable, and she took a step back on the path. He had a fiery red beard, split and braided into two long plaits. He was about her height, like most of the dwarves, but he was built like a boulder himself. He grabbed her shoulders, his fingers digging into her muscles and grinding against the bones. She let out a hiss of pain as he shoved her into the cave.

It was like walking into the maw of a huge stone creature. The vast openness of the sky was swallowed up, replaced with dark, lifeless rock. Moss hung from the ceiling like strands of hair. Around the edges of the room were tables laden with half-eaten dinners.

Pardrun held Thulan next to the tunnel heading deeper into the cliff like a throat winding deeper into the monster.

Mari stood near the wall, her brow drawn in a frown, holding a hammer so tightly her knuckles were white.

"We are here on a diplomatic mission from the Northern Lords," Sable repeated loudly, pushing warmth into her voice. The pressure on her shoulders lightened slightly, but then the fiery-bearded dwarf wrenched her pack off her back and dropped it to the floor.

He pulled her arms back, and another dwarf snatched the knife from her belt.

"Diplomatic!" She shoved the word at him, and he hesitated for a moment, but then tossed the knife into a pile with the rest of their weapons.

"Lenn," Thulan snapped at the dwarf holding Sable. "When did you start roughing up small women?"

He ignored her, and since the manacles were too large for anyone but Thulan, he pulled Sable's arms behind her and bound her wrists with rough rope. The cord crushed her wrists together, and the sharp fibers stabbed into her skin like needles.

The door to the outside swung closed, strangling out the light, leaving nothing but shadows. After a moment, she noticed that the moss on the ceiling glowed with a faint yellow light that let her make out the commotion in the room.

Sable twisted her wrists against the ropes. "There's no need for this!" She pushed *vitalle* into her words, trying to be heard throughout the room. "We come in peace with a message for the High Dwarf!"

Lenn clamped down on her shoulders again and propelled her toward the tunnel. When she got closer to Thulan, she could see the dwarf staring at the closed door, her shoulders hunched.

"Take them to the throne room," Pardrun growled. "Rion will be very interested to hear what they have to say."

Thulan blinked and refocused on the big dwarf. "Rion? We're here to talk to High Dwarf Dirthor, not his scrawny, spineless nephew."

Pardrun drew back and drove his fist into Thulan's face, sending her reeling into the wall.

"Stop!" Sable yelled, her fury pouring into the words.

Everyone in the room hesitated.

Leonis and Reese recovered first, both shouting and struggling to reach Thulan as she slumped against the rocks.

Mari ran over to Thulan, reaching for her arm to help her up, but Pardrun pushed Mari away.

Thulan staggered back upright on her own, shaking her head and moving her jaw gingerly. "You always did punch like a coward, Pardrun." She spit blood out on the floor. "Take these chains off me and try that again."

He grabbed her by her hair and twisted her toward the tunnel. "You've always thought you were better than the rest of us, Thulan. But if you want to survive the night, you'll stifle that smug attitude and bite your tongue."

Leonis grunted as a dwarf tightened the ropes around his wrists. "She *is* better than the rest of you."

The dwarf punched him in the gut, and the half-elf doubled over. "Silence!"

Leonis groaned and opened his mouth again.

"Silence is a good idea, Leonis," Sable said before he could speak.

"You four," Pardrun called out, "bring the prisoners, their weapons, and their packs. The rest of you"—he dropped a scathing gaze at Mari—"are on guard duty. Back to your posts."

"But—" Mari started.

"To your post!" Pardrun bellowed. With his hand still locked in Thulan's hair, he shoved her into the tunnel.

Thulan let out a grunt of pain, and Leonis growled as he was pushed after her. Lenn's fingers stayed clamped on Sable's shoulders as he propelled her forward, shooting pain up her neck and across her back no matter how she tried to shift.

The tunnel floor was smooth and clean, the walls curving up to meet at a ceiling not terribly far above Leonis's head. Balls of glowing moss, which must be nightmoss, sat in nooks at regular intervals, making any shadows diffuse and vague.

Specks of light flashed on the walls as they walked, glittering off of tiny silvery facets embedded in the rock. The sparkles and the glowing nightmoss might have given the tunnels an ethereal, dreamlike feel if it hadn't been for the painful hands of the dwarf on Sable's shoulders, the constant pushing, and the heavy tread of footsteps echoing off the walls.

The door outside fell farther behind them, and the walls of the tunnel narrowed occasionally, squeezing toward her like a closing fist. She drew in deep breaths, trying not to think about the endless rock around them.

More tunnels branched off before they strode out into a larger cave, busy with dwarves. The sight of the guards and their prisoners went through the chamber like a gust of wind, spreading murmurs, turning every dwarf to stare at them. Their expressions were uniformly dark. Sable's guard pushed her past a dwarf with streaks of grey running through her short beard and braided hair. The woman glared at her and spit on Sable's sleeve.

Sable flinched away, but Lenn pushed her forward again.

"Thulan," Leonis said, "you downplayed the level of hostility we were going to face here."

Thulan glanced back, her face surprisingly pale. "What is wrong with you?" she asked Pardrun.

The dwarf gave her a shove and didn't answer.

A few times Sable heard Thulan's name mentioned, sometimes in shocked exclamations, sometimes in mutters, but she never managed to pick out the speaker.

"An awful lot of dwarves seem to know who Thulan is," Reese said from behind Sable.

She caught a glimpse of him over the bright red head of Lenn. "And the Northern Corner doesn't seem to be deserted any longer."

They turned into a smaller tunnel, and the feeling of being encased in stone that had been inching its way up Sable's neck snaked out tendrils of dread. The rock ceiling closed in lower, heavy and smothering. The door to the outside world was lost uncountable turns behind her.

The farther they walked and the more hostility they encountered, the quieter Thulan grew, her unanswered questions dwindling away.

They finally entered a wide tunnel lit with moss lanterns that alternated yellow and red, making the walls shimmer with flecks of golden light. A beautifully woven rug ran along the floor all the way to a pair of thick wooden doors, which were pulled open to reveal a huge cavern.

Sable's guard pushed her behind the others into the long, wide chamber. Tall columns were carved like sentries all the way down each wall.

Between them, stunning artwork was on display. Richly colored, detailed tapestries, statues of dwarves carved to a perfect lifelikeness, enormous paintings of battles or dwarven life.

The far end of the room was raised several steps, and a thick throne sat on it, looking as though it was formed out of the rock around it. The front was smooth and throne-like, but the sides grew rougher near the base, shifting into uncut rock that spread seamlessly into the floor.

Dwarves stood along the outskirts of the room, clumped into small groups, looking bored until they caught sight of the prisoners. A few more stood near the throne, talking quietly. When one of them saw Pardrun striding toward the throne, he flicked his hands at the dwarves around him, and they moved quickly out of the way.

"My lord," Pardrun said, reaching the base of the dais and shoving Thulan down to kneel, forcing her head forward until she bowed to the throne. "We found a traitor bringing humans into Torren."

Thulan's hands were curled into fists. Every line of her body was tense.

Lenn dug his fingers into Sable's shoulders, driving her down until she crashed to her knees on the hard floor beside Thulan. Reese let out a growl next to her as he and Leonis were forced down.

Four guards with spears positioned themselves between the prisoners and the throne.

The dwarf on the dais lifted a thin hand to one of the braids in his beard, rolling the golden bead at the bottom of it between his fingers. Past the braid, Sable caught a glimpse of the pale skin of his neck. He let his hand drop and turned his hollow, sunken eyes to Thulan.

Sable tried to ignore the pain in her shoulders and her knees, focusing on weaving *vitalle* into her words. "We're here on behalf of the Northern Lords," Sable said, spreading her words out to the guards and the dwarf standing near the throne.

"Silence!" Lenn hissed, digging his fingers into her shoulders. She tried to twist away from him, but he held her like a vise.

Thulan caught Sable's eye. "Don't speak."

The dwarf on the dais stepped between the guards until he loomed over Thulan as she knelt. "Who do you think you are? Bringing them here?" His voice rang out through the cavern with a shrill edge.

Thulan twisted against Pardrun's grip on her hair until she could look up. "Rion? What are you playing at? You've known me since you were waist high, begging to be immortalized. What happened to your block-headed uncle? We have important—"

Pardrun released Thulan's hair and slammed his fist into her cheek, sending her sprawling onto the floor.

"Thulan!" Sable shouted, pulling against her guard's grip.

Leonis and Reese both tried to lunge toward her, but their guards held them back.

"You will speak to the High Dwarf with respect!" Pardrun snarled at Thulan. He grabbed the back of her collar and pulled her up to her knees.

She spat blood onto his boots, and his hand curled into a fist again.

"You hit me again..." Thulan's voice was frighteningly soft, but Sable could feel the tendrils of warmth in it. "And I swear to you, you will regret it for the rest of your life."

Pardrun let out a snort of contempt.

Thulan shifted to face the High Dwarf. "What happened to Dirthor?" she asked, her voice irritated, as though she weren't bloodied and bound, kneeling at Rion's feet.

"As if you don't know," Rion said coldly. His eyes strayed to a huge painting leaning against the wall. It was framed with strands of glowing nightmoss and depicted a serious dark-haired dwarf chiseling a huge, rough, glittering gem out of a rock wall. He was dressed in common clothes, a leather vest and cream-colored shirt, but the details in the drape of the fabric and the richness of the paint were magnificent.

Thulan's gaze strayed to the wall and lingered on the painting.

"High Dwarf Dirthor," Rion said, his eyes still on the painting, "was murdered in the attack by the humans. Crushed with so many other great souls when you collapsed our tunnels."

Thulan's brow creased, and she glanced at Sable, Reese, and Leonis.

"We always guessed there was a traitor helping the enemy," Rion said quietly, turning back to Thulan. "I wouldn't have guessed it was you."

"Thulan hasn't done anything," Sable said, shoving warmth into her words as she pushed forward against the grip on her shoulders.

The expressions around them stayed uniformly vicious.

"Quiet, Sable." Thulan searched the dwarves around them. "You all know me. You all know that my husband..." She turned back to the High Dwarf. "Brunn died in a collapse...my boys died...Why would I...?"

"Driven mad by grief?" a dwarf said from the side of the room. He wore a fine dark blue vest, and his black boots were polished until they shone. He walked to the bottom of the stairs leading to the throne and faced Thulan. "Looking for your own way to be immortalized? I don't know. Why don't you tell us?"

"Why is everyone talking about being immortalized?" Leonis asked.

Thulan ignored him. "Drusty?" Her eyes caught on the thick silver threads woven into his beard. "You've...done well for yourself."

"No one's done well, Thulan." Drusty glanced around the throne room. "Not after the humans came."

"What are you talking about?" Sable asked. "What humans came into—"

Lenn clamped his hand over her mouth, his rough fingers digging into her cheeks.

Sable twisted away, getting enough room between her mouth and his fingers to shout, "We're here to form an alliance! The humans are being invaded by a foreign empire who—"

Lenn's hand clamped down again, this time pulling her head back against his stomach, his palm crushing against her face.

"Then the humans can die," Rion shouted. "I hope they're crushed in their homes, their children murdered, their lives destroyed! I hope they die slowly, choking on dust, trapped in the dark!"

He jabbed a finger at Thulan. "You'll be immortalized, Thulan Bright Hue! When you die as a traitor alongside this human trash!"

CHAPTER TWENTY-FIVE

Lenn pushed Sable forward fast enough that she stumbled, held up only by his painfully tight grip on her shoulders.

The air was stale and laced with a damp chill that dragged cold fingers up her arms and along her neck. The world lay in absolute stillness, stirred only by the tromping tread of the guards driving them deeper into the tunnels. Their dim yellow lanterns of nightmoss penetrated the blackness only a half-dozen paces ahead or behind them, and every side tunnel they passed was nothing but a gaping black maw.

Thulan's angry protests had died as they were herded away from the crowded halls near the throne room. It hadn't been more than three turns since they'd passed through a well-lit guardroom, but it might as well have been a hundred for how isolated and remote this tunnel felt.

The tunnel sloped gently downhill, and they passed a metal gate on the left. It looked like a prison cell door, but the mosslight shining through the bars landed on piles of potatoes and apples. Another cell-turned-storage room opened on the right, filled with canvas bags like the huge sacks of flour Sable had seen delivered to Talia's bakery long ago in Dockside.

They moved downhill past a dozen more cells, stopping when Sable could just make out the end of the hall several doors past them. A dwarf pulled open the cell next to them, though, and the hinges gave out a long, grating creak. Pardrun pushed Thulan inside, and as soon as he let go of her, she spun toward him.

He didn't even wait for her to speak before slamming his fist into her face and sending her sprawling backward. He shook out his hand as he walked out of the cell. Leonis was thrust in next. When Lenn gave Sable a shove, her foot caught on the thick iron at the bottom of the cell door and she stumbled forward, crashing into Leonis's back.

Reese stumbled in behind her, and the door squealed shut, latching with a metallic clang.

The walls of the cell were rough-cut stone, arching up to a low rounded ceiling. The floor was relatively flat, empty except for what looked like a dirty old chamber pot. The cell was no more than four paces in any direction.

Thulan struggled up to a sitting position.

"See you at the end of third watch." Pardrun gave her a cold smile as he locked the door. "It's been a long time since we had a drop." His voice lingered almost lovingly on the last word. "I'm sure everyone will be looking forward to it."

He whistled to his guards, and they headed back up the tunnel, leaving the cell in pitch blackness.

Sable stood silent with the others for a long moment. The chill sank through her thin short-sleeved shirt.

"Well," Leonis said finally, his voice fading into the emptiness. "I think that went well."

"What are they thinking?" Thulan's voice burst from the darkness like an explosion. "Has everyone in Torren gone mad? A traitor? Me? And humans collapsing tunnels? It makes no sense. None of this makes sense!"

"Thulan," Reese interrupted her. "When is the end of third watch?"

"And what is a drop?" Sable added.

Thulan fell silent, and Sable's eyes picked out something that might be her outline in the darkness as she scrambled to her feet

"Third watch ends early in the morning," Thulan said. "Around dawn in the outside world."

"It's past sundown by now," Reese said, "so we have the night."

"What is a drop?" Sable repeated, louder.

Thulan cleared her throat. "A drop is an execution."

"Like a hanging?" Reese asked.

"They're going to hang us at dawn?" Leonis said mildly.

"No, not a hanging," Thulan answered, "a drop. There's a cavern with a chasm so deep we've never found the bottom. If someone's to be executed, they're taken to the bridge that spans the chasm and…"

Bone-cold tendrils of fear crawled up Sable's neck at the idea of a gaping black, bottomless chasm at her feet. "Dropped?"

Thulan shifted in what might have been a nod.

Sable squeezed her eyes shut, as though that would be better than the blackness of the cell.

"Are anyone's ropes loose?" Leonis asked.

Sable opened her eyes and found that the blackness was not absolute. By some trickle of light that she couldn't quite find, the vertical bars of the cell door were barely visible, along with Leonis's tall form standing near them, twisting as he pulled at his bonds. Sable tried to shift her wrists, but they didn't budge.

"Purnicious?" she called quietly.

There was no answering pop. Sable looked around the darkness, stretching her eyes wide, trying to see anything. Purn didn't appear.

Reese gave a grunt, and Sable could just make out his shape as his arms came free.

"How did you do that?" she asked.

"If you position your wrists right while they're tying them," he said, moving closer to her, his arm outstretched until he found her, "you can make them seem bigger than they are, and your captor won't tighten the knots enough. It doesn't work if they're being thorough, but our dear dwarf friends were agitated and not paying close attention."

He turned Sable around and began to fiddle with the ropes at her wrists. "Are you hurt?" he asked quietly, his voice close to her ear.

She shook her head before realizing the motion was lost in the dark. "No, but I'll be happy to get these ropes off." She felt the cord loosen and fall away. A deep ache ran through her shoulders as she pulled her arms forward, rubbing her raw wrists. She turned to face him. "Thank you."

His palms slid up her arms, warm against the chilly air. "You're cold." He pulled her close and wrapped his arms around her, the warmth of him softening the very edges of her fear.

She leaned into him. "Only because this place is freezing and dark and horrible."

"Don't worry about the rest of us who are still stuck in ropes and chains," Leonis said.

Sable started to pull away, but Reese tightened his grip. "Leonis is a capable fellow," he said. "He'll be fine."

She let out a little laugh and sank back against him. It took a few breaths before the fear that was growing in her chest worked its way out. "Purn isn't here," she whispered.

"She'll find you," Reese said. "I'm sure she's been listening to us this whole time, and there's nothing in the world that will keep that little blue creature away from you. Something as insignificant as a mile or two of rock and darkness certainly won't."

Sable straightened. "Darkness! She can't see around me because it's too dark." She pushed herself away from Reese. "Go help Leonis before he starts complaining again, and everyone stay away from me."

Reese joined Leonis by the door, and Thulan backed up to the wall.

"Purn," Sable said quietly. "If you come right next to me, there's room. It's dark, but there's nothing within arm's reach of me."

There was a little pop, and the top of Purn's head appeared at Sable's waist. "Oh, mistress! This place is horrible!"

Sable knelt down, and Purn threw her arms around Sable's neck.

"I can't see anything!" the kobold whispered.

"Give it a few minutes. There's a tiny bit of light from somewhere, once your eyes adjust." She squeezed her arms around Purn's bony shoulders. "It's better now that you're here."

"I have no idea how to get you out," Purn again whispered.

"Let's start by getting Thulan out of her manacles."

Purn nodded. Thulan clinked the chains so the kobold could find her in the darkness, and Purn groped her way over.

"Can you get us out of the cell too, Purn?" Leonis asked, rubbing his own wrists.

Reese had one arm through the bars near the lock. "We need the key. Maybe you could steal it from Pardrun?"

"The tall guard?" Purn asked. "He left, but there are two dwarves stationed up at the end of this tunnel." She paused. "Metal is hard to shrink, Thulan, but there's already a weak spot on your chains. Hold on." There was a moment of silence. "Pull your arms apart, hard."

The dwarf grunted, and there was a small metallic crack. Thulan's arms came free, each still wrapped in iron and dangling a bit of chain.

"It'll take a lot more time to get the cuffs off," Purn said, "but this seemed like a good start."

"You're a treasure, Purn," Thulan said, rolling her shoulders and joining Reese by the door.

"Can you shrink these bars?" Reese asked Purnicious. "I think we'd need to get rid of five or six to be able to squeeze out."

Purn walked over and set her hand on them. "It'll take a while. These are really dense. I heard you say you have until dawn, but it'll take nearly that long to do it. I'm not a fan of working with metal."

"Would it be faster to shrink the lock or the hinges?" Sable asked.

Thulan felt along the hinges. "Actually, the fastest would be if you helped me make a tool. If I have a thin, strong piece of iron, I can pop these hinges."

"Do you have any idea where they put our packs and weapons, Purnicious?" Reese asked.

She shook her head. "I followed you all, staying invisible, until that throne room, but when they took you away, the dwarf with the packs went a different direction, and I didn't want to lose track of you. So many people left the throne room after you, though, I had to wait, and while I could still see the area right around you, Sable, your guards were crowding too much for me to blink to you. By the time they left, it was too dark, and I was afraid I'd blink and end up inside a wall or skewered by an iron bar." She shivered. "I was working my way down the tunnel to you on foot when you called."

Thulan ran her fingers down along the bars, feeling along the bottom. "Maybe there'll be something useful on the floor. Everyone feel around. I need a piece of metal about the size of a finger."

Sable knelt. Her fingers ran over a thin layer of dirt and small jagged pebbles. She rubbed her hands over the floor, moving closer toward the wall, but found nothing.

Thulan muttered something under her breath about "blasted tunnels."

"I thought you'd be happy to be underground," Sable said to the dwarf. "But you seem even less enthused than the rest of us."

Thulan stilled. "After the boys and Brunn died," she said quietly, "every room I entered, it's all I could see. The roof falling, crushing the boys and keeping Brunn from reaching them before his own collapsed..." She fell silent. "I ran out of the cliff just to get out from under it all and couldn't bear to go back in. So I left."

The cell was silent for a long moment.

"And now?" Sable asked.

"I can still see it," Thulan said softly, "but it's less...vivid."

Everyone fell quiet until Thulan started feeling along the floor again.

"It's easier not to think of if we're talking about something else," she said pointedly.

"Excellent," Leonis said, brightly, "then why don't you explain to us in what way you could possibly immortalize anyone? Because, even though I'm at a complete loss to know what that means, if there was ever a time I wanted to be immortalized, it is now, right before my impending execution."

Thulan's hand paused in its movement along the bottom of the cell bars before she started moving again. "It's nothing."

Leonis sat back on his heels. "There is no place on earth where that would be an acceptable answer, but in a prison cell? With your closest friends? Who apparently know nothing about you? You cannot possibly expect us to—"

"Shh!" Thulan hissed, peering out into the hall.

Sable froze as Purnicious popped out of view. It was impossible that it could be dawn already, but her heart pounded, and the idea of the chasm gaped open again. She stared, eyes wide to try to catch any movement or mosslight from up the hall where the guards had disappeared.

Leonis stayed perfectly still. "Did you shush me so you don't have to answer?" he whispered.

"Shut up, Leonis." Reese stood and positioned himself between Sable and the bars. "Was that a door?"

Sable stood as still as she could, looking past his shoulder, but the hall stayed black and empty.

Water dripped somewhere far away in an irregular rhythm, and Sable found herself straining to hear it against the silence.

"You don't immortalize people anymore?" a voice asked quietly, not from the way back out of the hall where the guards had gone but from the cells at the end of the hall. "What do you do with yourself, then?"

"Mari?" Thulan stood and grabbed the bars.

A dark shape moved into view, followed by several others.

"You've never gotten along well with Rion," Mari said, speaking low, "but this feels like an escalation." She whispered something to the dwarves next to her, and two thick shapes moved to the hinged side of the door. "I brought the Bodem boys."

Thulan let out a breath that was half relief, half laughter. "Hello, boys."

"Never had to break you outta anywhere, Bristles," one of the shapes said.

"We'll expect payment," the other said.

"Something grand," said the first.

"More than grand. Enormous."

A soft clink sounded from the bottom hinge.

Sable, Reese, and Leonis moved closer to Thulan.

"Bristles?" Leonis asked.

Thulan ignored him and leaned closer to Mari. "How did you get here?"

"Pardrun is such a blockhead," Mari said. "I bet he doesn't even know that one of the cells at the end of the hall connects to an access shaft."

"From a prison cell?" Thulan asked. "That's a poor design."

"Not when you remember how many of the old High Dwarves dealt with uprisings." Mari said.

Thulan let out a low laugh. "Is this how Horren's line of descendants always escaped prison and returned?"

Mari's teeth flashed in the darkness. "Less impressive than his supposed magical bloodline, huh? I mouthed off to Pardrun a bit too much when we first came north, and he punished me by making me clean out and inspect every cell. The door wasn't hard to find." She shook her head. "Pardrun didn't even stick his head in a single cell, and none of his guards ever go past here. They don't need many cells these days. No one stays long. Rion's taken to fining everyone he's nervous about—which is almost everyone—and threatening to drop them if they don't come up with payment within a day. So far, everyone's paid." She paused. "Heard he didn't give you that same offer."

A second chink sounded near the top of the door, and one of the dwarves working on it gave a grunt of approval. "Could you hold the door, Bristles? Don't want this to get away from us."

Thulan moved to the door and gripped the bars as the two moved to the middle hinge.

"It was loud when it opened," Thulan warned them.

"Pardrun keeps the hinges dirty," one of the boys said.

"Says it's extra security," Mari said, her voice exasperated. "Says he doesn't have to waste guards here if all the cell doors are loud."

"He's always been such a conscientious leader," Thulan said. "How'd he get to be commander?"

"Kissing up to Rion," Mari answered. "How does anyone get anything these days?"

There was a third clink, and the Bodem boys moved to hold the bars as well. "It'll swing out into the hall enough to get you all out," one of them said, peering into the cell. "Especially since most of you are scrawny humans."

"And then you can explain why you're with these scrawny humans," the other added, his voice not entirely pleasant. "Lift a bit, Bristles, and the lock will protest less."

A faint, short grinding noise sounded as the hinges pulled apart, and a low metallic groan came from the lock as they swung the door off the hinges.

"I've never been so appreciative of your skills," Thulan told them.

Reese moved first, sliding through the door, and Sable followed through a space wide enough she could walk straight through. Thulan, though, had to turn sideways and squeeze.

Once everyone was out, the Bodem boys gently swung the door back into place and fiddled with the hinges for a bit.

"All done," one whispered.

"Then let's move," Mari said softly, "before anyone unpleasant shows up."

She led them downhill toward the end of the hall and into another cell.

Sable stepped up close to Thulan, hesitating before stepping through another cell door. "How do you know Mari?"

"She was one of my closest friends," Thulan said. "She worked door guard duty with Brunn, and her two boys were the ages of my sons. We can trust her." Thulan stepped into the cell.

Mari shuffled around near the wall before pulling open a part of the stone wall. The warm glow of mosslight came from a handful of lanterns set along the floor inside a roughly carved narrow tunnel. Sable drank in the sight of the faint light.

The walls inside were irregular, almost jagged in some parts. Tall enough for a dwarf or Sable to easily stand, but it certainly hadn't been made for anyone the height of Reese or Leonis.

"Give me your hands, Bristles," one of the Bodem boys said.

In the dim light, Sable could see that the hulking forms were mirror images of each other. Tall dwarves with thick black hair curling around their heads and down their backs. Long beards covering most of their chests, interspersed with a few leather-wrapped braids.

The one brother fiddled with Thulan's manacles for a few moments, and they clicked open. "We'll take 'em with us though. No point leaving them here to give Pardrun clues."

Mari stepped into the tunnel, and Thulan followed.

Reese moved to the door and hesitated. "This is the way out?"

"The way out will not be simple," Thulan said. "Come on or go back to the cell, but don't just stand there."

Reese glanced at Sable and ducked into the tunnel.

"Purn?" Sable whispered. The kobold's bony hand slipped into hers from the empty air beside her, and Sable squeezed it before following Reese into the tunnel.

"Once we start moving, keep quiet," Mari said while everyone filed in and one of the Bodems closed the secret door. "This tunnel runs alongside enough rooms that someone might hear us. And I really don't want to be caught sneaking around with a bunch of humans."

"I'm following you since Thulan trusts you," Leonis said, "but where exactly are you taking us?"

Mari held up her lantern to examine him. "Thulan, why does this one look elvish?"

"These are my friends," Thulan said bluntly. "If you trust me, you can trust them. And he asked a good question. Where are we going?"

Mari studied Leonis for a moment longer before turning away. "Through the old access shafts. To the better side of Torren." She headed down the tunnel.

"I thought Torren was the name of the city way down by the southern door," Leonis muttered.

"So did I," Thulan said.

CHAPTER TWENTY-SIX

THEIR FOOTSTEPS ECHOED in a muffled jumble of scuffs and thumps in the rough passage. The tunnel twisted and turned downhill at a steady pace, but their mosslight lantern gave off more than enough light to show their way.

Just like the other tunnels, tiny flecks in the wall reflected glimmers of light, flashing like stars as they passed.

Sable kept a grip on Purn's invisible hand as they moved lower. Eventually, Mari motioned for everyone to stop next to a narrow door. When there was no sound from beyond it, she cracked it open and peered into a dark space before motioning them all to follow.

Their lanterns lit a room with a long table surrounded by chairs. Each wall had wide columns carved into it, and when one of the Bodem boys pushed the door closed, it formed another column, indistinguishable from the others.

Mari picked up a bunch of cloaks piled on the table. "They'll try to fetch you for your execution at the end of third watch, which is only about seven hours from now, so we should have you out of the tunnels before then. We'd never be able to smuggle you back out the north door, but there are a few other exits. Rion's paranoid, and he's been closing them up, so we'll need to scout a bit to figure out which ones we can still use. Until then, you can wait at my home."

She handed each of them a cloak. "We don't have far to go. This is the third level, two lower than the throne room, and any path but the one we just took is long and winding. Most likely, no one down here has even heard of the commotion you all are causing yet." She rubbed the back of her neck nervously. "But news of a drop will spread fast, even through the convoluted levels of New Torren, and you humans aren't exactly easy to overlook. From here we'll be on public roads, so these may make you look a little less…human." She frowned up at Leonis and Reese. "Slouch."

Sable draped one of the cloaks over her shoulders and pulled up the hood.

"New Torren?" Thulan said.

Mari grimaced. "A few things changed while you were gone." She motioned one of the Bodem boys toward the only door, and he cracked it open and looked out. "Third watch started an hour ago," Mari whispered. "The tunnels should be clear."

"Why?" Thulan asked, but Mari had already stepped out of the room.

The passage they stepped into was indeed empty. It was smooth and wide, with lanterns set at long intervals, providing just enough light to see. Mari hurried them forward, taking turns quickly. When they reached a smaller tunnel branching off, she ducked into it. The Bodem boys lingered for a moment at the intersection, then disappeared.

Mari pulled open a rough wooden door. "Welcome to my humble home," she said as they filed in. She pushed it closed behind them and flipped the lock before leaning back on the door and taking a deep breath.

The walls were rounded and rough like a natural cave, peppered with reflective specks. The furniture was carved into the walls—shelves decorated with small metal sculptures, nooks that held balls of nightmoss, and seats scooped out of the stone creating recesses lined with brightly colored pillows.

"Well," Mari said in a normal voice, "the Bodems will investigate the escape route options, but it'll take at least an hour. I'd offer you places to sleep, but I imagine you have a lot of questions first." She looked at Thulan. "I have a good number myself."

Thulan stepped away from one of the sculptures and took a seat.

"How did Rion get to be High Dwarf?" Thulan asked. "Even if Dirthor died, what happened to the six or seven dwarves who should have been next in line for the throne? And why is the entire dwarf population up in the Northern Corner?"

"Yes," Sable said, sitting in a small nook on the wall. "What happened at the southern door?" She sank into the soft cushions that lined the seat. She felt Purn sit on the floor and press against her leg.

"And why are people blaming humans?" Reese added, resting back against the wall where he could see the room and the door.

Leonis looked at the rock surrounding them and sighed, moving to sit in another cushioned nook in the wall. "I don't care that much about what's happened to the dwarves, but I am very interested to know why the High Dwarf thinks Thulan could immortalize him and why those good souls, the Bodem boys, called her Bristles. Is it because her beard is bristly? I've always thought it was."

"My beard is not bristly," Thulan said.

"That's true," Mari agreed. "Thulan's beard is amazing and has been the envy of many a dwarf."

"From this moment, Mari," Thulan said, "ignore everything Leonis says and start explaining what's going on."

Mari crossed the room to a large shelf and poured water from a delicate silver pitcher into thin coppery goblets. "Well, after you left," she said, handing Thulan one of the cups, "which is something you need to explain, life went on like normal. Until nearly four years ago when we started getting reports of disturbances in the deeper tunnels."

"How deep?" Thulan asked.

"Down near the old sapphire quarry."

Sable took the goblet Mari offered her. The cup itself was light and thin, made of dimpled copper that shone with a rich light.

"Why was anyone down there?" Thulan asked. "Those tunnels were mined dry generations ago."

"Which is why, a month later when some children claimed they'd seen a human down there, no one believed them." Mari finished handing out the water and started cutting up a loaf of dark bread and a large chunk of red cheese.

"How on earth would a human get to the sapphire quarry?" Thulan asked.

"How would a human get into Torren at all?" Reese asked. "I've hunted in the woods outside the southern door for years, and I had no idea it was there."

"That was the question," Mari said, handing out small plates.

Sable bit into the red cheese, which turned out to be smooth and rich and mildly spicy. "This is delicious," she told Mari. "Thank you."

Mari smiled at her, considering her for a moment. "You're the first humans I've ever met. I have to say you're less fearsome than I expected." She took her own plate over to one of the last open seats.

"The children were right," Mari continued. "One of High Dwarf Dirthor's scouts found humans in the tunnels, digging at the edge of the quarry."

Thulan's eyebrows rose. "Along the fault lines?"

Mari nodded. "But the night we found them, there was a collapse along the Black Seam Fault."

Thulan's hand froze in the act of breaking off a chunk of bread. "How big?"

"All the way down it."

"That fault ran below the market, and the silversmiths."

"And the wet storerooms," Mari said, "and every tunnel leading to homes on the south side. We tried to clear the passages, but..."

"Grenn and her family lived in the south side," Thulan whispered.

"And Crell, and Worren." Mari's voice held an old, hollow sort of grief. "And three hundred other dwarves."

"The market was the only way out of those caverns," Thulan said faintly. "You couldn't reach any of them?"

Mari shook her head. "The next collapse came too soon."

Thulan's bread slipped from her fingers. "Next?"

"There were eight."

Thulan swore quietly.

"After the second collapse, we discovered a chasm had opened from a higher tunnel down to a cave past the quarry, where at least a hundred humans were living. Drusty was the first one to spot them."

"Drusty!" Thulan interrupted. "How did a mole like Drusty get fancy enough to stand below the throne and order people around?"

"Who's Drusty?" Leonis asked.

"That sniveling bootlicker who talked to us in the throne room," Thulan said. "He was a mid-level grunt in the Excavation Unit."

Mari nodded. "He's really leveraged his friendship with Rion." She sighed. "The Bodem boys fought at the quarry. Most of the humans only had pickaxes, and there were only a few fighters among them. The frightening part was the number of tunnels they'd dug. Three more were visible, headed in the directions where they'd found the softest rock."

Thulan let out a groan. "They dug along the veins?"

Mari nodded.

"What's a vein?" Leonis asked.

"A run of softer rock between the harder stone," Mari said. "They're stable unless you start digging in them and they begin to crumble. There are plenty of times when digging through a vein is the fastest way to get somewhere, but not from the quarry."

Thulan nodded. "The veins there separate three huge shelves. No dwarf in their right mind would have disturbed those areas. No one wants mile-long slabs of rocks shifting, even a little."

"But that's exactly what happened," Mari said. "The third collapse was the big one. The middle shelf slid, collapsing every tunnel crossing the Rocklen Seam."

"Including the southern door," Thulan said.

"All the way to the residential wing of the High Dwarf's caverns and the throne room." Mari sighed again. "That's when Dirthor died. Along with his wife, all of his children, his sister, and his oldest niece and nephew, who lived in the royal apartments."

"Leaving Rion next in line," Thulan finished.

Mari nodded. "Those were the worst collapses, but the next few days were a nightmare. The instability in the middle shelf shifted the top shelf, and the infirmary cavern was crushed, along with all the wounded who'd been brought there. Then smaller fault lines began shifting, one by one.

"Rion called for an all-out evacuation, stopping any rescue attempts and demanding everyone salvage as much of their possessions as they could and move north."

"He stopped the rescues?" Thulan asked.

"He executed two dwarves who refused to stop digging. Claimed every dwarf's responsibility was to save what they could and get to safety. Pardrun was the highest-ranking guard anyone could find, so Rion named him High Commander and gave him the power to execute anyone who didn't begin evacuating immediately."

"No one objected?"

"Everyone was so scared and stunned, I think many of them *wanted* to run." Mari looked down into the dimpled copper cup she still held in her hand. "Our group from the Nicked Chisel refused to go."

"What's the Nicked Chisel?" Sable asked.

"A tavern that served the best ale in Torren," Thulan said, keeping her eyes on Mari. "Brunn and I used to spend too much time and money there with Mari, the Bodem boys, and a dozen others."

"We hid in the tavern," Mari said. "Waited until most of the cousins had gone north and most of the rumbling had stopped, and then we..."

She glanced up at Thulan, then back to her cup. "There were twelve of us, and we worked for four days." She turned the goblet slowly, her eyes fixed on the warm copper. "For the first two days we could hear noises… calls for help from places we couldn't reach. By the third day those had stopped."

"No one else stayed to help?" Thulan asked quietly.

"We'd run across cousins fighting to clear a doorway, calling out to someone who occasionally called back. We helped when we could, but… Everything was destroyed. More than half of Torren was blocked off, another quarter so damaged it was unrecognizable."

She shook her head. "We finally came here to find that Rion had named this New Torren and begun clearing out the old throne room. He commissioned a new throne to be carved, sent a few dwarves out to gather whatever herds they could, and declared that our job was to rebuild and regain strength until we were strong enough to fight the humans."

"No one wanted to ignore him and go fight anyway?" Thulan asked.

"Some complained that Rion was hiding like a coward. But when the first people to speak out were branded traitors and arrested, less people objected. In the end, those of us who dared to not adore Rion were moved to lower levels and assigned to tunnel excavation crews. We spend our time grumbling and hoping Rion doesn't ever have an heir so we have a chance at someday getting a better High Dwarf."

"And then I showed up at the Northern Corner with some humans," Thulan said.

"I still don't understand how humans got in there," Reese said. "No people I know are good at digging. They've recently found gold in the Scale Mountains, and they take ages to dig a single mine. How did any get that deep into the Marsham Cliffs without you knowing?"

"We don't know," Mari said.

"The humans stopped at the quarry?" Thulan asked. "An hour's walk in the right direction from there would have led them to store rooms with ten times more wealth than the quarry held."

"I know. No one knows why they stopped, unless they thought the small sapphires left in the quarry were valuable."

"Maybe they did," Thulan mused. "Humans don't have many gems. Or much art, to be honest. The treasures just in Dirthor's throne room would put every human lord's wealth to shame."

"Most of those treasures were lost," Mari said. "Rion brought up what he could. You saw the Dirthor painting?"

"That huge one near the throne?" Sable asked. "That was High Dwarf Dirthor?"

Mari nodded. "He never kept it in the throne room. He claimed he wasn't quite that vain, but his wife, Brella, loved it. She had it mounted above the entrance to the arena and told him that as soon as he was dead or too old to know what was going on, she was gonna bring it in and place it next to the throne."

Thulan sank back in her seat. "Brella's the one who should have been painted. She ran things more than he did, I think."

"I think she liked that you picked Dirthor instead, though," Mari said.

Sable frowned and turned to look at Thulan.

Leonis leaned forward. "*You* picked Dirthor?"

"She could have charged a fortune for it, don't you think?" Mari said. "But she just gave it to him."

Thulan shifted. "I gave it to Brella. Dirthor never would have accepted it."

"You painted that?" Reese asked. "The one with the dwarf chiseling the gem?"

"Thulan!" Sable said. "That was magnificent!"

Mari looked at them, her eyebrows raised. "Haven't you ever seen Thulan paint?"

"She's painted my face for plays," Sable said, "and I've seen her paint props and backdrops, but nothing like that." She turned to Thulan. "You told me you worked for a silversmith."

Thulan paused. "I did, temporarily. The silversmith was working with me at night to craft a set of rings for my boys and Brunn."

"Bristles!" Leonis grinned at Thulan. "Paintbrush bristles! That sniveling High Dwarf wanted you to immortalize him in a painting." He looked at Thulan as though he'd never seen her before. "That's it. I insist you immortalize me."

Thulan ignored him. "So there's been no one else who challenged Rion for the throne? He must be a horrible leader."

"I'm sorry," Leonis interrupted before Mari could answer. "I know our lives are at stake here and time is precious, but we need to spend just a moment longer on Bristles. Tell me everything there is to know about her and her painting skills."

CHAPTER TWENTY-SEVEN

MARI GLANCED AT THEM, slightly perplexed. "Thulan was the premier painter in Torren. She had dwarves begging her to paint them or their families."

"Wait," Leonis said, "was Thulan rich?"

Thulan scowled at him.

"Still is, I'm sure," Mari said. "The banking tunnels weren't damaged, and they are very proud of the fact that they managed to bring almost all the wealth they were holding north. It took years to sort out who inherited the money of the dwarves who were killed. But since Thulan had no relatives clamoring for her money, I'm sure it's still there. She certainly wouldn't be living on this level if she had stayed in Torren." Mari paused. "Which means you must have really caught Rion off guard, Thulan. If he'd been thinking, he'd have fined you every coin you own before ordering you executed."

Thulan rolled her eyes and took a long drink.

"Do you have one of her paintings?" Sable asked Mari.

Thulan twitched.

Mari rubbed her fingers along the edge of her plate. "I do," she said quietly. "It's very dear to me."

Thulan lowered her cup slowly.

Leonis swallowed a bite of bread as he watched her. He set his plate aside and leaned his elbows on his knees. "Thulan?" He waited until she dragged her gaze over to him. "May we see it?"

Her expression turned pained, almost desperate. Finally, she twitched her head in a nod.

Mari left the room, returning with a panel of wood the size of a small window.

Leonis took it, holding it gently with both hands. His gaze swept over it until it locked on one place. His fingers tightened.

He didn't move or speak, and Sable and Reese crossed the room to him.

Leonis tilted the panel toward them, and Reese drew in a breath.

The painting was richly colored in reds and blues and a gold that almost glowed. This wasn't the detailed, stunningly lifelike sort of painting that hung in the throne room. This was motion and joy and wildness. A captured moment of pure delight.

Four young dwarf boys stood atop a boulder, their hands flung up in victory. Each had a short beard that ran along their jaw lines, curly and unruly beneath exultant smiles. Their cheeks were ruddy with exertion, and their eyes…

The panel trembled in Leonis's hands.

The two boys on the right had Mari's walnut hair and bright smile, but the two on the left…

The two on the left were perfect, boyish versions of Thulan.

Across the room, Thulan's eyes were fixed, unseeing, on the floor. Her thumb rubbed over the dimples of her cup urgently, as though trying to scrub something away.

"Beautiful, Thulan," Leonis said finally, his eyes locked on the boys. "They're beautiful."

Thulan gave a nod so small it was almost a flinch.

Mari stood on the far side of Leonis, looking at the painting with wet eyes. "This was just a month before…"

The expression on Thulan's sons' faces was so achingly familiar, Sable could hardly bear to look at it. It would be easier to go back a few minutes to when immortalizing someone in a painting was just another bit of banter between Thulan and Leonis, but the joy in the boys' expressions was like a light that Sable couldn't look away from.

Thulan kept her eyes pointed at the floor.

Sable took a deep breath to loosen the tightness in her throat. "Thulan," she said quietly, "would you like to see it?"

Leonis twitched the painting closer to himself.

Thulan slowly dragged her gaze over to the back of the panel. She stared at it for a moment, her cup shaking in her hand. "I don't know," she whispered.

But there was a deep longing in her eyes, and Sable reached forward and took hold of the corner. Leonis held the painting for a heartbeat before letting go.

Sable walked across the room and sat next to Thulan, taking her cup and holding out the painting.

Slowly, as though facing something terrifying, Thulan turned to look. A sob escaped her, and she pressed her hand to her mouth. She reached out and took it, the wood trembling in her grip.

Sable thought back to the conversation with Thulan long ago, drawing the exact words back to her mind. "Their names were Neron and Thon, right?"

Thulan nodded. "Neron was my oldest." She ran a finger over the taller boy's cheek. "Thon was the baby. Always causing trouble." There was a mischievous glint in the younger boy's eyes.

"He looks like he's ready to cause trouble," Sable said.

Reese stepped over and set his hand on Thulan's shoulder. "They look like strong, happy boys, Thulan." She didn't move, and he squeezed her shoulder before moving back to his seat.

Mari watched Thulan for a moment, then shifted her attention to Sable and the others. "Now that you know what you walked into," she said quietly, "why don't you tell me why you're here."

Sable leaned forward in an attempt to give Thulan a little privacy with the painting. "We were hoping to build an alliance."

Mari listened with growing uneasiness as Sable told of the Kalesh and the threat they posed.

"This Empire," Mari said quietly, "they live to the east?"

Reese nodded. "If you were to go to the top of the Marsham Cliffs and head east for several weeks, you'd stumble into the Empire."

"Or if you dug east," Mari said. "The sapphire quarry is about as far east as the tunnels run."

"What were the humans wearing?" Reese asked

"The Bodem boys said most were dressed like common workers," Mari said, "but the few fighters among them were dressed in black."

"The Kalesh soldiers wear black," Sable said. "But how could they have mined all the way here from the Empire?"

"They wouldn't have to," Mari said. "Above us, a desert goes as far east as we've ever explored. There are shafts that lead from the surface down into caves. Not many, and they don't lead anywhere particularly useful, but the Kalesh could have come across the surface and then descended in a shaft."

"And managed to stumble into a sapphire quarry?" Sable asked. "That feels lucky."

"It wouldn't be luck," Reese said. "If they thought there was a reason to explore those shafts, they'd send hundreds, thousands maybe. They'd send expendable workers down every hole they could find in the hopes that one of them would find something useful. Even if the rest of them died trying."

"Which they probably did," Mari said. "Most of those caves are isolated systems without anything worth mining."

Sable glanced at Thulan, who was still focused on the painting. She turned back to the others. "What would make the Kalesh even think to look?"

"They probably figured if there was gold in the Tremmen Hills, there might be some in the cliffs here too." Reese crossed his arms. "The Empire would absolutely waste thousands of people looking into something like that if they thought it might give them some wealth."

"The timing is off," Sable said. "The collapses here were nearly four years ago. I didn't hear of the Kalesh in Immusmala until two years ago, and even that was just as money lenders for merchants who wanted to mine."

"If they were offering loans two years ago," Reese said, "then they'd been there long enough to have learned the situation, decided it was real enough to pursue, and brought enough people from the Empire to fund the operation."

Sable sat up straighter. "If the Kalesh are the ones responsible for the collapse, maybe High Dwarf Rion can be convinced to join in the fight with us."

"He won't," Mari said. "There's no reasoning with him. But..." She ran her fingers through her beard. "The old group from the Nicked Chisel is all down here, and they just might listen. We've all grown a bit tired of doing what Rion wants anyway."

Thulan looked up from the painting for the first time. She wiped her hand across her eyes. "That's not the High Dwarf, but it's a useful group."

"Most of them lost someone in the collapse," Mari said. "They'd be glad to finally know who to blame and why."

Thulan tapped her fingers on the edge of the painting. "That's a very useful group." She looked at Sable. "We should talk to them."

"Do we have time?" Sable asked. "How long until the guards notice we're not in our cell?"

Mari stood and began taking empty cups and plates back over to the long shelf. "Pardrun's guards are lazy, so they'll just sit in their guardroom. They don't know about the access tunnels, either, and there are no other routes to the lower levels anywhere near the prison. So whenever they discover you're gone, they'll search the entire first level before coming lower." Mari paused at the shelf. "I could round everyone up. There's a tavern close by we meet in. It could take up to an hour to collect them all, though, so you'll have to talk fast."

"Thulan," Reese said, "can this group actually help us?"

Thulan set the painting down gently on a small table next to her and took an unsteady breath before turning to Reese. "At one time, they were the most influential dwarves in Torren," she answered. "Several were on the High Dwarf's council." She looked at Mari. "But if Rion moved you all to the third level, do you still have any influence?"

"With Rion, no. But outside the throne room…" Mari paused. "We still have some." She gauged the faces around the room. "What do you say? Want to talk to some dwarves who might want to fight alongside you?"

"Let's do it," Thulan said. "But do it quickly."

Mari brushed off her hands. "I'll wake my boys to help me. As long as you don't mind messy rooms, you're welcome to rest on their beds for a bit." She ducked back through the door leading into the rest of her house.

When she came back, Leonis glanced up. "I don't suppose there's any way we're going to see our weapons or packs again?"

"Slim went to find them," Mari said.

Thulan let out a breath that was almost a laugh. "You'll have your bow back soon, Leonis. Slim can steal anything from anyone. He's thoroughly disreputable but very effective."

Two younger dwarves filed into the room, both as tall as Mari but not as broad. They were older versions of two of the boys in the painting, but they still looked young and their beards were short.

The taller of the two boys gave Thulan a tentative smile. "Hello, Auntie Thulan." The younger smiled at her somewhat blankly.

Thulan swallowed and rose. She stared at the two boys for a moment before managing a shaky, "Hello, boys."

"Move, boys," Mari said. "You can chat with Auntie Thulan later. Merron, go find Tumm, Reckon, and tell the Bodem boys to meet us at the Chisel when they find an escape route. Linos, get everyone who lives near Brell. They have an hour—no, a half hour to meet at the Broken Chisel. Tell them the chance they've been waiting for is here, and if they don't get their fat heads there, I'll make sure Pan never sells them ale again."

The two boys nodded and, with curious looks at the humans in the room, slipped out the front door.

Thulan stared after them.

Mari came up beside her, setting her hand on Thulan's shoulder. "We'll hurry. Make yourselves at home. I'll be back as soon as I can." She squeezed Thulan's shoulder and left.

Thulan faced the door, even after it closed, and Sable moved next to her, looking for something to say.

"They're so old," Thulan whispered.

There was nothing to say to that, so Sable just stood next to her for a few minutes in silence.

"Did you ever paint Brunn?" Leonis asked.

"I tried to paint a picture of him when we first met. We weren't even as old as Mari's boys. Brunn was funny and clever." Thulan shook her head. "I gave up. Even then, when I barely knew him, there was too much of him to capture. I could never get the way he smiled right. Once we'd been married for ten years, it was hopeless. I didn't even have the skills to capture something as simple as his hands." She swallowed. "There was just too much to him," she finished quietly.

Thulan sank back down into her seat.

"Is it going to be worth it to talk to your friends?" Sable asked.

Thulan's brow creased slightly. "They're solid, trustworthy dwarves, and they'll listen to reason, which is more than I can say for Rion."

"How many of them are there?" Sable asked.

Thulan gave her an apologetic look. "Maybe twenty. If they're all still around."

"Twenty dwarves," Leonis said.

"That's twenty more than we managed with the elves," Thulan said.

Leonis sighed. "I know."

CHAPTER TWENTY-EIGHT

IT WAS LESS than a half hour before Mari returned, slipping into the door and closing it quickly behind her. "We've got everyone we could find," she said, "and we need to hurry. My friend Jennah did a little scouting. She heard talk of the execution on the second level." She shook her head. "News of you people is spreading quickly. The Bodems found us a good escape route. We'll talk to the cousins at the Chisel and then get you out of here before anyone comes this deep looking for you."

"Hope you're ready to give your speech now, Sable," Thulan said. "You'll finally get your audience."

"The same speech I was going to give the High Dwarf?"

Thulan shrugged. "I'd make it a bit more casual."

Mari looked around the room. "Put your cloaks back on. These dwarves are gathering because they trust me, and they love Thulan. We didn't tell them there were humans here. The less chance that bit of information has to get out, the better. How they'll react when they see you all… I don't know. Thulan and I will go in first, but—"

A series of quick knocks sounded at the door.

"Time to go," Mari said, her face still a bit nervous. "Stay together and come quickly."

She opened the door to find one of the Bodem boys standing there. He gave her a nod and motioned the others to come out. Leonis moved behind Thulan, standing almost protectively.

She scowled at him. "I'm not the one in danger around here."

"I believe Mari said we're in a hurry," he said without backing away.

Thulan leaned around him to look at Sable and Reese. "Stay close."

Sable turned, and her shoulder bumped Reese, who was immediately behind her. "Were you planning on *not* staying close?"

"I have no plans at all," he muttered. "How can I have plans with no weapons and no idea how to get out of this oversized hole?"

"It's a short walk," Mari said, waving them after her. "Let's get this over with." She stepped out the door, and the others followed.

At the first intersection, the other Bodem boy gave Thulan a brisk nod before falling in with them. At the second turn, a dwarf so thin he was almost wiry slouched against the tunnel wall. He saw them and stepped over to a door with a sign hung above it that vaguely resembled a broken chisel.

When he saw Leonis, Sable, and Reese, he hesitated but pushed the door open. "Everyone's in the back," he said quietly to Mari.

She nodded and stepped inside.

The wiry dwarf gave Thulan an appraising look and a roguish smile. "Still gorgeous, Bristles." He peered at Sable, Reese, and Leonis. "Mari wasn't kidding. You've gotten yourself into something dangerous."

Thulan patted his shoulder as she walked past. "It's not what you think, Slim."

He looked after her and shook his head. "That's a fine-looking dwarf." He glanced at Leonis. "Bet she's breaking hearts all over the human world, eh?"

Leonis stood speechless until Sable pushed him into the dim interior of a small, rather run-down tavern. The air smelled of garlic and onions, and the sticky floor grabbed at her boots as she crossed to the single mosslight lantern sitting on the bar.

Reese followed, his hand on her back. "I do not like this," he whispered. "There are no good exits, and even if we get out of this tavern, I have no idea how to get us out of the mountain. I hope you know what you're doing, Thulan."

Leonis crowded up close. "Why does everything we do seem to burrow us deeper into the caves?"

After the two Bodem boys filed in, Slim pulled the door closed and turned the lock.

Sable flinched at the noise, and both Leonis and Reese tensed.

"Did you happen to find our bags?" Thulan asked Slim.

An insulted look crossed his face. "They were in Pardrun's office. A blind tunnel mole could have found them. One of these scrawny humans could have walked in and picked them up, and no one would have noticed."

He stepped around the end of the bar and gave Thulan a pointed look. "The question you should have been asking was whether I managed to replace your packs with similar-looking ones that are actually filled with rocks and a few scorpions." He pulled their packs up from behind the bar, laying them on the counter and placing their weapons beside them.

Thulan grinned at him. "Nice to see your skills haven't waned over the years."

Leonis reached for his bow, and Reese immediately stepped past Sable to pick up one of his knives.

Slim held up a hand. "It'd be better if you didn't arm yourselves quite yet. I owe Mari a rather large debt, and so I'm willing to not kill you until she explains herself. I can't promise that the others in the back feel the same. If you walk in there armed, it might send the wrong message.

Low voices floated out from a door off to the side of the bar, and Mari straightened her shoulders. "Let's go, Thulan." She glanced at the others. "We'll call the rest of you in soon. When it's…safe."

She strode through the door.

"Thulan," Leonis said nervously.

"It'll be fine," Thulan said, with more determination than assurance. "They're good dwarves." She glanced between Sable and Reese and Leonis. "It'll be fine," she repeated, following Mari.

The Bodem boys and Slim were looking at the door with doubtful expressions.

"Is it going to be fine?" Leonis asked.

No one answered for a moment.

"If anyone can convince them to not kill you on sight," Slim said finally. "It's Thulan and Mari."

"That's…reassuring." Leonis leaned against the bar and rubbed his hands over his face. "Before we're all killed, I would like everyone to recognize that things went better with the elves."

"I always assumed Victis would attack us because of you," Reese agreed. "Didn't expect Thulan to be the death of us."

Slim set a tankard on the bar and glanced questioningly at the Bodem boys. They both nodded. "You humans drink ale?" he asked.

Leonis wrinkled his nose.

"No, thank you," Sable managed.

"Not dwarvish ale," Reese said. "Not when we need our wits."

Slim shrugged and poured cups for himself and the Bodem boys from a huge barrel.

Voices grew a little louder in the other room, and someone hushed them. Slim glanced toward the door, then moved the mosslight lantern behind the bar and out of view. "No point in inviting someone to investigate why there's light in a closed tavern."

"Why is the tavern closed?" Reese asked quietly. "Don't dwarves drink ale around the clock?"

"We do." Slim set his cup down with more force than necessary. "But the High Dwarf decided that the lower levels were less productive if they stayed up too late drinking, so he imposed a curfew."

Reese raised an eyebrow. "That's...bold."

Slim snorted. "It was stupid. The third level already thought he was a sniveling coward. If he's pushing for a revolt, he's headed in the right direction." He took a drink. "Of course, without the curfew, I have no idea how Mari would have smuggled three humans through the tunnels."

"For the record," Leonis said, "I'm only half human. The elvish half of me hasn't done anything to anger the dwarves as far as I know."

"Then they'll only half kill you," Reese said dryly.

Slim shook his head. "They'll kill all of ya. No one in Torren's fond of elves."

Thulan appeared in the doorway, her face grim. "C'mon in." She looked at Sable. "I hope you're ready to be persuasive. We don't exactly have a warm audience here."

"Do we ever?" Sable whispered.

Thulan sighed. "I swear we used to. C'mon. I'll introduce you." She glanced back at Reese and Leonis. "Let Sable come in first. She looks more likable than either of you."

Thulan stepped back through the door, and Sable took a bracing breath before following her.

The back room of the tavern was crammed with muttering dwarves seated around a handful of small tables and benches.

Every conversation in the room stopped when Sable stepped into view. Stools creaked as every dwarf turned to face forward. Reese and Leonis stopped in the doorway, and an angry rumble rolled through the room. Several dwarves pushed themselves to their feet.

"You agreed." Thulan set her hand on the closest dwarf's chest. "You all agreed to listen."

None of the dwarves relaxed.

"This is Sable, Reese, and Leonis," Thulan said, gesturing to each. "They've been as loyal of friends to me as any of you. For years." She tilted her chin up at the large dwarf in front of her. "I've traveled with them and lived with them and fought alongside them, Rudd. Sit down and hear what they have to say."

Rudd didn't move. "Brunn's memory is the only thing keeping me from killing all of you with my bare hands," he snarled.

"Good enough for me," Thulan said, patting his chest. "Sit down and listen."

The large dwarf dropped back into his chair, leaving his huge hands curled into fists on the table.

Others slowly sat back down, and Sable searched their faces for anything less hostile.

"Sable," Thulan said with a commanding note in her voice, "has something to tell you. If you don't like what we have to say when we're done, you can march us back up to that spineless Rion and stay as stupid and blind as he is. But I told these humans that dwarves are rational. Try not to make me a liar."

A good number of the scowls turned to include Thulan, but she ignored them, motioning for Sable to start.

Sable stepped forward, wondering if the dwarves could tell as easily as she could that Thulan's bravado was a thin mask.

Rudd sat close enough that Sable could have reached out and touched him. Not that she wanted to. His neck alone was as broad as her waist.

She offered him a smile that felt weak, wishing she could steal a little of Thulan's swagger. "Mari told us what happened in your tunnels." Her voice sounded wavery, and the dwarves' stools creaked again as they shifted in irritation.

She focused on Thulan's sons and husband. They hadn't been killed in the cave-ins caused by the Kalesh, but they'd been lost. She looked around the room. How many of these dwarves had lost loved ones in the destruction of their city?

"When I was fifteen," she began, "my parents were killed by black-clad raiders who showed up in our village and burned it to the ground." She pushed the truth into her words, and felt the warmth start to seep out into the room. It might as well have been warm water flowing around rocks for the amount it affected the dwarves.

"You'll find no sympathy from us," a female dwarf behind Rudd said. "We're all out. Especially for humans."

Something in the woman's tone reminded Sable of Braddick, and Sable took a step forward. "I don't need your sympathy. What I need is for you to understand that those black-clad raiders were soldiers from an Empire that exists to the east. An Empire that takes whatever it wants by force and is currently focused on the gold and riches we have in our mountains."

A stir moved through the room. Not of interest, exactly, but of something.

"Were any of you at the sapphire quarry when the humans were found?" she asked.

A few heads turned toward Rudd, whose mouth flattened into a thin line.

"There were workers and soldiers, were there not?"

Rudd didn't answer.

"And the soldiers were dressed in black, every bit of their clothing as black as night. As black as a dark, empty tunnel." She looked back at the dwarves, who were still glaring at her, and threaded her hatred of the Kalesh uniform into her next words. "They wore boots, tall enough to reach almost to their knees, tied in long strips of leather."

Rudd's eyes narrowed.

"Their swords," Reese said, taking a half step forward, "are one-handed short blades. They're made of a low-grade steel that dulls quickly. Much lighter and more brittle than the head of Thulan's hammer."

At the questioning looks of the other dwarves, Rudd gave a sharp nod.

"They use those swords because the imperial army is so massive, they don't waste their good steel on the common soldier. Against dwarven axes and blades, I would imagine they stood little chance."

Rudd nodded slowly. "So humans use inferior weapons. This is not news worth breaking curfew for."

"I'm sorry," Leonis said. "I didn't realize dwarves were afraid to break curfew."

Multiple dwarves bristled.

"The Kalesh Empire uses inferior weapons," Reese said, pulling attention back to himself. "But only for their disposable infantry. The troops they send on missions to scout out new areas and see what resources are available."

"Areas like the caves accessible from the grasslands above Torren," Sable said. "Yes, it was humans who destroyed Torren, but not the ones you think."

The room gave her their attention, and she began to tell them of the growing, approaching threat of the Kalesh. She infused her words with warmth, and slowly it began to wrap around the dwarves, winding its way through the room. Most of their faces looked like they'd been carved in stone, though, and her words did little to soften them.

She finished, and silence fell over the room.

"That's an interesting story," Rudd said. "If it's true. But one of the humans claimed they served the dragon. And we know you have a dragon in the south."

"You could understand them?" Reese asked.

Rudd shrugged. "Wasn't trying to talk to them. One fighter, the leader maybe, kept shouting about the dragon coming to kill us all and rule the world." He leaned back in his chair and gave a grim smile. "At least 'til he couldn't shout anymore."

Reese scanned the room as though seeking confirmation before looking at Sable. "Common soldiers and grunt workers wouldn't speak our language."

She paused. "You think there was a Tien Sark here?"

"I don't know. They don't waste them on teams searching for riches, but it certainly sounds like one." Reese turned back to Rudd. "He wasn't talking about the dragon in the south. They call their Emperor 'the Dragon.' All their battle cries have to do with dragons."

The large dwarf looked unconvinced.

"If we were part of the humans who destroyed the tunnels," Reese continued, "or had any idea what had happened here, why would we have come and knocked on your door?"

Rudd tilted his head. "Because humans are stupid?"

"They are," Thulan answered, "but they have a strong sense of self-preservation." She fixed Rudd with a piercing look. "And if you're stupid enough to think I'd befriend a human who destroyed Torren, then I might as well be talking to a bunch of rocks. You want a chance to fight the people who destroyed your home? We're offering it to you. But this isn't a leisurely visit." She glanced toward the door. "Rion plans to drop us at the end of the third watch, and it won't be long before someone discovers we're not in our prison cell any longer."

There was a rustle throughout the room, and Sable looked over to the collected dwarves. The audience was still far from receptive, but she pushed truth into the next words anyway. "We came here to ask you to help us in a fight that wasn't yours—only to find that it is yours. So you have a choice. Will you stay here like your High Dwarf wants or come fight the war you've been aching for?"

The dwarves in the room shifted, some of them muttering to each other quietly.

"The third level isn't the place where these decisions are made," one of the dwarves said.

Thulan's gaze raked across the room. "When I left, you were a family of driven leaders who convinced Dirthor to reorder his ruling council until he actually had a sense of what all our cousins needed. Some of you ended up sitting on that same council, helping to guide us to the prosperity we all enjoyed."

She looked around the dingy walls of the tavern. "Mari said you were down here because Rion had relegated you to the third level. I assumed he did so because he was afraid of the voice you had among the dwarves." Her expression took on a withering edge. "I had no idea you'd actually become spineless third-level dwarves."

Mari winced at the words, and the mood of the entire room grew more dangerous.

Sable forced herself not to take a step backwards, but she felt Reese move closer.

"You have no idea what we've been through," Rudd growled. "We're still here, trying to get back some semblance of what they took. We didn't turn tail and run as soon as things went badly."

Thulan put her hands on his table, leaning in close to him. "Brunn died in an accident," she hissed. "If there'd been someone responsible for it, if someone had murdered my husband and sons while they slept, I would tear the world apart to find them. I wouldn't be plodding along on tunnel excavation crews, groveling under an inept High Dwarf." She gave the room a contemptuous look. "The Broken Chisel is an appropriate place for you all to cower."

Rudd shoved himself up, sending his chair toppling back. Other dwarves shot to their feet, and Reese shifted to stand in front of Sable. He reached for a knife at his belt and found nothing.

Sable set her hand on Reese's back, looking around him. The room crackled with hostility.

"Pick your second," Rudd growled.

Thulan looked up at him, her face livid.

Mari swore under her breath and stepped forward.

"No." Thulan held her hand toward Mari. "I want Reese."

Mari stopped short, and the attention of every dwarf in the room shifted to Reese, their expressions varying from shock to contempt.

Reese gave Thulan an uneasy look. "What does a second do? Hand you weapons?"

Thulan let out an exasperated breath. "What's the point of a second if you're not fighting?"

Reese eyed Rudd. The dwarf wasn't as tall as Reese, but his arms were twice as big, his shoulders massive. "I thought I wasn't supposed to fight."

"That was in the throne room," Thulan said. "This is different."

Rudd's gaze, dripping with scorn, ran over Reese.

"Different how?" Reese asked.

"Name your second," Thulan said to Rudd, "unless you're just gonna stand there and admire mine."

Rudd let out a snort. "Callun."

A dwarf rose from a table farther back, his stool scraping against the floor. He was nearly as big as Rudd and looked equally angry. His wide chest was covered by a thick leather vest, and his beard, which was long and brown, had bits of bone tied into the braids.

Mari let out a small groan.

"You'll fight him," Thulan told Reese.

Reese warily watched the burly dwarf approach. "Weapons?"

"Nope." Thulan stepped back, giving the two dwarves space to step into the front of the room. Reese moved next to her.

Mari pulled Sable back into the doorway where Slim waited. "They're going to need some room."

Leonis lingered near Thulan.

"Get out of the way," she told him.

"You both have to knock them down?" Leonis asked, eyeing Callun as the big dwarf stepped around the nearest table. "Reese might as well fell a tree with his bare hands."

"Thanks." Reese shifted to face Callun.

"Knocking down is a good start," Thulan said. "Keeping him down will be the trick."

Reese squared off against the dwarf, gauging how Callun moved. "I think the knocking down is going to be hard enough."

"What if only one of you wins?" Leonis asked.

"Let's not let that happen." Thulan glanced at Reese. "It might not seem like it, but Callun is an old friend. Try not to make any injuries permanent." She looked between the burly dwarf and Reese. "But don't lose. And Callun is known for his punches. If I were you, I wouldn't let one land."

Leonis patted Reese on the back with a grimace. "Good luck." He moved over to stand next to Sable.

"I thought we'd gotten past the fighting part," Sable whispered to Leonis.

He crossed his arms, and his brows creased with worry. "We'd have been better off if she'd fought in the throne room," he said quietly. "She's more thrown off by everything that's happened than I thought she'd be."

Rudd stepped toward Thulan in the small open space near the front of the room. He towered over her. Callun and Reese spread out as much as they could, and while Reese was taller by a hand, the dwarf took up substantially more space.

"Remember," Mari said in a worried voice as the room fell silent, "it is after curfew. Keep it quiet."

The punch Rudd threw at Thulan was so fast, Sable didn't even know he'd moved until Thulan stumbled back into the stone wall. Callun charged in almost at the same moment, but Reese ducked his first punch and drove forward too, ramming his elbow into Callun's cheek.

The dwarf staggered, and Reese took a few steps backward. "Thulan?"

She shoved herself up, shaking her head, then barreled forward, slamming into Rudd's chest, sending both of them sprawling over the nearest table. Dwarves scrambled out of the way, hissing out quiet cheers and shoving Thulan and Rudd back toward the front of the room.

"Can Thulan beat him?" Sable whispered to Mari, who wrung her hands in distress.

"Maybe," she managed, the word sounding utterly unconvincing.

Thulan slammed into a wooden bench along the wall, snapping off the legs with a series of loud crashes.

"Shhhh!" Mari hissed, glancing back toward the hall.

Sable grabbed Leonis's arm beside her, digging her fingers in as Callun came for Reese again, swinging his huge fist with astonishing speed.

Reese dodged the first two punches, but the third caught his shoulder, sending him reeling and spinning backwards. He steadied himself on the wall and turned to find Callun closing in, his fist already flying forward.

Sable clenched Leonis's arm, almost afraid to watch until Reese ducked and spun, somehow catching Callun's leg with his foot and knocking the dwarf off-balance. Reese drove into the dwarf's chest. Callun crashed to the ground, his head striking the stone floor.

Reese grabbed Callun's shoulder while he lay dazed and heaved the dwarf over onto his stomach. Callun let out a groan, and Reese twisted the dwarf's arm behind his back and pinned it with his own body weight.

Reese looked over at Thulan just in time to see her double over from a punch to the gut. "Thulan! Stop playing around!"

Thulan glanced up at him, saw him pinning Callun, and flashed a smile.

Rudd grabbed for her shoulder, but she caught his hand, spinning and pulling him forward. She curled around until her back was against him, then slammed her head into his nose with a loud crunch. She twisted away, and Rudd clapped his hands to his face. Blood streamed out, running red down his beard as he stumbled backwards.

Thulan closed the distance and drove her fist into his temple. He crashed back on a table, his body falling limp.

"Now," Thulan said, leaning her arms on the table next to Rudd and breathing heavily, "if you're not a bunch of cowards, stop hiding down here and figure out a way to gather whatever dwarves haven't lost their spines."

The room fell silent. Sable scanned the dwarves, all of whom were looking at Thulan with begrudging respect, if nothing else.

Slim's head twitched toward the front room, and he disappeared through the door.

Reese released Callun's arm and backed away. The dwarf rose, rotating his shoulder and studying Reese.

"There's a war brewing," Thulan continued, "and I'll be there fighting the snakes who destroyed our home and killed our friends and family. You can come fight them with us or hide here and wait for them to come destroy these tunnels too. Your choice."

The dwarves shifted, but no one answered her.

Slim ran back in. "Rion knows you're gone. Time to go."

The rest of the room stayed silent.

Thulan gave the dwarves one last look that was half anger, half regret. "I'd thought better of you," she said and turned away.

CHAPTER TWENTY-NINE

Sable's aching fingers reached up for a handhold, and her leg burned as she climbed up onto the next shelf of rock. Her nightmoss necklace illuminated only the small section of the steep shaft in front of her, the rest winding up into blackness.

Above her, Thulan swore as her foot slipped, sending a shower of pebbles bouncing down.

Sable shifted out of the way, and below her Reese, Leonis, and Mari did the same.

"Sorry," Thulan muttered.

The flight from the Broken Chisel felt interminable. Slim had padded ahead of them, picking turns confidently as their path grew rougher and narrower, until now, where he climbed above them quickly, occasionally calling back encouragement.

They'd left the Bodems somewhere far behind, blocking off the route with some crates in an effort to make the path appear unused.

Sable's thoughts were as leaden as her feet as she pushed herself higher, churning between the elven king's refusal, the High Dwarf's fury, and the wasted time at the Broken Chisel. The old, familiar fear of the Kalesh coming, which she'd managed to ignore since leaving Tutella Island, resurfaced. The truth that there were no elven or dwarven allies coming felt like the final nail in the coffin of her hopes.

A breath of fresh, damp air blew past her, and Sable strained to see past Thulan and Slim.

The darkness above them looked different. Beyond the soft light of her nightmoss, the shaft around her was crowded with inky shadows, but a jagged gap above them all was velvety black, pierced with starlight.

"There," Slim called back. "That wasn't too bad, was it?" With a bit more scuffling, the dim glow of his mosslight disappeared.

Thulan followed him, and Sable scrambled up the last rocks until her head broke out into the cool air under a sprawling, star-filled sky.

She crawled out onto dusty earth and collapsed onto her back, breathing in deep lungfuls of the fresh air and staring up at the wide, beautiful, weightless sky. The ground beneath her was dry, and small rocks jabbed into her back, but she didn't care. Her arms and legs were exhausted, her back ached, and her eyelids were dry and gritty.

Reese climbed out and rolled onto his back beside her, letting out a groan.

Slim stayed sitting, peering up into the sky. "I never have understood why humans like having nothing above them."

"The sky never falls and crushes us." Leonis lay down, his breath coming fast.

"And it's beautiful," Sable added. "Look at the stars."

"They're nice," Slim admitted, "but you can't touch them. Anything shiny in a tunnel, you can get to, harvest, and put wherever you like. The stars are…they might as well not exist, they're so out of our reach."

"That's part of what makes them beautiful," Sable pointed out. "No one can take them away."

Mari climbed out of the hole and sat next to Thulan. "I don't think anyone will follow you out here, even if they track you this far. You can get back to the forest from here?"

Thulan nodded. "We're farther north than the door, right?"

"Quite a bit," Slim said. "We're almost to the keyhole valley."

"That far?" Thulan looked around.

There was no moon, but compared to the utter blackness of the caves, the huge plain they sat on was at least visible. Sable turned her head to the side. Flat ground spread out as far as she could see in any direction, looking as though the rocky dirt she lay on was all there was in the world.

In one direction, which Sable took to be east, the sky was dark purple instead of black.

Slim pointed the opposite way. "You'll brush the bottom edge of the keyhole if you head west. If I were you, I'd get moving. You don't want to be close if one of Rion's men pops his head out here."

Thulan frowned at Mari. "In all the mess that happened, I forgot to ask something. Last spring, a group of dwarves traveled through the human world toward the Scale Mountains. From what I could gather, they were looking for caves."

"That was Tel!" Mari straightened. "Did you see them? How are they?"

"I just heard they'd passed."

"They're not on an official trip," Mari said. "They petitioned to go, but Rion wouldn't allow it. Tel heard that there were extensive caves in the northern Scale Mountains and wanted to check them out. When Rion refused, he took some cousins and went anyway, but we haven't heard from them since."

"There'll be trouble if the dwarves try to live in the Scales," Reese said. "The Northern Lords own those mountains. I don't see them giving that up."

"They can have the surface of the mountains," Mari said with a shrug. "We'll take the inside." She turned back to Thulan. "If you run across him, tell him to be careful coming back here. Rion hasn't grown any fonder of him since he left."

Thulan pushed herself up with a groan, and Mari stood as well.

"Thank you," Thulan said, "for trying to help."

"I'll talk some sense into the group at the Chisel." Mari looked down the hole in the ground. "You made a good start. Weren't going to change their minds in a night anyway."

"They're too angry," Slim agreed. "But the fight helped." He gave Reese a smirk. "Callun can't say the humans are weak after one took him down."

"Does it matter?" Sable pushed herself to her feet, her muscles protesting. "One dwarf doesn't feel like enough. And just admitting a human isn't weak is hardly the same as helping us against the Kalesh."

"It's not just one dwarf. It's Callun," Mari said.

Slim stood and nodded. "You played that well, Bristles."

Thulan gave him a little grin. "It's all a performance. There was no doubt Rudd would pick Callun. Rudd's too showy to pick anyone less important."

"Important how?" Reese asked.

"If there were an organized government of the third level—" Mari said.

"Which is illegal, so there definitely isn't," Slim interrupted.

Mari laughed. "Definitely not. If one were to exist, though, Callun would be High Dwarf."

"The big one Reese fought? With bones in his beard?" Sable asked.

Mari smirked. "The bones are mostly for Rion's benefit. Our illustrious High Dwarf sees the bones and assumes Callun has turned savage and lost all his intelligence and leadership skills. Cal was one of the first to be sent to the third level in Rion's supposedly random assignments."

"All a performance," Thulan said.

"The cousins from the Chisel will spread the word of what's going on," Mari said. "It might take a bit, but I think we can make some headway." She turned to Reese. "How'd you drop him so fast?"

Reese grimaced from where he still lay on the ground. "A man name Braddick pulled that move on me twice. At which point I decided I needed to learn it myself." He shifted the shoulder Callun had punched. "I should have done it sooner."

Slim laughed. "Callun punched me once—"

"For stealing his ale," Mari interrupted.

"I didn't get up for an hour." Slim held out his hand to Reese.

Reese took it, and the dwarf pulled him to his feet.

"Thank you," Reese said.

"Thank you for knocking Callun down." Slim glanced back into the tunnel. "I haven't had anything to taunt him with in ages."

"Speaking of performances," Leonis said, "you certainly took your time with Rudd, Thulan."

She shrugged. "It worked better if Reese took Callun down first."

"You got slammed into a wall," Sable said, "just for show?"

Thulan grinned again. "Had to make him think he was winning."

"Are you hurt?" Sable asked.

Thulan shrugged, then winced and rolled her shoulder. "Nothing permanent. Let's get moving before it gets too bright."

Sable's toe caught on the thousandth rock, and she stumbled forward. The sun sat low behind them, casting their shadows in long, bumpy lines across the dry ground and spikes of grass. What she'd originally taken for an endless landscape turned out to only be endless in three directions. The fourth, directly in front of them, had a sharply defined end, which they were quickly approaching.

Past the edge was nothing but a grey haze.

It was disquieting to know they were walking toward the top of the towering Marsham Cliffs, a rock face that had always seemed unclimbable.

The ground rose into a rare low hill, and Thulan stopped at the top. "The Marsham Cliffs are tall here. There's a path down somewhere nearby, but the descent will take hours once I find it, and it won't be easy." She scanned the landscape ahead of them, then pointed to a long dark line ahead of them, running parallel to the cliffs a short way from the edge. "Looks like there are some bushes near the top of that valley. We can rest there for a few hours."

"That's a valley?" Sable asked.

"It's a keyhole valley—it has no inlet or outlet." Thulan started down the hill toward it. "It's open all the way down to the level of the forest outside the cliffs, but there's no way into it. The cliffs along the side are too steep."

The closer they walked, the wider the valley appeared and the more Sable could see the sheer cliffs plunging down. They were nearly at the edge, though, before she caught a glimpse of a green valley floor far below. The valley was at least five times longer than it was wide, with dense forest filling each end, the trees shrunk to a tiny size by the height. The center of the valley was wider, with a broad stretch of rolling knolls of grass cut through by a meandering stream.

"The dwarves don't use this?" she asked Thulan.

"We can't get to it." Thulan walked along the edge toward the bushes clustered at the very end. "At least not easily. The stone around this southern end and all the way up the western side is so hard it's painfully slow to tunnel through. A few have tried, because it would be the perfect place to graze herds, but they always abandon it before they get too far." Thulan reached the bushes and peered into them. "No one's ever found a passable way down. Werruk, a famous excavator, claimed that if you tunneled from outside the Marsham Cliffs directly through the narrowest part, you could reach the valley. But no one's interested in a route that requires us to leave the cliffs first."

Thulan found a gap in the branches and ducked through. Sable followed her between the dry, brittle bushes, coming out into a small clearing hedged in by foliage. Aside from the sky, nothing could be seen through the pale green leaves.

Thulan dropped her pack. "This will work."

Reese studied the space, then motioned for Sable to follow him.

"I'll keep watch outside," Thulan said, "but if no one's followed us yet, then Rion doesn't know which direction we went." She glanced toward the sun. "Get a few hours' sleep. We'll climb down the cliff this afternoon and have a real night's rest tonight."

"I can keep watch," Purn said, popping into view.

Thulan looked like she was going to object, but Reese nodded. "That's a good idea," he said. "Purn can stay invisible, and she needs very little sleep." He peered through the bushes and picked a flat spot on the ground where he dropped his pack.

"She does?" Sable asked, following him over to a nondescript side of the clearing.

"How do you know that?" Purnicious demanded.

"Because you're always awake." He lay back on his pack like a pillow, crossing his arms behind his head and closing his eyes. "You help Sable get comfortable as she goes to sleep, things miraculously get mended overnight, and you're always awake before me in the mornings."

Purn narrowed her eyes. "I'm not ever visible at night, wastrel."

"You still make noise, little blue monster," he said, not bothering to open his eyes. "Don't mess with my clothes while I'm sleeping."

Purnicious studied him for a moment, looking indignant. "Well, from now on, you won't see me *or* hear me."

He cracked an eye. "Everything that moves makes noise, Purn."

"Not me," she said firmly and popped out of view.

"So you're saying Purnicious should always be on watch," Leonis said, finding his own place to sprawl on the ground. "This sounds fine with me."

"I'm saying that Thulan, out of all of us, should get some sleep," Reese said.

"I'm fine," the dwarf grumbled.

Reese cracked an eye again. "Because nothing in those tunnels was exhausting for you?"

Thulan sat down with an irritated noise.

Reese looked up at Sable, still standing, and nodded to the space next to him. "This is the best spot." It was indistinguishable from any other part of this dull little enclosed space.

"Of course it is." She set her pack down next to his and lay down. When she rested her head on her pack, she caught a flash of green out of the corner of her eye.

Just past the skinny trunks of the bushes next to her, the ground disappeared and she could see the length of the keyhole valley spread out below her. The sides were light-colored cliffs towering like a wall around the silent, isolated land below. The sun, still rising in the east, only lit partway down one side, but the reflected light from the stones cast a gentle glow over everything below it. A flock of white birds took off from the cliff, catching the sunlight for a moment before they plunged down into the shadows toward the forest below.

"See?" Reese's voice was quiet next to her. "The best spot."

She turned to find him rolled onto his side, close beside her, looking over her at the valley.

"Did you know that place existed?" she asked.

He shook his head. "I've never been up the Marsham Cliffs. Didn't even know there was a way to the top that didn't involve scaling sheer rock walls."

She looked back at the valley. She couldn't see the near end, but her gaze traced the meandering little stream through the wide center of the valley. From this distance, the hills seemed to be covered in smooth, soft grass. The cliffs sat around it like a shield, like this was a little oasis of peace, a stronghold of some type of life she'd never quite found anywhere else.

An oak sitting by itself on a small rise caught her eye. Its canopy was broad and thick, and the image of her cottage nestled itself snugly under the very edges of its leaves.

She could almost feel the grass beneath her, hear the babble of the stream. "It's perfect," she whispered.

When she turned back, Reese was watching her with an expression she couldn't quite decipher.

"It feels wrong," she said quietly, "to want to live there. To want to block out the rest of the world with huge cliffs and just…live."

"No." He looked past her, down into the valley again. "It's wrong that the rest of the world is so hard that we want to run."

She closed her eyes and felt the world beneath her spin slightly, the exhaustion of the last day catching up with her. "What do we do now? Our talks with the elves and the dwarves were complete failures." The sheer hopelessness of their position rose, but she closed her mouth, unwilling to voice all those fears again.

"Maybe Atticus or Jae and Serene had more luck." There was so little optimism in his voice that Sable didn't bother to agree.

The idea of going to the Northern Lords to report how little they'd accomplished felt like nothing more than a burden. "How long will it take us to get to Barrowford?"

"That depends. The headwaters of the Black River are somewhere around here, and once we get there, if we find a boat headed toward Barrowford, and if we can convince someone to take us, the trip should only take a few days. Most likely, though, we have a long way to walk."

A flash of brightness caught her eye from above as Innov shot over the top of the clearing, streaking through the sky and skimming over the thicket. She plunged into the valley, trailing a blaze of light into the shadows until she was so small Sable could just barely tell when she flared her wings and pulled up, soaring low over the grassy valley floor.

Innov's golden light wheeled through the unreachable valley, and Sable let her longing grow. Her gaze traced the low hills and discovered little clearings in the forest until her eyes grew heavy and she drifted off to sleep.

CHAPTER THIRTY

Sable leaned against the rail at the bow of the wool merchant's boat, breathing in the elusive scent of the Black River and the hint of coming rain until the next gust of tailwind blew the musty scent of wool around her again. Behind her, the boat was packed with bales of wool. It was the third day of sitting next to the smell, and she sat as far forward as possible to get fresh air and watch the pine trees drift by.

Unlike the tangled forest near Immusmala, which grew rampant over the Tremmen Hills, or the luminous, vibrant trees of the Wildwood, the northern woods were quiet and unruffled. Tall trunks rose straight toward the sky, their bottom halves bare, giving each other space and revealing glimpses deep into the forests.

The closer they came to Barrowford, the more the shore was dotted with houses and towns. When they'd embarked from a village deep in the north, they'd been the only boat heading south. Now the waterway teemed with boats floating downstream or laboriously rowing against the current.

After their short rest at the keyhole valley, Thulan had found a path down the Marsham Cliffs, if a scratch in the rock that involved clinging to sheer faces and sliding down the steepest parts counted as a path. It had taken hours, and they'd reached the base near sundown, but that had been the hardest part of their journey by far. The warm night spent in a farmer's barn, a quick deal with the musty-wool merchant, and long days on the river left Sable replaying again the detached refusal of the elves and the hostility of the dwarves.

She watched the shore move by, bringing them closer to Barrowford and the gathered army and the coming war. A small part of her that was quiet but persistent was relieved that the dwarves and the elves weren't moving toward it too. At least for the beginning of the war, Sable didn't have to worry about seeing Cintis dead on the battlefield. Or Mari.

A rustle behind her was her only warning before an arm shot around her shoulders, pulling her back against something solid. The second arm followed and pinned her before she even had time to shout.

"Reese!" She dropped her weight, shoved her hips back, and flung out her arms out, breaking his grip. When it loosened, she spun, grabbing his arm with her left hand, drawing *vitalle* out of him.

He smiled down at her but didn't step back. "You're getting faster, Flame of the North."

She reached for the knife she kept at her belt but missed the handle and grabbed her own shirt instead.

His smile widened. "That's not the knife you're lifting."

She found the knife hilt and drew it, holding it up in the small space between them. Gripping his arm tighter, she pulled energy out of him until her palm grew hot. "You scare me to death every time you do that."

He eyed the blade and took a step back, twisting his arm out of her grasp. "You're definitely getting faster." He rubbed a red mark, shaped like her palm, on his arm. "And faster at getting the *vitalle* moving. That hurt."

"You take a great deal of pleasure in these little attacks, don't you?"

"What's more fun than grappling?"

She slid the knife back into its sheath.

He grinned. "And you showed me you can't get the knife out smoothly, so I'm not doing a good enough job training you." He considered her for a moment. "Draw it again."

"I can do it when there's no pressure."

"If you do it enough when there's no pressure, you'll be able to do it when there is. Put it back. Cross your arms. Now do it again."

He watched her as she drew and sheathed the knife a dozen times. "A hundred more times should be a good start."

"A good start?" She leaned an elbow on the rail. "How long until we reach Barrowford?"

"Soon. Draw."

She frowned at him.

"If you do it too slow," he said, "I'll assume you need more practice."

"You enjoy this too much," she said, pulling the knife out again.

He looked downstream at the busy river. "This is more fun than anything we have to look forward to tonight. I'm sure we'll need to give our report before dinner, and then, if we're especially unlucky, we'll be trapped in debates all evening about what the north should be doing and how unprepared it is."

She sheathed the knife and moved next to him along the rail, her shoulder brushing his arm. "Do you think Atticus will be back yet? Or Jae and Serene?"

He leaned into her. "Jae and Serene should be. The Greenwood isn't far. Atticus might not be there, though. He and Flibbet have a huge area to cover."

She turned her back to the rail so she could reach the knife easier and shifted so her shoulder was against his again. He looked down at her and smiled. "Draw."

"Do you object to me touching you?" She pulled out the knife. This time, her hand found it easily.

"Not at all. I object to other people touching you and you not being able to stop them."

"Like dwarves? Because I don't think the grappling techniques would have helped me with one of those." She thrust the knife back into its sheath.

"If you're grabbed by a dwarf, the *vitalle* is what you'll need to focus on. You won't be strong enough to break their grip." He reached toward her neck, and his fingers brushed her skin as he pulled the little sword necklace out of her collar. "Maybe I should have you practice your sword work too."

"Or maybe not. The knife and the grappling are growing more comfortable, but the sword is just awkward and long. If I promise to have Jae keep teaching ways to protect myself with *vitalle,* can I never do a sword movement again?"

"Oh, Jae's going to teach you no matter what. He just doesn't know it yet. But you should definitely keep working on your sword work. It's good for a lot of things. Balance, strength, reflexes."

"You have an unreasonable affection for them," Sable said.

"There's nothing unreasonable about it."

His face was so close she could see the little golden flecks in his eyes. "Draw," he whispered.

She grabbed the knife hilt easily this time, but his hand caught hers before she could unsheathe it. Sable tried to shift the knife, but his hand was still locked on hers. "I seem to have an obstacle."

"Hm," he said. "We need to work on how to break a hold."

Every time she'd purposely tried to move *vitalle*, she'd used her palms, but she closed her eyes and tried to pull some energy out of Reese's hand through the back of her own. She opened up a channel, and while it didn't flow as quickly as it would into her palm, a rush of warmth flowed out of his hand and into hers. She opened her eyes to find him smiling at her.

"Interesting." He didn't let go. "So it's not just your palms or your lips that can do that."

"You could kiss me right now," she said, leaning toward him. "See if I can still draw it in that way."

His smile turned suspicious. "I'd rather not have you test that skill on me again."

"Barrowford!" the merchant called out from the back of the boat.

Reese glanced past her to where a grey stone wall ran along a ridge above the next bend in the riverbank. Purnicious popped into view, perched on the rail next to Sable. Reese flinched at how close she was, and she gave him a smug smile.

He returned it with a frown. "I keep expecting you to interfere when I attack Sable."

Purnicious shrugged. "I don't think you're a real threat."

"If you did?"

She leaned forward, and her lips drew back, revealing little white teeth. "You don't want that."

"Good." Reese studied her, then reached out and shoved her backward off the railing.

"Reese!" Sable grabbed for her but missed as Purnicious tumbled overboard. "Purn!"

Before the Kobold reached the water, she popped out of sight and reappeared crouched on the deck. She sprang forward with her teeth bared, slamming her hands into Reese's feet. The laces of his boots cinched tight. Reese grunted, but Purn was already scaling up his legs, her bony fingers grasping wads of clothes as she raced up. His belt shrank, digging into his stomach. He doubled over, and Purn lunged for his neck, seizing his collar, strangling him with the shrinking cloth.

Sable stared at them, her hands reaching out for Purn. But Reese sank to his knees and ripped his collar open, drawing in a breath. He wrapped his hands around Purn's waist, his fingers nearly encircling her as he pushed her back.

She let go of his shirt and gripped his arms, her teeth still bared. He held her at arm's length, his gasps shifting to laughter.

"Reese!" Sable knelt next to them. "I can't believe you pushed her off!"

"I knew you were fast enough to not hit the water," Reese said to Purn, grinning at her, "but I didn't know you were that fast." When she didn't try to attack again, he loosened his grip. "You didn't even get a toe wet, did you?"

Purnicious flexed her fingers, breathing furiously through her nose. "*Don't* do that again."

He shifted and began to untie his boot laces. "I don't need to. Your reaction time is excellent." His smile faded. "But it's not enough. Your strangle move always breaks down when the fabric gets too thin. You'll slow them for a moment, but it won't actually strangle anyone."

"True," Thulan said as she and Leonis came up beside them. "Don't waste your time fighting along the edges. That's where he wants to keep you. Shrink something more essential, something that controls the rest of him."

"Like his brain," Leonis offered.

Purn's teeth flashed again. "That's an excellent idea."

Reese looked at her curiously. "Could you do that?"

Purnicious stepped closer. "Want me to try?"

"Please don't," Sable said.

"Fine." Purnicious wiped her hands off on her skirt. "For now, he can keep his big head that size."

Reese looked down at his torn shirt and the belt and laces that were now too short to use. "Any chance you'd like to fix all this?"

"I'll fix the shirt." She stepped forward and ripped the corner off her own yellow tunic. Instead of pulling back, Reese sat still and let her fiddle at his collar. When she stepped back, the rip was still there, but it was now lined with a frilly yellow ruffle.

Reese pulled his shirt out and peered down at it. "Perfect. Every time you see that ruffle, Purn, remember that your strangle move won't work on someone who really wants to hurt Sable." He reached out and patted her shoulder as he stood.

The kobold pushed his arm away. "I wasn't trying to kill you," she muttered. "Even if I wanted to."

Sable ran a finger over the yellow ruffle. "It's lovely."

He smiled and looked downstream. The boat had started into the wide turn, and Barrowford's wall stretched away ahead of them, enclosing a large city built on a vast, low hill. At the top, a squat stone fortress presided over everything. A broad bridge crossed the river leading to a gate with five flags hanging above it.

Reese gave a surprised hum. "All five lords are here." He pointed past the city to a long, open plain that was filled with military tents. "Maybe they're actually taking this seriously."

The army camp spread out like a blanket over the open space.

"So many soldiers," Sable said quietly.

"Still not as many as the Kalesh could bring," Reese said.

Sable set her elbows on the rail. Not enough soldiers, and no elves or dwarves coming to help. Everything was playing into the Empire's hands. No matter how they fought this, they'd just be chipping away at an army so vast they'd never beat it.

"We're fighting along the edges where they want to keep us." Sable pushed herself off the rail. "Maybe we're thinking of this wrong. The Kalesh want this to be a battle of numbers." She pointed at Thulan. "But what if we focus on the thing that controls the rest of it?"

"The Emperor?" Thulan asked. "Because that seems unlikely to do us any good."

Sable shook her head. "Vivaine."

Leonis straightened. "You want us to fight Vivaine?"

"No, I want to *use* Vivaine." Sable nodded toward the soldiers. "They're here to fight the Kalesh army, and the Kalesh army is controlled by the Tien Sark. But Vivaine is the mythological figure that the Tien Sark are enamored with."

"You think you're going to get Vivaine to call off the army?" Thulan said. "You've been optimistic in the past, Sable, but that's a little much."

"Vivaine is the reason the Kalesh attacked the north in the first place," Reese agreed. "She doesn't want to stop this war."

"If she even has any power right now," Leonis added. "You left her alone with a wounded dragon and stole all the influence she had over the merchants."

"Do you really think Vivaine hasn't recovered by now?" Sable asked.

"She's had that city in the palm of her hand for decades. One bad day isn't going to unseat her."

"It was a really bad day," Leonis said.

"Vivaine has certainly regained her footing," Sable said, "which actually plays into our hands. If she has any lingering doubts about what the city thinks of her, we can fix that. What Vivaine wants is to have power because she's loved. When she had to choose, she chose to be loved by the Kalesh instead of the north, and that damaged her hold on the south at the same time. But what if we could offer her all of it?"

"How?" Thulan asked.

"By having her do exactly what she was trying before. Have her broker a treaty. What the Kalesh really want is the gold. With the north fighting them, and now the south against them, they think they have to fight for it. But if it comes down to a fight, we lose." Sable shrugged. "So we give up the gold. At least some of it. Or even most of it. At this point, I think everyone in the north and south would see the wisdom in that. Vivaine can broker a deal with the Kalesh where they get a portion of the mines in exchange for peace."

"That's a..." Leonis glanced at Thulan. "That sounds nice, but your plan is a little short on details."

"I could list a hundred objections without even thinking hard," Thulan said.

"True," Sable agreed, "but Atticus will help us smooth all those out. He is going to love this idea. It's the answer. Focusing on the one thing that can control everything else. If we can do this, the north and Immusmala won't have gold, but how is that different from how we've always lived? And Vivaine gets to not only be admired by the Kalesh, but everyone here loves her too, because she stopped a war we were bound to lose."

"So," Leonis said, "your plan is to set Vivaine up as the hero?"

"If Vivaine being the hero stops all those soldiers from dying and keeps this land free of the Empire? Absolutely."

PART III

Here is where we will begin to see the looming danger. It's not quite recognizable for what it is. Not yet.

But keep in mind, with the lighting, that the danger is just out of sight.

-Stage notes from act two, scene eight of ***The Phoenix Rising*** by Atticus the Playwright.

CHAPTER THIRTY-ONE

SABLE PAUSED with Reese on the jetty before stepping out into the crowded waterfront. The space between the docks and the city was thronged with people, handcarts, and wagons as dozens of boats unloaded supplies. Shouting voices echoed off the city wall, muddled together into an incomprehensible clamor.

Innov soared away from the racket, away from the city wall, and out over the camped army.

"Durnek!" Reese called out. Near the next jetty, a Tutella monk looked over. It took a moment before he waved in recognition and started working his way toward them.

He broke through the crowd, and his eyes caught on the yellow ruffle on Reese's shirt. "You look…lovely."

"Thanks." Reese glanced around. "Is the entire north here?"

"Essentially. Three quarters of the north's forces are camped south of the city, and the rest are on their way." Durnek looked behind, nodding to Sable, Leonis, and Thulan. "Any news from the dwarves or elves?"

"Not good news," Reese answered.

Durnek sighed and motioned toward the city gate. "I'm headed to the keep with a message for Sam. I can take you with me or just take a report if you'd rather not get embroiled in hours of boring discussions."

"The second, please," Leonis said. "The elves say it's our fight, not theirs, and the dwarves want to kill us all themselves."

Durnek shifted his sack. "Why?"

Reese gave a quick summary of the situation with the dwarves. "There's a dissenting group that might be able to offer us some support, but we shouldn't hope for any official reinforcements from Torren."

Durnek nodded. "Not a totally unexpected answer, I suppose."

"Is Atticus here?" Sable asked.

"Got here about a week ago." Durnek pointed along the city wall away from the gate. "Follow this around and you'll see his wagons."

"Any news of the Kalesh?" Reese asked.

"No sign of any troops yet. The closest we can guess is that we still have a fortnight before they land in the south, but there were two more Tien Sark causing trouble in Steepdale and Ravenwick. Hopefully our army will be headed to the narrows by Tutella soon." Durnek blew out an annoyed breath. "There are dissenting voices about that, but they made Braddick the official general of the five armies yesterday, and he's in favor of making our stand there. I would guess we'll start moving out soon."

"I'm surprised they agreed on a general," Reese said. "Not particularly surprised they picked Braddick. Although I thought Lord Perric would fight harder to get one of his own generals in charge."

"He can't." Durnek glanced around the crowd, then stepped closer. "Two weeks ago, Perric dismissed every general and half the captains in his army. Claimed they were attempting a coup and he couldn't trust them."

"He got rid of all his generals right before we're headed into a war?" Reese asked.

"That was stupid," Thulan said.

Durnek nodded again. "His forces are an unorganized mess. The new leaders are untested and don't have the loyalty of the men."

"That's just what we need," Reese said, "a huge part of the northern army weakened."

"It was poor timing." Durnek shifted his sack again. "I should get moving. I'll pass on your report. If they have questions, I'll send someone to find you." The monk headed into the busy waterfront.

The crowd was thick along the wall in the opposite direction, and it was slow working through the soldiers carrying supplies toward the army. All along the city wall, bright awnings and tents were set up. Merchants hawked their wares, and entertainers sang or performed stunts.

"Is there a festival going on?" Sable looked up at the grey sky, trying to remember the last time she'd seen the moon. "The next full moon will be the Blood Moon Festival in Immusmala, but that's not for a week or two. Do they celebrate that here?"

"Blood Moon?" Reese asked. "That sounds cheerful."

"It's not cheerful," Sable said, "and now that I think about it, you wouldn't have it in the north. All the fires that spread on the grass of the Eastern Reaches at the end of the summer fills the eastern sky with smoke, so when the moon rises, it looks red. The main event of the festival, aside from the normal hubbub of merchants gathering, is the public trials."

Leonis grimaced. "That's my least favorite festival. Dozens of prisoners are tried publicly with the details of their crimes announced to the crowd."

"It's unpleasant," Sable said. "Only prisoners convicted of the most horrible crimes are tried. They've all received sentences of execution, but it's held off until the festival, where they can beg for the leniency of being sent to sea as a slave on a ship instead of being executed."

"Who decides that?" Reese asked.

"The three prioresses hear statements from people for or against the prisoners." Sable paused. "I suppose only two prioresses will this year, unless they've managed to choose a new Phoenix Prioress."

"If they've chosen a new one but Innov is still with you," Thulan said, "they are not going to be happy."

They rounded a corner of the city wall and found endless, neat rows of army tents. The light filtering through the gloomy sky lit the vibrant blue and red of Atticus's wagons like beacons in the midst of the colorless sea.

They started toward them, and Sable's attention was caught by a glimpse of firelight on a wide, flat-topped hill rising past all the tents. The light came from a jumble of jagged ruins on the top. It was the direction Innov had flown, but it was impossible to tell whether the light was the phoenix or merely someone's campfire.

Atticus's wagons and the road that followed the city wall made a little triangular campsite. Familiar benches sat along each wagon. The cook pot bubbled on its stand where the corners of the wagons drew close to each other, filling the space with a rich, savory scent. Inside the open window of the blue wagon, Leonis's tree glowed with its soft green light.

Atticus's wavy white head leaned close to Jae and Serene over a book, Jae's quill moving quickly across the page.

Sitting rather close to each other on the opposite bench were Terrane and Gwen. The large man sat by a hot flat rock, examining some small cakes that were cooking. Gwen wore a brilliant blue dress, shockingly colorful compared to the white she'd always worn as a Mira. Her hair and posture were still unnecessarily straight and orderly, but there was a touch of something softer about her than Sable remembered, and she rested her hand lightly on Terrane's arm.

He met Sable's eyes with a smile, then took in the group around her. He glanced at Gwen with a questioning look.

"You'd better make more, then," Gwen answered his unspoken thought, "because I'm not sharing my cakes with anyone."

"You're back!" Atticus said, rising. "Tell us you have good news!"

"We do not have good news." A flash of something bright in the window with Leonis's tree caught Sable's eye, and she looked over, expecting Innov.

Instead, tending to the leaves was the slim figure of an elf. She wore a simple dress of light green, and even inside the wagon, her hair managed to catch some of the sunlight coming through the clouds. Long locks flowing over her shoulders and down to her waist glowed like strands of warm copper and shimmering gold. She caught sight of Sable, and her face lit.

Sable took a step toward the elf. "Ayda?" She turned to Jae and Serene. "You brought elves!"

Jae held up a finger. "We brought one elf."

Ayda leaned out the window. "We saw your phoenix fly to the barrow a little while ago!"

"The barrow?"

"That big hill over there." Ayda waved to the ruins on the hillside.

"Are more Greenwood elves coming?" Leonis asked.

Ayda propped her elbows on the windowsill. "Definitely not. Serene and Jae expected an immediate answer, but elves with authority are tasked with keeping the elves' land…healthy. Stable. Keeping things the same, because if you change one thing in the forest, it causes ripples you didn't expect."

Atticus stood with his eyes focused past the wagons into the distance, not listening. He blinked when Thulan walked past him toward the cook pot. "So you found no allies at all?"

"None to speak of." The dwarf stirred the simmering soup. "It was a disaster from the moment Victis came to meet us," Thulan continued. "He's as miserable as he was when we first met him, and just when we were about to be rid of him, Sable invited him to dinner."

Jae let out a laugh. "You did?"

"It wasn't on purpose." Sable moved over to the bench along the red wagon and sank down. Reese sat next to her, leaning back against the wagon.

"You'd have loved dinner with Victis, Atticus." Leonis climbed up onto the roof of the blue wagon and pulled open the panel above his tree. "I have never sat through a more awkward meal or one more rife with political peril. Between Thulan and Sable, we're lucky to not be in an all-out war with the elves."

Ayda swung herself up onto the roof next to him and dangled her feet inside the opening for the tree. She looked at Sable curiously. "You met Victis Thornroot?"

"You know him?" Sable asked.

"By reputation." Ayda frowned. "He's said to be rather severe."

"He is," Thulan said, "to everyone but Sable, who is his very special friend."

Atticus settled into his favorite chair next to the fire, his eyes bright. "Tell me everything. Don't leave out a single detail."

Thulan launched into the story of their time with the elves, deftly skipping over Leonis meeting his father, focusing on dinner with Victis and Sable's attempt to convince the king. Sable listened, laughing at Thulan's dramatic descriptions of every painful moment.

As they talked, Sable let her eyes wander over the endless rows of army tents, following soldiers of the north in their different uniforms. Above it all, the wide barrow rose peacefully, if vaguely sad with its crumbling ruins.

Leonis took over the telling of the story once they reached the dwarves and, with the omission of the more painful conversations at Mari's home, told the encounter with enough liveliness that the dwarven tunnels felt like some grand adventure instead of the futile struggle it had really been.

Atticus rose and brought Sable a waterskin, sitting next to her on the bench. He looked across her at Reese. "You look like you've recovered."

Reese nodded. "I don't know what's in the Wildwood, but it only took one day there to feel back to normal."

Atticus raised his eyebrows. "That's interesting." His gaze lingered on the yellow ruffle on Reese's shirt.

"He's trying to prove some kind of point to Purn," Sable said.

"Well, when you're done proving it, there are plenty of shirts in the costume crates that will fit you." He lowered his voice so only Sable and

Reese could hear. "Sometime soon, you two will have to give me the true version of your trip." He focused on Thulan. "How is she?"

Sable searched for some of the pain Thulan had shown in the tunnels. But the dwarf was laughing at Leonis's retelling, looking like her normal self. "It was hard on her." Sable glanced at Atticus. "Did you know she's an amazing painter?"

The edge of his mouth curled up in a smile.

"Of course you did," Reese said. "Is there anything you don't know about us?"

"Probably." Atticus turned his attention back to Thulan, looking fondly at the dwarf. "Thulan is a very private person. It took her months to tell me anything about herself. I thought I'd found a treasure merely because she could act so well, but discovering that she could also paint—that was just the crown on her lovely head."

"We saw a picture she painted of her sons." Sable said quietly.

Atticus let out a slow, sorrowful breath. "I imagine that was breathtaking."

"And heartbreaking." Sable nodded her chin at the roof of the wagon. "And the trip wasn't just hard on Thulan. Leonis met his father."

Atticus's winced. "How did that go?"

"It went well, mostly. But he's aged, terribly. Cintis said it's from grief. He looks ancient."

Atticus slowly raised his eyes to where Leonis lay on the wagon. "Poor soul."

Whether he meant Leonis or Leonis's father, Sable wasn't sure.

Somewhere behind the clouds, the sun must have dropped low enough that the world was falling into shadows. In the west, bits of the sky were tinted with a reddish hue, and the warm light seemed to soften the entire world just a bit.

A glitter of light caught Sable's attention as a bit of flame rose off the barrow and shot up into the sky. Flashing a brilliant gold that made the clouds look like merely a backdrop for her fire, Innov soared over the army camp, making a long, lazy circle before angling down toward the wagons.

Sable held out her arm, and the phoenix flew in to land in a flurry of sparks. "Our whole trip was one failure after another, Atticus," Sable said, "but I have an idea of what we can do now."

There was a rustle of whispers along the road at the edge of the wagons as a handful of soldiers stopped to stare at the phoenix.

Sable heard whispered of "Issable" and gave the men a small wave.

Atticus sat back against the wagon, propping his feet up on a crate with a smug smile. "What is your idea, Issable?"

"I want to stop messing around with the Kalesh army and try to change the one person who could control it all."

He blinked at her, his smile slowly shifting into a thoughtful frown. After a moment, he put his feet back on the ground and leaned his elbows on his knees, staring into the campfire.

"I told you he'd like this idea," Sable said to Reese.

"Until he figures out all the problems with it."

"Oh, there are problems," Atticus said, still focused on the fire.

"But if it works…" Sable said.

The playwright nodded slowly. "If it works, it could change everything."

"We think there was a Tien Sark with the Kalesh who destroyed the dwarven mines," Sable said, "which means they've been involved with our land for years. Vivaine has a great deal of power she could wield over them. She spent so long working toward a treaty involving gold. If we can get her to revive that, with the Tien Sark admiring her as much as they do, then maybe she can convince them to stop fighting."

"Until the Emperor orders them to start again," Reese said.

"But the Emperor wants the gold," Atticus mused. "If he can get it without the expense of a war, he'll accept that deal. Aside from the gold, our land doesn't have much to offer him."

"The Empire wants one more thing," Reese pointed out. "Sable."

She drummed her fingers on the side of the waterskin. "That's a part I need a solution for, Atticus. If there's no war, maybe they can be convinced the daughter of the Ghost isn't a threat, but if the Emperor hated my mother as much as they say, I don't know of anything that will change the fact that they want me dead. And while the idea of faking my death is still one solution, it would be a lie, and I'm not a fan of lying." She looked between the two of them at their unspoken question. "And yes, whatever solution we find may need to include my sisters."

Atticus ran his fingers through his beard, still nodding. "We have a lot of steps before the point where we have to figure out what to do with you."

"For starters," she said, "I want the lords to keep me as ambassador and let me negotiate with Vivaine. What do you think the chances are they'll agree to that?"

Atticus grinned. "Slim, but we don't want them to agree right away. Where would the fun be in that?" He rubbed his hands together. "I need to write this out and think about it. This is an excellent idea."

"I'm surprised you didn't think of it first," she told him.

He gave a little laugh. "So am I." With a flash of a smile, he headed to the back of the wagon.

The sun set and the army camp fell into darkness. The world shrank down to the circle of firelight reflecting off the wagon walls and the soft green glow of Leonis's tree. Innov moved over to roost among the coals of the fire, and Sable sank back against the wagon, letting the familiar conversations wrap around her.

Serene came over and dropped heavily onto the bench next to Sable. "Do you still have the *Ghost of the White Wood* book?" At Sable's nod, she continued, "Can I borrow it? Melia's story has enough influence on what we're going through that I'd like to include it in our records."

"You're recording everything?" Sable asked.

"We've always tried to record interesting things that happen, but we've never been part of anything as momentous as this. I'm collecting as much information as I can, and Jae's writing it out."

"What will you do with it once you write it?" Sable asked. "Assuming we all survive. Go back to Stonehaven and rebuild the library there?"

Serene sighed and shook her head. "Without Merrick, we'll never get the wall to Stonehaven to keep the enchantments. They've probably begun to deteriorate already. What we need is a place that is completely safe. Someplace with more than a wall." She looked over at Terrane and Gwen.

"I've been talking to Flibbet," Serene said. "He knows a couple more people who can use *vitalle*, and we've been discussing how much we could accomplish if we worked together. Merrick always wanted a place where people could learn about their skills and share their expertise. But we've always been so divided. Northerners and southerners. Those who serve the priories or themselves. But now, the idea of working together feels…possible. A Mira and a northern firestarter are working on how their skills can be combined. Yesterday, Gwen got a bit of dead grass to smoke just by touching Terrane and channeling his thoughts."

Sable raised an eyebrow and looked at the two. "That's impressive."

"It is." Serene stretched out her legs and yawned. "But we need a place. A home. Something that we can call ours. For people like Jae and me, Gwen and Terrane. Maybe even Atticus." She glanced at Sable. "Definitely you."

A home. Sable's dream cottage suddenly shifted. What if it wasn't alone in the woods? What if it was part of a town, a community? What if her home sat next to Jae and Serene's? The cottage brightened as though the sun had just broken through the clouds.

Her home under the wide boughs of the oak and, not far away, other little homes and a sturdy, growing library.

Sable straightened. "How about in a beautiful valley with hills and grass and forests and a river, but no entrance, no exit, and sheer walls so high no one can scale them?"

Serene raised an eyebrow. "If there's no entrance or exit, how will we get in and out of it?"

"That's your puzzle to solve. It's a keyhole valley that Thulan showed us, a bit past the northern door into New Torren. It lays behind the Marsham Cliffs, separated from the forests by a solid rock wall, but if you can figure out a way in, I swear it's exactly what you want. It's like a…a stronghold that will keep out the rest of the world, where you can protect all the important things and return to with all the new knowledge you gather." Sable shook her head. "I'll have Thulan paint you a picture of it. You won't believe how perfect it is."

Serene's eyes drifted to the fire, and she nodded. "A stronghold…" she mused. "That is exactly what we need."

CHAPTER THIRTY-TWO

"Sable!" Atticus's voice cut through the quiet of the morning.

Sable rolled over on the thick pile of stage curtains and looked out the back door of his blue wagon. After weeks of sleeping on the ground, the last thing she wanted to do was climb out of the snug bed she'd burrowed into. Especially when the world outside was a dim and drippy grey.

"Sable!" he repeated. "Rabbit has news from the south. He's headed to the council and says he needs more voices who know Immusmala."

Sable sat up, keeping a curtain wrapped around her to ward off the chill. "Why?"

"You know as much as I do," the playwright said, impatience bleeding into his voice, "but he was in a hurry."

"If the Northern Lords will be there, I need something to wear. Something respectable enough to—"

He tossed a dress of creamy white linen into the wagon and pushed the door closed.

"And a cloak for the rain!" she called after him. "Not one of your ratty ones. Something Ambassador-like."

Thulan let out an annoyed grumble and pulled a curtain over her head. The space where Reese had fallen asleep last night was empty. Sable pulled the short-sleeved dress on, shivering under the thin fabric.

She grabbed a brush and pushed the door open, and chilly droplets of mist landed on her arms.

Atticus called for Gwen to get up in the other wagon and pulled something out from inside it, returning to Sable with a cloak. The fabric was a rich, deep blue oil cloth, the lining thick and soft.

She wrapped it around herself, nodding. "This works."

Reese came around the corner of the wagon from the direction of the river. His hair was damp, and a fat duck hung from his hand. He took in Atticus and Sable. "Isn't it a little early in the morning to be dressing her up for one of your schemes, Atticus?"

Atticus smiled. "Never too early for a scheme."

Gwen and Serene stepped down from the other wagon, wrapping their own cloaks around themselves.

"Where are we going?" Reese asked, setting the duck down by where Thulan would make her cook fire.

"Rabbit has news from the south, and I need to talk to the lords about staying the ambassador for a little longer," Sable said, stepping down the little stairs at the back of the wagon and pulled up her hood. "Looking the part can't hurt."

The cloak dragged on the ground, and Atticus looked at it critically. "Purnicious?" he called.

The bottom of the fabric shifted, shrinking away from the ground at the front corner. In moments, the entire hem was the perfect length.

"Beautiful work, Purnicious," Atticus said. "As always."

"Thank you." Purn's little voice came out of the space by Sable's feet.

Ayda climbed out the window of the wagon, taking a deep breath and turning her face up toward the sky. "Don't you like the rain?"

"The rain is lovely." Atticus peered into the wagon Sable had just left. "Having Sable look bedraggled and waterlogged is not. Where's Innov?"

"Probably out playing in the raindrops," Sable said.

Atticus gave the sky a quick frown before surveying the group. "If everyone's ready?"

He hurried them along the muddy dirt road that was already stirring with soldiers and into the city itself, where only a few early merchants and servants were moving about. Ayda traipsed along beside them, bright in the dim, damp light, spreading her arms to catch more of the misty raindrops, apparently unconcerned by the morning chill.

Barrowford had a different feel than Immusmala. Instead of buildings made of stone and brick, the streets were lined with timber-framed shops. Down the side roads that wound off from the main one, the houses and shops were mostly subdued, neutral colors, but on the wide avenue

Atticus led them up, the triangles and rectangles between the thick beams in the walls were painted in yellows and reds and blues. Awnings of vivid colors sheltered the edges of the street, covering tables that merchants were just starting to fill. The roofs of the buildings were steep, the gables carved with scrollwork and fanciful shapes. Small flags fluttered off lines flung across the street from building to building. Even in the dim light of the cloudy morning, the street was cheerfully bright.

The road widened just outside the wall of the fortress, and Atticus strode toward the gate, nodding to the guards, who motioned him into the courtyard. Inside the wall was a ring of connected stone buildings with nothing but arrow slit windows. A thick iron-bound door was open to the courtyard, with soldiers moving quickly through it. To the left of the door rose the keep itself, a fat, round tower at least twice as tall as the rest. Between the somber grey stone and the thin windows, the complex felt menacing and unwelcoming.

Until they stepped inside the entrance hall.

Torches cast a warm glow over the stone floor and walls, illuminating thick beams crossing the ceiling. A wide fireplace crackled with fire, driving away the chill of the morning, and the scent of fresh bread filled the room. Hallways headed off to either side, but straight ahead, the wall was filled with windows looking out into a misty courtyard of green grass and small pines.

Atticus led them through several hallways to the base of the tower. At the bottom of the stairs, Lord Loren and the burly form of Lord Perric appeared from deeper in the fortress.

"What's the news from the south?" Lord Loren asked.

Atticus shrugged. "I've heard no details."

"It had better be worth climbing all these stairs before I've breakfasted," Lord Perric grumbled.

The other lords and Braddick were already seated in the council room three stories up, serving themselves from the trays of bread and eggs the servants were hurriedly placing on the table. Rabbit stood near the windows, shuffling through some papers. He glanced toward the door and gave Atticus a small nod.

Lord Perric strode into the room, breathing heavily and glaring at them all. "What news from the south is so urgent we have to gather this early in the morning?"

Rabbit stepped up to the head of the table. "The Prioress Vivaine has been taken prisoner by the Sanctuary and is accused of betraying the city of Immusmala. Eugessa has called for her execution."

CHAPTER THIRTY-THREE

SABLE STOPPED in her tracks and stared at Rabbit. The idea of Vivaine even captured by anyone in Immusmala was ludicrous, never mind—

"Executed?" Atticus gripped the back of a chair.

Gwen snorted. "Impossible."

Ayda crossed the room and hopped up to sit on the windowsill, looking curiously at the room. "That's good, right? Isn't she evil?"

"Yes." Reese pulled out a chair and sat.

Serene sat and drew a small scroll, a quill, and a bottle of ink from her pockets and began scribbling notes.

Lord Loren took a seat near the head of the table. "Where is the prioress now?"

"We don't know," Rabbit said, "although the most reliable information says she's been confined somewhere in the Dragon Priory."

"Someone put her in her own prison cells?" Sable sat next to Reese.

The room turned to look at her with varying degrees of surprise.

"She has prison cells?" Lord Erick asked.

Sable nodded. "Under the priory."

"Why does a priory need a dungeon?" Lord Loren asked.

"To imprison theater groups." Atticus sat slowly, studying Rabbit with a troubled expression. "How sure are you of this information?"

"I wouldn't have woken everyone up if I wasn't sure."

Gwen still stood behind a chair. "No one could confine Vivaine to the catacombs against her will. Or anywhere else. Argyros would kill them."

"That's the other news," Rabbit said. "The dragon's gone. I have four different witnesses who saw him fly over the Sanctuary Wall a week ago, and no one's seen him since."

"Argyros can fly?" Sable asked.

Gwen shook her head, her brow creased. "Not that I've ever seen."

"This is the first good news we've heard in weeks." Lord Perric pulled a plate of bread closer to himself. "The dragon gone and one of the prioresses set to be executed. Too bad they're not executing them all."

Atticus tapped one finger rapidly on the table. He glanced at Sable and Gwen. "What does it mean that her dragon left?"

"I have no idea," Sable said. "The dragon was always uncomfortably close to her." She turned to Gwen. "Have any of the creatures left prioresses before?"

"They're called *denos,*" Gwen said. "Like Innov, sometimes they leave the Sanctuary while they're waiting for a new prioress to be chosen, but desert a living prioress? Never." She looked out the window. "Although Vivaine is the first prioress to have a dragon."

"It's true, then?" Lord Loren asked. "Vivaine hatched that creature?"

"The Dragon Priory always only had a dragon egg," Gwen said, "and no one even knew if it was real. Compared to a living unicorn or phoenix, having merely an egg kept the Dragon Priory in a position of lesser importance."

"Until Vivaine," Atticus said.

Gwen nodded. "Prioresses are almost always elderly, but when the last Dragon Prioress was weakening, Vivaine was only twenty-five. All the prioresses and abbesses gathered together to declare the candidates being considered to replace the ailing prioress, and Vivaine got up and left.

"She'd have been disciplined for insubordination, except when she returned an hour later, she was glowing white, holding a newly hatched silver dragon in her arms, as though she were carrying a baby. She walked to the front of the gathering and just stood there until the other two prioresses admitted they couldn't ignore a sign like that. They claimed Amah had blessed Vivaine, and they named her the Dragon Prioress."

All of Gwen's words had been warm.

Sable sank back in her chair. Vivaine would have taken a great amount of joy from the drama of such a moment.

"How did Vivaine know how to hatch a dragon?" Reese asked.

"Argyros had been talking to her for years," Gwen said. "She used to secretly visit the egg, which was kept down in the catacombs. At the time, the cells were used for storage, and the egg was kept in a special one, surrounded by treasures, because they believed it wanted to be kept somewhere cold and dark." She pulled her chair out and sat, her back stiff and her voice obstinate. "Argyros would never leave Vivaine. He's been devoted to her since before he hatched."

Gwen's words had all been warm until the end, when a thread of chilliness wound through them

Sable shifted to face her. "But?"

"There is no but," Gwen answered brusquely.

Sable leveled a disbelieving look at her.

Gwen folded her hands and studied her fingers. "In the last year, something shifted. It was subtle at first, but a few times, it seemed like Argyros was making decisions on his own, not always the one Vivaine would have chosen. She covered it well, but I was around the two of them too much not to notice."

Sable nodded. "It did feel like that."

"Did that worry her?" Atticus asked.

Gwen shrugged. "I don't know. Vivaine has always..." She glanced around the room. "Kept to herself. I've never been privy to her thoughts."

Sable raised an eyebrow at the admission. Vivaine had never let Gwen touch her? "Never?"

"She's very private," Gwen said.

Sable thought of the hours she'd spent with Gwen holding her arm, reading her mind. "Must be nice to get that choice."

"At Tutella Island," Reese said quietly, "when Argyros burned Tylar, that wasn't Vivaine, was it? It was the dragon."

Sable nodded. "It terrified her. She tried to hide it, but I don't think she had any intention of killing him. She knows her power comes from people thinking she's benevolent."

Serene paused her quill and looked up. "So maybe Argyros has outgrown the prioress."

Gwen shook her head stubbornly. "You don't understand how close the two of them are. The dragon can speak to her somehow. In her mind. I don't know if it's through words or impressions, but the two of them are constantly connected."

"It shouldn't be hard to find a dragon," Ayda pointed out. "Has anyone asked the trees? If something that powerful is in the forest, they'd all be talking about it."

Her words were met with silence.

"Maybe you could give that a try," Atticus said, "and let us know what you find."

Ayda beamed at him. "I would love to."

"The north should have a say in Vivaine's punishment," Lord Darien said, dragging everyone's attention away from the elf. "She's as much responsible for the attacks on the north as the Kalesh are."

"I agree," Lord Erick said. "However she betrayed the south, it is nothing compared to what she did to us."

Rabbit nodded. "Thus the urgency of this council. As Gwen and Sable can attest, Immusmala will celebrate the Blood Moon Festival at the next full moon, where prisoners who have been sentenced to death have a second trial with the chance to plead for leniency."

"You have a festival dedicated to sentencing prisoners?" Braddick asked.

"Among other things," Gwen said. "The biggest draw of the festival is that young couples pledge themselves to be handfasted. The trials are just a small part of it."

Rabbit tapped on his paper. "My sources near the Sanctuary say that Prioress Eugessa will try Vivaine before the entire city."

Sable tried to picture Vivaine, sullied and chained among the violent, vicious criminals.

"That's a bold move," Serene said.

"A killing move," Braddick agreed. "Either Vivaine is sentenced to death, or she debases herself before Eugessa, begging for mercy. That's not the sort of humiliation she'll recover from."

Sable shook her head. "There's no possibility for real mercy. The only option beside death is a life sentence on a galley. It's not humiliation. It's enslavement." She ran her fingers over the cuff of her cloak. If Vivaine was imprisoned, every hope of having her broker a treaty with the Kalesh crumbled. She glanced over at Atticus, but he was staring at the table, his face unreadable.

Lord Erick leaned forward. "Whole towns were wiped out by the Kalesh because she drew our soldiers south. Women and children murdered, livestock killed, crops burned. She has a great deal of blood on her hands. She deserves death."

Atticus twitched.

"Yes, she does," Reese said solemnly.

"Anyone can speak for or against the prisoner at the trial," Rabbit said. "If the north wants to make an accusation, they should send someone. Quickly. The festival is in five days."

Sable shook her head. "Except we don't want her to—"

"Send Sable," Atticus interrupted, not looking up.

Sable stopped short.

"No," Lord Darien said.

"Absolutely not," Lord Perric agreed. "This woman has no role in anything that is going on."

Sable kept her eyes on Atticus, trying to read his expression. Going to the festival to call for Vivaine's execution was the exact opposite of what she needed to do.

Atticus looked up, but not at Sable. He turned to Lord Perric. "Sable is the obvious choice, and you know it." Despite the angry looks Atticus was garnering from all the lords and despite the fact they were discussing Vivaine's execution, his tension from moments before had seemingly evaporated. He leaned back easily in his chair. "As things stand, no lords or generals can be spared. You are needed here with the army."

Sable was certain his composure was an act, but she scrambled to think of what he had in mind.

"Sable is familiar with Immusmala and the prioresses," Atticus continued, folding his hands. "The southern people know her and the phoenix. And when she speaks, they will listen."

The lords were looking between Atticus and Sable.

"Will you bring our accusations and call for her execution?" Lord Loren asked Sable.

Atticus met Sable's gaze, his posture still relaxed, but his eyes held the slightest hint of an appeal. The idea made no sense, but it was Atticus. She gave him a small nod and turned to Lord Loren. "If you name me as ambassador, I will deliver whatever message you send."

"But will you call for her execution?" Lord Perric pressed.

"There will be no calls for execution," Sable said. "Prioress Eugessa will announce what Vivaine is charged with and the penalty for it. The only thing the public can do is bring more witnesses for or against the accused. Then the priories will determine Vivaine's fate. Or, I suppose, Eugessa alone will determine her fate." Sable leaned her elbows on the table. "There is no love lost between the two prioresses. Eugessa has been looking for a way to unseat Vivaine for a very long time. I doubt Eugessa will offer Vivaine any mercy at all."

Out of the corner of her eye, she saw Atticus's fingers tighten.

"This is very good," Lord Loren said. "I thought Vivaine would never be made to pay for what she's done."

"So," Atticus said, "will you send Sable? She could leave today, and traveling by the river, she'll arrive before the festival."

The lords were quiet for a moment. Braddick looked critically at Sable but didn't speak.

"I have no problem sending her," Lord Loren said. "She can be compelling. As long as she swears to support the north's demand for justice, she has my vote."

"And mine," Lord Erick agreed.

"I don't see anyone else as disposable as you," Lord Darien said to Sable. "And since I would imagine the south is going to rid us of the wretched woman whether we speak up or not, I suppose I have no real objection. But you will be there as a representative of the north, not as your own person. Everything you voice will be the opinion of the north."

Atticus watched Sable closely, his gaze intense.

"I'll stand up at her trial and give whatever statement you want," Sable said.

Atticus let out an almost imperceptible breath of relief.

The room turned its attention to the last two lords.

"I suppose I have no objections," Lord Runess said.

Lord Perric nodded dismissively. "You're as good of a choice as any. We'll write out our grievances for you to read, but I doubt the south will care a whit about what the north has against their prioress. You'll be as superfluous there as you are here."

"Excellent," Atticus said, rising. "We'll get you ready to leave, then, Sable." He inclined his head to the lords. "Have someone draw up your letter, and we'll return for it shortly."

He held his hand out toward the door, and Sable stood along with Reese, Gwen, and Serene. Ayda hopped off the window as Rabbit gathered his papers, wished the lords a good morning, and followed.

Atticus strode down the stairs, his back straight and his pace fast, leading them out through the gate of the keep before he slowed and turned. He set his hand on Sable's shoulder. "Thank you."

Sable studied him. "What are you planning, old man?"

"I don't have a plan yet, but we need to hurry. People at the Blood Moon Festival are out for…well, blood."

"We?"

"I'm coming with you, of course," he said. "The whole troupe will go. Having the wagons will give us extra access to the festival, although we'll be too late to claim a good spot."

"I'm coming," Reese added.

"And me," Gwen said firmly.

Atticus nodded. "We need to hurry. Vivaine cannot be executed." His tone was firm, the words warm.

"Then why did you just ask me to support that very thing?" Sable asked.

"Because it's better left in our hands than someone else's." Atticus set his other hand on Sable's shoulder and gripped her tightly. A flicker of something raw and almost desperate flashed in his eyes. "She can*not* be executed."

His words were so hot they drove away the chill of the morning.

Without waiting for an answer, he turned and hurried down the street.

CHAPTER THIRTY-FOUR

THE NEXT HOUR was spent in a bustle of activity around the wagons. Rabbit was charged with finding a boat that would hold everyone and both wagons. Reese left to find Sam and tell him the news. The only person who wasn't busy was Ayda, who danced lightly along the roof of the red wagon, humming to herself and spreading her hands to catch raindrops.

Sable helped Thulan and Leonis pack the troupe's belongings while Purnicious blinked back and forth between the two wagons, helping to organize everything.

Atticus, who'd said almost nothing since the keep, strode away down a path between nearby army tents, muttering to himself.

Leonis waited until he was gone before crossing his arms. "So, just to be sure I understand where we now stand, not only are we going to try to make Vivaine the hero of everything, we first have to somehow save her from being executed when we all agree she is actually guilty of what they're accusing her of?"

"Guess she didn't quite regain her footing as you thought she would," Thulan said to Sable. The dwarf paused in her packing to look after Atticus. "I'm worried he's not going to be able to stay levelheaded about this."

Leonis frowned. "After everything Vivaine's done, he can't possibly still have feelings for her."

Thulan snorted. "He's loved her most of his life. That's not going to change merely because she's shown herself to be a murderer on a grand scale."

"He loves the evil woman?" Ayda said, lying on her stomach and peering down at them. "Why?"

Sable shook her head. "He used to, but now he knows she's not who he thought she was."

"No," Thulan said, "now he thinks he could help her rediscover who she once was."

"But he seems like a good man," Ayda mused, "and she seems cruel and heartless."

"Both those things are true." Sable turned to Thulan. "But he's not that naive."

Leonis paused in the act of lifting a small bench. He exchanged looks with Thulan. "Atticus is trying to save her. This could go badly."

Thulan swallowed. "Maybe he has a plan."

"He doesn't have a plan." Leonis took the bench to the back of the wagon. "He's just desperate, and things never go well when he's desperate."

"Our real problem," Sable said, "is stopping this early enough. If she's really put on trial at the festival, there's no way to stop the execution. The entire Sanctuary, the city, and the Merchant Guild will be calling for her head. Even Atticus can't take on all of them at once."

"Can't he?" Thulan asked, packing up her cookware.

Sable dropped a spoon into a basket of utensils. "What sort of plan could he have? It would have been impossible enough just trying to convince Vivaine to help us stop the war. It's doubly impossible if I have to do it while accusing her of murdering innocent people in the north."

"Then why did you agree to it?" Thulan asked.

Sable flung her hand in the direction the playwright had disappeared. "Because Atticus wanted me too!" She hesitated. "And because I need to get my sisters out of Immusmala, and this seemed like a good step in that direction." She glanced at Thulan. "But what plan can possibly have me both accusing Vivaine and saving her?"

Thulan heaved up her heavy cook pot and sighed. "There isn't one."

Leonis shook his head and grabbed another bench. "This is all going to go very badly."

The drizzle had stopped, but the sky was still gloomy by the time the wagons were loaded onto a long, low supply boat. It was impossible to see the sun, but it couldn't have been much later than midmorning when Atticus led Sable, Reese, and Serene back to the keep. Ayda, who'd watched all their preparations curiously, followed along.

"Are there any Tien Sark being held captive?" Sable asked.

"Sam says there were two," Reese answered, "but Braddick had them executed."

"Can't blame him," Sable said, "but now that we have Gwen, it would be nice to question one. I'd like to know exactly what they think of Vivaine. If we can somehow manage to get her in a position to be influential again, I need to know exactly what they're expecting from her."

"Maybe we'll run into another one," Ayda said brightly.

"As long as he's already captured," Reese said.

They reached the council room and found the lords and Braddick still there, now joined by Sam and several other officers.

Lord Loren looked up from the map they were poring over and pointed to a small scroll at the end of the table. "We've written out the accusations we have against Vivaine and our permission for you to read them in our place."

Sable nodded and picked up the paper.

Ayda crossed to the window. Their room in the tower was higher than any of the other buildings in the keep, and the distant hills were visible over the city.

"General Braddick will lead the combined armies to the narrows near Tutella Island," Sam said. "Where we'll make our stand."

"Good," Reese said, studying the small markers spread across the map labeled with the colors of the Northern Lords. The south held several black ones painted with a silver dragon.

Braddick picked up a black marker. "If the stories are true," he said to Andreese, "you threw a knife and assassinated the Kalesh ambassador while he watched a play."

Reese's hand twitched on the map.

"Ah." Braddick nodded. "Frankly, I didn't believe you had the mettle for it." He motioned to the paper in Sable's hand. "If this trial turns out to be a farce and the Dragon Prioress looks like she will survive the day, you are ordered to throw one of your knives at her before she can cause the north more pain."

"I'm not one of your soldiers, Braddick."

"You serve the north," the general said with a shrug, "so, according to the will of these lords, you serve me." He met Reese's angry gaze with a condescending one. "She burned your friend Tylar alive and murdered General Tanis. We all know you want to kill her."

Lord Perric nodded, moving to the window. "That is an excellent idea, Braddick." He turned to face the room, crossing his arms and leaning back on the sill. "If the trial is going poorly, Andreese, you will end things. Do it quickly, and don't miss."

"He won't miss," Braddick said. "Knife throwing is his one skill."

"If the Dragon Prioress is pardoned," Sable said, "and Reese assassinates her in public, they'll hang him. Right then and there."

"Then he should make some sort of escape plan," Braddick said. "I'm sure your theater troupe can come up with something."

"You're mistaken if you think I'm going to carry out your orders," Reese said.

"If you don't," Lord Perric added from the window, "and Vivaine survives, I don't suggest showing your face in the north again."

Something flashed in the window, and Lord Perric flinched. His mouth fell open, and he lifted his hand to his neck where a small shaft was embedded.

Lord Perric coughed and crashed forward to his knees.

"Get down!" Braddick yelled, ducking low against the table.

Reese grabbed Sable's arm and pulled her down to the floor. "Ayda!" he shouted. "Get out of the window!"

The elf had shifted on the window, her eyes blazing, her attention fixed across the keep. "The coward is running away."

Reese ran to the window, staying hunched low. "Where?"

Sable crawled over and peered over the windowsill. Ayda pointed to a man running across a flat roof on the far side of the courtyard, wearing the dark blue uniform of the city's soldiers. Sable felt Purn's hand on her arm.

Sable grabbed the kobold's unseen hand. "Purn! Follow him! But don't let him know you're there!"

There was a pop, and the feel of Purnicious's hand disappeared just as the man on the roof vaulted over the crenelations at the edge, dropping from view.

Ayda frowned at the empty roof. "What's Purnicious going to do?"

"She'll let us know where he goes," Sable said. "Or maybe Serene can track her."

"I could find her easily," Ayda said. "She's so exuberantly alive. She stands out among you humans like a bonfire on a dark night."

"What did he look like?" Reese asked Ayda.

"Cowardly. Who shoots a man from a distance then runs away?"

"An assassin. What did he look like?"

"Human," Ayda said.

Serene pushed her way through the generals and lords who'd rushed to Perric's side. The lord let out a wet, gurgling cough.

Reese took a deep breath. "Of course he was human. Did you see a hair color?"

"Darkish?" Ayda said. "But all your hair is darkish. None of it shines."

"Did he have tattoos on his neck?" Reese asked.

Ayda paused. "Maybe. His neck was dark too. Like it was hairy or he wore a tall, tight necklace."

Reese swore. "No one touch the dart! If it's Tien Sark, the shaft will be poisoned in an effort to harm any healer who comes to help."

Braddick ran to the hall, barking orders at the guards.

The roofs across the courtyard were empty.

Shouting came from somewhere inside the building. In a few heartbeats, an alarm bell started ringing, and soldiers began pouring out of every building.

Reese moved toward Perric, staying low. The others had backed away from the lord, who now lay on the floor, his body spasming and coughing. His eyes were fixed open in fear, and the whites had turned a bloody red.

Serene knelt with her hand on his chest, her eyes closed, her face creased in concentration.

Reese set a hand on Serene's shoulder. "It's too late. They call that poison *zat'roko,* bloodeye. It's very fast."

She pressed her hands harder into Perric's body.

His motions weakened, his cough coming in short bursts until he gave one last gasp and grew still.

CHAPTER THIRTY-FIVE

PERRIC'S BODY lay on the floor, empty and still. The arrogance and confidence he'd always exuded was gone, replaced by a face frozen in fear and pleading, his eyes a bloody red.

Serene swore and sank back, shaking out her hand.

Reese knelt and closed Perric's eyes.

Ayda sat in the window, her eyes fixed on the unmoving lord with an intensity that almost crackled. "He's dead?" the elf whispered. "That fast?" She looked around the room as though everyone in it had suddenly become something monstrous.

Braddick strode back into the room, crossing to the window and scanning the buildings outside.

Lord Runess stayed crouched on the floor, lower than the windows. "How did a Kalesh assassin get into your keep?" he demanded, glaring at Lord Darien.

Reese rose and looked out the window. "The Tien Sark can get in anywhere." He moved back to the table. "You can all sit. We'd be vulnerable in the window, but the roofs outside are too low to see us at the table."

Slowly, nervously, the other lords returned to the table. Sable took a seat next to Reese. She could just see Perric's head on the floor. Rubbing the side of her neck absently, she glanced outside. From the table, she couldn't see the other roofs, but she let out a breath of relief when Braddick pulled closed the windows, putting thick, wavy glass between the room and the outside world.

When he reached Ayda, she twitched away from him, hopping off the windowsill and letting him pull the last window closed. When Braddick moved away, she leaned against the wall between two windows, her back to the thick stone wall, her arms crossed, and her gaze raking across the room.

Lord Runess was the only person still crouched on the floor in the corner.

"Everyone can retake their seats," Braddick said, striding back to the head of the table. "We'll stay away from the windows until we've caught the man responsible."

"They've just assassinated the most powerful lord in the north," Lord Runess said, not rising. "Which makes me the next obvious target."

Reese shook his head. "If he'd wanted you dead too, he'd have waited until he could take out both of you while he had the advantage of surprise." He considered the other lords around the table. "Perric was the better choice, though. He wasn't only the most powerful lord, his death also leaves a huge vacuum in his territory. With his heir so young and no obvious trusted general to lead his troops, his territory is weakened, which affects us too. Without a clear leader of his army, unification will be slower and more chaotic."

"The *better* choice?" Braddick asked.

"From a Kalesh point of view," Reese added.

Braddick studied him. "Just how long did you spend in the Empire?"

"Long enough to learn to hate how they govern themselves and treat the people they conquer." Reese gave Braddick an annoyed look. "I promise you, there is no one in this room more opposed to the Empire than me."

"I'd hardly expect you to confess a secret admiration of them in present company," Braddick said.

Three soldiers and a healer came into the room, hurrying over to Lord Perric's body. Reese warned the healer about the dart, and she wrapped it in a cloth before removing it, then nodded for the soldiers to load the body on a stretcher.

"This changes things," Lord Darien said, watching them carry Perric's body from the room. "We have much to discuss." He glanced at Sable. "You have your orders. We'll expect a report from you on Tutella Island once the festival is over." He looked pointedly at Reese. "And we expect to hear the prioress has been taken care of."

The lord turned back to the table, and several voices began talking at once. Atticus motioned toward the door, and Sable trailed him out into the hall and down the stairs. Jae and Serene followed immediately, with Ayda and Gwen coming behind.

A few soldiers moved through the keep, hands on their weapons, opening every door they came to and ducking in to search the room.

"Can either of you track Purnicious?" Sable asked Serene and Ayda, who had stopped a few steps from the bottom. "I sent her after the Tien Sark. If we can find him, we can notify the city guard of where he is."

Serene nodded. "If I have a general idea where she is, I can probably find her."

Ayda closed her eyes. "That way." She pointed straight at a wall. "But far away. Maybe past the city wall."

"Are you sure?" Serene asked.

The elf opened her eyes. "Can't you feel her? She's so different from a human. She's like an elder tree, or one of the pools that's inhabited by a naiad." Ayda's eyes took on a distant look. "She's past the wall, definitely, heading up the nearest hill." She glanced at Sable. "Your phoenix is back in those ruins again on the barrow, if you're wondering."

"I wasn't," Sable said, "although now I'm wondering why she keeps going there."

Some footsteps on the stairs caught their attention, and Sam came into view.

"Do you have any monks near the western gate who can help apprehend a Tien Sark?" Reese asked.

Sam raised an eyebrow. "There are two, but I can send for more to follow us." He motioned for a servant to come over.

"I need to get back to the boat and make sure everything's ready to leave," Atticus said. He glanced at Gwen. "Are you coming with me?"

She hesitated. "If they capture him, they might need me."

Atticus gave them a worried look. "You all be careful. And hurry."

Reese and Sam set a quick pace out of the keep, through the city streets, away from the river, and toward the western gate. Reese scanned the crowd around them on the avenue. "I wonder how many Tien Sark are here," he said quietly.

Sam walked with his hand resting on his sword hilt. "I don't know. It could have been carried out by just one person."

"The man died so fast," Ayda said. "I've heard humans were fragile, but that...He was fine, and then...he was dead."

"Bloodeye works fast," Reese answered. "I'd imagine it would kill an elf quickly too."

Ayda frowned at the idea. "Can you not heal yourselves?"

"Very slowly," Serene said. "Not from something like that."

Sable glanced back at the stone keep. "It's bad timing with Perric dismissing all his generals a couple of weeks ago." She glanced at Reese. "Why would they risk a coup when we're on the brink of war?"

Reese shook his head. "I always thought Perric's generals were loyal. Most have served him their whole lives. I have friends in his troops, and if there were feelings of sedition among his generals, they hid it well."

"How did he find out about it?" Sable asked Sam.

"Within a couple of days, three different reports of secret meetings and a letter detailing the murder of him and his family, which was explicit enough that Perric imprisoned the men immediately and dismissed anyone close to them."

"Did the generals confess?"

"It would lead to their immediate execution, so no. They all claim the reports weren't true."

Sable frowned. "Maybe they weren't. Maybe someone wanted to destabilize Perric's troops."

Reese slowed to a stop, and everyone else drew up as well. "This is exactly what the Tien Sark would do. Plant a false report to weaken Perric's forces before they assassinated him. Then his death leaves a power vacuum." He started walking again. "If our assassin is a Tien, they may have been planning this for weeks."

They passed out of a city gate, gathering the two monks stationed there and leaving directions for the others that would be following them. Hurrying through the small number of army tents that wrapped this far around the city, they headed for the pine forest that covered the hills to the west where Ayda claimed Purnicious was waiting. Before they reached the end of the camp, the rain started again, and Sable pulled up the hood of her cloak.

"Be careful, Purn," she whispered.

Guided by Ayda, Reese led them on a circuitous path, entering the forest far from where Purnicious was stopped. He motioned for them to move quietly as they drew closer.

Sable felt Serene cast out. The group around them flared to pillars of heat, Ayda burning hotter by far than the rest of them. As the wave moved through the forest, it revealed the slight warmth of the trees, then, near the top of the hill they were climbing, the fiery heat of a human sitting on the ground and the blazing form of Purnicious.

"At the top of the hill," Serene said quietly.

Sable placed her feet down quietly in the damp pine needles, peering through the trees, looking for any sign of the Tien Sark. A little pop sounded, and Purnicious appeared ahead of Reese.

"He's at the top of the hill," the kobold whispered, "resting against a tree. Not asleep, though. He'll hear you before you get much closer."

"We could come at him from all sides at once," Reese said to the monks.

"I can reach him without him hearing me," Ayda said. "I'll walk on the breeze."

Sable looked at her. "Is that what you call it when you appear and disappear?"

Ayda nodded. "It's quieter and faster to walk on the breeze, but it takes a little bit of effort."

"What will you do once you reach him?" Reese asked. "He'll have at least a knife on him, if not a sword."

Ayda shrugged. "A knife can't hurt a tree. At least not easily."

"A tree?" Sable asked.

Serene took a step toward the elf, her face intrigued. "You're going to change?"

"Yes, and I'll pin him in place so you can talk to him."

Reese looked between Serene and Ayda. "What are you talking about?"

"I'll walk on the breeze so he can't hear me," Ayda explained, as though this was all obvious. "When I reach him, I'll change into a tree with my roots over him so he can't move, then you can come ask him whatever questions you have." Her brow creased. "I don't like him. I'll pin him tightly."

Reese stared at her. "You'll…change into a tree?"

"Elves in the Greenwood can do that," Serene said. "But it takes too long. He'll wake up long before you've finished changing."

Ayda waved her hand at the idea. "Oh, that won't be a problem." She turned to Purnicious. "Could you help me change back? I'll need something to anchor me."

"Turn back into an elf?" Purnicious's little brow creased. "I don't know how."

"Just set your hand on me and remind me that I can be an elf." Ayda crinkled her nose. "Sometimes I forget that."

Purnicious looked dubiously at her.

"It's easy," Ayda assured her. "The way you coax a piece of fabric to grow or shrink. Just coax me back to being an elf."

"I can try," Purnicious said, not sounding particularly confident.

"If it doesn't work," Ayda continued, unconcerned, "you can just leave me here. At some point, I'd appreciate it if someone went to the Greenwood and told my brother where I am. He'll anchor me back. But there's no rush. It's a lovely thing to be a tree."

"You can really become a tree?" Sable said. "So when we first met, and talked about being brave, and you said we should all be trees, you were speaking literally?"

Ayda nodded. "Of course. Weren't you?"

"No," Sable said. "Not remotely."

"Is this going to work?" Reese asked.

Serene shrugged doubtfully.

"It'll work," Ayda said firmly. "The man will be pinned. What you do with him at that point is up to you." Her brow furrowed. "At least, I'll pin him at first. If you take too long, I might forget he's there, and if my roots shift, he might be able to wiggle out. It wouldn't be fast, but once I've changed, you should come and do what you need to do." She gave them a bright smile. "This is fun!"

Reese held out a hand. "How long before you might forget?"

But Ayda turned and disappeared.

Reese swore, and Sable scanned the woods, looking for any sign of Ayda.

"Elves," Serene muttered, starting forward. "He's up at the top. See the tree with the twisted trunk? Just past that." She cast out again, and Sable felt the flare of Ayda's heat moving uphill. "Ayda's heading that way too."

"Spread out," Reese said, "and move quietly. I'll go around the back. We'll approach him from all sides. Gwen and Sable, hang back until Ayda pins him or we get him immobilized, we'll call you to question him." Reese and the monks moved quickly and quietly away through the woods.

Serene started forward slowly, and Sable followed her with Gwen and

Purnicious. Serene cast out again, and Sable felt Ayda's heat drawing close to the Tien Sark.

Sable caught a glimpse of the blue-clad soldier's legs sticking straight out in front of him as he leaned against a fat tree trunk. They moved closer, letting more of the man become visible.

Ayda appeared out of thin air standing over him, one foot planted on either side of his legs.

The Tien Sark grabbed a knife at his belt, but even faster than he could draw it, Ayda flung her arms up. Her fingers splayed out, multiplying and sprouting dozens of small branches. Her arms thickened, and her skin turned to silvery, smooth bark.

Sable's feet stumbled to a stop, and Gwen and Serene froze next to her. The Tien stared at Ayda in shock for a heartbeat, which was all it took for her toes to burrow down into the ground in long, probing roots and her legs to grow together, twisting to become a shimmering trunk.

The Kalesh man tried to scramble back, but the tree he'd been leaning against blocked him, and before he could pull his legs away, Ayda's roots slithered across them, pinning him to the ground. More roots darted out, wrapping around his waist and stomach before the ends dove into the ground, immobilizing everything from his ribs down.

Her branches grasped higher, growing almost faster than Sable could see. Her hair rose and spread, slithering up the branches and bursting into pale green leaves, vibrantly bright in the drizzly light.

The only elf-like thing left about the tree was her face, looking down at the man with a frighteningly emotionless expression carved out of wood.

He wrestled a small knife out of somewhere between Ayda's roots and, with a cry, stabbed it into her trunk.

The tip of the blade barely sank in, but the Ayda-face that had been smoothing slowly into the trunk suddenly jutted forward, her expression furious. A thin branch swung down and slapped his wrist. He yanked his hand back, but the branch caught it, wrapping and tightening like a snake around his arm.

"You," she hissed, the words drawn out in a frightening mix of Ayda's voice and the raspy creak of wood, "should not have done that."

Ayda's roots exploded with dozens of spines, sharpening into vicious thorns.

The Tien Sark yelled something in Kalesh, pulling back on his arm and thrashing his feet, but Ayda merely shoved his legs down against the ground. Her branch hardened into a corkscrew around his forearm, straightening his elbow, then pushing further until the man cried out in pain and leaned forward to get pressure off the joint.

One of her roots grabbed his other arm and locked it against his side.

The thorns along her roots pressed into him from all sides, their tips easily cutting through the fabric of his uniform and sliding into his skin.

The man froze, his breath coming in gasps, his eyes wide.

Ayda's silver bark grew rougher, glittering in the rain. Her face sank back and smoothed into the trunk until there was nothing but a shimmering tree.

CHAPTER THIRTY-SIX

SABLE AND GWEN followed Serene closer to the trapped man. Reese stepped into view on the far side of the tree, a knife in his hand, looking warily between Ayda and the Tien Sark. The Kalesh man tried to twist toward him but hissed when the thorns on Ayda's roots dug into his arms and stomach. Sam and the two monks appeared, forming a loose ring around him.

The man stilled, watching them all warily. His upper back and shoulders were still propped up against the huge pine where he'd been resting. Roots encased the man's legs and hips, reaching up past his waist. Another pinned one of his arms to his side and trapped the other, still reaching toward Ayda, in a corkscrew of wood. Small, sharp thorns pressed into him from every angle. He was dressed in the dark blue uniform of one of Lord Darien's men, but above his collar, rows of tattooed scales covered his neck up to his jawline.

"I see you've met Ayda," Reese said, walking closer and examining the way the tree held the Tien Sark. "I confess I wasn't sure she could actually do this."

A finger-thin branch swept down and smacked him on the back of the head.

Reese ducked. "My apologies for doubting you."

Serene stepped closer to Ayda, her mouth hanging open. "That should have taken…so much longer. I've read of elves turning to trees, and even the most skilled can only change slowly and with a great deal of focus."

Ayda's leaves quivered.

"Was that a laugh?" Sable asked. With the man tightly pinned by Ayda's roots, she moved close to Ayda's trunk and pulled his knife out. A small branch bent down and brushed her shoulder. Sable looked up at the spot on the trunk where Ayda's face had been. "You're welcome."

Sable pushed back her hood. Ayda's branches caught most of the drizzle, but the sound on her leaves was less like a normal rainy patter and more like the tinkling of tiny bells.

"What do you want with me?" the Tien Sark asked, his accent almost undetectable.

Reese squatted down next to the man. "We're going to ask you some questions."

"I have nothing to say," the man protested. "I just came into the woods to rest. The city's been so busy I needed a break. I'm not deserting my post."

Reese set the tip of his knife against the ground and rolled the hilt between his fingers, spinning it slowly. "Exhausted from assassinating Lord Perric?"

The man opened his mouth as though he would object.

"I thought a Tien Sark would have more stamina," Reese added.

The man searched Reese's face for a moment, then relaxed back against the tree with the ghost of a smile. "Then you know questioning me will get you no answers."

"She'll get answers." Reese nodded toward Gwen. "You probably aren't going to like it."

The Tien studied Gwen as she stepped forward. "Torture won't work."

Gwen knelt next to the man, setting her hand on his arm just above where Ayda's branch held him.

The man flinched, looking at her suspiciously.

Even with the man pinned beneath Ayda's roots, Sable held his knife tightly. The blade was only as long as Sable's thumb and barely wider, but still, the handle felt reassuring in her hand. "It's a sort of torture," she told him, "but you won't feel it. That's part of what makes it creepy."

He focused on Sable, his eyes narrow.

"I'll show you how it works," Sable continued. "What's your name?"

A muscle twitched in the man's cheek, but he kept his mouth shut.

"Talzek," Gwen answered.

He twitched back toward the Mira, trying to twist his arm away, but Ayda's branch still held it fast, and her thorns dug into his skin.

"See? Creepy," Sable said.

"Why are you here?" Reese asked.

Talzek glared at Gwen, still shifting his body against his bonds.

She gave him a contemptuous snort. "By the time you try not to think of the answer, you've already thought of it." She looked up at the others. "He was sent to weaken the north. He's been learning about the lords. He started the rumor about Perric's generals, and he decided Perric was the best lord to assassinate."

"How long have you been here?" Reese asked.

"A year," Talzek snarled.

Gwen shook her head. "About six months."

"Have you seen Zenivah?" Sable asked, leaning against the Ayda-tree.

Talzek turned his stony gaze to Sable. Little spots of blood appeared at the holes in his uniform where the root spikes dug in.

"He is upset that he has not." A smile curled up the corner of Gwen's lips. "He imagines her younger and more beautiful than she really is. Sort of fiery."

"She's not fiery," Sable said. "She's more like ice. Old, self-absorbed ice."

"She is dangerous," Talzek said, his teeth flashing in a vicious smile. "And you are nothing compared to her." His words were warm with fervor.

"You may be disappointed when you meet her," Sable said. "She is dangerous, but she is not the mythological force you believe. She's an old woman who's relied on lies and deception to gain power."

The Tien Sark's look stayed contemptuous.

"He thinks you're too simpleminded to understand her," Gwen explained. "He's not particularly impressed with any of us."

"We tracked him from the city," Sable said, "trapped him with an elf who turned into a tree, and now you're reading his mind. What do we need to do to impress this man?"

A blaze of light flashed overhead, and Talzek struggled harder against his bonds. Sable glanced up to see Innov flying past. The phoenix dove into the trees, weaving among the branches, leaving a trail of sparks. Sable held out her arm, and Innov alighted, showering her with embers that bounced and rolled down her cloak.

Under Ayda's branches, no rain reached the phoenix, but her back still steamed from her flight. Innov ignored the Tien Sark and the people and fixed her eyes on the Ayda-tree. With a thrust of her wings, she flew up among the branches and nestled in, a bit of fire perched among the silver branches. Ayda's limbs trembled slightly, making her leaves shiver with what looked like happiness.

"Issable, Flame of the North," Talzek said, his voice suddenly calculating.

"It's just Sable," Reese corrected him. "How many Tien are here?"

Talzek's eyes lingered on Sable for a moment before he considered Reese.

"Yes," Gwen said dryly. "You're catching up now. Answer General Andreese's question."

"I was under the impression you were no longer a general." The Tien Sark studied the rest of the group.

"There are only four Tien Sark here," Gwen said. "One is…" She paused. "He left him near Steepdale, so in Lord Darien's lands. He was the lowest ranking. His scales don't even go up onto his neck."

"The one we captured?" Sable reached out and touched Gwen's shoulder, thinking of the Tien Sark in Tutella's chicken coop.

Gwen nodded, and Talzek frowned at the word captured. "Talzek," Gwen continued, "was sent here to the north, in Runess and Perric's land." She tilted her head, pulling her hand off his arm long enough to slap it. "Pay attention, Talzek. Where are the other two?"

He shot her a vicious look.

"One on the Eastern Reaches," Gwen said, "but he's probably come farther west to more populated areas by now, and the last one was sent to Immusmala."

"Then at least one of you has seen Vivaine," Reese said grimly. "The one sent to Immusmala is probably the highest rank." He leaned forward and pushed Talzek's chin up, studying the tattoos on his neck. "You're a Third File? Who's in Immusmala? A Second?"

Talzek met Andreese's gaze with enough arrogance that Sable checked to make sure Ayda's roots were still pressing against him. The elf seemed to have relaxed her corkscrew on his arm enough that his elbow was now bent the slightest bit in the correct direction, but the thorns still pressed into his skin.

"The Tien Sark in Immusmala has tattoos all the way up to his ears," Gwen answered.

"Second File." Reese sat back. "The Empire is serious about Zenivah, isn't it?"

Gwen glanced at Reese with a smirk. "He thinks you're stupid for having to ask."

Reese considered the man. "What are your next orders?"

"He doesn't have new ones," Gwen said. "They haven't communicated. They were sent to embed themselves and learn. He's been waiting for a signal to meet the others."

"Four isn't exactly a battalion," Sable said.

"True," Reese agreed. "When are the rest of you coming?"

A cold smile twisted across Talzek's face.

Gwen drew back slightly. "Soon. He expects when he gets the signal to move south, it will be because they are here." She paled. "A lot of them. Hundreds. He expects a fleet of boats bringing Kalesh soldiers to Immusmala."

"How many boats?" Sam asked.

"So many," Gwen whispered.

"How many Tien Sark?" Reese asked.

The Tien Sark gave him that chilling smile and let his head fall back against the tree. He began to chant low words in Kalesh, the rhythm rolling out quiet and monotonous.

Gwen frowned. "He expects a ship of them." She slapped his arm again. "Talzek, how many Tien Sark?"

But the man closed his eyes and chanted a little louder.

"Always with the chanting," Serene said, annoyed.

Gwen pulled her hand off his arm and wiped it on his shirt, as though he'd been dirty. "He's focusing too much on the words. It's a sort of meditation. If you have more questions, I might be able to get a real answer out of him, but it will be hard, so pick your questions wisely." She stood and backed away.

Sam turned to one of his monks. "We should get him back to the city so the lords can question him. Go bring a unit of soldiers."

The man took off toward the city, and Sam looked around the group. "You all have an interesting way of doing things."

"Unsettling, isn't it?" Reese asked.

Sam nodded. "But effective." Sam brought his attention back to the Tien Sark. "I'd be interested to know if he has insight into the rest of his army. Their plans to move north, or what targets they'll hit."

A bit of warmth pressed against Sable's legs from Talzek's words. He was still chanting, but his voice had dropped almost to a whisper. His eyes were closed, and unlike the tepid feel of the earlier chant, this was growing steadily warmer, and she made out the word "*zabat*." She hadn't heard the Kalesh name for a rebel since Bastian had called her one.

"He doesn't," Gwen answered Sam. "He knows only what is common knowledge here in the north. He hasn't had any contact with any Kalesh in months."

Sable almost interrupted to ask Reese to interpret, but then she heard the word "dragon" clearly. Gripping Talzek's knife tightly, she took a step closer. His eyes were closed, and the words were so quiet, she leaned closer. He was no longer speaking Kalesh.

"...have come at the bidding of the Dragon," he whispered, the words warm against Sable's legs.

Sable started to pull back. Coming at the bidding of the Emperor was hardly interesting news. She was turning away when something caught her attention about his stomach. Ayda's roots still wrapped around him. The bark still pressed against his shirt, but something looked off.

"The dragon will rise, destroy the chaff, bring peace and gold, and she will reward those who have served her even before they knew her," Talzek continued, the words whispery soft.

Sable turned back to him. The dragon wasn't the Emperor. He was talking about Vivaine.

"The dragon has called us," Talzek said, the words fervently warm, "and we have come to her..." His whisper grew quieter.

Vivaine had called the Tien Sark?

Sable knelt next to him, straining to hear the next words.

"Sable!" Reese's voice cut into her concentration. "Get back!"

She glanced back at him. "He wasn't sent by the Emperor..."

Ayda's roots lay across the Tien Sark's stomach, and it occurred to Sable what looked wrong.

The thorns were gone.

There was nothing but smooth roots and small bloody holes all over Talzek's clothes. His clothes that were no longer pinned against the tree.

Her roots had loosened.

Reese lunged forward as Sable scrambled back, but Talzek wrenched his arm out of the corkscrew and grabbed her by the collar, twisting her until her back was pinned against his chest. His other arm tore free. In one smooth motion, he ripped his knife from her hand and pressed the tip against the side of her neck.

Reese froze a pace from Talzek, his knife gripped in his hand, his eyes fixed on the Tien Sark.

Sharp pain cut into Sable's neck, and her breath came in short, fast bursts, choked by her rising terror and the crushing weight of Talzek's arm across her chest. She dug her fingers into his forearm, but he merely tightened his hold on her.

A drop of blood rolled down her neck. She swallowed, and a flash of pain shot across her throat. The tip of the knife pulsed with the pounding of her heart.

Reese's eyes flicked to hers, and behind his fury she caught a hint of fear.

He looked pointedly at her hands and shook his head slightly.

"Not a step closer." Talzek's breath was damp and hot on her cheek. "Or you'll lose the Flame of the North."

Reese held her eyes. "Please, Sable, don't try *anything* we practiced."

She shoved away the thought of the blade and focused on Reese. Right, the grappling. Lying awkwardly on her back, she didn't have the leverage to break Talzek's grip, and she'd never get *vitalle* out of his arms faster than Talzek could plunge the knife into her throat.

She squeezed her eyes shut, and fury at her own stupidity shoved back her fear.

"Did Vivaine call you here?" Sable asked, pushing her anger and her fear into her words until they were blistering hot.

"Zenivah," he whispered, "desired our help."

Every eye watched the Tien Sark. Serene flexed her fingers, her face livid. Gwen's eyes followed the trickle of blood Sable could feel dripping down her neck. Sable glanced down at Ayda's roots, hoping to see them tighten, but they were perfectly still.

Sam started to ease his sword out of its sheath, but Talzek tightened his grip on Sable's shoulders. The monk froze.

Reese shifted his weight. "Let her go."

"I would not dishonor the Empire," Talzek said, the words warm, "by missing the opportunity to rid them of a *zabat* just to save my own life."

"Then why haven't you?" Sable asked.

"Merely weighing whether there is anything more valuable that I could trade you for." His words slid warmly across her skin.

"The chance to report everything you've learned to your superiors," Serene offered.

Talzek shook his head. "Nothing I've learned is that valuable. You people will be easily conquered."

"What do you want?" Reese asked.

Talzek took in a deep breath, his chest pressing against Sable's back. She gripped his arm, her mind racing to find some way she could fight back faster than he could move his knife.

One of Ayda's roots dug into Sable's hip, and she pushed *vitalle* into it, willing the tree to wake up, but the connection was through her dress and the cloak, and she could barely funnel any energy into the root.

She looked at Reese, desperate for a sign of what she should do, but his expression was set in a cold, helpless fury.

"I don't think there is anything at all I want," Talzek said slowly, the words perfectly warm and true, "more than I'd like to kill the Flame of the North."

The fury drained out of Reese's face, leaving a raw, desperate terror.

Talzek twitched, and Sable tried to pull away from his knife, but his arm around her shoulders was like an iron band.

The Tien Sark leaned his mouth close to her ear. "And so the flame went out," he whispered.

Sable's eyes widened, and she waited for the tearing pain of the knife.

It slid into her neck smoothly, almost gently, before hot, blazing pain lanced into her and a burst of blood sprayed Talzek's hand.

Reese lunged forward.

Before he could reach the Tien Sark, a pop sounded next to Sable's ear, and Purnicious slammed down onto Talzek's chest with a savage scream, her lips drawn from sharp white teeth.

Talzek hissed something in Kalesh, a note of terror in his voice as Purn's hand shot out. Her fingers scrabbled at the blade in Sable's neck.

The knife twisted in a burst of pain, then the pressure of the blade disappeared, and the blunt, empty hilt rammed into Sable's neck.

Behind Purn, Reese drove his knife into Talzek's stomach, and the Tien's body lurched.

Purn's cry turned feral, and she slammed her hand onto the man's neck. He cried out something in Kalesh, but his arm around Sable's shoulders loosened, and she scrambled away, grabbing her neck.

Hot blood pumped between her fingers, and the trunks of the trees around her tilted to the side.

Serene crashed down beside her, shoving Sable's fingers out of the way, clamping her hand over on the wound. Warm *vitalle* rushed into

Sable, penetrating deep into her neck like a hot iron jabbing into the wound. Sable gasped at the pain.

Purnicious knelt high on the Tien Sark's chest, and as Sable watched, the kobold's hand sank *into* his neck.

Blood poured out around it. He grabbed for her, wrapping his hands around her throat, but she leaned closer to him, baring her teeth in rage.

Reese wrenched one of Talzek's hands off the kobold while Sam tore off the other and pinned it to the ground.

Purnicious shoved her hand farther into the Tien Sark. *"Do not touch my mistress,"* she hissed.

Talzek snarled at her, and Reese drove his fist into the man's face. His nose spurted a gush of blood—until every drop of it disappeared.

The red blood on his face. The blood coating his neck and Purn's hand. Every smear, every splatter of the Tien Sark's blood. Gone.

Sable's hand flew up to her own neck where Serene's hands were still slick with Sable's own blood.

Talzek's skin turned bone white.

The kobold drew in heaving breaths, her blue fingers still sunk deep in his bloodless neck.

Talzek twitched and opened his mouth, but no sound came out. He stared at the kobold in horror until he sagged back, his eyes wide and unseeing.

Purn slowly drew her hand out. The gaping hole that had replaced half the man's throat was edged with tattered muscles and sinews and a bright white curve of bone.

But not a single drop of blood.

CHAPTER THIRTY-SEVEN

THE KOBOLD SAT PERFECTLY STILL, staring at the dead man. Her breathing slowed, and her fingers began to quiver. Reese shifted closer to her, but she shrank away without looking at him.

Serene let go of Sable's neck and sank back, her hands covered with blood.

Sable lifted her fingers to the wound. The shooting pain deep in her throat was gone, but there was still a gash in her skin, and it throbbed when she touched it. Her hands came away wet with blood.

Serene tore some fabric from her shirt and handed it to Sable. "Hold that on it," she said. "I healed the tear in your artery, but the rest is still open." She shook out her hand. "We'll clean it and bandage it when we get to the boat."

Sable pressed the fabric against the wound. "Thank you," she whispered.

Serene nodded, her eyes already on Purnicious.

Sable scooted closer to the kobold, the motion making the world spin. "Purn?"

The kobold's eyes were locked on the hole in the Tien Sark's neck. Sable reached out and took her arm, gently pulling her off the man. Purn's whole body shook as Sable gathered her onto her lap. The kobold buried her face in Sable's shoulder and let out a broken, jagged sob.

Sable wrapped her free arm around the kobold's bony shoulders, closing her eyes and trying to banish the thought of the knife sliding into her throat. "Thank you, Purnicious," she whispered. "I'm so sorry. I was so stupid. Thank you."

Reese climbed over the Tien Sark and knelt at Sable's side, his breath still coming fast and rough as he took in the blood dripping down her cloak and soaking her dress. He reached out with a trembling hand to lift her chin, pulling her hand and the bandage away. He stared at the wound, then looked at Serene, a terrified question in his eyes.

"The artery was just nicked," Serene said. "So I could fix it, but she still lost a lot of blood. She'll be weak, but I fixed the worst of it." When the fear in his expression didn't disappear, she added. "Don't worry, I learned from your wound. I won't close it up until we've cleaned it out."

Sable pressed the cloth to her neck again and swallowed, then swallowed again. Each time, a slicing pain spread across the side of her neck, but she did it a third time to prove to herself she couldn't still feel the blade.

Reese smoothed Purn's black curls and pressed a kiss to the top of her head. "Thank you," he whispered into her hair.

Serene climbed to her feet and looked down at Talzek's body. "You shrank his blood, didn't you, Purn?"

Purnicious nodded.

Reese let out a breath that was more exhaustion than anything. "That was brilliant."

"It was horrible," Purn whispered.

He kissed the top of her head again. "It was both."

"I'm sorry, Purn," Serene said, a note of apology in her voice, "but once you've rested, we need to get Ayda back to normal. If we're going to get to Immuomala, we need to go."

The kobold wiped her tears on her sleeve and nodded. "I can do it. All I did was shrink things." Her eyes flickered to the Tien Sark, then away again. "It was horribly easy."

Sable let her go, almost reluctantly. The moment the kobold was off her lap, Reese pulled Sable closer and wrapped his arms around her in a crushing hug. He buried his face in her hair, his arms shaking.

"New rule," he whispered. "No going near Tien Sark. Ever. Even if they're dead."

Sable sank against him. "Agreed."

Purnicious set one of her hands against Ayda's bark.

The very ends of her branches quivered, and Innov took off through the forest.

Purn closed her eyes, her brow furrowing in concentration.

The entire tree trembled, then, almost faster than Sable could follow, the branches drew back, leaves sank into the bark, and the tree blended and melted and brightened until Ayda stood in front of them, her hair glowing copper in the gloomy forest, her feet set on either side of the Tien Sark.

With her leaves gone, the rain pattered down to the ground around her, landing on them all.

Ayda face was upturned toward the rain, her expression vaguely mournful until she blinked and looked around. She caught sight of the dead man and twitched away from him, taking a few quick steps back. "I…" She paused at the blood on Sable's clothes and the cloth at her neck. "I forgot, didn't I? The rain on my leaves was like…like I'd been dying of thirst. I…forgot everything else." She took a step toward Sable. "I let him get to you?"

"No," Sable said. "I was an idiot and got too close."

Ayda glanced back at the Tien Sark's throat. "What happened to him?"

"Purnicious," Reese answered.

Ayda's expression grew distant. "I…remember that…a little."

"I've never met a kobold before." Sam said, his eyes fixed on Purnicious.

She sniffed and gave him a little wave. "You've been very kind to my mistress. Thank you."

Sam raised an eyebrow. "Anyone who's not had better watch out."

Serene turned to Sable. "Before he grabbed you, did you say Talzek wasn't sent by the Emperor?"

Sable nodded. "He said *The dragon will rise, destroy the chaff, bring peace and gold, and she will reward those who have served her even before they knew her. The dragon has called us, and we have come to her.*"

"Vivaine called the Tien Sark?" Gwen asked. "How? I thought they serve the Emperor."

Reese looked down at the Tien's body. "They do serve the Emperor. But if a woman with an actual dragon called for them…"

Ayda stood a few steps from Talzek's body, hugging her arms to her stomach. "Do all the Kalesh bring this much violence?"

"The Tien Sark do," Reese said, "and the army."

"Will they really burn the forests?"

"If it suits them."

Ayda's lips pressed together in a slight grimace, and she pulled her gaze from the Tien Sark. "My people don't understand that this is any different from the fighting you usually have," she said, rubbing her hand over her arm.

"If you spoke to the king," Sable said, "he might change his mind."

Ayda gave a quick, shaky nod. "My father will listen to me," she said, the words warm. She dropped her arms and straightened her shoulders. "There shouldn't be more men like this here. Your army is moving to the island in the great river?"

"Tutella Island," Sable said. "If we can manage to get Vivaine's help, there may be a chance to avert the war, but if not…"

"I will speak to my father." Ayda took a deep breath and looked around the group, her gaze catching on Serene. The elf disappeared from view and reappeared so close to her that Serene took a half step back. Ayda pointed up at the taller woman. "You write in your books all the time," she said, the words almost accusing. "Do not write down how fast I can change." The words rolled out with a hint of the authority Sable had felt before from Victis.

Serene raised an eyebrow at the sensation. Dressed in her long, dark cloak, she stood like a tall shadow looming over the bright elf. "Why not?"

"Because it would change things that I do not want changed."

"It's going to make recording this little encounter more challenging."

"Then don't record this at all," Sable said.

Ayda flashed a smile at Sable. "Exactly. We'll just keep all of this as our own little secret."

"Feels like a small price to pay for Ayda helping us get help from the Greenwood elves," Sable said, "and there's really no need to record my stupidity for posterity."

Serene considered the words, then shrugged. "All right. No record of this."

Ayda beamed up at her. "Thank you!" She stepped back and took in the group. "I don't know why my people don't spend more time with humans. You're entertaining." Her gaze caught on the Tien Sark, and her smile faded, and she sighed. "Most of you. When all this is over, I think I'll spend a few years as a tree. It's so much less troubling." Without another word, she disappeared.

Serene cast out, and Sable caught Ayda's heat moving deeper into the trees.

Footsteps and voices drifted through the trees from the direction of the city.

"If you're in a hurry," Sam said, "you should go before whoever that is gets here. The lords might have sent soldiers with my monks. I'll…" He glanced at the body. "I'll do my best to explain what happened here. Honestly, it might be easier without the elf-turning-into-a-tree part."

Reese rose and helped Sable to her feet.

"Thanks," Reese said. "See you at Tutella after the festival."

Sam nodded and started toward the coming voices.

The downward sloping gangway shifted under Sable's feet, and the deck of the flatboat ahead of her tilted a surprising amount for being docked. Even the water in the river was oddly sloped.

"Whoa." Reese's hand closed around her arm, pulling her away from the edge. "No falling into the river."

She concentrated on the wooden planks of the ramp in front of her, but her feet and head felt heavy. Worse, all the parts connecting her feet to her head felt heavy.

The walk from the woods where they'd left Sam with the body of the Tien Sark had been endless. At first, she'd felt just a little tired, but the farther they'd walked—and Barrowford seemed to grow larger with each step—the heavier she'd felt.

Her steps had lagged, and Reese had slowed along with her while the others had hurried ahead to make sure everything was ready to leave. Now, only steps from the boat, she felt like she was wading through water or waist-deep sand.

"Sable!"

She heard Atticus's voice from somewhere far away, and she looked up to find him, but turning her head quickly sent the world spinning again, and though she was sure she was staying upright, everything else slid quickly to the left.

"That's it," Reese said firmly, sweeping her up into his arms.

"I'm fine," she protested, even as she leaned her head against him. She closed her eyes, blocking out the dizzying way the world still spun.

"Yes." Reese carried her onto the boat. "You're fine."

"Sable?" Atticus's voice came again, closer this time.

Sable was lowered onto a hard wooden surface. She opened her eyes to blink up into the grey clouds and the white curls of Atticus's head. His face looked old and worried, and she managed a small smile.

"I'm fine," she said, although the words came out less clearly than she'd intended. She was lying on a wooden bench along the side of the boat. Someone called out a command to move the gangway, and the wood beneath her head rumbled, then oars splashed into the water and the boat rocked gently into the river. Atticus moved her hair out of the way to look at her neck.

"I'm fine," she repeated. "Serene fixed the bad part."

"Did you?" Atticus asked, looking over his shoulder.

He moved aside so Serene could kneel down. Sable's eyes slipped closed, and a warm, wet cloth rubbed across her neck. "Jae, where are my herbs?"

For a few minutes, Serene's fingers worked near the wound, then she wrapped a bandage gently around Sable's neck. "Try not to dislodge this," she said. "I don't want to wrap it too tightly around your neck, so just be careful."

Serene shifted her hand to Sable's forehead, and *vitalle* seeped into her like warm water. The tired feeling in her eyes washed away, the sluggish feeling in her brain cleared, and the heat spread down into her chest. Sable took a deep breath. Her arms and legs still felt heavy, but she let out a contented sigh. "Serene," she said, her voice a little steadier, "you are my favorite person."

"She is?" Reese asked, sitting on the bench by Sable's head. "I just walked with you all the way across the city, keeping you from running into walls, children, and three different merchant stands. What do you have against fruit merchants?"

Sable looked up at him. "Maybe I'm hungry, and you kept me from eating."

He held a little loaf of bread over her. "I would never."

She caught the scent of honey. "Is that Brother Matthew's honey bread?"

Reese nodded. "One of the monks gave us a basket for lunch."

She reached up for it but missed and grabbed his wrist.

"Who's your favorite person?" he asked, holding it out of her reach.

She squinted up at him. Instead of shifting to get the bread, she started to pull a little *vitalle* out of his arm. The trickle was slow and small, and she doubted she could pull more even if she tried.

"Resorting to magic to cheat," he said, lowering his arm. "No wonder you like Serene so much."

Sable took the loaf with a victorious smile. "Maybe I needed energy more than I needed bread."

"Well, then." He took her other hand in his. "Take as much as you need."

Sable took a bite of the bread. It was warm and soft and delicious, and she took another bite before even swallowing the first. "The bread is good for now."

"Our captain assures me," Jae said, coming over to them, "that we can reach Folhaven at midday on the day before the festival. We should reach Immusmala by that evening."

"Good. Before then, we have some things to discuss." Atticus drew up a stool.

The others pulled up a bench and some crates.

The pine trees along the shore moved by at a quick pace while the boat rocked gently. Sable felt her eyes grow heavy.

"We need to make sure Vivaine doesn't go to trial," Atticus said.

"Except she should be executed," Reese said. "She is the reason all those soldiers died at Immusmala and why so many lives and homes were destroyed in the north. She set that in action, knowing the cost of it all, just to keep her own city safe and herself in power."

"You're not going to convince Atticus of that," Leonis said from where he sat at Sable's feet, slumping back on the side of the boat with his legs stretched out. "It's Vivaine."

"It *is* Vivaine," Gwen said, "and that's why she can't be executed. No matter what she's done. The entire power structure of the city revolves around the priories. We are already missing a Phoenix Prioress. If we execute the Dragon Prioress too, it will completely unravel the south."

"That is part of it," Atticus agreed. "Merely putting Vivaine on trial will cause trouble. If she is executed, especially for crimes mostly committed against the north…" He shook his head. "That would be dangerously disruptive. But there are more problems than that."

"Like the Tien Sark," Sable said, not opening her eyes. "If Vivaine called them here, they'll protect her."

"I agree," Atticus said. "Even if there are just one or two in Immusmala, they might do something like assassinate Eugessa, which would bring us back to the same problem of a dead prioress. Our bigger problem, though, is the dragon."

"The one who left her and took himself out of the entire situation?" Thulan asked. "Or are you talking about a different dragon?"

"There is only one dragon," Gwen said.

Atticus gave a thoughtful hum. "That is the root of our problem. There are several ways this could play out.

"First, if the dragon has really left her, he is somewhere on his own, and the Empire will stop at nothing to find him and use him."

"No one could control Argyros except Vivaine," Gwen said. "She hatched him. She raised him. If she has lost control of him, then he'll certainly never put himself under anyone else's power."

"I don't believe he can be controlled," Atticus said. "At least, he soon won't be." He gave them a self-conscious smile. "I've made a hobby of researching dragons over the years. Flibbet and I have read all the books and stories we could find. Argyros is young. Incredibly young. Dragons live for hundreds of years, outliving even elves.

"If Argyros's wings have grown strong enough to fly," Atticus continued, "he's reached a sort of adolescence. While there are stories of hatchlings being influenced by people, once a dragon can fly, it's an independent creature. I don't think Vivaine can control him any longer, nor could the Empire. But people have struck deals with dragons."

"What deal does a dragon want?" Thulan asked.

"There are tales of offering servants or wealth, herds of cattle, even human sacrifices to get a dragon to ally with a particular land."

"That's exactly what the Empire would do," Reese said. "They'd worship it. The Emperor would sacrifice anyone and anything for that sort of power."

"But if Argyros cannot be controlled," Leonis said, "then Vivaine's death is irrelevant to our dragon problem."

"Except I think the idea that he left her is highly unlikely." Atticus ran his fingers through his beard. "When I used to report to her about the things we discovered in our travels—"

"When you snuck off," Leonis interrupted, "to have your secret relationship with the Dragon Prioress, which you never told your troupe about…Yes, go on."

Atticus ignored the interruption. "Argyros was always with her. He never liked me. It sounds odd to say, but I think he was envious of the fact that I'd known Vivaine longer than he had. If Vivaine ever drew closer to me than a few steps, he'd move between us." His words spread through the group like a cloud of warmth.

"Are you saying the dragon is in love with her too?" Thulan asked.

"I am not in love with her." Atticus's words were not entirely warm.

Sable cracked her eyes open to find Atticus pointedly not looking at her, but the rest of the group was.

"It's less of a lie than it used to be," Sable said.

"Argyros is not in love with her," Atticus continued in an annoyed voice, "not like you're thinking. He's devoted to her. As though they share some bond that connects them on such an intimate level that somehow they feed each other."

"That is what Narine and Innov were like," Sable said. "Narine could sense what Innov was thinking, and the two of them were noticeably stronger when they were together."

"It's the bond between the two of them that troubles me," Atticus said. "I don't know where Argyros is, but wherever it is, he won't stand to have Vivaine harmed."

"Then what should we do?" Serene asked.

"I'm still working on it," Atticus said. "But if we let Eugessa execute her, which none of us doubt she will attempt, I think there's a good chance that either Argyros or the newly arriving Tien Sark army may very well raze Immusmala to the ground."

CHAPTER THIRTY-EIGHT

Sable's eyes slid shut as the conversation continued. The bread sat warm and satisfying in her stomach, but her limbs felt like they were full of lead, and no matter how dire the conversation, all she could think of was how nice it would be to sleep for a day or two.

"But you are offering no alternatives," Serene said to Atticus, her voice exasperated. "If she can't be executed or exiled to a prison ship, what should be done to her?"

"Ideally? She should apologize for what she's done and ask for forgiveness. Eugessa should accept, and Vivaine should convince the Tien Sark to find a peaceful solution to our current situation."

Sable roused herself enough to give Atticus an incredulous look. "That's a realistic outcome."

"Stranger things have happened than someone repenting the errors of their ways," he said.

Sable let her eyes close again. "Not if that someone is Vivaine."

Everyone's voices droned on, growing more distant and more jumbled.

Reese's arm slipped under her shoulders, and she came awake as he helped her sit. "The captain says there's a storeroom in the back with a hammock, and Serene insists you need somewhere quiet to rest. Can you walk?"

Sable nodded but took his offered arm. Atticus was watching her with a worried expression, so she gave him a smile that was meant to be reassuring. From the crease that appeared in his brow, she hadn't succeeded. Reese moved her toward the back of the flatboat and a structure that took up the back quarter of the deck. He opened a door to a room with crates and barrels stacked along each wall. They moved down an aisle between them. Near the back of the room, a thin hammock swayed in front of a window looking out the stern.

Sable climbed gratefully into it.

"You'll feel better in a couple days," Reese said. "Trust me, it takes a little while to replace your blood after you've let it fall out somewhere." He folded a small blanket and offered it to her for a pillow.

"Thank you," she murmured, her eyes closing again.

She heard a little pop, and the blanket beneath her head suddenly thickened. She wanted to thank Purn, but the words drifted off before they made it out.

For a moment, there was nothing but the gentle creaking of the boat and the swaying of the hammock, and even that began to float away.

"Are you all right, Purn?" Reese asked quietly, his voice low to the ground.

"I'm fine," she answered coolly. "I'm not the one who almost died."

The room was quiet again.

"It's normal to not be all right."

Sable opened her eyes to see Reese squatting down to Purnicious's height while she stood with her back to him, her face creased with misery. Sable started to reach out for the kobold, but Reese set his hand on her little shoulder first, gently turning her around.

"No one would be all right after that," he said.

Purn's shoulders crumpled forward, and he pulled her into his chest as she burst into tears.

"I can still feel it," she whispered, clenching her hand into a fist against him. "I can still feel inside his throat."

He set his hand over hers. "You will. For a long time." He pushed her shoulders back slightly until he was looking into her face. "But every time you remember how horrible that felt, make yourself remember it was what saved Sable. If you hadn't done that, the next time you felt Sable, she'd have been dead."

Purnicious took a shuddering breath and curled up against him again. "How can you do this?" she whispered. "How can you keep fighting if it feels like this?"

Reese opened his mouth but slowly closed it again and looked out the window. He stayed squatting on the floor, his arms wrapped around her small shoulders while Purn cried into his chest.

The rocking of the hammock was irresistible, and Sable's eyes slid closed again. The room and the boat began to fade.

"Will I ever forget how…evil it felt?" Purn asked softly.

He didn't answer right away. "No," he said finally. "You won't."

Sable cracked her eyes enough to see Purnicious still leaning against him. "I'm sorry I put sparkly gold fabric on the cuffs of your favorite pants."

Reese let out a little snort. "I ripped that off weeks ago."

"I know." She looked up at him with the hint of a smile. "But you left a few threads, so last night while you slept, I put it on again."

Sable woke in the dark. The hammock swayed gently, and the boat was quiet. The window next to her was barely lighter. She could see a spattering of stars amid dark patches of clouds and black jagged tops of pine trees moving by beneath them.

Her body still felt heavy, as though lifting her arms would take far more effort than it was worth. She raised a hand anyway and ran her fingertips over the bandage on her neck.

How had she been so stupid? The Tien Sark had drawn her in, and she'd fallen for it, like an idiot. Just like Vivaine had drawn her south with the army.

Letting out a groan, she closed her eyes.

"How do you feel?" Reese's voice came out of the dark room.

She turned and could barely make him out leaning against the stack of crates next to the hammock, his legs stretched out under her. "Tired. How long did I sleep?"

"All day yesterday and most of the night. It's a few hours before dawn."

Sable lifted her head, but it felt like a rock, and she let it fall back into the hammock with another groan.

"Does it hurt?" His voice was closer and worried.

"No. Just heavy." The little bit of motion had made the world feel off-kilter. "I didn't think I lost that much blood."

There was a rustle, and Reese knelt by the hammock. His jaw clenched, and he reached out hesitantly toward her neck. "You lost…a lot."

She felt the smoothness of the blade again, the horrible spurt of blood, and she squeezed her eyes shut. "I was so stupid to get close to him."

His fingers brushed across her neck next to the bandage, splintering the memory, and she grabbed his hand, pressing it against her skin, keeping the feel of the knife away.

"Possibly the stupidest thing I've ever seen anyone do," he agreed.

She opened her eyes to see the hint of a smile on his lips. He started to pull his hand away, and she tightened her grip on it. "Please don't stop."

He studied her face. "I'll leave my hand there if you'll draw some energy out of me."

"I don't need—"

He started to pull his hand away with a slight smile.

"Wait. I'll take a little."

"Good." He sank back on his heels and shifted so his arm draped across her and his hand rested more easily against her neck. His fingers were warm, and she kept her hand on his.

She focused on where her palm touched his hand and drew a small stream of *vitalle* out of him, letting the warmth seep into her. It felt like sunlight.

"What were you thinking about when you woke up?" he asked quietly.

"My cottage. I told Serene about the keyhole valley, and she wants to create a place there. A secure place."

"A stronghold." His words were soft, with a tone Sable couldn't decipher. In the dim light, she couldn't make out his expression. "She told me. It's a great idea."

"She invited me to join them there," Sable whispered.

"Of course you should be there." His voice sounded firm, but his hand on her neck tensed. He relaxed it. "You're just as creepy and magical as the rest of them."

"I'm not anything compared to Serene. Or Terrane."

He let out a breath of laughter. "I can feel you pulling energy out of my hand, Sable."

The flow of *vitalle* had strengthened, and Sable cut it off quickly. "I'm sorry."

"Don't stop," he said firmly. "You need more than you've taken, don't you?"

She wanted to object, but she felt hollow, and the trickle of energy from him had started to fill the edges. "You'll tell me if it hurts you?"

"It won't hurt me." His breathing grew more ragged, and he rose up onto his knees and leaned over her, bringing both hands up to cup her cheeks. He was close enough above her that she could make out the same desperation she'd seen as the Tien Sark held the knife to her throat. "You can take anything you need from me. Every single thing I have, just..." His words were hot, and pain creased his face. He squeezed his eyes shut. "When he stabbed that knife into your neck..." His hands shook. When he opened his eyes, she could make out the pleading in them, even in the dark. "Don't ever make me see anything like that again."

"I'm sorry. It was so stupid—" she began, but he kissed her, smothering the rest of her apology.

He pulled back far enough to look at her. "Don't tell me you won't do it again, because we both know that if you think something's important enough, you'll run straight toward it, and I love that about you, but..." He kissed her again. "Be careful. And keep Purnicious with you every second of every day."

She nodded, and he drew in a shaky breath.

He leaned his forehead against hers. "I can*not* lose you." Each word was hot, pressing against her, seeping into her. He loomed over her like an inferno of heat, and her own body was like a chilled, empty husk.

He shifted until he grasped her hand, their palms pressed together. "Take everything you need from me. I need you to heal."

She nodded, and he sank back to his knees, still gripping her hand.

Slowly, she focused on their palms, and *vitalle* flowed into her, warming her hand, then her arm, soaking its way up to her chest. He gripped her tighter, and she closed her eyes, the heat from him beginning to warm the edges of the gaping chill inside her.

CHAPTER THIRTY-NINE

BLINDINGLY BRIGHT AFTERNOON light filtered through the small window, and Sable groaned, turning away and making the hammock swing.

"There's bread and cheese on the floor beneath you." Gwen's voice came from nearby.

The woman sat straight-backed on the floor, pointing underneath the hammock with the feathery end of a quill. She was focused on the three different books open in front of her alongside a scroll held open by an inkwell and a silver hairpin. Without looking up, she moved the quill back to the scroll and finished writing a neat note.

Sable rubbed her eyes and sat up, her head spinning slightly at the motion. "How long did I sleep?"

"Nearly all day." Gwen turned a page in her book.

Sable scooted forward until her feet touched the floor and lowered herself down, letting the boat spin slowly around her. She picked up the yellow cheese and took a big bite. "Has someone been with me the whole time?"

"Serene wants you watched. Something about severe blood loss and something else I don't remember." Gwen glanced up. "Are your hands cold?"

"A little."

The Mira frowned. "Ice cold?"

"More like 'I dipped them in the river' cold. Not ice cold."

Gwen dropped her attention to the books again. "You're probably fine, then. I was supposed to let Serene know if they were ice cold."

Sable laughed and scooted over to sit against one of the large crates, pulling the food close to her. "It's comforting to be in such conscientious hands."

Gwen flashed her a tiny smile. "Serene knows you're strong enough to handle a little blood loss. The pregnancy has just made her overly protective." She grimaced. "And seasick."

"Do people get seasick on riverboats? I can't even feel us rocking."

"I don't know. She was inside this cabin for a long time with you and started complaining that the wooden crates smelled revolting."

Sable sniffed the crate behind her. It smelled very faintly of cut wood.

Gwen shrugged. "I have no idea what she meant."

Sable took a bite of the bread and tried to see Gwen's books. "What are you reading?"

"Kalesh stories." Gwen trailed a finger down one page in a book, then flipped to the next. "These are the only ones Serene has found anywhere. All the ones in Stonehaven were taken by Vivaine, and the three lords in the south who had decent libraries were visited by Sanctus guards who paid them four times what the books were worth, buying every volume that mentioned the Empire. Said the priories were creating a public library so people could learn about our ally."

"A public library?" Sable asked. "For a population that can't read?"

"That was Serene's thought as well. Although she is very taken with the idea as a whole and keeps trying to think of efficient ways to teach people to read."

"So Vivaine wasn't just after books from Stonehaven," Sable said, "she was after Kalesh books."

Gwen nodded, pulling a different book closer. "But I don't know why. Did she just want to burn them in the Sanctuary?"

"What are these books about?"

"One is recipes, which is utterly useless. This one is a ships log from a Kalesh merchant ship that docked last summer. Somehow Flibbet got hold of it. It's mostly a very dry report about a very long voyage, but it also mentioned that the social unrest in the Empire will undercut profits on their next shipment." She picked up the last book, and Sable saw two more slim volumes underneath it. "This is a set of books Serene stole back from Vivaine. They have Kalesh myths and fairytales, most of which are as incomprehensible and nonsensical as our own. There are a few that might be about Zenivah, but they don't use her name. Since the three volumes tend to repeat themselves, I'm attempting to sort whether it's a single story or multiple."

"Are you finding anything interesting?"

"Not really. These are recorded by some historian who collected stories and decided to consolidate them into a single series of books. What I can't figure out is whether he tried to give faithful retellings or tweak things. Every story has the same feel. He writes…oddly. He speaks of a woman with a dragon who helped the Emperor, but the stories are just details of the uprising she quelled, nothing more informative than that."

Sable swallowed a bite of bread and leaned her head back against the crate, surprisingly exhausted by the exertion of sitting and eating. She rubbed her neck, feeling the thin scar. "It's oddly relaxing that you don't care at all that I almost died," she said seriously.

Gwen glanced up at her. "You throw yourself into stupid situations more often than a prioress throws herself into prayers, and you always survive. It's hardly surprising anymore." Her brow creased. "The dragon here is definitely not Argyros. He's always described as 'shadowed.'"

"That glittery silver dragon is a lot of things, but not shadowy."

"I agree, but every mention of Zenivah's dragon—or the woman I'm assuming is Zenivah—calls him a shadow beast."

"Personality-wise, it fits," Sable said around the next bite.

Gwen picked a book up and handed it to her. "What do you make of this?"

The page held a short verse with a sketch of a dragon underneath it.

With flowing hair and elbows jabbing
The Mighty Dragon Queen went stabbing
Through her foes with scaled feet crabbing
Carried by her endless shadow.

"Aside from the fact that it sounds like it was written by a child?"

"I told you his tone is distinct." Gwen held out another book, open to the last lines of a story.

And when she poofed into view,
her smile did not whicker as the sun does,
but her fury reigned down on one and all
and everyone like the shadow of her shadow beast.

"It's the wrong *reign,*" Sable said, "and I thought horses whickered, not suns and certainly not smiles."

"Neither of those is as awful as *poofed,*" Gwen said. "The one thing that is clear is this does not sound like a silver dragon. So why are all the Kalesh so willing to assume Vivaine is Zenivah when she has a silver dragon?"

"Maybe Argyros is actually really old, and he used to be tarnished." Sable flipped to the next page.

Gwen let out a low laugh that sounded so free and happy, Sable looked up in surprise.

The Mira smiled widely. "That's funny. Can you picture Vivaine polishing each scale?"

Sable took in the woman's face. Maybe it was that she was dressed in a rich green robe instead of the stark priory white, or maybe it was that her hair was a bit disheveled from a day of sitting on a boat, but something was different. "You seem…happier."

Gwen's smile turned slightly self-conscious. "I feel happier."

"Wouldn't have anything to do with a certain burly woodsman with a knack for lighting fires, would it?"

Gwen sank back against a crate, dropping her eyes to the books. "It's weird, isn't it? He's so…"

"Nice?" Sable offered.

"Rough," Gwen said with another smile. "But fearless."

"That's because if anything bothers Terrane, he can set it on fire."

Gwen laughed again, a surprisingly fond note in it. "True, but I meant he's not afraid of…"

Sable waited. "The Kalesh? The Northern Lords? The priories?"

"Me," Gwen said, impatiently.

Sable stared at her.

"He's not afraid of me," Gwen repeated quietly. "He's not afraid to let me touch him."

The room warmed with the truth of her words. "It never occurred to me how isolating your gift is," Sable said.

"It never once felt like a gift until Terrane. He says he's bad with words, and this way I can know what he thinks of me without him bungling it up."

Sable raised an eyebrow. "And what does he think of you?"

Gwen hesitated, then reached out her hand. Sable fought back the old feeling of invasion that Gwen's touch always brought and wrapped her fingers around Gwen's slender ones.

An image appeared in Sable's mind. Gwen, but brighter. More beautiful, smiling radiantly.

Gwen pulled her hand away, and the image faded.

"Wow," Sable said.

"Reese has the same overexuberant idea of your beauty compared to what you really look like," she said with a smirk, "and knowing how Reese feels about you, I should be terrified by Terrane's thoughts, but…"

Sable nodded. "But it's also nice to have someone really see you and somehow still think you're better than you actually are."

"It is."

The water lapped against the sides of the boat in a muted, distant sort of way, and Thulan's laugh came through the cracks around the door. Sable looked at Gwen, who had turned back to her books, thinking how odd it was to be sitting comfortably with the Mira she'd hated for so long.

"I need your help," Sable said. "Assuming we can stop the trial, how am I going to convince Vivaine to use her power with the Tien Sark to stop the war? Or am I crazy to think that could work?"

"I think it's likely we can stop the trial. This is Eugessa, after all. She's never successfully stood up to Vivaine in a council. She'll never be able to pull off a public trial and end up condemning her." Gwen sighed. "Although I can't wrap my brain around the fact that Vivaine caused all those deaths." She ran her fingers over the feathered end of her quill. "I lived with her for sixteen years, Sable. Worked with her nearly every day. I watched her struggle with hard decisions if she knew not everyone would prosper from her choices. And now, I'm supposed to believe she made deliberate, calculated plans that would end in innocent people's deaths?"

"You know what she did to Narine on Tutella. Vivaine hurt her when she was already weak and dying. Hurt her gravely, and intentionally."

"I *know*!" Gwen closed her eyes and rubbed her hand across her face.

"But..." With a pained expression, she leaned forward and grabbed Sable's hand.

Memories flooded into Sable's mind.

Vivaine, standing in the doorway of a small, simple room in the Dragon Priory, smiling with a more genuine smile than Sable had ever seen on her face.

"You are not cursed, Gwen," the prioress said, a note of gentle correction in her voice. "You are remarkable. Your gift is a blessing straight from Amah. Never let anyone tell you differently. Those who have were too blinded, too trapped in their little worlds to understand how magnificent you are. If it felt like a curse, it was only because you had no direction, but here, in Amah's house, you will help me to keep the peace, to discern what people are really planning, to head off dangerous men's schemes. If you can help me make wise decisions, the whole city can prosper. You can help so many people, Gwen."

"And we did." Gwen's voice broke into the memory, drawing Sable back to the boat. "I learned of assassination attempts, and we saved lives. I learned what people really wanted, and the negotiations Vivaine made for peace were good and strong, and the south prospered."

The memory shifted, and Vivaine stood at the end of the council table in the Dragon Priory, leaning on her hands, her head hanging forward until her silver hair covered her face.

"It's all bickering and tantrums," the prioress said tiredly.

Gwen looked down at her own clasped hands, hands which still had the smooth roundness of childhood. "But these are the most powerful people in the land." Her voice was small.

Vivaine sank into a chair, and Gwen looked up at her. The prioress's face was younger, smoother. There was something softer in it. "Sit, my dear. You are so much like I was when I was your age. Wanting to help the world but finding so much pain when you try. And people who don't appreciate what you can do."

Gwen sat on a chair, keeping her back straight and her hands folded neatly in her lap. "How do you not hate everyone?"

Vivaine let out a sigh that sounded rueful. "By remembering that they are still small. Most people's minds never grow enough to understand the larger story of the world. They are mired in their own little battles, and they are territorial over their own tiny scraps. Amah has tasked us with the unappreciated duty of looking out for their good, even when they can't understand what that good is."

Vivaine looked back over her shoulder at the thin door in the wall, which was cracked open. It swung out slowly, and Argyros's silver scales slid into the room. Gwen tensed, but the dragon paid no attention to her. He merely moved smoothly to the side of Vivaine's chair and set his shimmering head on her lap. The prioress's face softened, and she trailed her fingertips over the ridge of scales above his eyes,

"People fear what they don't understand, Gwen. They fear Argyros because he is different. They fear me because I can speak with Amah—"

"No one fears you, Holy Mother," Gwen protested. "They love you."

"People love Narine," Vivaine corrected her. "As well they should. She is goodness wrapped in flesh. But no one fears Narine. Were she to command the city to give food to the poor, they would murmur about what a beautiful idea it was and then go home. If I were to command them to do the same..."

"They would find some food and give it to the poor," Gwen finished.

Vivaine nodded slowly. "Narine is gentle, and the world loves her for it. But remember, Gwen, if you are nothing but gentle, you can never fully use the power Amah has blessed you with. Power, even the power to do good, requires a strength that gentleness does not have. Do not be afraid to show the world you are powerful. The more powerful you are, the more good you can do." She looked fondly at Gwen. "Find the biggest stage you can to affect the world from. Then you have the power to do real good."

Gwen pulled her hand away from Sable. "It was there...I know it was always there, this desire she had to decide for everyone else what was right, but you must understand that she did do good. She stopped fighting and kept truces and worked tirelessly for unity in the south. She was always trying to keep her people safe. So these actions she's taken now are...they feel like they've been made by someone else."

"Perhaps they were," Sable said. "You know Argyros has been getting more powerful. Maybe he's changed her. Maybe with Argyros gone, she'll have returned a little to herself." She paused. "She really never let you touch her?"

"She said she was honest with me and it was unnecessary to touch. She told me it was a sign of trust in her that I never try."

"And you believed that?"

"I was twelve years old, Sable, and she was the first person, the *only* person I'd ever met who wasn't terrified of me. Who looked at me like I was a treasure, not a monster. Yes, I believed her. I adored her. I would have died for her without a moment's hesitation." She paused, then continued with a flinty look. "It's not like she's the only one who avoids me. You flinch any time I get too close."

"I..." Sable stopped, both at the accusation, which was utterly true, and the blazing warmth in Gwen's voice.

"So no," Gwen continued, "I didn't think it was strange that she didn't want me to touch her. Before Terrane, no one has ever wanted me to touch them. At least Vivaine was kind about it."

Sable paused. "Do you wish you were back with her?"

"No, but…" She sighed and gestured to the books. "This is the first useful thing I've had to do since I left Tutella Island. When I was in the priories, I was involved, every day, with the most important things happening in the south. Here I'm a vaguely useful tool that is occasionally brought along but always held at a distance. I'm on the periphery of your little band of actors, and I'm not even a shadow in the picture the Northern Lords see." Gwen rolled the shaft of the quill slowly between her fingers. "It's…challenging to get used to being totally unnecessary."

"What do you want to do?"

Gwen stared at the crates for a moment. "I don't know. It's nice to not feel like I'm sneaking around stealing people's thoughts." She looked down at the books. "Research is interesting. Except there isn't much to be done. We don't have enough books."

Sable studied Gwen, wondering what the Mira had looked like when she had been young and frightened. It was hard to imagine the woman as anything but a towering force of self-assurance. "You were always so irritatingly confident."

Gwen's eyes narrowed, and she looked up at Sable with an annoyed expression.

"I was completely out of my depth when I started with Narine," Sable continued, "blindsided by how wholly and completely Vivaine had taken every single thing I loved, and then you were there. Controlled, composed. Untouchable. You could take every thought from me, and I could do nothing against it." She leaned her head back again. "The stupid part is that if Vivaine had just asked for my help, if she'd treated me the way she treated you long ago, I'd have helped her do anything."

"She couldn't," Gwen said quietly. "She was terrified of you."

"She was definitely not terrified."

"I have never seen her avoid someone as much as she avoided you. She would mentally prepare herself before you arrived. Her words were always guarded, if she spoke at all. When you left, she would visibly relax."

Sable stared at her. "But I was nothing. I had no power to do…"

Gwen nodded. "It took me an embarrassingly long time to realize she was scared you would catch her lying, and even longer to realize that only someone who lied regularly would fear that."

"She never lied in public," Sable said quietly. "I used to go to festivals just to feel the warmth of her words."

"It's easy to be honest about wanting to have the goddess bless people," Gwen said. "It's easy to make public speeches bland enough that every word is true, and yet you've said nothing at all."

Sable looked at Gwen thoughtfully. "You were never scared of me."

Gwen shrugged, and a smile curled up the corner of her mouth. "I didn't care enough about you to bother lying."

Sable laughed. "See? It's that sort of confidence that is utterly unnerving." Pushing back the residual reluctance at the thought, Sable leaned forward and set her hand on Gwen's.

The Mira's eyes widened, and her attention snapped up to Sable's face. Sable focused on the fact that Gwen was familiar, that this moment felt like sitting comfortably with an old friend.

I'm sorry I've been afraid to touch you, Sable thought. *It's been a long time since I was actually afraid of you, and I was foolish not to notice that I still treat you like I am.*

"It's all right," Gwen said with a smile. "I've known since the day I met you that you were slow."

Sable returned the smile and dropped her hand. "So how do I convince Vivaine to help us? Just focus on how much she wants to be loved?"

Gwen shook her head. "She'll sacrifice that if she thinks what she's doing is the *right* thing. The only way she's working with the Kalesh is if she thinks that somehow she's working toward a goal so good that whatever pain this land suffers, it's worth it for the good that will come of it."

"What could be that good?" Sable sank back on the crate and closed her eyes. "She's inviting the Kalesh here. Opening the entire land up to destruction. I know she doesn't think of the north as her own, but the south will suffer too. How can she cause pain to her entire world and still think..."

Sable's eyes flew open. "'Find the biggest stage you can to affect the world from.'"

Understanding dawned in Gwen's eyes.

"She isn't planning to have this be her entire world," Sable said. "She's setting this up so she is embraced by the Empire itself. She hasn't cared about finding a new Phoenix Prioress or keeping this small part of the world safe because she's planning to ride the fame and power of her dragon into the Empire as a living myth."

PART IV

A return to her home that was never home. Only a place to be escaped.

The colors are bright, but never quite comfortable.

Most of the shifts are subtle here. A slight darkening of the stage. A brighter focus on an uncertain future. A hope that isn't ready to be grasped. All are shifts, but all are subtle.

Until the end. There is no subtlety at the end.

-Stage notes from act two, scene twelve of ***The Phoenix Rising*** by Atticus the Playwright.

CHAPTER FORTY

SABLE'S LEGS only felt a little tired as she kept up with the slow roll of Atticus's red wagon. The road to Immusmala stretched through the Tremmen Hills ahead of them, winding through the vivid green forests and dotted with other travelers headed to the festival.

Innov perched on Sable's arm, and the warmth of the phoenix sank into her, buoying her spirits. Sable dragged her fingertip down the phoenix's feathers, drawing out orange flames. When she wiggled her finger deeper in, the core of the flames licked around her skin in shades of blue.

The phoenix peered around the forest, contentedly leaning into Sable's fingers. Until the phoenix twitched and focused on the woods ahead of them.

"Do you have a scheme to stop the trial yet?" Serene asked Atticus.

"No," Atticus said. "We need to talk to Vivaine, but getting into the Sanctuary is going to be tricky. They don't allow merchants or troupes in for this Festival, and we're arriving late enough that it's going to be hard to get a spot along one of the streets near it. Even if we can find a way in, I don't have a good enough standing with Eugessa to get to see Vivaine, nor do you. We have very few friends remaining in the city who have any influence at all. We have Sable, who has Innov, and maybe the phoenix can get us in—"

Innov launched herself into the air in a cascade of sparks, circled the wagon once, then flew off over the forest.

"Sable might have Innov," Atticus corrected himself with a sigh. "We are very lacking in the sorts of things we need for a scheme."

"Innov starts the Blood Moon trials," Sable said. "She lights the bonfire that sits by the stage." She looked toward where the bird had disappeared over the trees. "Of course, I don't know if she knows that the festival is about to start or if she'll play her part."

"Seeing as she just flew off in the direction of Immusmala," Leonis said, "maybe she has some idea what's going on."

Sable rubbed a hand over her skin where the phoenix had perched and scanned the sky for any flicker of light.

"If she arrives on her own, and not with Sable," Atticus said, "we lose the little bit of clout we had."

"Are you sure you don't have anything planned?" Serene asked.

"I don't have a scheme!" He ran his hands through his hair, making the waves stand up wildly. "*Eugessa*"—he said the name with contempt —"will control the festival. *Eugessa* hates Vivaine. There is no way *Eugessa* will let this play out any way but with Vivaine's execution. Which will leave *Eugessa* as the only prioress in the Sanctuary. A role she will die before giving up."

Atticus's words were warm, but everyone's expressions remained skeptical.

"You always have a scheme, Atticus," Serene said finally.

They started up a long, gradual hill, and without Innov, Sable's feet began to drag. She moved over to the wagon and started to climb up.

"I feel all right," she said before Atticus could ask. "This is just a lot of walking."

He shifted to the side, and she sat next to him, the wagon jolting and bumping beneath her.

Jae stepped up close to the side. "Another lesson?"

"Yes!" Sable made room for Jae to sit next to her, and Atticus watched them curiously.

"I've been practicing with Reese." Sable held out her hand, and Jae took it. "He claims he's not tired of having his hand singed." She focused on where her palm touched Jae's, and instead of pulling *vitalle* out of him, she opened up a channel between them, imagining it surrounding the area where their skin touched. That act, which he'd had her practice countless times on the boat, changed everything. Instead of struggling to force *vitalle* through the barrier of skin, the energy in both their hands was right there, like two ponds of water, almost touching, just waiting to be mixed.

She drew in a breath and pulled some *vitalle* from Jae's hand into her own. It moved almost without effort. On the exhale, she pressed it back out. Her palm warmed the slightest bit, but mostly the energy moved effortlessly between them.

Jae nodded. "Getting stronger and not much heat. Good."

He pulled his hand away and took a stub of a candle out of his pocket. "Sometimes, though, it's the heat we're after."

Sable sat forward. "You think I can light a candle?"

"I think you can do a great many things we haven't tried yet, but of all the things we can do to living and non-living things, making them hot is the easiest. You made a channel between you and me because we were two reservoirs of *vitalle* and you wanted to reduce the energy wasted in heat, but here it's the heat we want, so just push energy into it. You're going to overload it with *vitalle* until it catches fire."

He set his fingertip against the wick. Sable felt the small rush of heat, and the candle lit. He blew it out. "Don't be disappointed if it doesn't work the first time."

"It'll work," Serene said from beside the wagon.

"Who's teaching this lesson?" Jae asked.

"Clearly it should be me," Serene answered.

"Ignore her," Jae said to Sable, holding out the candle.

Sable took it and focused on where her fingertip touched the wick. She pushed *vitalle* into it, the tip of her finger growing hot as energy flowed out of her. The air around the wick warmed, and the top of the wax softened.

Jae glanced down at where Serene walked next to the wagon. "See?"

His wife frowned at the candle. "You just need more focus," she told Sable.

He shook his head. "Serene muscles her way through things like this because she can move more *vitalle* with less effort than anyone I've ever met. We mere mortals benefit from some tools. For instance, a lot of us find saying a word helps us focus."

"You don't need a word," Serene said.

Jae waved her words away and continued to address Sable. "Your powers are so closely connected to speaking, *I* believe it will be almost essential for you to use words, at least while you're learning. Eventually, you may be able to do it silently, but I would guess you'll always be able to do things more easily and precisely if you speak. Serene disagrees, but the first time she tried to light a candle, she set Merrick's entire table on fire with barely any effort, so she doesn't count."

He touched the wick. "*Incende.*" A flame flickered to life before he blew it out.

"What's *incende*?" she asked.

"It means burn. You could just say *burn,* but the more specific the word, the better you'll focus. We use words from an old language because *burn* can mean an assortment of things to us, while *incende* merely means to set something on fire with *vitalle.*"

Sable touched the wick again, taking a moment to gather her thoughts. It wasn't truth, exactly, that she wanted to put into her words—it was a command. Maybe a sense of what she wanted to be the truth. She wanted the candle to burn. Leaning closer to it, she focused on the point where her finger touched the wick.

"*Incende.*" She shoved *vitalle* into the word.

Heat poured out of her fingertip. The top of the candle blazed into a flame, and she flinched away from it. Melted wax streamed down, dribbling hot over her fingers.

She blew out the flame and shifted the candle between her hands, trying to avoid the running wax.

"See?" Jae said to Serene. "Words."

Sable's eyes followed the thin trail of smoke rising from the wick. "I just…" She peeled the cooling wax off her hand. The fingertip she'd used to light the candle was red, but she set it on the wick again. This time she focused more closely and with less force. "*Incende.*"

A small flame ignited, and a smile spread across her face. "I can start a fire!"

Reese looked impressed from where he walked near Serene. "We're working that skill into your self-defense training," he said.

Sable turned back to Jae. "What else can I do?"

Shadows from the trees lengthened across the road. Jae had climbed off the wagon hours ago and had already finished telling two long tales about sea monsters. Sable had lit the candle a hundred times, and she was considering abandoning the jarring trundle of the bench when they bumped over the crest of the hill and caught view of Immusmala. The forest ended, and the road ahead wound downhill through grass. A line of merchants and festivalgoers moved down the hill, across the river, and in through the city gates.

Past them all, the grass that had always looked smooth and free outside the city was torn up. The ground by the wall was trampled and brown. Snippets of green grew up from the earth around three large scorched patches where they must have burned the bodies of the dead.

Atticus kept the wagon moving, and they started down the hill.

Sable pulled her eyes away from the battlefield and looked over the city, everything inside her growing tense. Dockside was hidden by the huge hill that ran down the center of the peninsula, but her eyes caught on the white spires of the Sanctuary. "Every time we come back here, I like it less."

"This place hasn't been kind to you."

Her eyes lingered on the roof of the Phoenix Priory, and even from this distance, it seemed empty and lifeless. "Do you think Innov went home?"

Atticus glanced over at her. "Do you think she still considers the priory home?"

"I have no idea."

He straightened, his gaze catching on something over Sable's shoulder. "It would appear not."

Innov flew toward them from above the forest, a shimmering trail of sparks rippling behind her. She made a wide arc over the hillside, soaring out over the river and then up above the traffic on the road and toward the wagon.

"I do love that bird's sense of drama," Atticus said.

Sable leaned forward. "What is that?"

Something fluttered behind the phoenix. Something thin and gauzy like an abbess's veil, but long enough to cover an entire person.

Heads below them on the road turned to follow the phoenix as she soared up to the wagon, landing not on Sable's outstretched arm but on the front corner of the wagon's roof. The strip of gauze fluttered down, pinned between her talon and the wood.

It was definitely not a veil.

The thin tube of almost clear whatever-it-was crinkled as it settled down between Sable and Atticus, wide enough that they shifted away from each other. It had the slightest shimmer to it, reflecting minuscule bits of firelight as Innov's embers rolled down and bounced harmlessly off.

It wasn't smooth. A pattern was pressed into it that looked familiar, like seashells. Sable touched it, and it held its shape, moving stiffly away from her fingers.

"Is that..." Jae stepped up on the edge of the wagon to look more closely. "Is that a snakeskin?"

"If there is a snake that big in those woods," Leonis said, "we are never camping there again."

"It's not a snake," Reese said.

Sable yanked her finger back. Those weren't seashells.

"It's dragon skin," he finished.

Perfectly formed impressions of Argyros's scales were stamped into the thin skin, each overlapping the other. The brittle membrane, the exact tapered shape of Argyros's tail, fluttered against the wagon, sliding across the wood with a dry, slithery sound.

Atticus glanced ahead of them on the road, where travelers had paused to look up at the phoenix and the wagons. He reached up and tugged on the skin. "Sable, get Innov to let go."

She stood on the bench, grabbing the corner of the roof for balance. "Drop the disgusting dragon skin, Innov." She put her forearm against the phoenix's chest. Innov hopped willingly onto her arm, releasing the skin and letting Atticus fold it quickly into a whitish, crinkly bundle that he tucked under the driver's bench.

"Maybe Vivaine isn't the only thing the dragon sloughed off," Leonis said, looking at the skin with revulsion.

"You realize what that means, right?" Reese asked, looking at the others. "Snakes shed their skin when they grow."

Sable glanced uneasily back into the forest Innov had flown out of. "That is not good."

Atticus shook the reins, urging the horse faster. "I told you we shouldn't discount the dragon."

CHAPTER FORTY-ONE

"Will you stay on the bench?" Atticus asked Sable quietly as they neared the city gates.

"Because you want to display Innov?" Sable asked.

"Yes," he said simply. "And you look tired."

"I am tired," Sable said. "So if you're about to ask me to change into fancier clothes, you're out of luck."

Atticus considered her worn traveling clothes with a slight look of disapproval. "That will suffice, if it must. It's actually not you they should be looking at. The city loves Innov, and she's been gone a long time. After everything Immusmala has been through, and with the events that are looming tomorrow, the people could do with a little hope."

"I'm positive there is more to your motivations than that," Sable said, shifting Innov to her other arm, "but I agree."

They rolled under the city gate, the eyes of the city constables following Innov with expressions varying from eager, welcoming smiles to suspicious scowls. The wagons moved uphill with the crowd, and Sable waved to the occasional calls of "Issable" that rang out.

They climbed up to the Spine, the broad avenue running down the high center of the peninsula, and the wagons slowed. With no access to the wide-open plaza of the Sanctuary during this festival, every merchant and performer had shouldered their way into a spot along the busy street.

Atticus steered his bright red wagon toward the Sanctuary, inching through the milling crowd. The street was packed with people, but there was something not quite festive in the air. Faces turned toward Innov, but instead of the normal wonder, they looked almost desperate.

"Where are we headed?" Sable asked.

"Not sure. I'm hoping for a spot to park the wagons."

"On the evening before a festival?"

Atticus shrugged. "It doesn't hurt to try."

She gave him a disbelieving look "You expect me to believe we're not headed to the Sanctuary?"

"If you already knew, why did you ask?"

"Because I was hoping you'd be honest with me."

Someone yelled Atticus's name from the crowd, and he waved at them, but his smile was more muted than usual. More people noticed the carts, and he waved greetings to merchants and shop owners.

"Will we see the show about Prioress Vivaine and the Baledin?" someone asked.

Atticus paused at the request.

Leonis swung up on the corner of the wagon. "As is tradition for the Blood Moon Festival," he called out, "the Figment of Wits Traveling Troupe will be performing the comedy of Lord Blossombritches and the Haunted Larder."

Several cheers went up from the crowd, and Leonis grinned. Atticus turned his attention back to the road ahead of them.

"That's…" Sable paused. "A more lighthearted choice."

"It's a good choice," Atticus said quietly.

"Of course it's a good choice," Leonis said. "It's the one we perform every year. This will help them feel nostalgic toward their home and, indirectly, toward Vivaine. You're welcome." He climbed up onto the roof of the wagon and called out personal invitations to the merchants they passed, hurling friendly jibes into the crowd and turning the eyes of those on the avenue to Atticus's wagon.

Something struck Sable, and she scanned the crowd. There wasn't a single embroidered dragon, and the dress shop they were rolling past had no Kalesh styles in the window. "There aren't a million Kalesh dragons around anymore."

"Or soldiers," Atticus said.

He was right. Not a single Kalesh uniform was visible. She ran a finger down Innov's neck. The thought should have felt hopeful, but somehow it was just part of the shadow hanging over the city.

Seemingly in defiance of the uneasiness, every corner of the next intersection featured a white-robed abbess standing on a small platform. They each held a flowering bough over the heads of a young couple standing at their feet.

"There are a lot of betrothals this year," Sable said.

The nearest couple looked adoringly at each other as the abbess spoke the blessings of the pledging ceremony. Sable dropped her hand from Innov and looked away only to see three more couples waiting for the next available abbess. Her fingers started to tap on her leg. "What are they thinking?"

Atticus glanced at the nearest abbess. "I would imagine they're thinking they love each other and a betrothal makes a good deal of sense." A smile snuck through his beard. "Would you like me to pause the wagon so you can join them? I'm happy to wait."

Her fingers stopped, and she turned to stare at him. "We're on the brink of a war, Atticus."

"I'm sure that plays into it too."

She spread her hands out. "So they pledge themselves to each other? Because they're anxious to get their hopes up extra high before they're smashed?"

He looked at her with a raised eyebrow.

Sable's fingers started drumming on her leg again. "It's foolish."

"Is it?" Atticus scratched at his beard. "They love each other and they're choosing to move ahead in the hopes that things...work out."

The wagon rolled slowly past another couple. The young woman's cheeks were flushed as she smiled blissfully up at the merchant guard next to her. Sable's eyes caught on the sword hanging from his belt. In a matter of weeks, he could be lying dead on a battlefield.

She wanted to shake them both.

Instead, she took a deep breath, moved Innov over to perch on the side of the bench, and folded her hands on her lap. It was none of her business what these people did. If they wanted to act as though the world was all flowers and wine, they had that right.

The wagon passed the couple as the abbess finished her blessing and the young woman threw her arms around her betrothed.

Sable pointedly looked away, sinking back against the cart. "Things do not *work out*." Atticus opened his mouth to object, but she held up her hand. "When I met you, I was trying to get Talia away from Kiva and Ryah somewhere safe. Did either of those things work out? No. Want me to list everything else we've tried and failed at since then? Do I need to list the people who've died who shouldn't have?" She dropped her hand. "And you can't argue with me anyway. You're in love with a woman who is forever out of your reach, Atticus, so don't tell me that I should 'hope things work out.'"

The words hung between them as Atticus kept his eyes forward, his attention focused too intently on guiding the horse through the busy street.

"I'm sorry," she said. "That was uncalled for. I don't know why all these couples frustrate me."

"Yes, you do," he said quietly. "But you're right. I never did have any hope for Vivaine and myself. Not real hope, anyway. That would have required her to actually want it too." He rubbed a thumb over the reins. "But had she ever looked at me the way that young lady looked at that young man, or the way you look at Reese, even the goddess herself couldn't have stopped me from doing everything I could to make it work." His words were warm and wistful. "I think I would have risked everything else for that chance."

The heat of his words sank into Sable's skin. She looked ahead down the road, searching for the tall Veil Wall that surrounded the Sanctuary. Vivaine was there, in one of those small cells under the Dragon Priory, and she had been for almost a fortnight. "And if she looks at you like that today?"

Atticus twitched the reins, moving the horse a little to the side. "She won't."

The wagon trundled slowly through the crowd. More abbesses stood among the people, handing out blessings to couples.

"Vivaine and I aren't the point, though," Atticus said finally. "I've seen a lot of people fall in love over my life and learned the tales of hundreds more. In the best stories, they come together despite the gathering storm and weather it leaning on each other."

"That sounds very nice." Sable let her head fall back against the wall of the wagon. "But I'm tired of hoping for things I desperately want, only to watch them all fall apart. There are things we can make happen and things that are out of our hands. In all your scheming and planning, you never lose sight of what we can control and what we can't."

He was quiet for a few moments while Leonis continued to shout invitations to the crowd to come see the show tonight.

"Well," he said finally, "I can't think of a single thing we can control that will keep Eugessa from executing Vivaine. So maybe I'm ready to just hope things will work out."

CHAPTER FORTY-TWO

WHEN THEY REACHED the Veil Wall, having found no space to park the wagons, the gate was open. Unfortunately, a half-dozen Sanctus guards blocked it, only letting in workers carrying parts of the large platform being assembled near the front of the Dragon Priory.

"Can you get us in to see Vivaine?" Atticus asked Sable quietly.

The Sanctus guards were all looking at Innov, and one of the men's faces looked vaguely familiar. Sable gave the man a nod, and he nodded back.

"Probably not." She moved to the side of the bench. "But maybe I can get Innov in to see her, and we can tag along."

Reese stepped up to the side of the wagon, his arms folded. "You're not going in there, are you?"

"Depends on how friendly the guards are," she said quietly.

"Think they'll let me come with you?"

She glanced at his scowl. "Depends on how friendly *you* are."

"This place does not make me feel friendly."

He offered his hand, and she took it and climbed down. "I couldn't tell," she said with a small smile.

"Don't get captured and thrown in the dungeon with Vivaine," he said, neither breaking eye contact with the guards nor smiling.

"I'll do my best." She started toward the gate.

Thulan pulled up behind Atticus, and the crowd in the street trickled around the bright wagons curiously, most of them watching Innov.

Sable could demand entrance, but she'd never been good at the sort of authoritative tone guards would listen to. She could ask politely, but they were used to saying no. Deciding her best option was to look confident, she held the eyes of the familiar guard and started toward him, hoping whatever question he put to her would help her know how to proceed.

Innov launched into the air, flying toward the gate. Sable stopped, trying to keep the dismay off her face. Without Innov, she had no chance at all of walking through that gate.

But all six guards focused on the phoenix. Instead of soaring into the Sanctuary, she arced over their heads, showering them with tiny motes of fire.

In their posture, Sable saw the shift. She'd been around Innov for so long, she'd almost forgotten that feeling. That moment when the phoenix flew over and every heart felt the whisper of hope, a brush of lightness across shoulders that had been burdened for too long.

Sable focused on the guards. These weren't obstacles for her to pass but men who had dedicated their lives to serving the priories. Men who'd not only lost the Phoenix Prioress but were on duty for a festival where the High Prioress they'd most likely admired their whole lives would be put on trial.

Innov turned and passed over them a second time, her embers falling like a pure form of the blessing that prioresses always handed out. The phoenix came back to Sable, landing on her arm in a bright whirlwind of embers.

Sable stepped closer to the guards. "May I bring Innov in to see the Dragon Prioress?"

Whatever hesitation she expected, she did not find. The two guards in the center, neither of whom she knew, stepped aside immediately. "You can ask the Prioress of the Horn," one of them said.

"Thank you." She nodded back toward Atticus. "And may I bring one of the High Prioress's oldest friends?"

The guards looked at Atticus with a bit more sharpness, but the one Sable knew nodded, and before the others could object, Atticus climbed down from the wagon and came forward.

Sable forced herself to walk steadily under the thick Veil Wall and into the stone plaza, suppressing a shiver as she enclosed herself again inside these walls. Atticus walked at her shoulder as she headed toward the bustle of activity in front of the priories.

"That's a lot of guards," he said quietly, nodding his chin toward the Sanctus guards lining the front of the Dragon Priory.

Before they were halfway across the wide courtyard, a glittering white figure came striding toward them alongside a night-black unicorn.

Eugessa's hair was dyed a rich, coppery red. Her hand resting on her black unicorn's neck was ringed with gold and silver bracelets. The sun was low behind the Veil Wall, and the unicorn moved through the evening light like a shadow. Innov shifted her wings and faced him, her talons tight on Sable's arm.

For a moment, Sable toyed with the idea of ignoring the prioress and walking straight to the Dragon Priory, but Atticus hummed something that sounded like a warning.

"Fine," she said, adjusting her path to intercept the Prioress of the Horn.

When Eugessa was a dozen paces away, she motioned for the guards trailing her to wait, and the prioress approached Sable with a scathing look. "Leave Innov and get out," she said quietly.

The prioress's powdered face was as cruel as ever, but it was the unicorn that held Sable's gaze. He had always been dark, but tonight he absorbed the little light around him, reflecting nothing back. She could just make out thick muscles rippling under his sleek coat, chiseled and hard compared to the soft flesh of Eugessa's hand.

"I brought Innov to see Vivaine," Sable said, drawing her attention back to the prioress.

Eugessa's lips curled into a sneer. "Does your arrogance know no bounds? The *High Prioress* is being tried for her life, and you still cannot speak of her respectfully."

"Should I take lessons from you on how to treat Vivaine with respect?" Sable asked. "I could see you gloating all the way from Barrowford when you managed to finally get the upper hand on her."

Eugessa's eyes narrowed. "The beloved High Prioress is in isolation for a time of meditation and communion with Amah until tomorrow." The words were a cold lie. "There's certainly nothing consequential enough about you to merit the chance to see her," she said with far more warmth. She flicked a disdainful look at Atticus. "Nor her old lapdog."

Atticus kept his expression polite.

Next to the half-built platform in front of the priories, a line of workers stacked wood for tomorrow's bonfire. Innov shifted her attention from the unicorn to the growing pile.

"Leave the Sanctuary," Eugessa ordered. "You have no role here. If Innov stays, she can light the bonfire when it's time. If she inexplicably decides to stay with you, I will start it myself." She looked contemptuously between Sable and Atticus. "I can't officially ban you from the trial tomorrow, since it's open to even the lowest trash of the city, but I will warn the guards to keep a close eye on you lest you attempt to interfere in any way."

"I have a signed letter from the Northern Lords," Sable answered in a level voice, "charging me with the responsibility of speaking for the north at the trial."

Eugessa gave a dismissive sniff. "I'm sure you prepared a compelling speech, but no one cares what the north thinks. Your presence here isn't necessary. It has never been necessary." She leaned closer to Sable, her eyes vicious. "The High Prioress's exalted neck will dangle at the end of a rope for the crimes she's committed. If you try to stop that, I will see you hanged right alongside her." The words flowed over Sable almost hot with fervor.

Eugessa flicked her hand at the nearest Sanctus guards. "Please escort them from the plaza." Without waiting for a response, she started back toward the platform.

The unicorn stood with his attention fixed on Innov.

Sable had always thought that horses' eyes looked soft. Trusting. But the unicorn's nostrils flared slightly, and his eyes, which were a hollow, fathomless black, focused on the phoenix with so much intensity, Sable shifted Innov away from him.

"Cernus," Eugessa called, with more softness in her voice than Sable had ever heard. The unicorn remained looking at Innov for another breath, then followed the prioress, the feathered black hair around his hoofs swinging like tattered edges of his shadow.

The guards gave the creature a wide berth but approached Atticus and Sable with resolute faces. Sable glanced toward the Dragon Priory, but Atticus shook his head.

"We can find our own way out," he said to the guards, turning back toward the gate, where the colorful shapes of his wagons called like welcoming beacons. The men fell in behind them.

Innov shifted on Sable's arm but didn't leave.

They'd only taken a few steps when a veiled abbess came toward them. "Issable!" she called quietly. Through her veil, the woman's smile twisted to the side by a scar on her cheek.

"Pixy!" Sable hurried toward the woman and hugged her with her free arm. Atticus stepped up next to Sable. "Atticus, this is my friend Pixy from the priory. Pixy, meet Atticus the playwright."

"The mail courier!" Atticus said warmly. "Well met!"

One of the guards cleared his throat.

"Well met indeed," Pixy said. "I am a huge fan of your plays. Tell me you're doing Lord Blossombritches tonight and that you'll be close enough to the Sanctuary that I can watch from here."

The guard cleared his throat with a more pointed tone, and Pixy glanced over at him. "Relax, Gerard, you know you're not in a hurry to get back and attend the Mother of the Stabby Horn. This may be the nicest break you get all day."

Gerard gave a small smile.

The other guard frowned. "We have orders, Pixy."

"I just want to talk to Issable for a moment, Len. If you can't give me that, then expect there to be cookies missing from that box of apple butter crisps your mother will be sending you at harvest."

"At least walk toward the gate," Len said. "You know she's still watching."

Pixy made a face behind her veil but nodded. She fell in next to Sable as they started once more toward the gate. "It's nice to see Innov again."

"I'm as shocked as you are that she hasn't come back," Sable said. "Have they narrowed down candidates for a new Phoenix Prioress?"

"No," Pixy said, irritated. "The two prioresses could barely have a civil conversation before Eugessa tossed the Dragon into a cell. If you want my honest opinion, neither of them wants a Phoenix Prioress."

"They can't just get rid of a priory." Sable ran a finger down Innov's chest. "A third of the abbeys in the land are under the Phoenix."

"They have all sorts of excuses," Pixy said. "War, now Vivaine's treachery." She paused. "We still don't know who set the fire that killed Narine. Unofficially, Vivaine and Eugessa still blame you, I think, but that story didn't gain any traction here in the city, so they claim they're still investigating."

"It was Kiva," Sable said. "A dwarf named Pete who works for him was seen by multiple witnesses."

Pixy grew quiet. "Why would a merchant want to kill Narine?"

"I intend to ask him that."

"They'll never find anyone good enough to replace her," Pixy said. "I'm sure at some point, the position will be filled with a puppet. Until the Dragon was arrested, I thought it would surely be one of hers, but Stabby has been pulling off some surprisingly competent schemes."

"Stabby?" Atticus said, amused.

Pixy grinned. "I needed a name for her murder horse, and the prioresses are so closely entwined with their *denos*, the name really applies to both."

"Do you have a name for Innov?" Sable asked.

"Innov is beauty and life and hope and all the truly good things in life. She and Narine deserved their own names. Neither the Dragon nor Stabby have earned that right."

They were nearly to the Veil Gate, so Sable lowered her voice. "Speaking of the Dragon and the dragon, what do you think has happened to Argyros?"

"I saw him the day he disappeared. Vivaine was in the plaza, and the newest Kalesh Ambassador was here with her." Pixy leaned closer. "They say the old one turned his back on the Empire to help you do…something."

Sable nodded. "General Goll killed him for it."

Pixy sighed. "That is exactly the opposite of the way things should have gone."

"I agree."

"Anyway, the day the dragon disappeared, the new Ambassador was speaking with Vivaine in the plaza with several merchants. They were ripping into her, accusing her of all sorts of things, some of which I think may actually be impossible, but there was a crowd at the gate, and things quickly turned against Vivaine.

"Eugessa came out and bullied her way into it all, demanding to know what was going on." Pixy paused. "I saw Vivaine motion to Argyros. Just that little finger wiggle she gives him, but he was back on the stairs of the Dragon Priory, and he didn't come to her. He watched it all as more and more people turned against her, like he was waiting for her to fix it, but she couldn't.

"When Eugessa called for the Sanctus guards to take Vivaine into custody, there was a moment of silence, but no one objected. Argyros didn't interfere when they took Vivaine down to the dungeon cells—he didn't do anything. And then he was gone."

Sable glanced at Atticus. "I thought he'd disappeared before she was arrested. If he watched that happen and didn't stop it…"

"I know he's covered in scales and looks like a giant lizard," Pixy said, her voice low as they reached the gate, "but if you ask me, the expression on his face when they arrested Vivaine was one of contempt. My opinion is she lost him. He decided she was too weak and left her to her fate."

Atticus looked troubled by her words but gave her a slight bow. "It was very good to meet you." He glanced at the guards. "If you ever need an escape from your prison, I have been known to smuggle women out of the city and into a new life."

Pixy smiled at him through the veil, her mouth twisting against her ropey scar. "Very tempting, but I don't have the face for theater."

"There are many opportunities for a clever, interesting woman in the world," he pointed out.

"Time to be on your way," Len said from behind them.

Sable gave Pixy a quick hug again. "Be careful with yourself," she whispered. "Keep out of both Stabby's and the Dragon's bad graces."

"I'll do my best," Pixy said with a crooked grin. "Don't get caught in any more battles." She stepped back, and the guards ushered Sable and Atticus out through the gate.

When they reached his wagon, Sable set her hand on his arm. "I'm sorry we didn't get to see her."

He glanced into the Sanctuary. "We learned a good deal, though."

"No, we didn't. Eugessa wants to execute Vivaine. We already knew that."

"No, we assumed she did. Now we know." He climbed up onto his wagon. "And I've been reminded of how tenuously Eugessa holds all her power. The woman is a bully because she is always on the edge of losing it all. Tonight, I'll talk to some of the merchants and find out where the Guild stands. Eugessa's right—they won't really care what the Northern Lords say, but if we can get the city to oppose the execution, I think we can stop it."

The avenue outside the Veil Gate was wide enough to allow the wagons to turn around, but enough people were milling about that Leonis hopped down and began to call out cheerful directions to the crowd, ushering them back away from the gate.

As soon as there was enough room, Atticus and Thulan started the slow process of turning the bright wagons around.

Sable moved over to one side to give them room, and Reese came next to her. "Who were you just talking to?"

Sable glanced back through the gate, but the abbess was gone. "That was Pixy."

"So you went into the Sanctuary, had a short, surprisingly uneventful chat with Eugessa, and then visited with an old friend." He gave her a sidelong look. "Your plans don't usually work out that...peacefully."

"Eugessa did threaten to kill me if I interfered with her execution of Vivaine."

"That's more like what I expected." He brushed his fingers against the back of her hand. "Please be careful. Eugessa hates you enough to follow through with that."

Sable pushed her hand against his. "Don't worry. I refuse to have Eugessa be the tragic end to my story."

Atticus's wagon had turned far enough that it was sideways, blocking most of the avenue, when a familiar voice snapped out from across the avenue, demanding people move.

A short, wiry form squeezed past Atticus's horse, wearing a dark red vest over a pristine white shirt. He looked insulted that the congestion had the gall to be in his way.

Until his attention caught on the bright form of Innov.

Kiva came to a dead stop, his irritable expression wiped away by surprise that quickly turned to wariness. "Sable?"

CHAPTER FORTY-THREE

KIVA SCHOOLED his face into something less shocked and managed a smile that did not come close to reaching his eyes as he took in the entire troupe.

Sable twitched her arm, and Innov squawked and took off. An explosion of sparks washed out Sable's view of the wretched man for a moment. The usually beautiful cascade only reminded her of the fire that had killed Narine.

Sable strode through it. "You vile, loathsome coward." Her words blasted out across the cobblestones.

"Sable!" Atticus's called, but she ignored him.

Kiva raised his hands, his expression wary, and the huge form of Boone planted himself in front of Kiva. The few people who could see around Atticus's wagon craned their necks at the sight.

"Move, Boone." Sable's word shot out with so much force that he flinched, but he stood his ground. Reese was at Sable's side, one of his knives in his hand. Sable started around Boone in one direction while Reese moved in the other.

Kiva's gaze flickered between Reese's blade and Sable's face. "Let me explain."

"Leonis," Atticus said, steering his wagon until it blocked most of the crowd's view of Sable. "Let's keep the rest of the city out of this."

Leonis slipped past the wagon and called out something enthusiastic to the gathered people. Thulan started to climb down from her bench, but Atticus waved her back.

Kiva sidestepped toward Sable, keeping Boone between himself and Reese.

"Before your general kills me, Sable," Kiva said, "give me one minute to explain."

Everything about him made Sable's skin crawl. His shifty eyes, his narrow face that managed to taint every expression with cruelty. "Who says it's going to be Reese who kills you?"

Kiva's expression curled into the scornful, oppressive look that used to press down on her, leaving her too small to do anything but crawl away. "You don't have any weapons."

The old, familiar look rolled over her with no more force than a breeze.

"I don't need a weapon." Sable held Kiva's gaze, and his confidence faltered.

"Give me one minute." His voice tried to sound commanding, but she could feel the desperation in it.

"I don't have a minute's worth of patience for you. Use your last words wisely."

He looked her over again, a calculating smile curling up the edge of his mouth. "You've changed over the past years, Sable."

"Those are the wrong words." She took another step closer.

Kiva raised a hand as though he could hold her back. "Pete is no longer in my employ," he said quickly.

Reese moved to the side. "Because he killed Narine and got caught?"

Boone shifted to keep facing Reese.

"You're judging this all wrong," Reese said to the big man. "You should protect Kiva from her more than me."

Boone didn't budge.

"Where is Pete now?" Sable asked. "Because when we're done talking to you, we'd like a word with him."

"There was an accident at the docks." Kiva's eyes flashed between Reese and Sable. "Turns out dwarves can't swim."

"We can swim," Thulan growled.

Kiva looked up at her. "Apologies, Mistress Dwarf. I meant they can't swim when they have rocks tied to their boots."

"You killed him?" Sable asked. "Why?"

"Because he got caught," Reese answered.

"No. Because he was stupid," Kiva said. "Because, when he got a message telling him to kill Narine and make a statement of it, he believed it was actually from me."

His words were warm, but Sable shook her head. "Your minute is almost done."

"Pete and Boone were at the summit, yes," he said, the words coming out faster, "but not on the island. They've never been presentable enough for respectable company. Pete got a message written in—I admit—a hand that looked a lot like mine and sealed with my seal." Kiva's face darkened. "The seal was discovered missing the next day, and the aide who'd been tasked with keeping it safe is also no longer in my employ."

"Time's up," Sable said.

"Why would I kill Narine?" Kiva said, his voice desperate.

"Because you wanted her out of the summit."

"She was barely a part of the summit!"

"Then you wanted me out of it."

"You?" He laughed, but it held a frantic edge. "You were the most exciting thing that happened there. Yes, you're always misguided and overly dramatic, but the special sort of chaos you bring to a situation is a gift from the heavens. Do you know how easy it is to manipulate things once they've started to spin off course? The impossible thing is to shift anything in the midst of the rigid order Vivaine always imposes. I'd have loved you there for the entire time. You'd been there one day and I'd already struck two lucrative deals away from the council table."

His words had been warm the entire time, but Sable shook her head, her anger at him seething. "You expect me to believe someone else told Pete to kill her?"

"Narine was days—if not hours—from death!" He ran his hand through his hair. "If I wanted Narine dead, I wouldn't have *set her on fire*, Sable! A tiny dose of a mild poison would have sent her off in her sleep, and no one would have thought to question it. You know me. I do not create big, dramatic scenes. I take advantage of the chaos people like *you* create. That is what should have tipped Pete off. The message told him to 'make a show of it.'"

He shifted his weight, gauging Sable's reaction, his eyes flicking to the rest of the troupe surrounding them and sticking for a moment on Serene. "You know I'm telling the truth, Sable."

Every word he'd spoken had been warm.

Reese continued to circle to the side, and Boone shifted until his back was to Sable and Kiva.

Kiva held up his hands. "I had nothing to do with Narine's death." He said each word clearly, and they swirled between them, almost hot.

Out of the corner of her eye, Sable saw Reese glance at her, and she gave the smallest nod. He didn't lower his knife.

"Who did, then?" she asked.

"I don't know," Kiva said sincerely.

"Guess," she said flatly.

He paused. "Eugessa. Although it was more violent and cruel than I would have thought she had the spine for." Again, the words were true.

Sable stepped forward until she was only inches away from him and set her hand on the front of his richly embroidered vest. There was a small, snake-sized bulge in the lower pocket, and she shifted her body away from it.

"Have you done *anything* else," she whispered, "that would make me want to kill you?" Very gently, she drew a trickle of *vitalle* out of him.

His eyes widened, and he started to back up.

"Don't move," she said, anger still roiling in her chest, "and answer the question."

He swallowed. "I have not." He gave her the hint of a strained smile. "At least not since I tricked Talia into signing a contract with me."

She increased the flow of *vitalle* to a small stream, and he tensed. "That's enough reason, you know."

"Yes," he said stiffly, "but it's old news. And Talia seems content with the arrangement."

Sable's eyes narrowed.

He raised his hands again. "Speaking of your sister, she's coming over for dinner tonight. Would you like to come too?"

"Dinner? With you?"

"With Talia," he corrected her. "It is nearly impossible to get time with her away from Lady Ingred." These words were warm as well. "Consider it a gift. An apology for Pete's idiocy. Talia will be thrilled to see you, and I'm happy to make room for one more at the table."

Sable paused the flow of *vitalle*.

On the other side of Boone, Reese give her a disbelieving look.

"No." Atticus's voice came from the seat of his wagon, reminding her that the others were there.

"You're not invited," Kiva said, not looking at the playwright.

"You have plenty of other things to do tonight, Atticus," Sable agreed.

"As do you," the old man said.

"Not really," she answered.

Reese's shoulders sank in something like defeat. "Make room for two more seats at your table."

Kiva gave him a probing look. "Actually, I have someone you might be interested in meeting, General." There was a mocking twist to the title. "If the rumors about your familiarity with the Kalesh are not exaggerated."

When Reese didn't respond, Kiva glanced around, then lowered his voice. "I caught a Kalesh soldier sneaking through Dockside. It took fourteen of my men to capture him. Three of them are dead and one more will be by morning."

Reese studied him. "Tattoos?"

"Scales, up his neck and over his shaved scalp."

Reese's knife dipped. "All the way over his head?"

Kiva nodded.

Sable swallowed against the feel of the cold knife at her neck, resisting the urge to rub the skin over her scar.

"Where are you keeping him?" Reese asked sharply.

"The Hole," Kiva answered.

Reese glanced at Sable.

"A cistern beneath one of Kiva's buildings," she said.

"That might be enough," Reese admitted. "Guards?"

"Thirty men." Kiva looked at the two of them. "You want to meet him?"

"Yes," Reese said immediately.

Kiva studied him. "In return, I want to know who and what he is."

Reese considered the offer for a moment, then nodded.

"Then I definitely have an extra seat at my table," Kiva said. "I'm delighted to have the famous General Andreese as my guest."

"This is not a good idea," Atticus said.

Sable still had her hand on Kiva's chest. "Do you have any intention of harming Reese or me tonight?"

"No," he said bluntly, the word warm. "You're both too valuable to harm."

She dropped her hand. "There you go, Atticus. We'll find you later." Sable motioned down the street. "Lead the way, Kiva."

"I had…" Kiva paused and glanced toward the Veil Gate, then turned back to her. "This is more interesting than the business that brought me here." He held out his arm to Sable. "May I escort you, Issable, Queen of the North."

She resisted the urge to shove his arm away. "Where did you hear that name?"

He laughed and dropped his arm. "Everyone knows that name." He started around the horse hitched to Atticus's wagon. "Don't worry, without your phoenix, and dressed like a vagabond, no one will recognize you." He snapped his fingers. "Boone! Make a path through the crowd."

Atticus watched Kiva thoughtfully. "Be careful, you two."

"It wouldn't be a trip to Immusmala without a visit with Kiva." Reese set a hand on Sable's back. "Let's get this over with, and if you sense anything off at all, tell me immediately."

Sable nodded and started after Kiva and the enormous form of Boone. "I don't think he means us any harm, but I'm not sure what he does want."

"That's what worries me," Reese said.

Reese was at Sable's side, one of his knives in his hand.

CHAPTER FORTY-FOUR

Sable and Reese walked in the wake of Boone for several blocks before the crowd thinned and Kiva waited for Sable to come up next to him.

"I didn't expect to see you here," he said. "Are you here for Vivaine?"

The houses on either side of the avenue were enormous stone edifices owned by the merchants and wealthy families of the city. After so long in the north with their timber houses, they looked more impressive than Sable remembered. "The Northern Lords wanted someone to air their grievances against her."

Kiva raised an eyebrow. "And they sent you two?"

"They sent her," Reese said from behind them.

Kiva barely glanced in his direction. "But the loyal dog came along too."

"The soldiers of three northern territories," Sable said icily, "would leave their lords to follow Reese if he asked. You're usually better at recognizing people's significance, Kiva, and not insulting ones more powerful than you."

Kiva shrugged. "There is nothing in the world I could do to convince your dog to like me, Sable. I'm hardly going to waste energy pretending there's love lost between us."

"If only you'd offer me the same courtesy," she said.

Kiva let out a laugh. "I've been telling you how fond I am of you for years. I admit, though, I believe I've grown even more fond of Talia. She doesn't have your flair for disruption, but she is incredibly effective when she sets her mind to something."

"Pointing out that you own my sister is hardly the way to win my affection," Sable said, not bothering to hide her annoyance. "I'm worried about them enough already without you adding to it."

"You know I'm not lying," Kiva said easily. "Talia and I have developed an excellent working relationship that benefits both of us. That seems like something you would respect."

"Talk about something else," Sable said curtly.

"All right, tell me about the scaled man."

Reese explained the Tien Sark and the tattoos. "If they go onto his scalp, then he's the highest rank they have. He's not here to gather information like the others we've seen. He's here to lead something."

"No other Kalesh have come through Dockside," Kiva said. "I caught him early this morning and have been debating what to do with him. He doesn't look like the sort of man who will give us answers." He looked at both of them. "I assume the two of you know why someone so valuable to the Empire is here."

"We have ideas," Sable admitted.

Kiva didn't ask more as he continued down the street.

The grand houses around them were occasionally interspersed with expensive shops selling silver jewelry or silks. There was still a marked lack of anything that looked Kalesh.

Another thought struck Sable. There were no Kalesh styles, but there was also no gold. Aside from the little she'd seen on Eugessa, people's jewelry, even on a festival day, was mostly silver. After a year of mining near the city, even the wealthiest merchants didn't have any. She felt a flicker of irritation that even without taking over the land, the Kalesh must have managed to get most of it.

They passed an abbess on the street corner holding a flowering branch above a couple.

"What are they doing?" Reese asked.

"Sable hasn't told you about the pledging ceremony?" Kiva said, giving her an amused look. "Curious." He turned to Reese. "These young lovers are pledging themselves to each other."

"They're getting married on a street corner? In a crowd?"

"Pledging to be married," Kiva corrected him. "A betrothal formally expressing their adoration for each other and getting a blessing from the abbess. They'll be handfasted within the year." He motioned to another abbess up ahead. "Normally, pledging ceremonies are done in people's homes, with their parents, family, and friends as witnesses. But during the Blood Moon Festival, a couple can find any abbess to witness their love. Do you barbarians in the north not pledge yourselves to each other?"

"We call it an engagement," Reese answered, "and it's a private promise between the couple. No abbesses involved."

"Well, there's nothing we like more in the south than involving our priories in every bit of our lives," Kiva said dryly.

The street was lined with smaller merchant carts and performers there for the festival.

Sable's feet grew heavy, and she straightened her shoulders. Dockside was still a reasonably long walk, and she refused to let Kiva know that a simple walk down the street was tiring.

Boone turned, cutting between a silk merchant's wagon and an older woman playing a lilting tune on a lute. He started up wide stone steps made of black granite.

Sable stopped, staring at the huge house. The main edifice was grey, but pitch-black stone arched over the many wide windows and outlined the broad, intricately carved front door. The house was taller than its neighbors, and its roof was steep. From its attic, two large windows faced out like two haughty eyes looking over the avenue. From their height, they might even see over the buildings, all the way out to the sea.

The first thought that flashed into Sable's mind was that Talia would love a room with those windows.

"Welcome to my humble home," Kiva said.

Sable turned to find him watching her closely and realized her mouth was hanging open. She snapped it shut, and he smiled smugly. Too many questions vied for her attention for her to pick just one.

"Who did you steal this from?" she asked finally.

He headed up the steps. "Strictly speaking," he said over his shoulder, "*you* stole this from someone."

She climbed the black steps with Reese, following Kiva through the door held open by two servants. They walked through a short, narrow entry covered with carved wood panels, then into an entry hall with a soaring ceiling. Paintings hung in elaborate frames, and at the far end, a huge staircase swept up, splitting and wrapping around both sides to continue to the second floor. At least a dozen lanterns hung from hooks on the walls, giving the room a warm, welcoming feel that itched against Sable's skin.

"I think I'd remember stealing a house," she said, following Kiva through a door on the left side of the hall, into a long dining room set with a glittering array of dishes and goblets.

"If Sable stole it," Reese said from behind her, "doesn't that make all this hers?"

Kiva shook his head. "She traded it to me to pay off the last of her debt."

Sable frowned. "Lord Renwen's ledger included a house? I clearly overpaid."

"It included so much more than a house, Sable." Kiva strode through the room into a smaller study. It was at least three times larger than his room above the fabric shop had been. Along with an enormous desk that Sable could not imagine having fit through the door, there were four large upholstered chairs around a low table.

Kiva pulled a cord on the wall near his desk and then motioned them to the chairs. Sable and Reese both hesitated in the doorway.

He watched them for a moment. "You're guests at my house for dinner. We have a little time before Talia arrives and the festivities begin. You can stand there at the door like I'm going to bite you, or you can take a seat. I promise you these are the most comfortable chairs in the city." When neither of them moved, he shrugged, went to the farthest chair, and dropped into it with a dramatic sigh of contentment.

Sable crossed the room and sat across from him. The cushions were deep and soft, and she melted into it, letting out a short groan of pleasure.

Kiva grinned like a boy showing off a new treasure. "Talia likes these chairs too."

"How does a ledger get you a house?" Reese came and sat on the front edge of the chair next to Sable, leaning his elbows on his knees, his body tense.

Kiva took in his posture with amusement. "The very last time Sable worked for me, she was supposed to scout Lord Renwen's house and discover where he kept his business ledger, because it was reported to also keep financial records for every merchant in the Guild. Instead, she snuck into his office against my express orders and stole not his official ledger, but his secret ledger, the one that recorded how dozens of the city's most affluent merchants had cheated the Guild."

"Which you used to blackmail someone into selling you this house," Reese finished for him.

"Blackmail is an ugly word," Kiva said. "The ledger gave me the most important thing in any game. Knowledge. I have done my best to use that knowledge wisely."

A servant entered the room, dressed in a formal black tunic, carrying a wide silver tray piled with fruit and nuts. He set it on the table before them, then, with a pointed look at Reese and Sable, set down a bowl holding two steaming washcloths.

"Thank you, Turner." Kiva watched the man leave. "I think the best thing about all of this"—he waved his hand at the house around them—"is the help. I never would have found someone in Dockside who noticed my guests were too filthy to be presentable."

Sable studied him. She'd never seen him quite this...friendly. If it weren't Kiva she was looking at, this would feel like a visit to an old friend who was excited to show off his success.

"It was impossible to live in Dockside and not be too filthy to be presentable," she said. She picked up the washcloth, and the heat stung her fingers, but she opened it and pressed it to her cheeks. The damp heat felt luxurious, and despite a feeling of irritation that it was from Kiva, she scrubbed at her face, her neck, and her hands. The cloth came away embarrassingly dirty. She dropped it back into the bowl next to an equally dirty one from Reese.

"Where did the Tien Sark come from?" Reese asked.

"He disembarked from a ship bringing wool from the Eastern Reaches, but Rabbit had sent word a couple of weeks ago about the scaled tattoos, so we cornered him. It went...less smoothly than I would have hoped. I've been pondering what to do with him all day. I was headed to the Sanctuary to discuss it with Eugessa when I had the pleasure of meeting you two. I thought he might be an interesting addition to the trials tomorrow."

"After we talk to him," Reese said, "you should kill him. Definitely don't take him around the city in the chaos of the festival."

"He'll be well guarded," Kiva said. "He's merely one man, regardless of how resourceful."

"And Sable's only one woman, and yet you're clearly nervous that she's here."

Kiva laughed. "I am. And yet also very pleased. I had no idea I would get to show off my house to an old friend tonight."

Sable opened her mouth to point out, again, that they were hardly friends, but there was a strange warmth in his words.

A familiar laugh sounded from outside the room, and Sable sat up.

That wasn't Talia.

A slight figure dressed in priory white stepped into the doorway.

"Ryah!" Sable said, pushing herself out of her chair.

Her youngest sister stopped in her tracks, staring at Sable, before rushing across the room. "Sable!"

"Surprise," Kiva said dryly, still sitting in his seat.

Sable grabbed her little sister and wrapped her in a hug.

"You're here!" Ryah said, squeezing her. "How did you know to come?"

"I'm here for Vivaine's trial," Sable said, pulling back and holding Ryah by the shoulders. "You're getting taller." She also looked tired. Sable caught just a glimpse of shadows on Ryah's normally bright face.

Her sister smiled widely again. "I can't believe you're here!"

A shadow moved into the doorway, and Sable glanced over to see a man with a bare chest, bare arms, and a shaved head. Tattoos swirled across his scalp, not dragon scales like a Tien Sark, but long, arcing lines that reminded Sable of claws or fangs. They wrapped down his neck, slipping under a thick leather collar and covering his shoulders and arms.

"Evening, Tomm," Kiva said easily.

Sable stared at the gang boss for the Muddogs for a moment before looking back at Kiva. "Things between the Vayas and the Muddogs seem to have changed a bit since I saw you two together last."

"Your introduction of Tomm and me has turned out to be mutually beneficial." Kiva waved the man toward a set of glass bottles on a shelf near his desk. "Dockside has the docks, but the Bend has the packing warehouses. Between the two, there are all sorts of interesting smuggling operations just waiting to be discovered."

"You could be doing better things than smuggling," Ryah said.

"We could," Tomm answered, "but it wouldn't be as much fun."

Sable focused on Ryah again. She was dressed in a beautiful abbess's gown, more formal than their normal dress. "You look amazing. Why are you here? I thought Eugessa wouldn't let you leave the priory."

"It pays to perform favors for a prioress," Kiva said. "When I need something, Eugessa usually owes me, and lending me Ryah for an evening is a price she was very willing to pay."

"What do you need Ryah for? Blessing some illegal activity?"

Ryah looked at Kiva. "You didn't tell her?"

"Tell me what? He said he'd invited Talia to dinner."

Ryah's expression turned vaguely reproachful. "You didn't tell her any of it?"

"And ruin the surprise?" Kiva cocked an ear toward the doorway. "It's so much better to have it play out like this."

Talia's voice came through the door, laughing and bright. She appeared in the doorway of the study, smiling over her shoulder. She wore a long, cream-colored dress, thankfully devoid of any embroidered Kalesh dragons. Instead, threads of delicate blue swirled around the waistline like a belt of flowers. It was simple but stunning. Her hair hung down over her shoulders in the carefree way it always had when she and Sable had shared the tiny room in Dockside, and despite the fine dress, she looked more familiar and more achingly like herself than Sable had seen her in years.

Sable took a step toward her, and Talia turned. She caught sight of Sable and stopped in the doorway, her mouth dropping open.

"Sable!" Talia grabbed her skirt and rushed across the room. Sable stepped past Ryah and wrapped her arms around her sister. "You're here?" Talia pulled back and held on to Sable's shoulders, looking shocked. "How are you here?"

"Surprise," Kiva said again with a smug smile.

Sable heard Reese stand behind her, and Talia glanced at him. "Hello again, Reese."

He gave her a nod, looking cautiously at the people in the room.

Talia gripped Sable's arms. "I would have invited you if I'd had any way of getting a message to you."

"Invited me to what?" Sable said.

There was a shuffling sound from the door, and Reese tensed.

In the doorway stood a young man looking utterly caught off guard and wearing the formal uniform of a Kalesh soldier.

"Sable," Talia said, her voice nervous. "This is Niko."

"And the reason we needed an abbess tonight," Kiva said. "Who else would perform Talia's pledging ceremony?"

CHAPTER FORTY-FIVE

"PLEDGING CEREMONY?" Sable stared at Talia. "*Pledging* ceremony?"

Talia's hands tightened on Sable's arms.

"Surprise," Kiva said for the third time.

"If he says that again," Sable told Reese, "throw a knife at him."

"Gladly," Reese answered.

Sable looked between Talia and the young soldier who was quickly recovering his composure.

"Hello, Sable." The soldier's accent sharpened the consonants, much like Bastian's always had. "It's nice to finally meet you."

"It's..." Sable turned back to Talia, who was looking at her with an uncomfortable smile. "Finally?"

"Nikolas and Talia," Kiva offered from across the room, "have been spending time together since...when? At least since the mid-winter festival."

"Since mid-winter?" Sable asked. "You'd been *spending time* with a Kalesh soldier for the last six months of Narine's life? During which I saw you at least four or five times."

"I would have told you," Talia said, her discomfort changing to irritation, "but I was afraid you'd react something like this."

Sable took in Niko's uniform again. "After the Kalesh attacked the city, I didn't think any had the gall to stay around."

"I met Niko because his commanding officer, General Grigg, came often to Lord Trelles's house," Talia said, trying to keep her voice calm. "After the…" She paused. "*Events* involving Ambassador Bastian, General Grigg was promoted to Ambassador, and he's kept a small retinue here." She stepped back as Niko walked up next to her. Talia put her hand on his arm. "Niko was chosen to be one of them."

Sable stared at the two of them.

Ryah came over and linked her arm with Sable's. "I've met Niko before, and I like him very much."

Sable was opening her mouth to point out that Ryah liked everyone when Reese stepped forward.

"*Tel mordu es?*" he asked.

Niko blinked in surprise. "*Parrin, en ketuus Tallene.*"

"He speaks Kalesh?" Talia whispered, looking at Reese intently.

Sable turned to her sister. "Do you?"

"Enough to know he asked where Niko is from."

Reese studied the Kalesh soldier. "When was the last time you were there?"

"I was twelve when they took every boy from my village."

"Have you been back?"

Niko shook his head. "I have not."

Reese weighed the answer, then held out a hand. "I'm Reese."

Sable stared at him with perhaps more shock than Niko, who didn't hesitate before grasping Reese's hand. "I know." He glanced at Sable. "From what I hear, the two of you excel at finding trouble."

"That is almost entirely Sable," Reese said. "I follow her around, try to deflect the worst of it, and worry about all the things she refuses to see as dangers."

Niko laughed, the sound edged with nerves. "Then the sisters are more alike than Talia has led me to believe."

"From what I can tell," Reese said, "Ryah is the only safe one of the three."

Tomm snorted from where he leaned against Kiva's liquor cabinet. He tilted a glass toward Ryah. "Don't let the white dress fool you. She's drawn to dangerous situations like a prayer to the heavens. *I think someone in there needs help, Tomm,*" he said with a fake high voice.

"It was only that one alley," Ryah objected.

"And the warehouse. And that abandoned shop," Tomm added.

Ryah gave a guilty smile. "Those weren't that bad."

"Why are you going into dangerous alleys?" Sable asked Ryah.

"Sweet Amah, Sable," Ryah said in exasperation. "You're going to berate me? You insulted Vivaine until Argyros shot fire at you!"

Niko reached out and patted Reese on the shoulder. "I think you've got it the worst, *koleg.*"

"The world should be grateful that these three aren't together very often." Reese glanced at Kiva. "I hope your big fancy house is as strong as it looks."

"What's *koleg*?" Sable asked Talia.

"Friend." Talia looked curiously at Reese. "Your reputation of hatred toward the Kalesh seems undeserved."

"I have a deep and abiding hatred for the Kalesh government," Reese said, "but the soldiers are not the Empire."

A bell jingled from the dining room, and Kiva stood. "Dinner is served." He surveyed the room with a broad smile. "This is the best dinner party I've had in years."

There were three places set along each side of the table and one at each end. Kiva and Tomm took the ends, the burly Muddog looking remarkably at ease among all the wealth. Ryah pulled both sisters to the near side of the table, seating Sable in the middle seat and leaving Reese and Niko to sit across from them.

Servants filed into the room, bringing small bowls of soup, and Sable leaned closer to Talia. "How many people work for Kiva here?"

"Seven in the house," she said, "but hundreds if you count all his warehouses and other businesses."

Sable looked down at her dirty traveling clothes. "I would have changed if I'd known I was going to be spending the evening in such luxury." She looked at Talia's dress. "Or attending a pledging ceremony."

Talia looked across the table to where Reese and Niko were deep in a discussion, and Sable was surprised at the affection in her sister's eyes. "I'm sorry I didn't tell you about him," Talia said quietly. "I wanted to, but Lady Ingred didn't know about him—no one did. We were afraid if people found out, his commanding officer would reassign him, so we kept it quiet."

Sable resisted the urge to point out that she was the last person on earth who would have let the secret slip to a Kalesh general.

"I'm so happy you're here," Talia continued, grabbing Sable's hand. "I know I messed all this up, but I want you to know him. You'll like him. I want you to..." She shrugged. "I want you to be happy for me."

Sable looked across the table at Niko. The soldier laughed at something Reese said and, after a glance at Sable and Talia, answered him in Kalesh. Sable frowned at the two men. "Did you understand that?"

Talia narrowed her eyes. "No. It may be a mistake to let them sit together."

Niko's smile was quick and easy, and Sable had to admit she hadn't seen Reese this relaxed in a very long time.

"Niko has a reputation for being fair and honest," Ryah said. "Everyone around the priory likes him."

"What if..." Sable stopped and looked at Talia. "What will you do when he's sent back to the Empire?"

Talia's smile was tentative. "I'll get to see more of the world than I ever imagined existed."

"They'll let his wife travel with the troops?"

"They won't, unless he's been promoted to the ambassador's inner staff. They're allowed to bring family with them wherever they're stationed. Ambassador Grigg has told him that he's due for a promotion at the new year and all but promised him the open seat on his staff when one of the colonels retires."

The idea of Talia moving so far away Sable would never see her again was shoved aside by another thought. She looked slowly over at Niko. Talia wanted to marry a Kalesh soldier, but what if they discovered...

"I forgot." Sable looked at both sisters. "I didn't come south just for Vivaine's trial. I need to talk to you both. Alone."

"This isn't alone enough?" Talia asked.

"Definitely not. We need time with no Kiva, no Tomm, and, I'm sorry to say, no Niko." Sable gave Talia an apologetic look. "If you want to tell him afterwards, that's your choice, but...we should talk before your pledging ceremony."

Talia expression turned suspicious. "What's it about?"

Sable paused. "Our mother."

Both sisters' eyes widened.

Talia stood, pushing back her chair. "Excuse us. We need a few sister moments alone."

Without waiting for an answer from Kiva or anyone else, she motioned Sable and Ryah to follow her and swept out of the room. Sable and Ryah followed despite the curious looks of all the men. Talia moved quickly up the enormous staircase with a familiarity that left Sable feeling out of place. They climbed up three flights before arriving in one of the attic rooms that faced the avenue. The ceiling started high on the left side of the room and sloped steeply down until the wall to the right stood barely as tall as Sable. The walls were painted a delicate yellow, and a luxurious-looking bed was tucked up along the short wall. A chair upholstered in rich blue brocade nestled in front of the window.

The window itself was enormous. The sun had set, leaving the sky a clear, pale blue, and Sable could see over the dark roofs across the street to the city past them, cascading down the hill until it ended abruptly at the top of the sea cliffs. Beyond it, the sea stretched out endlessly, catching the airy blue of the sky and reflecting it back with a million ripples of darker blue.

A dozen framed sketches on the taller wall caught Sable's attention. The lines were quick and easy, the hills and cliffs and oceans drawn with the same longing that Talia had used on the walls of their hovel in Dockside.

"This is your room." Sable had meant to phrase it as a question, but the answer was too obvious.

Talia had a room in Kiva's house. A room utterly, perfectly suited to her. Sable stared at the drawings, barely seeing them, trying to wrap her mind around the truth of it all.

Her sister sank onto the bed. "Kiva claims it's the reason he picked this house, because he thought I'd love it." Her voice was amused.

Sable turned to stare at her. "He what?"

Talia let out a laugh. "Since when do you believe what Kiva says? He picked it because it is connected to an enormous warehouse on the back side that is walled in and fortified enough to withstand a siege. It has some secret bunker in the basement I've never seen and am not supposed to know about and two hidden entrances for his less presentable employees to use." She glanced at the wide window. "I do love this room, though."

"Do you ever stay here?"

"I've slept here twice. Both times, Lady Ingred was invited to some clandestine affair where no one could bring their own handmaids. Both times, Kiva had left me some supplies, and I spent the days drawing." She glanced at the wall. "I didn't know he'd framed them."

The frames were simple but elegant, and their mere existence sat uneasily in Sable's stomach.

"What does Lady Ingred have to be clandestine about?" Ryah asked from the window.

Talia snorted. "Both times, it was a dress designer revealing new styles.

Apparently the fashion business is rather cutthroat in this city, and a stolen design can cost a dressmaker thousands of silver." Talia focused on Sable. "What about our mother needs to be explained before I can have a pledging ceremony?"

Ryah sat next to Talia, her brow creased. "What is there about Mother that's this big of a secret?"

Sable pushed the door closed. "Purnicious?"

The kobold popped into view.

"Purn!" Talia squealed and dropped to her knees on the floor, wrapping the kobold in a hug.

"Hello, Purnicious!" Ryah said, taking her turn hugging the little creature.

"I need to make sure no one is listening to our conversation, Purn," Sable said.

The kobold gave a quick nod, but before she could disappear, Sable raised a finger.

"Purnicious, did you know about Niko?"

The kobold froze and glanced at Talia. "I...did see him a few times...but..."

"Purnicious didn't hide anything from you," Talia said. "I knew Niko before Purn left, but we didn't start spending a lot of time together until after she went away with you and Narine."

Purn looked up at Sable a little sheepishly. "I like Niko. He always treated Talia very nicely." She gave Talia a smile. "I'm happy for you."

"Thank you, Purn," Talia said, affectionately.

The kobold blinked out of sight, and Sable faced her two sisters. "Talia, how well did Niko know Ambassador Bastian?"

"Not well. He'd met him once or twice." She tilted her head. "Is it true that Bastian betrayed the Empire to help you?"

Sable paused. "Bastian betrayed the Empire to help our mother." At both sisters' surprised looks, she continued, "When Bastian was young, he was part of a force in the Empire sent to quell the uprising of a rebel known only as the Ghost of the White Wood. Who turned out to be a woman who carried an elvish bow and was named Melia. A name the Kalesh changed to A'Melia, the *A'* added to denote they thought of her as a spirit or a ghost."

At both sisters' stunned silence, Sable sank into the blue chair and started the story of how Bastian had captured Melia.

"A'Melia had an elvish friend named Evay, an elf who was bound to her by some sort of blood oath. The two of them together assassinated the Kalesh prince."

Sable moved through the rest of the story quickly. "During the battle here in Immusmala, in an attempt to barter with the Kalesh," she said, forcing out the words and looking at Talia apologetically, "I told General Goll who I am and traded myself in exchange for the Kalesh leaving our land alone."

"You what?" Ryah demanded.

"You didn't!" Talia whispered. "So they know about you now?" She grabbed Ryah's hand. "They know about us?"

"No. At least, I don't think so. There aren't that many people who know the three of us are sisters."

"Except Kiva," Talia said. "And Tomm, and Niko, and Reese, and Eugessa, and *Vivaine*!"

Ryah's eyes widened.

Sable sank back in the chair. "A good summary of the heart of our problem."

Talia shoved herself to her feet. "And if the Kalesh army finds out," she said, her expression turning accusing, "and Niko is pledged to me, they'll assume he knew!"

"Which is why I need to tell you now."

Talia's mouth hung open. "You...Are you saying that if I marry the man I love, it's going to get us both *killed?*"

"If I had known you were falling in love with the enemy," Sable said sharply, "I would have told you sooner. And if *Kiva* hadn't been an idiot and killed General Goll, they'd have taken me back to the Empire, executed me, and everything would be fine."

"How would that be fine?" Ryah exclaimed.

Talia paced across the room. "I can't believe you're telling me this tonight!"

Sable leaned forward, waving her hand at Talia's dress and hair and everything. "It's not like I had any idea I was coming to your pledging ceremony! Or that you'd been stupid enough to fall in love with a Kalesh soldier! How is this ever going to end well, Talia? He is the enemy of everything this land is about!"

"I fell in love with a good man!" Talia jabbed her finger down toward the dining room. "A man who was raised in a different part of the world, ripped from his home and his family at the same age I was, and conscripted into his enemy's army, where, through years of honesty and integrity, he earned the respect of his superiors and the men he fought with." She paused. "He knows Reese killed the Kalesh ambassador. You know what he said about that? That if he were in Reese's shoes, he'd understand the need to keep the Empire away."

The words were warm, and Sable settled back a little into the chair.

Talia ran her hand over her hair, looking wildly around the room. "I have to tell him."

Sable shook her head. "What if he runs immediately to the ambassador to report he knows where all three of A'Melia's daughters are?"

Talia spun, her face outraged. "He would never."

"He's served these people half his life," Sable said.

Talia planted her hands on her hips. "Would Reese betray you?"

Sable let out an annoyed breath. "No."

"And is Reese anywhere near the point where he would pledge to marry you?"

"It's not that simple, Talia."

"It *is* that simple, Sable. Over a year ago, I saw the way you and Reese were together. Since then, every time I see you, he is there, and the bond between the two of you is stronger. Any fool can see that." Talia pointed at Sable. "You softened to Niko not because you heard I was pledging myself to him, but because Reese softened toward him."

Sable opened her mouth to argue, but the accusation hit too close to the truth.

"Here you are tonight, together again, but not actually together. You orbit around each other as though you're connected, and yet you're...not."

Sable shoved herself out of the chair. "Some people realize when a situation is not ready, Talia. That no matter what you feel, there are things that need to be sorted out first." Her hands curled into fists. "You're not the only one suffering because of this situation, Talia. Not everyone throws away logic to try to build something that could be ripped away from them in a heartbeat."

Talia looked at her with a pitying expression. "Only the ones who want to be happy."

CHAPTER FORTY-SIX

Talia turned toward the door. "Excuse me," she said, her voice harsh, "I need to speak with Niko."

"And what, Talia?" Sable said. "Ask him to walk away from his life? To run into hiding with you in a land he doesn't know? Give up everything he's built? If he's as honest as you say, you're putting him in a horrible situation."

Talia stopped and turned to Sable, her fear replaced with the old stubborn set of her jaw. "Then he and I will figure it out together. Because no matter what happens with my life, I know I want it to be with him."

She yanked the door open and left.

Sable stood in the middle of the room, a hollow feeling growing as Talia disappeared down the steps.

Ryah stood and came over, slipping her arm around Sable's waist and leaning her head on Sable's shoulder. They stood quietly for a moment.

"I always knew Mother was special," Ryah said finally.

"She was amazing. I'll have her story copied and sent to you. You'll love it."

"Did..." Ryah's voice came out barely over a whisper. "Did Bastian tell you more about her? Sometimes I...can't remember much."

The shadow was back over Ryah's face, and a thin knife slid into Sable's chest at the sight. She'd left Ryah with Eugessa for far too long. "Bastian was in love with her. Spent most of his career trying to be the one from the Empire who found her. To warn her she needed to run again."

Ryah let out a sigh.

"Beyond that, though, I didn't have much time to talk to him." Sable blinked away the memory of Bastian's body on the ground.

"I always liked him," Ryah said quietly.

"So did I."

They were quiet for a moment before Ryah sighed again. "I need to go ask Tomm not to tell people we're sisters. I doubt he would, but I should ask, just in case."

Sable glanced down at Ryah. Maybe she hadn't seen a shadow there. The changes in Ryah were more complex than that. She looked older, more confident than Sable remembered. Still earnest and gentle, but somehow stronger. "After the trial, will you leave with me? Eugessa will not keep your secret, not if it will earn her favor with the Kalesh."

"I know." Ryah looked up. "But leaving the priory…what else will I do?"

"I don't know, but you're not safe here."

Ryah considered the words seriously. "I have to be with Eugessa tomorrow during the trial." A frown creased her brow. "She's going to have Vivaine executed. I've never seen Eugessa so…crazed."

"What do you think should happen to Vivaine?" Sable asked quietly.

"If she dies, or if she's imprisoned, or if she's stripped of her position in any way, that leaves only Eugessa in the priories." Ryah bit her lip. "For a time, I thought that maybe Eugessa was getting…better. Softer. For a short time last year, she would talk to me about her fears and the trials of running the priory, and she…" Ryah shrugged. "I thought she was getting better. But then there was the summit, and since then, she's been so closed off. More difficult and cruel than before."

Sable paused, thinking of Kiva's accusations about Eugessa killing Narine. "What happened at the summit?"

"I have no idea. I thought, on our way there, that there was hope. That she might not blindly support the Kalesh but might work with the north and the others. But then Vivaine grew more and more angry, and Narine —" Ryah stopped. "In all honestly, Sable, I think everything changed with Narine's death. Eugessa took it very badly."

"Sadly?" Sable asked cautiously.

"No. She was…unhinged. She was angry and vicious and impossible to please. There were days when everyone avoided her, and I was the only one near her for hours. It was…difficult. She was broken, Sable. Something about it broke her."

Sable let the warmth of Ryah's words wrap around her. She almost asked if Ryah thought Eugessa was capable of ordering Narine killed. But she couldn't bring herself to ask something Ryah never would have imagined. "Please consider leaving with me," she said instead. "I think you'd love the north."

"I'll find you after the trial, and we'll see." With a weak smile, Ryah headed down the stairs.

Sable moved back to the window. The sky was now a deep, rich blue, the ocean a glowing reflection of it beyond the silhouettes of the city roofs.

The room was slowly falling into shadows, even the yellow walls fading into gloom.

Faint noises from far below reminded her she should rejoin the others, but she lingered. If she ignored the fact that she stood in Kiva's house and just focused on the feel of the room, she could almost capture it. Almost feel the way things were long ago when she and Talia had shared a room. Everything had been hard and hungry, but there'd been a sense of home.

She stepped closer to the sketches on the wall, searching for the one she knew she'd find. It was hung near the window, low down, as though Kiva had thought it less important than the rest.

How could he not have noticed the effort that had gone into this one? The way the hills and vastness of the Eastern Reaches had been captured. The way the ocean only touched the bottom. The way the center of the drawing was a valley that, instead of holding a burned, broken village, had no more detail than a smudge of shadow.

The sound of the lute came muffled through the window, the tune delicate but sad.

In the darkening room, the open emptiness of the Eastern Reaches seemed to spill out of the picture, spreading around her.

A noise at the door made her turn.

"I wanted to make sure you were all right." Reese's voice was familiar and safe, drifting toward her with a subtle warmth, and he took a step into the room, looking into the corners as though he might find some danger lurking there. "And, honestly, it makes me nervous to have you in Kiva's house."

Sable took a step toward him but stopped. "Talia is telling Niko about Melia."

Reese brought his attention back to her. "If they're pledging to be married, that's something he should know."

"You trust him? We don't even know him."

"Talia knows him," Reese said simply. "And she trusts him."

"Talia also trusts Kiva," Sable retorted.

"No, she doesn't. She is guarded and careful around him. She's not outwardly hostile toward him, like you are, but she's…she's like the snake charmers who dance with the poisonous snakes. She smiles and dances around him, but she keeps him at arm's length."

Sable stared at him. "When did you possibly come to that conclusion?"

"From watching them every single time we've seen them together. You butt your head against Kiva every time you meet him. Talia plays him like that woman outside plays her lute. I don't think Kiva even notices half of it, or maybe he actually is fond enough of her that he doesn't care."

"So you don't have any problem with Talia telling Niko about Melia?"

"I have a problem with the fact that the information about Melia is less of a secret every day, and that puts you in more and more danger. But Niko seems like a good man." He held up his hand to stop her objection. "Purnicious agrees, as does Ryah. Kiva called Niko honest enough to be a useless acquaintance."

"You made all these assessments in the hour since we met him?"

"Why do you think I've been talking to him?"

"I…" Sable stared at him. "I honestly hadn't thought about it."

Reese stepped toward her. "Niko adores Talia. It's obvious. I knew men like him in the Empire. Good men who'd been conscripted into the army and were doing the best they could. Of all the people here who could know that Melia was your mother, Niko is the least objectionable."

Sable crossed back to the window. Lanterns shone in the street below, glowing over the people milling among the merchant carts. A small crowd stood listening to the old woman's lute.

Reese's footsteps came close and stopped behind her. "*Are* you all right?" His voice was just behind her, and she leaned back against him.

Only people who want to be happy, she heard Talia say again.

"No," she whispered. "Are you?"

He was quiet for a breath. "No." The word blazed with warmth.

His arms wrapped around her shoulders, pulling her tight against his chest.

There was a pop behind them. "I'm so sorry, mistress," Purn said, "but Talia and Niko have decided to go ahead with the pledging."

Sable sighed. "Was there ever any doubt?"

"We're running low on time for dinner and the ceremony," Purn said apologetically, "before Talia is expected back at Lady Ingred's."

Reese kept his arms around Sable for another moment before loosening them. Sable let her hands fall from his arms, and he stepped away. She turned toward the door, where a distant light lit the stairway headed down into the house.

"Then let's go make an already complex situation even more difficult," Sable said, starting toward the door.

"I think it's lovely," Purnicious said quietly, "even if it is difficult."

Reese followed Sable into the hall. "Purn, why is it you like Niko so much when you barely know him, but it's taken you years to like me?"

Purn popped out of sight. "Niko," she said primly, her voice coming from the empty air, "told Talia her clothes were lovely and once left a shirt of his to be altered by her tailor."

"I should have known that's all it would take. What gaudiness did you add to his shirt?"

Purn giggled from the stairway. "Nothing he'll ever find."

The smell of roasted meat and baked apples filled the stairway before they were halfway down. They returned to the dining room to find heaping platters of meat and fish and fruits. Sable and Reese took their seats again. Kiva's eyes followed Sable curiously while the rest of the table started serving themselves.

"Niko," Ryah asked, "do they do pledging ceremonies in the Empire?"

"I don't know about most of the Empire," he said, "but northern Tallene, where I'm from, is poor. When a couple agrees to marry, they go to a place that has special meaning to them and build a *vez'ska*, a small tower of stones balancing on each other. When you walk through the countryside, you'll come across them under a tree, or on a hilltop, or at a bend in the river. It represents the building of a life, one bit on top of the next, and you never know whose they are."

"How big of a rock tower?" Ryah asked.

"Not big." Niko looked around the table. He scooped a pile of smashed yams onto his plate and set a large roll on top of it. Next he added a flat fish filet, a slice of apple, and topped it all with a scarletberry. The entire tower was barely taller than his goblet. "This would be on the small side, but you don't find many more than twice this big."

"That's a beautiful tradition," Ryah said. "Do they do anything similar for the hand fasting?"

"That's a ceremony before family and friends, much like yours here."

The rest of the dinner passed with attempts at casual conversation, led mostly by Ryah.

When everyone had eaten, Kiva pushed his chair back. "Unless you want to rush through your joyous occasion, Talia," he said with a remarkably amiable tone, "we should start."

Talia met Niko's eyes with a smile.

"Does Lady Ingred know about Niko now?" Sable asked.

"She knows we're attached," Talia said, "but I didn't mention the pledging ceremony."

"Because you didn't want her to come? Or because you don't want her to know?"

Talia paused. "Both."

Everyone started toward the hall, and a servant brought Ryah the branch of a tree loaded with light pink flowers. It was thicker and fuller than any other branch Sable had seen by a wide margin.

"Kiva," Talia said. "That's beautiful."

"Only the best for my daughter," he said, his tone not completely ironic. He stepped up to her and offered his arm. "Am I enough of a father that I can escort you in?"

Sable clasped her hands together, struggling for the second time tonight not to shove his arm away.

"Actually," Talia said, "I was hoping Sable would escort me."

Sable looked at her in surprise.

"You've been protecting me my whole life," Talia said quietly, holding out her hand. "It would mean a lot to me if you'd walk in with me."

Sable took her hand. "Everything you do terrifies me, Talia." She looked into her sister's face, searching it. "But you have no reservations about pledging yourself to marry Niko?"

"Not a single one," Talia said simply, and the words flowed around Sable like a warm breeze.

Sable took a deep breath. "Then I'm happy for you."

Talia broke into a smile. "No, you're not—you're still terrified. But thank you for saying it." She linked her arm with Sable's.

Kiva stepped out of their way, and Sable thought, just for an instant, that there was an edge of disappointment in his expression, but he gave Sable a mocking smile and waved toward the entry hall with a flourish. "Then let's begin."

Sable walked with Talia into the wide entrance hall and over to the stairs. Ryah stood several steps up, holding the flowering branch above Niko on the bottom step. He watched Talia approach, and Sable's throat tightened at the adoration in his eyes.

Talia smiled at him, her arm tight around Sable's until they reached the bottom of the stairs. She gave Sable a fierce hug, then, before Sable was ready, let go and turned toward Niko, taking his hand and stepping up next to him.

Sable backed up next to Reese as Ryah began the traditional blessing, her voice clear and pure, her face beaming with happiness. "As you pledge yourselves to each other, may the fire of your love burn through the thickets ahead of you, clearing your path and easing your way. May you cling to each other when the world would tear you apart. May you find warmth from the cold in each other's arms. May you discover, as you see the world through each other's eyes, that this life holds incredible beauty, even in the bleakest times."

Talia stepped closer to Niko, and he put an arm around her.

Ryah smiled at them both. "Mother Perrin, who ran my abbey, used to have her own blessing, which I always loved." She closed her eyes. "Love does not follow our rules. It does not appear merely where it should, docile and modest. It breaks into lives the way sunshine breaks through clouds. Without warning and with wild, heedless abandon. It is a vibrant, glowing, burning thing."

Ryah's words were warm and rich, and Sable felt them stir a deep ache.

"We enter this world alone," Ryah continued, "our hearts walled in by loneliness every day. But then love comes, reaching across an impassible distance, touching the darkest corner of our unfathomable depths."

Reese shifted, his arm brushing Sable's, and her fingers stretched out instinctively, intertwining with his.

"And just like that," Ryah said quietly, opening her eyes, "we are no longer alone."

Reese's fingers tightened on Sable's.

Niko cupped Talia's face in his hands. "I love you, Talia."

She gave him a dazzling smile. "And I love you, Niko."

He wrapped his arms around her and dipped her backwards, kissing her fiercely, and Ryah beamed at them. "Amah's blessings upon you!"

Niko straightened, and Talia stood up, laughing.

Ryah hurried down the steps and embraced them both. Sable held

Reese's fingers for a moment longer before letting go. She moved up next to Talia and hugged her.

When Sable backed away, Niko looked at her uncertainly, but Sable stepped up and hugged him too. "I haven't seen Talia this happy in years," she said, "so thank you."

"I never had a sister," Niko said.

"And we've been short on brothers," Sable said. "I'm thrilled to have someone to help me keep Talia out of trouble."

Niko smiled. "We might need more help to accomplish that."

CHAPTER FORTY-SEVEN

"Well, that was heartwarming," Kiva said, leaning idly against the wall as Talia, on Niko's arm, descended his front steps to the avenue. "Don't you think?"

Sable watched them step out onto the torchlit avenue. "Why did you invite me tonight, Kiva?"

"It's not enough to see your sisters?"

She turned to him. "That was the bait, not the purpose."

Kiva didn't move from the wall, but he gave her a lazy smile. "I don't think Vivaine should hang."

"Because you've always admired her so much?"

"Because I think it would be bad for the city."

Sable studied him. "You're not the first person to say that, but why bother telling me?"

"Because you have a way with words, and tomorrow you could turn the crowd. If Eugessa thinks the people are against her, she'll relent."

"I've been tasked by the Northern Lords to support Vivaine's execution."

Kiva raised an eyebrow. "I have intimate knowledge of how well you carry out an assigned task if you believe there's a better way."

Sable leaned against the opposite wall. "What would you see done to her?"

Kiva shrugged. "Imprisonment of some kind. Sentenced to penance on the merchant ships would be fine. Eugessa has her heart set on execution, and hanging a woman who's been beloved by the south for generations is…too much. That sort of unrest is very bad for business."

"Ah, business."

"And unity," he continued. "The Kalesh will be back. Ambassador Grigg isn't trying to hide it. I doubt we have long before more troops arrive."

"The fact that you have a Tien Sark in the Hole confirms that." Her hand strayed to the scar on her neck.

Would it be better or worse to tell Kiva of the Zenivah myth? Maybe the south should know, but telling Kiva that Vivaine held that much power felt as safe as playing with his pet snake. "When can we see him?"

Kiva's eyes lingered on the scar on her neck. "Looks like that hurt."

She dropped her hand, swallowing against the phantom pain. "Only briefly. When can we see the prisoner?"

"Time is never brief when you're in pain. As far as our Kalesh friend, your dog said he'd be unlikely to talk, so I had his water laced with pera root tonight. Once that kicks in, we should have a few minutes before he gets sleepy. But there's no point getting there too early. So we have a bit."

"Good." Sable pushed herself off the wall, leaving him by his open front door and heading for the dining room.

Ryah stood at the window, looking after Talia and Niko. Tomm strode over and leaned against the wall next to her. Ryah was such a lithe white wisp of a thing next to his muscled arms and tattooed chest.

"How is Mother Perrin?" Ryah asked.

He paused. "She still has the cough."

"Is it getting worse?"

He didn't answer.

Ryah put her hand on his arm. "Take me. Now."

"Aren't you due back at the priory?"

"I want to see her," Ryah said, stubbornly. "If you won't take me, I'll go myself."

He gave her an amused look. "I never said I wouldn't take you. I'm always here to help you break a rule."

"Rules should be broken if they keep us from doing good," Ryah said decidedly, turning toward the door where Kiva stood. "Do you have any pall flower root?"

Tomm's eyebrows rose.

"Pall flower root is illegal," Kiva said.

"Which is why I'm asking you," Ryah said, "not someone more…law abiding."

A smile spread across Kiva's face. "I love your whole family." He nodded to a servant in the hall behind him, and the man hurried off. "Pall flower root is also expensive."

"I only need a little," Ryah said. "Tell me what I owe you, and I'll send payment."

"The Muddogs will cover the cost," Tomm said.

Kiva waved off the words. "We'll just call it a favor, Ryah."

Ryah gave him a grateful smile.

"No," Sable said firmly. "Ryah will owe you nothing."

"The Muddogs will cover the cost," Tomm repeated, his tone hard.

Kiva let out an amused laugh. "As you wish."

The servant returned, giving Kiva a small packet of paper. He held it out to Ryah. She started toward him, but Tomm strode across the room and took it first. "I'll send payment in the morning."

"Two silvers should cover it." Kiva leaned around him to look at Ryah. "Then you won't owe me anything but gratitude for my part in helping ease the pain of that sweet old abbess."

"She will owe you nothing," Tomm said. He turned to Ryah and fixed her with a stony look. "Nothing."

Ryah set her hand on Tomm's arm and gave Kiva a wide, grateful smile. "Thank you. Both of you."

"Any time you need anything, my dear," Kiva said, "don't hesitate to ask."

Tomm pulled his arm away from Ryah and took a step closer. He was easily a head taller than Kiva. "Watch yourself."

Kiva grinned up at him. "Sorry, Tomm, didn't mean to step on any paws."

Ryah let out an annoyed breath. "You two could have stopped while you were being nice." She crossed to Sable, throwing her arms around her. "I'm so glad you were here."

Sable squeezed her sister tightly. "Please be careful."

"I'll see you at the trial tomorrow." Ryah's face creased with worry. "Let's pray that Amah has a peaceful solution to all this."

"Let's pray somebody does," Sable agreed.

Ryah gave her one last smile, then headed toward the door. Tomm fell in behind her like a looming, burly guard.

Kiva glanced at Sable and Reese. "We'll leave for the Hole in a few minutes. I have some matters to attend to first." He waved a hand at the table and his office with a smirk. "Do make yourselves at home."

Reese walked into Kiva's office and inspected the bottles of liquor Tomm had been drinking from over the evening. He picked up one glass bottle. "Kiva certainly has done well for himself."

Sable came up next to him. The thick glass bottle was beautifully made, the liquid inside the color of dark honey. The words on the label were not in a language she could read.

"Kalesh aged cider." He pulled out the cork and smelled it. "This is expensive even in the Empire."

He poured tiny amounts into two small glasses on the shelf and handed one to Sable. "Sip carefully. It has a kick."

She smelled the glass, and the warm scent of apples and cinnamon burned up into her nose all the way back to her throat, making her cough.

Reese smiled at her. "See?" He took a sip and grimaced slightly as he swallowed.

Sable took a tentative sip herself, and her mouth was full of warm spiced apple until she swallowed and the liquid set her throat on fire. She breathed out, trying to cool it.

Reese held up the glass. "The colonel who ran my school in the Empire kept a bottle of this, unopened, on his desk the entire time I was there." His eyes grew distant. "It was Vann's greatest dream to break into Colonel Pollon's office, steal the bottle, and drink it."

Sable took another sip of the liquor, but it was so strong she set it back down on the counter, coughing. "Vann? The one you thought you saw during the battle?"

Reese nodded.

"Did he steal it?"

"The first time he tried, he was caught by a captain and flogged. The second time, he barely escaped. And the third…" Reese shook his head, smiling. "The third time, Vann had the bottle in his hand. I thought he was actually going to pull it off, but he was nervous and his hands were sweaty, so it slipped out of his grip and smashed on the floor."

"You were with him?"

"Couldn't let him go in on his own. He just stared at the broken bottle for a second, then pushed the glass out of the way with his shoe, knelt down, and licked the cider off the floor."

"Please tell me you did not do the same."

He shook his head with a smile. "I never wanted the cider in the first place. One of the colonel's drawers had a bit of silver, so we took that in an attempt to make it look like a random robbery. We shoved everything else off Pollon's desk and got out before the alarms rang." He smelled his cup again. "The room smelled just like this." He took another drink, walked to one of Kiva's comfortable chairs, and sank into it. He looked at the glass for a long moment, then set it on the table, leaned back, and closed his eyes.

Sable paced across the room, her eyes straying to the dining room, her mind trying to sort through the events of the night.

She was nearing Reese's chair when he opened one eye. "Ryah seems fairly comfortable ordering a gang boss around."

"I know," Sable said with a groan. "She needs to be careful."

Reese let out a little laugh, closing his eyes again. "She looks like she has it under control."

She drew to a stop at the side of his chair. "What?" He opened his eyes, and she jabbed a finger toward the door. "How could *Ryah* possibly have *Tomm* under control?"

Reese reached up and took her hand, pulling her toward him until she sat on the arm of his chair.

"I think it's time you faced the fact, Sable," he said, not letting go of her hand, "that your sisters are both as capable as you are of knocking a man completely off-balance."

Even the arms of Kiva's chairs were comfortable, and Reese's hand was warm, so despite the objectionable nature of his words, Sable didn't pull away. But she did narrow her eyes. "I absolutely refuse to face that fact. And I've never knocked you off-balance. Not once."

He snaked one arm around her waist and pulled her into the chair. She slid onto his lap, and he drew her closer until she could smell the spiced apple on his breath. "I didn't say a single word when you were deciding to come to Kiva's for dinner," he pointed out.

"I noticed." She shifted slightly to sit more comfortably. "It was weird."

He lifted his other hand to the side of her neck, his thumb brushing warm against her cheek. "And now," he said quietly, "I'm here with you in Kiva's ill-gotten house, and all I can think about is that I wish we could stay longer." He held her gaze. "If that's not off-balance, I don't know what is."

"I wish," Sable said, leaning into his hand, "I was like Talia and could just…just let an abbess wax on about love as though it really was strong enough to solve every problem." She closed her eyes against the warring emotions inside her. "I wish I could ignore everything else and do what I want."

"What do you want?" he whispered.

She opened her eyes and looked at his face, his familiar eyes. His hair was long again, and his beard had grown enough she knew he'd trim it soon. She set her hand against his chest, feeling his heartbeat. "You."

His arm tightened around her waist. "You've had me, Sable. From nearly the first moment I saw you."

"And you've had me—almost as long." At his raised eyebrow, she shrugged and smiled. "You were very grumpy at first."

"Of course I was grumpy. I woke up looking at a beautiful woman, but instead of being sweet, she kept arguing with me."

"It had nothing to do with the pain? It was all me?"

He grinned. "I'm fairly certain it was you."

Sable closed her hand, grabbing a fistful of his shirt. "Why can't this just be simple?"

"Something about your mother and a brutal Empire and certain death." He slipped his hand behind her neck and pulled her closer. "Things that I can't bring myself to care about right now."

She hesitated. "We'll care about them the moment we get out of this chair."

His eyes held hers, and her throat tightened at what she saw there. He leaned closer. "Then let's not do that."

She pulled his shirt, closing the last few inches between them, and closed her eyes. His lips touched hers, and she tightened her grip, forcing herself not to pull *vitalle* from him. Both of his arms wrapped around her, and she melted into him.

"If you two break my chair," Kiva's voice drawled from the doorway, "I will be very angry."

Sable started to pull away, but Reese tightened his arms. He broke off the kiss long enough to say, "Go away, Kiva."

"Our prisoner is only going to be talkative for a limited time." A sharp edge of irritation hardened Kiva's voice.

Sable rested her forehead against Reese's and closed her eyes. "I was led to believe I didn't have to care about any of that until I got out of this chair."

"I'm leaving immediately," Kiva said. "If you two are coming, the time is now."

Sable sighed and started to stand.

Reese kept his arms tight around her for another breath before he loosened them. "This prisoner better have very interesting things to say."

CHAPTER FORTY-EIGHT

The darkness covered the filth of Dockside in shadows, but night never lessened the stench of fish that clung to the streets and buildings themselves. The broken windows of the buildings near the Hole seemed to watch Sable with hollow eyes as she followed Kiva down the dead-end street. Reese walked next to her, scanning the boarded-up doors and inky black alleys.

Years of memories crept along with them, moving silently through the alleys, dressed in dark clothes, stepping carefully through the clutter, always mindful of the nearest hiding place and fastest way out. Memories that lived in the choking fear that the sort of people who walked brazenly down the middle of the road at night could catch sight of them and crush everything they had with less effort than it took to step on a roach.

"Are you going to tell me why you think this Tien Sark is here?" Kiva asked Sable over his shoulder.

"I haven't decided yet," she answered.

Kiva gave her an amused smile. "It's always entertaining when you try to be cagey. You fret too much over it." He glanced back at Reese. "The pera root should have loosened his tongue a bit by now. At least until it makes him sleepy."

Boone started up the stairs to a building Sable had always avoided. The Hole was a cistern in a building that had once held a slaughterhouse. When she'd first come to Dockside, after hearing the Hole mentioned, she'd snuck onto the low roof of a nearby building and looked into a room with bare walls, a bare floor mottled with dark stains, and a ceiling hung with rows of huge iron hooks. The metal was a dark brownish red that very well might have been rust, but Sable had never been able to banish the idea that they were all stained with blood.

The front door was pulled open by a disreputable-looking man who nodded deferentially to Kiva. Torches were lit inside, and a half-dozen of Kiva's men stood up from where they were playing cards.

"News?" Kiva asked.

"He's still sitting like a lump," one of the men said.

Kiva motioned to the door at the back of the room, and the man pushed it open, leading the way into a vast room that took up the rest of the first floor.

A ring of torches burned on pillars around a black hole in the center of the floor and the circle of men guarding it. More lanterns were slung on chains between the pillars, hanging over the cistern. The rest of the room held nothing but thick support columns and rows of hooks dangling from the ceiling.

"Please tell me you've never been here before," Reese said quietly, setting his hand on her back.

"Not inside."

From this close, it was obvious that the metal hooks were rusted from years of disuse. Rusted to the point where their points were slightly rounded, some so corroded they looked as though they'd crumble if she touched them.

A railing that had once surrounded the cistern now only existed in small sections.

"Do I need to point out how much I don't like this?" Reese asked her.

"Kiva wants me to speak at the trial tomorrow and convince them not to execute Vivaine," Sable told him. "He's not going to throw me in a cistern tonight. And he knows I'll be displeased if he throws you in."

"You're assuming he's rational."

"Only when working toward his own ends."

Reese lowered his voice further. "Did you tell Kiva about Zenivah?"

"No. It feels like something he'd exploit."

"I agree. But he's bound to learn part of it during the questioning."

She looked up at him. "Unless you question the Tien in Kalesh."

"If Kiva doesn't have someone working for him who speaks Kalesh at this point, he's a fool."

Kiva strode up to the most substantial section of the railing and looked down into the hole. Sable followed.

The pit was so deep she grabbed the railing at the wave of dizziness that passed over her. The smooth stone walls dropped down at least two stories. They were far enough uphill from the sea that the bottom of the cistern was dry, but the Tien Sark must be sitting nearly at the level of the ocean.

The Tien Sark sat against one side, his knees drawn up, his head resting back on the wall. He looked small. The scales tattooed on his head looked almost like a covering of very short hair.

Kiva leaned his elbows on the railing and looked expectantly at Sable.

Even with the Tien Sark so far below her, she gripped a rail to keep herself from rubbing the scar at her neck. "He doesn't look particularly chatty," Sable noted quietly.

"Ask him a question or two," Kiva said. "He'll talk. It'll work best if the conversation is casual. He'll respond less to hostile questions."

Sable ran through the questions she had, trying to decide where to start.

Reese looked over the railing. "*Draconek nadra,*" he called into the pit.

The Tien Sark looked up sharply.

"What does that mean?" Sable whispered.

"Glory to the Empire," Kiva said. At Sable's surprised glance, he gave her a lazy smile. "By all means, keep questioning him in Kalesh if you wish. Just remember to keep it chatty."

The Tien Sark still hadn't made any move to speak.

"What's your name?" Sable called down.

He considered the question. "Jrogen, First Talon."

"Hello, Jrogen. Have you noticed your name sounds a lot like dragon?"

He gave her a flat look.

Sable paused. "Wait, it sounds like dragon in our language. What is dragon in Kalesh?"

"*Dracon,*" both Reese and Kiva said.

She looked between them. "Ah. Well, then, his name still sounds like dragon."

"All their names do," Reese said. "When they join the Tien Sark, they choose new names having to do with dragons. Or their scales or claws or teeth or something dragonish."

Sable considered the man. "Is Zenivah a dragonish name?" He didn't answer. "Have you seen her?" Sable called down to the prisoner. "Or did you arrive too late?"

Kiva shifted his full attention to Sable.

She ignored him. "We met a couple friends of yours. One on Tutella Island, who, last I saw, was imprisoned in a chicken coop, and another outside Barrowford. He's…that encounter didn't end well for him. Both of them were upset that they hadn't seen Zenivah."

"They knew their roles," the prisoner said without any emotion in his voice.

"Have you heard she's imprisoned?" Sable asked.

The Tien twitched, and Kiva's eyes widened.

"You really did just arrive when Kiva picked you up, didn't you?" Sable said. "If you'd been in the city for even an hour, you'd have heard that she's detained. Much like you. Although I've been to the cells she's in, and they're nicer than this."

"I don't remember them being particularly nice," Reese said.

Kiva's attention locked on Sable, and she tried not to shift under his scrutiny.

Jrogen shook his head. "The dragon cannot be bound."

Sable shrugged. "I would guess he'd be harder than she was, but the dragon left her."

"*Nemzet,*" he said, the word derisive.

"Not impossible," Reese answered. "No one's seen the dragon in…" He glanced at Kiva.

"Nearly a fortnight," Kiva said.

Sable leaned a little farther over the rail. "Does the missing dragon mess up your plans? Does it change what you want?"

Jrogen let out a little chuckle and rested his head back on the wall. "It is not for me to want anything. It is what Zenivah wants."

"And what does Zenivah want?" Sable asked, keeping her voice casual. "Aside from her freedom?"

The Tien shrugged. "She will tell us in her own time. Our job was merely to come to her when she called."

Sable blew out a breath. "So she really called you?"

"The Great Dragon had prepared us. We were merely awaiting reports from the scouts," he said, "but when her call reached the Empire, we came."

"Great Dragon?" Sable said quietly. "The Emperor?"

Reese nodded.

"Did Zenivah bid the Emperor to send you?" Sable asked. "Does your Great Dragon serve her now?"

"Zenivah's message came to me, even before the Emperor heard." There was a note of pride in Jrogen's voice. "We do not need the approval of the Emperor when we have Zenivah's commands."

"What if the Emperor didn't want you to come?" Sable asked.

Jrogen tilted his head to look up at her, his brow creased. "Zenivah called us."

"How many of you answered the call?" Reese asked.

"All of us."

"You're the only one here," Kiva said.

"When Zenivah's message reached my hands, I rose from my chair and came. The others had to prepare the ships. They will be here soon."

"How soon?" Reese asked Jrogen.

The Tien Sark shrugged. "With Zenivah's call to hurry us across the water, it could be as early as tomorrow."

"What will they do when they arrive?" Sable asked. "Zenivah is no longer in power."

"They shall free her." He paused. "If they find her harmed, there will be much bloodshed." A laugh bubbled out of the man. "The Great Dragon will have sent many men to serve Zenivah."

"Is that funny?" she asked.

"You might want to hurry," Kiva said. "If he's started laughing, he's not going to be awake much longer."

"How many men is the Great Dragon sending?" Sable asked.

Jrogen closed his eyes. "The seas shall be covered with the armies of the Dragon." The words had a rolling cadence to them, interspersed with chuckles. "The waves shall rise up and flood the land."

"I've heard this one before." Sable closed her eyes, bringing to mind the words from the first Kalesh soldier they'd met in the woods outside Ebenmoor. "Like water engulfing the land and never drawing back."

Jrogen grinned at her, but his eyes started to slide shut. "There is no prison," he said, his words coming out slowly, "that can hold her once they arrive."

CHAPTER FORTY-NINE

SABLE STEPPED BACK from the railing. "Well, executing Vivaine seems like a bad idea, and leaving her alive might be worse." She looked at Reese. "We need to find Atticus."

"First," Kiva said, still leaning on the railing, "take a few moments and tell me about Zenivah."

She started to object, but Reese set a hand on her arm. "Seems like a reasonable request, especially when we're standing above his creepy prison hole surrounded by his men."

"Fine." Sable gave Kiva a warning look. "but if you decide to use this for any reason that flies in the face of what is good for this entire land, I'm going to kill you."

Kiva laughed. "It's that good, huh?"

"The Kalesh have an old myth about a woman who had a dragon. She put down an uprising and helped the Emperor conquer his enemies. Now they think Vivaine is the reincarnation of that woman. Or maybe that the woman is still alive. I don't know. But the Tien Sark worship dragons, and we've been thinking they found out she was here and came to serve her, which she was bound to take advantage of." Sable paused, glancing down into the hole. "But this is the second man who's told us that she sent for them."

Kiva stared at her for a moment. "So Vivaine is poised to take control of the Kalesh troops. She and I aren't on good enough terms for me to want to see her at the head of an invading army. Let me think on this tonight." He studied Sable. "What do you intend to do at the trial tomorrow?"

Sable considered the question. "I'm not sure yet. What are the merchants planning?"

"They're torn." Kiva studied the man below them, whose head had lolled to the side. "Some want her dead, some are unwilling to leave only Eugessa in charge of the priories."

He was silent for a long moment before he waved absently at them, still looking down into the cistern. "You're free to go. No one in Dockside will bother you."

"What are you thinking?" Sable asked him.

He flashed her a smile. "That this night turned out much more interesting than I expected. I very sincerely mean that it has a been a pleasure, as always, Sable." Without waiting for their response, he strode across the room toward a small door in the back of the building.

The sun was setting the next day when Sable crossed under the Veil Gate with Atticus and Reese, the jostling crowd only giving them room because Innov perched on her arm. The shadows of the wall darkened Atticus's face, casting the wrinkles Sable rarely noticed into deep lines.

"I wish we'd had the chance to talk to Vivaine," he muttered. "If she stands up for herself, it will make a difference. The merchants are divided. I spoke with fourteen merchants today, and they're evenly split between wanting to see Vivaine executed and not wanting to purely because it will leave Eugessa as the lone prioress."

"None of them supported Vivaine?" Sable asked.

He rubbed the back of his neck. "The battle significantly disrupted trade. The merchants in outlying cities and along the Eastern Reaches are too scared to bring their goods to Immusmala. Lord Trelles says that even if normal trade resumed today—which it won't—the last few weeks have caused him such a loss, he won't recover for months. And every single merchant knows it's Vivaine's fault."

The crowd was thick around them, thicker than at any Blood Moon trial Sable could remember, and she couldn't see anything over the heads in front of her but the tips of the priory spires, stark white against the blue sky. Every prisoner besides Vivaine had been tried earlier in the day, but not a soul had left the Sanctuary. Instead, the entire city seemed to be trying to fit inside the Veil Wall.

"Do you have a sense of which way they'll lean?" Sable asked.

"Trelles is of the opinion that her execution will make things worse, but I couldn't pin down whether he'll speak against it or not. If he does, he has enough weight to affect things, but I think it will all depend on how the trial develops. If Eugessa is convincing, I think they'll go along with the execution. If Vivaine manages to stand up to her..." He shook his head. "My guess is whichever prioress appears stronger will have more support."

Sable shifted her white cloak until it sat more comfortably on her shoulders. Atticus had picked out a light grey dress and the cloak for her to wear, and he'd been so pensive after talking to the merchants all day that she hadn't bothered to point out that wearing a white cloak while carrying the phoenix was more of a statement than she'd been prepared to make.

Not that she was complaining about the cloak itself. The fabric was light and airy with a slight shimmer. It flowed behind her with enough flair that she felt the constant urge to spin just to watch it flutter behind her.

Reese craned to see over the crowd and pointed ahead and to the left. Sable shifted that direction, moving diagonally though the mass of people.

The crowd milled to a stop long before they reached the platform where the trial would take place, and, with some direction from Reese, Sable held Innov ahead of her and worked her way through the crowd, exchanging greetings with the people who turned to see the phoenix. Without fail, they stepped out of her way, watching the bird pass with wondering expressions.

She heard a few whispers of "Issable" and at least one "Queen of the North."

They finally reached a wall enclosing a small raised hill and one of the larger trees in the plaza. The rest of their group filled the grassy space in front of the tree. Leonis hopped down from where he was standing on a stool set on the wall itself, motioning for Sable to step up on it. She did and found herself head and shoulders above the crowd. Reese climbed up and stood behind the stool, probably able to see almost nearly as much as she could.

They were very close to the wood stacked for the bonfire and not far from the platform, which was empty of everything but three Sanctus guards.

"Excellent spot, Leonis." Atticus stepped up on the wall next to Sable. "Anything interesting happen yet?"

"They poured some sort of fuel on the wood for the fire," he said. "Smelled strong for a few minutes."

"Like dwarven rum," Thulan agreed. "But sweeter. The flame is going to be impressive."

Atticus looked at the wood curiously. "Interesting."

"If it's highly flammable," Serene said, "one of the Mira could light it easily from a distance. Eugessa is looking to put on a show."

"When has she not?" Atticus asked. "Any sign of Vivaine?"

Leonis shook his head.

Atticus frowned at the stage. "I wish we'd gotten the chance to talk to her," he said again.

Innov shifted on Sable's arm, her eyes fixed on the bonfire stack.

"That's the fire Narine used to have you light," Sable told her quietly. "Do you recognize it?"

Innov shifted her weight and launched into the sky, not toward the wood, but across the crowd. In the dusky light, she blazed like a torch, and a ripple of faces turned to watch her. Hands reached up as a hush fell over the crowd. She flew faster, the breeze whipping the flames up between her feathers and leaving long tongues of flame trailing behind her.

Thulan let out a huff of amusement. "I wonder what Eugessa will do if Innov lights the fire too early?"

"Or better yet," Leonis said, "lights the stage on fire."

Innov skimmed the surface of the stage, making the guards step back out of her way, then spun in a tight circle around the bonfire wood. Sable tensed as a shower of sparks cascaded down over the pile, but nothing lit.

The wide doors at the front of the Priory of the Horn opened, and Eugessa stepped quickly out, looking annoyed as she scanned the plaza. Innov raced straight at the prioress and her unicorn, shooting low over their heads. Eugessa ducked, and the black unicorn tossed his head, slashing his black horn through a trail of sparks. The phoenix turned sharply and dove for the wood.

Eugessa snapped something at a Mira standing behind her, and the woman raised her hand toward the pile of wood, but Innov reached it first.

The phoenix flared her wings at the last moment and sent a jet of sparks onto the wood.

With a powerful thrust of her wings, she shot up into the air, and the wood beneath her erupted into flames.

The glittering gold from Innov burst outward, followed by huge tongues of blue and purple fire. The flames raced up into the sky, chasing the blazing phoenix.

Innov spiraled up away from the enormous flames, and the crowd let out a deafening roar, their hands raised as they shouted after the phoenix. The fire roared along with them like a raging windstorm, its light blindingly bright, casting hues of blue and purple across the white stones of the priories.

Eugessa stood stock-still at the door of her priory, glaring at the blazing inferno.

Innov, who'd risen so high she was almost lost in the sky, sped back down, swooping across the stage again and flying straight for Sable.

Still standing on the stool, Sable held out her arm, and Innov swirled around her, landing with a flourish.

A rush of warmth rippled out from the phoenix, soaking through Sable like she'd just stepped into a steaming bath. "So you did recognize it," she said to the bird with a grin.

"Innov," Atticus said, staring at the bird in adoration, "you are spectacular."

The phoenix shifted her wings and settled herself serenely on Sable's arm, apparently indifferent to the cheers filling the plaza and the fury on Eugessa's face.

Sable saw Eugessa snap her fingers at the people behind her and stride down the stairs of her priory. From somewhere behind the stage, a bell began to toll with a long, solemn rhythm.

Eugessa and her unicorn crossed behind the fire and appeared at the back corner of the stage, almost like she'd climbed out of the flames.

From the moment she was visible, the reason for the blue and purple flames was obvious.

The black coat of her unicorn was glossy in the twilight, and the blue and purple light shifted over it like living, glowing shadows.

Eugessa kept the unicorn between herself and the fire and stepped into the light from a line of lanterns along the front of the stage. They were shuttered along the side facing the crowd but shone brightly enough toward the prioress that the light caught on glittering threads in her robe and made her gold jewelry glow.

"She's finally learned a few lighting tricks from Vivaine," Leonis said quietly.

While the bell continued its long, slow notes, a Mira climbed on the stage behind Eugessa, staying a modest distance behind her. The Mira stood still, her hands held at her stomach, tucked inside her sleeves. Her cuffs and hems glittered with silver, and Sable heard Gwen give an annoyed growl.

"That's Isla," Gwen said. "She'll amplify Eugessa's voice."

"I gather you don't like her?" Leonis said.

"She served Vivaine for as long as I did. She's a power-hungry parasite. Certainly didn't take her long to switch loyalties to Eugessa."

Another Mira stepped up on stage, one Sable recognized from when Serene had tried to set the Dragon Priory on fire.

"That one can do stuff with the flames," Sable said quietly.

Gwen nodded. "Baila. She's not as talented as Terrane, but she could make the bonfire do some interesting things. I'm sure she was the one Eugessa was going to use to light it." She glared at the two women. "Did Eugessa take everyone from the Dragon Priory?"

Finally, three abbesses followed the Mira up the steps, one of them smaller than the others. Ryah took up her station with the other two near the Mira and fixed her attention on Innov.

Sable nodded to her sister, and Ryah managed a tiny, worried nod in return.

The bell rang out one long last note that faded slowly, stilling the crowd at the same time.

Eugessa raised her chin. Her eyes had been painted with copper powder that caught the light and glittered along with countless tiny gems tucked into her hair. "On this momentous evening," her voice rolled out over the crowd, "we gather for a very difficult task."

The words had the same volume and clarity as if Eugessa were merely speaking to another person, but Sable could feel the sound spreading far past where it should. It wasn't warm exactly, but a soothing, gentle movement brushed over her like a mother's hand stroking her hair.

It was subtle, almost unnoticeable, but familiar. It was the feeling Sable'd had every time she'd heard Vivaine speak to a crowd. The feeling — along with Vivaine's brightness—that had made Sable think she might actually be blessed by Amah.

"I didn't realize that feeling of comfort Vivaine always managed was manufactured by someone else," Sable whispered to Gwen. "Is there anything honest about that woman?"

"I…" Gwen's gaze flicked to Sable, then back to the Mira. "I thought Isla just made her louder. I had no idea the feeling didn't come from Vivaine."

"Did you?" Sable whispered to Atticus.

The old man watched Eugessa with an expression that Sable couldn't unravel. "I didn't know other people could feel it."

"It's not going to help her defense," Leonis said. "If she speaks on her own behalf and, for the first time, she can't pull that off."

Atticus's expression grew grimmer. "Eugessa has learned several tricks."

"…events of the battle cannot be overlooked," Eugessa continued. "And so today we must face the heavy burden of hearing the accusations that have been brought against the High Prioress and weigh for ourselves what shall be done."

She turned to the back of the platform, where the Dragon Priory was quickly falling into shadows. There were few lights in the windows compared to either the Phoenix Priory or the Priory of the Horn. Sable thought she could still make out dark streaks where Serene's fire had stained the stones.

Sable focused on the doors of the priory, waiting for them to open, but instead, there was movement in the shadows just behind the stage. Two Sanctus guards climbed steps onto the lit platform, escorting between them the dim, stooped figure of Vivaine.

CHAPTER FIFTY

THE CROWD FELL SILENT.

The two guards were tall and broad, and Vivaine looked brittle between them. Her prioress's robe was rumpled and dingy, the skirt smudged with dirt, the hem darker than the wood of the platform. Her hair hung limp around her face, long and grey. Whatever silvery brightness it usually had was gone.

Her steps were slow as the guards walked her to the center of the platform. A heavy chain hung between shackles on her wrists, so long that it brushed the ground. One of the guards knelt and locked the center of the chain to a ring anchored to the platform.

Sable glanced at Atticus. His eyes scanned the stage, took in the lights and the backdrop of the priories. He gauged the crowd's silent shock at Vivaine's appearance. He finally looked at the High Prioress, clenched his jaw, then returned to assessing the situation.

Eugessa stood tall, her hand resting on Cernus. The lights around the Prioress of the Horn were bright and white, the fire still burning with vivid purple flames. Vivaine's side of the stage was still lined with lanterns, but they gave off barely any light compared to the ones illuminating Eugessa, leaving the light around Vivaine more muddied.

"A bit theatrical," Leonis said. "There's no subtlety here."

"There's no way Eugessa keeps hold of all these moving parts," Thulan agreed. "Vivaine could have pulled it off, but not Eugessa."

Leonis nodded. "Vivaine would have put on a show worth watching."

"Before the prisoner speaks for herself," Eugessa said, "we will hear the charges brought against her."

Several merchants climbed onto the far side of the platform, where lanterns illuminated them with warm golden light, and Atticus made a disapproving noise.

Vivaine didn't pay attention to the merchants or Eugessa but looked out over the crowd. Her shoulders were slumped, her arms weighed down, her expression tired. Slowly, she turned her head to focus on Innov, perched on Sable's arm.

The High Prioress looked at them dully for a moment, then her fingers twitched, and the space between them shrank until she appeared to be almost within arm's reach.

One of the merchants began to list off things Vivaine had done before and during the battle, and Isla's power helped his voice spread over the crowd.

But Sable kept her attention on Vivaine.

The prioress's face was drawn, dark shadows smudging the skin under her eyes, and Sable braced for the brazen, hostile look Vivaine always fixed her with.

But her eyes weren't even on Sable. Instead, she looked over Sable's shoulder where Gwen stood, perfectly still. The High Prioress's expression grew slightly regretful, and Gwen drew in a shaky breath.

Vivaine shifted her focus to Sable for just a heartbeat. Her eyes were clouded, her gaze weightless, as though she wasn't completely present.

The prioress's attention drifted to Atticus, and something shifted in her expression. There was something almost sad about it, but not a reflection of Atticus's sorrow. There was no regret or nostalgia. It was more thoughtful than that. More brooding.

Atticus didn't move.

Vivaine held his gaze for a breath, then flicked her fingers.

She stood across the crowd again, alone on the platform, her attention shifting to some point above the heads of the crowd.

A second merchant began to list his grievances against Vivaine.

"Lord Trelles is going to speak," Atticus said quietly, pointing across the stage. At the far side, where the first set of merchants had mounted the stage, the broad form of Lord Trelles was visible. He stood with his arms crossed, watching the stage.

A much smaller man stepped out of the crowd and joined him. Kiva moved up next to Trelles, acknowledging the lord with a brief nod.

"And Kiva," Sable added. "Maybe their two voices will turn the mood of—"

Reese swore. Three of Kiva's men followed him out of the crowd, escorting Jrogen between them. The Tien Sark's hands were bound, but he appeared unconcerned by his situation. Instead, his attention was fixed fully on Vivaine.

"Clearly we didn't impress upon Kiva how dangerous that man is," Sable said.

"Idiot," Reese muttered.

Kiva watched the interactions between the merchants, Eugessa, Vivaine, and the crowd like a snake deciding which mouse to devour.

The third merchant listed the number dead from the battle, and murmurs rippled through the crowd. The mood of the plaza shifted. What had been curiosity and pity was now a steadily growing anger.

"After calling for peace for months," the merchant said, pointing a long finger at Vivaine, "she secretly allied with the Empire, and hundreds of our citizens are dead." For a moment, he let the words hang in the air and the rumble of the crowd grow. "It is with a heavy heart that the Merchant Guild upholds the judgment of our Holy Mother"—he bowed toward Eugessa—"that this woman be executed for her heinous crimes against the city."

The crowd murmured in agreement.

Vivaine showed no reaction to the words.

The merchants filed off the stage, and Lord Trelles started to step forward, but Kiva moved quicker, ascending the stairs and raising his voice. "I have some evidence to bring, Holy Mother." He motioned for his men to bring Jrogen on the stage.

"This man," he began, "is a highly trained soldier in the Kalesh Army, serving the Emperor himself, and he told me that he was called by Prioress Vivaine herself to come here and serve her. I was able to apprehend him before he could cause our city any trouble."

A wave of mutters rolled through the crowd.

Sable stared at Kiva. "He's speaking *against* Vivaine?"

The Tien Sark ignored them all, his focus still fixed on the Dragon Prioress.

Vivaine blinked as though just realizing where she was and turned slowly to look at him but didn't make any attempt to speak.

Jrogen leaned forward, straining against the hold of Kiva's men. "Where is the dragon?"

Vivaine flinched at the question.

"The dragon rejected her," Eugessa said, her voice spreading over the crowd. "Because of her corruption and greed."

Ryah's brow creased at that explanation.

"That dragon has nothing against corruption and greed," Sable said under her breath.

The Tien Sark shook his head, still looking at Vivaine. "If the dragon left you, it was because he refused to align himself with your weakness."

"What are your intentions here?" Eugessa asked the man, but he kept his eyes on Vivaine and said nothing. Eugessa questioned him several more times, but he stayed unmoving and silent.

Finally, she turned back to Kiva. "What is your conclusion about this man?"

"I believe the High Prioress called a foreign army to our land," he said. "It is with a heavy heart that I uphold your judgment, Holy Mother, that this woman be executed for her heinous crimes against the city."

Sable swore. "Of all times for him to actually tell the truth."

Eugessa offered him a benevolent sort of wave, and he had his men lead Jrogen off the platform.

"If there is anyone else who would like to speak for or against the accused," Eugessa said, looking blandly around the crowd, "tradition allows for it."

Lord Trelles had stepped back away from the steps, and Atticus sighed.

Eugessa pointedly kept her eyes directed away from Sable, but the crowd turned curiously in her direction. The Sanctuary had dropped into deeper blue shadows, and the torches near the priories didn't provide much light, leaving Innov to burn brightly under the branches of the tree.

"The Northern Lords have grievances," Sable said, pushing her words out. She didn't raise her voice, just fed *vitalle* into it and spread it out across the plaza.

Eugessa turned, contempt curling up the side of her mouth. "This trial concerns the city of Immusmala. The northerners have no voice here."

"After they came and died protecting this city from the Kalesh," Sable said, keeping her voice quiet, "you won't offer your allies a voice?"

The crowd muttered in agreement, and Eugessa shrugged. "The north has no say in the justice of Amah, but if you have words…" She waved a hand dismissively at the stage.

Leonis leaned toward Thulan. "Eugessa did not play that right."

Thulan shook her head. "Huge wasted opportunity there. Never put yourself on the side opposing a phoenix. Not in this lighting. That feels obvious."

Atticus offered Sable a hand as she climbed down off the stool. He gripped hers for a moment. "What are you going to say?"

"We wanted to talk to Vivaine, right?" Sable straightened her shoulders. "The Northern Lords handed me my chance."

She stepped down off the wall ringing the tree, and the crowd ahead of her parted, giving her a thin path forward. There wasn't much room, but Sable held Innov out in front of her and moved through the sea of faces illuminated by the golden light.

"Issable," someone said quietly, and Sable nodded in the general direction of the voice. She worked her way forward until she came to where the crowd was held a few paces back from the platform by Sanctus guards. The nearest guard glanced at Innov and let her pass. The stage was chest-high, and she had to cross the length of the front to reach the stairs Kiva had used.

The audience grew noisier as she walked.

Kiva and his men stood off to the side, the Tien Sark's eyes fixed on Sable with a burning hatred.

"*Zabat*," he hissed.

Sable flinched at the word and stopped to face him.

He knew. There was no doubt he knew she was Melia's daughter.

The thought should have terrified her, but instead, a tension that had coiled in her since General Goll's raven had flown toward the Empire loosened.

The rage in Jrogen's eyes was raw and almost uncontrolled—and directed at her.

She wasn't Melia. She wouldn't brazenly attack Kalesh soldiers or assassinate bloodthirsty Kalesh princes, but somewhere, almost hidden in the fury of Jrogen's eyes, she saw a tightly wound strand of caution. Maybe even fear.

She threaded a tendril of *vitalle* toward Jrogen. "Melia was my mother," she whispered. His eyes widened when the words came to his ears. "You shouldn't have killed her." The words were hot and fierce, and Sable held his gaze, the need to stand up against him and everything he represented flowing through her like fire. "You should never have come to this part of the world at all."

His response didn't matter, and she turned away to the more pressing situation.

Past the stage, above the Dragon Priory, Sable's eye caught on the bright white of the rising full moon. The sky around it was a deep, fathomless blue.

Not much of a Blood Moon, she thought idly before pulling the Northern Lords' letter from a pocket inside her cloak and climbing up on to the platform.

She stepped onto the stage and into the light from the shuttered lanterns.

The surface was smooth and stretched out wide and empty in front of her, much larger than it had appeared from the crowd. The lanterns on this side of the stage were definitely dimmer than Eugessa's side, and the glass on them had been tinted a little brown, so the quieting audience was lost in the shadows past them. The people were there, though, a mass of humanity waiting to see what she would say. Not faceless masses, but unknown souls here to witness the determining of a life.

Sable took in Eugessa's ill-concealed annoyance, then turned to Vivaine.

Even with her shoulders slumped and her back bowed, the High Prioress was taller than Sable. Vivaine kept her expression blank, focused past the crowd, and Sable had the urge to step right in front of her, force the woman to meet her gaze. See if there was any fight left in her.

But the crowd was waiting, so Sable turned away from Vivaine and held up the letter. It felt like a foreign thing, filled with words that were too simple for everything that was happening.

"The Northern Lords asked me to bring their accusations against Prioress Vivaine," she said, projecting her voice over the crowd. She opened the letter and read, but she couldn't keep her voice from growing formal, and she put no passion or warmth into it.

The letter detailed how Vivaine had lured their armies south, then sent troops in secret up the Black River to destroy their homes. Appalled exclamations rolled through the crowd at the news. As Sable listed the number of villages and homes destroyed, recounted the murders and slaughter of animals, the crowd grew uglier, and Sable felt the true weight of Vivaine's deeds settle on her again.

She reached the end of the letter, where Lord Perric had scrawled that the north demanded Vivaine's execution, and paused.

Sable changed the language to the traditional conclusion, keeping her voice impassive. "It is with a heavy heart that the Northern Lords uphold the judgment of the Holy Mother"—she nodded slightly toward Eugessa, who had the hint of a complacent smile—"that this woman be—"

Innov shifted, tightening her talons on Sable's arm, and the next words lodged in Sable's throat. The few times Sable had come to the Sanctuary for the trials when she was younger, these words had always sounded abrasive and heartless. Even when she'd understood the brutality of their crimes.

But in the face of Innov, they felt infinitely worse. They felt like the tearing away of hope. Like silencing the final peal of a bell.

They felt like death.

Keeping her eyes fixed on Innov, Sable let go of the letter, and it fluttered to the stage. She lifted a finger and ran it down Innov's chest, watching the play of the fire between her feathers.

"It is with a heavy heart," she said quietly, unwilling to truly release the words to the night, "that the Northern Lords uphold the judgment of the Holy Mother that this woman be executed for her heinous crimes against the city."

Her voice rang out across the plaza, loud and perfectly clear. She snapped her gaze over to Isla, who merely gazed over the crowd with a placid look.

"Do not," Sable hissed, sending the words across the stage straight to Isla's ears, "touch my voice."

Isla flinched and twitched toward Sable, her eyes wide.

"You're not the only one who knows this trick," Sable said softly. "If you want anyone to hear anything Eugessa says from now on, *do not touch my voice.*"

Isla yanked her focus back to the Prioress of the Horn.

"The priories thank the Northern Lords for their support," Eugessa said, her voice taking on a regal air. After the first few words, Isla had gathered herself enough to amplify it correctly. "Thank you."

The dismissal was pointed, and Sable glanced at Vivaine, but the High Prioress looked stoically over the crowd.

"How did you let it come to this?" Sable whispered, weaving the words only toward Vivaine.

The prioress's lips twitched with the slightest disdain, but she still didn't speak.

Sable had the urge to shake the woman. Instead, she planted her feet and settled Innov more comfortably on her arm. Eugessa glared at her for a moment before turning back to the crowd, asking whether there were any others who wished to speak.

The muddied lanterns at the front of the stage cast a dim glow onto Vivaine. The full moon behind her had a hard time lighting the dinginess of her robe. The abbesses with Ryah and the two Mira stood between the High Prioress and the bonfire, blocking much of that light.

Innov shifted on Sable's arm, and the glow lit Vivaine the slightest bit, taking the edge of the weariness and wrinkles off her face.

"What are you doing?" Sable kept her voice low, threading the words to Vivaine.

Vivaine kept her eyes focused on the distance. "Still not speaking for yourself?"

"Me?" Sable asked. "Why aren't you speaking for yourself? You have a chance. You can't still stand behind what you did. You can't have wanted all those northern women and children to die. Tell the crowd you were misled. Tell them the Kalesh deceived you. Tell them something. You know they want to believe you. And you know Eugessa isn't strong enough to stand against them or you. You could take over this entire farce with a flick of your fingers."

Vivaine stayed impassive, and Sable's frustration grew.

"You have fought tooth and nail for every single thing I've ever seen you want," Sable said under her breath, "and now—here—you do nothing?"

"Do not pretend you care," Vivaine said quietly. "Falseness is an ugly look on you."

"We have heard from the people of this city," Eugessa's voice rang out, "and even the lords of the north. The suffering brought to us by the prisoner has reached far beyond what any of us knew."

"I wish I didn't care," Sable said, struggling to keep her voice low. "I wish Innov weren't sitting on my arm insisting that even for someone as twisted and misguided as you, there should still be hope."

"Hope is a feeble, fragile thing," Vivaine said, "only propped up by power. If you lose power, you lose everything. Even Innov knows that."

"You are the only one who can stop the coming war," Sable said, filling her words with warmth. "You can tell the Tien Sark to find a peaceful solution. You can offer them the mines and stop the bloodshed that is coming. You can be the hero both here and in the Empire." Sable took a half step toward Vivaine. "Why won't you listen to me, for once?"

A hint of Vivaine's old strength crept into her eyes, and she spared Sable a glance. "Not everything in the world is about you, Issable. Your part in this little show is done. Take Innov, and step aside." She turned her eyes back forward.

The name Issable brought Atticus to mind, and Sable felt a twinge of pity for what he must be feeling. "I wish Atticus could see who you really are. He doesn't deserve the pain you've caused him."

Something in Vivaine's posture twitched, but she kept her focus stoically past the crowd. "Atticus has been useful over the years. He taught me everything I needed to know, but he's an old fool." Her words were harsh and warm. "He'll survive all this as miserably as he's survived everything else. Besides, he can take solace in the Flame of the North. He's as enamored of you as he always was of me."

The heat of those words pressed uncomfortably against Sable. "There is nothing similar in how Atticus feels about us."

Eugessa's words still droned on, but Sable ignored them.

A flicker of contempt crossed Vivaine's face. "There are many kinds of adoration, Issable. Everything for him is a performance. Atticus's whole life is a performance. He knows the power of it—loves the power of it. He knows that if you create the right story, you can rule the world." She was silent a moment. "The only thing he loves about me is the fact that I always controlled the story." Her eyes strayed to the playwright before she pulled them back. "Which is exactly what he loves about you." Her lips almost curled into a sneer before she schooled them again. "What Atticus truly craves is power, just like the rest of us. Now *step aside*."

"We gathered here tonight," Eugessa continued, her voice rich and amplified, "to see if there was anyone who would speak on the prisoner's behalf. If there were a reason to extend mercy to someone whom we've all been so deceived by. But all we have heard is more accusations. And now our path ahead is clear." She attempted to put some reluctance into her voice, but it rang false. "There has been no justification revealed for her crimes. The sentence of execution must stand."

Eugessa stepped away from Cernus and closer to the front of the stage, closer to the bright white lanterns. The unicorn tossed his head, his hooves stomping, striking the wood hard enough Sable could feel the vibrations in her feet. Eugessa's gown shimmered with silver threads as she moved to stand alone on the center of the stage, facing Vivaine. "Do you have anything to say for yourself? Anything to explain the horrors you've brought upon us?"

Vivaine kept her chin raised, looking out over the crowd. "I am guilty of nothing but keeping my city safe."

Isla didn't strengthen those words at all, and Sable doubted the people in the back of the crowd could hear.

"Then why are you now on trial?" Eugessa's words swept over the crowd. "Why has Amah's light abandoned you? Why has the dragon rejected you?"

"Amah does not abandon her servants." Vivaine's voice rang out louder, despite the fact that Isla still did not help. "She does not abandon those who truly serve her, nor does Isah remove his protection. We may encounter troubles and unbelievers who seek to destroy us, but those who are true to Amah would never turn on another of her faithful followers."

"I agree," Eugessa said. "We only root out those who have shown themselves, in the end, to be false."

For the first time, Vivaine faced Eugessa. Her posture had straightened, and while she was still dim, Sable tensed.

"Perhaps," Vivaine said clearly, "we should ask Amah which of us is right."

"Amah has already spoken," Eugessa said. "Anyone can see which of us she has blessed."

"We should not be so arrogant to presume we have heard her voice." Vivaine's tone was even, but it held an edge of defiance. "What are you waiting for? Pray for a sign, Eugessa." Vivaine wrapped the name in a curl of contempt, and Eugessa's expression flattened at the lack of respect. "Perhaps the goddess will actually answer you. Just this once."

The challenge rolled out, and the crowd turned toward the Prioress of the Horn.

Eugessa kept her scornful look fixed on Vivaine. "After everything we've heard, we hardly need another sign from Amah. But so that all may know what the goddess thinks of you…" She closed her eyes and raised her hands into the air.

Baila, the Mira, shifted closer to the bonfire.

"Amah, Goddess of Light," Eugessa began as Isla swelled her voice to fill the plaza. "Give us a sign. Show us your judgment on this woman who has claimed to serve you for so long yet has caused so much pain. You are not a goddess of pain. You are light and love and blessings." She paused, her arms still raised. Her jewelry glinted in the light, and she shifted her weight, sending glitters of light over her robe. "But you love goodness, and it says in the holy writings that you will burn the evil from the world. That to make us holy, you will purify us like a fire purifies gold."

The bonfire flared brighter, and a gasp went through the crowd.

Vivaine kept her steady gaze fixed on Eugessa.

"Show us, great Amah!" Eugessa cried out. "Show us your will! Is this woman an imposter who must be refined in flame?"

A huge burst of fire exploded from the bonfire, flames of blazing gold surrounding a tower of purple flame in the center, shooting into the sky with a deafening roar.

The crowd fell back, their faces—suddenly visible in the bright firelight—set in frightened exclamations.

Innov's talons tightened on Sable's arm.

Vivaine remained still and unimpressed.

Eugessa dropped her arms. "Now there is no question."

Vivaine turned back to the crowd and lifted her own arms. The chain caught them with a loud clank before they were any higher than her waist, but she raised her palms and her eyes toward the sky. "May Amah deal with me as she wills." Her words rang out crystal clear.

The entire plaza waited in silence.

By the light of the bonfire, Sable could see the tree where Atticus and the others stood. She tried to make out his expression, but he was too far away.

Suddenly, Serene stepped up onto Sable's stool, her face turned upward. She cast out. The pulse rolled through the crowd, shifting it into a sea of molten heat. Vivaine, Eugessa, the Mira, and the abbesses shot up into their own towers of warmth on the stage.

Behind them all, a torrent of heat hurtled over the Dragon Priory.

Sable spun toward it.

Silver scales, glittering with an icy brilliance, brushed over the high roof and dove toward the platform.

The crowd screamed and swarmed backward, shoving into each other as Argyros soared closer.

His wings spanned the platform, and his tail lashed out behind him, longer than his entire body had been. The tips of his scales were still silver, but the light didn't glide over them smoothly. Instead, it flashed between them, erratic and feral.

Argyros dove straight for Vivaine's back. The prioress stood perfectly still, her chin raised toward the sky, her palms upturned before her.

A hand grabbed Sable and pulled her toward the stairs. Kiva's eyes locked on the dragon, and Sable stumbled after him, Innov's talons clamped on her arm. They reached the stairs, and Sable ran down them, turning to see the dragon draw in a deep breath.

Sable caught a glimpse of Ryah across the stage, staring at Argyros in horror with the Mira and the abbesses.

Eugessa scrambled away from Vivaine.

Argyros opened his jaws, and rows of jagged, knife-like teeth caught the torchlight for an instant before he shot out a jet of flame.

It poured down on Vivaine, engulfing her and the entire center of the stage in fire.

Argyros snapped his mouth shut, and Sable ducked down with Kiva as the end of his wing blocked the sky overhead.

He soared away over the crowd, leaving nothing but a towering inferno where Vivaine had stood.

CHAPTER FIFTY-ONE

Sable crouched, staring up the stairs at the towering fire.

Kiva pulled on her arm. "Time to run, Sable."

Argyros pivoted in the sky and started back toward the stage.

Innov's eyes were fixed on the dragon, her talons tight on Sable's arm.

"Innov," Sable said, setting her hand on the phoenix's chest. "He's stronger now. You can't—"

The phoenix launched herself off Sable's arm and tore through the air, not toward Argyros, but across the stage.

On the far side, Eugessa hiked up the front of her robes and rushed for the far stairs. The Mira and the abbesses were pushing past each other to get off, but Eugessa plowed into the back of them, shoving the smaller women out of her way. Ryah stumbled to the side, falling to her knees.

Innov reached Ryah just as Argyros's flame slammed into that side of platform. The abbesses and Mira dove from the stage, their cries lost in the rushing flames.

Argyros tore through the sky over the stage. Only the very tips of his scales were still silver. The root of each was utter blackness. The reflected firelight glittered across him with frantic chaos. He soared up and over the Dragon Priory, disappearing from sight.

"Ryah!" Sable screamed, scrambling toward her.

Kiva wrapped his arms around her from behind. "Sable! Don't be stupid!"

Instinctively, she dropped her weight, breaking out of his grip as she'd practiced a hundred times. She scrambled up the stairs, but the fire raced across the wooden platform, the blistering heat blocking her like a wall.

Everything from where Vivaine had stood to the far side of the stage was engulfed in flame, blazing taller than Sable's head.

Sable ran to the front of the stage and jumped down. The crowd was still pushing away from the fire, shoving and crying out, trampling each other in their rush to escape. Reese raced toward Sable. Atticus remained on the short wall around the tree, staring at the tower of flames where Vivaine had stood.

Serene and Jae moved toward the stage, their hands outstretched, the flames closest to them shrinking down and guttering out.

Sable grabbed Reese's hand. "Can you see Ryah?"

"Innov reached her before the fire." He squinted into the blaze.

Sable caught a flash of a Mira's robe past the stage, and the flames near the back lowered.

Sable kept her eyes locked on the spot where Ryah had been.

Behind her, Atticus made a strangled noise. "Vivaine?"

The tower of fire where Vivaine had stood was lessening, and Sable drew back, not wanting to see the pile of ash that would be left.

But a figure moved in the flames. Tall and straight.

Baila, the Mira, rushed around the back of the stage, her hands outstretched.

The fire shrank, revealing long, glowing white hair and Vivaine's face. Her skin radiated light, every sign of aging and exhaustion burned away. Her expression was clear and smooth, her shoulders straight.

She lifted her hands to the sky as the last of the molten shackles fell to the platform.

The screams of the crowd died, and the plaza fell into silence, aside from the crackle of the fire, which was quickly being smothered.

Two flaming wings beat at the smoke farther over on the stage as Innov rose into the air. Sable scrambled up onto the hot, charred platform and ran through the choking air to find Ryah curled in a ball. The edges of her white robe were singed, but other than that, she looked unharmed. Terrified, but unharmed. Sable pulled her close, searching the dark sky for the dragon.

"Vivaine?" Atticus's voice came tentatively from the front of the stage. He stared at the High Prioress, his expression torn between wonder and horror.

Vivaine stood perfectly still until the fires died out, until the only light in the plaza was the bonfire and the few lanterns on the stage that had survived the destruction—and the brilliance of the prioress herself.

She was the pure, dazzling white of the full moon hanging in the sky behind her. As though a piece of the heavens had been born from the flames.

Sable squinted against the brightness of her robes.

In a rush of silver and black, Argyros streaked back over the roof of the Dragon Priory. Innov let out a sharp cry from the air, but the dragon didn't open his mouth. Instead, he flew straight for Vivaine, landing on the platform next to her, his talons digging into the charred wood. The silver tips of each scale glittered like blinding stars in gaping holes of black. His head, which used to be poised near her hip when he stood by her, now reached almost to her shoulder. She draped one hand on the scales crowning his head while he looked out over the crowded plaza. One of his eyes was an icy, steely grey, but a black scar lanced across the other, gouging deep into his brow and through a milky white, sightless eye.

Vivaine brushed her fingers over the silver-tipped scales on his head and let out a long, slow breath.

Ryah drew away from her, staring at Argyros as though she was looking at an abomination. "He's so cold," she whispered.

The charred wood sloughed off under Sable's hands and knees as she pulled Ryah toward the front of the stage.

The crowd stood frozen, watching Vivaine through raised fingers and squinted eyes.

"Do not fear." Vivaine's voice wasn't terribly loud, but it was clear and warm, and the plaza was so silent it sounded like a bell ringing through the night. "Amah holds nothing against souls who were led astray by those who do not understand—or willfully ignore—the goddess's ways." She paused, looking over the crowd with a benevolent smile. Sable expected the cold thread of a lie to be traced through those words, but she felt nothing but warmth. "Do not fear. All is well. Amah is still light, even when times seem dark. Isah does not abandon us, even as our enemies gather."

The light enfolding Vivaine reflected off Argyros's scales, as though she had pulled stars from the sky and nestled them into his back. He surveyed the crowd, and the light skipped across him with frenzied flashes of brilliance. Ryah scooted farther from them both, her breath coming fast and short.

"Are you hurt?" Sable asked.

Ryah shook her head. "The dragon is…Sable, he's so *cold*."

Thulan and Reese stood at the front of the stage, and Ryah crawled to them. Thulan helped her down and wrapped her in a hug, drawing Ryah back to where the others stood. Sable reached the edge, and Reese grabbed her hand, his eyes not leaving Vivaine as Sable climbed down and they backed away from the platform.

Across the stage, Sable caught sight of Jrogen staring at Vivaine, straining toward her against the men who held him back.

Vivaine's fingers still stroked the top of Argyros's head, but she raised her other hand in a blessing to the crowd. "Go out into the city. Tell the people what you have seen. Tell them that our hard times are drawing to a close and that Amah will guide us."

Some of the crowd started to disperse, but most stayed, still watching Vivaine.

"Zenivah!" Jrogen choked out, falling forward to his knees at the side of the platform. Kiva's men yanked him back, but he struggled to stay kneeling.

Vivaine graced him with an emotionless glance, then turned away.

Eugessa lay sprawled on her back on the stairs, her robe sullied with soot and smoke and maybe blood, her hair disheveled. She cradled her wrist against her chest and watched Vivaine with a mix of defiance and terror.

"The crowd was not to blame." There was no kindness now in Vivaine's voice. It cut across the stage, sharp as a blade. "You, though, should know better, little sister." The last word hissed out, and Eugessa shrank back.

The crowd stopped, whispers darting between them as their attention focused on the two prioresses.

"Even after all the ways Amah has blessed you," Vivaine continued, "you're still a blind, stupid child."

Eugessa's eyes grew flinty at the words. "Do not pretend this was from the goddess."

"You would not know the goddess's voice if it came from heaven wreathed in flame," Vivaine said. Argyros turned his head from where his good eye had been fixed on the dispersing crowd to face Eugessa.

The Prioress of the Horn pressed back against the side of the stage.

"Get control of your dragon, Vivaine," she snapped, "before he kills us all."

"If Amah wanted you dead," Vivaine said simply, "you'd be dead. She has chosen to let you live, stripped of all her blessings."

Every word the High Prioress had spoken had been warm with truth.

"She believes all of this," Sable whispered. "She actually believes Amah is doing this."

Atticus's frown deepened.

Vivaine sent the merest glance at the Mira Isla, who was huddled with the other women from the priories, then refocused on Eugessa.

When she spoke again, her voice spread out across the plaza. "It is Amah's will that you repent, denounce the arrogance you have lived under for so long, and serve the goddess with a contrite spirit."

"Serve you, you mean," Eugessa hissed.

"If that is what Amah is laying on your heart, then yes." Vivaine met the woman's hateful look with one of regretful benevolence. "You should have known better, little sister. You should have known that you do not have the power to stop…" She looked down at Argyros, running her hand down the side of his thick neck. "…Amah."

She caught sight of the crowd again.

"Go," she said firmly, although her voice stayed kind. "Night has fallen, and the Veil Gate will close. Spread the news of Amah's judgment through the city."

She motioned to the Sanctus guards lining the plaza, the white sleeve of her robe arcing through the night like a torch. The guards stepped toward the crowd, ushering them toward the gate.

Vivaine looked down at Argyros, a tender smile crossing her lips. "Let's go home." She turned toward the Dragon Priory but paused when she caught sight of Kiva standing near the side of the stage. He stepped back warily.

"The Merchant Guild has been blind as well," Vivaine said. "They have sought after money and power because they are weak. Tell them I will forgive them if they repent." She took a step closer to Kiva, and he stiffened. "But you, who brought lies against me here, will have no forgiveness."

Sable tensed as Argyros focused on Kiva, but Vivaine set her hand on the dragon's head. "Still, Amah is merciful. You have until dawn to leave my city. If you, or any of your family, are found here when the sun rises, Amah's justice will be swift."

Her gaze dropped to Jrogen, who still knelt.

"I believed what these faithless ones said, Zenivah," He kept his head bowed. "I deserve death for doubting you, but if you forgive me, great Zenivah, if you allow me the chance, I will serve you with every breath I take."

Vivaine turned disapproving eyes on the men who held him, and they dropped Jrogen's arms and backed away. He fell forward and pressed his forehead to the ground.

She took a step toward him. "I do not know who you are," she said gently, and the icy-cold lie cut through the smoke and the warmth of the summer night to slash into Sable.

"Liar!" Sable breathed, the word coming out loud and furious, and she shoved it toward the prioress.

Vivaine's pause was almost imperceptible, and she continued smoothly. "Rise, sir. Amah is pleased with your penitence and angered by these men who've kept you prisoner."

Her words had been so cold, Sable pulled back, shivering, and Reese wrapped an arm around her shoulder.

Vivaine held a hand out toward the Tien Sark. "Rise and allow me to offer you shelter for the night."

"She knows," Sable whispered. "She called him." She turned to look at Atticus. "She *knows*."

A flicker of pain crossed the playwright's face.

Jrogen rose and moved up the stairs, stopping a respectful distance from the High Prioress and bowing low. "You are gracious, Holy Zenivah."

Vivaine looked past Sable. "Regardless of whatever drew you away, Amah offers you this one chance to come home."

Sable looked over her shoulder to see Gwen considering Vivaine's words, her brow creased.

"The things you have done can be forgiven," the Dragon Prioress continued, "but it is time to decide who you stand with. The home you've always known or the quickly fading north."

Gwen shifted her weight forward.

Sable reached out and set her hand on Gwen's arm. *Don't stay where people know you for years and still hide from you.*

Frustration curled Gwen's brow, and she let out an annoyed breath but nodded, and Sable let go of her arm.

The prioress gave Gwen a very small smile that held a great deal of fondness and sorrow. "I don't know what lies they've told you to change you so much, but make sure they value you as they should. You should not be disregarded. Your skills should not be wasted by ignorant fools."

Gwen tensed, but Vivaine's gaze finally made its way to Sable. "Will the north repent and stand with Amah? Will you surrender your arms and plead for peace with the Empire?"

Sable shook her head. "Peace will only come if you stop the Kalesh attack. Command your Tien Sark to stop this war. Then we can discuss peace."

Vivaine sighed. "If you had spoken your own thoughts from the beginning, perhaps your voice would be worth listening to. But you chose to be the voice of the north, and so you will be treated as such. Will you offer the north's surrender?"

Sable stepped forward. "Vivaine," she pushed her desperation into the words, "you could stop—"

"I will take that as a no," Vivaine interrupted coldly. "If you are not here to surrender peacefully, you are banished from the city. If you, or any with you"—her gaze flickered emotionlessly to Atticus—"are here come daybreak, it will be seen as an open declaration of war by the north, and you shall be killed on sight."

Vivaine turned, scattering glinting light over Argyros's scales, and moved toward the same stairs the Sanctus guards had escorted her up only an hour ago, shackled and weak.

Sable sent a thread of *vitalle* toward Vivaine. "I know what you've done," she whispered. "I know what you are doing."

Vivaine paused, her head turning slightly to the side. "Then you know," she whispered back, "that you are utterly powerless in the real story here. Play Queen of the North while there is a north, Issable, but do not think Amah will spare you if you stand in her way. You are no queen. You are nothing but a blade of grass, common and frail. If you stand in Amah's way, you will be trampled."

CHAPTER FIFTY-TWO

Vivaine moved off the platform at a measured pace, Jrogen's black uniform and darkly tattooed scalp trailing after her like a shadow.

Eugessa lay sprawled on her back, staring up at the twinkling sky. She moaned and held one arm tight against her chest while a dark, bloody stain spread over her right shoulder.

"Ryah!" she snapped. "Help me up, girl!"

Ryah took a step forward.

Thulan set a thick hand on her shoulder. "That woman doesn't deserve your kindness."

"If it has to be deserved," Ryah said, "it's something other than kindness."

Eugessa tried to roll over onto her side but gave another gasp of pain. The other abbesses hung back, but Ryah walked along the side of the stage, squeezing between it and the low burning bonfire.

The prioress watched her approach with a vehement nod. "You've made the right choice, child. You swore to serve Amah, and I am her vessel."

Ryah reached the stairs and held out a hand to Eugessa. The larger woman grasped it, and Ryah heaved her up until Eugessa was standing, leaning heavily on the side of the stairs.

"If you were Amah's vessel," Ryah said, "when I look at you, I would see reflections of her. But when I look at you...all I see is you."

Eugessa stared at her while Ryah held the woman's hand for a moment longer.

"In all of Amah's teachings, she wants more for us than grasping after power," Ryah continued. "I hope you find that."

"Insolent girl," Eugessa snapped, pulling back her hand. "After all I've given you, you think you'll find better with Vivaine?"

"No," Ryah said, dropping her arm to her side. "I haven't seen Amah reflected in the High Prioress for a very long time." She lifted her eyes to the spires. "My whole life, I thought if I could just get here, I would find Amah. I would sit at the feet of the women who knew her and learn to hear her voice." She dropped her eyes to Eugessa again and continued, her voice sorrowful, "But, if I'm honest, I felt closest to Amah when I was traveling with the troupe, not as an abbess, but just as a person, listening to people's pain and sharing my own. Your priory is full of people who hide their weaknesses and strive to look perfect." Her brow creased. "But I think Amah is met in the flaws and the pain and the hopelessness."

"You know nothing of Amah's blessing," Eugessa said, her voice scathing.

"I know very little of Amah in any way," Ryah agreed softly. "But if the blessings I find here will turn me into a woman like you, I'd rather not be blessed."

Eugessa's expression curled in seething fury. "Get out of this holy place." She swiped her hand through the blackened soot on the stage and wiped from Ryah's shoulder, across her chest, and down onto her stomach in a long, black smear.

Ryah stiffened, and Thulan growled and started toward the two of them.

"You don't deserve to wear the white," Eugessa snarled.

"Do any of us?" Ryah asked quietly. "Goodbye, Eugessa." She walked soberly back toward the front of the stage.

Thulan waited at the corner, fury simmering in her face. When Ryah reached her, the dwarf motioned to the black streak with forced carelessness. "I think she improved it."

Ryah gave her a weak smile.

On the far side of the stage, Kiva was giving quiet orders to his men, sending them hurrying toward the Veil Gate.

Sable pushed a thread of *vitalle* at him. "Kiva."

He snapped his head toward her. When he saw how far away she still was, his eyes widened. "I'll keep Talia safe," he said, his voice grim, the warmth of the words flowing across the thread of *vitalle*.

"Swear you'll get her out of the city before dawn," Sable said.

"I'm not doing it for you, Sable. Vivaine *will not* touch her." With one last dark look back at the Dragon Priory, he strode for the Veil Gate.

"We need to go," Jae said, drawing Sable's attention back to their group.

Sanctus guards were ushering the last of the crowd out the gate.

Sable felt Serene cast out. The wave lit the people around her, blazed Innov into light where she perched on the stool under the tree, and warmed the few abbesses and guards still moving around the platform or trailing after Eugessa into her priory.

Serene turned slowly in place. "Where did the unicorn go?"

The dying bonfire sent flickering firelight over the front of the priories. The full moon added a white shimmer to some of the stones but left whole sides of the buildings in dark shadows, any of which could have concealed the black creature. But Serene's casting should have lit him up like a torch.

"I haven't seen him since Argyros appeared," Jae said.

"He must have gone back into the priory," Ryah said, peering into the shadows. "I'm surprised he didn't wait for Eugessa, though."

"Are those two as close as Vivaine and Argyros?" Atticus asked.

Ryah nodded. "They're fond of each other. Cernus is the only...well, he's not a person. He's the only creature Eugessa actually talks to. I've found them together, Eugessa's head against his neck, talking to him with a vulnerable sort of expression I've never seen her use anywhere else."

"Does he talk back?" Gwen asked. "I always had the feeling Argyros talked back to Vivaine."

"The way she spoke to him always seemed very one-sided." Ryah glanced at Sable. "Did Innov talk to Narine?" She paused. "Does she talk to you?"

"She does not talk to me," Sable said, "and I don't know if she talked to Narine, exactly, but Narine seemed to understand her. And Innov can certainly understand us."

"Mysterious magical creatures aside," Atticus said, eyeing the approaching guards, "it's time we moved along. Between Vivaine's orders to be gone and the fact that the Kalesh army is arriving at any moment, we have a very limited time to get out of the south."

Atticus's wagons moved slowly up the long hill ahead of the rest of the troupe, traveling away from Immusmala. The full moon bleached the grass and the top of the trees to silvery-greys and the dusty dirt of the road to a pebble-speckled white. Sable walked alongside Thulan's wagon, debating whether the jouncing of the wagon bench would be preferable to the long climb. Innov perched on her arm, though, and the warmth of the phoenix and the stillness of the night was enough to keep her walking.

To the west, huge clouds piled up over the Tremmen Hills, their rounded tops smooth and soft in the moonlight.

Ryah sat next to Thulan on the wagon, and between the dwarf and Leonis, she was slowly catching up on everything that had happened in the past few weeks.

Sable glanced back at the torchlit city. "Did anyone else notice that Vivaine's dragon is considerably blacker than it used to be?"

The wagon trundled up the hill, creaking and crunching along the road.

"Overall, I'd say that entire trial didn't go well for us," Leonis said finally.

They reached the top of the hill, and the road wound into the forest ahead of them like a silver river through the shadows. The clouds over the hills drew closer, and a damp wind stirred the grass on the hillside behind them.

Innov shifted on Sable's arm, peering into the deep shadows to their right.

Sable yawned, and Reese frowned.

"Atticus," he called, "we should find a campsite."

"We're not far from wherever Innov found the dragon skin," Leonis pointed out, "so let's not go wandering in the woods. There's a clearing off the side of the road not too far ahead. We should be able to reach it before the rain gets here. We can sleep there and get moving again early."

Innov took off and flew along the edge of the road ahead of them until she veered into the woods, her golden light illuminating a thin trail.

The wagons drew closer to it, and she flew back out, circling them once, then flying back in.

"I think—" Sable began.

"Don't say she wants us to follow her," Leonis interrupted. "I'm not interested in sleeping near some huge dragon skin."

"Of course she wants us to follow her." Sable moved to the beginning of the path. Innov sat on a tree branch not far in, looking back at them. "The wagons will fit, Atticus."

Sable started down the thin road, and Reese fell in next to her. Slivers of moonlight lanced down through the canopy above them, leaving irregular patches of light on the trail, but beyond that, the only light was from Innov. The branches of the trees murmured above them as the wind picked up.

"The wagons will fit," Leonis said from the road, "until they won't anymore. How are we going to get them out if the trail narrows too much?"

"Then leave the wagons here," Sable called back. "Or stay here yourself. Innov has never once tried to lead us anywhere, and I'm following her."

"We're not leaving the wagons unattended on the road in the middle of the night," Leonis protested.

The wind gusted by, carrying the scent of rain.

"Especially with a rainstorm on the way," he added.

Serene and Jae moved into the path, and Gwen followed. Serene cast out, and her wave rolled through the forest around them, showing only the huge warm columns of the trees and smaller flashes of heat from little forest creatures.

"Looks safe enough," Serene said.

"Will your magical casting out thing show a creepy pile of dragon skin?" Leonis asked.

"No," Serene answered. "But a pile of dragon skin is hardly something to be afraid of."

"I'm not afraid," he said, indignant. "I'm merely pointing out that the local dragon is hardly a sweet, gentle creature. Wherever he goes to shed his skin is probably not a sweet, gentle place."

Just past Innov, Sable could see a larger patch of moonlight. "Atticus," she called back to him. "There's a clearing ahead where we could leave the wagons."

After a moment's hesitation, Atticus turned his wagon onto the road, and Thulan followed with hers, both of them ignoring Leonis's grumbling.

Innov waited at the far side of the clearing while they pulled the wagons in.

Leonis scanned the trees. "There isn't even a path out of here."

"Where are you taking us?" Sable asked Innov.

The phoenix spread her wings and half hopped, half flew to the next tree. There was no path, at least not that Sable could see in the darkness.

"This way," she called back.

Thulan unhitched her horse, and at Leonis's exasperated sigh, she shrugged. "Good of a place as any to spend the night."

Leonis pulled his bow out from under the wagon bench, muttering, while Atticus and Thulan settled the horses and took two lanterns off their wagons.

When everyone was ready, Sable followed Innov in a generally straight line through the forest, wading through the knee-high ferns while their feathery leaves tangled and caught on each other. Huge rock formations rose out of the darkness near them, turned golden by Innov's light. Overhead, clouds smothered the moon.

They walked until Sable could make out the distant crashing of the surf. "We're almost to the coast," she called back.

"Don't walk us off a sea cliff," Leonis said.

Serene cast out again, as she had every few minutes, and ahead of them, the forest of warm tree trunks stopped abruptly.

Above them, rain began to patter on the leaves.

"How much farther is Innov taking us?" Leonis asked. "Because we're going to be soaked before we make it back to the wagons."

Instead of moving toward the coast, Innov flew into the gap between two looming rock outcroppings. The circle of golden light from the phoenix lit a bit of a very thin winding trail.

Sable followed her while a gust of wind rushed between the rocks, bringing with it cold, pelting raindrops. Sable wrapped her white cloak around herself.

Innov landed ahead of her on a rock, her light illuminating the mouth of a cave. Sable hurried toward it until Serene cast out. From somewhere deep in the cave, a blazingly hot form flared into existence, and Sable pulled to a stop.

"There's something in there," Serene warned. "Something…big."

"If it's the dragon," Leonis whispered, "I want the chance to say 'I told you so' before it kills us."

"It's not the dragon." Ryah squeezed around the others and took a step past Sable. She glanced at Innov, who was waiting on the rock by the entrance, her fiery feathers steaming and sizzling in the rain. Her golden light fell across the dry ground right inside the entrance. "You could feel him? From the road?" She started into the cave.

Sable grabbed her arm. "Who's in there?"

"It's Cernus. Can't you feel him?"

Sable peered into the pitch-black cave. "The unicorn? No, I can't feel him." Her hand tightened on Ryah's arm. "How can *you* feel him?"

"He's…" Ryah paused. "He's not hot, not like Innov. But he's not icy like Argyros. He's…complicated. Like he wants to be warm, or maybe he *is* warm, but it's smothered." She glanced at Sable and shrugged. "No one else feels like him." She pulled her arm out of Sable's hand and looked over her shoulder at the others. "It's all right. He's curled up against the back wall. Innov, show them."

The phoenix launched off the rock and flew into the cave, illuminating it with honey-gold light.

The cavern was bigger than Sable had expected, the rough walls and ceiling glittered with specks of light as Innov moved past. Two dozen paces away, where the sloping roof of the cave met the uneven floor, the inky black shape of Cernus was visible, lying on the floor. Innov flew closer, alighting on a jagged stone near the creature.

"Is he…dead?" Leonis whispered.

"No." Ryah walked closer. Innov's light outlined the curve of Cernus's back as he breathed slowly but didn't move.

"Ryah," Sable said quietly, moving into the mouth of the cave, "please don't go near the vicious black unicorn."

The others crowded in behind her, out of the rain, but didn't move farther in.

"If Amah and her prioresses are supposed to be good," Thulan said, "why are two of their three creatures violent and evil?"

"They were good gifts once," Ryah said. "Innov was life and hope. Cernus was purity and peace, and Argyros was strength, or the idea that strength can begin with something small, like an egg—" She stopped and looked around the cave with a sudden sense of wonder. "Is this—"

"What is that?" Leonis interrupted. To the right, the cave drew back into a long, low alcove where something hazy lay piled on the floor.

Reese took the lantern from Thulan and walked carefully closer. The nearest part of the pile shimmered. "The rest of Argyros's skin."

"This is the Cave of the Mothers!" Ryah spun slowly, her expression awestruck. "The cave where the first prioresses were given the phoenix, the young unicorn, and a dragon egg. This is where Argyros would have felt safe enough to shed his skin, and where Cernus came when…" She paused. "Why would he come here? He's always been protective of Eugessa. Leaving her there to face Argyros's fire feels…weird."

"He left before that," Reese said. "The last time I saw him was when she declared that Vivaine would be executed."

"Maybe the idea of one prioress killing another was too much for him," Ryah said quietly. "Maybe the tension between him and Eugessa was because she was growing more violent."

"Regardless of your old story," Sable said, "Cernus has never seemed interested in peace or purity. He's huge and intimidating."

"Cernus wasn't always shadows and darkness." Ryah stepped quietly toward the unicorn. "When he was young, he was a frosted silver. The records say he gave off his own light, and his horn glittered with strands of pearly white."

"What happened to him?" Thulan asked.

Ryah gave a small shrug. "He's old. Maybe they darken with age." She stepped closer and reached out a hand toward Cernus's back. Before she could touch him, he tossed his head, his glittering horn swinging through the air in her direction. She froze and pulled back.

"Thulan," she said quietly, "do you have any apples left?"

"I have one," Thulan answered, "but it's for me."

Ryah held out her hand. The dwarf let out an annoyed breath but pulled an apple out of her pack and walked close enough to hand it to her. Ryah set it on the floor near the back of Cernus's head and backed away. "We'll be safe in the Cave of the Mothers tonight. Nothing will harm us here."

"Is she looking at the same cave we are?" Leonis asked. "Everyone else sees the huge, disgusting dragon skin and the terrifying unicorn, right?"

"It is a nice cave," Reese said. "The way the ground slopes, we won't get wet no matter how long the rain lasts. I don't see any signs of hill cats or bears."

"Well, that's reassuring," Leonis said dryly.

"We can sleep by the door and take turns keeping watch," Reese continued. "The unicorn doesn't look like it wants anything to do with us, and it's a very long walk through the rain back to the wagons."

Thulan sighed. "I'm lighting a fire." She moved to the edge of the cave and found a pile of dried sticks blown into a nook.

Ryah stayed watching the unicorn. Innov still sat on the rock near him, and Sable moved up next to her sister.

"Why is he here?" Sable asked.

Ryah's brow creased. "He's broken. Can you feel it?"

Sable looked at her sister. "What do you mean by that?"

"The way people can feel broken when they're grieving," Ryah said thoughtfully. "Or the way they can feel a bit shattered when their hopes have been dashed. Cernus is…cracked." She shrugged. "Broken."

Sable fully faced her sister. "I have never felt anyone else feeling broken."

Ryah let out a sigh. "Nobody ever does. I thought maybe you might. Some of it feels a little like something you'd recognize. Hope feels warm, and hatred feels cold."

Sable stared at her. "You can feel everyone's emotions?"

Ryah paused. "Not everyone's. Most emotions aren't strong enough to feel. But some…" She looked back at Cernus. "But he's very broken. He feels like he's splitting apart. Like the whole world is splitting apart and the only thing filling the rift is pain and terror and loneliness."

Sable set her hand on Ryah's shoulder. "Have you always felt this?"

Keeping her eyes on Cernus, Ryah nodded slowly. "As long as I can remember."

Reaching up slowly, Sable set her fingers on Ryah's cheek and turned her sister's face toward her. Ryah's eyes looked weary. Old.

"You can feel other people's pain?" Sable whispered.

"And their joy," Ryah said. "But that's rarely as strong as their pain or their fear."

"Sweet Amah!" Sable breathed, wrapping her arms around her sister and pulling her close. "When you said Argyros was cold, this is what you meant."

Ryah nodded into Sable's shoulder. "He's always been a bit…cool. Like he's frosted. But tonight, Sable…" She shuddered. "He was full of hatred. Ice cold. A cutting, gnawing cold. And Vivaine…"

"What about Vivaine?" Sable asked.

Ryah pulled back and lifted wide, frightened eyes to Sable's. "It's how she survived the fire. She was so terribly cold, it couldn't hurt her."

CHAPTER FIFTY-THREE

It was Reese's hand on Sable's shoulder that woke her. She knew it before she opened her eyes and saw him motioning for her to stay quiet. She twisted to look toward the back of the cave where Cernus had lain last night, but she couldn't tell if he was there in the blackness.

Reese leaned close to her ear. "Will you come with me?"

Behind him, the rocks outside were glistening with grey light. She rubbed the sleep out of her eyes and nodded.

She could just make out his smile as he offered a hand to help her up.

He didn't drop her hand but led her out of the cave and deeper into the rocks.

Behind them, framed by the entrance of the gully, the full moon hovered low over the forest. It lit half the rock faces with a depthless pearly-grey and left the others in black shadow. The rain had stopped, and the sky had cleared. Only a handful of stars were bright enough to be seen in the moonlight.

The gully narrowed, and Reese stopped at a thin game trail leading up the rocks. He let go of her hand. "The beginning is the steepest part," he said quietly.

Sable peered up the trail. The moon lit the first few feet clearly, and though it was steep, it wasn't impossible. She turned to find Reese beside her, watching her closely. "Are we going to run into bears or hill cats up this trail?"

Reese shrugged, not looking away from her. "You're the one who can sense these things. Are there any near us?"

She glanced up the trail again. "Say something true."

He shifted closer, and his voice was low and rough next to her ear. "I love watching the sunrise with you." The words blazed out, flaring him into a tower of fire so close to her that his heat merged with her own. The warmth swept her up like a storm and had almost faded before she remembered to check for animals on the path. She cleared her throat and turned around, looking pointedly at the night sky above them. "Is there a sunrise coming soon?"

A smile curled up one side of his mouth. "Are there any animals nearby?"

"Nothing here but you and me."

He lifted his hand to brush his thumb across her cheek. "So what are you waiting for?" he asked with a glint of amusement in his eyes.

She swallowed and tried to school her expression into something casual. "Every time I want you to say something true," she said, starting up the path, "you try to be distracting."

"Judging from your reaction," he said from behind her, his voice smug, "I succeeded."

She gave him a smile over her shoulder. "Where are you taking me?"

"Please watch where you're going," he said. "If you fall down these rocks, the rest of the group is going to be angry with me."

Sable refocused on the steep path ahead of her. The first dozen feet were definitely the steepest. Past that, the trail switched back and headed up the outcropping at a more leisurely slope. In minutes, Sable climbed out onto the broad top of the rocks. A warm summer breeze swirled over the rocks, sending shivers through the bits of grass that grew from crevices.

The outcropping rose like a moonlit island above the rolling forest. The tops of the trees below were kissed with moonlight like the crests of waves, the low spots between them lost to blackness. Ahead of her, the forest ended at the sea cliffs and the ocean began, glittering like an endless shimmering carpet.

She stood in a world of black and silver, every object steeped in a strange, stark beauty. Every familiar shape shifted into something slightly *other*. As though she were seeing a secret side of the world usually masked by sunlight and color.

Reese stepped up close behind her. "Do you like it?"

"It's perfect."

"Good." He took her hand and walked forward, picking his way over the rough surface of the rocks until he reached a flat area. He considered the level section of rock. "It *is* perfect."

He let go of her hand and crouched down.

The sky to the east wasn't really brighter, but it was the tiniest bit less black than the rest. Sable turned slowly, taking it all in. Over the forest to the south, the sky was lighter as well, most likely lit by the lanterns and torchlight of Immusmala, which was hidden by a swell of trees.

A quiet clatter brought her attention back to Reese as several stones tumbled out of his arms. He knelt next to them and selected one of the largest, positioning it on the flat surface in front of him.

Then he picked up a smaller, flatter stone and carefully placed it on top, adjusting it to find a stable arrangement.

The moonlight painted the edge of each stone silvery-grey. Sable took a step closer, staring down at the two stones.

The beginnings of a rock tower.

"Reese," Sable whispered.

"Niko's pledging ceremony was better than Immusmala's, don't you think?" The words were said lightly, but when he held out a stone to her, his eyes burned with an unasked question. "No offense to Ryah," he said quietly, "but I don't feel the need to invite an abbess to this."

Sable stared at the stone, her heart thrumming so strongly she wondered if he could feel it vibrating through the rocks beneath them. "Reese…"

He reached his other hand out and took hers, drawing her down next to him. She sank to her knees. She stared down at the stacked rocks.

The beginning of a pledge.

"What if everything falls apart?" Her words came out raw and scared. She could feel his eyes on her.

He turned her palm up and set the stone in it, cupping her hand in his own. "I don't know. I don't even know what today will bring." He swallowed. "But I know I love you."

The words blazed through the night like a fire, pressing against her skin with a flaming heat, wrapping around her. Through her.

His hands trembled against hers. His eyes held a raw, desperate longing. "I know that I want to be with you every day for the rest of my life."

She gripped the stone and let her own longing rise up, let it drown the endless litany of things that could go wrong.

The beginning of the tower was a small, tremulous thing, and the sight made something flare inside her.

Everything about her life was small and tremulous, and she was tired of it.

The tower should be taller. Stronger. It should stand here, every day and every night, to witness the moon and the ocean and the trees in all their changing seasons. It should watch the sun rise day after day for a thousand years.

Regardless of what came, she wanted it to stand.

The tight knot that had tangled around the idea of Reese for so long showed itself for what it really was: brittle, grasping strands of dread and worry. Fear spun into cords that bound her. A plaintive voice hounding at her with its endless warnings of what pain might come next.

It wasn't just Reese. It was everything. Fears about the future. Fears about the Empire and Kiva and Vivaine. The list circled endlessly in her mind.

And she was tired of it.

The fire inside her was small but fierce, and she breathed in, fanning it brighter. She lit every cord of fear that was tying her down, and every cord burned away. She took a deep, gasping breath, and it was filled with a terrifying freedom.

But it was *freedom*.

She focused on the rock tower, her hand shaking.

Regardless of what came next, she wanted it to stand.

She pulled her hands out of Reese's and placed her stone on top of the others. The rock trembled, but she adjusted it carefully, shifting it until it perched steadily on the others.

She turned to find Reese watching her, searching her face, the burning longing still in his eyes.

He was too far away.

He was always too far away.

She moved closer and set her hand on his chest, feeling his heart pound against her palm. Her other hand slid along the side of his neck. His beard brushed against her palm, sending a shiver up her arm.

"I am tired of not being close enough to you," she whispered. "I am tired of feeling like I have to wait until the world is safe to be with you."

He wrapped his arms around her waist. In a smooth motion, he pulled her tight against his side. "I'm also tired of you not being close to me."

"Good." She tangled her fingers into his hair and poured everything inside her into her words. "Because I love you." The heat filled the air, and his arms pulled her close. She pushed against him, and his beard tickled her skin as she drove away the last of the space and kissed him.

Warmth swirled around them. She felt her lips begin to tingle, and she clamped down on the desire to draw *vitalle* out of him. Instead, she pushed energy into him, focusing on every inch of him she could feel, pressing tiny tendrils of warmth into his body.

He gripped her tightly for a long moment, then pulled back, his breath coming fast. "What were the words Ryah said? The ones for the pledge that her abbess taught her?"

"I don't remember," she said, kissing him again.

He lifted a hand to her chin and held it gently as he pulled away. "I know you remember," he whispered. "They were good words."

She leaned her forehead against his, closing her eyes. They were good words, but it took more effort than it should have to focus her mind on Ryah's blessing.

"Love does not follow our rules. It does not appear merely where it should, docile and modest. It breaks into lives the way sunshine breaks through clouds. Without warning and with wild, heedless abandon. It is a vibrant, glowing, burning thing."

She opened her eyes to find him nodding slowly.

"I have always loved the sunrise," he said, "because it breaks through the darkness. Even when it's so cloudy I can't see the sun, when dawn comes, the world gets brighter. It doesn't matter what the weather is or what the day holds—the moment when the light comes always feels new. Hopeful. I want to stay in that moment forever." He brought his hand to her cheek. His words were hot, and though there was nothing but moonlight around them, his eyes brightened. Then his skin, then the strands of red woven through his beard and his hair.

She drew in a breath. It had been so long since the truth someone spoke had been so fervent it didn't just warm them but made everything about them more vibrant.

"That's how I feel about you," he said. "Sometimes I think I always loved sunrises because part of me was waiting for the time I'd find all that in you."

Sable's fingers tightened in his hair, drinking in his heat. Something tight and painful and fierce grew in her chest.

"Finish the words," he whispered. "Please."

The tightness in her chest tried to climb up her throat, but she whispered the next words. "We enter this world alone, our hearts walled in by loneliness every day. But then love comes, reaching across an impassible distance, touching the darkest corner of our unfathomable depths."

His arms pulled her even closer. "And just like that," he said, "we are no longer alone."

She took in the familiar expression in his eyes. A look she'd seen a thousand times, even before she'd admitted to herself what it meant. "It always felt easier to be alone," she said. "It was safer. Until you."

A glitter of brightness soared up out of the gully. Innov flew to them, spiraling once. Glowing embers rained down, cascading over their heads and shoulders, falling onto the stones, where they burned bright in the darkness for a moment before winking out.

The phoenix spun and soared toward the ocean, her flight wild and free.

"The blessing of a phoenix seems better than an abbess," Sable said.

"It does." Reese watched Innov glide toward the east. The sky past her was now a light purple, nearly every star washed out by the coming sun.

"Let's finish our tower," Sable said, "before the sun rises and the day pulls us away from here."

Reese kept his arms tight. "I've decided the tower isn't important."

She picked up a rock, offering it to him. "But I want to build it. A monument to our place. A place no one else may ever find. Something that will hold this moment forever."

He let out a noise something between a groan and a growl and pressed his lips to hers, hard and long, until she lost track of what else she wanted. "Fine," he said when he pulled away. "But you're getting up to watch the sunrise with me every day from now on."

She raised an eyebrow. "For the rest of our lives?"

"Any morning I wake you, for the rest of our lives. Without complaint about how unnatural it is."

"I steadfastly refuse to give up my right to complain, but any morning you wake me, I'll watch the sunrise with you."

"We have a deal." He loosened his grip.

They built the tower in silence, brushing shoulders against each other, piling stone on top of stone under the lightening sky. The tower was almost to Sable's knee when Reese placed the last of the rocks he'd gathered and stood.

Sable looked around at the pebbles nearby. "We need something small and pretty for the top."

There was a tiny pop next to her, and a clear stone rolled across the ground to stop by her feet. The surface was smooth, but cracks ran through the interior, glittering in the growing light.

Sable picked it up. "That is perfect."

Reese looked at the empty air next to Sable with a raised eyebrow. "Thank you, Purn." When the kobold gave no answer, he leaned closer to Sable. "A blessing from that kobold might be more impressive than one from a phoenix."

"I heard that, wastrel." Purn's voice came from next to his legs.

Sable set the clear stone on top of the tower, then stood next to Reese, facing the east as the first edge of the sun crept over the horizon. She took his hand. "I love watching the sunrise with you too."

He hummed a sound that didn't sound quite like an agreement. She glanced at him and caught the hint of a roguish smile before he swept her into his arms. She let out a shriek and grabbed his shirt as he turned away from the rising sun and carried her toward a bench-like shelf of rock. He sat, settling her onto his lap. "We'll watch tomorrow's."

CHAPTER FIFTY-FOUR

Atticus's voice called for them from below, a note of irritation coloring his tone. Sable unwound herself from Reese, pausing when she heard Ryah's voice rise above the others in the gully.

"She sounds…" Reese tilted his head to listen. "More combative than usual."

Sable stood. "I forgot we have a rogue unicorn down there." She paused, looking at their stacked rocks. In the daylight, the small tower looked almost otherworldly. "Do you think it will last?"

Reese stepped up behind her. "Maybe. It's reasonably steady for being as tall as it is." He wrapped his arms around her and kissed her neck.

"You don't care if it lasts, do you?" she accused him, laughing at the way his beard tickled her neck.

"It's a stack of rocks." He turned her around to face him. "A useful stack, though. It served its purpose."

"Which was?"

"Distract you from all your worrying and planning long enough for me to trick you into accepting my proposal."

Sable squinted up at him. "I don't remember an actual proposal. I certainly don't remember accepting one."

He shrugged. "You stacked rocks. That seals it. It's an unbreakable vow."

"Niko said nothing of the sort."

"Sable!" Atticus's voice snapped from the gully. "Get back here! Innov is being difficult."

Sable paused. "Maybe we should go." She headed back toward the path that ran down to the cave. "I think the tower will be there for a hundred years."

"In a hundred years, we'll come back and see."

"Are you going to carry me up here when I'm that old?"

"The way you collect magical creatures, you'll probably have something like a griffon at that point, and we'll just ride it here."

Raised voices came from the gully, and she quickened her pace.

When they reached the cave, everyone was standing outside it except Ryah, who was just inside the entrance.

"We can't leave him here without anything," she said.

"We don't have any food," Thulan said. "You gave him the apple already."

"He's a horse," Leonis said. "Or a horse-like thing, and the world is full of grass. I'm sure he can find food for himself."

"It's not the food." Ryah caught sight of Sable. "Sable! Tell them that there's something wrong with Cernus. He still hasn't moved. Innov knows something is wrong."

The unicorn was still curled in the back corner of the cave with Innov perched on his shoulder.

"I'm surprised Innov is there," Sable said. "When we saw Cernus in the Sanctuary before the trial, he and Innov looked like they were about to attack each other."

"Really?" Ryah asked. "Cernus and Innov have always gotten along well." She stopped. "I think they can communicate. With Argyros too. It didn't happen often, but whenever Innov came to the Priory of the Horn, I swear she came to…talk to Cernus. If phoenixes and unicorns talk."

"Whatever is happening," Atticus broke in, "we need to move. The sun rose hours ago"—he cast an accusing look at Reese—"and we are still very close to a city that is firmly under Vivaine's control. Not to mention that we have a long trip to Tutella Island ahead of us. The Tien Sark are moving quickly, as is the rest of the Empire." He scowled at Sable and Ryah. "The only ones *not* moving quickly are us."

"Come here." Ryah grabbed Sable's hand and dragged her toward the unicorn, ignoring Atticus's huff of irritation.

Innov illuminated the entire back of the cave with a warm golden light that shone off Cernus's sleek coat. From only a few steps away, Sable could see the unicorn's head curled around, almost hiding from the rest of the cave.

Regardless of the fact that the creature did nothing but breathe, Sable nodded. "Something is wrong with him."

"You can feel it?" Ryah asked.

"No, but Innov tends to be drawn to people—or animals—who need help. Hope. There might not be anything physically wrong with him, but something is wrong."

"He's broken," Ryah said, "like some part of him has been torn out."

"Something with Eugessa?" Sable asked.

Ryah nodded. "He left when she declared Vivaine would be executed." She sighed. "Things have been tense with Cernus since Narine died as well. Since the summit, he and Eugessa were…I don't know. Something was wrong."

"Kiva thinks Eugessa ordered Narine killed," Sable said slowly.

Ryah turned to her, shocked. "She would never!"

"Really?" Sable asked honestly. "If anyone would know, Ryah, it would be you. Could she have ordered it? A dwarf who worked for Kiva actually started the fire, but he was ordered to by someone else. Kiva thinks it was Eugessa."

Ryah shook her head, her expression horrified. "No. Absolutely not. She loved Narine." Her eyes grew distant, flickering among memories. "No." The words sounded more like an argument than a declaration. "She…wouldn't."

"What is it?" Sable asked.

Ryah's gaze sharpened again, and she sank to her knees. "Oh, sweet Amah." She reached out toward the unicorn but paused and closed her hand into a fist. With obvious effort, she opened it again and set it on his back. Cernus twitched at her touch, and Ryah flinched, letting out a pained breath.

Sable set her hand on her sister's shoulder. "Ryah?"

Ryah twisted her shoulder away and shook her head. When she looked up, there were tears in her eyes. "The evening Narine died, Eugessa was inconsolable."

She tensed, and her attention snapped back to Cernus. "You were in the garden," she said to him, her voice low, filled with pain. "I remember. You tore up the flowers, and Eugessa barricaded herself in her room. I could hear her crying, and even from inside the house, I could feel your fury."

Cernus's breath came faster, and he shifted his head, the vicious tip of his horn catching the morning light.

Sable took a step back. "You can talk to him?"

"He understands us." Ryah's voice was so soft Sable almost couldn't hear her. "I can feel how much the memory hurts him."

"Because Eugessa had ordered Narine's death?" Sable asked it as a question, but it needed no answer, and Ryah did nothing but bow her head.

"He feels betrayed," Ryah whispered. "The brokenness, it's Eugessa's betrayal."

"He left because she'd announced she was killing Vivaine," Sable said.

Ryah nodded. "Eugessa broke the vow they had to each other to serve the people and Amah. He knows she killed Narine, and he knows she wanted to kill Vivaine." She was quiet for a long moment. "He loved her. He still does, but his bond with her is broken."

"Sable." Atticus's voice came from the mouth of the cave. "We need to get moving."

Sable moved around Ryah to squat down next to Innov. "I envy you," she said quietly to Ryah. "I'd love to know what Innov feels."

"She is grieving for Cernus but helping him feel less hopeless."

"We can't do anything better than that." Sable stood. "Let Innov care for him. We need to go."

"You'll leave her here?" Ryah asked.

Sable let out a little laugh. "I don't leave or take Innov anywhere. She goes where she wants." She held out her hand and helped Ryah stand. "The two of them probably need to decide what they're going to do now that neither of them has a priory."

Ryah stepped closer, peering into Sable's eyes with a probing look.

Sable leaned back. "What?"

A smile started on Ryah's lips. She glanced at Reese, standing watchful at the mouth of the cave, one hand on a knife in his belt.

She let go of Sable and walked over to him, setting her palm on his chest. Rising up onto her tiptoes, she kissed him on the cheek. "I'm happy for you two." She stepped back, letting out a little laugh. "Not as happy as the two of you are, but still happy."

The sun was high in the eastern sky before Atticus's wagon creaked back onto the road heading north. Thulan's followed, and everyone else fell in, walking alongside the dwarf's wagon. Sable's pants were damp to her knees from walking through the ferns, and the normally hard-packed dirt gave slightly under her feet.

The road was not empty. Dozens of festivalgoers leaving Immusmala dotted the road ahead of them, and a small cart drawn by a mule trundled along behind them.

"How long have you felt what people feel?" Serene asked Ryah. "And what does it feel like? Does it feel like your own emotions? Or can you tell they belong to someone else?"

Sable walked on Ryah's other side, watching Serene examine her sister as though she were a fascinating new book. "Get ready for a lot of questions," she told Ryah. "And tests and experiments as Serene tries to figure out exactly what you can do with your unique talent."

"I didn't even know for a long time that it was unique," Ryah said. "People talk about understanding what others feel all the time. I thought everyone could actually feel it."

"Sable can feel people's words, and Ryah can feel people's emotions," Leonis said. "I wonder what your other sister can feel?"

Ryah blinked at him. "I have no idea."

"As far as I know, Talia is normal." Sable looked ahead of them, thinking of how fond Kiva was of Talia. And how much Lady Ingred relied on her. There was almost something there. Some thread she couldn't quite follow.

"Talia can do something," Reese said from next to Sable. "She's like one of those trackers who can almost talk to wild animals."

"She can talk to animals?" Sable asked slowly.

"Well, she can talk to Kiva."

Sable laughed. "I agree on the 'Kiva is an animal' aspect of this conversation, but I have no idea what else you're talking about."

"When Talia went to work for Kiva," Reese said, "she was completely naive, right? But she walked into a world of spies and Kiva himself and wasn't eaten alive. When she didn't come with you and Atticus, you said she was perfectly comfortable with Pete and Boone. The two thugs you'd been cowed by for years. Boone is not the kind to stand and chat with someone in an alley."

Sable frowned at him but couldn't disagree.

"Then she went to work for Ingred," Reese continued, "with no knowledge about what a merchant's spoiled daughter would need, and years later, she's still Ingred's personal attendant—the personal attendant of a woman who you've said is fickle and demanding and rude. That kind of woman goes through help at an alarming rate."

"That's true," Sable agreed. "The first time I saw Lady Ingred, she had snuck into Lord Renwen's, rudely interrupting my plan to steal Renwen's ledger, and complained that she'd had to fire her personal secretary because the recently married woman had the gall to get pregnant."

"Was Lord Renwen as rich as Lady Ingred's family is?" Ryah asked. "I never met him."

Sable shook her head. "Renwen's wealth was nothing compared to Ingred's. He was a newcomer to the guild who was making a name for himself. She must have thought of him as an investment, or a novelty, because everything about the man was pale and limp. Like a dead fish."

"She toyed with him because she's bored, impulsive, and fickle," Reese said. "And yet Talia has managed to make herself a permanent companion. After all this time, she is still there and still trusted. I don't know what Talia can do, but it's not normal to survive all that without a scratch. Not to mention that she has Kiva wrapped around her finger." He paused. "*Kiva.*"

"But Kiva has a weird attachment to Sable as well," Leonis pointed out.

"I've noticed," Reese said, "but it's not the same. Kiva and Sable play this constant game of who can manipulate whom. Every moment of their relationship is combative. But everything Kiva does toward Talia is about protecting her. No one needed Sable's skill in the Sanctuary to know he meant it when he said he'd do anything to keep Talia safe from Vivaine."

Sable frowned. "Talia can be very likable when she wants."

"Can you name another person Kiva likes?" Reese asked. When she didn't answer, he shrugged. "I don't know what Talia can do. Maybe she doesn't even know what she does, but she does something. She can talk to the animals, Sable."

"Next time we see her," Serene said, "let's ask." She turned back to Ryah. "Can you feel all of us right now?"

"If I try." Ryah looked around apologetically. "It's a lot to take in when there are so many people around. I usually filter it out."

"What's Thulan feeling right now?" Leonis asked.

"Annoyed that you'd ask," Thulan answered.

Ryah smiled at the two of them. "She's content. I think because we're all together."

Thulan let out a grunt that could have been irritation or agreement.

"It doesn't feel like emotions, really," Ryah continued. "I don't feel contentedness from Thulan. I feel...wrapped in a warm blanket. Relaxed. And it's definitely not my emotions, it's...not outside me exactly, but not inside either."

"That is exactly how Sable explains how the truth feels," Serene said. "How far away can you feel someone?"

"That depends on how many people are around." Ryah pointed to the wagon ahead of them. "If I were alone, I could maybe feel as far as Atticus in his wagon. But with all of you around me, there's too much commotion." She paused and looked into the sky over her shoulder. "Innov is easier to feel. She's so blazingly hopeful and bright."

Innov flew into view over the trees and fluttered down to land on the back of Atticus's wagon.

"Cernus and Argyros I can feel strongly too. From the mouth of the cave last night, I could feel Cernus's pain so strongly it drowned out the rest of you."

Sable glanced behind them. "Can you feel Cernus now?"

Ryah shook her head.

"Ryah's gift and Gwen's seem similar," Jae said. "In that they both sense something internal to other people."

Serene nodded. "We should come up with some tests for them to see how similarly they work."

Serene and Jae fell into a discussion about testing ideas, and Sable leaned closer to Ryah.

"How is Atticus feeling since Vivaine?"

Ryah looked ahead toward his wagon. "You know how I told you Cernus felt broken?" she said in a low voice. "Well, when we got close to the cave, I was confused, because it was so much like what I'd been feeling from Atticus." She shook her head. "He's...not doing well."

CHAPTER FIFTY-FIVE

Sable looked thoughtfully at the red wagon Atticus drove, then quickened her pace until she could climb up on the bench next to him.

He greeted her with a worried look. "Feeling weak?"

"Is it too hard to believe I just wanted to ride with you for a while?" Sable asked, leaning back against the wagon.

Atticus narrowed his eyes. "I'm not interested in discussing what happened at the trial last night."

"Then let's discuss this morning," Sable said. "Don't I get any sort of congratulations from you for throwing all logic to the wind for the sake of love? I'll even take an 'I told you it would make you happy' if you can't manage anything else."

His expression softened. "I did tell you," he said wryly, "and if you'd listened to me sooner, you'd have been happy sooner. You should remember that next time you feel the need to argue with me."

Sable smiled. "I doubt I will."

"What do you have planned next?"

"I don't know. We'll figure it out together as things play out. I don't have a real plan." She looked down the road ahead. "Which is terrifying."

"Exhilarating, you mean," he said with a smile. "A plan based purely on hope that things will work out."

She met his smile with a disbelieving look. "You may enjoy jumping into a situation and improvising everything that comes next, Atticus, but I'd rather have someone write out the lines for me."

He shook his head. "Every magnificent moment you've had has been because something gave you a push and you went completely off script. You should trust your own voice more than you do."

The wagon shifted behind her back, bumping and creaking over the hard road. The sound was so familiar that for a moment she was overcome with—not homesickness. She couldn't be homesick when she was here with the people who felt like home. But it felt like homesickness. Or maybe nostalgia for this home before it had all become so dangerous.

But the danger wasn't going to lessen, and so she straightened her shoulders. "Jrogen, the Tien Sark Kiva brought to the trial, recognized me as Melia's daughter."

Atticus nodded. "That is not surprising."

"No, what's surprising is…" She blew out a breath. "He was afraid of me. That's the first time I've seen a Kalesh leader afraid of anyone."

"He should be frightened of you."

Sable snorted. "No, he should be frightened of you. You're the one who taught me how to…do all the leader-like things."

Surprisingly, he didn't argue with her.

"Meeting you changed my life, Atticus." She kept her eyes fixed on the road ahead of them, watching as each clomp of the horse's hooves brought a bit more of the world ahead into view. "The day I met you was the first day since my parents died that I tasted freedom. If you hadn't taken pity on me when I hid in the shadows at the side of your stage, I'd still be trapped in Dockside, smothered under Kiva. I might not even understand that the Kalesh were coming, but if I did, I would merely see them as another prison. Someone else powerful coming to trap me in too small of a space and make me be…not be me."

Atticus kept his hands on the reins, not interrupting.

"Even knowing that sitting by you makes me want to talk," Sable said with a smile, "I still want to talk to you, and that is saying something, because I do not like people making me do something."

"I hadn't noticed," he said mildly, keeping his gaze forward.

"I think you know already how dearly I love you, Atticus, regardless of how many times you draw me into your crazy schemes." She set her hand on his arm.

He smiled sadly. "But you want to point out you were right about Vivaine."

Sable sighed. "No, I want to tell you that I'm terribly sad you weren't right about Vivaine. Until the last moment, I'd hoped…"

They sat in silence as the wagon rolled on.

"Remember I told you about a layered audience?" he said. "When your story is intended for more than one group and can have a different meaning for each? Eugessa merely put on a show for the crowd. An amateur move. Vivaine, though"—he let out a long, defeated breath —"played all her layers perfectly."

Sable looked at him curiously. "All I know is that her performance wasn't for my benefit. She told me as much flat out."

He nodded. "Her original, clearly feigned weakness and Argyros's fiery dramatics were partially for the crowd. A story that dramatic will spread faster than…well, faster than fire. The whole south will know it in a matter of days. Won't be much longer than that before it reaches the north. But that was the simplest layer."

The chaos of the trial began to fall into a sort of order as he spoke. A purpose to the moving parts.

"On a second level, it was a message to Eugessa, the Mira, and the abbesses that Vivaine is unequivocally in control of the priories. At this point, anyone who still serves Eugessa will only do so with Vivaine's permission." He paused. "That alone is a frightening goal. I have not seen Vivaine so anxious to visibly rule the Sanctuary before now. She did rule it, but it was always subtle."

"This was not subtle," Sable said.

"No." He ran his fingers through his beard. "But the third layer is the truly troubling one. It was her real goal, and that was for an audience of one."

The final piece fell into place. Sable had accused Vivaine of not taking control of the situation, but she'd been perfectly in control the entire time. She'd played the crowd perfectly, crushed Eugessa, and taken back the loyalty of the Mira. And her final audience…

"Jrogen."

Atticus nodded. "That whole performance was to prove that she controls a dragon and is immune to its fire."

"Which feeds the Kalesh myth about her." Vivaine had done, in a single event, what Sable had wanted to undo for weeks: shown herself to be the Zenivah the Kalesh wanted.

A question nagged at Sable. "How did she know a Tien Sark would be there? He was only there because Kiva brought him. Something I tried to dissuade him from."

"I doubt she knew for sure, but a display that big? One prioress executing another?" He glanced at Sable. "We rushed down from Barrowford for it. If there had been any Tien Sark anywhere closer than that, they would have come to the Sanctuary to witness it. We know there are a few around. I'm sure they were there."

Sable glared down the road ahead of them. "Just once I would like to beat Vivaine at this game. Just once I would like to outthink her instead of perfectly playing some role in her games."

Atticus let out a breath that was too pained to be a laugh. "So would I."

The wagon trundled along the road, creaking and groaning. The horse's hooves clopped quietly in the soft earth. They crested a hill, and the road wound away ahead of them, dotted with a few travelers and wagons.

"She said something about me," Atticus said finally, still not looking at Sable. "You two talked on the stage, and she said something about me."

Atticus has been useful over the years. He taught me everything I needed to know, but he's an old fool. Vivaine's voice had been so brutally harsh.

Sable's hand twitched on his arm, and he sighed.

"I know you remember her words, Sable. Tell me what she said."

He'll survive all this as miserably as he's survived everything else. Besides, he can take solace in the Flame of the North. He's as enamored of you as he always was of me.

"No," she said quietly.

He finally looked at her, and the hollowness in his eyes made Sable grip his arm tighter. "Was it that cruel?"

There are many kinds of adoration, Issable. Everything for him is a performance. Atticus's whole life is a performance. He knows the power of it—loves the power of it. He knows that if you create the right story, you can rule the world. The only thing he loves about me is the fact that I always controlled the story. Which is exactly what he loves about you. What Atticus truly craves is power, just like the rest of us.

"She doesn't know you," Sable said. "She thinks everyone in the world sees life through the same twisted lens she does." She slid her hand down his arm and grasped his hand. "Atticus, believe me, she doesn't see you for who you are."

He looked back down the road for so long that Sable pulled her hand off him and sat beside him quietly.

"She didn't kill anyone." His words were dull.

Sable paused. "The whole point of that trial was that she did."

He shook his head. "When Argyros came and lit the stage on fire. She didn't kill anyone. She could have had him kill Eugessa. Ryah, the other abbesses and Mira, they'd all be gone." His eyes were unfocused, staring down the road unseeing. When he spoke again, the words were odd. Discomposed. "Instead, she put on a show."

He blinked and shifted his head slightly toward Sable. "What did she say about me?"

"She said nothing about *you*, Atticus." Sable sat back, her arms crossed. "She knows nothing of you."

The old playwright's face settled into a troubled frown, but he turned his attention back to the road and didn't ask again.

CHAPTER FIFTY-SIX

SABLE STOOD on the darkening road, peering one direction, then the other. The night was growing steadily darker, the stars blotted out by clouds and the trees turning the forest floor into a shadowed maze of trunks and ferns. The campsite between the wagons clanked with preparations for the night.

There was a tiny pop next to her, and Purnicious appeared.

"Where's Talia?" Sable asked.

"Ahead of us," Purnicious said, looking thoughtfully down the road.

"With Kiva?" Sable asked.

Purn shrugged. "I can't see her as clearly as I can see you. There are people around her, but I can't tell who. She's hours ahead of us."

"Do you think she's all right?"

Purn closed her eyes in concentration. "It's hard to tell from this distance. If she was closer, I'd know more." She looked up at Sable. "I'll go check, unless you need me tonight."

"Are you sure you're not too tired?"

"All I've done today is ride in a wagon," Purn said with a smile. "I'd love to see how she is."

Ryah's laugh came from behind them near the wagons, along with Leonis's jibing voice.

"At least you only have one distant sister to keep track of now," Sable said.

"It's nice to have Ryah close by," Purn agreed. "Even more than that, it's nice that she's not in the priories any longer. It was always scary not to be able to feel her when she was inside those buildings." She cocked her head to the side. "I can feel Ryah more when she's close to you. Actually, I can feel Ryah and Talia more clearly when they're together."

"Then we should work toward getting all three of us together," Sable said. "You'd know everything there was to know."

The kobold smiled up at her. "I'll be back by morning."

"Thank you, Purn. And be careful."

The kobold disappeared with another pop, and Sable looked up the dark road. Talia was at least out of Immusmala. It was a step in the right direction, even if she was still with Kiva.

The softest rustle behind her was the only warning before Reese's arms grabbed her from behind. She stifled the yelp of surprise and stopped herself from trying to break his grip.

"You clearly forgot everything I taught you," he said in her ear.

"Maybe I don't want to get away from you." She leaned back on him. "Purn went to check on Talia."

"I heard. I was in the process of sneaking up on you when she interrupted."

"It's an odd game you two play."

Reese hummed in agreement. "She's a quiet little thing. Walked up behind me earlier, and I didn't hear her until she was only steps away—" He dropped his arms and moved next to her to face down the road, back the way they'd come.

"Is something out there?" Sable whispered.

"I thought I saw something down the road." He listened for a long moment. "There's a lot of game in these woods, though, and enough other travelers. It's probably nothing."

She almost asked him to say something true, but she thought about how Serene and Jae cast out so effortlessly and closed her eyes instead.

Instead of using the words to create heat and waiting to feel what warmed around her, she just sent out a wave of…questioning. Searching. A pulse that spread the way sound rippled through the world.

Beside her, Reese flared into heat. Immediately afterward, the group moving around the campsite blazed to fiery forms. The ripple rolled out, and she very faintly caught the warmth of the trees, the forest between them dotted with smaller balls of heat. Rabbit- and squirrel-sized creatures, a handful of larger animals grazing nearby. A large bird in a nearby tree.

Her eyes flew open. "I did it! With no words! There are a lot of animals in the forest."

He let out a short laugh. "That's a good thing. Any people?"

"The largest thing is a…deer, maybe. Grazing in that direction." She pointed off to the side of the road.

His chest vibrated with a thoughtful hum. "Good."

"Do you think anyone would follow us from Immusmala?"

He was quiet. "I don't know. With Purnicious gone all night, I think I'll set up a watch with Thulan."

The road was dry and hard under Sable's feet as they rounded the last turn before Tutella Island five days later. According to Purnicious, Talia and Kiva had arrived earlier that day and were already on the island. Here on the western bank of the river, rows of army tents filled the mouth of the long valley leading into the hills. Soldiers moved everywhere, leading horses, carrying supplies, marching in lines, standing around cook fires as their dinner simmered. The fine dust the wagons had been kicking up on the road for the last several days filled the valley like a beige fog.

"Looks like the whole army made it." Leonis pointed across the river where a far greater number of tents covered the ground.

Reese studied the soldiers ahead of them on the road. "There are uniforms from all five lords."

Sable walked alongside the wagons over the bridge onto Tutella Island, and despite the nearby armies, the wooden bridge and the clear water felt like they were welcoming her home.

The two monks guarding the bridge let them through, and the coziness faded as the wagons rolled into the forest. The trees might have been as silent and serene as usual, but there were so many soldiers moving along the road that it was impossible to tell. The gate to the town was open and choked with uniforms of every color hurrying into and out of the town.

Durnek waved to them from the side of the gate. "There's a large house reserved for you on the square," he called over the heads of the nearby soldiers. "Just to the right of the gathering hall."

Atticus nodded and led the wagons carefully through the traffic.

Ryah stepped up beside Sable. "That was Eugessa's house at the summit."

Sable nodded. "I hope this visit here goes better than that one did."

"So do I," Gwen agreed, coming up next to them.

They moved slowly up the road between the now familiar timbered houses. The sun had set behind the Scale Mountains, and some of the wavy glass in the windows already glowed with ripples of candlelight.

"I'm not sure what I'm doing when all of this is over," Sable said quietly to Ryah. "But the monks have offered me a home here. If I stay here for a bit before I find something more permanent, would you stay with me?"

"Here?" Ryah's eyes swept across the street. "I would love to!"

Sable nodded. "So would I."

They walked into the main square, and Sam's voice called from the wide doors of the gathering hall. "Reese!" Sam wove through the crowd. "We heard about the dragon. Rabbit's been getting ravens from Immusmala daily. Vivaine is firmly in control again, and Eugessa has been seen only once, and she looked haggard and dirty."

"Is Terrane here?" Gwen asked.

"He's in a house one street off the square." Sam pointed down a narrow street. "Blue front door, lots of flowers by the stoop."

Gwen nodded and headed in that direction while Sam took in the rest of the group. "A council will start shortly in the gathering hall. You are all invited. By me if anyone asks." He grimaced. "The lords and Braddick may control the army, but this is still my island." He gestured to the large house. "Make yourselves at home. As much as you can under the circumstances."

"Your island?" Reese asked Sam.

"You know what I mean." Sam waved away his words.

"Oh, it's your island, General," Reese said with a grin. "I've just never heard you admit it before. The lords must have really annoyed you."

Sam scanned the soldiers moving around them. "They just push every boundary. Always looking for a way to take a little bit more. It's infuriating." He refocused on Reese. "I could use your help. We're sorely lacking in rangers, so we're blind to what is going on around us. The men who followed Tanis are scattered in the different armies. Since they know this area from when you and Tanis camped up in the hills, I thought we could convince the lords to let us have them to expand our rangers. I'm nominating you to lead them."

Reese took in all the soldiers moving around the square. "How many scouts do you have out right now?"

"Barely any," Sam said. "Everything is in chaos. Three-quarters of the army arrived in the last day. Tonight's council is focused on trying to formulate some sort of organization." He squinted at Reese and Sable. "The lords weren't pleased about the fact you left the Tien Sark dead in the woods outside Barrowford. They wanted to question him. It might be wise if you pick a quiet corner and spectate. The lords are actually working together fairly well. I'd like to not give people reasons to be angry."

"Sounds good to me," Sable said. "If Rabbit's already gotten news from Immusmala, I doubt we have anything new to report."

Sable pressed the steaming cloth to her skin and groaned at the luxurious heat. She rubbed away the grime off her face and neck, then moved to scrubbing her arms.

Purnicious popped into the small washroom behind her, holding a pile of clothes. "Atticus sent these."

"Purn!" Sable pulled the cloth away from her face. "I made you a bed!"

The kobold looked at her blankly.

"There is this little nook in the room I'm staying in, and it is perfectly Purn-sized. I collected blankets and a pillow, but honestly, you might need to fluff it a bit." Sable smiled down at her. "The blankets are splendidly, garishly colored though."

Purn's eyes lit. "Which room?"

"Second door on the left." Sable wrung out the cloth and hung it to dry, then dipped her hands back into the wooden basin. "Let me guess what Atticus sent for me. Some sort of simple but elegant dress that will make me look like I'm noble, but not pretentious. Something to help the lords unconsciously think of me as a woman of influence." Sable dried off her hands and picked up a brush to start working on the tangles in her hair.

"A pair of comfortable traveling pants, a sensible dark blue shirt which will look beautiful with your hair, and a vest that I barely had to bellish at all to make perfectly flattering."

Sable stopped with the brush halfway through her hair. "Really?"

Purn nodded. "It looks like something you'd pick out for yourself."

"That's…" She pulled at the brush. "Any ideas why?"

The kobold shrugged. "There's a commotion going on near the gathering hall, though, so you might want to hurry."

Sable pulled on the clothes, which were remarkably comfortable and remarkably similar to the traveling clothes that she usually wore.

"Have you seen Talia?"

"She's in a house off the square, but Kiva's been there all day," Purn said with a wrinkled nose. "She's not happy to be here, but she's safe."

Sable nodded. "I'll go see her as soon as I can."

"I'm going to go see my bed!" Purn said, and disappeared.

Sable walked downstairs to the main room, where Jae and Serene were sorting through quills.

Reese sat near them, a bit cleaner too. He took in her clothes, and when he saw the knife she'd put on her belt, he gave an approving nod.

Sable crossed the room to where Atticus was peering at a handful of books on a shelf. "Dare I ask what I'm supposed to be?"

He gave her an innocent look. "Isn't that the sort of thing you'd pick for yourself?"

"It is, which makes me nervous."

"I thought about our conversation from the other day," he said, "and it really is true. All your most magnificent moments have been when you've been pushed to the point where you have taken charge of the situation and spoken, using words that were truly yours. Not something scripted for you. Whatever happens here, I, for one, would like your voice to be heard. So…" He gestured to her. "Be yourself. Or a cleaner version of yourself that doesn't look like you just traveled for days. But still yourself."

She studied him, but his words had been warm. "And if you come up with interesting roles you want me to play?"

"I'll be sure to mention them to you," he said with a smile, motioning to the door. "Shall we?"

Outside, the square sat in a dusky blue as two monks lit lanterns. The doors to the gathering hall were open, and light spilled out onto the cobblestones while voices tumbled over each other.

A monk stopped them just inside the door, and Atticus paused to talk to him.

Sable waited in the entrance, looking over Atticus's and Serene's shoulders. The hall wasn't as crowded as it had been the last time Sable had been there. That night, Vivaine had hosted a dinner for everyone at the summit, and there had barely been space to move. Tonight, only a dozen people sat around a table on the far side of the fire pit that filled the center of the floor. No fires were lit on the warm evening, but torches and candles were placed everywhere, brightening the huge hall and the solid wall of books along the back.

"If you would hear me out, my lords," a man was calling over the noise. "I have information about the gold mines you are going to find interesting."

The voice caught Sable's attention. She'd heard it before, but it wasn't one of the lords. It was a voice from a wholly different time and place. A voice that didn't fit here. She couldn't see the man's face but caught a glimpse of pale skin and limp beige hair.

Behind her shoulder, Reese made a displeased noise. He moved closer to her, setting a hand on her back, which didn't quite fit either. The voice was from long ago. Before Reese.

"Who is that?" she asked him, shifting to see around Atticus.

"We don't own any of the mines," Lord Darien said. "You should take your report to the south."

The man laughed, an easy sound that rang false. "No one actually owns a mine." It was the pompous tone that clicked the voice into place.

Sable stretched up onto her tiptoes to get a full view of the man's face —a man who looked like a well-dressed dead fish.

She grabbed Reese's arm. "It's Lord Renwen!" she whispered.

Reese's attention turned away from the door. "The Renwen you stole the ledger from that got Kiva his gaudy house?"

"The beautiful house that I just lost?" Kiva said from behind them. "Yes, that Renwen." Sable looked back to see him studying the pale lord. "Nice to see old friends, isn't it, Sable?" he asked without a hint of pleasure.

"Whether you're referring to yourself or him," she said, "the answer is no."

He didn't look amused. "I'd lost track of good old Renwen for a while. He's been spending time in the north since he fled Immusmala."

"Does he know you're the one who ended up with his ledger?" Sable asked.

Kiva shrugged. "I guess we're about to find out." He started to push past her.

Sable grabbed his arm. "Where's Talia?"

"We have a house off the square." He set his hand on top of her own.

"Would you like to accompany me to the table? I'm sure we can find seats together. It would be lovely to have your special insight on everyone's words."

Sable pulled her hand away from him. "I'd rather light the fire pit and jump into it."

He grinned at her, winked at Reese, then started toward the table.

Serene stood in his way. She held her book in the crook of one arm and rolled one of her spiky quills between her fingers.

He paused. "I heard of your work in the Sanctuary when you almost burned down the priory." He gave her his calculating, oily smile. "You're an interesting woman."

"She's a dangerous woman," Jae said from her shoulder. "The kind of woman people will be reading about hundreds of years from now. Long after leeches like you are forgotten."

Tiny lines of fire formed along Serene's quill, sparking and hissing.

"History does not look kindly on people who prey on the weak for their own benefit," Jae finished.

"History is kind to those who win." Kiva's gaze dropped to the flames snaking over her quill. "Nice trick." He turned sideways and moved past her.

Reese set his hand on Sable's arm. "Does Renwen know you're the one who stole his ledger?"

"I don't think he knows I exist," Sable said.

"Let's find seats." Atticus started forward. "This should be interesting."

Lord Renwen hadn't changed much. He was still gaunt and waxy. He still managed a towering confidence and civility that felt like a wash of thin paint over a cold, calculating mind.

"The interesting thing about the gold mines," he said casually, "is that everyone thinks they are producing—" He stopped short, but not at the sight of Sable. Renwen's gaze fell on Kiva, and the facade cracked. A flash of pure, unbridled hatred filled the lord's eyes before he blinked and it was gone. "Everyone thinks they are producing gold." He finished, turning his attention back to the lords.

"The gold mines aren't producing gold?" General Braddick asked from his seat at the head of the table. "What are they producing?"

Vacant seats were spread around the huge table, and Atticus, Jae, and Serene sat on the far side. Both Jae and Serene opened books and readied their quills. Sable found a seat on the near side between Reese and Lord Loren.

"The mines are producing nothing." Renwen slid several papers down the center of the huge table. "These are maps of every mine working as of a month ago. And next to each you can see the value of the gold that has been extracted."

Runess picked up one of the maps. "Why is production down? Which month is this from?"

"Every month since each mine opened."

"You mean to tell us that not one mine has produced enough gold to be profitable?" Lord Darien asked.

"Impossible," Kiva said flatly.

"How much gold have you seen in Immusmala lately?" Renwen asked.

Kiva paused. "There's barely any left in the city because the Kalesh took so much."

"Wrong." Renwen pointed to the maps. "The Kalesh only took a little. Only a part of this amount. They believe the lion's share of the gold is hidden around Immusmala, while the merchants think the Kalesh took it all. But the truth is, it doesn't exist."

Kiva shook his head. "How did you get this information? No one has information on every mine. The owners keep all those numbers too close to the vest."

"I'm a resourceful man," Lord Renwen said, animosity lacing his words. "If I set out to learn something, nothing will keep me from digging up every secret there is. The numbers are correct."

Renwen's words moved across the table with a surprising amount of warmth. Atticus, Serene, Reese, and even Kiva glanced at Sable for verification. Lords Loren and Erick did as well.

She gave a very slight nod, but Renwen's gaze had followed theirs and landed on her with a heavy intensity. "I make it a habit of discovering the people, in any situation, who actually know what is happening." He looked around the table once, then returned his attention to Sable. "This is the actual amount of gold the hills have given up."

The words were still true, but for a moment Sable didn't register the importance of them. Lord Renwen's eyes ran over her, scraping across her skin as though he were mining her for information. She sat stiffly in her chair, trying to keep her face neutral.

"This can't possibly be true," Kiva said. "I talk to merchants every day.

There are reports of fifty times this much being harvested just in the last few months."

"Have you seen these reports?" Renwen asked.

"Not specifically. The merchants keep the numbers vague. Which I don't blame them for."

"They keep the numbers vague because every single mine owner thinks his mine is the only one not producing. So he creates false reports exaggerating his worth lest he lose face among the Guild."

"But there were other reports," Kiva objected. "Not related to any mine in particular. Reports on exploratory shafts, pebbles of gold in the rivers. Small veins that were believed to connect to larger ones." He tossed the map back down. "Those I have seen. Dozens of them. Everyone has seen them."

"Indeed," Renwen said. "They were fake. Every single one."

"How do you know?" Lord Darien demanded.

Kiva crossed his arms. "Falsifying numbers is something Lord Renwen is intimately acquainted with."

Renwen gave him a cold smile. "When you know what to look for, the clues are not hard to spot. Then you just follow the trail to see who caused all the problems in the first place."

The hint of a mocking smile curled up the corner of Kiva's mouth. "And what did you find?"

"If you're going to say there is some vast conspiracy to fabricate reports about the mines," Lord Runess said, "that feels unlikely."

"Not a vast conspiracy," Renwen said, pulling his gaze from Kiva. "Every single trail, when I followed it long enough"—he raised a long, pale finger—"led back to a single point."

His words had remained warm the entire time, and she caught Atticus and Kiva glancing at her again. Renwen noticed, and his own attention slid over to land on her again. When she didn't object, Atticus turned a probing look back to Renwen.

"Who?" Kiva asked.

Renwen leaned forward and set his finger on the nearest map, on the very tip of the city of Immusmala. "Her holiness, the High Prioress Vivaine."

CHAPTER FIFTY-SEVEN

THE GATHERING HALL erupted into scoffs and questions and derision.

Sable turned to Reese, who was staring down at the nearest map.

"Is that true?" he asked quietly.

"Renwen believes it is." From across the table, she caught Atticus's eye and nodded. The playwright sank back in his chair.

"Prioress Vivaine spread false reports about gold that doesn't exist?" Lord Runess demanded.

"She did," Renwen said simply.

Reese swore under his breath.

"Why would she do that?" Lord Darien said. "The gold is the reason the Kalesh are here. If the Kalesh conquer us, she will lose all her power. She's too intelligent not to know that."

The table broke out into a half-dozen separate conversations as lords and generals shouted over each other.

Sable threaded some *vitalle* across the table to where Atticus, Jae, and Serene sat. "She found out about the Zenivah myth," she whispered, "and lured them here with reports of gold."

Serene tapped her fingers on the table, the motion growing quicker and more irritated. Jae's quill paused, and he glanced up with a defeated look before returning to his book. Atticus let out a heavy sigh.

"Thank you for the information." General Braddick's voice carried over the room as he stood. "The council will take this information into account. May we keep the maps?"

Lord Renwen gave an agreeable nod. "Of course, General. If you are in need of more details, please let me know. My people are camped across the bridge should you require anything."

Braddick crossed his arms, considering the man.

"Is it safe to assume a man of your talents has information about things in the south unrelated to the gold mines?"

Lord Renwen gave him a thin, complacent smile. "I make it a practice to know as much as I can about as many things as I can."

Braddick nodded. "Find Lord Renwen a house in Aedis," he said to the monk guarding the door, then turned back to the pasty lord. "We're breaking for dinner, but afterward, join us again." It wasn't phrased as a question.

Lord Renwen gave Braddick a slight nod. "At your service, General."

Kiva's eyes narrowed as he watched Renwen head for the door.

"We reconvene in an hour," Braddick said, leaning on the table. "Our best estimate is that we have a fortnight to prepare for what is coming. We have a great deal to do." He pushed away from the table and strode toward the door.

The rest of the table stood, breaking into smaller groups of quiet, tense conversation.

Sable stood to find Kiva approaching her. "That was interesting," he said. "Judging by your face, he was telling the truth?"

"He believes it's the truth," Sable answered. "Take me to Talia."

He raised an eyebrow at the command. "Of course, Queen of the North," he said dryly. "Would you and your dog like to join us for dinner again?"

"I just want to make sure my sister is all right." Sable motioned toward the door. "After you."

Kiva grinned at her. "Yes, Your Highness."

Renwen, who still stood talking to the monk at the door, looked up as Kiva approached. "How is Master Hull's house treating you, Kiva? Did you find the secret door in his cellar to the expensive bottles of wine?"

Kiva barely came up to the lord's chin, yet he met the man's gaze with complete composure. "I did. And I drank most of it."

"And how is dear Lady Ingred?" Renwen's face stayed nonchalant, but his tone hardened.

Sable caught the slightest confusion in Kiva's expression before he smoothed it out.

"There aren't many things I miss about Immusmala," Renwen continued, "but she and I were close once. I assume you knew that already." The latent threat in his voice was chilling.

Kiva gave him a breezy smile. "I did. And Lady Ingred is still lovely and beautiful. And incredibly useful to me."

Renwen's jaw ticked, but he turned his attention to Sable. "I don't believe you and I have been introduced." He glanced behind Sable. "Although you travel with Atticus the playwright, so it's not terribly difficult to deduce that I have the honor of speaking with the Flame of the North." He gave her an oily smile. "My real question is why is it that I make such an auspicious person so nervous?"

"Anyone who has things in common with Kiva makes me nervous," Sable said.

"Kiva and I have nothing in common," Renwen said bluntly. He gave Reese a bored glance. "And you must be the general who saved Immusmala. I expected someone more impressive."

"I expected you to look like a dead fish," Reese said with a shrug. "Sometimes expectations aren't met, sometimes they are."

Renwen gave a little laugh, but his eyes were sharp and calculating. "It's odd that you knew anything about me at all, seeing as I don't believe your path and mine have ever come close to each other."

"Let's keep them that way," Reese said.

"I believe we're past that point." Renwen took in Kiva and Sable. "Looking forward to seeing you all when we reconvene." Without waiting for their answer, he motioned for the monk to lead the way and strode out of the gathering hall.

Kiva watched him go. "Resourceful fellow, there," he mused. He turned to Reese. "Best add Renwen to your list of people who have something against Sable. It won't take him long to figure out how she fits into the ledger theft."

Reese nodded, keeping his eyes on Renwen as he disappeared into the soldiers moving in the square. "I'll put him on the list right below you."

Kiva grinned. "Come on, I'll take you to see Talia."

Torchlight lined the square, and northern soldiers moved efficiently through it, their varying uniforms all darkening to black when they stepped away from the firelight. Sable started down the stairs outside the door and found a knot of soldiers gathered around a familiar handcart just off to one side.

"Flibbet!" Atticus called.

The merchant's blond head peered through the soldiers. "Atticus! Finally!" He lowered a bundle of arrows he'd been holding up. "I have some business to attend to, gentlemen. I'll be around the square later tonight and all day tomorrow if you are interested in striking a deal."

With a few complaints, the soldiers ambled off, and Flibbet motioned them over. "What took you so long?" Flibbet asked Atticus, tucking items away. "I have something you need to hear."

Kiva looked curiously at the little merchant.

"And you need to hear this before the council continues tonight," Flibbet said. "Because I don't know what it means."

Sable turned to Kiva. "I'll see Talia later. How do I find her?"

"We're in the house with the pointy roof and the red front door, just outside the square. She's probably holed away writing to Niko again." Kiva shook his head. "It took Niko himself to get her to leave, you know. She flat-out refused until he begged her."

"That's not surprising at all," Sable said. "Tell her I'll come by later."

Kiva nodded, then, with a lingering curious look at Flibbet, headed across the square.

Reese moved over to Flibbet's cart and pulled out the spyglass. "You still have this?" he asked the merchant.

Flibbet stopped short and looked at him. "I do," he said slowly. "Interested in a trade yet?"

Reese put it back down with a slight smile. "I still have nothing worth trading."

Flibbet gave a noncommittal hum and closed his cart. "Where can we all talk that's more private than here?"

Atticus led them over to their house. Flibbet tucked his cart in a nook along the side before following them inside, where Thulan, Leonis, and Ryah were immersed in a loud game involving black and white pebbles.

"Some monks brought food," Thulan said, motioning to a counter along the wall. "Good men, these monks."

Sable filled a plate with some dark bread and flaky fish while Atticus told the peddler and the others about the gold mines. "And, according to Lord Renwen, the source of all the lies about the gold was Vivaine."

Those who hadn't heard already stared at him in confusion, and even those who'd heard Renwen explain it shook their heads.

Thulan sat up. "This is why the Kalesh were in the dwarven tunnels! Because Vivaine convinced them this land was full of treasure!"

Jae set his plate at a table on the side of the room while Serene stacked their books and quills off to the side.

"It doesn't make sense for Vivaine to lure the Kalesh here with lies about the gold," Jae said. "Once the Kalesh are entrenched here, even if she convinces them she's this mythical Zenivah, she'll still lose control of this land. I can't imagine her plan was to go from ruling the south without peer to being a pawn of the Empire."

"Unless she didn't know the myth of Zenivah early on and didn't intend for the Kalesh to hear about the gold," Sable said. "Maybe she had some other plan. Something involving the merchants, and the Kalesh crashed her plans."

"What plan would she have, though?" Serene said. "I can't think of a reason to lie to an entire land about there being gold in a place no one had ever thought there was gold."

Everyone looked at Atticus, who had been holding a piece of bread, looking unseeingly into the empty fireplace. He put the bread onto his plate on the mantel without taking a bite, then turned to them and shrugged. "Maybe Renwen is mistaken. Maybe Vivaine isn't part of it, and it started how we thought it did, as merchants looking for ways to gain more wealth. Maybe no one expected it to grow out of control like this."

"Or it's just all nonsense," Thulan said.

"No," Flibbet said, setting his own plate on a small side table in irritation. "It's not nonsense. It is very, very troubling." Seeing everyone's eyes on him, he stood, rubbing his hands together, and paced across the middle of the room.

"Out on the Eastern Reaches," he began, "is an isolated community made up of a large number of Kalesh refugees."

"There is?" Reese asked. "Where?"

Flibbet waved his hand in a vaguely eastern direction. "That way. I'd only been there once, long ago, but it's grown since then. I traveled there after leaving Atticus in the hopes that they might know something we don't." He paused. "And they did. I met an old man who'd escaped the Empire when he was young." He glanced at Atticus. "When he had lived there, he'd only known half the Zenivah story. He knew about her and how she helped the Emperor, but that was it. He had never heard the part about her having a family, or her enemies killing them and trapping her in a rift, or any idea at all of her prophesied return."

Serene pushed her plate aside and opened her book to a new page. "How long ago was he in the Empire?"

"Forty-five years ago."

She made a note at the top of the page.

"When did he learn the whole story?" Atticus asked, as though he didn't want to know the answer.

"The same time the rest of the town did," Flibbet said, "twelve years ago when a traveling theater troupe stayed there for a month, working on a new play."

Atticus let out a pained breath.

"The troupe claimed they were writing the play themselves," Flibbet continued. "They'd adopted a story from here in the north and were weaving it into the Zenivah story. In the northern tale, a woman had been wronged by her chieftain, and she'd tried to kill him. But instead, his men had found her, and a wildcat she lived with, and trapped them in a gully and caused a rockslide to fall and crush her."

Jae straightened. "I know this story! There's a canyon in the Wolfbane mountains that the wind howls down, and they say that's her voice claiming she'll come back and seek her revenge on the clan." He slapped his hand down on the table. "I knew the Zenivah myth reminded me of something!"

Atticus put his back to the room, setting his hand on the mantel as though he needed the support. "How do you know that story, Jae?" There was a low dread in his voice.

"A book in Stonehaven."

Serene looked at her husband curiously.

"It was shelved with those old folktales from the north," he explained, "the ones with the snow trolls and the ice worm."

Atticus turned slowly to Flibbet. "And the newer refugees knew the full myth?"

The peddler nodded. "Any refugees who'd left the Empire in the last ten years knew Zenivah had promised to return."

In the firelight of the room, deep shadows etched themselves around Atticus's mouth and between his brows.

"So," Sable said, "that theater group changed the myth twelve years ago?"

Ryah pressed her hand to her chest. "Atticus?" she said softly.

He didn't turn. "What did she say about me on the platform, Sable?"

Sable froze with a bite of fish halfway to her mouth as the room's attention swung to her. Vivaine's words rose painfully to her mind, and Sable almost refused again to tell him. But she didn't need Ryah's skill to feel the anguish radiating from Atticus.

Sable set the piece of fish down. "She said you valued power."

He shook his head. "The exact words, Sable."

"Atticus…"

"Please," he said quietly. "Every word."

She picked up a crumb of bread, rolling it into a little ball between her fingers. "'Atticus has been useful over the years. He taught me everything I needed to know, but he's an old fool. He'll survive all this as miserably as he's survived everything else. Besides, he can take solace in the Flame of the North. He's as enamored of you as he always was of me.'"

The others shifted uncomfortably, except Atticus, who stayed facing the mantel.

"I told her there was nothing similar in how you felt toward the two of us, and she said, 'There are many kinds of adoration, Issable. Everything for him is a performance. Atticus's whole life is a performance. He knows the power of it—loves the power of it. He knows that if you create the right story, you can rule the world. The only thing he loves about me is the fact that I always controlled the story. Which is exactly what he loves about you. What Atticus truly craves is power, just like the rest of us.'"

Atticus swore and turned to the room. "Anyone know if there are Kalesh prisoners on the island?"

"I heard some soldiers say there were in a house near the wall," Flibbet said.

"Show me." Atticus strode toward the door. "Reese! I need you to interpret for me."

Reese glanced at Sable as he rose.

"It's been a while since he got cryptic with us." Thulan pushed herself to her feet.

Leonis nodded. "It was overdue."

Sable rose too, but Reese set his hand on her shoulder, his expression firm. "If you come, swear to me you will stay far out of reach of every single prisoner."

"Reese!" Atticus called from outside. "I need you!" His voice held a note of desperation.

Reese didn't move.

Sable glanced out the door. "I promise."

His look didn't soften, but he nodded and followed Atticus into the night.

Flibbet led everyone to the edge of Aedis and pointed to a small house along the wall. Around the back, three Tutella monks guarded a cellar. At Reese's request, one pulled open the heavy door with a long, low creak. A single torch illuminated five soldiers slumped against the walls in the rough stone room. Two monks walked down first, their hands on the hilt of their swords.

Atticus followed, motioning for Reese to come with him. Sable stopped on the stairs, staying behind Thulan. The air in the cellar was damp and warm, smelling of bodies kept inside for too long. The ceiling was held up with stone pillars. The prisoners looked at them with dull expressions. Their hands were tied, and their black uniforms were caked with dirt, but they looked fed, and a bowl of clean water sat near the door.

Atticus strode into the center of the room as though he were striding onto a stage. "Where did you first hear the story of Zenivah's return?" His voice was loud and confident, but not unfriendly.

Reese stepped down into the cellar as well, scanning the prisoners, keeping his hand on a knife. "*Tel priy pokutu Zenivah krona?*"

The soldiers glanced at each other but didn't answer.

Atticus approached one.

"Atticus," Reese warned.

One of the monks moved closer, but the prisoner didn't move.

Atticus squatted and set his hand on the man's foot, looking at him intently. "Where?"

"*Jesi sviat,*" a soldier said.

"A fall festival," Reese said. A few others spoke up, and Reese nodded. "They heard it from festivals, street performers, traveling theater troupes." He listened to one soldier. "It became a popular play in the capital and spread across the countryside. The show was everywhere for a few years."

"That sounds a lot like something Atticus would be a part of," Sable whispered to Thulan. The dwarf's expression was dark, and she didn't answer.

"It has songs—" Reese began.

A soldier started a lively tune, and after a few words, others joined in. It started quiet, but slowly grew.

"The scales like moonlight break the dark," Reese said, "scatter the black, end the night."

Atticus stood slowly, taking in the prisoners, his face pained.

The rest joined in, and the cellar rang with the men's voices as it rose to a victorious ending. The soldiers ended with a cheer somewhere between enthusiasm and defiance.

When they quieted, Reese continued, "The day returns, the light returns, the queen returns forever."

"That was...catchy," Leonis said from next to Sable.

"So the story was a play?" Atticus asked.

Reese asked in Kalesh, and one of the soldiers shrugged and answered. They spoke for a moment before Reese turned to Atticus. "A couple of years after the show became popular, an ancient scroll was found in a monastery in the western province where Zenivah was from, telling the tale of the woman and her dragon."

Atticus took a step backwards, shaking his head as though he could erase the words.

"That province created a holiday for her," Reese continued. "People eat something called dragon bread." He paused. "Then, a few years ago, they heard rumors of a woman with a dragon who lived in a land of jewels and gold, far to the west."

Atticus reached out, almost blindly searching for a pillar to lean on.

One of the prisoners said something defiant, and the others nodded.

"Zenivah is coming," Reese translated quietly.

Atticus turned to everyone waiting on the stairs. "She isn't just controlling the story. She wrote it."

CHAPTER FIFTY-EIGHT

THE NIGHT AIR was cool as Sable stepped out of the cellar holding the Kalesh prisoners and into the alley that ran along the wall. Atticus followed the rest of them out and paced across the street, running his hand through his hair.

"You learned more than we did in there," Reese said. "Care to explain?"

Atticus stopped, his shoulders slumped. "She was right. I taught her everything she needed," he said, staring at them. "Everything."

"About what?" Sable asked.

Thulan sighed. "Everything about spreading stories."

Atticus met Thulan's eyes, and his shoulders sank further. "I've reported to Vivaine for decades about the world. When we met, she would ask me about the troupe. How I picked plays the audience would respond to. What made a compelling story. Why we used Leonis's glowing tree on our stage. How it was that we were always among people's favorite troupes. I thought..." His eyes dropped to the ground. "I thought she was just interested."

"You think Vivaine started the second half of the myth," Sable said. "That Zenivah had been wronged and trapped and would return."

Jae nodded slowly. "She had a primed audience."

Atticus leaned back against the city wall, and his head dropped forward. "The Kalesh already knew a myth about Zenivah—she just added interesting new parts." One of his hands gestured weakly to the cellar door. "With songs to make sure it spread quickly."

"But twelve years ago?" Sable asked. "What was she planning twelve years ago?"

"Expansion," Thulan answered. "Vivaine had been the undisputed leader of Immusmala for decades already by then, but what was there to gain past that? The north? A loose collection of bickering territories? Or a huge Empire to the east who already revered dragons?"

"But they wouldn't have known about her," Atticus said. "So she hired a troupe like ours and planted a seed in the western edge of the Empire. Started a story, one designed to spread quickly. One that felt ancient and timeless but fit the Empire of today. One that would feed off their unrest.

"And then," he said heavily, "a few years later, an 'ancient' scroll was discovered in a monastery on the western edge of the Empire—the edge closest to Vivaine—that told the same story. A story that hadn't existed before the troupe started to spread it. The scroll took the tale and grounded it in history. Added to its weight."

Serene straightened. "This is why she stole all the books from Stonehaven! Because we had the wildcat story."

"And when you're trying to prove your version is real," Thulan said grimly, "you have to get rid of anything that is older."

"But why?" Sable asked. "Why go to all this work? Why waste twelve years—"

"Probably more," Atticus interrupted. "Twelve years ago, her troupe created and started spreading the story. How much time before that did it take to learn about the Empire and…find a theater troupe willing to go to the Empire who could get this rolling. They must have had a reasonable amount of skill."

"All right, more than twelve years, then," Sable said. "Why spend all that time when she could just walk into the Empire with her dragon and they'd worship her anyway?"

"Because then she might be a novelty," Atticus said. "A thing to admire, a pawn for the powerful in the Empire to use. But now, she is no pawn. She is the goddess they lost long ago. The woman whose only peer is the Emperor himself."

"Not even him," Leonis pointed out. "In the original myth, the Emperor wanted to marry her, and she refused him. She's the woman who's too exalted even for an Emperor."

"So the story of the gold was just to lure the Kalesh to this part of the world," Thulan said.

"A poor choice." Reese leaned back against the wall. "The Empire isn't going to be happy when they find out there isn't any."

"Won't matter," Leonis said.

Thulan nodded. "The gold was just the glittery backdrop to get the Kalesh to look at her stage."

Atticus sighed. "The gold wasn't the story. The gold was like Leonis's tree. Anything sparkly or bright works to get people's attention. Vivaine is the real story. The Kalesh will believe they came for some gold and found a goddess instead. She'll go from prioress of an insignificant city to essentially Empress of the Kalesh Empire. Without seeming to seek after it at all."

"I liked it better," Jae said, "when we thought she was just haughty and opportunistic."

"We should get back to the council," Atticus said, straightening his shoulders and putting on a voice that was too strained to sound businesslike. "The lords should know what we're facing."

He started down the alley, and the others followed.

They neared the square, and Sable saw the house Talia and Kiva were staying in. "You don't need me in the council meeting, do you?" she said to Atticus. At the absent shake of his head, she added, "Then I'm going to check on Talia."

He continued toward the square while Reese and Ryah followed her to a house on the square significantly smaller than Sable's. She knocked on the bright red door, and it was opened by Talia herself.

"Sable! Ryah!" She stepped aside and motioned them in. "Hello, Reese!"

The house was snug and tidy. A little fire burned in the wood stove heating a kettle. Talia looked tired and pale.

"Oh, Talia," Ryah said, hugging her sister. "How are you? How is Niko? He's still in Immusmala, isn't he?"

Talia nodded. "He and I were at the trial together, and the moment Vivaine threatened Kiva, he rushed me out of the Sanctuary and made me swear I'd leave." She sighed and sank into a chair. "He's still there, of course."

"What are you going to do?" Ryah asked.

"I have no idea. I haven't even gotten a letter from him yet. I don't even know what he's thinking right now."

"Well," Sable said, sitting next to her. "If he's anything like Reese, his letter will go on about how he'd rather have you safe than with him, and then you can write him back aggravated at the nobility of the sentiment."

Reese took a seat in a chair on the other side of the small room and shrugged. "She's not wrong."

"But he'll be miserable, even if he won't admit it," Sable continued, "and then the two of you will find a way to come back together."

"How on earth is that going to happen?" Talia asked. "He's a Kalesh soldier, Sable, and the entire north is gearing up for war with them."

Sable squeezed Talia's hand. "Niko loves you, and you love him. Add to that the fact that you are more stubborn than anyone I've ever met, and it's just a matter of time until you're reunited."

Talia managed a weak smile. "I hope so." She glanced at Reese. "Purnicious stopped by earlier and told me about a certain rock tower that was built by a certain couple on their way out of Immusmala." She turned back to Sable with an amused look. "I thought people who could see how hopeless a situation was didn't do things like that."

"Only the ones who want to be happy," Sable answered.

Talia grinned at her. "Very wise."

The faint scent of mint and chamomile spread through the room from the tea kettle. Talia leaned back with a sigh. "If only Vivaine and the Empire would settle down and stop all the fighting, maybe we could all be happy."

"Vivaine isn't stopping any time soon," Sable said, launching into an explanation about the gold mines and the Kalesh myth of Zenivah.

The kettle was boiling when Sable finished.

Talia rose to pull it off the heat. "Everyone has underestimated her for years." She pulled four simple cups from a shelf and began to fill them.

"We need to figure out what she'll do next," Sable agreed. "And not underestimate that too."

"It seems obvious at this point," Ryah said. "She's attained what she wanted. The Kalesh know about her, and any Tien Sark at the trial will have pledged themselves to her by now. Like Atticus said, they won't really care that they're not finding gold, not when they've found Zenivah." Ryah sighed. "She'll just let the Kalesh take over the north and try to get them to take her to the Empire."

Talia set the kettle down slowly. "I don't think so."

Sable felt a hint of amusement at this seriousness in Talia's voice, but when she carried tea to Sable and Ryah, her eyes were sharp and surprisingly calculating.

"She'll continue to play to her strengths," Talia mused, holding out a cup absently to Sable.

"Which strengths?" Reese asked, looking at Talia.

"Well," Talia turned to get the last two cups, "sitting back and letting the Kalesh take the victory in the north does not sound like her." She handed Reese a cup.

"That's true," Ryah said. "But what else could she do?"

Talia sat in her chair with an elegance that made Sable straighten her posture. Whatever expression had made her look young before was gone, replaced with a resolute confidence. "Well, Vivaine's goal is to convince the Empire she's the equal to the Emperor."

Sable stopped with her cup lifted, staring at her sister through the swirl of steam. "She'll need to prove to them that *she* can create an Empire."

"An Empire?" Ryah asked.

Sable lowered her tea. "She's not just going to let the Kalesh take over the north."

Talia tapped a finger on her cup. "No, however this war goes, at the end of it, you can be sure it isn't going to look like the Kalesh conquered us. It will look like Vivaine."

Sable stared at Talia, torn between astonishment at the shrewd look in her sister's eyes and her absolute certainty that Talia was right.

"But..." Ryah began, her face troubled. "I know Vivaine has done horrible things, but I believe she truly wants to do good. I have seen her upset when there's a problem and she can't work out a solution that is good for most of the people involved. She thinks she can help people."

Talia shrugged. "That's a compelling reason to want power. If she believes she can do good in the small city of Immusmala, how much more good could she do if she ruled the Kalesh Empire?"

Sable groaned. "That is exactly what Gwen says about her. She sees herself as the person who can see what the world needs. She thinks she's been given the responsibility to guide it. And yes, more power, to her, means more of a chance to do good."

"But for Vivaine to win the north," Reese said, "she'll have to use Argyros."

"Where is the good in that?" Ryah asked. "She can't think that killing people with her dragon leads to any goodness."

"She can," Sable said. "She'll believe the vast good she could do if she had power in the Empire will overshadow whatever pain she'll cause here."

Reese gave a defeated sigh. "We can't even stand against the Kalesh if they *don't* bring the dragon."

Talia turned her attention to Ryah. "Kiva told me about the dragon at the trial. I can't believe how close Vivaine came to killing you."

Ryah wrapped her arms around herself. "It was less terrifying than you'd imagine, at least once Innov reached me. She was like a…shield. I felt utterly safe, even though I could see all the dragon fire past her."

Talia frowned. "Kiva thinks Vivaine has lost control of the dragon, but that sounds to me like he was doing exactly what she wanted."

"They felt different than they used to," Ryah said. "Before, Argyros treated her like a mother. But after the trial they felt like…equals."

Talia looked curiously at her. "They did?"

Sable sat forward. "Did you know Ryah can feel what other people are feeling?" she asked Talia.

"Feel how?" Talia asked blankly.

"I can just feel it," Ryah said. "For instance, Reese is feeling like the ground, which was already shaky, has just fallen away completely. Sable feels mostly shocked at how quickly you put all that stuff about Vivaine together, and you…" Ryah gave her a sad smile. "You feel like your heart was left back in Immusmala and now you're supposed to try to live without it."

Talia tapped a finger on her teacup, looking like she wanted to argue.

"She's not being poetic," Sable said. "She actually feels it."

Talia turned an annoyed look at Sable. "You're surprised I put together all that about Vivaine? I've been working with Kiva and Ingred, learning how to navigate a world where every single person wants something. If I couldn't figure out what people were planning, I'd have been chewed up and spit out ages ago. What do you think I've been doing all this time?"

"Honestly," Sable said, "I've never really been able to wrap my brain around it."

"Talia," Reese said slowly, "what do you see when you look at Kiva?"

"Besides a conniving, greedy, manipulative leech," Sable muttered.

Talia frowned at her. "Kiva's parents died when he was young, and Eugessa took all their belongings. He spent years on the streets. He was small and weak, and while he's never told me the details, I don't need Ryah's skills to know he was treated violently for a long time. He caught a vayakadyn snake and tamed it enough to use against his enemies, and that was how he kept himself safe." She shook her head. "So I don't see what you see, Sable. I just see a man who will do anything—absolutely anything—to not be weak again."

"Wanting to keep yourself safe, I understand," Sable said, "but stealing, destroying, and killing to do it… It's his methods that make him horrible, Talia, not his motivations."

Reese propped his elbows on his knees and studied Talia. "What does Kiva think you're good at?"

"This." Talia waved her arm around the room. "He says I'm good at seeing what people are really after and what they'll do to get it."

"Maybe you have a skill along those lines," Sable said.

"It's not anything special. I just listen to what people say, compare that to what they're actually doing, and then it's easy to piece the rest together. People's motivations are rarely a secret."

"They are to me," Sable said. "Which is how I always end up walking into whatever trap Kiva or Vivaine set for me."

"No matter how many times they catch you," Reese agreed.

Sable smiled at him. "It hasn't happened in a little while." She turned back to Talia. "What does Vivaine want?"

"To be loved," Talia answered without hesitation. "*Revered* and loved. She wants to be idolized."

"What does Argyros want?" Reese asked.

Talia shifted her shoulders, as though she was trying to stave off a shiver. "He wants to be feared and to be free. Once, I saw Vivaine begin to say something to him that sounded like a command, and the scales on his neck actually stood up a little. She backtracked immediately and softened it to something like an entreaty, and he relaxed, but…" She shifted again. "I don't envy anyone who tries to control him. Vivaine included." She shrugged. "I honestly don't think I have any sort of special skill here, but Kiva is always inviting me to meetings to tell him what I discover about people."

Sable let out a laugh. "Well, that proves it above anything else. Kiva has access to countless people as shifty and conniving as he is. He has no shortage of people who can figure this stuff out. If he's choosing you, it's because you're markedly better than they are."

Talia looked down into her teacup for a moment before meeting Sable's eyes again. "I don't want to rehash our long running fight, Sable, but I think you're wrong. Kiva is lonely. Deeply, permanently lonely. I know you hate the arrangement he and I have, but I honestly think he thinks of me as a daughter at this point, and that is why he invites me to things. I think he likes the company. He likes yours too. Did you see how happy he was to have you over for dinner?"

"Do not try to make me feel sorry for that man," Sable said. "He treated us like slaves for years, and he does the same to countless others still today. Just because we've proven ourselves to be more useful to him in these positions doesn't excuse the rest of it."

"I know," Talia said, irritated. "I'm not blind to who he is or what he does. I'm just saying, he's not as one-dimensional as you make him out to be."

PART V

There is a quickness in these scenes, an urgency, even with all the great distances to cross and all the last desperate attempts to make.

The brightness in this part is hard to capture. The still before a storm. The moment between dawn and the coming clouds. Not too bright, but not yet shadowed.

The trick is to let the unexpected pieces fall together perfectly. Solidly.

Because when the breaking comes, then we know it broke something it should not have. Something that should have remained whole.

-Stage notes from act three, scene one of ***The Phoenix Rising*** by Atticus the Playwright.

CHAPTER FIFTY-NINE

Sable stepped out into the cool night with Reese behind her. She lingered on the doorstep, listening to Talia and Ryah chatting easily together. Despite the fact that the house was temporarily Kiva's, the main room seemed to glow with light and warmth. The bright red door swung shut, leaving Sable outside in the lantern-lit street.

"Ryah will be safe there with her," Reese said.

"Everyone seems more convinced of that than me." She glanced toward the window. "I don't know that I like leaving Ryah so close to Kiva."

"He'll keep her safe." Reese stepped in between Kiva's house and Sable. "He wouldn't risk alienating Talia or you by letting anything happen to Ryah."

Sable started to object, but he held up his hand. "I'm not saying she would be safe with him forever, but for a few days, she can keep Talia company. The two of them will be happier together."

The idea was irritating in a way Sable couldn't quite name, and she leaned to the side to see the window past his head.

He shifted to block her view with the hint of a smile. "I love it when you feel protective but thwarted. You always look like you're about to do something crazy."

She focused on him, and a bit of the irritation drifted away. "I thought you didn't like it when I do crazy things."

"I don't like it when you do *dangerous* things." He stepped closer. "Yes, crazy and dangerous are often the same thing with you, but your crazy plans keep things interesting."

She set her hand on his chest. "Seeing as I feel this way almost constantly, you must be in heaven."

"I am," he said, his smile growing. "Someday we'll have a quiet, calm life somewhere and I'm going to have to invent problems to get you to look like this."

She laughed, but it faded quickly. "Will we ever have that life?"

"I don't know," he admitted, "but it's what I want, so I'm going to live as though we will." His words were warm as he raised his hand and lifted her chin. "Not to sound too much like Talia, but I don't want to miss out on this right here because of what might come in the future."

"Even if what's coming is a dragon?" Sable whispered.

"Especially if what's coming is a dragon." He kissed her, and she leaned against him, grabbing at his warmth and steadiness, drawing it into herself, using it to drive back the constant whirling fears.

"Sable," he murmured around the kiss. The word was slightly pained.

She yanked back, and the *vitalle* was cut off. "I'm sorry!" She grimaced, taking a step back. "I keep forgetting. I just…I always want your strength. I always want your steadiness."

He stepped forward again, wrapping his arms around her and pulling her close. "You can have anything you want from me." He rubbed his lips together, his eyes creased in a smile. "Just don't try to kill me."

"Sable!" a voice called from the square.

Reese let out a low growl. "My new dream is that someday we'll have a quiet evening to ourselves."

Flibbet hurried down the block toward them, his blond hair catching the torchlight. The little peddler had a bounce to his step as he waved a small book in the air.

Sable dropped her arms and started to turn, but Reese made a disapproving noise and kept his arms around her waist.

"Reese!" Flibbet said cheerfully, walking up to them. "How are you?"

"Interrupted," Reese answered.

Flibbet let out a bright laugh. "It looks more like you two are done being interrupted. Or interrupting yourselves? Hard to decide which it was, isn't it?" He looked at them expectantly.

"I…" Sable glanced at Reese, who seemed equal parts lost and annoyed.

Flibbet stepped closer and dropped his voice. "How much do you think we weave ourselves? Sometimes it feels like the knots are made by something vastly more powerful than us, but then when you trace each thread, it *looks* like it's just us."

"...Are we weaving?" Sable asked.

"I don't know!" Flibbet exclaimed. "Are we?"

"This interruption right now is just you," Reese said. "If you went and wove somewhere else, this whole conversation wouldn't have to happen."

"Exactly!" Flibbet agreed with some vehemence. "And yet here we are!"

"Is there something you wanted, Flibbet?" Reese asked, irritation leaking into his voice.

"No, there's something *you* want." He held the small book out with a flourish, and Sable took it. "When I was in that community of Kalesh refugees on the Reaches, they had a small library. This was in it, and I immediately thought of you."

Sable tilted the book toward the nearest torch. It wasn't a book in the traditional sense. The front and back covers were merely worn pieces of leather sewn onto a slim stack of papers. The first page was filled with neat, official-looking writing, titled *Deaths and Damages Attributed to A'Melia, the Zabat, Known as the Ghost of the White Wood.*

Sable looked up at the old man. "My mother?"

Flibbet grinned and glanced at Reese. "A worthwhile enough interruption?"

"What do you want in return?" Sable asked. "I don't have much."

"It's not a trade," Flibbet said. "It's a gift from the town. I told them I knew Melia's daughter, and after demanding to hear all about you, they asked me to give you this." He grew more serious. "The news of Zenivah's return made them all nervous. They say the Emperor doesn't need more power. But the return of the Ghost of the White Wood—that was a different thing. Even the oldest among them looked hopeful at the news. They said if anyone could beat Zenivah, it was the Ghost."

"They clearly don't grasp who Vivaine is or that I am not the Ghost of the White Wood," Sable said.

Flibbet shrugged. "I told them the truth of what I knew of you." He wiggled his fingers in the air. "Weaving, weaving. The threads just keep growing and tangling into the tapestry. Your threads are rather pronounced, my dear." He glanced at Reese. "Yours as well, and it's very exciting to see." He rubbed his hands together. "Very exciting. Even the cart doesn't want to trundle off somewhere new." His hands paused, and he focused suddenly on Reese. "Maybe because of you..."

"Me?"

Flibbet looked back toward the square, rubbing the back of his neck. "That is still open," he mused. "But sometimes they just stay open."

"What's open?" Sable asked.

Flibbet turned again and looked at Reese, somewhat suspiciously. "I like being here," he said flatly.

"Right here?" Reese asked pointedly. "Right now?"

Flibbet waved a hand around, encompassing the whole island. "I never get to see these things unfold. I usually just drop off a little something and have to move on." He pointed a finger at Reese. "Don't be in a hurry."

"About what?"

Flibbet paused, and his eyes narrowed and darted back toward the square. "About *anything*," he whispered.

"I'll do my best," Reese said slowly.

Flibbet studied him for another moment, his expression dubious. "Good, because I really would like to stay—" He tilted his head to the side, as though listening, then gave a little huff of surprise. His face spread in a smile, and he offered them a small bow. "Have a lovely evening. I'm afraid I have some business to attend to." He strode toward the square, his steps quick.

"I actually thought he had been getting less strange," Reese said.

Sable flipped the book open. "This is the Empire's official version about A'Melia, but look." She held the book up toward the torchlight, and Reese looked over her shoulder. "There are notes written all over in the margins, but it's too dark to read them."

"I suppose you'd like to go somewhere with good lighting and read through that," Reese said, resigned, "instead of taking the walk along the wall I was about to invite you on."

Sable turned inside his arms. "I do love the wall."

He looked down at the book. "As do I. But I am curious to see what that says. And the wall is an excellent place to watch the sunrise."

"Sunrise on the wall it is, then," Sable said.

CHAPTER SIXTY

THE MAIN ROOM of the house was mostly quiet, and mostly dark, except for near the table where Leonis and Thulan played the game with the pebbles. Sable dropped the book on a well-cushioned couch, then went to light the nearby candles.

"Everyone knows an elvish archer is worth five humans, at least," Leonis was saying. "And a dwarf is worth one short human, so—"

"That is the stupidest thing you've ever said," Thulan interrupted. "An elf is worth more than a human, fine, but not more than a dwarf."

"Have you ever seen elven archers? They can shoot you from so far away you can barely see them. And they can move silently and invisibly, so they can appear right next to you."

"They appear next to me and meet my hammer," Thulan said. "If an elf is worth five humans, so is a dwarf."

"But Reese beat your best dwarf," Sable pointed out, lighting three candles on a small table next to the couch.

"Well, then, Reese is worth five humans, too," Thulan said.

Sable sat and picked up the book while Reese watched over Thulan's shoulder as she tossed a handful of pebbles.

"The only reason an elf is equal to a dwarf," Thulan said, picking out several of the pebbles and starting a pile in front of her, "is because elves use creepy magic to make themselves stronger while dwarves rely on hard work and muscle."

"Doesn't matter anyway," Reese said. "Neither elves nor dwarves are coming."

"Then who else can we get to help? An army of kobolds?" Leonis let out a laugh that dwindled into a thoughtful look.

Sable tensed and glanced around the room.

Thulan's hand paused over the pebbles. "I'd take an army of kobolds."

"Just think of what a unit of them could do," Leonis said, lifting his hand to his own throat. "Purn by herself was terrifying enough with that neck thing." He shivered.

"Leonis!" Sable snapped.

Reese smacked him on the back of the head. "Shut up." He walked over to the couch and dropped down next to Sable with an irritated breath, stretching his feet out and interlacing his fingers behind his head.

"He just hit me!" Leonis said to Thulan.

"Someone needed to," she answered.

Sable waited for a moment to see if Purn would appear, but there was no sign of her.

Reese closed his eyes. "He's an idiot, Purn," he said quietly.

"We've always known that," Sable agreed.

There was no answer from the space around them, and Thulan called Leonis's attention back to the game.

"Sorry, Purn," Leonis said quietly.

Sable opened her book. Under the title, she could now make out the small note.

Translated and annotated by Arn, bard of the west, friend of Melia and Evay, Zabat in his own right, even if the Empire, in all their denseness, never noticed.

Sable nudged Reese with her elbow. "Don't fall asleep. Look at this. Arn names himself a rebel like Melia and Evay. When the Empire calls her 'an irritating pebble in the shoe of the local commanders,' he points out that the reward of eight thousand silver that she eventually built up contradicts that statement."

Reese cracked an eye. "Eight thousand? That's impressive."

After an official-sounding declaration of A'Melia's status as a wanted criminal, the report was broken into incidents where the Ghost and her elven cohort, Evay, had either damaged imperial property or killed imperial soldiers.

The book was laid out chronologically, with the location recorded in the first entry being near the site of a small uprising that the Empire had quelled.

Small uprising = peaceful village, Arn's note in the margin read. *Quelled = razed to the ground, murdering every man, woman, and child they found.*

The report detailed how soldiers leaving the uprising were accosted in the forest by a woman who appeared to move with inexplicable speed, and eleven soldiers were felled with elven arrows. The single remaining soldier, when he reached the nearest outpost the next day, claimed a woman with black hair had appeared in front of him and warned him that the Empire's sins would revisit them tenfold if they didn't leave the area.

That first reward was set for fifteen silver for capture of the woman or the female elf seen with her.

"Wake me up when the reward reaches a hundred," Reese said.

It took six months for Melia's reward to reach one hundred.

The beginning of Melia's vengeance against the Empire was filled with a dozen bloody ambushes, until the Empire retaliated by destroying the three towns nearest to where she was thought to be.

From that point, something changed. Instead of killing Kalesh soldiers, A'Melia and Evay targeted the Empire's supply lines, destroying important bridges, setting fire to storehouses of goods, burning an outpost to the ground. And the locations became more erratic. Occasionally, after a brutal attack from the Empire on some village, the Ghost would lead survivors on a mission of vengeance. But, as Arn's notes pointed out, none of the deaths during that time could be directly attributed to Melia.

The deaths that the Empire claimed were by elvish arrow, Evay took the credit for and declared they were purely out of self-defense. It was clear to anyone who knew her that she considered Melia part of that self.

Sable flipped through the report, reading Arn's notes with a painful sort of curiosity. The longing she'd felt when she was near Bastian resurfaced. She read further, torn between wanting to know every detail and a horrible, growing sense of loss.

Melia had done so much, been so many places, and Sable had known none of it.

Not only was her mother gone, but maybe Sable had never had her to begin with. Years of fighting an Empire she'd never mentioned. Years of dedicating herself to a cause that Sable hadn't known existed. Years of traveling and fighting with a friend who was closer than a sister, whom Sable had never met.

The report ended at the dramatic events with Bastian and the assassination of the Imperial Prince Turrn. The official report painted Bastian as the great hero who stopped a coup, but Arn corrected it to match what Sable had learned in *Ghost of the White Wood*.

Arn had written notes at the end.

> *Eight thousand silver is an insult, frankly. The disruption caused by Melia and Evay reached across the entire Empire. I have heard of rebellions as far away as Tuurees and Blackdraw that rally around her name. The Emperor himself holds Melia up as an example of the enemy who would destroy the Empire.*
>
> *I have no knowledge of where Melia and Evay are now, nor do I want it. They deserve whatever freedom they have found.*

The Eastern Reaches, Sable thought dully. Melia went to the Eastern Reaches, married a man named Stephen, and then pretended none of this had ever happened.

With a surprising amount of frustration, she read Arn's final words.

> *I can only wish that a dozen more of them would arise from the people and destroy the Empire once and for all. Of course, the unrest they caused still ripples today. Perhaps its echoes will crack the Imperial stone that hangs around our necks and shatter it into dust.*
>
> *The publicly posted wanted notices do neither of them justice and were clearly drawn by an enemy who only knew them in battle. They were sisters, through and through. At their best when they were together.*
>
> *Melia was quick to smile and fearless when she believed she was in the right. Evay's humor was as dry as a desert wind. I found her endlessly amusing. Truth be told, I miss their smiles and the easy way they had with each other. Wherever they are, I'm sure they're keeping each other safe.*

Sable resisted the urge to let out a derisive breath. Where Melia had gone, Evay had certainly not followed.

She turned to the next page and froze.

There, in black and white, sat a stunningly lifelike drawing of Melia's face.

Her hair was black and long, her dark eyes filled with an intensity

Sable had rarely seen in them. Her mouth was set in a stubborn line, her features achingly familiar.

A noise almost like a whimper escaped Sable, and Reese twitched awake.

Sable touched a fingertip to Melia's cheek.

Reese drew in a sharp breath and sat upright. "How do they know what you look like?" he whispered, the words surprisingly frightened.

"It's not me," Sable said quietly. "It's her."

Reese looked between the picture and Sable. "No wonder Bastian recognized you."

Thulan and Leonis walked over, looking curiously at the book.

"I don't think you should ever visit the Empire, Sneaks," Leonis said. "They'll kill you on sight."

Thulan nodded. "That's quite the resemblance. Although there's a little of Ryah in the eyes, don't you think?"

Leonis made a noncommittal noise.

Across the top of the page were the words *Zabat A'Melia - 8000 strietyn.*

Sable turned the page, and everyone stared at the next image.

It was an elf, a female elf with a thick braid falling over her shoulder, narrowed eyes, and a thin, angry mouth. She was beautiful in the elvish way, haughty and distant.

Her hair should have been colored a deep russet brown, but her features were set in the exact expression they'd had when she'd looked at Sable.

"That's..." Leonis trailed off.

"Evay," Sable breathed.

Staring off the page at them was the angry elf who had stood at the king's shoulder while Sable had begged them for help.

"Humans are not worth protecting," the russet-haired elf had said. *"They die too easily."*

"She knew," Sable whispered. "She knew who I am."

"Of course she knew," Thulan said. "You are the spitting image of Melia."

"She asked me if I could shoot a bow." Sable stared at the picture.

"Human lives are short and violent," Evay had said. *"There is enough to grieve in the world without binding ourselves to those who will be dead in a few seasons."*

She turned to Leonis. "You knew her. Did you know her name?"

"I didn't," he answered. "I'd never seen her before that day." His brow creased. "Now that I think about it, she looked different than the others, but there are plenty of elves I don't know. And…I was distracted."

"At least now it's clear why she was so angry," Reese said, leaning back on the couch.

"How is it clear?" Sable demanded. "My mother's closest friend—the woman closer than a sister—is an elf I'd never met, and when she did finally meet me, she hated me on sight? What could have happened between them?"

"It wasn't hate, Sable," Thulan said, sinking down into a chair. "I was a bit distracted as well with Leonis and his father, but now that I think about it, she wasn't angry. She looked at you the exact way Victis looks at Leonis."

Leonis nodded slowly. "Hadn't thought about it before, but that was guilt and grief if I ever saw it."

"You told me once that your mother would go on long hunting trips," Reese said. "That it was the only time she took her elvish bow, and that it was the only time your father seemed comfortable letting her out of his sight."

Sable studied the picture of the elf. "You think she went with Evay?"

"What was she like when she came back?" Reese asked.

Sable thought back to the last trip her mother had taken, just weeks before her death. "A little sad. Happy to see us, but sad in a way I never quite understood. I just thought she loved getting out in the world for a while. It took her a few days to settle back into normal life."

"It makes sense that Evay would stay away from your mother most of the time," Thulan said. "A foreign woman with an elven friend would hardly be something that would go unnoticed on the Eastern Reaches. Or anywhere else, for that matter. With the Empire looking for her, they wouldn't have done something that stupid." She gave Sable an apologetic look. "And they wouldn't have told Melia's young daughters about Evay either. Children aren't the best at keeping secrets."

Sable nodded slowly. "But she would have known about us. If she was spending time with my mother, she had to know about us." She studied the elf's image, the hostile look in Evay's eyes feeling like some accusation pointed directly at Sable. "When we were in the Wildwood, she knew exactly who I am, and she convinced the king not to help."

"Yes, but she looked older than this," Leonis said.

Sable almost argued that it had been a lot of years since the Empire would have made the images before she realized Leonis's point.

Evay did look older than this. The drawing was of an elf without a single sign of age. Her face was smooth, her eyes clear. In the Wildwood, Evay had looked...not old, but worn. There had been a tightness in her skin, creases at the edges of her eyes. Sable had taken her to be some sort of elder, but maybe it hadn't been centuries that had aged her.

Elves lose something when one they are close to dies. Victis's words came back to Sable. *Years. Centuries sometimes.*

Sable looked at Evay's picture. If she'd really loved Melia that much, then she valued humans a lot more than she'd shown. And if they'd been sisters, through and through...

The longing came back. Evay knew Melia better than Bastian had known her. Better than anyone had.

Reese's head sank back onto the couch. "I know that look, Sable. You're going back to the Wildwood."

"I'm going to talk to her," Sable said, pointing at Evay. "I need to talk to her. To meet her. To find out what she knows." She looked up at Reese. "And maybe...if I can convince her to help..." She shrugged. "If I can get through to her, well, Leonis's father said it would take a more influential elf than him to change the minds of the elves. She's an influential elf."

"You already talked to her," Leonis said. "It didn't work."

Sable looked at the picture for one more moment, then flipped the book closed. "It will this time. I'll get Evay to see that she needs to help us, and she's going to tell me *everything* there is to know about my mother."

Thulan shook her head. "I think you have a lot to overcome with—" She stopped, staring out the front window. "What the...?" She strode to the front door and yanked it open. "Decided to use your brain for once, Drusty?" she called as she marched into the dark square.

"Drusty?" Leonis asked, glancing at Sable and Reese. "Wasn't that the dwarf Thulan called a 'sniveling bootlicker' who was serving the High Dwarf?"

They moved to the door Thulan had left open. She strode across the square toward three other dwarves. One was the same black-clad dwarf who'd stood with the High Dwarf and accused Thulan of treason.

"What opened your eyes, bootlicker?" Thulan called out.

"That answers that question," Leonis said quietly.

"Thought we might find you here, coward," Drusty said. "Snuck out like a rat, didn't you?"

"Was I supposed to stay and be executed without cause?" Thulan walked straight up to Drusty, stopping inches from him. They were the same height, and Thulan seemed unconcerned that Drusty was broader.

The dwarf held his ground. "Seems Callun and the rabble down in the third level managed to learn some information about the humans who attacked us. Wanna explain how that happened?"

"Callun?" Thulan said. "Big dwarf? Bones in his beard? No idea where he'd learn that. He's got twice the brains of your pathetic High Dwarf Rion, though. Maybe he just used his head."

"I know they broke you out," Drusty said. "The old band you used to prance around with like you were the most sparkly gems in Torren."

"I didn't realize gems prance. And how could the good cousins from the third level possibly get past Rion's crack unit of guards?" Thulan crossed her arms. "This doesn't explain why you're here, Drusty. Can we hope that Rion crawled back in some hole and Callun sits on that ugly new throne? Can we hope that there's a chance of a future for the dwarves?"

"High Dwarf Rion is still on his throne," Drusty snarled. "And Callun is still a third-level grunt. But enough people heard his story that Rion decided to investigate."

"I'd say he made a good decision, except he sent you here."

"Get out of my way, Thulan." Drusty shouldered past her. "I am here to discuss things with the council of humans. Something you clearly haven't been invited to."

Thulan paused just a moment before following. "It hasn't been interesting until now." She strode after the other dwarves to the gathering hall.

"I am not missing this," Leonis said, slipping past Sable with an eager smile. "Do you think they'll fight right in the middle of the council?"

CHAPTER SIXTY-ONE

Sable glanced at Reese. "Thulan wouldn't fight here, would she?"

Reese started down the stairs. "If she does, I want to be there." He glanced over his shoulder. "Bring your new book. You should tell them about Evay."

"They don't even know about Melia," Sable objected.

He shrugged. "Maybe it's time they should. The enemy knows. Our people should too."

The monk outside the gathering hall was familiar, and he waved Sable and Reese in after the others before closing the door again.

"...and we bring greetings from High Dwarf Rion," Drusty was saying in a pompous voice. He and the other two dwarves stood at the head of the table, addressing General Braddick. "The dwarven nation has become familiar with your impending doom and is here to negotiate an alliance."

Thulan positioned herself close to the dwarves, her arms crossed.

Braddick's gaze flickered briefly to her before returning to Drusty. "We were under the impression that the dwarves were uninterested in allying with us."

"That was before we learned that the Kalesh Empire is also our enemy," Drusty said. "The cowards are responsible for the destruction of our capital city and the death of hundreds of dwarves. Rumor has it you'll be facing up to fifteen thousand Kalesh soldiers and have barely half that yourselves."

From Braddick's face, the numbers were accurate. Sable glanced at Reese. "Fifteen thousand?" she whispered.

He frowned but didn't argue with the number.

Sable moved up next to Thulan. Atticus gave her a questioning look from where he sat with Serene and Jae near the foot of the table. She held up the book, wondering if Flibbet had shown it to him, but from Atticus's blank expression, he had no idea what it held.

Braddick studied the dwarves. "The prowess of dwarven warriors is legendary. How many do you have to offer?"

"That depends entirely on what we're fighting for," Drusty answered.

"Vengeance isn't enough?" Thulan muttered.

"We have little time for games," Lord Runess said from his seat next to Braddick. "Name what you want."

"The Scale Mountains," Drusty said simply.

There was a moment of silence.

"You want a mountain range?" Lord Darien said. "An entire mountain range?"

"You're not doing anything with it." Drusty held out his hand, and one of the other dwarves handed him a rolled parchment. He stepped forward and spread it out on the table, showing a map of the entire range from the northern snowy peaks all the way to the Tremmen Hills near the sea. "Nor can you do anything with it. The southernmost hills hold the possibility for some gold, but the range from the Black Hills north, while riddled with caves and tunnels, holds nothing you have the capacity to mine. Any gems or precious metals will be difficult to attain."

In the midst of Drusty's warm words, most of the heads around the table turned to Sable with questioning looks. Renwen, who sat near the far end, narrowed his eyes at her.

"He's telling the truth," she said.

A mutter went through the room as lords and generals leaned toward each other for quiet discussion. Several rose to see the map better.

Drusty shifted to face Sable with a furious expression. "You dare question my honesty?" he hissed. "I am the ambassador of High Dwarf Rion, and I will not have the honor of the dwarves impugned by you."

"Wrong move," Thulan said in an undertone. "If you want to win, you want her on your side."

"I do not need the support of some nameless human," Drusty muttered.

Thulan gave him a contemptuous look. "She's the Queen of the North."

"There is no Queen of the North," Drusty said, but his tone was less confident.

"You do not want to risk that," Thulan said.

"If the resources in the Scales are difficult to attain," Lord Runess said loudly over the conversations in the room, "why do you want them?"

"It would be difficult for *you* to attain," Drusty corrected. "You have neither the knowledge, the tools, nor the disposition to spend years underground mining the resources in those mountains." He leaned forward. "The surface of the Scale Mountains is poor grazing land. There are no significant waterways. The range itself is of no real value to you. The dwarven realm, though, was critically damaged by the Kalesh Empire's inept mining. What we require is a large, stable system of caves where we can build a new city. The Scales provide that. We gain a home. You lose nothing, but gain the assistance of the dwarven troops in your war."

"Which is also your war," Braddick said.

"True. If you refuse us the Scales, we will find our own way to make the Kalesh pay for what they've done. If, however, we can come to a mutually beneficial agreement, it will be profitable for us all." Drusty gave a humorless smile. "Except the Kalesh."

"How many troops do you offer?" Braddick asked.

"Wait," Lord Darien said. "The Scale Mountains belong to Lord Loren, Lord Erick, and me. Whether or not this alliance is created is up to us."

"None of the rest of you are giving up the opportunity to mine gold," Lord Loren agreed.

"The effort you will expend to mine it will outweigh the gold you will find," Drusty said, his words still warm.

"How do you know this?" Lord Erick asked, but he glanced at Sable.

She nodded again.

"A detachment of dwarves explored the Scales last year," Drusty said. "We have records from long ago about the tunnels and resources there, but we needed to verify they were correct."

"You sent a scouting mission to explore our land?" Lord Darien asked.

"Merely of an exploratory nature," Drusty answered.

"By that he means that High Dwarf Rion didn't know it was happening," Thulan said. "The current High Dwarf is consumed with hatred for the humans who destroyed our city. Some other, more forward-thinking cousins realized we needed a new home more than revenge." She looked at Braddick. "If you can offer them both, the dwarves will be behind the effort one hundred percent."

Braddick leaned on the table. "We haven't yet heard how many dwarves that would be."

"Every dwarf we can spare," Drusty said. "Seven hundred at least, and we will provide dwarven blades and axes to arm a hundred more humans."

Braddick nodded slowly, and the Northern Lords exchanged glances.

"I think we can come to an agreement," Lord Runess said.

"Once we discuss it." Lord Darian stood. "Any agreement here will be between Loren, Erick, the dwarves, and myself. You aren't involved, Runess, unless you have some stake in the Scale Mountains we don't know about."

"You're fools to not take their offer," Thulan said.

The table turned to her with irritated faces.

"You know you get nothing out of the Scales," she continued, "and seven hundred dwarves is worth thirty-five hundred more human troops."

"That's my math," Leonis whispered smugly over his shoulder to Sable.

"You know he's right," Runess said, "and you know you're all going to agree. Just get it over with."

The other Northern Lords exchanged glances.

"Even with the dwarves, we are still outnumbered," Loren pointed out.

"We may be able to help with that," Sable said, stepping forward to the table. "We just received some new information that may give us an opening with the elves in the Wildwood." She set the book down, opened to the image of her mother. "This is A'Melia. A famous rebel who fought the Empire and killed the current Emperor's brother. She was also my mother."

Atticus leaned forward and peered at the book, along with the rest of the table. The hint of an approving smile touched his lips.

Looking around the table, Sable gave a quick overview of the story of the Ghost of the White Wood, then turned the page to Evay's picture.

"We met this elf in the Wildwood," Sable said. "It's Evay, and now that I know who she is, I can persuade her to help us."

General Braddick looked unconvinced.

Sable picked the book up. "Make the deal that you know you need with the dwarves, and I'll be back within a fortnight…quite possibly with elves."

"You are not a part of this council," Braddick declared. "And having a book from the Kalesh Empire is no reason for anyone to listen to you. Human or elf."

"Everyone will listen," Thulan said. "She's the Queen of the North."

From the corner of her eye, she saw Atticus rub his hand over his mouth to banish a smile.

"She's nothing," Braddick said derisively. He leaned forward, and his gaze pierced Sable. "You've already tried this exact same thing and failed."

Sable picked up the book, holding the general's eye. "No, last time I gave the speech *you* wanted me to give, and no one heard it. This time *I'm* talking, and, if nothing else, they will listen."

CHAPTER SIXTY-TWO

THE LITTLE STREAM babbled at Sable's feet, catching the sunlight as the shadow of a scuttling cloud darted away through the Wildwood. The sun was high in the sky, falling warm on her hair and shoulders, but a few fingers of wind stretched down into the clearing. The trees around her emanated greenness and life the way a fire gave off heat. She could almost see it radiating through the air.

It was the same stream she, Reese, Leonis, and Thulan had camped by last time they'd come to see the elves, but this time felt different. This time, Sable was not at a loss to think of what she wanted to say. She took a bite of a green apple Reese had found, the sour dryness sharp enough to cut through the endless circle her thoughts had moved in since Tutella Island. Starting with the speech she'd give Evay, then the counter to all the possible objections the elf could have, and ending with the ever growing list of things Sable wanted to know about her mother.

She looked across the little stream, another question coming to mind. In *Ghost of the White Wood*, both Evay and Melia could "step," a magical process where they crossed a long distance in a single step. Sable cast out and felt a mild warmth to the grass on the far side and the heat of the trees. If Melia had learned to step…

Leonis walked into the clearing. "I called Victis personally and tried to convey you're here too, Sneaks, but trees aren't great at conveying details." He looked back into the woods behind him. "Although I'm sure he already knew we were here."

"Think he'll bring those leaf packets with him?" Thulan asked from where she sat leaning against a large tree.

"Please do not ask him for one," Leonis said, pained.

The glade fell quiet, and Sable turned back to the water.

Reese came up, stopping close beside her. "Are you ready for this?"

"No. I'm terrified."

His eyes followed the water as it slipped over the small rocks and swirled in the smoother parts. "She loved your mother, and you loved your mother. That's a solid starting point."

She leaned her shoulder against his. Over the trees, the clouds were sailing eastward like a fleet of ships, and she watched them until they disappeared behind the trees. She took another bite of apple, her thoughts churning until she heard the little echo of Narine's voice.

What are you afraid of, Issable?

She shied away from the question itself, noticing instead how odd it was that the name Issable had never sounded wrong in Narine's voice. It had been the same with Sable's mother. To her father, she'd always been Sable unless he was very serious, but her mother had always spoken her full name fondly.

Evay would know her as Issable.

And there was the fear.

It had been twelve years since she'd heard her mother speak her name. That life felt more unreachable than the clouds. There were times when it was hard to remember her mother's face or voice. Times it felt like the cord that had once bound them together had stretched and frayed until it was only a thread.

"I'm afraid it won't be enough," Sable said quietly.

"To convince the elves to help?"

Something flashed in the woods in the corner of her eye. She expected to see Innov perched in one of the branches, but when she looked, there was nothing. She glanced up to see Innov soaring high up near the clouds like a piece of the sun that had broken free of the rest.

"No. I'm afraid the fact that it's me won't be enough to make her listen."

Leonis cleared his throat from behind them, and Sable turned to see Victis standing at the edge of the clearing. He was dressed not in the formal clothes he'd worn to take them to see the elvish king but in the green and brown mottled tunic that Sable had seen other elves wear.

"Greetings, Flame of the North," he said with a slight nod. "I hope you have brought a new petition for the king. It will not go well if you merely repeat the same request."

She felt his words fill the clearing, but they were merely a gentle pressure instead of the smothering power he wielded sometimes. "I'm not here to see the king."

He considered her words. "Who would you see?" The question sounded resigned, or possibly like a warning.

Sable swallowed down her nervousness. "Will you take me to Evay?"

"If you insist, although I warn you, she's not anxious to speak to—"

"I insist." Sable attempted a smile to soften the demand, but it felt tense.

He looked at her as though he might object again but instead merely nodded. "Evay is not fond of company. I will take you to her, but we will leave your companions at the home of Parseis." He glanced at Leonis. "Your father is anxious to see you again." He set his hand on the nearest trunk, and his expression grew distant before he motioned for Sable to walk with him and started back into the forest.

Innov flew high in the sky, showing no inclination of descending to offer moral support. With a bracing breath, Sable joined Victis.

The closer they got to the elven city, the more Sable's hands grew damp with sweat and the more the apple felt sour in her stomach. Instead of walking past the elven houses like they had before, Victis took them around the outskirts on a small trail.

At a branch in the trail, Cintis stood leaning against a tree, smiling widely. "Your visits are getting more and more frequent," he said to Leonis.

"Thulan missed you." Leonis clapped Cintis on the shoulder.

"I missed her as well." Cintis grinned. "Did you bring more dwarves?"

"You wouldn't be able to handle the happiness," Thulan said.

"Parseis is thrilled you're all here." Cintis waved them down the smaller path.

"You'll be all right?" Reese asked Sable.

She nodded, the movement feeling jerky. "I doubt I'll be in any danger."

Victis's brow darkened. "We allow no harm to come to our guests."

"Even emotional harm?" she asked with a grim smile. At Reese's worried look, she tried to make her expression more hopeful.

"Where's Sable going?" Cintis asked Leonis.

"To speak with Evay."

Cintis's eyebrows shot up, and he looked at her with consternation. "Oh."

"If you're not back in a couple of hours," Reese said, "I'm coming to find you."

Victis gave an almost inaudible snort of derision. "That effort would be in vain. But if Sable is occupied longer than that amount of time, I will make sure you receive word."

Victis held his hand out for Sable to proceed down their original path, and she fell in beside him. The wind whipped across the top of the canopy, but down on the path it was mere gusts, shoving Sable's hair forward and brushing past her neck and arms. The hint of autumn coolness raised goosebumps on her skin, and she rubbed at her forearms to banish them. She and Victis walked in silence until they reached another fork in the road.

Victis stopped. "You will find her down this path." He pointed to the thread of a trail leading off into the woods. He paused, and while nothing particular changed in his stiff expression, she sensed a warning. "Much like Leonis's father, Evay has suffered deeply."

"We've all suffered deeply, Victis."

He considered her with a probing look. "Hers has increased since she saw you. I understand that humans sometimes heal from such deep grief. For an elf, it is merely a long death."

She looked down the tiny trail, wondering if this was the sort of place her mother had gone with Evay. "We don't heal from it. It breaks a piece off us, and we just learn, after a very long time, to cut ourselves less often on the jagged edge." She took a step down the path, but Victis set his hand on her arm.

"Her jagged edge still cuts her," he said quietly. "Every day."

Sable faced him. "Every day, I live without a mother, a father, and the childhood I lost that night. Don't make the mistake of thinking humans suffer less than elves."

He didn't look away from her, but he let his hand drop. "May your conversation bring you more healing than grief." Without waiting for an answer, he turned back the way they'd come.

The path ahead of Sable wound into a tight stand of aspens whose light green leaves trembled with each gust of wind. She followed the path as it twisted around the trunks and came out into a small clearing with a single oak tree in the center.

The wind tossed the treetops into a flurry of motion, and the noon sun poured into the clearing with a brightness that made her squint. The lower branches of the oak bowed down to the ground to form one of the smallest homes she'd seen yet.

Past it, she heard a rustle of motion and a soft *thwump*. She walked cautiously around the house until she saw the stiff back of Evay, her thick braid hanging down her back. The white bow in her hand arched as she drew, aiming for a rotting stump at the far end of the clearing.

Thwump. The arrow crowded in next to six others, grouped so tightly Sable could barely tell them apart.

Evay pulled another arrow from the quiver on her back and nocked it, drawing again.

Sable's gaze locked on the elvish bow. Her mother had defied the Kalesh in those final moments, her posture just like this.

The words she'd planned to say were strangled out by the sight. When they finally crawled up her throat, she could barely manage a whisper, but the emotion behind it drove the sound across the clearing.

"I know who you are."

Evay flinched, then breathed again before loosing her arrow. It hit the very edge of the stump. She lowered the bow but didn't turn.

"You know who I am, too," Sable said, the words coming clearer. "Don't you?"

Evay ran her hand along the smooth, curved surface of the bow. "You've looked exactly like her since the day you were born. How could I not know her face?"

Sable's feet rooted to the ground. "You were there when I was born?" She'd meant it as an accusation, but the words came out too small.

Evay turned toward her, every muscle of her body taut. Her gaze lagged behind, and when she finally swung her eyes up to meet Sable's, they were hollow with pain.

The sunlight cut harsh shadows down Evay's face into the tortured lines snaking up from her brow and knifing down at the edges of her mouth.

"I was there," Evay said, the quiet words barely reaching Sable, "with Melia and you the day you were born. And so many days after."

There was love in those words. Deep, heart-wrenching love that could have sounded sweet, but the sentiment tore into Sable. The rift between the past and this moment ripped wider, leaving a bottomless, bleeding chasm. She took a step closer, all her reasoned words crumbling away.

"And yet," Sable whispered, shoving the words toward Evay, "the day I came to you here in need, *in dire need*, you refused me."

Evay flinched.

"I came here weeks ago," Sable said, jabbing a finger toward the lush green ground, "thinking I had no friends, no connections. Knowing there would be no sympathetic ear among the elves, but I came anyway because we desperately need help. And yet who was here? My mother's *dearest friend*." Sable hurled the words at Evay, and the elf recoiled as though they'd physically hit her. There was an edge of childishness to the accusation that Sable couldn't quite root out, but suddenly she didn't want to. Something inside her felt childish. Vulnerable. Betrayed.

"The friend who was *closer than a sister*." Sable blinked back tears, furious that they dared to wet her eyes. "Don't stand there and speak as though you loved my mother, as though you ever loved me. You stood next to the king and played me for a fool in front of the entire Wildwood."

Sable's anger at Evay tangled with years of anger at everything that had happened. "How could you hide who you are? How could you turn the entire wood against me?"

A flicker of matching anger filled Evay's eyes. "You have no idea—"

"I needed you!" Sable flung at her. "You knew who I was, and what I needed, and you chose to walk away!"

Evay started to shake her head, her expression growing more angry. "You do *not* understand—"

"Did you walk away that night too?" Sable demanded. "The night the Kalesh burned down our home and killed my father and my mother right in front of me?"

Evay took a furious step toward Sable, and when her foot landed she was only an arm's length away. A puff of air blew Sable's hair back and she forced herself not to pull away.

From this close, Sable could see every wrinkle creasing the elf's face and trace the strands of white in her hair. A savage rage burned in Evay's eyes. "I would give everything I have ever had to have been there that night!"

Sable's own ire rose to match hers. "Then where were you?"

Evay's jaw clenched as she drew in a breath. When she spoke, there was an old bitterness in her voice. "Taking a letter to your grandfather."

Sable blinked. She stared at Evay, speechless for a moment. "I don't have a grandfather." Even as she said it, another layer of the lies she'd believed began to unravel. Evay's words had been perfectly warm.

"Not any more. But at that time, Melia's father still lived in a small village in the northwest corner of the Empire. It took her a month to travel to him, but I could step so much farther than her, I could be there and back in a fortnight." Evay's gaze shifted to the trees over Sable's shoulder. "That trip, I took a carved fox from Stephen, some silver, a drawing of you girls, and a letter." Her eyes grew unfocused. "I had spent time with the elves of the Wildwood for years by then and they watched over Melia from a distance, but by the time they reached you that night..."

"My mother told me my grandparents were all dead." It was the least important reaction to everything Evay had said, but her mind grabbed ahold of it anyway.

"One of many, many lies Melia told you." Evay's voice took on a resigned edge. "It was easier when you were too little to tell anyone her secrets. In those days I saw you often. Melia would bring you out of town, or I would step in at night when the windows were shuttered. When you got too old to keep a secret, I stayed at a distance, and visited when you slept. More babies came and the times to meet grew fewer, but we managed."

Part of Sable wanted to turn and run from the clearing, block out all these painful words that were pouring into her—but they *were* pouring in, like rain falling on part of her heart that had been parched and dying for years. And so she forced out a question. Any question to keep Evay talking. "Where did you live?"

"I visited the forests and traveled the Reaches. I lived wherever I wanted."

The bow Evay held was pale white wood, except for a rust-colored stain just above her hand. Sable had only seen it strung once, the night her parents died, but it had hung above her parent's mantle her entire childhood.

"That's hers, isn't it?"

Evay dropped her eyes to it, her thumb rubbing at the edge of the stain.

Sable blinked away the memories of the elves stepping out of the darkness moments too late, of elvish arrows toppling the Kalesh soldiers, their bodies falling across the bodies of her parents.

Evay took a deep breath. "I didn't reach Pelrock until a week after the attack. Even the largest piles of ash had stopped smoking. I found her bow and I found your tracks." Her eyes focused on Sable, shadowed by failure and grief. "I tracked you to the sea. I saw the other tracks with yours, the adults who'd taken you there, but none of them were Melia's." She shook her head, the motion almost desperate. "She wouldn't have gone to the sea, she would have come to find me." She shifted toward Sable. "I ran up against the sea and it was like an impassible wall. Melia was gone. You girls were gone. And…" She tried to shrug, but the motion was more like a shudder. "I couldn't…"

Those first days had been numb and horrific, like a walking nightmare. Sable's parents were dead, her home burned to the ground. Every night was full of terrified dreams of black-clad monsters. Survivors from some other town had found her and her sisters, and she'd just followed their directions, mindlessly, as they all moved toward the sea, piled into some boats, and headed for Immusmala.

"If I'd known you existed," Sable said, her voice caught between harshness and wretchedness, "if I'd known you were coming back, we would have waited."

Evay didn't look away. "I know."

"Those people left us on a street in Immusmala. Just left us! Do you have any idea—" Sable's throat tightened around the words and she took a step forward.

She pointed a shaking finger at Evay. "I was fifteen years old. I could keep a secret. Especially one that my mother's life depended on—and you told me *nothing*!"

Evay flinched, but stood her ground. "You grew, and you got older, but when was the right time? There were rumors of soldiers who might be Kalesh, nothing close, but it still worried us." She shook her head. "How could we decide when was the right time?" A knowing look came into her eyes. "Surely you faced the same problem raising your sisters."

The question reminded her too much of Talia and Sable dropped her hand to her side. "I shouldn't have *had* to raise my sisters."

Evay shrugged, the motion surprisingly helpless. "We thought we were protecting you, and protecting Melia."

Sable shook her head, trying to ignore the words, but they were too much like how she'd treated Talia. And the truth was, it wasn't the distant past Sable was angry about. All of that was so long ago, and so tangled up in such harrowing pain that this was just another gouge scraped through one possible life that had already been utterly destroyed.

Her real anger, her still bleeding wound, was much newer.

"Why didn't you say anything when I was here?"

Evay's eyes ran over Sable's face. "I saw you with Victis, and I thought you were…" She pulled the bow closer to her chest. "I thought *she* was back…until you spoke to Artis. You don't have her voice," she whispered, "and it was like she was ripped away again."

She swallowed and took a bracing breath. "I don't know if there is anything you could have said at that moment that would have made it better, but when you said you were walking straight toward the same death she'd suffered, I…" She shook her head as though she were shaking off something that clung to her. "All I wanted to do was to get as far away from that pain as I could."

A little sympathy bled into Sable, but she ignored it. "Which is exactly what you did."

Evay took another deep breath, and met Sable's eyes. "It is. Part of me was terrified for you, and I…" She paused. "That day, after you left, I told myself that I'd been protecting you. That it was better for you this way, but that was a lie. I was only trying to protect myself. You needed me, and I abandoned you. I betrayed Melia, and I'm sorry."

Her hand twitched on the bow, almost reaching toward Sable. "You're just like her, you know. She would have walked up to the elven king and demanded his help, and when she was refused she would have stood in that glade and argued with him, just like you."

The words were warm around Sable, but they also dug into her, like little needles itching under her skin. "I didn't even know her. She was never that…brazen. She was just my mother."

Evay slid her hand down to the dark stain on the bow, rubbing her finger over it. "Brazen. Yes. But I never saw her as happy as she was when she lived with you girls and Stephen. She used to say she had no idea life could be that sweet."

The words flowed into the chasm that had been growing since Sable had read *The Ghost of the White Wood*. The distance between the memories she'd held of her mother, and the truth of who A'Melia had been. Slipping into the emptiness left by the fact that her own mother had been a stranger.

"She told me," Evay said, "more than once, that she wouldn't give up life with all of you for anything in the world."

Sable drew in a shaky breath. "The Kalesh soldier who caught her said she had wasted her regretful little life." The memory of her mother's defiance in that moment blazed in Sable's mind. "She told him it had been more than she deserved, and she regretted nothing."

Evay's fingers froze on the bow. "Was she—" The words cut off in a choked breath. Her eyes lifted to Sable's with a look of terror. "Was she scared? At the end?"

"No." Sable reached out and touched the bow with her fingertips. "She was fierce and defiant and furious."

Evay dropped her head forward, covering her eyes with her hand. She stood, breathing raggedly for a long moment before she looked up again. Her eyes were wet, but there was a spark of ferocity in them. "Good."

That single word resonated in Sable's chest, and the edge of her fury toward Evay softened. The things she'd intended to say at first rolled back into her mind, and she loosened the grip she'd been holding on her anger, letting it begin to drift away. "I met Bastian."

Evay's face sharpened. "Did you kill him?"

Sable started to shake her head, but stopped. "I suppose I did. He loved her, you know."

"I think he did from the moment she appeared in front of him, holding a knife to his throat and demanding he act like a human being."

Light flashed over the trees across the clearing, and Innov soared into view. She circled the oak tree, then flew toward Sable's outstretched arm.

Evay's gaze locked on Innov as she landed in a flurry of sparks. The glow of the phoenix softened the elf's face, and caught at the bittersweet emotions in her eyes.

Innov's warmth poured into Sable and she took what felt like the first deep breath she'd taken in days.

"Melia would have killed to have a phoenix on her arm." Evay's eyes trailed over the flickering flames that licked out between Innov's feathers. "Victis introduced you to the king as Sable."

Sable nodded. "My mother always called me Issable though. You can too, if you want."

Evay looked at her with a serious, probing expression. "You're not the girl you were back then. If half the things Cintis tells me are true, you've earned the right to decide who you are." She thrummed one finger over the still taut bow string, making it vibrate with a low hum. "I am sorry. I should have helped you last time you were here. The answer to what you really want to know, is yes."

Sable looked at her questioningly.

"Yes, I still love her—and you—enough to help," Evay said with a sad smile. "And yes, I can change the elves' minds."

CHAPTER SIXTY-THREE

THERE WAS no council this time. Evay led Sable to the elven king's house, and before Evay could call out a greeting, a voice came from inside.

"Has the time come already?" The king's voice held none of the authority it had carried the last time Sable had spoken to him.

Evay strode into the king's house, motioning for Sable to follow. Inside, the floor was carpeted with soft, thick grass. Shelves were nestled in among the branches, a few small tables or desks scattered across the round room. The foot of a bed of reeds was visible on the far side. The trunk of the elm that rose in the center was ringed with a bench, and the king leaned back against the tree, making no effort to rise. His eyes were fixed on Evay with an undecipherable expression.

"Sable," Evay said, "you've met Corelis before."

Sable waited for a more formal introduction, but Evay just sat in a delicately carved chair, motioning for Sable to take a seat as well.

"First she comes with the indomitable Victis as her ally," Corelis said with the hint of a smile, "and now, more surprisingly, with you."

"She is Melia's daughter," Evay said simply.

Corelis kept his eyes on the other elf. "She was Melia's daughter last visit as well." There was a complexity to his voice that Sable couldn't unravel. He seemed to be waiting, not happily, but resignedly. "At that time, you said she was not worth the heartache she would bring."

"That was an old pain speaking," Evay answered.

"And what is speaking now?"

Evay paused. "A different sort of pain. But this decision is more right."

"What does Victis say?" Corelis asked.

"He will say yes," Evay said, her voice firm.

"I will not order any to fight," he said, "and neither will he."

"Each decision should be made freely," Evay agreed.

The king finally turned his eyes to Sable, watching the embers fall from Innov's tail and fade away in his grass. "Victis told me when you returned, you would find a way to secure what you need. I told him no human could do such a thing, but Cintis tells us your true name is Flame of the North, though I've heard whispers that it is Queen instead."

Sable felt a flicker of irritation at Leonis for spreading the name even here. "My true name is Sable," she said. "The titles others give me—that one in particular—are just words."

"Words have power," Corelis said, considering her, "as you well know." He rose. "I cannot say I am glad to have met you, Sable, Queen of the North. I fear your path still has a great deal of pain, and now my people will share it. But for today, you have the hospitality of the elves. Those who will fight will be ready to leave at dawn."

Evay inclined her head and motioned for Sable to follow her out.

Sable stepped outside, squinting into the bright sun of the clearing. "Leonis told me the Wildwood doesn't care about elves from other places, but they seem to care about you."

"I'm not quite a part of the woods," Evay said, "But I've lived here, on and off, for nearly thirty years." She glanced across the clearing to where Victis stood. "Most of the elves here cannot step nearly as well as I can. Or nearly as far. Victis is the only one who comes close. Because of that, I've traveled with him on several occasions outside the wood, and fought beside him several times." She gave Sable a small smile. "As you know, once you've befriended Victis, all sorts of other elves welcome you too."

The commander of the guard's attention was fixed solely on Evay, his expression a mix of anger and something Sable couldn't name.

Evay strode across the clearing, stopping in front of him. "Come with us," she said bluntly.

She was standing closer than Sable would have dared, her chin lifted to face the commander of the guard.

Victis didn't back away. "I do not think they're worth it."

"Based on the many humans you've met?" Sable asked.

Evay gave him a grim smile. "A good point. You never spoke to

Parseis's wife, regardless of the fact that your friend loved her, so she doesn't count. Aside from her, you've met…who? Only Sable. Who, in the course of a single evening, convinced Victis the Grim to escort her into the Wildwood and introduce her to multiple elves, including the king."

Victis's expression didn't soften. "And yet you ask me to fight other humans who are trying to destroy everything. How exactly do you decide which ones are worth it?" The question was asked with enough authority that Sable shifted her shoulders against the pressure.

Evay showed no sign of noticing. "I'm on the side of the ones who are standing against cruelty."

Victis gave no response.

"Have you never had to save your forest from an elf who wanted too much?" Sable asked.

"With human conflict," he said, "I do not have the benefit of hearing the judgment of the trees."

His words squeezed around Sable, and her irritation flared. "Then I suppose you'll just have to decide whether you trust Evay's."

Victis kept his gaze on Evay, weighing the words.

"Yes, Victis," Evay said, her voice low but hard. "Do you trust me?" There was more challenge in her voice than Sable had heard anyone level at him.

Something in his expression loosened into annoyance. "Yes." The word was curt.

"Then stop wasting time and gather everyone you can. I'll tell my story once, and only once." At Victis's cold look, a smile quirked up the corner of her mouth. "It's a chance to order elves around. Don't act like you don't want to."

His expression didn't change, but he strode toward a small group of elves walking past the clearing.

Sable grinned at his back. "I didn't know anyone spoke to Victis that way."

The elf watched Victis leaving, a slightly mournful expression on her face. "He only commands the elves who are part of these woods." The smile crept back into her lips. "It aggravates him that his voice has no impact on me."

"None?" Sable asked. "It has an impact on me."

"Oh, I can feel the authority, it just has the wrong effect."

Sable nodded. "Makes me want to argue with him. I don't like people telling me what I should do."

Evay laughed. "Something we both learned from Melia." She turned her attention to Sable. "I assume you came here with Leonis and some companions?"

"They're with Leonis's father."

"I'll bring you there while I help gather elves. I should have told them all before what Melia and I did and what we knew. If the Empire is here, the elves need to know what is coming."

A thousand questions rose to Sable's mind. Everything she'd thought of to ask Evay and several that hadn't occurred to her until now.

Evay looked at her with an amusement that held an edge of sadness. "That's exactly what she looked like before she burst out with more questions than anyone could ever answer."

Cintis entered the clearing from a small trail and headed for them. "Reese sent me to check on you," he said with a slightly mocking grin. "He doesn't trust we can keep you safe."

Evay raised an eyebrow. "I can't wait to meet the man who feels this protective of you. But for now, Cintis, will you take her to her friends?"

He nodded.

Evay turned back to Sable. "I am not exactly a part of the woods here, but they will listen to me. I imagine it will take most of the night to tell them everything Melia and I went through and everything they can expect from the Kalesh." She paused. "Tomorrow at dawn, Cintis will bring you to us, and, if nothing else, Victis and I will come with you."

It was still pitch black the next morning when Cintis cleared his throat from the doorway of Parseis's house. "Between Victis and Evay," he said quietly, "a good number of elves have agreed to join you."

"How many?" Sable sat up on the mattress of rushes the elves had brought for her, rubbing her eyes. "And how early is it?"

"All but three of the king's guard," Cintis said, "every archer from the rangers' unit, and almost every retired guard or archer. And dawn is not far off."

Leonis propped himself up on his elbows. "Really?"

"I told you," Parseis said from his own pallet across the room. "You just needed someone more influential than me to convince them."

The sky was brightening, but the shadows still lay thick under the trees by the time Cintis brought them to where Evay and Victis stood together, bows on their backs, a short blade sheathed at Victis's hip. Instead of a clearing filled with elves, the two stood in a quiet stretch of forest.

Sable glanced at Reese, who was scanning the forest around them, the hint of a frown on his face. Leonis, though, was looking wide-eyed through the trees.

"It should be known," Victis said, his voice thick with command, "that the elves serve no man. When the battlefield is settled upon, we shall select our portion and defend it. But we will not serve under a human leader."

Sable glanced at Reese.

"No one would expect you to," Reese answered. "We're grateful you'll fight alongside us. Everyone knows the strength of an elvish archer."

Victis nodded. "Then let us begin."

He started through the trees, following no path that Sable could see. Around her, countless shapes moved through the forest, appearing between trunks before slipping back into the shadows.

"So many," Leonis whispered to Thulan.

She glanced around the woods. "It's unsettling."

"What it is," Leonis said, starting forward, "is me winning. How many dwarves have you managed to bring?"

"You did nothing to get these." Thulan pointed at Sable. "This is thanks to her."

"Doesn't matter. Elves are winning."

"That depends on what constitutes winning," Evay said. "Numbers or total fighting prowess?"

Leonis looked at her blankly.

"Last night, seven hundred dwarves marched through the northern edge of the Wildwood, heading for your coming war."

Thulan smacked Leonis on the back. "Seven hundred, see? I don't know how many shadows are tiptoeing through the woods here, but not seven hundred. Dwarves are winning."

"Three hundred and forty-seven," Evay said, looking at Thulan in amusement. "But an elf is easily worth two dwarves in battle."

"That's debatable, but even if it were true, it still only puts your force at six hundred and ninety-four dwarves strong," Thulan replied. "We're winning."

"By a hair," Leonis said.

"By a neatly braided beard," Thulan said. "And winning is winning."

Leonis continued to object against the math, but Thulan remained adamant.

"I've never met a female dwarf before," Evay mused quietly to Sable. "She's exuberant."

"Don't tell her that," Sable said.

Evay glanced at Reese. "The bond between you two is remarkably strong. Tell me how you met."

"As soon as you tell me how you met my mother," Sable countered. "I read *Ghost of the White Wood,* and it mentions a blood debt. Did she save your life?"

Evay looked back ahead of them through the forest. "She did."

Sable frowned. "What endangers an elf that a human could best?"

The elf lifted the side of her tunic, showing a silvery scar on her stomach. "An infected wound."

"Arrow?" Reese asked.

Evay nodded. "My people live far to the north in the Empire in a forest of frost pines, known as the White Wood." She motioned to Melia's bow. "The wood of the pines is, unsurprisingly, white. The Kalesh had reached all the way to the human town by the same name at the edge of the wood. We weren't worried that they'd find their way into our valley. No human could have. But, as my father liked to say, I was curious to the point of death, and I used to scout along the edges and see what a mess the humans were making of things.

"One morning I got too near a Kalesh soldier, who mistook me for a deer."

Sable raised an eyebrow. "Because you're shaped so much like a deer?"

"Because they're reckless and stupid and shoot at anything that moves." Evay shook her head. "The wound bled—a lot. I had the energy to step away, but I landed, very dizzy, on a steep riverbank, and before I could figure out which way was up, I was tumbling downstream. The last thing I remember thinking was that bleeding to death had at least been warm. Drowning was icy cold."

Evay glanced at Sable. "I knew nothing until I woke up in a shallow cave with Melia bent over me, packing my wound." Evay gave a slight grimace. "It hurt, and she was human, and I was…not kind. But she told me to stop whining and shut up so she could work. Whatever she did next hurt so much I passed out again.

"She spent two weeks with me in that cave. It was fall, so she fished and gathered nuts and apples for our food. I was barely alive, and it took me several days to notice she was furious. More than furious.

"She'd been following the soldiers who'd shot me for a month, ever since they'd burned her village to the ground. Her father was one of the few survivors, and he was badly injured. The Kalesh were staying in the area, and so was she, until she could get her revenge."

Evay looked up through the trees. "My people don't meddle in human affairs. At all. But Melia had hatched a plan to burn down the Kalesh outpost. Their captain was the man who'd ordered the raid on her home. He was vicious and bloodthirsty to the point that even his own soldiers balked at some of his commands.

"The outpost was just being built, and they'd conscripted local people to help with the work, so Melia joined the crowd and packed bundles of kindleweed in a small gap between the walls."

"What's kindleweed?" Sable asked.

"Just what it sounds like. A weed with hollow stalks that dries out even before it's harvested. It catches fire fast and burns slow and hot. Some of the local people saw what she was doing and added more of their own.

"Melia worked out everything with the town while I recovered. The night of the harvest festival, the townspeople brought kegs of ale to a field near the outpost, drawing out the regular soldiers. Melia was going to light the building with flaming arrows, but her bow was awful. A rickety thing that warped when it was pulled and had so little power she'd have had to stand on their doorstep to hit them."

Evay's eyes grew distant. "I like to think it was that moment that I made my decision to fight with her instead of stand with my people, but the truth is it had happened already. Sometime in those weeks while she helped me heal and I listened to her rage against the Kalesh, or tell me of her parents and nephews, or plan her revenge, she'd become a friend. And so I went back to my people, got Melia her own elvish bow, and she and I went to the outpost together. The first two arrows that lit the building were fired at the same time."

Sable risked a glance at the elf. "Were there Kalesh inside?"

"A few," she said quietly. "The captain tried to run out the front door, but Melia shot him in the chest with a flaming arrow."

They walked past a few trees before Evay began again. "When my people found out what I'd done, they were furious. The Kalesh were circulating reward notices for Melia and her elven partner. The elders of the

White Wood cut all ties with me, but I'd already decided that I was going to help Melia.

"In those early days, she didn't see herself as anything special. She just knew that a single woman, especially with the help of an elf, could move quickly and quietly and cause the Kalesh a great deal of pain, and that's all she wanted. It took a long time before she realized how powerful she'd become. When possible, she didn't hurt the common soldiers of the army. She'd target ruthless leaders or damage supply lines, anything to disrupt the relentless destruction the Empire caused.

"And then, finally, when she was almost worn out with all the fighting, Bastian unwittingly offered her the chance to kill Prince Turrn, whose cruelty was legendary. Even if she'd known beforehand that it was the last thing she'd do against the Empire, she'd still have done it in a heartbeat." She looked at Sable. "If she'd known that during our escape, she'd meet a man named Stephen and that she'd be in love with him before he was done hiding us in his attic or guiding us to freedom through noxious bogs in the dead of night, she'd have tried to kill Turrn years earlier.

"And," Evay said quietly, "even if she'd known that settling down with him and having a family would mean the Kalesh would eventually find her, I think she would have done that too." She looked at Sable. "Until I saw your face when you were talking to the king, I hadn't remembered what she was like then. All I could think of was that she was gone. But I saw you standing there facing Corelis, and I remembered her…alive." Her brow creased. "I didn't want to. The anger of her being gone was familiar and safe. Remembering what she was like alive is…painful. But also good. I would give anything to see her again." She drew in a breath and met Sable's gaze. "I'm sorry. I should have come find you girls."

That statement deserved an answer, but Sable couldn't manage to find one before Victis appeared, stalking toward them.

"I suppose you'd like to talk with the dwarves," he said, his voice disapproving.

"Are they close?" Thulan asked.

"At the next stream," Victis answered, annoyed. "I had planned to skirt their path, but if we meet up with them and lead them through the woods, maybe they won't trample quite as much of it."

CHAPTER SIXTY-FOUR

"At the next stream" turned out to mean "at the far edge of the woods, which we won't reach until sundown."

While Thulan complained about the distance, Sable told Evay everything that had happened since Melia had died, explaining how both Talia and Ryah had arrived in their current situations.

"Bring me to meet Kiva when we arrive at the island," Evay said grimly.

"Gladly," Sable said. "Maybe you can convince Talia to get away from him."

When Evay learned that Reese had been to the Empire, the two of them began discussing places they'd been. Sable walked between the two of them. The forest around them was still elvish—the trees seemed to listen and give off a brightness that made normal trees seem lifeless. The wind from the night before had calmed, and when she caught glimpses of the sky through the canopy, it was a clear blue.

The air felt tranquil. Innov flew through the forest, a flickering golden speck in the distance, growing brighter as she wove through the trees toward Sable. She landed with a spray of sparks on Sable's arm, and the phoenix's warmth seeped into her.

The motion of the elves around them in the woods had become more obvious. They were scattered as far as she could see on either side and behind them.

It wasn't until Thulan stopped talking mid-sentence that Sable noticed the low, thrumming rumble.

"Finally," Thulan said, lengthening her stride and moving past Sable.

The sounds grew until it was obvious that it was songs accompanied by the sounds of a camp being set up. The elves around them faded into invisibility, but Cintis, Victis, and Evay moved forward with Sable and the others.

They reached a stream to find the clearing on the far side swarmed with dwarves. More moved in the trees past it. Small cook fires popped up, and the air was full of the shouts and laughter of hundreds of dwarves.

"Look at them all!" Cintis said, watching the commotion with wide eyes.

Leonis sighed. "I'm not sure I'm ready for hundreds of dwarves again."

Thulan planted herself at the edge of the stream, her arms crossed. "Rion was stupid enough to put you in charge, Pardrun?"

The huge, dark-haired commander of the guard stopped for a heartbeat at the sight of Thulan then turned away. "No one cares what you think." He motioned to dwarves carrying heavy packs. "Cooking supplies along the riverbank."

"Why do you still have a job?" Thulan asked. "You can't keep a dwarf, two humans, and a half-elf locked up, even when they're shackled and caged."

"I know you had help from the tunnel worms on the third level," Pardrun growled. "As soon as I prove it, some dwarves are gonna drop."

"Even now that you know I'm not a traitor and shouldn't have been imprisoned in the first place?" Thulan asked.

"Doesn't matter. They defied the high dwarf's orders. Not a smart set of cousins."

"Smart enough to steal prisoners out from under your nose," Mari said, walking up to the stream and carrying a bundle of weapons under one arm. She grinned at Thulan. "Or so I hear."

Pardrun glared at her, but Mari splashed across the stream and clapped Thulan on the back. "Hello again, Sable, Reese, Leonis." She took in Cintis, Evay, and Victis. "You picked up some elves."

"Can you imagine if we'd showed up at the Northern Corner with Victis?" Leonis asked with a grin. "I'd like to see Pardrun take him into custody."

Mari's eyes widened. "You're Victis! You're the one who makes the best food Thulan has ever eaten."

Victis blinked at her, his severity momentarily broken by shock.

"Are you cooking tonight?" Mari asked eagerly.

His jaw twitched. "No."

"Too bad," Mari said. "Thulan went on and on about it."

"We're not supposed to talk to them about it," Thulan said. "It's rude."

Mari's brow creased. "Really?"

Victis refocused on Pardrun. "I assume you are the leader of your company. I am Victis, son of Turris, Commander of the King's Guard."

Pardrun sized up the severe elf, then nodded. "Pardrun, son of Ror, Commander of the Dwarven Royal Sentinel Force."

"Dwarven Royal Sentinel…" Thulan's voice trailed off, incredulous. "It's the guard. Just the guard. I don't even think it's capitalized."

Pardrun's face darkened, but before he could speak, another familiar dwarf approached carrying a blanket wrapped around a bundle of swords. The braids in his beard were decorated with bits of bone.

Reese caught sight of him and stiffened.

"High Dwarf Rion renamed it," Callun said. "Stupid, eh?"

"It's not wise to disrespect the High Dwarf so publicly," Pardrun warned. "Someone's going to think you're after his job. It's no secret you think you could do it better."

"That muddy rock could do it better," Callun said, nudging a stone with his boot. He turned his attention to Thulan. "Nice to see you again, Bristles."

"It's nice to see all of you." Thulan waved at the entire commotion of dwarves setting up camp. "Wasn't sure I would."

He shrugged. "Just had to fight a few things out first."

"Put the weapons with the rest, over past the wagons," Pardrun ordered him. "You too, Mari."

"I'll get right on that," Mari said, pulling a thick war hammer out of her bundle and turning to Thulan. "Picked this one out for you."

Thulan took it slowly, looking the hammer over. "Isn't this Slur's?"

Mari nodded. "Lost him in the collapse. He woulda been happy to have you carry it."

"She does not get a hammer!" Pardrun shouted. "Those are for arming the dwarven army, not some deserter who's thrown herself in with the human weaklings."

"I can see why the High Dwarf put that one in charge," Evay said.

"Tact and prudence like that will be invaluable when we're all trying to fight together."

Callun didn't bother to hide his smile. "Pardrun, the Weapons Master's told everyone to stack their weapons along the far side of the road. It looked muddy, though."

Pardrun glared into the crowd of dwarves making camp. "What? Can't that idiot do anything right?" He stormed off through the dwarves.

"You have a Weapons Master?" Thulan asked.

Callun shrugged. "Someone said we did. I don't know who it is or where they are. Figured it sounded like something that would get Pardrun to leave. Didn't want him around since he was bound to not approve of this." He set his roll of swords on the ground and pulled one out.

Without pausing, he strode into the stream, heading straight at Reese, who shifted in front of Sable, his hand going to a knife in his belt.

Callun's grin widened at the motion. "Figured we'd run into each other somewhere out here. Picked this out for you. Seemed like the right size." He flipped the sword and held it out to Reese, hilt first.

Reese stared at it. "Is that stonesteel?"

"Is there any other kind of steel?" Callun asked.

"Yes." Reese took the sword and turned it slowly, his eyes running over the blade. "A lot of other kinds, and none compare to this."

It looked to Sable like a perfectly normal sword, but judging from Reese's reverent expression, it was something much more.

Reese glanced back at Callun. "How hard did you hit your head when we fought?"

"Not hard enough to forget how fast you took me down. The sword is yours on one condition: You teach me that move."

Reese brought his attention back to the blade. "Agreed."

"Good." Callun clapped Reese on the shoulder with a huge hand, hard enough that Reese staggered to the side. "The cousins from the Broken Chisel are set up in the woods over there. C'mon." He splashed back into the stream, glancing back over his shoulder. "Everyone's invited. Even you elves. Gotta find a way to get along with you sometime."

"I'm afraid I have duties to attend to," Victis said stiffly and turned, disappearing into the trees.

"He was afraid Callun was going to come right out and invite him to dinner." Thulan grinned, hefting her new hammer and splashing into the stream.

"Let's go," Cintis said, grabbing Leonis's arm and pulling him forward.

"They're only fun until they capture you and throw you in a dark cell," Leonis complained, but when Cintis dropped his arm and jumped across the stream, stepping only on a few of the largest rocks, arriving dry on the other side, Leonis followed.

Sable glanced at Evay. "Care to join the dwarves for the evening?"

Evay watched Callun's huge back as he walked away, and she shrugged. "Could be interesting."

When they reached a cluster of dwarves gathered around a small campfire, Slim, the wiry dwarf who'd helped them escape, was leaning easily against a tree at the outskirts.

"Bristles," he greeted Thulan with a rakish smile.

"Give it up, Slim," Mari said, patting his shoulder as they passed him. "Never going to happen."

Slim sighed. "She even looks good out here in all the colors and glaring light, eh?" he said to Leonis.

Leonis shook his head in disbelief and walked past without answering.

"Who's he talking about?" Cintis whispered.

Sable recognized several dwarves from the Broken Chisel sitting around the fire, including the huge Rudd who'd fought Thulan.

"Bristles!" Rudd greeted her, waving her over. "Come sit! Have some ale! We didn't drink last time we saw you. That was the problem."

Sable, Reese, and the elves paused at the edge until Callun waved to them from near the fire. "No one's bringing you ale all the way out there."

"What if we don't want ale?" Leonis muttered.

Callun shooed dwarves off a log near the fire.

"Do we not want ale?" Cintis asked, sitting next to Callun.

Sable and Reese followed Leonis and Evay until they all sat in the midst of the dwarves. The expressions around them ranged from skeptical to curious to the occasional friendly nod.

Callun took a drink from a metal cup, then passed it to Cintis. The elf sniffed the cup, then took a sip. He blinked at the flavor and let out a little cough, then took another sip.

"Not terrible," he said, passing it to Leonis.

Leonis held it away from himself and passed it to Evay. "Yes, terrible."

Evay smelled the cup as well. "Smells like human ale."

"Human ale!" Rudd exclaimed. "This is Pan's Golden Ale from the Broken Chisel, not some watered-down piss water."

She took a drink, grimacing. "It has a kick."

Rudd laughed as she passed it to Sable. The ale smelled strong, and she sipped it carefully. It was thicker than water, with something that tasted almost like citrus until sharp jabs of bitterness and spice shot across her mouth. She swallowed it, and it burned down her throat.

She coughed and handed the cup to Reese, who took it with a stony face. "Have you had this before?" she asked.

He shook his head. "The dwarves I traveled with didn't share with me."

She almost asked when he'd traveled with dwarves before she remembered that after his parents had died, a holy woman had taken most of his possessions, then used the rest to pay a band of dwarves to take him to his aunt's house. They'd taken him partway, then abandoned him on the Eastern Reaches.

"Smelled like this though," he said quietly. He glanced at the dwarves around the fire, considering Thulan, Mari, and Callun. "Guess it's time to replace that memory with a better one." He lifted the cup and downed the rest of it.

Callun gave an approving nod, and the dwarf on Reese's far side slapped him on the back as he let out a long breath. Someone took the cup and refilled it.

Mari climbed to her feet on the far side of the fire.

"You all should have seen it!" She pointed at Thulan. "Bristles had just knocked on the North Door, standing next to three humans." She waved her hand at Leonis. "Well, two and a half humans. Pardrun's head was about to explode with fury, except…it's Thulan. You could actually see the wheels spinning in his head as he slowly and painfully considered the dwarves on his side—wisely not including me—before he decided twenty dwarves should be enough to take her and opened the door."

"Aside from you, there were only ten," Thulan corrected her.

Mari waved off her words. "Everyone knows Pardrun can't count. But you all saw Reese and Thulan fight in the Broken Chisel. Pardrun's twenty dwarves might not have been enough if any of this crew had fought back. They let themselves be taken, and Pardrun still was terrified. He didn't even throw a punch until after Thulan was shackled, and he still looked scared she might hit him back."

A round of cheers and laughter rang out.

"In the throne room, I heard he punched her again," one of the other dwarves said. "She told him if he did it again, he'd regret it for the rest of his life. My aunt said he looked like he might wet his trousers right there."

"That's not how I remember it," Sable said quietly to Reese.

Reese laughed. "Oh, he was scared."

"Thulan," Sable said suddenly, "Pardrun did hit you again. When we got to the cell."

Heads around the fire turned to look with shocked faces at Thulan.

She finished a long drink of ale, then wiped her mouth. "I noticed."

Callun grinned at her. "Please let me be there when you make him regret it."

A small smile curled up the corner of Thulan's mouth. "I suppose I owe you that much for convincing everyone to come join the fight."

"Make sure the elves get to watch," Evay said. "I just met him today and I already want to hit him." A round of laughter and cheers met the sentiment, and several large dwarvish hands slapped Evay on the back.

Next to Sable, Reese laughed, and she leaned against his shoulder, her own smile feeling wider than it had in weeks. "Dare we hope things are actually starting to go well?" she asked him.

He slipped an arm around her waist. "It does feel…hopeful. At least I assume this is what hope feels like. Can't remember feeling it before now."

She laughed and dropped her head onto his shoulder. "The only downside I can think of is that we'll have to deal with Pardrun when we arrange things with the dwarves."

"Nah," the dwarf next to Reese said. "Rion may have put Pardrun in charge, but Rion's not here. You have something you need the dwarves to do, you come talk to Callun."

Reese looked over the huge dwarf with the bones in his beard. "Won't that cause trouble between Callun and Pardrun?"

The dwarf next to Reese grinned. "We can only hope."

CHAPTER SIXTY-FIVE

THE SUN HAD SET and the green of the forest had deepened to blue, but, through the thinning trees, Sable caught sight of swatches of orange clouds in the western sky. Instead of stopping to set up camp, as they'd done at sunset every other day, the long column of dwarves and the silent shadows of the elves continued through the forest.

Victis reached them as the trees ended. Pardrun came too, scowling at the fact that he was followed by Callun.

"Not a bad-sized army," Evay said.

Sable followed her gaze. The forest ended not far ahead, and a small rise of grass hid anything farther from sight. But the sky above the grass was hazy and dark. "Is that smoke?"

"From a decent number of campfires," Evay said. "How many humans did you think you'd have?"

"Six thousand," Reese answered. "If all the lords brought their full armies."

Six thousand northern soldiers. If Leonis and Thulan's estimations were correct, adding the dwarves and elves was the equivalent of several thousand more humans. Sable glanced over her shoulder at the lines of dwarves walking behind them. That number seemed high, but no one had argued with their estimates. So that put the northern forces at close to ten thousand strong.

Sable turned back to the smoky haze visible ahead of them. That was a little closer to the expected fifteen thousand Kalesh.

Innov flew high overhead, an isolated, glittering light against the darkening sky.

They climbed the small rise until they could see the land ahead. It dwindled into more blues than greens, laid out like a map.

The Black River reflected the lighter blue of the sky, cutting a bright line through the land to their right. Not far down from where they stood, Aedis was clearly visible on Tutella Island, the dark figures of monks moving like dots along its walls. Past the island and the river was nothing but hills, the road there too winding and thin for an army to use.

Laid out straight ahead of Sable was what was rightly called the narrows, a grassy plain stretching from the Black River to densely treed hills on the left. Ahead of them, to the south, the narrows widened into a broad greenish-blue valley that followed the river south.

The narrows looked like a funnel. The Kalesh coming north between the river and the hills would be slowly crowded into a thinner plain until, here next to the island, it was pinched small enough that the northern army blocked off any access further north.

Just this side of the narrowest point where they'd make their stand, Sable took in the squares of army tents standing stalwartly across the plain in squares, like some military quilt. There were far more of them than there had been when she'd left.

"That's more than six thousand," Evay said.

Reese nodded, counting the squares of tents. "More like eight."

Behind her, the column of dwarves filed over the hill, their marching feet thrumming the ground. To her left, the elves slipped out of the trees like a mist, more of them than Sable had expected moving onto the grass.

"The dwarves claim the land at the far side," Pardrun said, pointing to the edge of the narrows just before the hills began.

Callun rolled his eyes. "Claim is a stupid word. We're not conquering anything." He turned to Reese. "The dwarves will camp in the space between the northern army and the trees. Your leaders meet on the island?" At Reese's nod, Callun slapped him on the shoulder. "I'll see you there tomorrow."

He whistled back at the line of dwarves and started across the hill. The column of dwarves followed him.

"A selection of dwarves who are actually in control will meet you at the island tomorrow," Pardrun said, glaring daggers after Callun before striding away.

Reese rolled his shoulder. "I want to support Callun in that little rivalry, but he's going to break my shoulder one of these times."

"We will make camp in the trees," Victis said, motioning to the forest along the base of the first hill. He gave a series of signals to one of the elves, and the whole elven army shifted to move along the tree line toward the hills.

Pardrun caught up with Callun and shouted something at him, which Callun ignored.

"I will attend your meetings on the island myself," Victis said, his brow creased in disapproval at the dwarves. Without another word, he disappeared after the elves.

Sable stood on the hillside with Reese, Thulan, Leonis, and Evay. There were more humans than she'd expected, and the elves and the dwarves were actually here, actually helping. None of which was as encouraging as she'd thought it would be.

She looked south, as though she could see the distant Kalesh army. "Is all of this enough?"

"I hope so." Reese started down the hill toward Tutella Island. "Because I have no idea where we can find more soldiers."

The next morning, Sable leaned her elbows on the thick stone wall of Aedis, standing next to Reese. The black sky above lightened to a deep purple at the horizon, the stars disappearing one by one as the first sign of dawn stretched toward her. The river shushed by, only a sound in the dark shadows beneath the wall, and the timbered homes of the monks behind her were still wrapped in quiet and shadows.

They stood silent for a long time until the purple lightened to violet and pink, the colors shifting so gradually it was impossible to tell if they were changing or if she was just imagining it.

"Time feels like it's stopped," she said, "and at the same time is racing forward."

Reese leaned his chin on his hand and hummed in agreement. "I hate the waiting part."

Her eyes ran along the lines of soldiers. "I keep thinking that from

Argyros's point of view, our army is laid out in nice little units for him to set on fire."

He let out a frustrated breath but nodded. "Since Vivaine's trial, I have been in at least a dozen conversations brainstorming how an army can fight off a dragon. No one has a single good idea." He glanced into the southern sky. "So we keep coming back to the hope that Vivaine doesn't want to start burning soldiers alive."

"Another plan based purely on hope," Sable said. "This is starting to feel like a habit."

"When I pointed that out, Atticus gave me the speech about all plans being based on hope."

Footsteps sounded on the wall, and Sable glanced past Reese to see Sam approaching. The monk stopped next to them and looked out over the army. "Rabbit got a raven. The Kalesh army is leaving the mouth of the Black River. They'll be here in eight days."

The timeframe wasn't unexpected, but she glanced into the dark sky of the south, half expecting to see a cloud of dust.

She picked up a loose pebble from the seam in the wall and rolled it between her fingers. The edges were sharp, but she squeezed it until it dug into her fingers, letting the jab of pain push back the looming fear.

"How many?" Reese asked.

Sam paused. "Twenty-five thousand."

Sable's fingers froze.

Reese turned slowly to look at him. "What?"

"Reinforcements from across the Eastern Reaches." Sam's voice was grim. "We dispatched some dwarves last night to bring down some hillsides along the western bank of the river. The army won't be able to move up that direction. They'll have to come up on the eastern side, which means they still have to get through the narrows here. It's not unreasonable to think we can hold it."

"Any sign of Vivaine?" Sable asked.

Sam answered the real question. "No sign of the dragon with the army. Last report had it in Immusmala with Vivaine. As far as we can tell, she's had little to no contact with the army itself."

"And the Tien Sark?"

"They're leading it. Someone Atticus says you met in Immusmala. A man with scales all over his scalp."

"Jrogen." Sable sighed. "Why didn't Kiva kill him when he had the chance?"

"Because it's Kiva," Reese said. "And he never does the right thing."

The sky had lightened to a buttery yellow near the horizon, and the army was now visible laid out just north of the narrows. Reese tapped his fingers on the wall, looking thoughtfully toward the dwarves. "How justified do you think the dwarves' reputation for building things quickly is?"

"According to Thulan," Sable said, "they can put 'scaffolding up across a rock face with a mining bore, a sluice, a hopper, and a disposal vent in two days.' Whatever those things are."

Reese pushed himself off the wall. "Can you find her? I have an idea. I need some paper. And Serene and Jae. And Evay. And anyone else with creepy magical powers you can think of."

"Like me?" Sable asked.

He gave her a quick smile. "Your magic is the creepiest of all. It's the only one that's tried to kill me more than once."

He and Sam headed for the gathering hall, while Sable went back to the house off the square. She sent Purn to find Gwen and Terrane, then knocked quietly on Serene's door.

Jae answered. "Morning," he whispered.

"Reese says he needs Serene and you and anyone else 'with creepy magical powers' I can find."

Jae glanced at the window at the end of the hall, which was still dim. "This early?"

Sable shrugged. "Something about dwarves building weapons to combat the dragon and the twenty-five thousand Kalesh that are now on their way."

He stared at her for a moment, digesting the number. "Serene," he said over his shoulder. "Time to get up."

She groaned and pushed herself up, and when she stood, Sable was surprised to see a small bump in her shirt.

About to turn down the hall, Sable stopped. "It looks like there really might be a baby in there! Has it been a really long time since I saw you, or do your black robes just usually hide that?"

Serene rubbed a hand over the bump. "It just appeared over the last week or two. The bump showed and the nausea left at about the same time."

"You look less tired," Sable said.

"Those are the sorts of compliments people keep giving me. How bad did I look before?"

Sable laughed. "It wasn't how bad you looked—it was how cranky you were."

A small smile curled up Serene's lips. "I wasn't that bad, was I, Jae?"

"Or course not, dear," he said with a perfectly straight face, but when he turned to close the door, he grinned at Sable. "We'll be right down."

Sable collected Thulan on her way down, and when they stepped out into the square, Gwen and Terrane were waiting and Evay was walking toward them from the direction of Talia's house, looking surprisingly tired.

"Did you get any sleep?" Sable asked.

"Not much," Evay said with a smile that still held a touch of sorrow. "I had eleven years of catching up to do with your sisters. We didn't even scratch the surface, but it was a start."

"And you met Kiva," Sable said.

Evay glanced back toward the house. "I don't trust him."

"Do you think we should find a different place for Talia and Ryah to stay?"

"It's not that. He's protective of Talia. It's everything else I don't trust him about."

Reese came out of the gathering hall with a rolled-up paper. He took in the assembled group.

"The problem is the dragon." He handed the paper to Thulan before leading everyone out of the square. "Atticus says there's almost no way to fight them. They're too armored for arrows and swords. Of all the stories he's ever found, the only way people ever beat dragons is to somehow negotiate with them or outwit them."

"The only negotiation that will stop this war is our surrender," Serene said.

"And no one outwits a dragon during a battle," Jae added. "I've read those, they're stories of individuals escaping a dragon's lair or something."

Reese nodded. "Neither outwitting nor negotiating is an option for us. And a dragon is the most dangerous when it's flying. Because then it's fast and impenetrable and breathing fire."

The river was covered with a fine mist as they climbed aboard one of the three ferries between the island and the armies. Thulan sat on the deck and spread out the paper, displaying a detailed drawing of some sort of contraption.

"Is there a limit to how much fire they can breathe?" Sable asked.

"If there is, it's a big enough limit that we'll be mostly dead before he reaches it," Jae said.

"This is the most depressing conversation I've ever heard," Gwen said.

"Yes," Terrane agreed, his voice thoughtful, "but all that fire…"

"It's not like you're going to be able to play with it," Gwen pointed out. "We'll be running for our lives."

Reese paused to look at Terrane. "What could you do to his fire?"

"Probably nothing. If he catches something close to me on fire, I could put it out, but I doubt I can keep him from spraying fire everywhere else. How wide was the stream?" Terrane asked.

"Stop sounding so excited about it," Gwen chided him. "He set half the stage on fire."

"Because the stream was wide?" Terrane asked, undeterred. "Or because it spread?"

"The stream wasn't much wider than his head," Reese answered. "The parts it hit ignited immediately, but the surrounding wood caught quickly just because it was hot fire on dry wood."

Terrane nodded slowly. "So not because something splashed."

"What would splash?" Gwen asked.

"There are different ideas on what dragon fire is," Terrane said. "Some say it's fire ignited in their throat and just the flames are propelled out. Some say they shoot out a burning liquid."

"How did you learn so much about dragon fire?" Jae asked.

Terrane shrugged. "Who doesn't want to learn about fire?"

"I would say it was just fire," Reese said. "But to hit us, he has to be relatively close. From what he did in Immusmala, I'd say he needs to be within about ten paces."

"Which is fine for him, because he's armor plated," Serene noted.

"Not everywhere," Evay said. "His eyes are vulnerable to an arrow."

"We should remember he only has one good one left," Sable said. "Innov gouged out the other. If Innov could blind the other eye, that would slow him down too."

The ferry bumped up against the riverbank, and Thulan rolled up the paper. "Argyros's scales might not stand up against big rocks. This is a torsion sling. It should fling rocks pretty far."

"The Kalesh call it a catapult," Reese said. "I never saw one in action, but they taught us the design."

Serene raised an eyebrow as she climbed off the ferry. "You're going to throw rocks at him?"

Reese nodded. "Big ones. Some catapults throw multiple rocks connected by chains."

"With enough accuracy to hit a flying dragon?" she asked.

Reese looked at Thulan. "That's the question. Is it possible?"

"Beats me," Thulan said. "But there are cousins who will know."

"The answer is probably no," Reese said. "Which is where you come in, Serene. I need you to figure out a magical way to ground him. If we can hold him still, for…well, a bit, we could attack with the catapults."

"That's your plan?" Gwen asked. "Knock the dragon down, then have the dwarf machine hit him with rocks?"

"Do you have a better one?"

"Yes. Convince Vivaine not to attack us with her dragon."

"Well, you work on that plan," Reese said, "and I'll work on mine."

"Back up to the part where you want me to ground a dragon," Serene said. "How am I supposed to do that?"

Reese shrugged. "Magic."

"That's your idea?" she said, annoyed. "Magic?"

"Yup. Figure out how to knock Argyros out of the sky. If you can get him to land somewhere specific, even better."

Serene stared at him, then looked at Sable. "Is he serious?"

"He looks serious," Sable said.

They were passing through Lord Loren's forces, and soldiers called out greetings to Reese and occasionally to Sable.

"I can move energy," Serene said. "I can't knock things out of the sky."

"Drain the energy out of Argyros, then," Reese said. "No energy, no flight."

"Right," she answered, "and then I'll drain the Black River by drinking it."

"Well, then just take energy out of his wings," Reese said blithely. "Or even just one wing."

Serene opened her mouth to argue, but stopped, her brow creasing in thought.

"It's not my job to figure out how to work your magic," Reese continued. "My job is to find people who can make rocks fly."

Reese turned again, striding forward as the first sign of the dwarves came into view ahead of them. Thulan hurried ahead with him, calling out questions to the dwarves she passed. They finally found Callun with a group of dwarves sitting around a morning campfire.

Thulan strode into the middle of them. "We need a torsion sling," she announced, elbowing a dwarf out of her way and spreading the drawing on the ground.

The dwarves were quiet for a moment, considering the drawing.

"The arm could be longer," one dwarf said, "if we could get the tension high enough."

There were mutters of agreement.

"Can you build this?" Reese asked.

"How soon?" Callun asked.

"The Kalesh will be here in eight days."

"Where's the lumber?" Callun asked.

"I'll get men working on it as soon as you tell me if it's possible."

One of the dwarves took a thin stick from the fire and marked a few places on the drawing. "It'll need reinforcements here and here."

There were grunts of agreement.

"We could make one of these," Callun said. "Once we have the wood."

"Excellent." Reese slapped him on the shoulder. "I need twelve."

The dwarves looked up at him with looks ranging from incredulity to flat refusal.

"There is no way—" Callun started.

"You can have as many humans as you need to help you work," Reese said. "You fix the design and teach them how to assemble it. I'll make sure there's enough lumber."

The dwarves studied him but didn't object.

"How accurate will it be?" Reese asked.

"I couldn't hit anything as small as a person," Callun said.

"How about as small as a dragon?"

Any dwarf that hadn't been paying attention was now.

Callun crossed his arms. "How big is the dragon?"

"Bigger than a carriage, smaller than a house," Reese said. "Wingspan to match."

The dwarves blinked at him.

"If it comes," Reese added, "Serene and these other magical folks will do their best to ground it. Then I'd like to hit it with some big rocks."

The dwarves followed his gesture and squinted at Serene suspiciously. Mutters traveled through them, and Sable waited for someone to complain that no one had told them there were going to be magic wielders or dragons.

One of them shook his head. "Weighted nets."

There was a moment of silence, then nods.

"Not rocks," another agreed. "Big weighted nets. Made of chains."

"Draw them up and I'll get someone working on them," Reese said, clapping Callun on the shoulder again. "Just tell me what you need to keep the dragon from setting us on fire."

The sentiment was met with troubled looks.

"A mountain over us would solve that problem," someone muttered.

Reese smiled at them. "I'll send a bunch of woodsmen over to get specifications for the lumber you need. Keep me posted on the twelve catapults."

He turned and started back toward Aedis.

"It'll be more like six," Callun called after him.

"Twelve it is!" Reese called back. "Thank you!"

CHAPTER SIXTY-SIX

THE SMALL BIRDS skimmed across the river, darting after insects as though this early morning were no different than any other. As though it weren't only a week before the Kalesh army arrived.

Sable leaned on the wall of Aedis again, trying to focus on the birds while Jae concentrated beside her. The morning was still, the sun not yet high enough to reach down to the water. A chilly wind blew out of the north, and she wrapped a cloak around her shoulders.

Jae held his hands out in front of him, his fingers stretched, straining. Despite the chilly wind, Sable could feel warmth around him, spreading over the river.

He waited until the birds rose higher in one of their soaring loops before he shoved his hands down with a sharp motion.

The birds plummeted down, screeching. They recovered just above the water and scattered up the river, leaving the sky empty.

"How did you do that?" Reese asked.

"I made a boundary layer of air," Jae said, "and then moved it."

"Not to point out the obvious," Leonis said, "but you dropped a few small birds, and not even down to the water. That doesn't feel like it's going to translate well to a dragon."

"It should," Jae answered.

"He can do it harder and faster," Serene said, "but he doesn't like hurting the birds."

"It's not even about harder," Jae said. "For the birds to fly, and for Argyros to fly, the air needs to move across their wings. If you can stop that from happening, they can't fly."

"So you're going to get rid of the air?" Leonis asked.

"No, I'm just going to make the air move with him. If it's not flowing over him, he'll fall...if I can make it big enough to cover his wings."

Thulan and Leonis looked skeptical.

"I thought Serene would be the one who could bring down a dragon," Thulan mused.

"Nobody's brought one down yet," Jae said.

Sable looked over the army. The beginnings of eight catapults stood along the front lines, facing south, their tall beams of wood sticking high above the tents around them. "Will those hit him when he falls?"

"We have them aimed at three different zones," Thulan said. "If Jae can get him to fall in one of those areas, we should be able to target him pretty quickly."

"There are a lot of 'shoulds' in this conversation," Leonis remarked. "What happens if Jae brings him down somewhere else?"

Jae and Thulan exchanged looks.

"We'll improvise," Thulan answered.

"Maybe Argyros won't show up," Leonis said, "and you can just use this to knock arrows out of the air."

"This is too big of a stage," Sable said. "I can't imagine Vivaine won't make an appearance." She looked at Jae. "Could you teach me to do the air thing?"

"It took me two months to get a small amount of air to move. Creating the boundary layer is complicated—"

"It's nearly impossible," Serene corrected him. "Moving air takes a delicacy I cannot manage. Somehow he's taking *vitalle* and...*not* moving it. He traps it, like it's not actually energy, and then while it's still trapped, he makes the whole thing move."

Jae considered the words. "Sort of."

"It's a whole lot better than nothing," Reese said.

Sable and Reese left them on the wall, climbing down out of the chilly breeze into the protection of Aedis's buildings. They threaded their way between the half-timber houses toward the main square.

"You know," Sable said, linking her arm in Reese's, "until Serene finds a way to actually build in her stronghold valley, the monks did offer me a home here on the island."

His eyes traced the steep rooflines around them. "When you foolishly pledged yourself to Vivaine that one time—"

"The time I saved your life?"

"The time you rashly jumped into another dangerous situation without thought to your own safety, yes, I almost joined the monks."

Sable pulled him to a stop. "You did?"

"I was furious that you'd just become an abbess. It didn't feel totally out of the question to become a monk."

"What stopped you?"

"Sam, actually. I told him I wanted to join, and he told me he didn't accept pledges made out of anger. He told me about Tanis and said I should go investigate my options. If, in a year, I still wanted to join, he'd be happy to have me." He reached up and brushed her hair back from her cheek. "But within that year, you'd written me that first letter, and…that was the end of joining the monks."

They started walking again, and Sable squeezed her arm around his. "You're welcome for sending that letter."

"You're welcome for bringing it to you." Purn's voice came from behind them in the alley.

"You know, Purnicious," Reese said, not turning, "sometimes it'd be nice to actually be alone with Sable."

"Any time my mistress would like some privacy, I'm happy to oblige her."

Sable glanced back at her. "Can you, though? Really?"

"Kobolds can give their masters and mistresses space," Purn said primly. "We are able to leave and not pay attention. I'd always hear if you specifically called me, though."

"Do you have to obey Talia and Ryah the way you obey Sable?" Reese asked thoughtfully.

"I don't have to, exactly," Purnicious answered, "but we're connected. They're her family, and so I want to help them."

"Ah," he said as they reached the edge of the square. "So when Sable and I marry, and I'm part of her family…"

Purnicious sighed and popped out of view. "Don't remind me."

Near the center, Flibbet stood next to his cart, chatting amiably with a few people, including Evay. Sable crossed the cobblestones to join her, and Reese looked into the cart, examining the goods Flibbet had on display.

"I take credit," the little peddler said, motioning to Evay and Sable, "for bringing the two of you together again." He leaned against the side of his cart, and it gave a low creak. "Yes, yes." He waved his hand. "The cart helped too. That little *Ghost of the White Wood* book I gave Sable has been very useful."

"I'm impressed you found the real story," Evay said. "I bet only a handful of people in the Empire know the truth."

"Then they're not dedicated enough to look for it," a voice said from the far side of Evay.

Sable leaned forward to see the thin, pale, fishy face of Lord Renwen.

"It takes work..." He gave Sable a bland smile. "But if you look hard enough, you can always find the truth."

She forced herself to smile back at him. From this close, she could see a worn edge to the collar of his silk shirt, and she'd spent enough time with Purnicious to notice that the elbows were slightly thin and could use a few swipes of the kobold's hands. He looked older and more worn than when she'd stolen his ledger for Kiva.

"Our pasts are hard to keep hidden," he said to Sable, "don't you think?"

Evay's posture stiffened at the tone of his question, and she turned to study the pale lord.

"Pasts are complicated," Sable agreed. "Sometimes they were barely ours. Sometimes we were only tools for other people."

"Yes, mindless tools, merely looking out for their own survival." He sighed and peered into the cart. "The real question is, can we ever stop being merely tools?" He looked back at her. "I hear you've known Kiva for a very long time."

Both Evay and Reese crossed their arms.

"Much longer than I would have liked to," Sable answered.

Renwen gave a noncommittal hum. "Any idea who he's sending covert messages to in the south?"

Sable paused. "How do you know he is?"

Renwen smiled lazily. "I make it my job to know what's happening around me." His words warmed the cool morning air. "Especially when dangerous men, who often have their fingers in the events of the world, start to send ravens in the middle of the night." He shrugged. "I suppose it's not unreasonable to think the former merchant is corresponding with his connections in the south. He did lose everything when Vivaine banished him." There was a smugness in his voice but no sign of dishonesty. He picked up a quill and studied it idly. "But why, I wonder, is he being so secretive about it?" He set the quill back down and turned to

Flibbet. “A fine collection of goods, sir, but I don’t think I need anything else today.”

With that, he sauntered away.

Flibbet looked curiously at Sable. “What was that about?”

“When I worked for Kiva, I stole something very valuable from Lord Renwen.” Sable watched the lord walk casually out of the square. “I guess he figured that out.”

“I don’t like him,” Evay said bluntly.

Reese gave a hum of agreement. “I don’t think he blames you, Sable. I think he’s after Kiva.”

“Me too. He wasn’t lying, though,” Sable said. “Kiva’s been sending secret messages.”

Along the front of the cart was a newly carved banner that read “Trinkets and Treasures.” Sable ran her fingers over the smooth lettering.

“Purnicious did that,” Flibbet said, beaming. “Isn’t she amazing? She’s fixed two cracks and filled in a gouge that’s been plaguing one of my wheels for ages, all in exchange for fabric. The cart adores her and is willing to give her anything she wants.”

“Everyone adores Purn.” Sable glanced into the cart. “She’d love any fabric scraps you have.”

Flibbet held out a bright red bit of ribbon and a tassel that was made of rich browns and golds. “Will she take cords and ribbons instead?”

“I am sure she will,” Sable took them and tucked them into her pocket. She looked at Evay and Reese. “Let’s go ask Kiva who he’s sending secret messages to.”

Reese paused, leaning over Flibbet’s cart again.

“I traded the spyglass,” Flibbet said, a peculiar expression on his face.

“Ah,” Reese said, straightening but not masking his disappointment. “I hope you got a good trade for it. That was a good glass.”

“I…” Flibbet glanced at his cart. “I did. I think.”

“Good,” Reese said with more politeness than truth. He turned away from the cart. “Let’s find Kiva.”

They found the man walking out the front door of his house.

“Who are you talking to in the south, Kiva?” Sable asked as they crossed the street to meet him.

He paused in the act of closing the door. “Good morning to you too, Sable.” With a glance at Evay that was a bit more cautious, he nodded to her too. He gave no indication of noticing Reese.

“Sending ravens in the middle of the night,” Sable continued, “looks suspicious. You might not have noticed, but we're preparing for a war with the south."

He started to shut the door, but Talia appeared.

"Sable," she said, "isn't it early for you to come fight with Kiva?"

"It's never too early," Sable answered. "Tell us about the ravens, Kiva. Or deny them, if you think you can pull that off and make me believe it."

"Amah's pointy nose, Sable, it is too early." Talia looked at Evay. "Would you like to come in for tea before these two start arguing?"

"I would love to." Evay patted Sable on the shoulder and joined Talia inside.

"Who'd you hear about the ravens from?" Kiva asked curiously.

"That's not a denial," Sable said.

"I know you've been a vagabond for the last several years." Annoyance crept into Kiva's voice. "But some of us have spent a great deal of time, energy, and money establishing ourselves. When Vivaine kicked me out of Immusmala, I lost a lifetime of effort." His face turned grim. "I liked my house, Sable. I liked my chairs. You can walk away from any place and carry your whole life with you in a little pack. I am desperately trying to figure out if I still even have any of my life left."

"And this requires secret ravens?"

"I haven't slept much in the past weeks and have gotten a great deal of work done in the middle of the night." His words were warm. "But I will agree, as you so eloquently said, we're preparing for a war with people coming from the south, if not the south itself. It's not a war with the merchants of Immusmala, or my creditors, or my debtors, but the good monks of the island still aren't keen on sending any information that direction." He gave her a lazy smile. "I didn't want to cause the good monks any undo worry, so I sent them myself. At night."

Everything he'd said had been warm, but she'd hardly expected an outright lie. She studied him for a minute. "Did the ravens carry any information I would dislike?"

He laughed, stepping forward and setting his hand on her shoulder. She shoved it off. "You'd dislike almost every bit of business I conduct, Sable." He moved to the side, gesturing back toward the square. "I'm afraid I have some of that business to attend to right now. Lovely as always to chat with you, Queen of the North." He started up the street.

"Have any of your contacts in the south mentioned where Vivaine and her dragon are?" she asked.

"Still in the Sanctuary, last I heard," he said over his shoulder.

"When was that?"

He paused. "Would have been two nights ago." He turned back to look at her. "Do you really think I'd still be here, that I'd still have Talia here, if I thought Vivaine was on her way with her dragon?"

Sable narrowed her eyes.

"We have an army to deal with, Sable," he said, heading up the street again. "That's a big enough problem without looking for more."

Sable watched him go. He'd been truthful, but something still felt off.

"Renwen told me about the ravens," Sable said, watching for his reaction.

Kiva stopped short and faced her. "Renwen…" He looked thoughtfully down the street, his eyes distant for a moment before he refocused on Sable. His usually unruffled expression looked ruffled. "Told you. Personally?"

She nodded.

"That's…" Kiva's hand strayed to the small pocket in his vest, the one with a small, snake-sized bulge. He tapped a thumb gently on the pocket. "That's interesting."

"Not really," she said. "You destroyed the man's life. I'm sure he'll return the favor if he gets the chance. If he's anything like you, the only thing he cares about is who owes whom."

Kiva's troubled expression didn't change. He nodded toward Reese. "Bump that man higher up on your list of people who have grudges against Sable."

"He's still sitting right below you," Reese answered.

Kiva didn't smile. "Might want to reverse those." Still frowning, he headed toward the square.

CHAPTER SIXTY-SEVEN

Later that same day, afternoon sunlight streamed into the front windows, warming the front room of the house.

Leonis tossed a handful of black pebbles that skittered across the table. "There's a big island outside, Sable," he said, not hiding his annoyance.

Sable spun around at the mantel and paced back across the room. Aside from Leonis and Thulan, everyone was busy somewhere else. Lunch had come and gone, Reese was closed in with the monk Durnek and the scouts, Atticus was off who knew where, and the clicking of the pebbles was like a dozen tiny clocks ticking too fast.

"You could go into the square, right out the front door," Thulan agreed, "and pace until your legs fall off."

Sable reached the far wall and faced Thulan and Leonis. "That's it. It's time to go see the troops."

"You don't need to do that," Leonis said. "They're already here and unified."

"Not me. *We* are going." Sable circled her finger to include herself and them. "Because these soldiers are days away from a battle, and the only thing we're good for is raising morale."

"*We*"—Thulan wiggled her fingers between herself and Leonis—"are not the Flame of the North."

"No, you're the famous actors who are always with me and who people recognized years before anyone ever saw me. You're also well known among the dwarves and elves, so I need you. I'm going to see if Reese is done yet. Leonis, find your lute and get ready to sing something happy, then you two find Evay and meet me in the square."

"One of my strings broke," Leonis said.

"Because he tries to cover his poor singing voice with overly enthusiastic strumming," Thulan explained.

"Then don't bring your lute," Sable strode over to where Innov perched on the back of a chair, and the phoenix climbed onto her offered arm. "But the two of you are coming with me."

"Remember how nice she was when we first met her?" Leonis asked Thulan, pushing back his chair. "She never used to boss us around."

"It's the Queen of the North thing." Thulan scooped the pebbles into a pile in the center of the table and stood. "It's gone to her head."

"I heard Brother Matthew made his honey bread this morning," Sable said over her shoulder, walking out the door. "Find some of that too."

"That's the first good idea she's had," Leonis said.

Sable headed to the gathering hall under the hot sun. Inside, Reese stood at the end of the long table with the monk Durnek and a handful of rangers, all studying a map. They all wore pine green uniforms that had been mottled with darker browns until they looked like shadowy patches of forest. Reese's and Durnek's had captain's stripes of solid green stitched onto their left sleeves.

"We'll expect reports by midnight tomorrow," Durnek said as Sable moved close to the table. He picked up a small satchel and dumped its contents onto the table. A dozen bundles of twigs the size of apples rolled across the map, each one wrapped in a band of colored thread. "The string denotes the color of the smoke. Blue for warning. Red for emergency. Be careful out there."

The rangers took the bundles and turned away from the table, greeting Sable and Innov with nods and quick greetings before filing out of the hall.

Sable moved forward until she could see the map clearly. The line of their own troops was shown with small wooden blocks. To the south, a jumble of black markers represented the Kalesh army. "Still seven days away?"

Durnek nodded.

Reese still leaned over the map, but he glanced up at Sable, taking in Innov on her arm. "You look like you're about to go find trouble."

"I'm insulted. I just want to take Innov to the troops. I thought they could use some inspiration."

Reese pushed away from the table. "Sounds good. I'd like to see the progress on the catapults." He picked up his sword and scabbard from a nearby chair.

"We're going to our own troops, not the enemies'," Sable said. "Are you worried they'll attack you?"

"Me? No." He buckled on the sword belt. "But if there's trouble, you'll find it." He gestured for her to lead the way.

"You'd be disappointed if I didn't," she said. "We're going to come back in a few hours, and you're never going to have drawn your sword, and you're going to be sad."

"One can hope."

Leonis and Thulan waited in the square with Evay, Gwen, and Terrane. Leonis and Gwen each held a satchel of honey bread.

"Are we bringing a parade?" Reese asked.

Sable nodded. "I thought we could show some unity between elves, humans, and dwarves."

Gwen held her satchel open so they could each take a small loaf. "So you thought you'd show them Thulan and Leonis arguing?"

"They won't be arguing," Sable said, pointing at the two of them. "They'll be good friends who are there to promote unity and teamwork among the races."

"Unity and teamwork." Leonis took a loaf, then hung his bag over Gwen's shoulder next to her own. "We are all about teamwork."

Gwen threw the satchel back at him and started toward the docks.

They crossed the river, and Sable walked with Reese into the straight pathways between the tents. Soldiers paused in their tasks to watch Innov pass, and Sable exchanged a few greetings with them. She'd expected them to look nervous, but mostly they looked bored. Captains emerged from the crowds to get updates from Reese about the Kalesh. The soldiers watched Evay and Thulan with curiosity.

They walked across the narrows along the front edge of the army, every so often seeing the tall pieces of lumber from the beginnings of catapults jabbing up into the air. They moved slowly, chatting with soldiers and officers.

The final catapult sat in a gap between the human tents and the dwarven army. One of the tall beams was broken, and half of it hung awkwardly to the side. On the ground a little way away, a team of humans and dwarves worked on its replacement.

Thulan and Reese headed over to talk to them while Terrane studied the catapult. "We should shoot burning things out of these."

"Is there anything you think shouldn't be set on fire?" Gwen asked him.

He smiled at her. "You."

"How very sweet," Sable said, watching the soldiers gather along the side of the human camp. "Doesn't everyone seem bored?"

At the sight of Innov, some of the dwarves began to gather as well, but there was a sharp division between the two armies. A good number of humans and dwarves cast curious or suspicious looks in Evay's direction as well.

The army of the dwarves was spread out along the edge of the forested hill that marked the side of the narrows, and Sable caught a glimpse of movement inside them where the elves were staying secluded.

A captain wearing Lord Loren's colors stood near her, and she stepped closer to him. "How are things between the humans, dwarves, and elves?"

The man straightened. "We're working together to get the catapults made. I know this one is a bit behind schedule, but they say it will be fixed by sundown."

"I mean on a more personal level. There doesn't seem to be much interaction between us and them."

The captain glanced at her. "Just don't really know what to do with them. They stay in their camp, we stay in ours. Everyone seems happy."

Sable turned to survey the soldiers around them. "Are the men bored, Captain?"

"At this time of day, a little. We run 'em ragged in the morning, and they rest until later in the afternoon."

"Hmm." Sable walked out into the clearing, moving to the open space near the catapult. The base of the structure was a platform the size of a large wagon. It sat on a very slight rise, so when she climbed up onto it, she could see over the tops of the nearest tents.

She twitched her arm until Innov shifted, giving off a spray of embers and capturing the attention of more eyes. Slowly she took in the humans, the dwarves, and the trees where she imagined at least a few elves were watching.

"How about a contest?" she called. She pushed *vitalle* into the words and spread them as far in each direction as she could.

Heads shifted as more people focused on her.

"We have three armies here. Care to see who's better at a little game of Capture the Catapult?"

At the general murmur of interest, she motioned for Reese, Leonis, Thulan, and Evay to come closer.

"Teams of four," she called out. "No weapons. Your goal is to get past these four and touch the platform of the catapult before you are knocked down."

Leonis and Thulan strode over and positioned themselves along the back. Reese and Evay came more slowly.

"Who's brave enough to try?" Sable called out, spreading her voice across the gathered soldiers. "Test yourselves against Andreese," she gestured toward Reese, "who led the forces in the south against the Empire and won." Reese raised an eyebrow, but she grinned at him. "And Evay, an elf who caused the Empire so much trouble over the years there is still an enormous reward out for her capture."

"Thank you for pointing that out among all these strangers," Evay said under her breath.

Both the human and the dwarf camps were paying close attention now, so Sable continued, "Thulan is renowned for her fighting skills."

"Among small groups of people in obscure parts of the world," Leonis added loudly.

"And Leonis," Sable finished, "is entertaining. He's your weak point, people." She pointed down at Leonis's head. "Focus your attack here."

"All true!" Leonis called out. "But I do bring something essential." He held up a loaf of bread. "The prize. First one to touch the catapult gets the last loaf of Brother Matthew's honey bread." He set the loaf down on the catapult. "Best bread you've ever eaten. Who wants it?"

Reese unbuckled his sword and set it on the back of the catapult, along with the two knives he had in his belt, and looked up at Sable. "The point of this is?"

"Showing them how well elves, dwarves, and humans work together." Sable said quietly. "So you all need to work together well. And don't get beaten too quickly, or my beautiful example of unity will fall very flat."

She tossed up her arm, and Innov shot into the air, spinning around the catapult and landing on the very top of the tallest beam.

"Who's first?" Sable called.

A group of four soldiers, all wearing Lord Darien's colors, stepped out into the grass and faced the catapult.

"Good luck!" Sable called as she climbed down off the catapult and backed up to a tent on the human side of the space.

The first set of four soldiers were on their backs quicker than Sable would have expected, but a second took their place.

It took until the fourth wave for a group of dwarves to step forward, but between Evay's ability to move so fast Sable was almost sure she was using magic, Thulan's grappling skills, and the ease with which Reese could knock people down, Leonis merely had to hold off the fourth attacker, taunting them loudly, until someone showed up to help.

There was motion along the tree line, and a group of elves appeared out of the trees but didn't come closer. Among them, one particularly stern face watched the next group of humans line up.

While the dwarves were getting themselves up, Sable strode forward and climbed back on the catapult, holding her hands up. "Well done, brave defenders. While you catch your breath, I'd like to nominate my own team of attackers."

She searched the dwarves. "Callun! Bring that boney beard out here and take your chance to repay Andreese for that time he knocked you on your back. Remember that?"

Dwarven heads turned toward Callun, who grinned at her. "I do remember that." He pushed his way out of the line of dwarves and positioned himself in front of Reese.

"Thank you, Sable," Reese said. "My shoulder still aches from where he punched me last time."

"Don't let him punch you this time, then," she answered, moving across the catapult platform, looking at the elves. "Victis! Why are you hiding over there? Surely the commander of the elven guard has some skills he could put to use. Unless you find Evay too intimidating?"

She fully expected him to refuse, but Victis paused for only a moment before stepping forward. Dwarves moved out of his way as he came to stand across from Evay.

"Too bad Sable didn't pick an elf who'd be a challenge," Evay said lightly.

Victis didn't answer.

"I need two more," Sable scanned the crowds, looking for obvious choices. She caught sight of another tall dwarf. "Pardrun!" she called out. "Another commander of the guard! I do believe Thulan owes you for that one extra sucker punch you pulled when you arrested her. Care to come get that now?"

Pardrun strode out onto the grass until he stood only paces from Thulan. He was at least a head taller than her, but Thulan gave him a wide smile. "I've been waiting for this," she said.

"Are you going to find me my own personal enemy?" Leonis asked.

"Who could possibly hate you, Leonis?" Sable said, looking toward the humans. "I need a northman to represent—" She caught sight of a familiar face. "Well, this is a treat! The great General Braddick is here, folks. Who wants to see the long-time Harvest Moon champion fight?"

Braddick's mouth was set in a firm line of refusal until a loud cheer went up from the human camp. After another moment's hesitation, he removed his sword and handed it to a captain standing next to him.

Reese turned to look at Sable. "Callun and Braddick? Really?"

She patted him on the shoulder as she climbed down. "I have complete faith in you."

Victis motioned the other three attackers closer. They spoke together for a moment before spreading out to face the defenders.

Sable backed up against the tent again to watch.

Other attackers had attempted an organized assault, but this was the first group who managed to pull it off. The initial flurry of attacks was too fast for Sable to follow, but she clearly saw the fist that Thulan drove into Pardrun's cheek, sending him sprawling backwards.

That was the only part of the defense that went well.

Ignoring Leonis all together, Braddick joined Callun in attacking Reese, and they knocked him down and dragged him away from the catapult within a couple of heartbeats.

In a blur of motion on the other side, Victis tangled with Evay for a breath, then appeared behind her, one hand resting on the catapult. Almost instantly, Braddick and Callun slammed their hands down on the platform as well.

A cheer erupted from all three camps, and Innov launched into the sky at the commotion. Sable climbed back up on the catapult, clapping and waiting for the crowd to quiet.

Callun held out a hand to Reese and helped him up. Thulan did not offer the same courtesy to Pardrun, who was still lying dazed on the ground.

"Well done!" Sable called out with a broad smile. "You bested our heroes! They were already weary from many previous attacks, so it's not as impressive as it could be, but a win is a win." She handed the bread to Victis and looked back at the crowd. "I think our brave defenders have done enough. From now on, the winning team will defend the catapult for the next round. Plus, there's a new rule: Every group must have at least one human, one dwarf, and one elf." She glanced down to where Pardrun was struggling to sit up. "I believe you have a few moments before the commander of the dwarven guard is ready to defend, so make your groups."

She climbed off the catapult and moved off to the side. Reese stayed talking to Callun and Braddick, and Evay looked amused by whatever Victis was saying. Around the clearing, humans and dwarves approached each other tentatively. At Victis's signal, a dozen elves came out of the trees.

Sable watched Innov fly overhead as the crowd next to her moved closer to the catapult, leaving her alone along the tent line.

There was a tiny pop next to her.

"That went well, don't you think?" she asked Purn.

The kobold's voice came out of the air next to her. "Mistress, there's a man behind the tent. He's been watching you, and I don't like him."

Sable cast out. The tent behind her was empty, but just past it, a figure burned with heat.

"How long has he been there?"

"I noticed him before you went up to speak just now. But everyone else is moving away, and he's still here. He has a knife. Should I get Reese?"

The heat of Purn's words faded, and so did her sense of the man. "Does he look like a Tien Sark?"

"No, he's dressed like one of Lord Darien's men, and I heard him muttering about getting closer, and he has no Kalesh accent."

Sable started toward Reese, but she was blocked by the backs of a crowd of soldiers. She threaded *vitalle* toward him. "Reese!"

He looked over at her, but she could barely see him through the soldiers.

Sable pointed over her shoulder. "There's someone behind the tent," she said, sending the words to him, "and Purn thinks he's—"

Purn grabbed Sable's leg. "He's coming!"

Sable turned to see a man rush around the side of the tent, a knife in his hand, barreling toward her.

CHAPTER SIXTY-EIGHT

"PURN!" Sable yelled. "The knife!"

The blade disappeared instantly, and when the man was mid-stride, something Purnicious-sized and invisible wrapped around his legs. He stumbled forward, falling and dropping the knife handle. Reese called her name, and she almost ran, but the man's face had gone from vicious to panicked as Purn's invisible body clambered over him, drawing strands of grass over his arms and legs, twining them together and binding him to the ground. He got one leg free, but the rest of him was trapped.

Sable dropped to her knees and wrapped her hand around his neck. She didn't squeeze—she just opened a channel and began to pull *vitalle* out of him. His eyes widened in terror, and he made a choking noise.

"Why?" Sable demanded. She cut off the flow of *vitalle* so he could talk but left her hot palm on his throat.

He stared up at her and clamped his mouth shut.

"Gwen!" Sable shouted, shoving energy into the word.

Reese burst through the crowd and stopped, taking in the net of grass pinning the man's leg and arms to the ground. Some of the soldiers he'd pushed past turned to look, nudging each other at the sight.

"Are you all right?" Reese asked, kneeling down next to Sable and looking her over.

She nodded. "Thanks to Purn. Do you recognize him?"

Reese shook his head.

Now that the threat was contained, Sable's fear shifted to anger. When the man kicked his feet, she started to draw a little *vitalle* out of him again, just enough for him to feel. He froze, his eyes wide with fear.

"Don't move," she said.

Gwen pushed her way through the gathering soldiers.

Sable motioned her over. "He's not talking."

Gwen knelt down and set her hand on the man's forehead, and Sable released his neck. "His name is Dun, and he was paid by a man to kill you."

Dun's face paled, and he tried to pull away from Gwen. But she shifted to hold both sides of his head and kept him still.

"Who?" Sable asked.

Gwen shook her head. "He doesn't know his name. He's tall and pale."

"Pale?" Sable reached over and touched Gwen's shoulder, thinking of Lord Renwen. "This man?"

Gwen nodded. "That's him."

Sable looked at Reese. "Guess Renwen found out who stole his ledger —" A slice of fear cut into her. "Are there more assassins?" she asked Gwen.

Gwen closed her eyes. "He knows nothing except that he would be paid five silver for killing the Flame of the North."

"Evay!" Sable called as the elf pushed her way through the crowd. "This man was from Renwen! If he targets Kiva too, Talia's in danger!"

Evay's expression, which was already grim, grew more vicious. She raised her head and looked toward Tutella Island, focusing on something Sable couldn't see. In a breath, she disappeared.

The soldiers around her shoved themselves back from where she'd stood.

"Is this man even part of the army?" Sable asked Gwen.

She nodded. "His home was destroyed when the Kalesh came through. He feels…desperate."

Mutters ran through the soldiers gathered around them, whether more from the assassination attempt, Evay's disappearance, Gwen's mind-reading, or the fact that Dun was bound to the ground with grass, it was hard to tell.

"Purn," Sable whispered, "get to Talia and make sure she's not hurt." She felt a little squeeze on her hand, then it disappeared.

"Someone tie this man up," Braddick commanded from near the man's feet. "Who's his commanding officer?"

When no one answered, Gwen glanced up. "Captain Hyren."

Braddick looked at her suspiciously. "I want Captain Hyren brought to the island. Get this man to the prison, now!"

Leonis peered over Braddick's shoulder. "Are you feeling protective of the Flame of the North? Because that feels like a new development."

"Lord Renwen paid this man to kill Sable," Gwen said.

Braddick frowned. "Then somebody find Renwen too."

He looked at Sable as though he might ask if she was hurt, but she stood, brushing her hands off. Instead, he pointed at her. "Come to the gathering hall and give your report. Now." He strode toward Tutella Island.

A handful of soldiers crowded around the man on the ground, and Reese took Sable's arm and pulled her back. He rubbed his hands over his face. "You said you wouldn't find trouble."

"I did not," she answered. "I said you wouldn't draw your sword, which has turned out to be true."

The soldiers pulled Dun up, breaking him out of the grass net.

"Come on," Sable said to Reese. "We need to get back to Talia. Will you come with us, Gwen? If they find Renwen, they might need your help interrogating him."

Gwen nodded, but Reese set his hand on Sable's arm. "I don't think the soldiers realized before now that you and your"—he glanced at Gwen and the grass Purn had used—"friends have more impressive things you can do besides hold a phoenix."

With Dun gone, the crowd had shifted their attention to Sable and Gwen. There was an unfamiliar wariness in their expressions.

Innov chose that moment to soar down from the sky, and Sable held out her arm for her to land. The spray of embers took the edge off the mistrust from the troops but didn't banish it entirely.

Sable searched for something to say to the soldiers that explained the magic they'd just seen, but before she could, a voice called out from the crowd.

"Shows what happens to someone who tries to hurt the Flame of the North!"

Sable looked for the speaker, who sounded a lot like Leonis when he played Epophus, but she couldn't see the half-elf. Mutters of agreement ran through the soldiers.

"Shows what happens when anyone threatens the north," a dwarven voice answered from a different part of the crowd, although Sable couldn't see Thulan either. "The ground itself fights back."

That earned a few more cheers, and a soldier Sable didn't recognize threw a fist in the air. "Long live the north!" he yelled.

This was met with a round of cheers, and the words echoed through the troops.

A few "Flame of the North!" cries were sprinkled in, and at least one "Queen of the North!"

"Let's go," Sable said quietly, starting toward the nearest tent, but Leonis stepped out of the crowd and hurried over to her.

"Someone back in the crowd announced you were attacked and killed, and the rumor is spreading," he said. "Best to prove that wrong before it gets worse."

Thulan shoved her way through the soldiers as well and grabbed Sable's arm. "Up on the platform, Your Highness. Quickly. You do not want this sort of rumor getting away from us, or we'll spend the next week trying to convince the world you're alive."

Sable shook her head. "Talia could be in danger."

"She has Evay and Purn," Reese said.

"She's probably the safest person in the world right now," Leonis said, putting a hand on Sable's back and propelling her toward the catapult.

That was true, and Sable pushed her worry aside as she climbed up onto the platform. The crowd quieted around her as more and more soldiers caught sight of her. She held Innov up, casting around for something to say.

"She doesn't look dead," someone called out.

Sable offered the man a shallow bow. "That's kind of you to say. You don't look dead either." It earned her a few laughs before the crowd settled back into an expectant silence.

She tried to think of something to say about Renwen's attacker, but none of that really mattered, so she switched back to her original goal of the day and let her words spread out across everyone she could see.

She looked from the large crowd of human soldiers to the camp filled with dwarves to the knot of elves. "For most of my life, I thought *my people* only included my two sisters. The rest of the world could burn for all I cared. Until I met a half-elf and a dwarf, a famous playwright and a soldier from the north. And then I met an elf who was family before I even knew her. My world, my family, is so much bigger than I ever imagined it could be."

Victis was watching her with his usual sternness, and she smiled at him. "I am continually shocked to discover that I have things in common with those who, on the surface, seem nothing like me."

She looked over the army again. "You all know the Kalesh won't see any difference between human settlements, elven woods, or dwarven tunnels. It's time we stopped seeing the differences too." She ran a finger down Innov's chest, watching the flames dance between her feathers.

"I'm not going to lie," she continued quietly. "The army coming for us is huge and well armed, and I'm often overwhelmed by those facts."

She looked up at the troops, taking in how the different uniforms of the north were mingled together. While none of their faces looked familiar, she had spoken with enough northern soldiers to feel like they were.

"I have thought," she said slowly, "for the past few months, that it's Innov here who keeps me hopeful." She shook her head. "But looking at you all now, I realize it's you. It's the soldiers whose homes were destroyed and families were killed who are still here fighting. It's those of you whose families are still safe but unprotected because you are here. It's dwarves who left their tunnels to stand alongside humans, even after humanity almost destroyed them. It's the elves who could protect themselves and leave us all to die, but instead they see the value in all of our lives."

She took a step closer to the front of the platform. "It feels impossible to hope we can beat the Empire. But I would have thought this"—she gestured to the entire army—"was impossible too. And yet here we are. Together."

The attention of every soldier was on her, and looking at all of them, she did feel a swell of hope. "The Kalesh love dragons," she said. "If Vivaine comes north, they may have a real dragon with them, but whether they do or not, they intend to burn down the north until there's nothing left."

She ran a finger down Innov's chest again. A cascade of fire rained off the phoenix. "But you can't burn down a phoenix. You throw fire at a phoenix, and all you do is make her stronger.

"The north is changing." The heads around Sable nodded. They looked at her with confidence and a dauntlessness that she drew in, pouring it back out through her words. "We have allies, and friends, and we are burning with a fierce new fire that they can't put out.

"They think flames are for destruction, for crushing the hope and will of anyone who stands against them."

Innov beat her wings and tossed her head, and Sable raised the phoenix up a little higher.

"But we know there's a different kind of fire. There is fire that burns inside you and drives you to do things that should be impossible. Drives strangers to stand together and defend each other. It breathes life and meaning and strength into everything it touches."

Sable's words swam around the catapult, rich and warm, spreading out through the soldiers of all three armies.

"The Kalesh will try to burn us down, but we know that's not how it will work. We know that if they throw fire on the north, all they will do is make us stronger."

Murmurs of agreement rolled through the soldiers, echoed by deep, rolling hums from the dwarves. Even the elves nodded.

"Seeing all of you together gives me hope that no matter what the Kalesh throw at us, in the end, we will find the north still living. Still standing. Still burning!"

"Still burning!" someone cried.

"Still burning!" thundered back a thousand other voices.

The roar of their cheers shook the wood under her feet and startled Innov so much that she shot up into the air, making the cheers redouble.

Sable watched the phoenix spiral up until she was barely a speck in the wide blue sky. She looked back down at the soldiers, unable to keep a smile off her face. Slowly, they quieted.

There were a few knots of humans, elves, and dwarves broken into groups of four scattered throughout the crowd, and Sable looked at them questioningly. "Who's ready for a few more rounds of Capture the Catapult?"

Sable and Reese walked back into the gathering hall to find most of the lords and generals milling around the table.

Kiva caught sight of her and strode over, motioning her away from the door to an empty corner of the room.

"Talia and Ryah?" Sable asked.

"They're fine," Kiva answered, leaning his hip against a table. "The official statement on the situation is that your attacker is in a holding cell and no other attackers have been found. Lord Renwen is also missing."

"You're entirely too calm about this," Sable said. "What's the unofficial version?"

"Between you and me?" Kiva shrugged. "Yours was the second attacker. Boone caught the first breaking into the back of my house this morning." His words flared against her, hot as an open flame, and despite his casual tone, his fingers tapped on the table with barely controlled fury. "Talia was the only one home."

Sable stiffened, but Kiva shook his head, the motion twitchy. "She doesn't even know it happened. Boone removed him and got the truth out of the man before taking care of him. And then I paid Renwen a visit."

"You said Renwen was missing," Reese said.

The usual mask of unconcern Kiva wore cracked. "He is now." The words were blisteringly hot.

It wasn't the heat that made Sable draw back—it was the raw ferocity in his eyes. "You killed him."

Kiva pushed himself off the table and stepped toward her, but Reese put his hand on Kiva's chest, stopping him.

Kiva leaned against Reese's hand, keeping his eyes fixed on Sable. "Renwen sent someone after Talia, *specifically,* just to cause me pain," Kiva hissed. His hand strayed to the pocket of his vest where a small bulge shifted slowly. "I have never taken such pleasure in watching Vaya bite a man."

A drop of Vayakadyn venom in someone's food would cause a slow, painful death spread over a matter of days. A bite directly from the snake…

Once, in Dockside, she'd found a small crowd gathered near the water where the sea snakes were often found. She'd wormed her way through until she'd caught a glimpse of a man splayed out on the broken cobblestones. The old woman next to her had whispered, "Vayakadyn," as his body convulsed. Sable had hidden behind the others, unable to watch but unable to leave, covering her ears against the horrible sounds.

It had taken several agonizing minutes before the man's screaming had stopped. The telltale black tongue had lolled out of his mouth, and Sable had fled.

The bulge shifted in Kiva's pocket.

Sable set her hand on Reese's arm. "Please move away from his vest." She met Kiva's vicious look. "What did you do with the body?"

"Dumped it in the river."

She opened her mouth, wanting to point out that he'd be missed, that someone might have seen.

Kiva spoke first. "He sent a man after Talia. Don't pretend you think I overreacted." He tilted his head toward Reese. "Your dog's not upset either. The man was a threat."

Next to her, Reese didn't disagree.

Kiva backed up a step and smoothed his vest. "Renwen only hired two men," he said, his voice more even. "The one who came after you is being taken care of as we speak—unofficially, of course. But permanently. You don't have anyone else to worry about." He glanced at Reese. "Next time I warn you someone's a danger, take it seriously."

Reese studied the man. "Are you sure there's no one else?"

Kiva's lips curled into a vicious smile. "I'm sure. Now come to the table. The lords are waiting for your 'official report' about the attack." He turned and walked away.

Sable stayed where she was, watching him rejoin the others at the table.

"I know Talia is probably safer with him than anywhere else," Reese said quietly, "but still…"

Kiva greeted someone, his manner as calm and unruffled as always.

Sable shivered. "Yes. Still."

CHAPTER SIXTY-NINE

THE SOUND of Sable's and Reese's footsteps echoed quietly through the little alley as they headed toward the square, leaving the wall and the now risen sun.

"You'll be with the scouts and Durnek for the morning?" Sable asked.

Reese nodded. "The reports from last night are that the Kalesh are still three days away, which means they're close enough that I want to redistribute our rangers. Make sure the army really is simply marching north and not sending any smaller units anywhere sneaky."

The square was mostly empty, with only a few soldiers moving into or out of the gathering hall.

Reese stopped and cupped her cheeks with his hand. He kissed her with more fervor than she'd expected, and she grabbed a fistful of his shirt to help keep her balance. He pulled back just far enough to look at her. "Thank you for watching the sunrise with me."

She smiled up at him. "I believe I'm contractually obligated to do so any morning you wake me up."

He kissed her again. "Good. I'll see you at lunch." He stepped back, but she held his shirt for an extra moment before letting go.

"Lunch," she agreed.

With a parting smile, he headed for the gathering hall, and Sable looked around the square. Some motion down the main road leading out of it caught her eye. Talia and Ryah were leaving their house, and Sable called out to them.

"Excellent!" Talia said as Sable came closer. "We need extra hands."

"Yes!" Ryah said. "Come help us!"

Ryah wore a simple linen dress that looked perfectly natural on her, but surprisingly, Talia was wearing something similar. "Do what?"

"Brother Matthew needs help making batches of his honey bread." Ryah linked her arm in with Sable's and started down the street away from the square. "And since Talia worked in that bakery for Kiva, we volunteered to help, and Matthew says that he's finally found someone who's not blockheaded about dough."

They wound their way through the narrow streets of Aedis, past timber-framed houses, and Sable listened to Ryah and Talia describe the different monks they'd met and who was, in fact, blockheaded about dough. At the end of one of the streets, set up almost against the wall of the town, they entered a long, low building with multiple chimneys, each trailing a feathery line of smoke into the sky.

Inside, the air smelled of honey and yeast and warm bread. Long tables were crowded with monks kneading dough, and four large stone ovens gaped open along the back wall.

"Talia!" a monk called from across the room. "Oven three needs you!"

"That's Brother Matthew," Ryah explained, waving to the monk and drawing Sable to a table close by. Heat radiated out of the nearby oven, but it was empty.

"You realize I'm blockheaded about dough." Sable looked at the open sacks of flour and the bowl of honey on the table.

"We just do whatever Talia tells us," Ryah said, rolling up her sleeves.

Talia squatted down in front of the oven, stirring the wood burning beneath it with a poker then adding a few more split logs. She dusted off her hands and stood. "First, we need to measure out some flour."

Talia moved along the table, measuring out flour and salt into bowls without hesitation. She set Ryah and Sable to mixing a wet, sticky mess of ingredients together with wooden spoons and sprinkled more flour into the bowls as she watched their progress. Sable's arm was tired long before the shaggy mass formed into the nice ball of dough that Talia had achieved several minutes before. Sable shifted to kneading it while the conversations of her sisters ebbed and flowed around her.

Ryah's eyes were bright as she shared a story about the impoverished baker who'd sold bread to the little abbey she'd lived in for so long. "He never had access to any good flavorings. All he had were the scraps of fish he could get from the fish packing plants. Rolls wrapped around bits of fish, loaves topped with smoked fish, hard biscuits with lumps of shredded fish. Not good fish, either. Stinky, fishy fish. They were all disgusting, but Mother Perrin couldn't bring herself to say no to the man, so she bought them, and we'd spend dinner pulling the bread away from the fish and plugging our noses in an effort to not have to taste it."

"Why not just leave the bread plain?" Talia asked, laughing. She had a smudge of flour on one cheek, and Sable's fingers stopped on the dough as she remembered all the years in Dockside when Talia would return to their dingy room from the bakery, dusted with flour, her cheeks too thin and her clothes too worn.

The woman standing across the table now was so different, and yet somehow exactly the same. She'd grown taller, and she managed to stand, even in a plain dress and elbow deep in baking, like some sort of elegant woman.

"He said a true baker could create delicacies with whatever flavoring he had available." Ryah shook her head. "Proving, I suppose, that he was no true baker, because by Amah's shiny bum, it was all disgusting." Her smile was sparkling, and she let out a laugh so much like she had when she was tiny that Sable pressed her lips together, trying to keep her own smile from turning teary.

"The bread isn't going to knead itself, Sable," Talia said.

Sable looked between her two sisters and blinked.

Ryah dropped her dough and reached out for Sable's sleeve. "Are you crying? We didn't starve or anything. Just had to eat stinky fish bread."

Sable set her hand on Ryah's. "It's not the bread. I'm just…" She looked across the table at Talia. "I'm just happy to be here with both of you. I wasn't sure this day would ever happen."

Ryah wrapped one arm around Sable, giving her a squeeze. "I never doubted you would find a way to get us back together," she said, and the words were warm. Then her face sobered. "Although I admit it would be nicer if it weren't happening on the brink of a war."

Sable blew out a breath. "I agree."

Talia held up her own beautifully formed ball of dough. "You may be the Flame of the North, but you're terrible at baking. This is what you're aiming for, in case you thought that disaster you're working on is getting close," she said with a smile. "Pick up the pace, big sister. We have a lot more bread to make, and people need to eat, even on the brink of war."

CHAPTER SEVENTY

SABLE WIPED the mud off her boots on the reed mat inside the door of the gathering hall while Reese waited to do the same. The downpour of the night before had rolled past, but the sky was still cloudy. At least a dozen candles were set on the table as a few monks and several officers worked in the gloom.

"Three of the scouts haven't returned yet," Sam said, looking up from a pile of papers spread out on the table in the gathering hall. "And the ones who have say the army is still on pace to reach the narrows tonight, but not until late. We'll need to be ready for an attack in the morning."

"Which scouts aren't back yet?" Reese asked, crossing to the table.

"The scouts from the western bank won't return until this afternoon," Durnek said, "but three from the eastern patrol are late. With the amount of rain that fell last night, it could be the streams are flooded and it'll take them a while to circle around. We sent out two more to check."

Reese pulled one of the maps closer. "No one else reported anything off?"

"Not a thing," Durnek answered.

Two blue lines were drawn on the map, streams flowing from the hills to the east of the narrows down to the Black River. Reese studied the hills past them. "Do you need me this morning?"

Sam lifted his quill. "No. Why?"

Reese slid his finger to the other side of the wide river and tapped the sketch of the cliffs on the western side. "I don't know," he said slowly. "I'd like to head up this hill. Get a different vantage point of the narrows."

"What are you looking for?" Durnek asked.

"Anything we're missing," Reese answered. "Be back by this afternoon."

"Want company?" Sable asked.

"Always." He smiled at her and headed out of the hall. "Innov won't be joining us, will she? I'd like to be a little more discreet than she tends to be."

Sable glanced up into the sky. "I haven't seen Innov since yesterday. Ryah said she saw her flying along the river yesterday afternoon, but no one's seen her since."

A wide valley ran up into the hills to the west of Tutella Island, surrounded by steep slopes. "Which one are we climbing?"

He pointed to the steepest and tallest of them, a little downstream.

"I'm going to regret coming with you, aren't I?"

"No." He shot her a smile. "You're going to thank me. The view from up there is amazing."

They were barely a third of the way up the steep slope before Sable fully regretted her decision. Reese followed a game trail through the trees that moved relentlessly higher, forming switchbacks over the steepest parts.

"It's misleading that you called this a hill," she called up to Reese. "Cliff might have been more accurate. Escarpment maybe."

He flashed a smile back at her. "There's a good place to rest not far ahead."

"Not far" was also misleading, and by the time the trail wound out of the trees onto the top of a rock outcropping, Sable's legs were burning.

Reese sat on a large rock, and she dropped gratefully down next to him. The breeze came in gusts, blowing chilly swirls across her skin, which was damp with sweat.

From this height, they could see down onto Tutella Island. The southern end of the island was below them, its forests interrupted by the regimented trees of the orchard and the cleared garden with the chicken coop. At the northern end, the buildings of Aedis were surrounded by their thick wall.

Across the river, the narrows spread out like a blanket. The distinct units of the army were clearly visible, drawn in a line straight out from Aedis to the far tree line, each lord's army a patchwork of tents. Dusty trails led through the grassy flatland, worn in by the soldiers and the supply wagons moving slowly through the troops. Eight catapults stood like rickety towers along the frontlines.

"How do the catapults work?" Sable asked.

"Each one has tested well. They're planning to test them all together this afternoon."

"That's cutting things close."

He nodded. "I'm impressed they got any done at all."

"Didn't you demand twelve?"

He gave her a small smile. "They needed a goal."

Past the northern army, the dwarves were still clumped together more like spots of lichen on a rock than an organized fighting force. The only sign of the elves was the newly made trails leading uphill from the dwarves into the forest.

Reese studied the land to the south of the army, but some of it was hidden by a small rise along the river.

"We don't need to go all the way to the top," he said, "but there's another lookout higher than this."

"What are you looking for?" Sable asked.

"A sense of what the Kalesh will think of the area. I think we've predicted how they'll attack, but it never hurts to run through it again. We can—"

His attention dropped down to the slope below them, away to the right.

Sable looked in the same direction and saw nothing but trees.

"What is it?" she whispered.

He didn't answer for a moment. "I heard something."

Sable strained to hear anything beyond the chittering of squirrels and the small cheeps of the birds that flitted in the treetops. "The road south of here is guarded, right?"

"Guarded and watched," Reese said. "The trails through the hills were filled with rockslides. They're impassible."

Still, he didn't take his attention from the hillside beneath them.

"We're not about to be attacked by a bear, are we?" she whispered. She cast out, sending a ripple out around them. The only warmth she felt was trees and a few small animals, but compared to the size of the hillside, she couldn't feel particularly far.

"If it was a bear, it was far enough down the hill I'm not worried." He listened for a moment more. "Let's move higher."

The hillside did not grow less steep, and before they'd reached Reese's lookout, Sable was damp with sweat again and breathing heavily.

It wasn't an outcropping of rock this time but a smooth, flat bit of earth at the top of a short cliff. There wasn't much room between the trees and the drop-off, and Reese sat down on a patch of grass not far from the edge, his own breath coming quickly.

"If it weren't for the army and the impending war," Sable said, sitting next to him, "this would be one of the most beautiful things I've ever seen."

The breeze blew across them unimpeded, almost too chilly to be refreshing.

The narrows were now laid out like a map below them, the army perfectly visible, every rise and fall of the grassy flatland shown clearly in the mid-morning sun. Little dots that Sable knew were deer grazing far from the army moved slowly enough that they looked like statues. The near side was bordered by the river and the band of trees that crowded up against the water.

The army was set up along a rise running from Tutella Island all the way across the plain to the steep hills along the eastern side. From this high, countless hills past the narrows were visible, steep and rocky and all but impassable for a large army.

Sable pointed to the valley that wound out of view south of the narrows. "Are you sure they'll come through there?"

"The Black Hills south of here funnel anyone coming north to that point. The other paths are too steep and narrow for supply wagons and too winding for soldiers on foot to move quickly through."

He stopped and tilted his head. "I thought I heard something again." He moved to the front of the ledge, staying perfectly still and looking down into the forest. Finally, he shook his head and came back next to her. "Maybe your bear is following us."

She stared at him. "That had better be a joke."

He smiled. "Bears don't track people. The berries are ripening, and there's a decent chance a bear or two is nearby, but they want food, not you."

"That doesn't make me feel any better."

He turned his attention to the south end of the plains. Sable lay back and closed her eyes against the bright sun landing warm on her cheeks. The wind skimmed past above her, and the thin grass felt surprisingly comfortable.

Reese let out a quiet breath that sounded almost like a sigh, and she opened her eyes to find him squinting toward the trees on the far side of the narrows.

"What's wrong?"

He shook his head. "Nothing." The word was said absently.

It also had a thread of coldness in it, and she nudged him with her knee. "You don't expect me to believe that, do you?"

He glanced at her, a self-conscious smile touching his lips. "Sorry. I just…" He turned forward again.

She sat up next to him, searching the distant hills for any sign of… anything. "What's wrong?"

"Nothing important." He gestured to the narrows. "That spyglass would have been useful right now."

Sable imagined using it to look down at the narrows, wondering how much she'd see of the army from here.

Reese went back to studying the view, and Sable took in the forest around them. The rich green of the pines pushed up toward the sky, which was quickly clearing of clouds. The nearest pine had a gash in its trunk old enough that the bark had created a gnarled ridge around it, leaving the center full of honey-colored sap frozen in glittering beads and long, shimmering drops.

"He had one." Reese's voice was quiet, and Sable tried to remember what they'd been talking about.

"Vann," he added.

"Your friend in the Empire?"

He nodded. "He had a spyglass." His look grew distant, but it had a hint of amusement. "He used it exclusively for spying from rooftops, looking for ways he could cause our instructors trouble." He refocused on the narrows. "I've wanted one ever since."

Sable reached over and set her hand on his leg. "I'm sorry it's gone."

There was a little pop behind them, and Sable glanced back to find Purnicious looking oddly nervous. She held out her hand, and Sable blinked at what she was holding.

"Hi, Purn," Reese said without looking away from the narrows.

Purnicious cleared her throat. "It's polite to look at someone when you greet them, wastrel."

His brow creased in irritation as he turned. "Then maybe you should appear in front of people instead of behind—"

Purnicious's little blue hand held out the silver spyglass.

Reese paused for a moment, then faced her completely. "*You* traded Flibbet for it?"

The kobold gave the spyglass an impatient shake. "Are you going to make me hold it all day? It's heavy for its size."

He reached out and took it, the motion slow and almost wary. "What did you trade for it?" Holding it carefully, he climbed to his feet, pointing it toward the narrows.

"I'm entitled to trade or sell any of my own possessions," she said primly.

"Purn," Sable said, smiling down at her, "did you just give Reese a gift?"

"I would never do such a thing," the kobold answered blithely. "It's obviously mine, since I traded for it. But it's awkward to carry, and since he's around all the time anyway, I thought he could carry it for me. Then it will be nearby when I need it." She waved her hand at him. "It's like he's my pack mule."

"Ah," he said, slowly scanning the land below them. "How often do you intend on using this yourself?"

"Every once in a while, I'm sure," she said. "Don't lose it."

Reese pulled the spyglass away from his eye and ran his fingers over it. "This really is a nice one." He turned and set his hand on Purn's shoulder, his huge hand covering the entire short sleeve of her yellow blouse. He leaned down and kissed the top of her head. "Thank you."

She ducked her chin, and Sable caught a pleased smile. "It's not yours," she reminded him. "It's still mine."

"Then I'll just have to stay near Sable forever," he said, straightening, "so that I can carry it for you."

Purn crossed her skinny blue arms, rubbing them against the chill. "I figured that unpleasant situation was already a given." Her voice was not entirely unhappy. "So I thought I'd at least get something out of it."

He paused, studying the short-sleeved yellow shirt and bright green skirt she was wearing. The skirt had strangely shaped patches of lighter green sewn into it, and neither piece of clothing was warm enough for the chilly wind.

"Purn," he said slowly, "where's your favorite purple cloak?"

She dropped her arms to her side. "Unlike you," she said, a little crease in her brow, "I don't wear the exact same clothes every day."

He squatted down in front of her. "Did you trade your favorite purple cloak to get me a spyglass?"

She shifted.

"I'll take this moment to remind you," he said with a slight smile, "that Sable will tell me if you don't answer truthfully."

Purn gave him an irritated look. "Just look through the dumb glass, wastrel, and don't be smug." With a sniff, she popped out of sight.

CHAPTER SEVENTY-ONE

Reese pointed the spyglass toward the narrows. After a few moments, he offered it to Sable. "Look how clear it is."

She stood and held it up to her eye. The distant grassy plain leapt closer, and she swung the glass across the narrows until a grazing pair of deer filled the circle of her vision.

"This is…" One of them lifted his head, and she could make out small antlers. "Amazing." She turned her attention to Aedis, but the town looked blurry.

"You can focus by turning the front end," he said.

With a small twist of the cylinder, the little city sharpened into crisp details. A white wagon trundled in through the gate as monks walked up the road from the ferry. Sable traced the road from the gate up to the house with the bright red door. "I can see Talia's house."

Purn popped back into view. "Evay was there earlier, but she must have left. Talia and Ryah are talking about how happy they are to have met her."

"Can you always hear them?" Reese asked.

"Not like with Sable, but from this close, I can hear what's happening around them if I try. It's easier at times like now, when they're both together."

Sable handed the glass back to Reese and sat again, leaning back on her elbows. "How are you, Purn?"

"Tired." The kobold sat on the rock next to her. "I've been helping Evay make arrow fletching. They don't have to gather as many feathers if I can bellish them, and each arrow uses such a small piece it's not too hard. But we've made a lot." Purn's smile was a bit wearier than normal.

"Make sure you're getting enough rest," Sable said. "The elves can probably charm birds into giving up their feathers."

"I'll be fine," the kobold answered. "It is nice to sit for a bit, though."

Sable glanced at Reese. "Maybe it's Purn you heard below us on the mountain."

"No." He aimed the glass at the far hills. "She's been close behind you all day."

Purn's irritated huff served as a confirmation of this. "You can't hear me when I blink."

"But you don't blink often," he said, still focusing on the narrows. "You almost always walk near Sable. Why is that?"

"Blinking takes more energy." Purn paused. "Or rather, it takes the same amount of energy, but I spend it in a single step, so I often have to rest before blinking again. For days like today, when I don't know exactly where you're headed, I might end up blinking to the wrong part of the mountain, then have to blink again to get back to Sable. It's easier just to walk."

"I should have Reese teach me how to hear you," Sable said. "I never have any idea where you are."

"You're not supposed to," the kobold said, annoyed. "We're secretive, magical beings."

Reese let out an amused breath. "Maybe other kobolds are. You're as easy to track as any other creature out here." The smooth motion of the spyglass came to an abrupt halt.

Purn shot him a glare.

"I think you're secretive and magical, Purn," Sable said.

"Thank you," she answered. "Your opinion is the only one that matters."

Reese aimed the spyglass north, tracing the river, and Sable settled onto her back. Lying flat, the wind didn't bother her, and the sun was warm enough that she grew sleepy. She heard Purnicious lay down next to her.

Sable focused on the scattered bird sounds of the forest and the soothing warmth of the sun, almost keeping her thoughts from running toward the coming battle.

"Sable," Reese asked quietly. "Did Evay say the elves were spreading south in the trees?"

Sable opened her eyes, squinting into the sun. "No, but I haven't asked her."

He took a step forward, focusing on the tree line at the far side of the narrows. "There's something in those trees."

Purnicious sat up.

Sable pushed herself up as well. "Something like people or something like a herd of deer?"

He didn't answer, but the spyglass started moving again, running along the distant tree line. He drew in a sharp breath, focusing on a single point.

"Kalesh!" He scanned farther south, his hands gripping the spyglass. "So many of them in the trees."

Sable scrambled to her feet, peering across the narrows as though she could see the Kalesh. "Near the elves? How'd they get there?"

"Just now getting close to the elves." Reese swore. "That's where the missing scouts would have been."

He swung the glass to the south. The valley the Kalesh were expected in was still empty. "Purnicious! How fast can you get to Aedis?"

She looked up at him with wide, frightened eyes. "I could get there in two blinks, if I really try."

He looked down at the city. "There are monks on the wall. Tell them I sent you. Tell them there are Kalesh in the tree line to the east of the narrows. They need to warn the elves and get the army ready. Now."

Sable shook her head. "Purn, that's too far to blink."

The kobold moved to the edge and looked down. "I can do it. I'll hit the lower outcropping first, then from there to the wall is…a long distance, but I can make it."

"Hurry, Purn," Reese said, dropping the spyglass. "We'll follow as fast as we can."

Purn disappeared with a pop, and Sable moved to the edge to look down at the outcropping of rock they'd rested on below. It was so far below them Sable fought off a wave of dizziness. The kobold popped into view and staggered to the side before pausing and facing the town below her.

"Can I see that?"

Reese handed Sable the spyglass, and she pointed it toward the nearest monk on the wall. Just as she brought him into focus, the small dark form of Purnicious appeared at his feet.

The monk took a sharp step back, and Purnicious grabbed for the wall, sagging down to her knees even as she pointed up the hill at Reese, then across toward the battlefield. The monk hesitated only a moment before running toward the nearest stairs.

Purnicious sank down to sit in the middle of the walkway, her head hanging down in exhaustion. Sable handed Reese back the spyglass, and he looked through it at Purn for a moment. "She'll probably be recovered long before we get there," he said, dropping the spyglass. "She's sturdier than both of us put together. Ready to run down a mountain?"

"No." The narrows no longer looked like a beautiful grassy plain. The forest along the far side was dark and foreboding, almost as though she could see shapes in the trees. "Are there enough Kalesh there to hurt the troops?"

He didn't answer immediately. "Not terribly, but they shouldn't be that close without us knowing."

"Do you think the missing scouts are…" Reese knew all the men who went out each day. She couldn't quite bring herself to finish the question.

"They're too capable to have missed this," he said grimly, starting toward the path downhill, breaking into a jog.

She ran after him into the woods.

When they reached the lower lookout, Reese pulled out the spyglass again, searching the far trees. They'd jogged the entire way, and Sable dropped gladly down onto a rock, trying to slow her breathing.

"Can you see anything more?" she asked.

He shook his head, pointing the glass toward Aedis. "But Purn's message did some good." He followed a line from the town toward the army. "There are a lot of runners moving through the troops."

"Which means most of our friends are probably running straight toward the fighting." She closed her eyes and took in deep breaths. "I thought I didn't have to worry about Thulan and Leonis and Sam until at least tomorrow." And Serene and Jae, she added to herself.

"Any sign of Purn?" Sable asked, refusing to think of any more names, and focusing on the fact that at least Ryah and Talia would stay safe.

He turned back to where she'd been on the wall. "Yes, she's standing on the very top of the wall." He pulled his eye away from the spyglass and shifted his attention to the hillside below them. "Here."

Sable took it and found Purn standing not just on the wall but up on the parapet along the outer edge, waving her hand.

"Purn?" Sable called.

The kobold's arms stopped, and she pointed lower down the hill, agitated.

"What's wrong with the hill?"

"Sable…" Reese's voice came from closer to the edge of the rock face.

"Purn is pointing below us on the hill." Sable paused. "No, above us. I have no idea where she's pointing."

"There's something below us," he said, his voice low.

Sable looked over to see him turning slowly, scanning up the slope around them. He moved closer, taking her arm and pulling her back toward the trees.

She looked toward the wall of Aedis again. "Purn's gone!" she whispered.

There was a pop next to them and Purnicious appeared, dropping to her knees. "Kalesh!" she gasped, falling forward onto her hands. "This hillside!" She lifted one hand enough to wave in every direction. "Everywhere."

Reese leaned down and scooped her up like a child, moving toward the trees. "How many? And which direction?"

"So many," she whispered, her head sinking down onto his shoulder.

Sable cast out, and three spots of heat, hotter than the trees around them, lit up down the hill. Above them, five more blazed up, spread through the trees.

Her wave spread past them, and even though it was fading, she caught the hint of at least a dozen more. "Three below us and five above," she whispered. "And a lot more past them."

"They're all over this hillside," Purn said.

"How close?" Reese asked.

"It'll take them a few minutes to reach us," Sable answered, "if they know we're here."

He nodded. "Which way is the clearest?"

Sable pointed down to the left.

He took a step that direction, then froze.

Across the narrows, Kalesh soldiers raced out of the trees toward the troops. Even from this distance, the battle cry raised in the northern army was audible.

Reese glared down at the tiny running Kalesh soldiers who hadn't reached the army yet. "What a waste. The Empire will throw away hundreds of men for nothing more than an irritation."

"Why?" Sable asked.

In answer, a tiny bit of fire shot out of the Kalesh troops, arcing toward the catapults. It fell short, but more burning arrows took its place.

"Let's go," he said, turning back to the trees.

Purnicious let out a gasp, yanking her head up and twisting to look across the outcropping.

Reese faced the trees on the far side. "Are they here?" he whispered.

But Purn wasn't looking at the trees.

Her wide, purple eyes stared, terrified, at where the river disappeared toward the south.

She shrank down, her bony fingers clutching at Reese's shirt. "*He's* here."

The breeze dragged cold fingers across Sable's neck as a flash of silver glinted in the sky.

Dragon wings stretched over the river, light from Argyros's scales shattering the sunlight into shards of ice.

CHAPTER SEVENTY-TWO

Reese shifted Purn to one arm and raised the spyglass in his free hand.

Sable squinted at the dazzling form of Argyros. "Where's Vivaine?"

"Not riding him." Reese blinked against the brightness. He swore, looking back at the army. "They're not ready."

Even without the spyglass, Sable could see that the army camp was now full of chaotic activity. The dwarves and a band of northmen had engaged the Kalesh soldiers who'd attacked from the woods. The nearest catapult to them was smoking, but it was swarmed with northern soldiers and there was no sign of flames.

Knots of activity formed around every catapult, and other soldiers slowly formed lines, facing the grassland.

All this in response to the tiny Kalesh attack. From the army's point of view, Argyros wouldn't even be visible.

"They don't know!" Sable stepped forward until she could see the army better. "Where's Jae? They need Jae!"

"The catapults aren't ready!" Reese said.

The dragon winged closer, brushing over the trees along the river.

"Where is Vivaine?" Sable repeated, scanning the area for any sign of brightness away from Argyros.

"There!" Reese pointed the spyglass toward a shining white figure that flared to life on a small rise in the middle of the narrows.

A handful of arrows shot out from the northern army but fell far short of hitting her.

Reese gave Sable the glass, and she focused on the prioress.

Vivaine came into focus, growing brighter by the moment. Her shoulders were back, her chin raised, her face set in a look of benevolent regret.

"Vivaine!" Sable yelled, threading the sound across the huge distance between them.

Reese grabbed her arm, hissing for her to be quiet, looking through the trees around them.

The yell had been pointless anyway. Vivaine was easily ten times farther than Sable had ever pushed her voice. The prioress gave no indications she'd heard anything.

Argyros banked away from the river, soaring over Vivaine's head, aiming for the forest where the elves were stationed.

Sable swore, casting around for some way to reach the prioress.

There was nothing around them but trees.

Sable slammed her hand into the rough bark on the nearest trunk, grabbing at the energy inside it. The *vitalle* moving ponderously through the tree surged into her palm like she'd opened a valve, searing across her skin. She held the spyglass to her eye with her other hand.

"Vivaine," she hissed, fueling the thread of her words with the tree's *vitalle*. The heat focused into a narrow thread, darting through the air, away from the hillside, over the river, and slamming into the High Prioress.

Vivaine flinched and snapped her attention to the hills.

"Call him off!" Sable thrust the words at the woman.

Vivaine's face shifted out of focus and grew until it filled the spyglass. Sable dropped it and saw a dizzying tunnel of color and light around Vivaine, who now appeared merely a dozen paces away. Despite the fact her image hung in mid-air past the hillside, grass swayed around her feet.

She stared at Sable, coldly composed. "The north has been given plenty of opportunities," she said, a note of regret in her voice. "It is you who brought us to this."

"Call him off," Sable repeated. "Is this what you want? To be known as the woman who slaughtered an army who couldn't even fight back?"

A curl of disdain touched Vivaine's lips. "You always miss the real point of things until it's too late. I should expect it by now, yet somehow it's a constant source of disappointment."

Argyros neared the elves in the woods.

"Vivaine," Sable said, fear bleeding into her voice. "Please don't do this."

"We need to move," Reese said. His eyes were locked on the dragon, his breath coming fast. Purnicious buried her head in his shoulder.

But Sable's feet were rooted to the ground as Argyros reached the forest. Elves poured out, bows up, arrows hurtling toward the glittering silver dragon. Every one of them ricocheted harmlessly away.

Sable tensed for the spray of fire, but Argyros merely twisted in the air and headed down the line of the army.

The High Prioress didn't even glance at the dragon. "You've had an extraordinary amount of luck up until now, Issable."

Sable dragged her gaze back to the glowing woman.

"More than I'd expected," Vivaine continued. "But I won't allow there to be more bloodshed than is absolutely necessary. Unfortunately, you've proven time and again that spilling yours *is* necessary." Her look turned almost sorrowful. "Maybe it's a mercy that you don't see these things until they're upon you. It'll save you a few moments' pain." She raised her hand toward Sable, almost like a blessing. "When he's done here, Argyros will come quickly. You will not suffer long."

She flicked her fingers, and the image of her shrank away until she was a tiny bright shape on the grass of the narrows.

Sable stumbled a step forward, searing pain ripping across her palm as she pulled it away from the bark. She glanced down to see her entire palm burned dark red, ringed with white blisters.

On the battlefield, soldiers still scurried around the catapults, trying to ready them.

But Argyros reached them first. He blasted a spout of flame at the first one, leaving a trail of blazing lumber as he passed.

It took only a couple heartbeats for him to reach the second and set it aflame.

The ranks of the soldiers began to break and run north.

Vivaine still stood tall and straight, alone on the grass.

Sable grabbed Reese's arm with her good hand. "She's not targeting the soldiers."

Purn lifted her head and looked toward the dragon.

Reese watched Argyros for a moment, then the color drained from his face, and he swore. He grasped Sable's shoulder, spinning her towards him. "Look at me!"

His eyes bored into hers, but Argyros's scales glittered like knife blades in the sun, and she twisted her head to see him set the last of the catapults on fire.

The soldiers scattered beneath the dragon's shadow. Thousands of small figures dressed in the familiar uniforms of the north.

Each catapult was a towering bonfire, and still, Argyros didn't target the soldiers.

"Don't watch, Sable!" Reese's voice pleaded with her, even as it shook with horror and fury. He lifted a hand to her cheek, turning her face back to him. Tears stood in his eyes. "Don't watch. Look at me."

Out of the corner of her eye, Sable saw the glittering form of the dragon keep on his course.

Toward the river.

And Aedis.

Sable tore away from Reese's hand and spun toward the island.

Argyros's silver wings soared over the wall, his shadow falling over the snug timbered homes.

"Innov!" Sable screamed.

No arcing trail of light appeared.

Argyros flew low over the tiled rooftops and opened his mouth. With a sound like a raging wind, fire poured out, engulfing a cluster of houses. Lighting building after building.

Flames tore through the roofs, raking a furrow of destruction across the town. The houses directly in his path disintegrated into ash, while those alongside it exploded into flame.

Argyros spun in the air and blasted the town again, razing another line of buildings.

Sable yanked the spyglass up, searching for the red door.

A monk ran through her field of view, looking over his shoulder, racing away from flames. Smoke billowed through the air in impenetrable clouds of sooty black. House after house, each homey and familiar, seemed to hunker down as the fire blazed closer. Terrified people rushed along streets, mouths open in shouts or screams Sable couldn't hear.

Fire was everywhere. For a moment she was a child again, standing helpless in the root cellar door, watching her house go up in flames.

She blinked and another house on the island blackened with smoke. The wall burst into flame and the neat flower patch next to it shriveled.

One end of the gathering hall burned, spreading closer to the hundreds of books inside.

Sable ran the spyglass along the road leading to the red door.

It came into view, closed and shockingly unharmed.

She stared at it, willing it to open. "Talia!" she whispered.

Flames exploded across her view.

The brightness seared her eye, and she ripped the glass away to see the center of Aedis consumed in blinding fire.

"Talia!" she screamed. "Ryah!"

Purnicious buried her face in Reese's neck again. His skin was white, his eyes locked on the blazing town. Argyros turned for another attack, and Reese's expression shifted from terror to fury.

He put his hand on Sable's shoulder, pushing her toward the trees. "We need to move." The words came out hard, and his hand on her back forced her to walk forward, the image of the blazing island seared into her mind.

"Purn!" Sable's throat was so tight she could barely get the word out. "Where are they?"

The kobold was curled into a ball, her hands over her ears.

Sable staggered to a stop. "Purn!" She pulled the kobold's shoulder until she could see her face, scrunched up, soaked with tears.

Purnicious shook her head, a fast, twitchy motion. "I can't..." Her voice broke. "I can't feel them."

The words were warm with truth, but they rushed through Sable like a wave of icy water. They pooled around her, frigid and empty.

Reese braced his hand against a tree, his breath coming fast. "No one survived that, Sable." His jaw clenched. "No one."

No one. Not just Talia and Ryah.

Atticus. Leonis and Thulan. Jae and Serene—the baby.

Evay. Sam. Every single monk.

Their faces swam past her.

No. She shoved the thought away. Some of them must have run to the fighting.

The assurance sounded hollow in her own mind.

"We have to move," he said numbly. "Quietly." He headed off the path, not downhill, but along the hillside, keeping to the rocky areas between trees.

Sable kept pace with him, her legs moving on their own.

"Purn?" she whispered again.

The kobold's body shook with sobs. She lifted her head from Reese's shoulder, but her eyes were bleary with exhaustion. She let out a whimper. "They're gone. I'm sorry, mistress. I can't..." Her face creased in concentration again. She gave one last weak whimper, and her eyes glazed over. She slumped senseless against Reese.

"Sable," Reese said, his voice tightly controlled, "I need to know where the soldiers on our hill are."

Sable stopped and focused on him, taking deep, gasping breaths. Her fingernails dug into her palms, and the burns on her left hand screamed in pain. She moved to the nearest tree and pressed her left palm against the trunk, ignoring the way the bark bit into her blistered skin. The pain felt right. Fitting.

She closed her eyes and funneled the *vitalle* from the tree into her search. The heat shot out around her like a wave, washing over the towering warmth of the trees, rushing through the forest.

A constellation of blazing human shapes sprang to life on every side.

They were terrifyingly close, and her eyes snapped open. "Dozens," she said, her voice low. "All around us."

He scanned the woods. "How close?"

"The ones above us are closest, but they're in every direction."

He moved quickly to a cluster of younger pines. He pulled the limp kobold quickly off his shoulder.

"Purn!" he said. "Purn, go invisible!"

She moaned but popped out of sight.

His hands still gripped her invisible form, and he tucked her between three small tree trunks. "Find us when you're stronger," he whispered.

Brushing off his hands and standing, he looked at Sable, his breath still unsteady. There was a fury in his eyes, but his words were firm. "Any direction worse than the others?"

Sable shook her head. "They're all bad."

"Then we'll head for the one path I know." He grabbed her good hand, and she could feel his shaking.

They started to run downhill, back toward Tutella Island, and Sable cast out every minute, giving him whispered directions. They rushed around a tangle of bushes, and Reese skidded to a stop at the top of a deep rocky ravine.

Motion caught Sable's eye past the trees at the end of the gully, and she cast out, focusing her attention down the hill. Not far below them, two lines of soldiers flared warmly, marching toward the island on what must be the river road.

"The road's full," she whispered. "How are there so many Kalesh here?"

"What's around us?" he asked.

She cast out again, and figures sprang up around them in every direction. She shook her head. "They're everywhere."

"The closest?"

She pointed past the bushes they stood next to. "Coming this way." She gripped his hand. "There's no way away from them, Reese!"

He swore. "If they see us, they'll kill us."

Up ahead of them in the sky, a thick rolling river of smoke flowed away from the island on the wind. Roaring flames and human shouts filtered through the woods. The ocean of fear inside her began to shift to fury at Vivaine.

"We surrender," she said. "Tell them who we are. No common soldier's going to kill the Flame of the North or General Andreese."

"I'm not a general anymore."

"They probably don't know that. They won't kill us. They'll take us prisoner."

Reese stared at her. "Vivaine will be happy to kill us."

Sable looked back at the smoke. "Then we take her with us."

Reese swore again but started around the bushes toward the approaching Kalesh. "Stay behind me."

PART VI

This begins in darkness, and the clouds linger. They overshadow everything.

There is not hope as much as "beauty from sheer tenacity" as Flibbet would say.

But the darkness remains always at the edges.

And now is the time to ready the flames.

-Stage notes from act three, scene eight of ***The Phoenix Rising*** by Atticus the Playwright.

CHAPTER SEVENTY-THREE

THREE KALESH WALKED out of the trees ahead of them. Two archers and a more weathered older soldier wielding a sword.

Reese let go of Sable and raised both his hands.

The archers immediately raised their bows at him, but Reese said something in Kalesh, and they paused.

Unlike most of the Empire's soldiers, these didn't wear masks. The two archers were young and severe, but Reese's words seemed to cause them a little confusion.

The older soldier's face hardened, and he continued toward them.

Reese held his hands out wider. "*T'je A'Sable! Docera zabat A'Melia,*" he said, the words urgent. "*Plan z'Sevver!*" He turned his attention to the older man. "*Docera zabat A'Melia!*" Reese repeated. "*Viz'na a Jrogen, il Tien Sark.*"

All three soldiers tensed at Jrogen's name.

Past the trees, Sable heard a blazing, rushing sound as Argyros raked the island with fire again.

The older man walked up to Reese and placed his sword across Reese's neck. "*Keto'zsi?*"

"He's General Andreese," Sable said over his shoulder, fury making her words come out hot, "from the Battle of Immusmala."

Reese held the man's gaze as the soldier studied him.

"We know Jrogen," Sable said, emphasizing the name, "the Tien Sark.

And we know Zenivah." She stepped to the side, looking over Reese's outstretched arm. Ignoring his growl of warning, she glared up at the soldier. The man was so tall Sable barely came up to his thick shoulders, and the fact that she had to look up so much to meet his gaze somehow flared the last of her fear into anger. "Take me to Zenivah," she ordered, biting off each word and pouring *vitalle* into them.

The soldier's sword faltered at Reese's throat. One of the archers said something in Kalesh and lowered his bow. There was a brief argument, but eventually an archer took a long coil of rope from a small pack on his back. He took the knives out of Reese's belt and bound his wrists together.

Sable held out her hands, and the archer left a short space between her and Reese, then wrapped the rough rope around her wrists. Her burned palm scraped against her other hand, and a blister ripped open. Wetness dribbled down her fingers.

The archer picked up the other end of the rope like a leash and pulled, dragging Sable and Reese forward as he started downhill.

She caught a glimpse of the sky over the narrows, and from the thin trails of smoke, the only thing Argyros had burned there was the catapults.

A huge roaring sound came from just above them, and bursts of flames appeared through the trees across a huge stretch of the hillside. A flash of Argyros's scales flew over, and the Kalesh soldiers flinched. The swordsmen in the back snapped a command, and the man holding the rope broke into a run.

They ran all the way down the hillside until Sable's breath came in gasps, each laced with the dry taste of smoke. Behind her, she heard Reese breathing heavily too. When they reached the road along the Black River, the entire hill above them was in flames. There was no sign of Argyros.

A line of boats sat moored along the riverbank, and the soldiers shoved her and Reese into one, rowing them across the river and onto the bank on the other side.

The wind dragged the smoke from Aedis and the burning hillside south, feathering it across the sky, covering everything in a thin, rusty haze. It turned the leaves of the trees a muted green and tinged the blades of grass with brown, as though they were dying.

The smoke carried the acrid stench of death, and the ramifications to the north began to sink in.

Every Northern Lord had been on the island. Every general. With the battle only a day away, they had been closeted away in strategy meetings all day each day.

The dwarven emissary Drusty and his delegation lodged on the square.

Victis spent each day in the city, sometimes with several other elves. The elf's stern face brought to mind another one.

Evay.

Sable twisted her wrists against the ropes. The roughness scraped her skin raw, but the pain was physical and real and for a moment took her attention from the gaping emptiness inside her.

No, Evay would have gone to help with the fighting.

Most of Sable's friends would have, and she clung to the thought.

The afternoon sun poured through the smoke, and she saw again the red doorway through the spyglass, just before the flames hit it, and tried to figure out some way that Talia and Ryah hadn't been there.

Kiva had probably been there too. He'd at least been on the island. In all their time there, she hadn't known him to leave.

She'd never seen Kiva scared. Not terrified the way he must have been in his last moments. He didn't have the eyes for fear. Not the way Ryah did. His wouldn't have been wide and terrified. He wouldn't have shrunk down the way Ryah always had—

The ground shook under her feet, and she realized it was trembling from the rhythmic thrum of tens of thousands of black boots. It was like approaching a wide beach with endless roaring sounds that stretched out in every direction.

The path turned out of the trees, breaking out into the dusky light, and Sable stumbled to a stop behind the archer.

A sea of soldiers filled the valley. The soldiers trampled the grass over a low rise on the way toward the narrows.

After a quick discussion in Kalesh, their captors set a fast pace toward the front of the troops, hurrying them past row after row of marching soldiers until a large group of officers riding horses came into view. Sable searched for any sign of bright white robes. If Vivaine had joined the army, she'd stand out like a star in the night sky.

There was nothing but an unbroken sea of soldiers.

The voice of the archer leading them spoke in a groveling tone as they reached a huge grey horse. Sable looked up to see a shaved head covered in tattooed scales.

"Flame of the North," Jrogen said, his Kalesh accent roughing the edge of the words. "I did not expect to see you again."

Jrogen took the front of their leash and pulled Sable up next to his leg, dragging Reese forward as well.

"I thought Zenivah killed you today." Jrogen kept his horse moving forward and tightened the rope until she was up against his saddle. His horse's hooves dug into the dirt close to her feet.

Reese let out a growl from right behind her.

"I wonder if she knew you weren't in the city?" Jrogen said.

Sable shifted away from the horse, but the rope was too tight. "She knew."

"It looks like Vivaine took away your big fight," Reese said. "You marched all this way for nothing."

The Tien Sark raised an eyebrow. "Zenivah broke the backbone of the north today, and not a drop of Kalesh blood was spilled. It was a good day."

"Did she attack with or without your permission?" Reese's voice sounded as casual, as if he were discussing strategy with Sam. "Because I don't think you would have targeted the city. If someone handed you a dragon, you'd have wiped out the troops."

"The troops are the stronger military target," Jrogen agreed. "It's less messy to restore peace when most of the fighting men are gone. You can execute the more troublesome leaders." He glanced at Sable. "And the *zabats.* Then the rest of the people fall into line quickly to become a profitable society."

"Ah, yes. The final goal," Reese said. "A profitable society."

Jrogen studied Reese as the horse walked forward with the rest of the army, forcing Sable and Reese to stay alongside it. "You were trained at the *Trotzin Pellon* school in Empire, were you not?"

Reese paused, then nodded.

"For how long?"

"Two years, before I grew tired of the ugliness of the Empire and came back home."

"Two years and four months," Jrogen corrected him. "You scored well on assessments. Your work was not exceptional, but solid, and your record, aside from a few pranks, was spotless."

"I'm honored," Reese said slowly. "People are usually only this interested in Sable."

"Her value is merely from her mother. Yours, however, is more interesting." Jrogen studied him again. "Well trained, years of work with armies in the north and the rebels until you actually led the army at Immusmala…and yet you allowed yourself, and your precious Flame here, to be captured by a few scouts." He paused. "I find that odd, General."

"It's just captain now." Reese turned his attention to the crowd of horses in front to them. "And it's been a challenging day."

Jrogen made an unconvinced sort of noise but refocused on Sable. He reached down and grabbed her chin as he twisted her face up toward him.

She yanked away from him, but he tightened the rope, pulling her arms up until he could take hold of her wrists. He lifted her as though she were no heavier than a child. Her feet left the ground, and he dragged her up the side of his horse. He shifted back and sat her sideways in front of him. The front of his saddle had no horn, merely a ridge of leather that made her lean uncomfortably toward him.

He grasped a fistful of her hair and turned her to face him again.

Reese glared up from next to their legs, looking like he was planning how best to rip out the Tien Sark's heart.

Sable met Jrogen's gaze. His expression was ruthless. Thin lines were etched into his brow and in the aggressive set to his eyes. He was older than she'd thought. His dark eyebrows were flecked with grey.

"I saw A'Melia once," the Tien Sark said. "When I first met you in Immusmala, I didn't see the resemblance. Your face is like hers, but the Ghost was a fighter. I was with Captain Bastian's troops when he caught her. I saw her marched through the army. I even saw her riding away with that elf." He paused. "I wish a tenth of my soldiers would fight with the spirit she did."

"Maybe you shouldn't have ripped them from their homes, then," Sable said, "and forced them to fight in your endless wars."

His mouth twisted into a thin smile. "There's the fight." He glanced down at Reese. "She has A'Melia's eyes. Looks like she wants to kill me with her bare hands."

"I'd like to see that," Reese said.

The Tien Sark let go of her hair and slipped his arm around her waist, pulling her tight against him. "I heard that A'Melia died weeping and begging for her life," Jrogen said, offhandedly.

Sable turned toward him, pouring heat into her words. "You heard wrong. She stood defiant and unafraid to the end."

He considered her words. "That's hard to believe. Not many do."

She leaned closer. "Will you?"

His smile was all teeth, like a wolf. "I very much hope so. What is your relationship to the northern army? The Flame of the North I understand—merely the phoenix you stole from the south and an outgrowth of your stage presence." He glanced at the sky. "Have you lost your bird?"

"Maybe she's off blinding Argyros's other eye."

"So you don't actually control her. Zenivah didn't believe you did." He grabbed her chin again, and his fingers dug into her cheeks. There was something invasive in his eyes, something probing and gauging. "Why do you feel the need to call yourself Queen of the North when it's obviously not true?"

"Get your hand off me."

He dropped his hand, shifted his weight, and slammed his black boot into the side of Reese's face.

Reese fell to the side, landing on his knees. The rope around Sable's wrists yanked her down, and her stomach crashed into Jrogen's solid arm. The horse shifted to the side but kept walking, dragging Reese forward on his knees until he struggled to his feet.

Jrogen took hold of Sable's chin again and wrenched her head back until she looked at him. "Why do you feel the need to call yourself Queen of the North?" he repeated. "Consider carefully how you answer my questions."

CHAPTER SEVENTY-FOUR

SABLE CLENCHED her hands around the rope, letting the slicing pain in her burned palm distract her from his grip on her jaw. "I don't call myself that," she said from between clenched teeth. "I don't know where the title came from. Why do you feel the need to hurt an unarmed prisoner?"

He let go of her chin, and his hand slid down to her arm. His fingers squeezed. "Women," he said slowly, "are weak." He looked at her as though that was an answer.

Sable didn't pull her arm away. "Vivaine is a woman."

"Zenivah is one with the dragon. Any frailty she had was burned away when she joined with him." He loosened his fingers. "You, though, are not one with the phoenix." His lip curled. "I don't believe you rose out of the fire today—you were just lucky enough to not be killed by it. You are as weak as any other woman. There is no honor in hurting you. And there is no point. I can threaten the man you depend on, and you will do anything I ask."

"You are reading this so wrong," Reese said. "It's going to get you killed."

Jrogen shot his foot out toward Reese's face again, but this time Reese dodged and took the brunt of the kick on his shoulder.

The Tien Sark wrapped both arms around Sable's waist, holding the reins loosely in his hand.

Her hands were tied, but her arm was against Jrogen's chest and stomach, and her leg lay along one of his. It wouldn't be as easy as using her palms, but with this much connection…

She concentrated on where her shoulder leaned against him. So slow he wouldn't notice, she began to draw *vitalle* out of him, letting it trickle into her with the vague hint of warmth. It wouldn't kill him, but with enough time, she could weaken him. Or at least slow his kicks.

"Our scouts say you amassed an army of eight thousand humans, along with several hundred elves and dwarves," Jrogen said, his tone casual. "How close was that to the true number?"

Sable glanced down at Reese, and he gave the slightest shrug.

"Fairly close." She focused on where the side of her leg pressed against his, opening a long, thin channel. She drew *vitalle* in slowly, making sure to keep it from moving fast enough to create any heat.

"How did you convince the dwarves and elves to help?"

"I asked them," she said coldly, keeping her eyes forward. From the height of the horse, she could see ahead of the army as they slowly climbed a low rise. Past the untrampled grass ahead of them, a towering column of smoke still rose from Tutella Island, along with thinner trails from where the catapults must have stood.

He yanked her hair again, turning her head so he could see her. "You in particular?"

"Yes." She leaned closer to him, pouring the *vitalle* she was taking out of him into her words. "You're going to find that the pleasure you're taking in controlling me is not worth the price you're paying."

He let out a breath of laughter that blew in her face. "There is no price." He leaned so close his nose was almost touching hers. "You try anything against me, I will kill him."

She held his gaze. "I'll kill you back."

He smiled. "I was wrong—you're exactly like A'Melia."

He kept a fistful of her hair, and she began to draw *vitalle* out of the parts of his hand she could feel.

"I'm not sure there's enough of the north left for you to be worth anything as a bargaining chip, but your value to the Empire is…more significant. Although before I could return with you, I'd need to also find your sisters." Sable flinched, and his smile widened. "Did you think Zenivah wouldn't tell me about you? I know all about your family."

Sable's gaze flickered toward the pillar of smoke.

He followed her gaze. "Ah, perhaps I do not need to find anyone." He tightened his grip on her hair and peered into her face. "Are your sisters dead?"

Her hold on the channels between them faltered, and the *vitalle* stopped. He took in her expression for a moment before loosening his fingers and lowering his hand. "That simplifies things."

She turned away from him, blinking back tears that were equal parts anguish, fury, and exhaustion. She reopened the small streams of *vitalle* flowing between them and fed it into her hands, trying to heal the burn on her palm, and absorbed it into the aching hollowness in her chest.

They were nearing the top of the rise, and no matter where she tried to focus, the tower of smoke drew her eyes back. The rust-brown remnant of everything the island had been, peeling away from the ruins and drifting out to disappear on the wind.

Every home, every book and map and comfortable chair.

Every soul.

She scanned the sky as though she'd see the glitter of Argyros's wings.

"Where is Vivaine?" Her voice came out rough.

"Zenivah will return to us before we reach Barrowford. For now, she has responsibilities in the south. Now more than ever." Jrogen's tone was easy, but his shoulders had slumped slightly, and he straightened them.

"Her name is Vivaine." Sable turned to look at him. "Does your Emperor really need this much help to hold his position? So much that he'll risk working with a woman who would gladly take his power as her own?"

"The Emperor needs no help." The cold lie of his words cut into Sable.

She let out a short laugh. "Didn't Vivaine warn you not to lie to me?"

Jrogen's expression took on a hint of confusion.

Reese let out a breath that was almost a laugh. "Vivaine's been keeping important secrets from you."

"There are no important secrets here," Jrogen said. "You overestimate your own value and the value of your insignificant little corner of the world."

"You're here," Sable pointed out. "At the head of a larger army. We must have some importance. Unless the Emperor makes a habit of sending you to insignificant corners of the world." Sable focused on where her side touched him and opened the channel between them the slightest bit further. For a moment she felt a line of heat between her arm and his chest, and she tensed.

Jrogen stayed perfectly relaxed. "It wasn't the Emperor who called me here."

She felt a flicker of irritation at his blind devotion. "I forgot. Vivaine called you, and you leapt up to obey her command."

The words came out dripping with contempt and she regretted it instantly. Reese's attention dropped to Jrogen's foot, and he shifted away as far as the rope would allow. The Tien Sark kicked out, but the motion was slower than before, and Reese deflected it with his arm.

The muscles in Jrogen's jaw clenched, but before he could do anything else, Sable spoke.

"Do you think," she said, trying to keep her voice even, "at the end of this, she will give *you* the dragon because you obeyed her? Or are you just happy to be close to it?"

"Ah," he answered. "You misunderstand. I did not obey Zenivah. When she called, the time was right, and so I came."

Sable shook her head. "You said, 'Our job was merely to come to her when she called.'" At his raised eyebrow, she added. "I have a good memory for words. You said you came because she called you."

"I came *when* she called me. Every path has a time, a life of its own. If it is rushed, it tires itself out and dies. If it is drawn out too slow, it never grows. When Zenivah called, the path had reached the right moment."

"She's using you, just like she's using everyone else. She doesn't care about the Empire or the Emperor or anything you care about. She is after power."

"Aren't we all? The dragon is a weapon." The corner of his mouth curled up, but there was a warmth to his words that had been missing. "Or a tool. Like the gold. Like you. By midwinter, the Jaw will be vacant."

Sable glanced at Reese to see if the last words had made any sense to him.

"The highest seat in the Tien Sark," he explained.

"When I return and present the Emperor with a conquered land full of gold, the reborn Zenivah, and now A'Melia's daughter, his power will increase, the Empire will grow more stable, and I will be the undisputed successor to the Jaw."

"Is it disputed right now?" she asked.

"Only slightly. Tesok is too old and slow to have come when the time was right, despite his fervent adoration of Zenivah."

Sable looked over the army moving inexorably north, mulling over this idea. If Jrogen wasn't driven purely by fanatical devotion to Zenivah but was also after his own advancement, that changed things. Opened a crack between the Tien Sark and the mythical woman.

Characters are never driven by only one thing... She could hear Atticus say. *If you can find the secondary things that drive them, you'll find the way their hearts and paths can be changed.*

The memory of the playwright's voice squeezed around her like a vice, and for a moment she couldn't breathe. She clenched her hand around the rope, driving the rough fibers into her burned palm, letting the sharp, physical pain drive back the tightness in her throat.

"There's a fatal flaw in your plan to follow Vivaine." She forced the words out in an even tone, making herself focus on Jrogen and pointedly keeping her eyes away from the smoke. "Two, actually. First, the gold is not real."

He raised an eyebrow. "I have held the gold in my hand. I assure you it is real."

"You have held a little," Sable said, pushing the truth into her words. "But a little is all there is."

Jrogen shook his head. "Zenivah warned me you were persuasive, and she's right. I almost find myself wanting to believe you."

"The fact that Vivaine didn't tell you why I'm persuasive is more telling than anything else about this conversation. She views you purely as a tool."

He gave an amused smile. "I prefer to be thought of as a weapon. It is not only implausible that there is little gold, but it's a bit too convenient for the north for your claim to be convincing. You'll need to come up with a less obvious lie if you expect to change my mind."

"You don't understand how fierce her attachment to the truth is," Reese said. "I promise you, she wouldn't waste your time or hers on a lie. There is very little gold. I've seen the accounts of the mines. Vivaine lied to you."

"You actually expect me to believe that, don't you?" Jrogen looked between the two of them. "Interesting."

"That's not the biggest obstacle you have," Sable continued. "Your second problem is what will happen when you bring Vivaine back and the Emperor discovers she's a fraud. She created the rebirth myth to manipulate the Emperor and your entire land so she could gain power there."

Jrogen shrugged. "Myths are for the masses. She has a dragon. She can call herself whatever she wants."

"You're bringing a very dangerous woman back and offering her exactly the power she wants. I doubt she'll stop before she unseats even your great Emperor."

"I grow tired of your voice," he said. "Speak again, and Andreese will pay the price."

Sable turned away from him, and her eyes caught on the smoke. The red door flashed through her mind, surrounded by flames, and she closed her eyes against the tears that threatened to rise again. Instead, she pushed all her focus into the channels between Jrogen and herself, drawing *vitalle* slowly out of his chest, his legs, and his arms where they wrapped around her waist.

Jrogen shifted, leaning a little more heavily on her shoulder. His hands held the reins loosely.

She breathed out, and like she'd done in the woods, she cast out a little wave of awareness without speaking. Jrogen's body burst into a wall of heat next to her, no dimmer than Reese's.

She wasn't weakening him, not on any real level, but it was still utterly satisfying to take something from this man whose every action was so callously brutal.

The warmth seeped out of him, and she gathered it deep inside her, crowding out the hollow feeling that had split open today and building a knot of heat and power, growing it until it felt like a tiny fire glowing inside her.

As the army moved slowly north, she kept her mind on the growing flame and away from the smoke and the emptiness and the death.

CHAPTER SEVENTY-FIVE

THE FRONT of the Kalesh army reached the top of a rise as the sun was near setting, and a sharp, shrill whistle sounded, repeating down the long train of soldiers until the entire army ground to a halt.

The narrows stretched ahead of them. The tower of smoke rising from the walls of Aedis had separated into thick strands, and the western sun slogged through them, turning them a grimy reddish-brown.

The scar left by the northern army was clearly visible across the grass. Once straight rows of tents were disheveled and clogged with the supplies left behind. Only a few figures hurried through it. Beyond it, the grass was flattened where the army had retreated, moving out of sight to the north.

Jrogen looked over the scene, then glanced down at Reese. "The few who haven't scattered will regroup near Barrowford, don't you think?"

Before Reese could answer, the Tien Sark pushed Sable in the back, sending her sliding down the side of his saddle. Reese grabbed her arm to keep her from falling to her knees, and she stumbled against him.

Jrogen snapped out a command, and a soldier took the end of the rope. The Tien Sark dismounted, and when he reached the ground, he left his hand on his saddle for just a moment longer than necessary.

"Feeling weak?" Sable asked.

Jrogen ignored her question, and their guard, who had a row of scale tattoos visible on his neck, led Sable and Reese to a small tent set between larger ones. Three Kalesh stood outside of it, two of whom had scales tattooed on their necks. The guard dragged them inside, and another guard followed. The tent was empty except for a pair of metal shackles attached by very short chains to a metal ring hammered into the ground.

With a quick motion, the guard force Sable to her knees, cut her ropes, and locked her wrists in front of her again, this time in the cold metal. Her skin ached where the shackles pressed against her bruised wrists.

When Reese was chained next to her, one of the guards left, and the other took up a position at the flap of the tent, facing them.

"Was Jrogen's condition thanks to you?" Reese asked quietly.

She turned her hand over to show her palm, which was still blistered but much less red. "I wanted to put his energy into something besides kicking you."

He let out a quiet laugh and leaned his shoulder against her. "I appreciate that."

Sable closed her eyes and drew in a breath. As she blew it out, she pushed out a wave of warmth. Kneeling next to her, Reese flared hotly, along with the guard at the door. Outside the tent, another guard was stationed at every corner. The wave rolled farther out, and soldier after soldier appeared as pillars of heat for as far as she could sense.

"Four guards outside," she said quietly. "And about a million soldiers."

There was a commotion near the door, and their guard reached out to take two small loaves. He brought them to Sable and Reese, then resumed his post.

The crust was tough, and the inside was dusty dry. "I miss Brother Matthew's honey bread." Sable moved her legs so she could sit, but it was uncomfortable with nothing to lean on, and she lay down on her side. The ground was hard-packed dirt, and a small rock jabbed into her shoulder until she shifted.

The army camp was full of noises and voices as the soldiers settled in for the night, every word spoken in a language she didn't understand.

"We've been in better places," she said quietly.

Reese shuffled around until he was sitting facing the entrance of the tent. "A few."

"Have any brilliant escape plans?"

"Guarded by Tien Sark and surrounded by an army? No."

"Me neither." She closed her eyes and shifted again.

The knot of fire she'd taken from Jrogen had spread and faded, leaving her hollow. As thoughts of the island flooded her mind, chains clinked, and Reese's hands closed around hers.

A tear leaked out of her eyes. "They're all gone," she whispered. "What do we do?"

Reese gripped her hands. "I don't know," he whispered back, the words rough.

She held on to him as the thoughts she'd been pushing back all day washed over her, until the ground beneath her cheek was soaked with tears.

She must have fallen asleep, because the first rumble dragged her up from a nightmare of fire. The hard ground beneath her vibrated slightly with a second boom, and the canvas at the front of the tent brightened as though someone held a torch outside it.

Reese was on his feet, kept hunched down by the short chain, before Sable even sat up.

A soldier called from outside, and the guard posted with them threw open the flap. A distant yellow glow shone from somewhere deeper in the camp.

Kalesh voices shouted in all directions.

"What are they saying?" Sable asked.

Reese leaned over to try to see out the tent flap. "Some oil caught fire."

A third, louder explosion thundered through the night, and the entire front of the tent lit. Their guard stepped outside.

There was a little pop, and Purnicious appeared next to Sable. In the light now glowing through the tent canvas, her eyes were wide, and she had a boney hand pressed to her mouth to keep from laughing. "If that one was that loud," she whispered, "the next—"

A concussion slammed through the air, thrumming through Sable's chest. The ground shuddered, and Purnicious squeaked and popped out of sight. The light outside flared bright enough that it looked like the sun was rising.

"Purn?" Sable said slowly.

The kobold reappeared, hunched down, both hands covering her mouth.

"What did you do?" Reese asked.

Purn dropped her hands, and a giggle slipped out. "A few days ago,

Thulan taught me what the oil smells like that they put on flaming arrows, and I found some barrels of it. The four wagons holding them were all close together, and so I shrank a few tiny holes in the bottom of the smallest barrel. After the oil had dribbled out on the ground, I tossed a burning stick into the puddle. I thought if I just lit the smallest barrel, it would make a good distraction, and then they'd be busy trying to move the larger wagons away…" She grinned. "I guess they didn't get them away fast enough."

"Distraction from what?" Reese asked.

"Your escape! It took us some time to reach you, so there's only an hour or so until dawn. We need to hurry!"

"Who's us?" Sable asked.

Purn flashed a grin at her. "You'll need to see it to believe it."

Reese held up his shackled hands. "We have a little problem, though. You're not fast at shrinking metal."

Purn pulled a little key out of her pocket with a flourish. "That's why I stole this."

She unlocked their shackles. Outside the tent, the burning oil showed the silhouettes of their guards.

"There's an entire army out there," Reese said quietly. "How are we going to get through it?"

"Very secretively. I'll be right back." Without another word, Purn popped out of view.

Reese moved to the tent flap, peering outside while Sable listened for anything more from Purnicious. Outside the tent, the army was in an uproar.

Sable cast out. The guards who had been behind the tent had shifted around the sides to see the fire. Just as the wave faded, something alive but larger than a person moved toward her.

"Reese," she whispered.

Purnicious popped back into view, right next to Reese's legs. She grabbed his hand and drew him back from the tent flap and held up a small knife. "No one should see us if we do this right."

Reese took the knife. "We can't just walk out of here."

"No, you'll ride. Get ready." Purn popped out of view.

In the back of the tent, a small slit appeared in the canvas. Purn's blue finger poked through and dragged down until she reached the bottom. She lifted the flap to the side and motioned them out.

Sable leaned her head out. There was no guard to her right, and she could only see one shoulder of the guard at the corner to her left.

"My goodness, that's a lot of fire!" a familiar voice said loudly. "Is that from the dragon?"

Sable paused. "Is that Flibbet?" she whispered.

"Hurry!" Purn grabbed her hand and pulled her through. Sable crawled out of the tent and ran behind the wagon, keeping it between her and the guard. Reese followed a moment later.

This wagon was much, much bigger than the handcart Flibbet usually had. It had four large wheels, and posts rose from each corner, hung with thick curtains. Sable peeked through a gap in the fabric and saw a jumble of objects that she couldn't make out inside the bed of the wagon.

"Or did the elves start the fire?" Flibbet asked loudly. "I hear they're very sneaky."

The guard gave a grunt that wasn't quite an answer.

Purn ran her fingers down the rip in the tent, mending it in a breath. She glanced toward the Kalesh guard before tugging Sable and Reese around to the far side of the wagon.

Clearly carved on the side of the wagon was a banner reading "Trinkets and Treasures."

"You had time to decorate this one too?" Sable asked Purn.

The kobold shook her head and hinged open a long panel of wood. "Same cart," she whispered. Behind the panel was a hollow nook stretching from one wheel to the other. "Get in."

"What do you mean, same cart?" Sable reached in, and her fingertips just brushed a back wall.

"Sure hope that fire doesn't spread," Flibbet said amiably to the guard. "At least not to the food wagons."

"Move along," the soldier said.

Purn motioned them in.

"Don't see a better option." Reese scooted in, shifting to lie on his side and facing out. Sable shimmied in after him, backing in until she was pressed up against him. "This is cozy," he said quietly.

Purn peered in at them, then swung the panel closed with a click, and they fell into darkness.

CHAPTER SEVENTY-SIX

THE SECRET COMPARTMENT was anything but cozy as soon as Flibbet's wagon started moving. The wooden wheels creaked and jolted over the uneven ground, and the entire cart groaned like it was about to fall apart. Sable shifted her shoulder against the hard wood, trying to turn more onto her back, but the space wasn't quite long enough for her to stretch out her legs, and she ended up back on her side.

"When I said my new dream was to have a time alone with you," Reese said quietly, right behind her ear, "I was imagining something more comfortable than—" The wheel closest to their heads slammed down into some sort of rut. "This."

Past the creaks of the wagon, Sable began to hear more voices. "I think he's taking us deeper into the army."

Wherever Flibbet was taking them, the wagon jostled through a commotion of voices for what felt like an hour before it pulled to a stop. In the distance, Sable could hear bells ringing out an alarm.

"Sounds like they discovered we're gone," Reese whispered.

Loud Kalesh voices shouted near the wagon.

"Want to make a trade?" Flibbet asked cheerfully. "Oh…yes…go ahead, just…pull the curtain back…make yourself at home."

The wagon rocked slightly, and the wood above them scraped with the sound of objects being pushed aside.

"Is there's something in particular you're looking for?" Flibbet said, his voice coming from the side of the cart.

"You have people?" a Kalesh voice asked harshly.

"Ah, people," Flibbet answered. "No. I don't trade people. Not even dwarves." He chuckled. "Look here, I do have some nice water skins or a belt. I have socks too. Long marches are murder on the feet. Would you like—"

The man snapped something in Kalesh, and footsteps came alongside the panel right in front of Sable. She held her breath as things bumped and scraped across the wood above her.

Something solid like a knee knocked against the wood right by Sable's head, and she flinched. Reese's arms pulled her back.

"*Smetch,*" the Kalesh voice said, dropping something heavy in the wagon.

Sable flinched again.

"He says it's trash," Reese whispered in her ear.

"*Sess smetch,*" he repeated. "Move. You go."

"Of course, sir," Flibbet said politely. "Perhaps next time we'll strike a—"

"Go!"

"Yes, sir." The cart creaked as Flibbet climbed back up into the driver's bench. "I know," he said quietly, accompanied by the sound of him patting the cart. "I was kidding. We wouldn't really have traded with a man like that."

"Is he talking to us?" Sable whispered.

Reese was saved from answering by the cart rolling ahead again, filling the air around them with squeaks and groans.

Eventually, Sable could see a little daylight through a crack near her feet. The sounds from the army were all on the far side of the cart now, and Flibbet started to whistle a jaunty tune as he turned sharply and bounced down a steep slope.

They jounced on the rough ground for long, painful minutes before he finally pulled the wagon to a stop. The sounds of the army were muted by a closer sound. The rushing of the river.

They sat silently for a few moments. Finally, the wagon creaked as Flibbet climbed down. His footsteps came over to the panel, and he swung it open. Sable blinked into the morning brightness, taking in the peddler's wide smile as he squatted next to the compartment. "This is more fun than I've had in years!"

Sable stared at him. "Fun?"

"Well, excitement at least, if not fun."

"Is it safe to get out?" Reese asked.

"Oh, yes! Come out, come out! I'm sure you need a stretch." He offered Sable a hand.

The wagon was parked along the edge of the Black River next to a rowboat. The riverbank rose above them, the dense forest broken only by a steep, thin trail. Beyond the trees, Sable could hear noises of the army preparing to march.

As she watched, the trail coming down from the army closed up, the thorny brambles on either side stretching to cover it. The little form of Purnicious appeared next to the bush closest to the wagon, and at her touch, branches grew across the path. When it was covered, Purn sank down to her knees.

Sable squatted next to her, setting her hand on the kobold's shoulder. Purn tried to smile at her, but her face was drawn with exhaustion. "There's no other path down here," she said tiredly. "We should be safe for a bit."

"Are you all right?" Sable asked.

The kobold nodded. "Just tired."

"How did you get here?" Reese asked Flibbet.

Sable glanced at the peddler. "I thought you were on the island with —" She stopped before she had to list any names.

"Our warning worked," Purnicious said quietly, "at least a little bit. With the news that Reese had seen Kalesh archers, people left the island to try to help. When I woke up and knew you'd been captured, I went to see who could help. The army was fleeing north, but I found Atticus, Thulan, and Leonis attempting to direct people to Barrowford."

Sable breathed out. "All safe?"

Purn nodded. "Jae, Serene, Gwen, Terrane, and Evay were there too. Serene and Terrane put out the fires on the catapults."

Sable stared at her. "*All* of them are safe?"

Purn nodded, but she hunched down a little lower, and tears filled her eyes.

Sable gripped her shoulder. "Talia and Ryah?"

Purnicious shook her head. "I keep trying, but…" She swallowed. "I think if they'd survived long and suffered at all, I would have felt it," she whispered. "It must have been quick."

Sable sank back onto the ground, pressing her hands to her face. The thought of their last moments washed over her. Their house hadn't been the first one hit, and the noise of Argyros's attack had been thunderous, even from the hillside.

They would have known what was coming. She drew in a gasping breath, her chest clenching at the terror they must have felt.

The memory rushed in from long ago: her sisters, young and paralyzed with fear, clinging to each other in the doorway of the root cellar as the only home they'd ever known burned to the ground.

The helplessness of that night flooded into Sable. She'd been powerless to do anything but watch the fire, watch the Kalesh kill her parents.

She dropped her head, and her fingers raked into her hair, clutching fistfuls of it, sending sharp pain across her scalp as tears flooded her eyes.

Argyros's fire had gutted Aedis, and the only hope Sable could find was that Talia and Ryah had been able to cling to each other at the end.

Reese's knees hit the ground next to her, and his arm wrapped around her. The feel of him breaking the grip of her thoughts, giving her space to draw in another gasping breath. She curled forward, and a sob wracked her body.

Purn's small hand came to rest on Sable's back, and that tiny gesture opened the hollowness inside her, and the tears came pouring out.

"Some of the monks survived," Sable heard Purn say quietly to Reese in a quavering voice. "They think about half. A good number of them had given up their houses for the different delegations, so they were living with the army. Sam and Durnek were with the troops too."

"Who didn't make it?" Reese asked.

Purnicious sighed. "No one's seen any of the Northern Lords or the dwarven delegation." She paused. "Or Victis."

Sable's head dropped further.

"The elves didn't take that well," Purn continued. "Sam asked if they'd regroup with the north at Barrowford, but they wouldn't answer."

"The dwarves?" Reese asked.

"Callun said they're going to Barrowford. Others were angry about that, but Callun told Atticus it would be fine, whatever that means."

Sable looked up, rubbing her hands across her face.

Flibbet gave her a sorrowful look. "I'm so sorry, my dear, but we should get across the—" He stopped, looking at the tiny rowboat, then back to his large wagon. "Ah, I guess maybe not quite yet." The wagon creaked, and Flibbet reached inside and pulled out a bundle. He came over and unwrapped it on the ground, revealing a few small loaves of bread and some apples.

"Thank you," Sable managed. It didn't feel quite like her own hand reaching out and picking up a loaf. She had it almost to her mouth when she smelled the honey. Her hand froze, and she blinked away the sight of Brother Matthew's bakery. Her stomach turned, and she dropped her hand to her lap.

Reese shifted to sit next to her and took an apple. "Thank you for coming for us," he said to Flibbet. "How did…" He looked up at the wagon. "How did you know we'd need that?"

Flibbet's eyes sparkled. "I woke up yesterday morning, and the cart was…" He gestured to the wagon next to them. "Do you have any idea how long it's been since it changed size? Decades!"

The oddness of the question wiggled its way into Sable's mind, and she glanced at Reese, who looked like he was at a loss of what to say.

"Your cart changed size?" he asked. "And found a horse?"

"Yes! But why? I had no idea. And then it wanted to leave the island. At first I thought we were just going to visit the soldiers, and maybe one of them had something really big to trade, but, when we crossed the river, it pulled me south."

"The cart did?" Sable asked, trying to follow the conversation.

"The cart did!" Flibbet let out a chuckle at her skepticism. "Normally, I would pretend it was something else, but at this point, any doubt that I had that the cart fully supports you is long gone. Look at it!"

Reese's expression mirrored Sable's thoughts about the little peddler's sanity.

"I admit I was angry." Flibbet patted the side of the wagon, and it let out a little squeak that almost sounded smug. "We were headed straight for the Kalesh army, after all. And then…" His smile faded. "When the dragon came, and Aedis was destroyed, I thought maybe it had just saved me and left all those people…" He sighed. "But that wasn't true either. Once Purnicious found me, I knew the cart was just headed for you the whole time. So I played peddler in the Kalesh army until we found you."

Sable stared at him. "The cart?"

Flibbet waved his hand in a dramatic fashion toward the words Purnicious had carved onto his little hand cart, which were duplicated perfectly here. "The cart."

Sable and Reese both turned to Purn, who shrugged. "I don't know what's happening, but that is exactly what I carved on his little handcart."

"Regardless," Flibbet said, rubbing his hands together, "the cart brought us together, and now we can head back north." His gaze caught on the rowboat again. "Maybe if we don't look at it, it will change back to a handcart," he said uncertainly.

"Did you leave this boat here?" Sable asked.

Flibbet shook his head.

"Well, whoever left it, we're going to use it," Reese said.

Sable took a deep breath and glanced across the wide, smooth water. "As of yesterday, there were a lot of Kalesh over there."

"I can find paths around them," Reese said. "We can move fast. I think we can reach Barrowford in six days. It'll take the Kalesh army at least ten."

"But then what?" Sable said, the hollowness inside her creeping up again. "Wait for Vivaine to burn Barrowford to the ground too?"

"I guess the answer to that depends on how much of the army is still together," Reese said quietly. "If the lords and most of the generals were on the island, the troops who make it to Barrowford will be unorganized and leaderless."

Sable set the bread back down and picked up an apple. "Jrogen said Vivaine went back south. I'd guess she'll stay there until whenever the next battle is happening. She can't afford to leave Eugessa there alone. Not with the open enmity between them now."

Flibbet looked up from selecting his own piece of bread. "You didn't hear?" He scratched uncomfortably at his blond beard. "Eugessa's unicorn disappeared, then she got sick. Vivaine declared it was heartache from the unicorn leaving her, but...an official raven came from the Sanctuary yesterday morning. Eugessa's dead."

Sable stopped with the apple halfway to her mouth. "Vivaine killed her?"

Flibbet shifted. "That's what I thought, but Rabbit says that when Eugessa died, her tongue was black."

"*Kiva* killed her?" Reese glanced at Sable. "Or Vivaine wants us to think he did. Maybe she used vayakadyn venom on Eugessa just like she did on Tanis."

She shook her head. "Kiva had no reason to kill Tanis, but he's wanted to kill Eugessa for…his whole life." She glanced at Flibbet. "She cared for his parents when they were dying, and after they were gone, Eugessa took all their possessions and turned Kiva out onto the streets." She paused. "She stole a ring from his mother, a butterfly with blue stones on it.

Stealing that back for him was the price he set on Talia's freedom." She swallowed. "Way back when he first got his claws in her." She blew out a breath and blinked back tears. "He's worked with Eugessa for years, but I always thought he was just biding his time."

Flibbet tilted his head curiously. "A butterfly ring?"

"A silver butterfly ring," Sable said. "It wasn't even high quality. But Eugessa thought it was a gift from Amah for her generosity in caring for the dying, and Kiva thought it was his birthright that she'd stolen." She rolled the apple between her hands. "Kiva just lost everything tying him to Immusmala. No matter what happens, he's not going back. Shall we guess what he was planning when he sent ravens south in the middle of the night?"

Reese tapped a finger on his loaf of bread. "Of course, no matter who killed Eugessa, the result is the same. Vivaine is now the only prioress. She has complete control of the south. If she uses Argyros in battle again, the north will surrender, too."

The fabric that the food lay on was a faded blue with a patch of slightly darker blue peeking out from under the apples. The color was close enough she might not have noticed, except the seam between the two was unraveling. Sable set her apple down and ran her fingers over the frayed edges of the fabric. "It always comes back to Vivaine. She's always the thread holding everything together."

"*Please* don't say you want to go talk to her," Reese said.

"Not this time, but…" She pushed bread and apples out of the way to look at the seam. "'If you create the right story, you can rule the world.'" She looked up to find both Flibbet and Reese waiting for her to continue. "That's what Vivaine told me when she was on trial.

"It's taken her years of hard work to patch all these lies together and do it subtly enough that she ended up with a plausible story. Yet…" She pulled the two pieces of fabric apart gently, and the hole widened along the seam. "Lies always unravel."

She sat back. "What if we helped it unravel faster? What if we could convince the Kalesh that she lied to them both about the gold and about who Zenivah was?"

"That would change things," Reese said. "But you told Jrogen, and he wasn't convinced. If *you* can't change someone's mind, I don't know anyone who can."

"Jrogen is going to be a challenge, but he was right about one thing. He said myths are for the masses." Sable smiled, and it had a savage edge.

"So we give the truth about the Zenivah myth to the masses. We let them discover how she's trying to manipulate the Empire."

"In the next ten days?"

"The beautiful thing about spreading a true story," Sable said, "is that it takes no preparation. You just tell it without worry that it will hold up to scrutiny or match up to other stories. It's the truth. Once they find out she's actually trying to manipulate the Empire and dragged them here for her own pursuit of power, the truth of Zenivah will spread like wildfire."

"That sounds nice," Reese said, "in the way Atticus's plans always sound nice, but how do we go about spreading the story among the Kalesh troops?"

"Ah!" Flibbet turned toward the wagon. "This is why you're still big."

Sable exchanged glances with Reese.

The peddler nodded. "And why I have five copies..." He looked meaningfully at Sable and held up his hand with his fingers spread. "Five!"

"Copies of what?" Sable asked.

"The original story with the wildcat," Flibbet said. "Serene was trying to figure out how to distribute them." He grimaced. "I think we found it."

"You'll give them to the Kalesh soldiers?" Reese asked.

"The right soldiers," Sable clarified. "Ones who will talk to everyone about what they say."

"Yes, yes." Flibbet started tying the bundle of bread and apples back up. "The cart will get them into the right hands." He stood, handed Sable the bundle, and pushed the curtain aside on his wagon. Leaning into it, he started rummaging through the jumble of wares. "If you're headed off without me, you'll need—ooh, look! A pack with some blankets and a waterskin and—" He stopped, focusing on the side of the cart where he'd been leaning. Lifting up the pack, he backed away from the wagon, waiting expectantly. The wagon sat perfectly still and quiet. "I was going to give it to them freely anyway," he said with a petulant tone before handing the pack to Reese. "Is there anything else you need?"

"No, this is great."

Flibbet sank back against the wagon, looking wistfully at the pack.

"Are you sure you're willing to go back into the Kalesh army?" Sable asked him.

"Oh, I don't mind that. Plenty of fine people in that army, like everywhere else. Just..." The peddler gave them a plaintive look. "Just don't do anything too exciting until I get back to you. Don't win the war. Or tame

Vivaine's dragon. Or whatever it is you have in store for the ending, all right?"

Sable raised an eyebrow. "I don't have any of that in store."

He pushed away from the wagon, and it let out a long, chirpy creak. Flibbet chuckled and patted the wagon. "I couldn't have said it better myself." He climbed up onto the driver's bench. "Purnicious, dear, could you clear those bushes back out of my way? We have Kalesh hearts to change!"

Purn popped over to the bushes and started to shrink the branches until Flibbet's wagon had enough room to pass.

"Thank you," he said to her, then pointed at Sable and Reese. "Nothing big until I get back!" Without waiting for an answer, he urged the horse up the riverbank and back toward the Kalesh army.

CHAPTER SEVENTY-SEVEN

"SAY Flibbet can actually spread the story throughout the Kalesh army," Reese said, reaching his hand down from the next rock ledge. "That's only going to change the way the common soldiers see Vivaine. It's not going to convince anyone like Jrogen."

Sable grabbed his hand and climbed up next to him, pausing to catch her breath. Their trail, which would more correctly be called a steep ravine, was cut deeply into the hillside and so overshadowed with trees that Sable couldn't see anything outside of it. It felt good to climb, though. To move. To burn up some of the tangled mess inside of her with action.

"I agree," she said. "Jrogen's different. But he's not only here for Vivaine."

Reese started up again, working his way up what must sometimes be a stream bed. "No, he's here to do something impressive enough that he earns the Jaw."

"Exactly. It's the secondary thing that drives him that Atticus talks about. We can't affect whatever devotion he has for Vivaine and her dragon, but he needs something pivotal to take back to the Empire to earn him that seat. So, let's think about the things he wants. First, Vivaine. If he can return the fabled Zenivah to the Emperor, that makes him look good. The solution to that is to convince Jrogen that what he needs to take back to the Emperor is the truth that Vivaine was trying to manipulate them all. Jrogen helps the Emperor save face, and he looks good."

Reese paused, looking along the side of the ravine. "Somewhere around here…"

Purnicious popped into view perched on top of a large boulder just above him. "Are you looking for a teensy, rough trail that looks incredibly slow to travel along, but not nearly as slow as this ravine? Because there's one just past this rock."

"I'm looking for paths that are guaranteed to not have Kalesh soldiers meandering down them." Reese climbed up and looked past the boulder. "And yes, this is it. If we keep moving, we should get to sleep near the Greenwood tonight."

Sable followed him through a narrow gap next to the rock and found a game trail winding into the woods. It was narrow enough that they'd have to walk single file, but the trail meandered peacefully between the pine trees, and if she disregarded the fact that there might be Kalesh soldiers somewhere on this hillside, it was really quite beautiful.

"Ayda never did bring any elves to Tutella," she said, "but maybe that's for the best. One less group that Vivaine hurt."

"Speaking of Vivaine," Reese said, starting down the trail, "how are we going to prove to Jrogen that she made up the myth?"

"I think she'll have to admit it herself."

Reese stopped and turned around. "You're going to get Vivaine to admit that?"

"Can you think of anyone else he'd believe it from?"

"That's not what I asked."

Sable looked through the trees, the beginnings of her plan still nebulous enough she couldn't quite see the answers. "It'd have to be approached just right, but…it's not out of the question."

"If anyone can do it," Purnicious said, popping into view on a low branch ahead of Reese, "it's you, mistress."

Reese began down the trail again. "I agree, but Jrogen is here for more than Vivaine."

"True," Sable agreed. "The second thing he wants, which is really tied in with the first, is Argyros. Even if we can prove Vivaine isn't Zenivah, she still controls a dragon, which is all Jrogen cares about. So, we need to show him that she doesn't really control the dragon."

"But does she?" Reese asked.

Sable stepped over a large root crossing the path. "I don't think so, not completely. After the trial, when Argyros landed next to Vivaine, she looked relieved. I thought, at first, it was because she'd missed him. But…

if I hadn't seen Purnicious in a fortnight, I wouldn't have just stood there calmly. Even if I was in the middle of a dramatic production, like Vivaine, I wouldn't have been able to hide my happiness that she was back. Vivaine seemed…merely relieved that everything was going well."

Purn shrugged. "I'm far more likable than that horrid dragon."

"You are," Sable said, "but I used to think Vivaine felt as fondly of Argyros as I do of you. I'm not sure that's true. Or if it is, it's buried under other complicated things, like her fear that he's not hers any longer."

Purnicious looked thoughtfully down at them. "That's…a little bit sad."

"I was going to say that made more sense than the fondness," Reese said.

"Regardless," Sable answered, "the bond between them feels fragile. I think, if Argyros felt Vivaine was trying to control him, it might fall apart. If Talia is right—" Her voice caught, and she swallowed before she continued. "If Talia was right, and Argyros wants freedom, I don't think he'd join the Kalesh. I think he'd leave."

"There was a lot of 'I thinks' in there," Reese said quietly. "And no matter how fragile the relationship between him and Vivaine is, he did come back for her at the trial."

"I know. But if Vivaine could be pushed to the point where she showed her hand, where she had to blatantly admit that she's using him for the power he offers…"

Reese stopped walking again. "Does every idea you have involve Vivaine admitting what she's been doing? Publicly?"

"On stage, if I can manage it." Sable gave him a self-conscious smile. "I haven't mentioned that she needs to admit she lied about the gold."

He crossed his arms. "You realize this sounds less plausible than most of Atticus's plans?"

Her smile widened. "Yes. He's going to be proud of me for thinking of it." She looked up at Purn. "Speaking of Atticus. If he and the others are going north with the rest of the army, they're probably a day ahead of us. Could you catch up with him?"

The kobold nodded. "I could reach him tomorrow."

"Perfect. He should know what Flibbet is doing and what I want to do. We'll meet up with him in Barrowford, but he likes to have time to prepare for things like this."

"And he might like to know we're no longer Kalesh prisoners," Reese noted.

"Right," Sable said. "That too."

Purnicious looked at Reese. "Is there anywhere nearby with a view? If I'm going to blink, I'll need to see where I'm going."

Reese nodded. "Not too far ahead."

"That means we have a long time," Sable said. "Walk with me, Purn, and I'll tell you everything I want you to tell Atticus."

Purn blinked over to Sable's side.

"You haven't brought up the most troubling thing about Jrogen," Reese said, still standing in the path with his arms crossed. "If he wants something to impress the Emperor and you take away the gold, Vivaine, and the dragon, he has only one thing left. You."

Purn reached up her bony blue hand and took Sable's.

"I know," Sable said slowly. "And that's the part I don't have an answer for yet." She glanced down at Purnicious. "Maybe Atticus will."

At least an hour later, they reached the base of a rock outcropping taller than the pines around it.

"From the top of that," Reese said to Purn, "you can see a very long way."

Purn craned her neck up and nodded. "Be careful while I'm gone, mistress."

"I will, Purn." Sable knelt down next to her and hugged her. "You be careful too."

The kobold stepped back and squinted up at Reese expectantly.

"You're waiting for a hug from me too?" He didn't sound totally displeased and knelt down. Her hands reached up, but instead of hugging him, she ran her fingers along the collar of his shirt and the shoulders, shifting the fabric. He let out an annoyed hum but didn't move as she swiped her hands down the sides of his beard as well, trimming up the edges.

"My mistress has no one to look at for days besides you." She inspected him and sighed. "I suppose that's the best I can do."

He flicked the end of her nose. "Get out of here, you little blue monster."

She grinned up at him. "You're welcome, and I'll miss you too." With a pop, she disappeared. Sable caught a glimpse of her on the top of the rocks before she blinked out of sight again.

Reese stood and looked at the rocks for a moment before he tilted his head.

Sable was starting to push herself up when he said, "Do you hear that?"

She froze. The breeze rustled through the trees and some little bird was pecking on some tree trunk nearby, but she heard nothing else.

She cast out, but aside from the warmth of Reese and the more subtle heat of the trees, she felt nothing,

He held out a hand and pulled her up. Slipping a hand around her back, he leaned close to her. "That is the sound," he whispered, "of you and me. Finally alone."

That afternoon, Reese paused on the trail, taking his bearings. He reached out and took Sable's hand, leading her off the trail. In a few moments they reached an opening in the trees, looking down over the hillside.

There below them was Aedis. Or what remained of it.

There was nothing inside the walls but blackened rubble and smoking piles of ash. Not even skeletons of beams or walls.

Sable's eyes traced the devastation. Faintly lighter paths marked where the cobblestone roads wound through the ash, but the house they'd stayed in on the square was gone. The great hall. Narine's house. Brother Matthew's bakery. Every timber framed building, and patch of flowers, and lamppost for the nightly torches. Every single thing, gone.

She searched for where the house with the red door would have stood, but it was impossible to pick out which lump of charred cinders was the right one. There was no red. No color of any kind but black char and white ash. Even the inside of the town wall itself was stained black.

Reese gripped her hand tightly, and he drew in a breath that shook slightly. "The town…it feels almost like another person Vivaine killed. I…I really thought we might settle there for a little while, once this was over."

Sable nodded. "It feels like another person lost. All the homes and the hall —" She turned to look at Reese. "All the books." Loss and anger warred inside Sable, and she clenched Reese's hand. "Vivaine has so much to answer for."

He nodded grimly and led the way back into the woods.

"Sable…" Reese's voice dragged her up from a deep sleep.

She opened her eyes, but the forest around them was still black. This close to the Greenwood, the trunks were wide, dark towers rising into the night. "It cannot be close to sunrise."

"No," he said, sitting up, "but you want to see this."

A bit of golden light lit the sides of the trunks near her.

"Innov?" She lifted her head to see the glittering form of Innov alighting on a branch a little way into the forest. A wave of relief rolled over her just at the sight of the bird. "She's back," she whispered. The phoenix didn't move any closer though. "What is she doing?"

"Waiting for him, I think."

A shadow moved behind Innov. A big shadow. It stepped closer to Innov, and light glinted off a sharp spiral horn.

Sable sat up, wrapping her blanket around her against the chilly night air. "Is that Cernus?" she whispered.

"Unless you know of another black unicorn."

Sable climbed to her feet, keeping the blanket around her shoulders. Innov flew to a tree at the edge of the small clearing, and Cernus followed, slowly. He stopped under Innov's branch, her warm light highlighting the curve of his shoulders and catching in strands of his dark mane.

"Hello, Cernus," Sable said cautiously.

The unicorn gave no indication that he'd heard her.

"Innov," she said, "if there's something you want here, you're going to have to be a bit more direct than usual, because…"

Cernus dropped his head down and tore a tuft of grass from the ground.

Innov flapped her wings, letting out a shower of sparks that rolled down his shoulders and neck until they bounced across the forest floor. She took off and flew to the tree closest to Sable, landing on a low branch. Shifting her wings a bit, she nestled herself comfortably down to sleep.

Sable moved over next to the phoenix, running her fingers down the bird's neck. "Where were you?" she whispered.

Innov looked at her with her round orange eyes but did nothing more than lean slightly into Sable's hand, pushing a bit of warmth and comfort into her.

"I wish," Sable began, but the words caught in her throat. She swallowed. There was no point in wishing things were different. "I'm glad you're back," she said honestly.

Cernus continued to nose around the tree, grazing as though he was perfectly at home.

Reese considered the unicorn, then the phoenix. "If Innov is unconcerned, I guess I am too." He lay back down, patting the ground next to him. "You should get more sleep. I'll be waking you up to see the sunrise soon enough that you're going to be cranky about it."

Sable sat by him but kept watching Cernus. There was something about the creature that was different than when she'd always seen him with Eugessa. Something less severe.

Reese pulled on her arm until she sank down next to him. "First a kobold, then a phoenix, now a unicorn." He wrapped an arm around her. "Maybe you *are* going to tame Vivaine's dragon."

It felt like only moments later when Reese jolted up. Sable's eyes flew open as he rolled to his feet, drawing his knife and holding it out toward a figure standing only a few paces away in the darkness.

"Do you think that would stop an elf who wanted to hurt you?" Ayda's voice said curiously.

Reese swore and lowered the knife. "What are you doing sneaking up on us in the middle of the night?"

"I wasn't sneaking up on you. The trees were talking about a unicorn and a phoenix." She paused. "Where did you find a unicorn as broken as this one?"

Ayda stood like a sliver of pale yellow in the darkness. Her dress was long and very subtly golden, and strands of her hair reflected a bit of Innov's firelight.

"Is he broken?" Sable asked, the echo of Ryah's words catching her off guard.

"Corrupted, maybe," the elf mused. "There's something wrong with him."

Cernus watched Ayda from the far edge of the clearing but made no move to come closer.

"He's from the priories in Immusmala," Sable said. "The same place Innov is from, and the dragon."

Ayda sat, curling her legs beneath her, and Innov flew down next to the elf. "I saw what the dragon did to your island. It was…wrong." She reached out gently to touch Innov's neck. "My father did not listen to me about sending warriors to help you. In fact, not a single elf listened to me, except my brother, who was no better than I at convincing anyone that the Kalesh are worth fighting. But I suppose, in the end, it didn't matter." She tilted her head. "Where are you going now?"

"Back to Barrowford," Sable said, lying back down and pulling up her blanket. "Vivaine and the dragon and the Kalesh are headed there, and… we're trying to come up with some ending that isn't the north being totally overrun."

Ayda beamed at her. "I'll come help!"

Reese dropped back down. "Great, we'll leave in the morning. After we get whatever sleep there is left to get. If anyone else shows up, just tell them to be quiet and we'll greet them in the morning."

"He doesn't sound excited," Ayda said to Innov. "He'll be more grateful when we befriend that dragon and end the fighting, won't he?"

Innov shifted her wings and pushed her neck against Ayda's fingers.

"Well," Reese said quietly, keeping an arm around Sable. "I guess a day to ourselves was better than none."

CHAPTER SEVENTY-EIGHT

AHEAD IN THE WOODS, Ayda chattered to Innov, who occupied her new perch on the elf's arm, and occasionally directed a question at Cernus, who walked next to her through the woods. In the five days they'd traveled together, neither creature had ever seemed to answer her, but Ayda kept up a constant flow of words anyway. The forest was red with the evening's glow, and Innov's light grew more pronounced as the shadows lengthened.

"Will we reach Barrowford before it's completely dark?" Sable asked Reese.

"We should." He looked through the trees at the quiet forest. "I know there's an army coming and a crazed woman with a dragon, but...we could forget all that and just stay in the woods. I'm fairly certain I could make us some sort of house. It might have a leaky roof and drafty walls, but it could be worth it."

Sable linked her arm into his. "Don't tempt me."

"I can fix a leaky roof," Purnicious said, appearing with a pop not far in front of them. "Or anything else he does shoddy work on."

"Back so soon, Purn?" Reese asked.

"It's been six days, wastrel." Purnicious moved to the side and fell in next to Sable.

"Hi, Purnicious," Sable said, resting a hand on the kobold's black curls.

"Atticus and the others are camped near Barrowford's gate." Purnicious gave Ayda a friendly wave. "It's not far ahead. Cernus looks...better."

"He does," Sable answered. "He seems less vicious than he used to be. Actually, he acts like a normal horse."

A patch of orange clouds was visible ahead of them, and before long, they came to the edge of the forest. The sun was behind the hills, but the clouds above were brilliantly lit and the world around them tainted a rosy gold. Ahead, a few torches flickered along the walls of Barrowford, and in the flat grassy stretch between the forest and the city lay an army camp full of bustling activity.

Just to their left, the steep sides of the barrow rose, its mostly flat top sitting at the height of the tall forest pines behind them. Innov took off from Ayda's arm and flew toward it. Cernus, after a moment's hesitation, started up a small game trail scratched into the hillside.

"I want to see what's up there," Sable said.

"I was hoping you'd say that," Reese said, starting up it. "What's happening with the army, Purn?"

"Braddick is still in charge," she answered. "All of the Northern Lords are dead, and none of their heirs are old enough or capable enough to lead, so the army has just started listening to Braddick for everything."

"How many soldiers made it up here?" he asked.

"About four thousand," Purn said. "Atticus says the rest probably returned home after they saw the dragon."

"Can't blame them," Reese said, "but four thousand isn't much against the twenty-five thousand Kalesh coming."

Most of the slope was just steep and rocky, and they quickly made their way to the flat top of the barrow. Tall grass brushed against their shins as they stopped to take in the view. The clouds had faded to a light, wispy blue, and the world around them was growing darker. Not far off, near the center of the barrow, the huge rocks of an old ruin stood jumbled on the ground. Innov perched on one of the larger rocks, and as Sable drew closer, she could see a large hole beneath.

"I heard people telling Atticus that this hill is the burial ground of a great man," Purnicious said. "He and his wife fought off monsters, and when they died, they were buried here and the hill raised above them. This was supposed to be a monument to their greatness. The bodies of the slain beasts were said to be buried with them, and people say the barrow is haunted by their spirits."

"Are there tunnels in it?" Sable asked.

Purn peered into the hole. "Not that I heard of, but that looks like it goes pretty far down."

The hole was mostly blocked by the pile of fallen stones. A single tree stood at one edge, its roots tangled in the rocks. One particularly wide stone had been pushed up as a root nestled under it.

"Look at that!" Ayda said. "See how strong trees are?"

More torches were being lit along the walls of Barrowford, and Sable walked to the front of the barrow. The slope dropped steeply down, and the narrow plain between herself and the city was filled with army tents. The city itself was an oval, completely surrounded by the tall stone wall. Inside it, Barrowford was lit with torchlight, its avenues busy with people. At the highest point in the city, the stone fortress was also alight with torches.

Off to the right, the wide bend of the Black River glowed faintly as it wound through the darkening land, reflecting the lighter blue still lingering in the sky. Three different bridges arched over it at different places.

"The Kalesh will come from that direction," Reese said, pointing over the river. "Or else they'll come up along this side. There are countless bridges between Tutella Island and here where they could cross."

"Either way," Sable said slowly, "they'll end up down on the plain below us, won't they?"

Reese nodded.

Sable stepped to the very edge. "This is it. This is our stage."

She could make out the shapes of individual soldiers in the army camp below, especially those starting campfires. "Purn, could you go tell Atticus we're here? We'll come find him as soon as we can."

The kobold blinked out of view.

"You think you can get Vivaine up here?" Reese asked.

"I do," Sable said.

Innov soared past her, flying out over the camp. Cries went up from the soldiers, and Sable watched the phoenix as she spiraled high into the air. The trail of sparks behind her showered down, glittering and flickering longer than usual as they fell toward the troops.

Sable drew in a deep breath of the cool evening. "I love it when she does that. Almost makes you think hope is a tangible thing."

Innov reached a point high in the sky, then soared in a wide arc and dove down toward the barrow. Sable wondered for a brief moment if she was headed toward Ayda, but the phoenix hurtled straight down at Sable, making one quick loop around her before landing on her arm.

The cheers from the troops below rolled out like a ripple in a pool, and a surge of people moved toward the barrow.

"Are you going down there?" Ayda asked, peering down at the crowd.

Sable nodded. "After everything else, if this can give them a little hope, it seems like a good thing."

Cernus had backed away from the edge, and Ayda backed away with him. "I'll wait up here and find you later."

Sable moved to the trailhead that led down the slope toward the camp. "Coming?" she asked Reese.

"I think they're here to see the Flame of the North," he said, "I'll be right behind you."

"They'll be just as happy to see their old general," Sable said, "and the Flame of the North is now quite attached to you. Let's go down together."

He hesitated only a moment before coming up beside her and offering her his arm.

The trail switched back twice as they descended, and the crowd grew larger and louder.

At the bottom, the path ducked through a hedge of dried thickets before spilling out right into the crowd itself.

The roar that greeted them was deafening. Calls of "Flame of the North" were echoed with "Queen of the North," and Sable tried to smile at the faces around her.

One soldier pushed through the others. "Back to stop Vivaine?" he called over the crowd.

"I'm certainly going to try," Sable told him.

A narrow path stayed open in front of Sable and Reese, and they worked their way through the crowd, Reese returning salutes as he kept one hand on Sable's back.

"Your Majesty!" a deep voice called out the wry greeting, and Sable strained to see a dwarf pushing himself through the crowd, the bones woven into his beard catching the firelight.

"Callun!" Sable greeted him.

Mari stepped out behind him with a grin, then Cintis.

"You're all here!" Sable looked between the four of them and the humans around them who seemed unruffled by their presence. "Even the elves?"

Cintis nodded. "Many of us came. We decided we're just the north, no territories, no elves or dwarves or humans. Just the north. All equally angry about the dragon."

Sable grinned at them. "That is wonderf—"

"Still burning!" a soldier yelled.

"Still burning!" thundered a hundred other voices.

Sable stared at them as the words echoed again through the crowd.

"It's become a bit of a motto," Mari said, speaking loudly over the crowd. "Ever since your speech on the catapult."

"Even after Aedis?" Sable asked.

Cintis leaned closer. "Fire only makes a phoenix stronger, you know."

"Atticus did this, didn't he?" she called back, but her words were lost in the roar of the crowd.

Sable shook her head. "He wasn't even there when I said that," she muttered, but she held her arm up so more people could see Innov, and the soldiers cheered until every face around her was lit with hope.

She lifted her eyes to Innov. "Still burning," she agreed quietly.

Reese grabbed Cintis's arm and pulled him closer. "Can you take us to Atticus?"

The soldiers around them continued their cheers, and Sable set her hand on Reese's arm. "No," Sable shouted over the cheers. "Braddick first."

CHAPTER SEVENTY-NINE

THE SEA of soldiers only thickened as Sable and Reese made their way through the army camp toward the city gate. Slowly, the clothes shifted from uniforms to civilian clothes as they reached the wall and moved into the city.

The wide avenue heading straight into the city was packed with people, and faces peered out of windows everywhere Sable looked. The expressions turned from worry and curiosity to wonder as they caught sight of Innov.

Reese called out to a city guard, and the man pointed up toward the wall.

Soldiers stood at the base of a set of stairs climbing the inside face, but they made no move to stop Sable, and she started up. The cheers continued, spreading farther the higher she climbed. When she could see over the roofs of the nearest houses, she caught sight of more crowds in the nearby streets.

"Why Braddick?" Reese asked quietly. "It's obvious you've won the support of the troops. It's a formality to get Braddick to see that."

"A formality that I would like to make very formal," Sable answered. "Let's hope he also sees the obvious, and we can move on to other plans."

By the time she reached the top of the wall, night had truly fallen. Torches lined the wide walkway along its top, illuminating soldiers standing guard. Barrowford itself was a map of lantern-lit streets. She paused at the top of the stairs, catching sight of Braddick off to the right.

He waited at the beginning of a slightly elevated portion of the wall, two steps higher than where Sable stood, with his arms crossed. He was tall enough that with the added height, her head would barely come up to his chest when she reached him.

"I guess he's not ready to admit to the obvious," she said quietly.

She crossed the wall and looked over the parapet, holding Innov up. The army camp was dark by comparison with the city, but when the phoenix fire came into view, the throng of soldiers exploded with cheers. She could make out cries of "Still burning!" and a surprising number of "Queen of the North!"

She walked toward Braddick, shifting Innov to the arm next to the parapet, letting the embers from her occasionally bounce off the top of the crenelations and trickle down the outside of the wall. When she reached Braddick, she stopped a few paces back from the steps. He stood with his chest thrust out and his lips turned down at the edges in contempt. There was something different in him, though. A weariness.

"I have a plan to stop Vivaine," Sable said, speaking just loud enough for him to hear over the crowd, "and to make the Kalesh leave, but I need the troops."

"I'm not handing the armies of the north over to a woman with no experience at war," Braddick said, the words blunt.

"If all goes well, General, they won't need to fight. Do I have your support?"

Braddick's mouth twisted into a humorless smile. "No, you don't have—"

"She could take them from you right now," Reese interrupted. "You know she could."

The general slowly closed his mouth.

"I could," Sable said, "but the troops respect you and follow you, and I would rather not introduce any more instability into the north than we already have." She met Braddick's eyes and poured truth into her words. "We've lost enough already. If you give me a chance, I might be able to end this before we lose any more men." She took in the exhaustion lurking in his eyes and the slight dip in his shoulders. Tutella Island had humbled him a little. "Do I have your support?"

Braddick's eyes dug into her as he weighed his options.

"You're not my queen," he said.

"That's not an attitude that's going to earn you much love from the people, Braddick," Reese pointed out.

"She's *not* a queen," Braddick repeated.

"I'm not looking for a lifelong vow of loyalty, General," Sable said. "I want your word the troops will do what I ask while I try to resolve this situation and you will be a supportive voice instead of your usual combative one."

The muscles in his arms twitched.

"I just need the troops positioned correctly," she said. "How many days until the Kalesh reach us?"

"Four."

"Well, then, you'll be relieved of any promise to me in five days. Whether I succeed or fail." When she spoke again, she tried to put aside their past enmity. "Do I have your support, General Braddick?"

"If you fail, and if the dragon doesn't kill us all, we need to be positioned to weather a siege."

Sable nodded. "You'll have a say in where every northern unit is placed and the fortifications we'll be building."

He still stood with his arms crossed, but one of his fingers tapped on the broad muscle of his arm. "Five days," he said slowly.

"Only five days," she answered. "Are you the general who will lead the army through them?"

Innov shifted on her arm, and a shower of sparks shot out from her, some of them cascading over the parapet and down toward the troops, and the cheers came again.

Braddick took one more breath before uncrossing his arms. He came down the steps until he was standing in front of Sable and pressed his fist to his chest in a salute. The sound of the cheers crashed against the wall, and Sable swore she could feel it in the stones.

Still saluting, Braddick leaned forward as though giving her a slight bow. "If you are responsible for the fall of the north," he said, his voice a low growl, "you will pay dearly for it."

Sable twitched her arm, and Innov launched into the air and out over the army camp.

"Good." She gave Braddick a small smile. "That's the attitude we need."

Sable stopped at the corner of Atticus's red wagon, in the last shadow at the edge of the troupe's campsite. The light from the cook fire lit the worn benches and seats, each familiar knot and scar like a part of the troupe itself. An idle complaint from Leonis floated down from the roof of the blue wagon where he lay pruning leaves of his tree. Thulan's offhanded retort was like a line from some well-loved play.

Still, Sable lingered on the edge, her hand on the rough corner of the wagon.

"Are you all right?" Reese asked quietly from behind her.

She opened her mouth but couldn't answer.

Atticus relaxed in his favorite chair near the fire, his old, slightly wrinkled hands flipping through a book just as they had a hundred nights before. But there was something in the space around the troupe. Something too empty. Too distant.

She didn't move, but Atticus glanced up and caught sight of her. He snapped the book shut and rose, a wide smile on his face as he strode through the campsite as though it were just a normal night.

He beamed at her, pulling her into an embrace.

She hugged him back, expecting that to banish the strangeness, but when he stepped back, leaving his hands on her shoulders, it was still there, still threaded into even the small space between them.

"I know Purnicious said you were fine," he said, looking her over, "but it does me good to see you with my own eyes." He paused. "I'm so sorry about your sisters."

Sable swallowed and nodded.

Past him, Thulan's eyes closed for a moment before she opened them and refocused on the soup.

Leonis's hands paused on his tree, and he sighed.

Sable turned back to Atticus and tried to smile, but the distance was still there. "Something's changed." The words came out a bit hesitant, and there was the sharp prick of tears in her eyes. She blinked them back, looking over his shoulder. "What's changed? What's wrong?"

He let out a quiet breath. "It's not us."

She took a step back. "I didn't do anything."

He dropped his hands, but they didn't fall to his sides. He fiddled with his fingers, as though he wasn't quite sure what to do with himself. When he spoke, though, his words were warm. "It was inevitable that you'd outgrow the troupe at some point. Although now that we come to it, I do feel like it came too quickly."

"Outgrew the..." She caught Thulan and Leonis watching her. "What are you talking about?"

"It's not a bad thing," Atticus said, although his eyes looked a little wet. "We're just a group of actors, you see, and somewhere along the line..." He gestured faintly toward the barrow. "You stopped acting."

The heat of his words filled the space around them.

She swallowed down the tightness in her throat. "You're hardly just actors."

"We dabble in other things," he admitted with a smile that came a little easier. "But at our heart, we're actors. You are, of course, welcome on our stage any time for any reason. But...you've moved a bit beyond us at this point."

Thulan and Leonis gave no sign of agreeing or disagreeing, but they looked more resigned than surprised by the words.

Sable opened her mouth to object, but there was no denying the warmth in Atticus's words or the way they expressed something she'd felt shifting for a while now.

"The one thing that hasn't changed," Atticus said fondly, "is that you're still family and anywhere we are, you will always have a home, so stop standing on the edge and come in. Both of you."

Atticus walked back to his seat, and Sable followed him into the light. She sat on the bench along the red wagon, and Reese settled in close beside her.

"He nails those speeches," Leonis said to Thulan. "Every time."

"I think he plans them ahead of time." Thulan gave Sable and Reese a nod. "Nice to have you two back."

Atticus sat and watched Sable, a smile playing across his lips.

"Are you trying not to comment on my fiery entrance?" she asked.

"It was exceptional." The words burst out of him like he'd been holding them in for days. "But I'm trying not to gush because I know you didn't do it for dramatic effect."

She grinned at him. "Maybe a little bit on the wall with Braddick was for effect, but the trip down the barrow wasn't planned." She glanced around the campsite. "Any chance Jae and Serene are nearby? Or Gwen and Terrane? Or Evay?"

"They usually show up around this time looking for food," Thulan said. "Unless they're blind and deaf, they know you arrived, so I can't imagine they'll stay away."

"Good," Sable said, "because we're going to need everyone's help to stop Vivaine." She pointed up toward the dark barrow. "And we need to turn that into a stage."

Atticus rubbed his hands together. "I love everything about this plan already."

"Did Purnicious say you found Cernus?" Thulan said.

"And Ayda," Sable answered. "She wasn't interested in pushing through the crowds with us, but I'm sure she'll find her way here at some point."

"What does the unicorn want?" Leonis asked.

"To graze, apparently," Reese said. "At least that's all he's done so far."

"That's much less dramatic than either Innov or Argyros lately," Leonis said.

"True. What exciting things did we miss?" Sable asked.

"Callun is the official commander of the dwarves now," Thulan said. "I suppose technically Rion is still High Dwarf, but assuming any of these cousins get back to Torren alive, I'd wager my beard that'll change."

The small campsite still felt a little jagged, but while Thulan and Leonis spun tales of their trip to Barrowford and Atticus interjected corrections of what had really happened, the edges of it smoothed a little. Sable sat back against the wagon, leaning against Reese's shoulder and letting them all talk.

She could almost picture Ryah sitting beside Thulan, laughing along with the others.

Before the soup was ready, Evay appeared at the edge of the campsite, and Sable stood and crossed over to her. The elf's eyes had dark circles under them, and the creases between her brow had grown deeper. She wrapped her arms around Sable, and her body shuddered as she took in a breath.

"I can't believe they're both gone." Sable's voice caught on the words.

"Purnicious says they didn't suffer," Evay whispered, as though she was clinging to the thought as tightly as she clung to Sable.

Sable nodded against her shoulder. "I keep telling myself that."

Evay clutched her for another breath, then stood back. "Thank you," she said, the words fervent, "for introducing me to them. I'm so glad you came back to the wood."

Sable wiped her hand across her cheek. "So am I."

They sat and talk turned to the number of soldiers who'd deserted the army. It was lower than Sable had feared, but still a good number had never reached Barrowford.

"We saw Aedis," Sable said quietly. "There's nothing left at all."

"Some of the books survived," Atticus said.

"How?"

"Sam and a few monks were inside the gathering hall when Argyros attacked, and they managed to make a line, pulling books off the shelf and throwing them out behind the building, along the town wall. They saved about half of them before the hall caught fire too much. The building burned fast, and the pile was far enough away that only the books on the near edge were singed. The rest smell like smoke, but they're whole."

"That's some consolation," Sable said, "even if it's a small one."

Atticus nodded as Jae and Serene appeared with Ayda traipsing along beside them, followed quickly by Gwen and Terrane.

Sable waited until everyone had taken their seats and Thulan had handed out bowls of soup before starting. "When I confront Vivaine, I want to use the barrow as our stage."

"Bold," Terrane said. "I like it."

"You're going to like it even more when I tell you that I want the entire base surrounded by fire. Think you can make that hedge of thickets burn hot enough to keep everyone else back, but not make so much smoke people can't see the top?"

"I can't believe you even had to ask," he said.

"Great. Now I'd imagine that—"

"What are you doing?" Gwen interrupted.

Sable paused. "Besides trying to explain my plan?"

"What are you doing talking about this right here? If you think Vivaine doesn't have spies in this camp, you're an idiot."

Sable felt Serene cast out, and on the other side of the wagons was enough activity that it was impossible to tell if anyone was actually trying to listen.

"I think we can get a little space blocked off." Reese pushed himself up. "There have to be a few soldiers around who'd like to guard the space around the Queen of the North while she consults with her…" He waved his hand at the troupe. "Court," he finished with a grin.

"Stick with Flame of the North," Sable said.

Atticus shook his head, his eyes bright. "Keep it vague, let them call her whichever they like."

Reese disappeared, and everyone fell to eating, except Ayda, who wrinkled up her nose at the smell of the soup and sat on the ground, picking long blades of grass.

"How many spies do you think she has here?" Sable asked Gwen.

"Enough to know everything that's happening." Gwen tapped her spoon on the side of her bowl, glaring into the soup. "She had enough to know where everyone would be on Tutella Island, didn't she?"

"Wouldn't have taken more than one to figure out where the north was headquartered," Serene said.

"It doesn't matter how many," Gwen snapped. "The point is that she knew. She always knows, and yet you're going to try to go against her. *Again.*"

"Of course we are." Sable rested her bowl on her legs. "Are we supposed to just roll over and let her take over the north?"

"If it keeps hundreds or thousands of people from dying? Maybe!"

Sable set her bowl down on the bench next to her. "Do you actually believe that?"

Gwen ran a hand through her hair, leaving it disheveled. "I don't know." She looked at each of the faces gathered between the wagons, ending with Terrane. "She's going to kill all of you. And I don't want to see that. Maybe…" She looked back at Sable. "Maybe if we work with her, maybe we can calm her down and figure out something that's a peaceful solution."

"You know we're past that," Sable said.

Gwen pushed herself to her feet. "Well, I can't sit here and listen to you all plan your own deaths." She looked down at Terrane. "I want nothing to do with any of this."

She strode away, and Terrane stood and started after her.

"Terrane," Sable said. "I really need your help."

He paused, watching Gwen disappear around the wagon. "But you don't need Gwen's?"

Sable let the question hang in the air. "She'll come around. And I have a lot of fire I need controlled," she said finally.

Terrane sighed and sat back down. "Fine, tell me what you need."

CHAPTER EIGHTY

REESE CAME BACK into the campsite, giving directions to a few guards, who stationed themselves along the street that ran past the wagons. They stood in the middle of the road, funneling passersby to the far side.

"That enough space?" Reese asked.

Serene cast out, and Sable could feel a ring of soldiers surrounding the wagons, creating a nice empty space around them.

"Should work," Serene answered.

"Great," Reese said, "Let's pull the benches in a bit closer, and we should be able to talk relatively freely—" He paused, looking at Gwen's empty seat.

"Gwen was not optimistic about our chances," Leonis said, pulling an end of his bench closer to the fire.

"If anyone else feels the same," Sable said, "it's understandable."

No one answered, but they all moved closer together until they sat in a tight circle.

"All right, then." Sable took a deep breath. "As Gwen pointed out, the immediate danger we all face is Argyros, and Vivaine will definitely bring him to meet with me."

"Do you think she'll bring Jrogen too?" Reese asked.

"I don't. I'm offering her a stage, and she's not going to share that with anyone she doesn't have to. We'll plan it for dusk, which she'll love because she can make herself brighter than everything around her. I'm sure she'll bring guards, but they'll hold back. She'll want it to look like it's just her and Argyros versus me." Sable glanced up at the dark shadow of the barrow. "I'd like to be prepared for those guards without looking like we're prepared. Anyone know anything about the tunnels under the barrow?"

"A few cousins explored them," Thulan said. "We found an entrance on the western side of the barrow. The tunnels go through a few catacombs, then climb up to those ruins on the top, but the exit is blocked by a boulder-sized rock in the ruins."

"Can you move it?" Sable asked.

Thulan blinked at her. "I thought calling it boulder-sized would convey how heavy it is."

"We have hundreds of dwarves here. Are you saying they can't move a rock? Just far enough for us to access that tunnel?"

"It's not just the rock. The ruins are...well, they're ruins. We'd have to excavate the ruins. It'll involve scaffolding and a long lever."

"No scaffolding. I need subtle," Sable said. "I'd rather that Vivaine didn't even know there were tunnels there."

"Well, then," Thulan said, "you need to find something both subtle and strong enough to shift a really big rock. Know anything that can do that?"

Sable looked over where Ayda sat weaving strands of grass together into a chain. "Trees are that strong."

The elf looked up.

"Want a job?" Sable asked her. "You'd get to be a tree."

Ayda's face lit up. "Yes!" Her smile faded a bit. "Although my father would be livid." She glanced at Serene. "No mention of me in your records, right? If humans and elves start interacting more, and he finds out I interfered..."

Serene shook her head. "No one wants to be famous. Flibbet asked me the same thing. Something about threads and interfering and not wanting to read a hundred years from now that he'd stepped in."

"A hundred years from now?" Sable asked.

Serene shrugged. "It's Flibbet, I have no idea what he was talking about. But I promise, Ayda, no mentions of you, or him, in my records."

Ayda clapped her hands together. "Then I'd love to help!"

"But," Sable said, "you have to pay attention and do your job while you're a tree."

Ayda considered the words. "For how long?"

"Long enough to shift a rock." Sable turned to Reese. "Assuming Ayda can get you enough room to climb out, would you be in the tunnels? If anything goes wrong, I'd like someone there to keep Vivaine's guards away from me."

"I'll be there too," Evay said.

Thulan nodded. "I'll round up some cousins, and we'll get a nice little party. A few of Vivaine's guards shouldn't be a problem."

"The thing we can't protect you from," Reese said, "is the dragon. You'll have Innov with you, right?"

"I will." Sable looked up into the dark sky. "Or I hope she'll come. But I think I can get Argyros to leave." Her eyes caught on the beams sticking up from the city walls. "What are you building up there? More catapults?"

Thulan shook her head. "Ballistae. They are supposed to shoot huge crossbow bolts—but they don't work."

"Will they in four days?"

"Nope." Thulan let out an annoyed breath. "The humans started building them while we were all south at Tutella, and the design has a flaw. If we put enough tension on it to shoot the bolt, two different support beams snap. They need to be redesigned and reassembled. It would take a fortnight to get them ready, if all went well. We have some cousins working on a faster solution, but no one is hopeful."

The machines looked menacing on the wall, and Sable hummed. "That's disappointing." She tapped her fingers against her leg. "Tell the cousins that even if they can't get them working, make sure they at least look impressive."

She turned to Jae. "How is your 'knock a dragon from the sky' trick coming?"

"I'm better at it than I was a week ago," he answered.

"Great, you stay on the walls. If we can get Argyros to go for the ballistae, hopefully you'll get a shot at him."

"And what happens if Jae brings him down?" Thulan asked.

"Actually," Jae said, "if I can bring him down, I can keep him down. I've been experimenting with birds, and by controlling the air around them, I can keep them from taking off again."

"For how long?" Sable asked.

Jae grimaced. "Probably not particularly long."

Sable nodded. "In the end, only Vivaine or Argyros himself will be able to get him out of the fight, so just do the best you can." She glanced around the group. "And...just try to stay away from his fire."

"Brilliant ideas like that are why we keep her around," Leonis said to Thulan.

"Avoid dragon fire…" Thulan patted her vest as though searching for something. "If only I had something to write such sage advice down on."

Serene leaned forward, ignoring both of them. "What do you want me to do, Sable?"

"I need you to do the most important fire of all. I want a division between our army and the Kalesh. A big fiery one. If things take too long with Vivaine, I don't want any Kalesh officer getting antsy and attacking. Think you can make some sort of line between the armies that can keep them apart?"

Serene nodded. "If Terrane helps me set things up."

"Good. His fire is for show, for keeping all eyes on the barrow, but yours will keep the army safe if it's needed." Sable glanced at Jae. "And you're keeping the dragon grounded."

The corner of Atticus's mouth quirked up. "We'll call you our Keepers."

"Keepers?" Jae asked.

Atticus nodded. "And when this is all over, you're the ones who will keep the story and make sure it's never forgotten."

Jae glanced at Serene, and she shrugged.

"It works," she said.

"Excellent," Atticus said, rubbing his hands together. "Keepers it is, then."

Hours later, the campfire was merely a pile of ashen coals, and Sable still sat on the bench with Atticus and a lantern as he scribbled down a list of things to take care of over the next few days.

Reese had left to organize a unit of soldiers to keep watch around the wagons at all times, and the rest of the group had wandered off to sleep.

Sable leaned her head back against the wagon, running through her ideas again. Details were mostly fleshed out, and Reese and Thulan had mapped out a good layout for the northern troops, but there were too many unknowns, and her brain swirled in circles around them all.

"There are a lot of layers to your audience," Atticus said.

Sable nodded.

"The trickiest part," he said, "will be remembering which part of the audience is important in each part. It's an amateur mistake to be focused on one audience when you should be speaking to a different one."

Sable tilted her head to look at him. "If I forget which audience I'm talking to at each point, this whole thing will fall apart and we'll all be killed by the Kalesh."

He bobbed his head in acknowledgment. "On stage, though, things can get complicated."

She reached over and patted his arm. "I swear I will pay attention to my audiences, Atticus." She pulled her hand back to her own lap and closed her eyes.

The scratching of Atticus's pen stopped, and she cracked her eyes open to find the playwright giving her the same fond smile she'd caught on his face more than once during the evening.

"What?"

"I never would have guessed the young woman I caught sneaking around by my stage would one day be a queen."

She closed her eyes again. "We both know I'm not really a queen. I don't think royalty has council meetings outside between colorful wagons."

"Maybe they should," Atticus said easily. He was quiet for a long moment. "What if the people want you to be queen?"

"Atticus." She opened her eyes and sat up. "This Flame and Queen thing was your idea from the beginning, and I admit it got us more attention than I ever expected, but—"

"It's far more than that now," he said. "You've made it far more than that. The people of the north need a leader. A good leader. Will you leave them to Braddick? Or one of the men like him who'd happily step in and take over? Or do you want the north to splinter apart again into factions that squabble amongst themselves?"

"No," Sable started, "of course not, but—"

"You are the one who unified them," Atticus said. "I gave you a name, but you took it, grabbed them by their hearts, and made them see what they could be. They love you, not because of Innov, but because you keep inspiring them to be more." He held up his hand to stop her argument. "You united them, and *you* stood up to their enemies. And now, even when everything seems more dire than it's ever been, you're planning to stand up to their enemies again."

He set his hand on her arm. "You had begun to do everything a queen should do for her people even before the north knew your name."

"I have walked into every trap Vivaine has set for me," Sable pointed out.

"And you've broken them open," Atticus said. "You've disrupted her plans. You've wounded her dragon. You have been the one obstacle that Vivaine cannot seem to overcome."

Sable looked at the pile of coals glowing with a dim red light. "There's a part of me that feels responsible for Vivaine, even though that doesn't make sense," she said quietly. "Responsible for not stopping her sooner, for not seeing what she was really like. She talks to me in a way she doesn't talk to anyone else, and if I'd really understood her sooner or asked the right questions, maybe…" She sighed. "I can't stand by and let her trample an entire land. I'm not standing up to her because I think I'm the Queen of the North, it's just… I think that if anyone has a chance to stop her—to really let the truth about her be known—it's me. And if there's a chance I can keep these people safe, I have to try."

A smile curled up the edges of Atticus's mouth.

She pointed at him. "Do not tell me that is a queenly attitude. You and I both know that I have no idea how to be a queen."

"I don't need to tell you. You already know it, and it isn't something you'd have to do alone," he said, and the words wrapped warmly around her.

"The bigger question is whether I want to be queen." She watched the red light flicker across the coals as fingers of a breeze ran over them. "I know that sounds ridiculous. There are people who would literally kill to rule the north. But what I want is a little cottage in the woods. Somewhere quiet. Somewhere people won't have expectations of me. Which…doesn't sound like a queen."

He tapped his pen on his paper. "That is one of your dreams," he said finally, "and one I'd like to see you attain."

"But you think I have other dreams, too? More regal dreams?"

He sighed. "I think you have dreams of righting wrongs. And taking people like Kiva out of power. Dreams of holding someone like Vivaine in check." He met her eyes, and his expression was almost apologetic. "Those dreams will be harder to live, but that is what I've seen you passionate about."

She leaned back against the wagon.

"You deserve the quiet cottage in the woods if that's what you truly want," Atticus said. "But unlike most people in the world, you're being offered the chance to see your other dreams brought to life as well. I'm not saying you should choose one or the other, but I think you have more dreams than the cottage to weigh before you decide. The people are already asking you, though. When all of this is over, you should have an answer for them."

CHAPTER EIGHTY-ONE

FOOTSTEPS at the tent flap pulled Sable's attention from the map spread in front of her. Sam moved inside. Past him, the side of Atticus's wagon flickered blue in the lantern light.

"We've received three separate reports," Sam said. "All confirm the Kalesh are camped a half-day's march south, and they've all crossed to this side of the river."

Reese leaned forward and moved the black marker painted with the gold dragon up the map. The marker had been getting steadily closer over the past three days, and he now set it down in the plain next to Barrowford, facing the northern army's markers. "Then by noon tomorrow, they'll be here." He glanced at General Braddick. "They'll be funneled the right way?"

Braddick nodded. "The barricades are both finished. They'll be brought to this point near the base of the barrow and stopped—or at least slowed—by the trench. Although that's not as deep or as long as I'd like it. The men are still adding some spikes to them to make them more of an obstacle. I'm sure the Kalesh scouts have seen it and planned for it, but the smart thing for them to do is settle the army down and then get to work clearing the path they need the next day."

"Good," Sable said.

"The first battalion," Reese pointed at one of the northern markers situated outside the city wall, "is low on arrows. The fourth has had their path to the city gate partially blocked by the bulwarks we placed here. If it comes to a fast retreat, they'll be vulnerable."

"I'll have the bulwarks adjusted," Braddick said. "And I have civilians making arrows."

Sable looked over the map for the hundredth time, then stood and faced Braddick. "Are you satisfied, General? If I fail tomorrow, you are positioned well for the siege?"

His eyes ran over the map, and he nodded. He took a step back at the table and considered both Sable and Reese. "I have not hidden the fact that I don't think your plan will work, but I acknowledge that you've worked with the army and the city and left us in as good of a place as we can hope."

For the first time since standing on the wall, he raised his fist to his chest and saluted both of them. "If your attempts fail tomorrow, be assured that the north will learn what you attempted. They will understand your courage. I will see to it myself."

Reese straightened and pressed his own fist to his chest.

The general's words had been warm, and Sable found herself smiling at the man for possibly the first time ever. "Thank you, Braddick."

With a nod, he left, and Sam went with him, already discussing the fourth battalion's bulwark.

With their tent empty, Sable crossed to a cot along the back wall and sank down onto it. Cot was perhaps not the right word for it after Purnicious had been around it for three days. What had originally been a layer of strong canvas hung across a wooden frame had turned to a thick, cushioned mattress piled with multicolored pillows, big enough for at least two people to share comfortably.

Sable had put together a smaller bed for Purn next to it, and found two interesting scraps of fabric for the kobold to work with. The result was an orange and purple explosion of blankets and pillows that Reese poked fun at every chance he got, and Purnicious adored.

It wasn't a cottage in the woods, but when they'd set up the tent as a command post for Sable and Reese, Purnicious had taken it upon herself to make it as comfortable as she could.

The benches along the walls were cushioned, three ornate lanterns had appeared one morning, hanging from the ceiling, and daily the rugs on the floor grew larger and softer.

Sable leaned back on a pile of pillows and closed her eyes. The world spun slightly, and despite the fact that the fate of the north would be decided tomorrow, her exhaustion finally overwhelmed her worry. Sounds of Reese tapping his fingers on the map sounded far off, and she let it slip away further.

Until a quiet pop sounded in the tent.

Sable kept her eyes closed. "Hi, Purn."

"Report for General Andreese!" Purnicious's little voice snapped off with an official sort of tone.

Sable opened one eye to see Purn standing next to Reese, her little blue fist at her chest in a salute, looking entirely too serious.

"I'm not a general," Reese pointed out. "You're looking for Braddick."

She wrinkled her nose. "Not for this."

"Please no bad news, Purn," Sable said.

"It's not bad," the kobold answered. "Destructive maybe, but not bad."

Sable shifted to her side and opened both eyes.

"All right, Purn," Reese said, "what do you have to report?"

Purn's face split into a wide grin, and she spread her arms in a dramatic motion that encompassed the entire tent.

Several dozen small pops happened in quick succession, and several dozen kobolds appeared out of thin air, filling every bit of space on the floor.

Sable sat up, pulling her legs onto the cot as two kobolds materialized right next to her. Reese grabbed instinctively for his knife.

"I found us some help," Purnicious said proudly. "When I left you two after Flibbet helped you escape, I realized we were close to that creation of kobolds I'd visited way back when I was first looking for you, wastrel—I mean, General. So I stopped by and told them that we needed help. It took them a bit of time to decide to come, but they arrived this afternoon."

The two kobolds next to Sable stood watching her warily, their hands held in front of them as though they were ready to do something drastic. The female had long, wavy hair the blue of the ocean and skin like a green apple. The male was more like a tower of fire, with cheery red skin and a beard of oranges and yellows.

"Hello," Sable said cautiously.

The kobolds nodded, just as cautiously.

"No one can know but you two!" Purn declared. "That was their requirement. I'll ask them to do whatever you'd like, but after this, no one will see them, not even you."

"Our lips are sealed." Reese looked over the room, a smile growing on his face. "In the whole history of the world, I'm not sure any army has had a more dangerous unit than this."

Purn grinned again. "What do you want us to do?"

"The thickets!" Sable stood, and several of the kobolds flinched back. She moved slowly to the map, and one of the kobolds popped into view standing on the edge of the table. His skin was dark forest green, and his violet beard was streaked with grey.

"Sable," Purn said, "this is Crisis, the creation's elder. Crisis, this is my mistress, Sable, and General Andreese."

Crisis gave them a small nod.

Reese turned to Sable. "I'm suddenly so grateful you bonded with a kobold named Purnicious instead of Crisis."

The kobold elder grinned. "It wasn't always my name. Had to spend a few decades earning it."

Sable pointed to the barrow. "Well, Crisis, we want a ring of thickets around this entire hill, but currently they only cover these two sides well. Along this whole area, there are gaps. Most of the thicket is dead. Could you…bellish the dead branches and fill in the gaps?"

Crisis glanced at Purnicious, his brow twitching down in disapproval.

Purn shifted. "They don't call it bellishing," she said, and there was a slight blush to her blue cheeks. "The real word is *augmea.*"

"I prefer 'bellish,'" Reese said.

Purn looked up at him in surprise, but the rest of the kobolds did nothing but continue to watch them warily.

"So," Reese said to Crisis. "Could you bellish the thickets so we can have a complete ring?"

The elder ran his long green fingers through his beard and nodded. "What do you want them for? Protection?"

"We want to set them on fire," Sable said.

Another kobold popped up onto the table, his orange eyes bright. "Fire? Where?"

"That's Blaze," Purn said, wincing slightly. "He's a lot like Terrane."

Crisis set a hand on Blaze's shoulder. "What else do you need?" the elder asked. "Growing thickets won't take long."

"Our trench isn't long enough, or deep enough." Reese pointed to a line on the map between the two armies.

"Anyone working in it tonight?" Crisis asked.

Reese shook his head. "They usually quit at nightfall."

"Digging holes isn't much work either," a kobold muttered. "I thought we'd get to infiltrate the enemy."

Reese straightened. "You could shrink all their swords! Or arrowheads! Or all their supplies!"

The kobolds grinned and nodded.

"We could shrink all their shoes," one offered.

"Or their pants!" One laughed.

The kobold next to him smacked him on the head. "No one wants a bunch of humans running around without pants."

"There are twenty-five thousand soldiers," Purn said. "That's a lot of anything to shrink."

Sable drummed her fingers on the table. "Not their shoes—we don't want to stop them from getting here. But once they do…" She looked up at Reese. "What was Vivaine's prophecy about her return?"

"You're asking me?"

"You interpreted it in the chicken coop." Sable closed her eyes and drew the words back to her mind. "'She is coming closer, rising from the flames of the setting sun. The ground will tremble, the seas will rise, the swords of her enemies will turn to dust in their hands. The unfaithful will drown in their fear, and she will cleanse the land of their wickedness.'"

She opened her eyes. "We don't want to stop them from coming, because I want them to see Vivaine and me, but if they go to attack the north, I wouldn't be sad if they got a healthy dose of fear." She looked at the kobolds around her. "What would it take to make a sword blade crumble in someone's hand when they hit something? Not every sword even, just those belonging to all the officers."

It was nearly midnight before the kobolds popped out of sight, Purn disappearing with them to begin their work. Reese put out the lanterns, dropping the tent into darkness.

Sable took his hand and drew him to the cot, collapsing down on the pillows and pulling him down beside her. "You're leaving before dawn tomorrow, aren't you?"

He ran his fingers down a lock of her hair. "We need to get into the tunnels before it's light. And we need to get Ayda in place. I'd rather Vivaine didn't see any of that."

"You'll wake me before you go?"

He was quiet for a long moment. "If I have to say goodbye to you in the morning, I might not leave. We'll think of it like every other morning. I'll get up early, and you sleep."

Sable sighed. "You'll be careful, right?"

"Sitting in my tunnel all day? Surrounded by some of the most competent fighters I know? Yes, I'll be careful."

She waited for him to say the obvious, but he stayed quiet, his fingers running slowly through her hair.

"You're not going to tell me to be careful too?" she asked.

"You're going to face down Vivaine and her dragon. I'm pretty sure you can't do that carefully."

The memory of flames consuming the red door came back to her again, and instead of pushing it away, she let the image fill her mind. Let the flames light the anger that had been growing steadily inside her, let it drive back the grief, just for tonight. And tomorrow.

No, there was no way to confront Vivaine carefully, but the time for being careful was long past.

"She killed my sisters." The words came out in a whisper, but the heat blazed through the space between them.

She gripped handfuls of his shirt in her fists and buried her face in his chest. Vivaine had sent her dragon, then stood on the narrows and watched as Argyros burned them alive.

Her arms shook with fury, and she saw not the flames, but Vivaine's uncaring, cold eyes. "She killed my sisters." It wasn't a call for sympathy. It was a declaration, a judgment.

The heat blistered against her cheeks, and she smelled the fabric of his shirt singe.

"I know, and she should pay for what she's done." Reese put a finger under her chin and lifted her face up toward his. The cool air of the tent washed across her.

She could barely see him in the darkness, but everything about him was so familiar, she didn't have to see him to know his expression.

"I love you." His words swept around her with so much heat the tent warmed. "I have loved every minute I've ever spent with you, and I want a million more. I want *years* more." He pulled her close and kissed her, long enough and hard enough that when he pulled away, her head spun.

She opened her mouth to answer, but he kissed her again.

"Don't promise me you'll try to be careful," he whispered when he pulled back. "Don't promise me anything. You will do what you need to, no matter what, and I love that about you. You wouldn't be *you* if you didn't. I just wanted to make sure you know how much I love you and how much I hope tonight is not the last night I see you."

She buried her face in his neck and clung to him, trying to banish every thought of what tomorrow could bring.

"Me too," she whispered.

It was still pitch black in the tent when Reese slipped out of the covers. He pressed a kiss to Sable's forehead, and she reached for him, but there was nothing except the swish of the tent flap and he was gone.

She crawled into the warmth he'd left and buried her head under the blankets.

CHAPTER EIGHTY-TWO

SABLE WROTE the last word of the short paragraph, took a deep breath, and held the letter up by the lantern, reading over the message. The parchment was too big for the little she needed to say, but there was nothing to add. She signed the bottom, blowing on the ink.

When it was dry, she rolled it up and dripped some wax over the seam. It blobbed onto the parchment, looking more like a spill than an official seal.

"It seems like a letter like this should have something more impressive than a glob of wax," she said.

Purnicious popped up onto the table and took the scroll. She set a finger on the seal, and it smoothed out. Then, with her brow wrinkled in concentration, she ran her fingertip over the newly formed circle.

When it was done, she held it out for Sable to see the small, fiery shape of a phoenix carved into the wax.

Sable took it and examined it. "That is amazing."

"It's not as pretty as what Miss Talia could have drawn," Purn said quietly, "but it should be clear to Vivaine that it's from you."

The little kobold held out her hand. "Shall I deliver it now?"

Sable shook her head. "I'd rather you stayed with me today, Purn. There's someone else who should deliver it anyway. Someone Vivaine might listen to. C'mon." She pushed herself up and walked out of the tent and over to the small campsite between Atticus's wagons, where she could smell breakfast cooking.

Even this early in the morning, the road was crowded with soldiers hurrying past. At the sight of Sable, a number of them paused. A few of them looked familiar, and Sable couldn't shake Gwen's warnings about the number of spies Vivaine could have in the camp.

Sable turned away from them, ignoring the feeling she'd lived under for too long now—that Vivaine was always watching.

Atticus looked up. His gaze caught on the message in her hand, and he started to rise, but Sable walked to the other bench and stopped in front of Gwen.

The Mira looked at the scroll for a moment, then shook her head. "Rethink this."

"I have thought about it a thousand times," Sable said. "Will you take her the message?"

"We have talked about this," Gwen said, standing and raising her voice. "You cannot defeat her dragon."

Heads on the road turned, and more soldiers paused to watch.

Sable lowered her own voice. "I'm not trying to—"

"Only Vivaine or Argyros can break their bond," Gwen snapped. "Not you!"

Sable drew in a breath and let it go slowly. She held out the message again. "Will you take this to her? You know you're the one she'll accept it from."

Gwen stood for a moment, her mouth twitching as though she was deciding between a dozen scathing retorts. Instead, she snatched the scroll from Sable's hand.

"You're responsible, Sable," Gwen said, pointing the scroll at Sable's face, "when everyone here is killed." She stalked out of the campsite.

The soldiers on the road moved quickly out of her way. A few slipped away too, and whether their movements were suspiciously spy-like or just the normal efficient speed of soldiers on a task, Sable couldn't tell.

She let out a sigh, ignoring the disapproving looks she could feel from everyone else in the campsite. Without waiting for them to point out how poorly that had gone, she headed back to her tent.

It wasn't quite midday when the first lookout on the city wall rang a warning bell. Sable stepped up to the parapet next to Braddick, shielding her eyes from the sun. A dark line came into view on the farthest rise she could see and slowly turned into a wave of soldiers and horses spilling toward the city.

"Right on time," Braddick said quietly.

"No dragon yet," Sable remarked. "Do you see Vivaine?"

The general pulled out a spyglass and focused on the troops. "No one dressed in white."

"Knowing her," Sable said, "she'll wait until everyone's settled to make her grand appearance."

Braddick pulled the spyglass away from his eye and looked down at Sable. "Isn't that the plan for your entrance as well?"

She gave him a small smile. "It is."

The afternoon trudged slowly onward, each moment marked by the thrumming march of Kalesh boots. The army flowed forward, filling the entire plain, funneling closer together as they reached the barricades the north had raised, and coming to a final stop at the wide trench that blocked their path.

"The trench is significantly wider than it was yesterday," Braddick said, glancing at her suspiciously.

"Is it?" Sable asked mildly.

The bulk of the Kalesh army stood out in the wide plain along the river, but the barricades had driven the front away from the riverbank, and so instead of facing their forces toward Barrowford, they'd been turned until the front lines faced the barrow.

"Do you see Jrogen?"

"There's a man at the front with tattoos covering his head."

"Good. Keep your eye on him, please."

Braddick gave some orders to a soldier nearby, and that man fixed his own spyglass on the Tien Sark.

As Braddick had predicted, the Kalesh army began to set up camp, even though there was still an hour until sundown.

"Tomorrow they'll attack the barricades in earnest," the general said. "It won't take them more than a few hours to breach them and be able to head straight for the city."

"By tomorrow the barricades will have served their purpose," Sable said.

A constant stream of soldiers reported to Braddick and were sent away with new orders, and Sable waited, watching the sky over the Kalesh army.

The sun was low over the western hills when the first glitter of silver appeared, flying out of the forest near the back of the army.

Sable straightened, and Braddick handed her his spyglass. It took her a moment to find the dragon and another to focus the glass. The sharp glints of lights from Argyros's scales were painfully bright, and a small, white figure sat on his back.

She lowered the spyglass, the metal feeling suddenly slippery in her hand. Argyros flew over the Kalesh army, ripples of silver and black chasing each other across his scales. The closer he came, the more Vivaine glowed, her white robe and her hair reflecting the sunlight with blinding brightness.

The activity on the wall around her shifted, like a window closing between her and the soldiers. Vivaine came closer, and the other people and problems faded into the background until there was no one left but the two of them.

Sable held the spyglass out to Braddick. "Thank you."

He took it slowly, his eyes still on the dragon. "I don't envy you."

She wiped her palm on her pants and straightened her shoulders. "Good luck, General."

He turned to look at her and pressed his fist to his chest. "Good luck to you too, Sable." He glanced back at the dragon, who had angled toward the barrow. "You pull this off, and I'll call you Queen of the North myself."

Sable wove almost numbly through the urgent, hurried activity of the army camp. The chilled feeling of isolation grew stronger as she headed toward Atticus's wagons. Dark clouds piled up in the western sky, drowning the world in blue shadows, bringing dusk earlier than she'd expected.

She found Atticus pacing between the wagons, wringing his fingers. He stopped at the sight of her and opened his mouth, then closed it again.

Past him, Argyros landed on the front edge of the barrow, glittering like starlight in the gathering gloom.

Innov perched on the back of a chair, her own small light golden and warm. Her attention was fixed on the dragon as the white form of Vivaine dismounted and stood beside him. Innov shifted, her wings rustling with an agitated feel.

Sable moved close to her, the phoenix's presence feeling like a small balm against what was coming. "Ready?" Innov twitched her feathers and stepped onto Sable's arm.

She heard Atticus step up close behind her. "I'm not changing into anything else." She turned to face him. "No costumes. No dresses or braids." She motioned to the traveling clothes she wore, the hem of her pants browned with dirt, the cuff of one sleeve frayed where it had escaped Purn's notice. "Just me."

"And me," he said.

Sable shook her head. "Atticus…"

"I can read audiences better than you, and I know her better than you." The words sounded rehearsed, and he held both hands up to stave off her answer. "Whatever illusions I had about her disappeared when she massacred an entire city." That, on the other hand, was full of warmth and enough heartache that Sable's objections died on her lips. He dropped his hands. "I want to be there at the end of this. No matter what happens."

He stood tall and steady in front of her, but the campsite was growing steadily darker and creases by his mouth and between his brow seemed to gather the shadows. He looked wearier and more worn than when she'd met him. Of course, back then, he'd been Atticus the famous playwright. That name sounded different in her mind than his name did now. Atticus. The man whose presence and steady faith in her had become something she'd moored herself to for…a long time now. The man who'd become a second father.

She let the warmth of his words, of all the words he'd ever spoken, drive away the chill around her and nodded. "I want you to come."

The corners of his mouth turned up in something too pained to be a smile. "Then lead the way."

Much of the northern army was now housed inside the city, and the remaining tents had pulled back close to Barrowford's wall in preparation for the coming siege, so it took only a few moments before Sable and Atticus neared the edge of the camp where nothing would stand between them and the barrow.

Until Kiva stepped out from behind the last tent.

Sable stumbled to a stop.

His deep red vest was covered in dust, his white shirtsleeves soiled and stained. His hair was disheveled, his face so thin it was almost gaunt.

Dark shadows lurked in every crevice and wrinkle, and his eyes glittered with so much hatred that she took a step back.

Green flashed by his stomach, and she stepped back again, grabbing Atticus and pulling him away from the bright green coils slithering around Kiva's fingers.

His small venomous snake, no thicker than a thumb, stretched her head toward Sable and hissed.

Innov's eyes were fixed on the snake, her talons gripping Sable's arm tightly. Sable looked back up at Kiva, her shock at his appearance warring with the shock that he was still alive.

"I'm coming with you." Kiva's words were harsh.

Sable shook her head. "No."

He shifted closer, and Sable dropped her eyes back down to the snake, whose thin tongue flicked out to taste the air.

"Vivaine killed Talia," Kiva hissed, and his hand trembled, "and so she's going to die."

Sable kept her eyes on the snake. "Unless you've found some antidote to that thing somewhere in the north, get it away from me."

"There are no snakes like this in the north," he said. "So no antidote." He did take a step back, and Innov's grip loosened. "Which is why," he continued, "a single bite is going to kill Vivaine. It will take only a few minutes, and she'll die in terrible agony, as she should."

Sable shook her head again. "There are bigger things at play than you or me, Kiva. I need to talk to Vivaine."

"And I need to kill her."

The look in his eye sent a chill down her back. She'd seen it before. His decision was made, and there was nothing that would stop him.

He would walk up to Vivaine and attack. It would never work. Argyros would kill him and the tiny snake before he got close, but the damage would be done. Any chance to negotiate with Vivaine would be lost.

She cast around for something to change his mind. Anything that would hold weight in his mind.

"You owe me!" The words burst out almost before Sable had finished the thought.

Kiva's eyes narrowed. "I do not."

"That ledger I stole for you changed your life." Her words sounded almost as desperate as she felt, but she pressed on. "You gave me my freedom. That was worth pennies to you compared to what you gained. You owe me for every good thing that's happened to you since that day." She shoved warmth into her words. "I *need* to talk to Vivaine before you do anything. Promise me you'll wait. Swear to me—on Talia's memory. You owe me at least that much."

He ran his thumb over one of the snake's coils, and his hand still trembled, but he gave a sharp nod.

"Say it out loud," Sable said.

"I swear, on Talia's memory, to wait until you're done with Vivaine," he said, the words full of warmth. "And then I'm going to kill her."

Sable examined his face, looking for a loophole, but he looked too furious to be trying to trick her. Too discomposed. "Then welcome to the party."

The three of them walked out onto the empty plain between the city and the barrow. A detachment of soldiers from the Kalesh army moved quickly up the switchback trail of the barrow, much as Sable had expected.

What was less expected was the small white horse-drawn wagon that trundled up with them. Something about it nagged at Sable's memory.

"Have you seen that before?" Sable asked quietly.

Kiva shook his head.

Atticus squinted at it. "No. The walls look like they're covered in stone. Who makes a wagon out of stone? Poor horse."

"It looks familiar," Sable said. "What does Vivaine need a covered wagon for?"

They drew closer to the barrow, and Sable searched for any sign of Terrane or evidence of the kobolds around the thickets at the bottom, but in the evening light, she couldn't see anyone.

"Is everyone in place, Purn?" Sable asked quietly.

"Yes," Purn's voice said from by her leg.

Kiva twitched and looked toward Purn's voice but didn't say anything.

They started up the trail, and a wind picked up from the west, bringing the smell of storms. Already, the world was dark enough that Vivaine stood like a pure white candle flame at the top of the barrow. Atticus's eyes stayed on her as they climbed.

When they reached the top, Argyros and Vivaine had taken up their station not far from the path at the front edge, clearly visible from both armies and the city itself.

Sable closed most of the distance to her, flanked by Atticus and Kiva, stopping a few steps from Vivaine.

Below the barrow, the northern army was lined up behind their defenses or stationed along the wall. The space between Sable and the city felt enormous, but the Kalesh army was closer. They'd drawn up behind the trench, and she had the fleeting thought that the top of the barrow was probably within range of an arrow.

She set the thought firmly aside and turned her attention to the hilltop around her.

The ruins sat just as they had the other night, with one obvious change. A new, silver-barked tree now grew among the others, positioned over the edge of the hole leading down into the tunnels.

A shadow gaped beneath the Ayda-tree, much larger than the entrance to the tunnels had been before, and Sable thought she saw a flicker of motion. She turned away before she drew any attention to it.

One of Vivaine's guards finished parking the wagon a dozen paces back from the edge but still close to the prioress and then joined the others in creating a wide arc around them, separating everything at the front of the barrow from the ruins.

Another dark figure moved away from the wagon, and this one was not a guard.

Atticus let out a sigh.

Still dressed in her long, dark green dress, Gwen stepped up behind Vivaine and took her place at the High Prioress's shoulder.

"Gwen…" Sable said.

The Mira folded her hands at her stomach and tucked them inside her sleeves. "Don't try to look surprised, Sable. You never were a very good actress."

CHAPTER EIGHTY-THREE

Sable pulled her eyes away from Gwen and found Vivaine's face set in a look of fondness, but it wasn't directed at the Mira or Sable.

"Atticus," Vivaine said gently. "Come use your skill on a stage worthy of it."

His hands were still hanging relaxed by his side, but Sable could feel the tension radiating from him. "The Empire?" he asked, the words light.

Argyros's one eye bored into Atticus as well, and his lips curled back just enough to show savage white fangs.

"Do you know of a bigger stage?" Vivaine asked. "Imagine what we could accomplish together."

Atticus took a half step forward, a nostalgic look in his eyes. "Remember that wine we stole? From that cranky old abbess?"

Vivaine smiled. "Sister Paulin. That was a lot of years ago."

"It was the worst wine I've ever drunk," he said, returning her smile with a small one of his own. "Do you remember what we toasted to?"

A growl rumbled deep in Argyros's chest at the familiarity in Atticus's voice.

Vivaine set her hand on the dragon's neck, and he quieted. "Saving the world. And that's exactly what I'm doing."

Innov shifted, and Sable noticed she wasn't focused on Argyros but on the white wagon. The walls and roof were made of white stone, and a thick wooden door was barred along the back.

"These people," Atticus motioned toward the city, "are the world, Vivaine."

"These people chose to fight," Vivaine answered.

Sable looked past the wagon at the guards, searching for Jrogen. But there wasn't a single scaled tattoo to be seen. In fact, the guards here looked more like Sanctus guards than Kalesh soldiers.

"You know what was beautiful about that afternoon with the wine?" Atticus asked. "The freedom to lie in that field and enjoy it. The freedom to dream of what we could do and where we could go. Don't take that from these people. Don't crush them under the Empire—"

"I am redeeming the Empire," Vivaine said, her words rolling over his with a bright fervor. "Do you know how many people they control? I can soften it, make it kinder. Safer. Even for these people here. There may be a few difficult years, but in the end, I can create a world that is truly peaceful, Atticus."

Vivaine's cheeks reddened slightly with the zeal of her words, and they rolled across the top of the barrow like a hot summer wind.

"These people—" Atticus began.

"You have always dreamed too small." Vivaine drew herself up. "You think on the scale of individual people, Atticus, and so you will never truly affect the masses. You could do great things, but you limit yourself with your narrow vision."

Argyros growled again, and Vivaine dropped her hand. "And so you will suffer with everyone else."

"Is there no way you'll end this peacefully?" Sable asked, stepping forward. She hesitated before offering the most obvious solution. The simplest and fastest. Somehow, the last time she'd offered, when she'd thought Reese was dead and the rest of the land was safe, it had been easier.

She ran a finger down Innov's chest, drawing in the phoenix's warmth as she forced herself to say the words. "You could take me back to the Empire. Have your grand entrance with the daughter of A'Melia and just…call off this battle. Leave the Empire out of this land."

Motion behind the guards caught Sable's eye as a dark shape moved in the shadows near the Ayda-tree.

"It's cute that you think I didn't already consider taking you," Vivaine said.

Sable tried not to look at the movement, wondering why Reese would give away the position he and Evay and the dwarves had taken so early.

But when a figure moved out of the darkness, it was decidedly bigger than a person.

The black unicorn's coat was barely darker than the shadows among the ruins. Vivaine twitched as Cernus stepped between two of the guards, who drew aside to let him pass, and up to the wagon. He sniffed at the corner and huffed against the stone, and something fell into place in Sable's mind.

The white stones looked exactly like stones from the Sanctuary.

Innov's attention was on the wagon as well, almost as though she were about to fly over to it, and Sable ran the back of her finger down the phoenix's chest to soothe her.

"You know…" Vivaine's voice pulled Sable's attention back to her to find the prioress's mouth curled in disdain as she took in Sable's clothes. "When I started the Queen of the North nonsense, it was merely to anger the Kalesh. To get them to hate you more."

Sable's finger froze on Innov. "You started that?"

Behind Vivaine's shoulder, Gwen had fixed her attention on the wagon.

"But you took it so much further, didn't you?" Vivaine said. "My people tell me you've been all but crowned." Vivaine set her palm on Argyros's neck, and Sable could feel the warmth flowing between them. "No. The daughter of Melia who dared to call herself queen needs to die here. Today. In front of the world."

The words were blisteringly warm, and Sable had to force herself not to step back.

"Because," Vivaine said simply. "I don't need you. Your sisters, the two remaining daughters of A'Melia, will be returned to the Empire, where Argyros will sacrifice them on the steps of the palace as proof of my power."

Vivaine waved to a guard. As the man approached the wagon, Cernus backed away, his dark shape blending in with the growing shadows. The guard pulled the bar off the wagon door and pulled it open. Kiva made a strangled noise. Purnicious's gasp rang out from the air next to Sable.

The door swung open, and in the small, cramped interior Talia stood, facing the door and pushing Ryah back behind her.

The breath rushed out of Sable, and she grabbed Atticus's arm. "Purn!" she whispered.

There was a pop, and Purnicious appeared with one hand on the wagon. She hissed and stumbled back, holding her palm where it had touched the stone.

"It was hard to figure out a way to capture your sisters in something your kobold wouldn't discover," Vivaine said. "And something your kobold couldn't enter."

"Tutella Island," Sable said, remembering the view through Reese's spyglass. "I saw that wagon on the island, just before Argyros attacked."

"I'm not stupid enough to destroy something this valuable," Vivaine said.

Kiva, who'd been frozen, took a step toward the wagon. Then another.

"Kill him," Vivaine said, a touch of pity in her voice.

Three guards moved forward, but one fell instantly, a black-fletched arrow sunk in his neck.

Evay materialized in front of the other, her face livid, another arrow loosing from her bow and taking down another guard.

Chaos erupted from the ruins as Reese and the others streamed out. Half the guards rushed to engage them while the others ran to protect the wagon.

Evay loosed arrow after arrow, and Kiva ducked under the sword of another guard and stabbed him with a knife. The guard fell, but he was replaced by another.

A dozen more soldiers ran out of the darkness behind the ruins, these dressed in Kalesh uniforms, and Sable caught sight of Jrogen's shaved head.

"Did you think I wouldn't expect your friends?" Vivaine asked, almost tiredly. Behind her, Gwen watched the fight, a flicker of surprise crossing her face before she smoothed it.

Under the Ayda-tree, Jrogen swung his sword, but when Reese stopped it with the stonesteel sword he'd gotten from the dwarves, Jrogen's blade cracked and crumbled to dust.

All around him, other Kalesh blades broke apart the moment they hit anything. The soldiers stopped, stunned, until Reese and the others pressed their attack again.

Evay dropped guard after guard, and Kiva reached the open door of the wagon before a Kalesh arrow caught him in the back of the leg.

He stumbled forward and fell half into the open door.

Evay spun and loosed another arrow.

Sable vaguely noticed an archer falling as she stepped toward the wagon, still trying to wrap her brain around what she was seeing. "Talia! Ryah!"

"Sable, stop!" Talia cried. She had backed up against the far wall of the wagon, pressing Ryah even farther behind her. Their eyes were glued on the floor.

"Stay back, Sable," Kiva said, his voice eerily calm. He'd sunk to his knees outside the wagon door. The arrow in his leg shifted, and he grunted in pain as he slowly pushed himself forward.

Sable moved closer, and Innov's light lit the inside of the wagon. A coil of green scales glimmered on the pure white floor.

The tiny snake hissed as it slithered closer to Talia.

"Kiva." Talia's voice was high with fear.

"Don't move, Talia," Kiva said, his voice still soothing. "Come here, Vaya. I know you got jostled, but just come back to me, girl. It's okay."

Sable took another step, lifting Innov to give them more light.

Kiva tried to crawl into the wagon, but his leg gave out under his weight, and he slammed his stomach down onto the floor.

The wagon creaked, and Vaya twitched closer to Talia.

The tiny green snake began to draw itself back.

"Do *not* move, Talia!" The calmness in Kiva's voice cracked.

Vaya wound herself into a coil, and Kiva lunged forward, slamming his arm down in front of the snake. Her tiny jaw opened, and she sank her fangs into his skin, then recoiled, the entire strike almost too fast to see.

Kiva let out a gasp of pain, and the snake coiled again, almost cowering away from him. He pulled his arm back against his chest, lying on his side on the floor of the wagon.

"Kiva?" Talia said, her voice trembling.

"Don't move." He held out his other hand. "Don't move. She has… enough venom for…two bites."

The snake was coiled again between Kiva and Talia, hissing.

From the corner of Sable's eye, she saw Reese and Jrogen grappling with each other. Reese's sword was gone, and the Tien Sark quickly got the upper hand. Everywhere around Reese, the number of black-clad soldiers far outnumbered Sable's friends.

"C'mon, Vaya," Kiva said gently. "Come here. It's all over now. Come on, beautiful." His arm spasmed, and the snake jerked back. He gritted his teeth and reached his good hand out toward the snake. "C'mon, girl," he whispered. "Come home."

Slowly, her tongue flicking out, the little snake slithered onto his palm.

His body shuddered with pain, but he kept his hand still until she was on it.

Talia stood frozen in the corner, her hand pressed to her mouth.

Kiva's breath came heavy and fast, and he pulled the snake up near his chest. "Can't leave you here if I'm gone. Sorry girl." He ran his fingers down along the snake's side, the motion surprisingly gentle. He shifted a little so he could reach her with both hands and, with a quick snap, broke her neck.

Her coils slackened and slid off his hand until he was holding a limp green body by the head. He tossed her toward an empty corner of the wagon. Then fell back.

Talia rushed forward, kneeling next to him, her hands hovering over him. "What do I do? Kiva, what do I do?"

He looked up at her, and Sable thought she'd never seen him actually smile until that moment. He lifted one hand to brush Talia's cheek. "You're alive," he whispered.

Talia looked down at his arm where two drops of blood were leaking out of the tiny punctures. Long lines of black traced up his skin. She blinked back tears. "You have the antidote, right? Where is it? I'll get it. Just tell me what to do."

"Go find Niko," he whispered, the words labored. "Trust me, my girl, you don't want to be alone."

His face crumpled, and he curled forward, a groan of pain ripping out of him.

"Sable!" Talia cried.

Outside the wagon, everything had gone still. Sable glanced over to see Reese pinned to the ground under Jrogen. The others were held down and vastly outnumbered among the ruins under the Ayda-tree. Evay stood with her back to Sable, her bow drawn, keeping three guards back.

Vivaine watched the wagon with a distant look, as though nothing of consequence were happening. From near Vivaine, both Atticus and Gwen watched with wide eyes.

"Sable." Kiva let out a wet, torn sort of cough.

She turned back to him. His arm under Talia's fingers was grey. Dark streaks were spreading up his neck, and his breath came in gasps. Any time now, his screams would start. She braced herself for it. For the long minutes it would take him to finally die.

"Give me a knife," he rasped before a spasm rocked his body.

His own knife lay on the ground just outside the wagon, and she hurried to pick it up, handing it to him.

He tried to take it, but his fingers stiffened into a claw, and the blade dropped. He curled forward, and his eyes met Sable's, desperate and pleading. "Please," he whispered. "End it."

Sable picked up the knife. "I don't..." The blade shook in her hand, and she moved forward. His arms were curled against his body, his chin clenched down over his neck. "Kiva..."

And then Evay was there, kneeling in front of Kiva, pulling the knife from Sable's grip, turning his head with a strong hand and sliding the blade gently into Kiva's neck.

Talia scrambled back, letting out a sob, but Kiva just sighed.

His head fell to the side, his mouth open, revealing a slowly blackening tongue.

CHAPTER EIGHTY-FOUR

EVAY GRIMLY SQUEEZED Talia's hand, then disappeared from the wagon and reappeared outside, picking up her bow and facing the guards again, who were too wary of the elf to have stepped forward.

Sable gripped the door frame. "Are you…all right?" she whispered

Talia dropped her face into her hands. Ryah's eyes were locked on Kiva's body, but she gave a jerky nod.

"Atticus?" Sable called.

He came to the wagon, holding a hand in toward Ryah.

"Stay with them?" Sable asked quietly. He nodded, and she pushed herself away from the wagon and turned toward Vivaine.

"Purn," Sable whispered, "light it."

Purnicious popped out of sight, and in a breath, Sable heard a low rushing wind.

Vivaine glanced over the side of the barrow and raised an eyebrow. Sable didn't have to look to see the golden glow spreading around the base of the hill. The plains near them lit, and even the sides of the tents and the city wall grew lighter.

Another line of fire lit in the trench blocking the Kalesh army from reaching Barrowford. The long rows of sharpened spikes the northerners had filled it with burst into flames, and Sable caught sight of Serene near the far end, holding her hands out toward the fire.

"Dramatic," Vivaine said, her voice as calm as ever. "But all it does is assure that everyone will be watching as I accept your surrender. With two armies and a city as witnesses, kneeling before me should be a sufficient gesture."

Sable stepped closer to the woman. "You misunderstand the point of our meeting. I'm here to accept your surrender."

Vivaine let out a laugh. "You grow more audacious all the time." Her smile faded. "Shall I have Argyros force you to kneel? I'm not sure there will be much left of you when he's done, but it will still serve my purposes."

Gwen shifted, her expression clearly saying that she'd predicted all this.

Sable ignored her. "I'm here on a peaceful diplomatic mission, Vivaine. It would be unwise to do anything violent."

"Why?" she asked.

"Aside from the bonds of human decency," Sable said, "which I know you are lacking in, we're in range of the ballistae. You and I are too small to target, but Argyros is not."

Vivaine looked at the wall of Barrowford, and without any visible communication, Argyros leapt off the barrow and soared toward the city.

"Think they can hit him while he's flying?" Vivaine asked.

Sable's eyes followed the glittering dragon as he arced through the night sky. "It's only a matter of time," she said, pouring *vitalle* into her words, "before everyone figures out your lies." The warmth of the words filled the air, and the wind blew over the top of the barrow and grasped at the heat, pulling it away.

Sable's eyes ran over the city, focusing on the thousands of soldiers who waited there, trying to protect the north. The elves standing with them. The dwarves. The people in Barrowford hiding tonight in their homes.

She turned to look at the Kalesh army too. Was Niko there somewhere?

"I will certainly not surrender, and even if you do, the war will drag on a bit. I'm afraid a peaceful resolution here is too quick." Vivaine stood at the edge of the cliff, a steady white glowing figure, watching Argyros soar lazily over the city. "I need the world here in disarray a little longer."

"So that the Kalesh don't learn too quickly that you lied about there being gold here?" Sable asked, shoving more warmth into her words. "You need time to get to the Empire and embed yourself there first, don't you?"

"See?" Vivaine sounded almost pleased. "You're slow, but you see things eventually."

"How long ago did you decide to make up such a lie?"

Argyros breathed a river of fire at the first ballista, and it exploded in flames. Soldiers fled away from it along the wall.

Vivaine shrugged. "You can't spend time with merchants without realizing that people will do anything for money. Or even for the rumor of money."

"Or power," Sable said.

"So often they are the same thing."

The dragon reached the second ballista, but the walls had cleared of soldiers, and when this one lit, there was no one to run from it.

"But you don't want gold," Sable said.

"Amah desires hearts and souls, not wealth."

"What will happen when the Kalesh discover you invented the myth of Zenivah's return?" Sable funneled all her anger into the words. The whole top of the barrow felt warm with them. The wind dragged the warmth away and it spread, but she poured more in. "A woman with a wildcat who was killed in a rift?"

Vivaine blew out a breath, her nostrils flaring. "That stupid troupe. If I'd have had Atticus make the story, I'd have gotten something unique, not a copy of some useless dead woman's story."

Sable watched Argyros fly toward the third ballista. "And you chose the Zenivah myth in the first place because of the black dragon. How long have you known that Argyros would turn black as he grew?"

She looked fondly over at him. "Argyros always knew. The silver is just the brightness of childhood. He'll shed it little by little as he ages."

"What happens when the Empire learns it was all based on a story from here in the north?"

"They won't."

Sable shrugged. "People love stories. I wonder how far that particular story has spread in the past ten days? I know you have a good grasp of just how fast a tale can travel when the people are primed to hear it."

Vivaine turned to Sable, drawing herself up to her full height.

"How long did you prepare the Empire before you sent your fake myth into it?" Sable asked. "Years? Decades? How many people did you send? I only needed a single eccentric peddler and five copies of the story."

A muscle twitched in Vivaine's jaw. "This Kalesh army is dispensable.

If they know the truth, they can be removed. The resources of the Empire are endless. The beautiful thing about stories is there is always a way to spin a new one. The right tale can change any mind. Atticus taught me that long ago."

Sable shook her head. The warmth danced around her, almost like a net, almost like a current of water, snaking out. "You have too many lies, Vivaine. What will you do when they all fall down?"

"They won't."

Sable tapped a finger to her lips. "What was it you said to me at Tutella? 'You always miss the real point of things until it's too late. I should expect it by now, yet somehow it's a constant source of disappointment.'"

Vivaine's lips curled in contempt. "The only thing that could actually destroy what I've built is if I admitted the lies to the Kalesh myself. And you will never get me to do that."

Sable ran a finger down Innov's chest, feeling the threads of warmth that spread out across the top of the barrow, ensuring each guard and Tien Sark had heard the conversation. Following the threads down toward the plain, feeling how they drew energy from the raging fires below before they stretched out to the Kalesh army, and the northern army, and even to the walls of Barrowford itself.

She gave Vivaine a smile. "I just did."

The prioress spun to look out over the armies. In the blazing light from the fires, a thousand faces at the front of the Kalesh army were visible, all silent, all facing the barrow. Argyros flew over the wall, lighting the second to last ballista on fire, but the faces of the north were all focused on her and Vivaine.

Sable turned back and caught Jrogen's expression as he still held Reese on the ground. The Tien Sark's eyes were cold and calculating.

Over the wall of Barrowford, Argyros twisted suddenly. His wings thrashed against the air, but he plummeted down, crashing onto the top of the wall a short distance from his target.

A section of the parapet crumbled.

Argyros let out a roar and staggered back upright, his wings fighting as though he were in an erratic wind.

Vivaine's eyes locked on the dragon. "Will you never stop causing me trouble?" she breathed. "These people can be silenced. You cannot stop Amah's will. You cannot stop me." Her hands curled into fists at her side, and she brightened. Tendrils of light from the fire snaked up the hillside and swirled around her, muddying the whiteness of her gown with redder hues. "Why are you still demanding my attention?"

Argyros let out a furious roar and shot fire along the top of the wall. The ballista burst into flames. His wings flapped uselessly, but he turned his head into the city and blasted fire toward the nearest homes.

Sable stepped forward, pressing even more *vitalle* into the words, heating the air until it felt like the fire surrounded them, shoving the words toward the city. "How long until Argyros realizes that you're just using him for his power? Keeping him small and controlled? How long until the Emperor himself hears of your treachery? Will he send his Tien Sark after you next?"

On the city wall, Argyros paused.

"The Emperor will never know!" Vivaine snapped.

Sable's gaze flicked to Gwen, who'd come up close behind Vivaine again. The Mira brushed her fingers against the back of Vivaine's shoulder, glanced at Sable, and gave a slight nod.

Sable let out a breath and fed more *vitalle* into the thread winding through the sky to where Argyros sat on the wall, the last ballista forgotten as he stared across the plain at Vivaine.

"Wrong answer," Sable said. "You forgot your audience, Vivaine. That's an amateur mistake. The Emperor isn't here."

Vivaine jerked her head toward Argyros, as though listening. "I'm not using you!" she said, but the words had a cold edge. "Of course I'm not."

"Do you think he can feel that you're lying as easily as I can?" Sable asked, making sure the words reached the dragon.

Gwen set her fingertips on Vivaine's shoulder, but the prioress didn't turn.

"Argyros!" Vivaine called. "Don't be drawn in by her lies."

"Do you think he's figuring out that he's just an accessory to you? Something to make you look brighter? A weapon for you to use to gain yourself more power? What does he get? To be paraded around as your pet?"

Gwen held Sable's eyes and nodded again.

"Everything you two do is focused on you," Sable continued. "Even now he's dutifully destroying your enemies. I thought dragons didn't like to be caged. How have you managed to hide from him, for all this time, that he's nothing to you but a tool? Because if I can see it, I can't imagine he can't."

"Argyros!" Vivaine called again. "Come to me!"

"Or," Sable said, still threading the words all the way to the dragon, "stop bending yourself to her will, and be free."

Argyros sat on the wall of Barrowford for a long breath before he stretched out his neck and let out a deafening roar that shot fire into the air as he thrashed his head.

"Argyros!" Vivaine cried, the word desperate.

The dragon roared again and launched himself into the air, his claws tearing apart the top of the wall. His tail lashed out, catching the corner of a tower, and the stones shattered. The tower teetered for a moment before crashing down.

Argyros roared a third time, and the anguish and fury in it shook the ground under Sable's feet.

"Come to me!" Vivaine commanded.

Gwen took hold of the prioress's arm. "You've lost him, Vivaine."

The prioress spun, yanking her arm away. "Don't touch me!"

Gwen dropped her hand. "He's gone. It's over."

Vivaine whirled toward Sable. "It is not over! I will get him back, and you will burn for this. The north will burn for this. You haven't won. You are alone, and your friends are beaten."

Under the Ayda-tree, the guards had rounded up Reese and Thulan and Leonis. Two more guards pinned an angry dwarf that sounded like Callun.

"Not all my friends," Sable said. "Purn, see if you can wake Ayda up enough to join the fight."

A moment later, the silver trunk shifted and stretched until a long, elvish face peered out of it. Ayda took in the sight in front of her, and an explosion of branches snapped down, lashing around the Kalesh, wrapping around throats and arms, peeling guard after guard off of their prisoners.

Reese struggled to his feet as Jrogen was lifted off the ground, thin branches wrapped around his neck and torso. The Tien Sark's fingers scrabbled at the silver bark until Reese slammed his fist into the man's face and Jrogen went limp. The soldiers Ayda couldn't reach were still free, but the numbers were more even now.

Vivaine let out a long hiss.

The prioress still stood next to Sable, breathing heavily, her hands clawed at her side. "You will *burn* for this," Vivaine whispered. "Amah has called me to greater things, and you are *nothing*! You are no queen. If you were, you'd have something to fight me with. Something to stop me.

A real army to sacrifice instead of this pathetic handful of northmen. I can crush you in a day. You have nothing to leverage. I have countless soldiers at my call."

Her voice rose with a fanatical edge. The fire below them just over the edge of the cliff still blazed, and Vivaine drew the light up in a river, swirling it around her. "Amah has called me, and I will serve her until my last breath! She has given me the north and the Empire, and you cannot stop me!"

Every word from Vivaine's mouth was scorchingly hot.

The prioress raised her arms. Light from the fires below raced up the side of the barrow like a waterfall flowing in reverse. Strands of yellows and oranges streamed over the edge, swirling around Vivaine. The heat from the fire came as well, not with a searing heat, but with enough warmth to make the air feel like noon on a midsummer's day.

Vivaine grew brighter, wreathed in the gold and scarlet of flames.

Sable lifted a hand to shield her eyes. Vivaine burned as brightly as she had when she'd stood on trial in Immusmala, wreathed in Argyros's flames, but there was no fire. The light merely writhed across the surface of her clothes and her skin like a thin facade.

Vivaine's arms stretched higher. The prioress's usual benevolent expression grew cold and imperious as she turned to face the watching armies.

Then she began to rise into the air.

Sable took a step back, wrenching her gaze to Vivaine's feet, but they were firmly planted in the grass.

She wasn't rising—she was growing.

In a single breath, the prioress was nearly as tall as the wagon. She held her arms out toward the armies, as though offering one of her blessings, and a ripple went through the masses below.

Vivaine grew taller, and Sable's mind scrambled to grasp what was happening as the woman transformed from a prioress into a glorious, terrible goddess.

Sable took another step back before the obvious truth occurred to her.

Not a goddess. The image of a goddess.

Sable cast out, and the normal-sized physical shape of Vivaine burst into warmth inside the image. The huge figure, created from the light, had warmth of its own, but it was misty. Insubstantial.

The front lines of the Kalesh army fell to their knees.

"No more lies, Vivaine." Sable crossed the space between them.

Innov took off, soaring into the sky as Sable wrapped her hand around Vivaine's arm.

"I am Zenivah," the prioress breathed. "I have been reborn to bring peace to the world."

Sable opened a channel between them. Vivaine's body roiled with *vitalle,* and it gushed into Sable's palm like a molten river. She grimaced at the pain and clamped her other hand down on Vivaine's arm, opening a second channel.

Energy blazed into Sable, and she directed it through her arms, down her sides, and into her legs, funneling it out into the ground. The paths were ragged, and flickers of pain danced along them.

But the towering golden image thinned until the real prioress could be made out inside it.

Vivaine let out a roar, animalistic and enraged, and clenched her hands into fists, drawing more light up the hillside. The image solidified slightly but remained a gauzy echo of what it had been.

Sable's arms felt like they were filled with fire past her elbows, and her grip weakened.

Vivaine wrenched her arm away, cutting off the flow of *vitalle*. Coolness washed across Sable's singed palms, and she let out a gasp of relief. Her breath came fast, and she curled her hands by her stomach, the skin on her palms feeling like they were still burning.

Vivaine spun toward her, grabbing Sable's shoulders, leaning close. Her breath was hot and fast, her eyes wild.

"I am Zenivah!" she screamed, spittle flying out of her mouth. "And I will never stop! You have nothing that can stop me!"

The benevolent facade that had masked Vivaine for so long shattered, and Sable looked into her frenzied face, searching for something to reach for, some connection to reality to draw the woman back from the edge.

There was nothing but raging fury.

"I am not a queen," Sable said. "But even if I were, I would still have no army to sacrifice, no followers to offer up in an attempt to thwart you. But you have none of those things either. We each have one *single* thing we have the right to sacrifice."

Vivaine squeezed her eyes shut. "The light!" she muttered. "The light will show them!" Her robe and her hair brightened.

Sable searched the woman's face, but there was nothing left to grab hold of. No way to bring her back.

She caught sight of Reese just breaking free from the last guard and turning toward her. He held up a hand to block the brightness.

Sable closed her eyes and pictured him the morning they'd made the stone tower, clinging to the way he'd looked at her. "I love you," she whispered, threading the words over to him. "Keep my sisters safe."

She cut off the thread before he could answer. She'd never be able to do this if she had to hear his voice.

Instead, she opened her eyes, squinting at Vivaine. She forced her hands to open and wrap around the woman's arms. Sable's blistered skin screamed in agony, but she only gripped tighter. She felt the warmth of the firelight encasing Vivaine. It was separated from the prioress's body by a thin space, but Vivaine's control was irregular. Heat rippled across Sable's hands with the brighter strands of light.

"It's not only light you can control, is it, Vivaine? You can control the heat too. But not well. Not like the light. You survived Argyros's flames, but they were his, and I think he helped you pull off that trick." She leaned closer to Vivaine. "I'm not immune to *real* fire. Are you?"

Vivaine's eyes snapped open. The woman was old, and thin, and it was nearly effortless to push her the few steps toward the cliff.

Sable pulled the woman close until their faces almost touched. "The only thing I've ever had the right to sacrifice," she whispered, "is myself."

With a final leap, Sable jumped over the edge, dragging Vivaine with her.

She caught a flash of Reese, running toward her before they fell.

Vivaine screamed and thrashed.

Sable let go of her, and they separated.

There was a moment where everything seemed to pause, a moment of weightlessness before heat blasted up from the fire. The ground rushing toward them was so bright Sable twisted away and closed her eyes. Even the sky seemed to be on fire.

She curled into a ball until there was nothing but fire and pain and blackness.

CHAPTER EIGHTY-FIVE

Everything hurt.

Sable flinched against the heat of the flames—but there was nothing around her except softness. And darkness. And silence.

She groaned and felt a jolt of shock that sounds still existed.

"Sable?" A hand was against the side of her head.

She cracked one eye open to see Reese's face hovering over her. Everything around him was dark.

He let out a long breath and set his forehead on hers. "I have never been so furious at you," he whispered.

Sable managed to get the other eye open and realized he was sitting next to her on what must be a large bed. "How did I…?"

"Innov." Reese tilted his head toward something behind Sable where Innov perched on the back of a chair, spreading her light over a small table set with a bowl of water and a neatly folded washcloth. "She flew down and wrapped herself around you before you hit the fire."

Yes. There had been wings in the fire.

"Thank you, Innov," Sable said quietly.

The phoenix shifted her wings, sending out a rain of sparks, but made no other acknowledgment.

Yes, the fire had been full of wings and smoke and white robes…

She looked back at Reese. "Vivaine?"

Reese shook his head. “Gone. I don’t know if it was the fall or the fire that killed her, but…”

“Argyros?”

“There’s been no sign of him. Gwen says he told Vivaine she could stay and die, weak and alone.”

Sable lifted her hand up to his arm and discovered that even though her shoulder ached, everything seemed to move normally. She stretched her legs, and aside from a sharp ache in her back, everything just felt a little bruised and battered.

“Serene says you don’t have a single broken bone.” He pulled a very short lock of hair in front of her face. “Your hair did not survive as well.”

She raised a hand and ran it through her hair. On her left side, it was barely longer than her chin. She refocused on him. “You don’t look furious at me.”

“I am. But it’s sort of drowned out by relief.”

“Ah.” She smiled at him and reached up to run her fingers through his beard. “I’m happy to see you again.” He was still wearing the clothes she’d seen him in on the barrow, although they were dirtier, and there was a tear on one shoulder.

Her gaze caught on a tapestry behind him on the wall, and she looked around the room. There were only a few candles lit, leaving the ceiling mostly in shadows, but the walls were covered in paintings and tapestries, and the blanket she was under was a thick brocade fabric. “Where are we?”

“The residential wing of the fortress.” He glanced around. “It’s no leaky-roofed cottage in the woods, but it’s not too bad. Seemed more comfortable than our tent.”

She smiled at him, but there were too many questions spinning in her head. “How long did I sleep? What happened to the Kalesh?”

“It’s only been half the night, so they’re still here. What they’ll do when dawn comes, I don’t know.”

She started to push herself up, and he gave a hum of disapproval but wrapped an arm under her shoulders and helped her sit.

“Where’s Jrogen?”

“In a cell under the keep.”

“I need to talk to him.”

“You need to rest. We can talk to him after you’ve had some more sleep.”

She shook her head but stopped when the room started spinning. "No, before daylight. Will you take me to him?"

Reese raised an eyebrow. "Well, unless you want to talk to Jrogen about some topic I'm personally going to have an issue with, I think you should change that night shirt for something a bit more…solid."

She looked down to find herself in nothing more than a thin white shirt barely reaching to her knees. "Where are my clothes?"

"Very charred. I don't know if Purn threw them out or is fixing them." He rose and went to a carved wooden wardrobe along the far wall. "But, lucky for you, the city loves you. It's been less than seven hours since you hurled yourself off a cliff, and yet some noblewomen in the city discovered you have no 'appropriate' clothes, and there have been gifts coming in for you all night." He opened the door to show a row of dresses hanging neatly.

"Gifts?"

"Apparently the Queen of the North has a dress code."

"When did I become Queen of the North?"

"I believe the actual ceremony is being planned for a fortnight from now, but the official document from the leaders of the five territories is being prepared to present to you when you're up and about."

Sable stared at him. "For what?"

He gave her an amused look. "Offering you the position of queen of the newly united north. I thought that was obvious." He pulled a light yellow dress out of the wardrobe. "Purnicious liked this one best. She said it was simple enough that you might be convinced to wear it, so she's already fit it for you."

The dress was made of plain linen, and embroidered around the waist in orange thread was a pattern that looked like flames.

"It is pretty." Sable glanced around. "Where is Purn?"

"Here!" Purn popped into view, standing next to her on the bed and beaming. "I was under strict instructions to let everyone know the moment you were awake. It's so good to see you awake, mistress."

Sable blinked at her. "Who's everyone? And aren't I the only one who can give you strict instructions?"

"Put that dress on the end of the bed, wastrel," Purn ordered. "And you heard my mistress—she wants to see Jrogen. Go make that happen while she gets dressed."

Ignoring Reese's objections, Purn shooed him toward the door, and when he was out, she turned to give Sable an appraising look. "We have a little work to do."

Sable stood, and though her legs felt a little shaky, she crossed the room to the tall mirror in the corner. The nightgown she wore was reasonably clean, except where the soot had rubbed off her skin onto it. Her legs and arms were smeared with ash, and her hair was singed on the left side until the ragged ends hung above her shoulder.

"A little?" she asked.

"Just a little," Purn said, bringing over a bowl of hot water and a cloth. "Let's start with the soot, and we'll end with the hair. I can get it long again, although it might take a bit more time than we want to spend right now. I can figure out something though."

Sable tilted her head, looking at the shorn locks. "What if we made it all short?"

Purn tapped her chin and looked in the mirror. "That would be faster. And if you don't like it, I'll lengthen it for you later."

"Perfect," Sable said. "Let's get me presentable enough that when I order Jrogen around, he takes it seriously."

When Sable emerged from the room into a stone hallway with Innov on her arm, two of General Braddick's men were stationed outside the door.

Reese pushed himself off the wall across from her and stopped, his mouth hanging open the slightest amount. His gaze traveled up the dress and took in her hair. It hung just above her shoulders, and his gaze caught on the braids holding Sable's hair back from her face and the thin silver ribbon Purn had woven through them.

She smiled up at him. "I take it you like the new hair?"

"I love it." He looked down at the dress again. "I will never doubt Purn's abilities again. I swear I left you filthy and half-singed just minutes ago."

She turned to one of the guards, but the world spun a little, and she reached out for Reese's hand.

"You sure you should be walking?" he asked, coming up beside her.

"I'm sure we don't have enough time for me not to." She looked up at the guard. "Could you take me to Jrogen's cell?"

The soldier shifted. "My apologies, but General Braddick would never allow that."

"Allow?" she said, raising her eyebrows.

"I mean he would be displeased if I brought you somewhere as unseemly as the dungeons. The prisoner is being retrieved and brought to the Great Hall."

Sable looked at Reese. "Do you know where that is?"

"Not even remotely."

The soldier gave her a smile and a quick salute. "We'll escort you there if you're ready."

He led them along the stone hall, down a set of stairs, and through more hallways until they reached a set of wide wooden doors that were open to a broad room with a raised dais at the far end. A huge fireplace sat on each side in the middle of the wall, a blazing fire crackling in each. The floor was mostly empty except for a tall chair situated on the dais and benches along each side wall.

Atticus, Thulan, and Leonis stood near one of the fires, and when they caught sight of her, Atticus threw up his hands. "The phoenix rises!"

Innov started at the shout and took off, flying over to land on the edge of the mantel.

The playwright strode toward her, smiling widely, and wrapped her in a crushing hug.

She smiled into his shoulder. "I'm not a phoenix, Atticus. I'm just a woman foolish enough to jump off a cliff into a fire."

He stepped back but kept his hands on her shoulders. "That was the death part. This is the rising from the ashes."

"That was the most dramatic thing I have ever seen, Sneaks!" Leonis said. "Vivaine was wrapped in fiery light, the barrow was ringed with fire, Innov tore out of the sky, leaving a streak of embers, and you…you dove into it all!"

Atticus stepped back, still smiling widely. "Did you know that in some old stories, the phoenix doesn't merely burn out? Instead, when it is ready to be reborn, it builds itself a pyre, climbs atop it, and lights itself on fire." His eyes were bright with excitement.

Sable couldn't keep her own smile off her face. "I'm glad you find so much symbolism in my act of desperation."

"Oh, there are all kinds of symbolism. There's so much I already have the outlines for two different plays, and I'm toying with a third." He still smiled, but a shadow hung over his expression.

Sable reached out and took his hand. "Atticus, I'm sorry about…her. About your…" She let out a breath. "Vivaine."

His smile faded, but he squeezed her fingers. "She was never mine."

"That's not what I meant."

"I know, but perhaps it's the important thing for me to remember. I don't even know if the woman I thought she was ever truly existed."

"Even at the end," Sable said. "Even when she was..." Vivaine's crazed expression came back to Sable's mind, and she sighed. "Even then, she actually believed she was doing something good. She just couldn't see how tainted it had all become. She must have started out, once, with a desire to do real good. With something that was actually admirable. She must have."

"I'm not sure that's true," Atticus said with a sad smile, "but thank you for saying it."

Heavy footsteps came from the passage outside, and twenty guards poured into the hall, surrounding General Braddick, who had his hand clamped on Jrogen's arm. The Tien Sark's wrists and ankles were shackled, and there was a purpling bruise on his cheek.

Atticus, Leonis, and Thulan stepped away, but Reese stayed at Sable's shoulder.

Braddick turned toward where Sable stood by the fire, pulling Jrogen with him. The guards spread out around them, keeping their eyes fixed on the prisoner.

General Braddick stopped a few paces from Sable and drove his knee into the back of Jrogen's legs, and the Tien Sark crashed forward onto his knees.

"The prisoner's execution is set for dawn," Braddick said, "on the city wall, in view of his army."

Jrogen kept his chin raised. His shoulders were pushed back, and his arms strained against the shackles.

Sable stepped up until she was only a few paces from him. "Well, now we know that you can face your death defiant and unafraid." She gave him a small smile. "Just like Melia did."

A muscle in his jaw twitched.

She folded her arms, tapping her fingers on the smooth yellow sleeve of her dress. "I could let them kill you, but then I'd need to find another messenger with as much clout and as much motivation as you to take my message to the Emperor."

His eyes narrowed almost imperceptibly. "Why would I be motivated to be your messenger?"

"You're not. You're motivated to earn that seat in the Tien Sark. The

Jaw, right? But to do that, you need something to impress the Emperor, and the things you came here for don't exist. There is no gold, and Zenivah was just a woman who was manipulating the Empire for her own power."

She raised a finger. "But you can bring back something different: the news that you've saved the Emperor himself from a woman who manipulated everything from the gold to your own mythology, all to gain power. A woman whom your rival—what was his name? Tesok?—supported fervently."

Footsteps by the door made her glance over to see Evay, Talia, and Ryah slip into the hall. When they saw the number of guards, they quietly joined Atticus, Leonis, and Thulan off to the side.

"There's nothing here for you," Sable said to Jrogen. "You can take your army home, tell the Emperor what happened, and manage to look very good in the process."

Jrogen's expression was still defiant, but his arms relaxed slightly against his chains. "A'Melia's daughter is here." He pointedly looked at Talia and Ryah. "Daughters."

Sable reached down and grabbed his chin, turning his face back toward her. "You talk about my sisters again," she said, pouring warmth into the words, "and I'll have General Braddick kill you right here. I'm the daughter who matters, you understand?"

She pushed so much ferocity into the words that Jrogen tensed but nodded.

Sable let go of his chin and stood. "You've met me, Jrogen. What do you think of me?"

"You're weak, and everything that you've earned has been through luck." His words were said easily, but they were a cold lie.

Sable let out a breath that was mostly a laugh. "Well, then, there's your answer to the Emperor. The daughter of A'Melia is weak and not a threat to him." Her smile faded. "So, will you be my messenger?"

Jrogen considered the question, his face still hard, then gave a sharp nod.

"Swear to me," she said, "that you will take your army, turn around, and leave this land the fastest way you can. You will harm nothing and no one on your way. You will not stop in the south. You will not stop for more than a single night until you get back to the Empire."

He nodded again, but she shook her head.

"Say the words."

"I swear," Jrogen said, "to take the Kalesh army back to the Empire as quickly as possible and harm no one and nothing in the process." His voice was calm, but the words were warm.

"And?"

"I will tell the Emperor that there is no gold and Zenivah was merely a crazed woman trying to manipulate him. The dragon is gone, and there is nothing of value in this land. Not even the daughter of the fabled Ghost."

"Then you have your life. General Braddick, make sure this man is returned to his troops by daybreak. We wouldn't want any of his officers to take it upon themselves to launch an attack on the city."

"You can*not* honestly trust him to keep his word," Braddick said.

"I know when he's telling the truth." She turned back to Jrogan and motioned to where Evay stood silently in the shadows on the side of the mantel. "And there'll be elven archers following you until you get on your ships. If you break your word, you're a dead man."

Jrogen's gaze flickered to Evay. He nodded.

"Good." Sable leaned forward. "Then get off our land."

PART VII

And now the brightness at the end.

It still grows slowly at the start, the first bit of sunrise. But it is coming.

Not an ending so much as a new beginning.

-Stage notes from act three, scene fourteen of ***The Phoenix Rising*** by Atticus the Playwright

CHAPTER EIGHTY-SIX

SABLE TOOK A DEEP BREATH, watching Jrogen be escorted from the hall. The air smelled of the pine burning in the fireplace and the faintly dry smell a stone building always had. Maybe it was the pine or maybe it was the vastness of the hall, but for a moment she felt as though she stood on a hillside, watching the last of a storm roll away into the distance. It felt fresh and new, as though the battered land and wounded families damaged from the tempest were just resting, waiting to be tended and healed.

The moment the footsteps faded in the hall, Talia and Ryah rushed over. Both sisters had washed and wore simple dresses that fit like borrowed clothes.

Ryah threw her arms around Sable, her eyes teary, while Talia embraced them both.

Sable pulled them close for a long moment before stepping back, leaving her hands on their shoulders. "Neither of you are hurt?"

"Are *we* hurt?" Ryah asked. "You jumped off a cliff. Into a fire!"

Sable opened her mouth to object, but catching sight of Talia's beaming smile, she paused. "You look happy."

"She got a letter from Niko," Ryah said. "He's on his way north."

Talia's smile widened. "Since the Tien Sark are here, the Empire recalled Ambassador Grigg to the capital, so Niko resigned!"

Sable glanced at Reese. "Kalesh soldiers can resign?"

"The actual term is 'deserted,' I suppose," Talia said, "but that doesn't sound nearly as courageous as the fact that Niko went up to Ambassador Grigg and told him he loved me and was coming north to find me, and the ambassador would have to kill him to stop him."

Sable raised an eyebrow. "How was that received?"

"The ambassador said he couldn't believe Niko had waited so long, since Niko had been a lovesick mess since I'd left. Then said if it wasn't too much trouble, if Niko could answer the last pile of correspondence before he left, it would make the ambassador's day better."

Sable stared at her. "Well, that's unexpectedly good. When will he be here?"

"Three or four days." Talia's fingers toyed with a thread at her cuff. "Before everything on Tutella Island, Kiva had told his people to sell whatever he had left in Immusmala and bring it north. They were told to extend an invitation to Niko if he wanted to come."

"So," Sable said, "Niko's coming north with a lot of money that now no one owns."

Ryah tilted her head toward her sister. "Talia owns it."

With a small shrug, Talia nodded. "Last winter, Kiva declared that if anything happened to him, his fortune was mine to do with as I pleased." There was a bit of sadness around her smile.

Sable let out a breath that was half laugh, half surprise. "It's infinitely better that you control the wealth than him." She set her hand on Talia's arm. "You know I'll never forgive Kiva for a lot of things, but he saved your life more than once, and now he's made sure you'll have everything you want. So I admit that he was not as one-dimensional as I thought. You were right."

Talia blinked at her. "It might be more miraculous that you said that than that you survived diving into a fire."

There were more footsteps in the entrance to the hall, and Jae, Serene, Gwen, and Terrane entered.

Atticus pointed at Gwen, then at Sable. "You two planned that whole argument the other day, didn't you? So Vivaine's spies would report that Gwen was angry enough to come to her side."

Gwen gave him a little bow. "It was easy to act like I thought Sable's plan was stupid. I did think it was stupid. There was no way she was going to know if the bond between Vivaine and Argyros was broken unless I could read Vivaine's mind. Since I didn't think Vivaine would let me close if she thought I was on Sable's side, it seemed like the thing to do."

Sable grinned at her. "I almost laughed out loud when you told me I was a bad actress."

"Well, I'd just spent all day trying to convince Vivaine I'd truly joined her, and you looked completely unruffled to see me there."

"I was nervous she'd done something terrible to you." Sable waved to Gwen's whole person. "When I saw you in one piece, I was so relieved."

"You didn't look surprised at all," Gwen said. "Atticus's reaction is what sold it."

The playwright shook his head. "You stepped up next to her, Gwen, and I swear I heard my heart break."

Gwen smiled fondly at the old man. "Don't worry. Sable convinced me weeks ago that you people are my real family now."

"That's what she does," Atticus said, glancing at Sable. "She convinces people of the truth. Which leads us to the interesting situation we find ourselves in now." His look turned expectant.

Sable glanced at the others and saw similar expressions. Her head felt heavy, and the thick softness of the bed called to her, but they were all here and this needed to be addressed at some point.

She leaned against Reese, and he wrapped an arm around her shoulders. "All right," she said. "Let's talk about it."

Atticus opened his mouth.

"First," Leonis said, his voice bursting with excitement, "go sit on the throne!"

Sable glanced at the chair up on the dais. The tall back and the thick arms were carved wood, the seat encased in a thin red fabric that didn't look at all comfortable. "Not unless you find three or four cushions for it." She looked around the hall with its stark stone benches. "Actually, I'd sit anywhere with comfortable cushions."

Serene raised a finger. "The library!"

"Where's that?" Sable asked.

"Not far. It's cozy, and there are comfortable chairs." Serene smiled widely. "And so many books."

"But..." Leonis looked around the room plaintively. "I wanted Sable to sit on the throne."

"There's a very throne-like chair in the library, too," Jae said. "Lord Darien used it to hear people's petitions more often than this hall."

"If there's a throne," Leonis said, "then lead the way!"

Sable held out her arm, and Innov flew over to her. Sable ran her fingers over the phoenix's feathers, drawing out some of Innov's warmth into herself.

Atticus fell in next to Sable as they walked into the hallway. "I've seen the document the north is preparing, and it does offer you a throne."

"He wrote the document," Thulan said from behind them.

Atticus waved away her words. "I may have helped with wording a little. It's quite good, really." He grinned. "Historic even."

Serene pushed open a heavy wooden door not far down the hall. The papery smell of books greeted Sable as she stepped into a room not even a quarter the size of the Great Hall, but this one was as welcoming as the other was cold. Dark-stained bookshelves stood along every wall from floor to ceiling with only a few gaps for windows or paintings. Outside was nothing but darkness. Rain splattered against the windowpanes, but the room itself was lit by the glow of a dozen candles and a dozen more small lanterns hanging from a thick-beamed chandelier.

The center of the room was open, the floor covered with a thick rug woven with reds and golds. Around the edges, chairs and small tables were situated. The far side of the room was raised up one step with an ornate high-backed chair centered between two windows.

"It is like a throne!" Leonis clapped his hands. "Sneaks?"

Sable ignored him and headed to a closer, more comfortable-looking chair upholstered with deep blue fabric.

Serene crossed to a table covered with open books and pages of notes. She sat, fitting into the light and the books and the pages of writing as though they had been made for her.

Innov hopped off Sable's arm and perched on the back of the blue chair. Sable picked up a small wine red pillow tucked in the corner of it and sat. It was soft but too deep, and her feet barely brushed the floor. She shifted but merely sank deep in. The sense of freedom she'd felt at Jrogen's departure evaporated, replaced by something more ill-fitting, and she wrapped her arms around the pillow, holding it against her stomach.

"Is the library always so well lit in the middle of the night?" That wasn't the question she wanted to ask, but the real one was too shrouded in the discomfort of this chair and this entire fortress.

"Serene and I were here when Purnicious told us you were awake." Jae joined his wife at the table. "It's a good library. Not as big as the one at Stonehaven or the Dragon Priory, but still, it's remarkably well stocked."

Reese sat in a chair next to Sable, his feet reaching the floor just fine, and everyone else either took seats or moved over to look at the bookshelves.

"It's beautiful," Sable answered.

Between the dark wood and the candlelight and the rows and rows of leather-bound book spines, it *was* beautiful. And snug and inviting. Thulan took a seat in a stuffed leather chair across the room, and Sable's eyes caught on a map hung behind the dwarf, nestled between two small shelves. It was the north, drawn out in great detail and well labeled.

Sable fiddled with a tassel on the corner of the little pillow.

Barrowford was a small mark on the map. Tutella Island just a dab of brown in a long blue river. She found Steepdale, but then her eyes wandered across little sketches of hills and forest, brushing past names of towns she'd never heard of, sweeping over the vast area encompassed by the northern territories.

The incongruity of the entire situation leaked out of the map and swirled through the room.

"Doesn't anyone else find this strange?" Sable shifted in the oversized chair again. "Why are the ruling families in the north so interested in creating a queen? How can people who've spent generations vying for more power suddenly want to hand it all over?"

Atticus sat on a chair across from her and leaned forward, propping his elbows on his knees and steepling his fingers. "That would be odd, but that's not the situation we have. As of this moment, every territory has lost their lord and most of their generals. In three territories, the succession is clear, but the next in line is too young to rule, which is always precarious. The other two are disputed."

Atticus tapped his fingers against each other. "But it's more than that. The leaders of the north have lost the trust of the people themselves. As far as the people are concerned, the lords led them to the brink of war, but you united everyone and saved the north. The ruling families are rightly afraid that they are on the verge of losing everything, and so they're ready to swear fealty to you in return for receiving their own territory as one of your dukedoms."

"So they're shoring up the little power they have," Sable said, running the tassel through her fingers. "That makes more sense."

"It's not a bad idea," Jae said. "For them or for the north as a whole. The people supporting you the most strongly are the families of the lords who agreed that the north should unite. All of their opponents are viewing the unification as a point of contention. It benefits the entire north to keep people in positions of influence who publicly support unity."

Reese nodded. "Not to commend the Empire for anything, but Jrogen pointed out that when they're trying to establish a new government, keeping the old one at least partially intact makes the process smoother. As long as you can count on their loyalty."

"Which I believe we can," Atticus said. "The ideas they've come up with—"

"Wait." Sable held up a hand. "I have conditions."

Atticus paused.

"No, Sneaks," Leonis said firmly. "You are doing this all wrong. First, you become queen." He made a dramatic hand wave toward the throne. "Then there are no conditions. You say something, it is law."

"Leonis," Sable said, letting her head sink back on the chair, "if you get to sit on the throne, will you shut up?"

His eyes widened. "Yes!" In a few long strides, he bound over to the throne and up the single step. He stood surveying the room with a raised chin before sitting regally. "You may call me 'Your Majesty.'"

"I'm gonna call you an idiot," Thulan answered.

"You were saying about conditions?" Atticus said to Sable.

"Yes." She leaned forward. "I've been thinking about what you said, Atticus, about how I have more than one dream. My cottage is one, and…" She gave Reese a small smile. "It's a really good one. But you're right that I want other things. I want to stop people like Vivaine and the Kalesh, and I would have done it even if the north never noticed me and even if it had cost me my life."

She took in the familiar faces around the room. "I've talked to enough people here to know that a unified country is good for them, and an end to the constant skirmishes between territories is a good thing. Men like Tanis and Sam and Reese have been looking for a chance like this for a long time, and if it takes me to have it happen, then I'm willing to do whatever needs to be done. But you know I have no idea how to rule something. So my conditions all revolve around the idea that I need help."

She looked from Thulan to Evay. "First, I want emissaries set up between humans, elves, and dwarves. Good emissaries," she added to Thulan, "who actually want to talk to humans. Not like Pardrun."

"No problem," the dwarf answered. "Rion won't be High Dwarf for long. Callun will pick a good emissary."

Sable hesitated. "Seeing as I'm not the queen of anything yet, I can say that personally, I'm very in favor of this change. I'm sure the official statement from the north will acknowledge that it will recognize whichever High Dwarf Torren chooses."

Thulan grinned. "When Callun heads back, I'm going too. There's no way I'm missing the fight that's brewing."

Sable looked at Evay. "Will the elves agree to an emissary?"

"They will, and I'll volunteer," she said. "I get antsy staying in the woods too long anyway, and with all of you here"—she gestured to where Ryah and Talia sat together—"I'm sure I'll be here often anyway."

"Perfect," Sable said. "My second condition is—"

"Wait," Reese interrupted. "I have one." He gave Sable a smile that held a little bit of a grimace. "If you become Queen of the North, I don't want to be king."

"Doesn't anyone else find this strange?" Sable shifted. "Why are the ruling families in the north so interested in creating a queen? How can people who've spent generations vying for more power suddenly want to hand it all over?"

CHAPTER EIGHTY-SEVEN

THERE WAS a moment of silence in the room.

Sable shifted to face Reese more fully. "You...don't want to marry me?"

"No," he said quickly. "I do want to marry you. I'd marry you if the only perk was getting to live in that leaky-roofed cottage in the woods we talked about. But I don't want to be king, and the north doesn't want me to be king. They want you to be queen. There has to be something else I can be." He gave her a half smile. "I doubt Queen's Huntsman is a real thing."

"Thou shalt be her royal consort!" Leonis decreed from the throne. "And thus thou shall have no real power."

"Bad idea." Thulan shook her head. "He'll have no real power, but everyone will know the queen is smitten with him, so he'll still be swarmed with people trying to manipulate the throne through him. All the politics, none of the power."

"But I could tell them to go away," Reese said, "and it wouldn't be official rudeness from the queen, right?"

"Strictly speaking, yes," Atticus said, "but—"

"Perfect," Reese said. "Consort it is."

Sable looked around the room, running the tassel of the pillow through her fingers again. "Can we do that? A queen and a consort?"

"You really don't understand the concept of a queen, do you?" Thulan asked. "You can do anything you want."

"You cannot do anything you want," Atticus said. "At least if you want to be a good queen, but the north has never had a monarch. Actually, no part of this world has ever had a monarch. In that sense, you can make the position whatever you want. You want a consort? Have a consort."

"All right," Sable said, "Reese gets to be the royal consort. Next—"

"While we're all naming conditions," Serene said. "I have one. It involves the Keepers."

Sable glanced at her, Jae, Gwen, and Terrane. "Is that the official name?"

Serene shrugged, smiling. "It works. I've talked to Callun, and he's willing to lend us some dwarves to tunnel through the Marsham Cliffs to that keyhole valley."

"The Stronghold Valley," Jae corrected her. He looked around the room with a hint of pride. "It's been named."

Sable felt a twinge of longing at the idea of the valley.

"True," Serene continued. "Callun says the dwarves never considered it part of Torren. Since the north only extends to the Marsham Cliffs, and the"—she glanced at Jae—"Stronghold will be past that, it seems the valley is up for grabs. So we're going to grab it."

Sable cleared her throat and looked back at the map behind Thulan. "We need a different name than 'the north' too, don't you think?"

No one answered.

Atticus rubbed his hand along the back of his neck. "There have been…proposals."

"Like what?" Sable asked. "When did anyone have time to make proposals?"

"Recently," he said vaguely.

"Atticus hath used the journey from the Island of Tutella," Leonis said, projecting his voice to fill the room, "to speak with many, many, many fellow travelers. What you are about to hear is his fault."

"You're not supposed to be speaking," Atticus reminded him.

"What proposals?" Sable asked again.

Atticus cleared his throat. "There's really only one. And it's gained enough popularity that I think it's pretty much decided."

The others around the room were watching Sable with varying levels of amusement.

"And it is?" she prompted him.

"It shall be called," Leonis called from the throne, "Queensland!"

Sable laughed. "Shut up, Leonis. What is it really?"

There was a moment of awkward silence.

"It's really Queensland," Atticus said. "From your dubious look I can tell that I have not impressed upon you how fervently the north admires you, Sable. They loved you even before you stopped the Kalesh and saved them from Vivaine and her dragon. There is an opportunistic cousin of the late Lord Loren who has already commissioned several songs to be written about you."

"Songs?" she asked.

"Leonis has one half written too," Thulan added. "It's terrible."

"It will be epic!" Leonis boomed. "Grown men shall weep into their ale at just the first words!"

"It made me weep hearing you try to sing it," Thulan muttered.

"Anyway," Sable said, turning back to Serene. "I agree your valley—"

"The Stronghold," Jae corrected her again.

"I agree the Stronghold is outside of the north," Sable said.

"Queensland," Leonis declared.

Sable threw the pillow at him.

His regal expression didn't waver as it bounced off his face.

"And," Serene said, dragging everyone's attention back to her, "it will stay independent forever. If we're to have a place we can learn and record history and teach each other, it can never be controlled by any monarch." She gave Sable an apologetic look. "So if one of your conditions is that you also get to remain a Keeper, we'll say no. It's queen or Keeper."

"Remain?" Sable asked.

"You are one. You've been one of us since the beginning." Serene's expression was full of regret. "But it would be wrong to tie us to a throne. It's too much power in once place."

Sable's gaze moved back to the map. There was no marking on it for the valley, of course. The map makers wouldn't have known it was there, but she knew where it sat. Could picture the green grass and the tall walls protecting it from everything else.

Up until this moment, she'd harbored an undefined hope of balancing both things, queen and Keeper.

"You'd still be a Keeper in spirit," Jae said quietly, "but not in name, and the queen will not command us to do anything."

She let out a breath. They were right. The throne should not be able to control a group of people with so much power. Nor should they control the throne.

And the cliffs of the Stronghold would do more than just protect Sable if she went there. They would also keep her from doing all the things she could do as queen. From righting the wrongs, checking the power of those who would abuse the people beneath them.

She nodded, the motion more difficult than she'd expected. But she kept her voice even. "I agree."

She blew out another breath and straightened as much as she could in the oversized chair. "Which brings me to my last condition. Gwen, I know you're one of the Keepers, but would you stay at court as an advisor? You spent years with Vivaine, navigating the politics of the south. I could use your insight."

Gwen straightened at the request, but she didn't answer.

"I want your insight," Sable clarified. "Not your powers. You told me once that you'd spent so much time reading people's minds, you were now good at telling what they were thinking even without touching them. I will never ask you to sneak around and spy for me. You're the only one who decides what to do with your gift."

"Good," Gwen said, crossing her arms and giving Sable a slight smile. "Because if you tried, I'd tell you I'm a Keeper and not under your rule."

Sable didn't smile back. "There's more, though. If you're willing, I'd like to make public what you can do."

Gwen's smile turned frigid.

"And what I can do." Sable glanced at her sisters. "And what you two can do. If I'm going to have a court, it won't run on secrets."

"We deem that dream to be unrealistic," Leonis proclaimed.

"Actually," Atticus said thoughtfully, "if you were bringing a proposal to the queen and knew she could tell if you were lying, her advisor could read your mind with a touch, and her sisters could tell both your motivations and your emotions…would you try anything deceptive?"

Leonis tapped the arm of the throne. "We deem that perhaps we would not," he said more quietly.

"I agree to your idea," Gwen said. "I'm tired of secrets."

"I'm tired of hiding," Talia said.

"And I'm tired of pretending I don't know what everyone is feeling," Ryah said.

"Excellent," Sable said. "Then it's settled. Atticus, it's your job to figure out how best to get that news out to the world."

Sable pushed herself out of her chair and rolled her neck. She walked to the nearest bookshelves and ran a finger along the book spines. She paused on one entitled *Maps of the Northwest*. The book was surprisingly thick, and she wondered how many of the places in it she'd heard of aside from Barrowford.

The bookshelves stretched above her to a high ceiling, lost in shadows. Rain spattered in irregular bursts on the window nearest to her like little snaps or hisses, and she pulled her hand off the books, wrapping her arms around herself. The room wasn't cold, but the air felt too…open. Too vast. Empty somehow.

Not just here. The whole fortress was thick stone and filled with people who were expecting her to be—

She brought her focus back to the books in front of her, taking a deep breath before her thoughts could grow any more disquieted.

Queen. They expected her to be queen.

The word felt bigger than it should. Heavier.

She cleared her throat and started down the row of books again. "Reese mentioned the crowning is being planned for a fortnight from now?"

"Yes," Atticus said. "So much of the north is here already, it seemed easier than returning after everyone had gone home."

She looked at them all. "Where will the capital of Queensland be?"

Atticus waved his hand at the fortress around them.

"In Barrowford?" Sable nodded. "That makes sense."

Atticus tugged on the end of his beard. "Well, this city is being renamed as well."

"To what?"

"It shall be called—" Leonis began in a resounding voice.

"Leonis!" snapped Thulan.

The half-elf paused, then slumped back in the throne. "Queenstown," he said in his normal voice. "It'll be called Queenstown. Thulan, you take all the fun out of life."

"Queenstown?" Sable asked. "Are you serious?"

"The people picked the name themselves," Atticus said.

"The wedding should happen at the same time as the crowning," Thulan said to Atticus before Sable could voice the incredulity growing inside her. "Maybe immediately before. That feels better than after, don't you think?"

Sable looked over to Reese for support but found him watching her intently, his fingers tapping on his thigh.

Atticus nodded. "Yes, the young woman marrying for love, then accepting the crown. I like it." He pointed at Reese. "They love you almost as much as they love her. The soldiers especially. You should wear a formal uniform, not from any particular territory, just something that looks official—"

Reese pushed himself to his feet. Ignoring Atticus, he crossed the few steps to Sable, stopping so close to her that she set a hand on his chest and tilted her head up to see him. He felt warm, his presence stirring the air, driving back the chill emptiness.

He put his hand over hers, pressing it against him until she could feel his heart beating under her palm. His other hand slipped along the side of her neck, and he leaned closer.

"Will you marry me?" His words came out low and almost rough.

His heartbeat thrummed under her hand, and her smile got lost somewhere in the way he smelled and in the desperate edge of his expression.

"I…" She managed a small, quizzical smile. "I stacked the rocks with you, Reese. I thought my answer to that question was clear."

"No." His fingers slid into her hair. "Will you marry me right now? Right here?"

Her mouth dropped open, but he continued, "A royal wedding is a political thing, but I don't want to marry the queen. I want to marry you—I wish I'd married you ages ago. Whatever happens from here on, I don't care. I just want to be with you. Every day."

He leaned down and kissed her. She slid her hands up around his neck and pushed against him, letting his warmth and solidness drive away all her fears.

Atticus cleared his throat. "I love the sentiment here, but your wedding will be a political event, and you need to use it as such. You need to set the stage, as it were, for what your marriage will be like, and the people will want to be a part of it."

Sable pulled back from Reese, looking up into his eyes. She untangled one hand from his hair to wave off Atticus's objection. "Then we'll do another public one later." She kissed Reese again. "I want to marry you. Right here, in a library, in the middle of the night. Surrounded by…" She gestured around the room.

"Your family," Atticus offered.

Sable looked at all the familiar faces and nodded. "Our family."

Reese, who hadn't looked away from her, smiled and pressed his lips to hers again, this time long and fierce.

"Do we need to let you two have the library to yourselves for a few minutes?" Thulan asked dryly.

"I'm not leaving my throne." Leonis flung one leg over the arm of the chair.

Sable finally broke away from Reese, despite the quiet hum of disapproval that sounded in his chest, and looked around his shoulder, picking out Ryah standing in the far corner of the room. "If only there were someone here who had done handfasting ceremonies before."

"Me!" Ryah clapped her hands and bounced up onto the balls of her feet. "I can do it!" She glanced down at her borrowed dress. "As long as you don't mind me looking like this."

Purnicious appeared next to her with a pop. "I can fix that!"

Another pop left nothing but empty air. It only took a few breaths before Purn reappeared, holding a dress. She held it up proudly.

Ryah's mouth dropped open. "This is... Where did you get this?"

The dress was long and white, vaguely like the one Ryah had worn when she'd left Immusmala, but if it was the same dress, the black stain that Eugessa had made across the front was gone, and the dress was no longer plain and restrained, the way abbesses' robes were. This was exquisite. There was a high waistline that was embroidered with a row of flowers in purple threads so light they were almost white. The sleeves were long and made of fabric as thin as mist.

"I know you said I could get rid of your dress," Purn said with a slightly apologetic wince. "But the fabric was so pretty, and it had a lot of potential, and...I know you love the priories, even if Eugessa and Vivaine turned out to be hateful hags. So I thought I'd work on it a little, and if you ever wanted it again..."

"Purnicious!" Ryah said. "It's the most beautiful thing I've ever seen."

"There's a large closet behind that door," Serene said, motioning to a corner of the room, "if you want to change."

Ryah grabbed Talia's hand and dragged her toward the closet. "You're in charge of my hair."

Purnicious looked at Sable. "You look beautiful already, mistress, but..." She turned an exasperated look at Reese and his torn, dirty clothes. Sighing, she motioned for him to come down to her level.

He squatted in front of her, and she traced her blue fingers across seams, tightening them up, fixing small tears, brushing away smudges of dirt.

"You know," she said as he endured her bellishing with a surprising amount of patience, "this changes everything."

"How so?" He lifted his chin at her direction and didn't move as she trimmed up his beard with her fingertips

"Once you're married, you'll officially be part of my mistress's family." She traced along the collar of his shirt. "Which means I'll have access to everything you own and can bellish it however I want. Like taking a boring collar like this and making it worth looking at." She dragged a finger down his chest, making a deep notch in the fabric. She paused, then reached forward as though ready to make the cut deeper.

"Purn," he said, the slightest warning in his voice.

"Fine," she said. "Give me your arm so I can fix the sleeves."

He held out one arm, and she set to work, her long blue nose almost touching him as she fiddled with seams.

"How is you bellishing all of my clothes any different from what you've been doing?" he asked.

She grinned up at him. "Now I don't have to sneak around to do it."

He watched her work for a minute. "But you still will, won't you?"

She gave no answer besides a smug smile. "Other sleeve, wastrel."

"Purnicious," he said, offering his other arm, "does this mean this is the last time you're going to call me wastrel?"

She finished with the sleeve and looked him over, then reached up a little blue hand and patted his cheek. "Absolutely not."

He grabbed for her hand, but she popped out of view.

When he stood, Sable stepped up closer to him, running her hands over the shoulders of the shirt. "She does do a good job."

"I only let her do it because it makes you happy," he said, smiling down at her.

"You know you couldn't stop me." Purn's voice came from nearby.

Talia returned, followed by Ryah in the white dress, her hair braided.

"Purn," Ryah called, looking around the room, "I need one more thing."

The kobold popped into view, and Ryah knelt next to her.

Thulan walked up to the throne and kicked Leonis's foot off the arm. "Help me move this thing out of the way."

With a dramatic sigh, Leonis stood, and the two of them carried the throne over to the side of the room. Ryah took its place, motioning for

Sable and Reese to join her. The others dragged chairs across the floor, facing them all toward where Ryah stood on the step.

Purnicious popped into view, holding up three strips of fabric, each as long as she was tall.

"These are perfect!" Ryah said, taking them. "How did you get them so perfect?"

Sable moved closer to look at them and caught the tired smile on Purn's face. "You just made these, didn't you?"

The kobold shrugged. "It wasn't terribly hard."

"I'm sure it was harder than you'll admit," Ryah said, "but I promise that's all we need."

Purnicious stepped up to Sable and took her hand. "I am very happy for you, mistress." She gave Reese an almost shy smile and took his hand too, bringing it over to Sable's. "I'm happy for you both and happy for me that we're all going to be family." Her large purple eyes grew wet, and she blinked quickly before giving their hands one final squeeze and popping out of sight. Sable glanced back to see her reappear, sitting in the deep blue chair. Her feet stuck straight out, barely clearing the front of the seat, but she beamed at them.

Innov took off from the chair and flew over to Sable's arm, her eyes fixed on the dangling strips of fabric.

Ryah held one out to Reese. It was a deep, rich blue, the color of the sky when the first brush of sunrise began to sweep away the stars.

Sable took the next. It was soft and smooth between her fingers. What she'd first taken to be merely a dark green caught the candlelight, and the color gained depth. The solemn green of the endless pine forests was woven through with highlights of lighter green. Threads of gold flitted through the fabric like tiny glitters of sunlight.

"In the south, especially in abbeys under the Phoenix Priory," Ryah began, giving Sable a smile, "weaving a handfasting braid is traditional to symbolize the weaving together of your two hearts and lives."

"Is the third piece for Purn?" Leonis whispered loudly.

Thulan elbowed him in the side, and he grunted.

"The third piece," Ryah said with another smile, still looking at Sable and Reese and holding up the gauzy, shimmering gold fabric that fluttered slightly, "is the love that brings you two together."

"Gold," Thulan whispered. "It's Innov."

"If either of you speaks one more word," Atticus said sternly, "I will have Serene remove you from this room. By whatever means necessary."

Thulan and Leonis exchanged smirks but closed their mouths.

Ryah leaned to look at Thulan over Reese's shoulder. "It is Innov, in a way. It is hope and goodness and trust and love, all rolled into one thing, somehow terribly complex, but also…perfectly simple." She motioned for Sable and Reese to face each other.

Sable turned to Reese, and he took her free hand while they held their ribbons of fabric close to each other.

Ryah knotted the gold fabric around the other two just below Sable's and Reese's hands, binding all three strands together. "Tonight, in this place, before your family and friends, you bind yourselves to each other. Using nothing but the love you share, you take your two separate lives and join them into one."

"Do you vow," Ryah asked them, "to love each other well through the bright seasons of life and cling to each other through the storms?"

Beneath the knot, the three strands hung close, brushing against each other. Above the knot, though, the green came to Sable's hand alone and the blue to Reese's. The two bits of fabric felt too isolated. Too distant.

Sable shifted her hand, laying the green across Reese's palm and setting her own hand on top. He smiled, and his fingers wrapped around hers, the fabric pressed together between them.

"Do you vow to care for each other in the long, weary days of sickness," Ryah asked, "and offer your own strength and courage to the other when their next step feels too hard?" She began to braid the blue, green, and gold fabric. The colors wove together, the separations between them dissolving as they formed into a single cord. The gold glowed in the light from Innov, but as the three pieces intertwined, the gold in the greens was drawn out, and similar threads Sable hadn't noticed glittered in the midst of the rich blue like tiny bits of firelight.

Sable looked up to find Reese watching her with such fierce intensity that the rest of the room fell away.

"Do you vow to love each other through poverty and wealth," Ryah's voice continued, "through heartache and joy, through the steady years and the changing ones, for every day of your lives, from now until you step into the Golden Lands?"

His grip tightened around her hand and the ribbons, but he lifted his other hand to brush his fingers along her cheek. "I do," he said, the words searingly hot.

She lifted her free hand to his chest and poured all her emotions into her promise. "I do." The air around them and between them swirled with heat.

"Life brings changes and heartaches and joys," Ryah said as she wove the ends of the fabric together. "A million tiny splinters will try to work their way into the cracks between you, snagging the fabric of your love, tearing holes and leaving gaps. Some will be easily brushed aside. Others will burrow in fast and deep. But it is the hard, brave, powerful work of love to draw them back out, to heal each other's wounds, to offer light and hope in the darkness."

At the bottom, she took the gold fabric and knotted the braid together again. Then she wrapped it twice around Sable's and Reese's hands.

"With this cord, you are bound together," Ryah said. "May you cling to each other and find joy and hope and courage for the rest of your lives."

Sable slid her hand up behind Reese's neck and pulled him toward her through the warmth. He stepped nearer, and with the happy cheers of the others filling the library, she kissed him, feeling the heat of him and their vows swirling around them.

She drew it all closer, pouring the heat into them both and pulling him tighter until there was no distance left between them.

CHAPTER EIGHTY-EIGHT

"Sable," Reese whispered, his voice slipping through the darkness. "Wake up. I have a wedding present for you."

She curled her legs up closer to her chest and reached behind her to where he usually slept—until she realized his voice had come from in front of her, where he was squatting next to their bed.

"Don't go back to sleep." She could hear the smile in his voice. "You have to wake up to get it."

Their room was shrouded in shadows. A low bed of coals in the fireplace gave a hint of red to the edges of the tall, carved bedposts and the wardrobe behind Reese.

"What are you doing awake?" she asked.

"Getting things ready." He leaned forward and kissed her forehead. "Get up."

"Ready for what? The wedding isn't until tonight."

"True, but this isn't a fake-wedding-for-the-masses present, it's a real-wedding-to-the-woman-I-love present." He lifted up a dark bundle. "I have clothes ready for you."

"The real wedding was a fortnight ago," she protested, but she pushed the covers back and drew in a breath at the chilly air that brushed across her skin.

"Some presents require time." He offered her a warm, soft wool shirt.

She pulled it quickly over her head. "Do they require being up in the middle of the night?"

"Just being up before the sunrise."

She stopped in the act of taking a pair of thick pants from him and looked out the window at a perfectly black sky. "The sun is not even close to rising."

"It will be by the time we get there." He held up a cloak. "It's a bit chilly out. You'll want this."

She pulled on the pants and her boots, then stepped up close to him while he wrapped the cloak around her shoulders. He was already dressed in his own, and she slid her arms inside it.

She rose up on her toes and kissed him. "We could just stay here where it's warm, you know."

"We could." He wrapped his arms around her and leaned into her kiss. "But you'd rather go."

"I would?"

He nodded. "So stop being distracting. We need to go." Taking her hand, he started toward the door.

"But I miss my warm bed, and you're usually so easy to distract," she said. "Am I losing my touch this quickly?"

"Oh, you're distracting." He pulled the door open. "But this is a really good present."

Sable stepped into the hall, greeting Nat and Coren, two of the guards who'd been assigned to protect her. When Reese started down the hall, both guards fell in behind them, all the way outside.

The night was clear, and a full moon hung in the west, casting silver-grey light across the courtyard. A breeze rolled over the wall of the keep, blowing past her cheeks with the sharp, cool edge of fall. Sable pulled her cloak tighter as Reese led them to the stables, where four horses were saddled.

"You're coming with us?" Sable asked the guards.

"Of course they're coming with us," Reese answered for them. "Do you have any idea the number of people who'd be lined up to kill me if I took you out of the city alone on the morning before we're married and you're crowned queen?"

"Out of the city?"

"We'd hardly need horses if we were merely walking down the street." Reese brought her to a black horse being held by a sleepy-looking stable hand.

Sable mounted, then turned to Nat, who swung up on his own horse. "Where are we going?"

"She's not the queen yet," Reese reminded the man, climbing into his saddle. "You're under no obligation to answer her questions until tonight."

Tonight.

Sable shook off the heaviness that settled on her whenever the coronation crossed her mind. The ceremony was as much of a formality at this point as the public wedding. The families of each of the late Northern Lords had already sworn loyalty to her, a royal council had been formed, the power and responsibilities of each duchy had been spelled out and agreed to. She'd spent every afternoon and every evening of the last two weeks in the council room or the library working out the details of what Queensland would look like.

And if she was honest with herself, it wasn't terrible. There was something satisfying in starting with a problem and being able to solve it fairly, and hopefully swiftly. While it probably wouldn't last indefinitely, the sense of unity among the people and the leaders was so strong that a great deal was being accomplished.

But that truth did nothing to loosen the knot of tension that had been tightening inside her for the past fortnight.

Sable pushed back the thought and turned to Nat. "Do you two even know where we're going?"

"Leave the good men alone," Reese said. "They've been sworn to secrecy, and, at least for today, they'll follow my orders over yours." He glanced at the eastern sky still black with night. "We need to get moving."

The guards at the gate swung it open for them to pass.

"How far are we going?" she asked.

Reese's only answer was a smile over his shoulder as he led them into the city. Their horses' hooves clattered on the cobblestones until they passed out of the southwestern gate and the road turned to packed dirt. Reese kept his horse at a walk, and Sable rode next to him as they entered the forest. The crisp night air carried the scent of pine on blustery gusts that continually tried to wriggle the chill through her cloak.

The forest was quiet except for the occasional hoot of an owl and the rustling of the trees. Moonlight angled down, brightening the woods enough that they made good time, moving from one patch of silvery light to the next.

Even with the fitful wind jostling the treetops, down among the trunks, the forest felt blissfully untroubled. Her eyes traced meandering paths that wound through the trees past small clusters clumped together as though meeting up for a leisurely conversation and past lone trunks grown larger and thicker than their neighbors. She tried to draw in the relaxed informality of it all.

Because it was the formality of the coming night that was the problem, bringing with it something that reminded her almost, but not quite, of the stage fright she'd felt the first night she'd performed on Atticus's stage.

Everything she'd done for the north up until now had been impromptu. Just an answer to whatever problems she faced. But this was so planned, down to the last excruciating detail.

They'd ridden for at least an hour, turning onto increasingly narrow trails, and a few birds had begun to tweet in answer to the purpling of the sky when a whistle sounded out of the woods ahead of them.

Sable straightened in her saddle, but one of the guards whistled back, and Reese moved on without any sign of concern. Sable cast out. Past their four horses was nothing but trees until a half-dozen shapes flared up, spread out in a line across the woods in front of them.

"You did plan this out, didn't you?" she asked Reese. "How many guards are involved in this little outing?"

He just smiled, and they came out moments later into a clearing where two of the soldiers waited. Reese dismounted and held out a hand to help her down. "You should probably get used to them. I doubt they'll let you wander the country with no protection from now on." When she was on the ground, he kept hold of her hand and started across the clearing. He glanced up at the light purple in the eastern sky. "Not much farther."

"You know I never believe you when you say that," she said.

But it turned out to be just a quick walk through a few more trees before they stepped out onto the broad top of an outcropping of rock. The land ahead of them dropped down, then spread out like a blanket of pines. The horizon was a pale yellow and the world light enough that here and there, nestled among the dark evergreens, a leafy tree was visible, its leaves lightening to autumn yellow or deepening to a vibrant red.

The sky arched cloudless overhead, purples and blues and pinks seeping into it from the coming sunrise, one color bleeding seamlessly into the next.

Reese took a seat near the front of the outcropping and pulled on her hand until she looked away from the view and sat next to him. The wind blew over the treetops below them and across the top of the rock, and he moved closer and wrapped his cloak around them both. "Warm enough?"

She shifted closer to him until she could feel the warmth of his body, then drew her knees up inside the cloak as well. "It's perfect."

The shushing wind brushing across the tops of the pines set them swaying and bending, rippling across the top of the forest like a restless sea. Sable closed her eyes and let the calm of the moment work its way into the knot inside her and loosen the tangles.

They sat in silence as the light grew. There had been so little quiet lately, and her mind shuffled from duchies to coronations to new building proposals for an actual palace in the center of Barrowford.

Queenstown, she reminded herself.

She pulled the cloak tighter around her and leaned on Reese, who sat relaxed and steady next to her. She closed her eyes and breathed in the morning air and the familiar scent of leather he always had. Her lungs stretched with the air as though she hadn't breathed deeply in weeks.

"See?" he said. "Nothing better than a sunrise."

"It's more than the sunrise," Sable said, putting her head on his shoulder. "I still don't know how you do this."

He kissed the top of her head. "Do what?"

"Sit here, doing nothing, and somehow make all the tension inside me start to calm."

"Maybe you're not the only one with magic."

"You definitely have some. At least over me."

They sat quietly again as the brightness grew in the east, gliding effortlessly, fluidly through the vast, open sky, chasing the purples and blues onto the slopes of the rocky Scale Mountains behind them.

She and Reese became merely two tiny figures, but instead of calming her as that thought usually did, the ceaseless swirl of doubts seemed to leak out of her, knotting even the stillness around them into tangles.

"The coronation is tonight," Reese said finally. "You're going to keep feeling like this until you decide whether you'll accept the crown."

"Feeling like what?"

The corner of his mouth curled up, and he set a hand on her fingers, which were rubbing quickly over a frayed section in the hem of his cloak. "Like if you fret enough, something will change."

She stopped her fingers, but the uneasiness didn't relent. "I am going to accept being queen. Of course I am. It's just…"

"You never really accepted that you were the Flame of the North." There was nothing accusatory in his voice, just the warmth of truth. "And yet you were. But being queen is different. If you don't believe you are queen, there will be countless others who will be happy to step in and take it all from you."

Her thumb brushed across the soft frayed edge of the fabric.

"I've never been queen," he said with a small smile, "but when Tanis died, the first soldier who called me 'general' almost got punched in the face. I was not a general. It was Serene who, ever so gently, told me to stop wilting and keep doing what I had been doing all along. Leading the men against the Kalesh."

Sable gave a small smile. "I can imagine her saying that. She'd probably tell me the same thing, wouldn't she?"

"Probably. A queen is the woman who will climb up on the catapult, see what her people need, and then work to give it to them. The only thing changing tonight is that by wearing the crown, you will never have to waste time again convincing people to listen to you."

Sable's thumb slowed against the fabric. "That's true."

The sky continued to lighten, and Sable mulled over the past two weeks. They really had been like days of standing on the catapult, assessing the problems around her and finding solutions.

She breathed in the morning air, and now it felt right. Clean. Wild. Free. And the worry of the coronation whittled away with the passing breeze.

When the sun was fully above the horizon, Sable nudged Reese. "This is so beautiful that if it weren't for the hour ride to get here, I'd say we should come more often."

"Good." He stood and held out his hand to help her up. "Because I still need to give you your present." He kept hold of her and led her toward the side of the outcropping, looking pointedly down over the edge into the woods.

The tallest trees only came about halfway up the rock face, and the forest spread away from them, unbroken for hill after hill—except for a small clearing not far from where they stood, which held just enough room for a small yard, a neat square of turned earth for a garden, and…

A cottage.

"Reese..."

"Before you're crowned queen tonight and get a palace and an entire country as your own," he said with a small smile, "I wanted to give you the one thing I've always wanted to give you. A home that is just yours and mine. Welcome to your cottage in the woods."

CHAPTER EIGHTY-NINE

THE SUN only brushed the tops of the pines with light, leaving the clearing washed in blue-tinged shadows. The roof was covered in red tiles, the walls crossed by dark timbers and filled with stucco already a rich creamy color.

As Sable watched, a puff of white smoke rose from the chimney.

"Reese…" She blinked, half afraid that would drive it away, back into her dreams. "It's perfect. How…?"

"You can thank Sam. The Tutella monks own small houses scattered across the north that they stay in when they're traveling, and I convinced him to sell this one to me. It hadn't been lived in for a while, so it took the workmen until yesterday to get it ready." He let out a little laugh. "The roof leaked."

"How did you pay for it?"

"Labor. I'm the official contact between Tutella Island and your royal court for the next five years." He pointed over the trees. "A short ride on horseback in that direction is a small town with a delicious baker and a brand-new outpost of your royal army so that any time you want to be here, we'll send word, and it will be ready the moment you arrive."

Sable's eyes traced the little rows of overturned earth in the garden and the trellis that leaned up against the wall.

"Reese. It's perfect."

He gestured toward a narrow path to their left. "There's your way down."

She nearly ran onto the path, following it back into the trees, down the steep slope, and through the forest until it spilled out into the grass alongside the garden.

Sunlight threaded through the trees, slanting into the clearing and setting the tiny drops of dew glittering. Another sunbeam brushed the side of the cottage, drawing out the rich browns of the timbers and turning the stucco to a buttery yellow.

Smoke now wafted steadily from the chimney, not the thick white of a new fire, but the gauzier grey of a well-burning hearth.

She breathed in the smell of the damp earth and the hint of woodsmoke and the wild, untamed freshness of the forests and the open hills. Turning, she threw her arms around Reese's neck. "It's everything I wanted," she whispered.

"And everything I wanted. There's excellent hunting in these woods and a river nearby full of fish." He scooped her into his arms, starting toward the front door. "Our spontaneous wedding in the library sparked an argument between Leonis and Thulan as to whether elves or dwarves have better wedding vows."

She leaned her head against his shoulder. "Of course it did."

"It turns out that both of them have some good points, but did you know dwarves don't have a wedding ceremony? They have hearth vows. A husband makes a cave for his wife, and the first time he brings her across the threshold, he recites a vow."

Reese paused outside the front door, a solid piece of wood painted a dark, rich red. "It was a bit too dwarvish for my taste, but with some surprisingly helpful suggestions from Leonis and Thulan, we rewrote it to have less references to ale and caves and beards."

"You did?"

He nodded and shifted her in his arms, clearing his throat. His eyes flickered to her face, then back to the door.

She set a hand on his cheek. "Are you nervous to say it?"

"Yes," he said with the hint of a smile. "You're the one who memorizes lines, not me."

"Are they good words?"

"They are." He glanced at the door, and his smile widened. "I don't have enough hands to both hold you and open the door."

She reached out and pushed the door open, and he turned to fit them through it.

Bright morning sunlight filtered in through the trees and the wavy glass of the windowpanes. Dark timbers crisscrossed the walls and made neat beams across the ceiling. A stone fireplace set into the wall on the left crackled cheerily and warmed a kettle hung over the flames.

Bundles of herbs hung drying near the fireplace, giving off the faint scents of lemon and mint. A couch, just big enough for two people, was pulled up close to the flames. Across the room, a table and some chairs were nestled under another window. On the far wall, a doorway led to a room with a bed piled high with pillows and blankets.

Sable's gaze moved from the tidy pile of wood stacked near the mantel to the two mugs hung on pegs on the wall to the thick russet cushions on the couch. "It's like Narine's house on Tutella Island," she whispered.

Reese nodded, and when she met his gaze, his eyes held slight worry. "I didn't know if that was good or bad."

She closed her eyes, taking in a deep breath of the room, feeling it settle around her like a blanket. She opened her eyes to smile at him. "It's good. Any reminder of Narine is good."

Letting out a breath that sounded relieved, he carried her to the couch and sank into it, shifting her to his lap but keeping his arms around her.

"I notice that this is not big enough for guests," she said with a smile.

"No guests," he said firmly. "I thought we could come at least once a fortnight for a night or two. If we set the precedent now, in the beginning, everyone will just accept it."

"Sounds perfect." She ran her finger along a thin line of stitching at the edge of his collar. Day by day, his clothes had been growing more polished, more formal looking. So far, he hadn't complained. She looked up to find him watching her with an intensity that stopped her hand. "Do I get my hearth vow? And is it like another marriage vow?"

"I suppose. But this time, we're alone, which is always better." He lifted one hand to her face. "Today, I offer you my hearth." His words began a little hesitantly, but they held a hint of heat. "Though the house is cold, if you'll stay by my side, we'll light a fire and fill our home with comfort and light."

The words grew warmer.

"While the fire burns bright," he said, brushing his thumb along her cheek, "if you'll stay by my side, we'll eat and drink and build our life together." The warmth of his words pressed around them, seeping into Sable's skin. "When the flames burn low, if you'll stay by my side, we'll have the strength to face whatever darkness comes. And when the flames go out," he finished, "if you will stay by my side, I will hold you until the end."

She leaned closer and kissed him. "Every day," she whispered. "I'll stay by your side every day until the end."

"You really got me a present?" Purnicious asked suspiciously. "Why?"

Reese stood by the door of their room back in Barrowford, waiting for her. "I was feeling generous. Are you coming to see it? Or would you like me to give it to someone else?"

Purn looked at Sable, her brow furrowed. "What is it?"

"I have no idea," Sable said, not trying to hide her amusement. "This is the first I've heard of it."

"I could hardly talk about it with Sable," Reese said. "You'd have heard every word. Are you coming?"

"He gave me an entire cottage this morning," Sable said to the kobold. "If I were you, I'd see what this is."

"How far away is it?" Purn asked.

"Not as far as the cottage," Reese said. "We don't have unlimited time today, though. They'll be tracking us down soon to prepare for the wedding and coronation. If you don't want your gift now, you'll have to wait at least until tomorrow. Maybe longer."

Purnicious narrowed her eyes. "Fine, but if this is some sort of prank, I will get you back."

He smiled at her. "This way." He held a hand out for Sable, and she took it as he opened the door. They moved into the hallway, and even though it was empty, Purnicious popped out of sight.

"It all started," Reese said, "when the first of the city's tailors showed up looking for Sable, who was of course locked in some meeting somewhere. Since no one is quite sure what style the new queen will like, he was dropping off some samples of fabric in case she saw something she liked."

"Ooh." Purn's voice came from behind them. "And you saved them for me?"

"The next day," Reese said, turning down a smaller hallway that led toward the servants' quarters, "three more tailors came, and that was only the beginning." He paused at a door. "Do you have any idea how many tailors there are in this city?" he asked Sable.

Sable shook her head.

"How many?" Purn whispered from the air beside them.

"A lot," Reese said, pushing open the door.

Purnicious gasped.

Inside was a room with shelves covering every part of the walls not filled with windows. Sun streamed in, landing on four large tables. Every surface and every shelf were filled with neatly folded samples of fabric.

They stepped in, and Reese pulled the door shut and leaned back against it, looking around the room with another smile. "What do you think, you little blue monster?"

Purnicious popped into view next to Sable, her mouth hanging open. She approached the nearest table, reaching out her hand to brush a velvety green cloth.

"It's..." She lifted her eyes and popped out of view, reappearing sitting on a high shelf with her legs hanging down, examining the edge of a delicate blue lace. She looked around the room, her eyes wide. "Look at all of it," she breathed. "Look at the colors! Brocades richer than anything Kiva ever wore! Silks, linens!" She blinked and reappeared standing on a table under a window, pulling out a swatch of brilliantly white cloth. "Ryah would love this!"

The kobold clasped the fabric to her chest, spinning slowly, taking in the entire room.

Reese picked up a bit of purple fabric from next to the door, holding it up, and Purn squealed.

"My cloak!" She disappeared and popped into view with her arms flung around his neck. "How did you get my cloak back?"

"I'm entitled to trade or sell any of my own possessions," he said in a perfect imitation of Purn's prim voice.

She pulled back from him, beaming. "Thank you! I am going to make you so many things!" She looked back over her shoulder. "This is the best present!"

Reese patted her on the back. "You're welcome, Purn. Do I get to pick my own fabric out?"

She drew in a deep, joyful breath and gazed around the room as though taking in the greatest treasure she'd ever seen. "Absolutely not!" she said cheerfully.

"I miss the cottage already," Sable said quietly to Reese as another servant, a tailor, and a steward-of-something-or-other hurried into the already crowded room that had been set aside for preparations.

"So do I." Reese frowned at the uniform hanging from a peg on the wall. "Why'd they have to pick black?"

"Black is neutral," Passtel, the royal tailor, answered, inspecting one of the seams on the sleeve. His fingers were long and thin, like his arms and his legs and his neck. And his nose. "It carries the solemn weight proper for such an occasion."

"Is this what Queensland's soldiers' uniforms are going to be like?" Reese asked. "Because I am against the black. First, it looks Kalesh. Second, it's not good for camouflage. They should be greens and browns."

"I have no idea what the army is planning." Passtel sniffed. "This is for a wedding, not a battle."

"All right." Thulan's voice came from the doorway. "Everyone out. The soon-to-be queen and her soon-to-be powerless consort need to get dressed."

Passtel began to object, along with several of the other people busy carrying clothing or shoes or trays of jewelry into the room, but Thulan pointed out the door. "Out!" she commanded.

The room began to empty, but Passtel stopped next to the cream-colored dress hanging by itself. "I adjusted the waist," he began, addressing Sable, "but I haven't seen it on you. Once you're dressed, I will adjust—"

"I promise she doesn't need a tailor," Thulan said. "Out."

"It'll be fine, Passtel," Sable said, trying not to smile. "I'm sure it will fit perfectly."

Thulan shooed the tailor and the last servant out of the door, then closed it behind them. She turned to face the black uniform, her brow creasing in distaste. "Let's all be thankful you don't have to wear that."

Reese glanced at her. "What else am I supposed to wear?"

"This," Purnicious said, appearing with a pop on top of a table so the steel-grey uniform she was holding could hang down to the floor. The fabric was a smooth, rich wool trimmed with crisp lines of stormy blue edging.

Reese stepped closer to it. "Oh, that is so much better. Where did you get this?"

Purn's wide smile sank to an insulted frown. "I made it, of course."

Reese's hand stopped in the act of reaching toward it. "What's wrong with it? What weirdness did you sew into it?"

"Doesn't matter," Purn said smugly. "You have to wear it *no matter what*."

"I most certainly do not. The inside is bright pink, isn't it? Or the cuffs are lined with lace?" He reached for a sleeve.

The kobold pulled the uniform away from him and pointed at him with her other hand, her bony blue finger so close to his nose that he backed away. "You said I could dress you."

"When?"

"When we were escaping after the summit at Tutella Island. After we'd been in Tanis's camp."

Reese stared at her. "That was months ago!"

"Doesn't matter. You said, 'The day the Northern Lords submit themselves to a southern woman is the day I'll let Purn dress me.'"

Sable rubbed her hand across her mouth to hide her grin. "I do remember you saying that. We were in the woods, just before we met the trolls."

"I remember that," Reese said slowly. "I was talking about Vivaine."

"Doesn't matter," Purn said. "You said 'a southern woman.' Sable is a southern woman. Today, I get to dress you, and you're wearing this." She held the uniform forward again. "I have been waiting for this moment since the first time I heard Sable called Queen of the North!"

He looked at it suspiciously, but everything Sable could see was perfectly respectable grey wool.

"It's nice," Sable said. "Nicer than the black one."

"It is nice," Reese said, taking it slowly as though it might bite him. "On the outside."

Thulan watched the entire exchange with her lips pressed together, obviously trying to suppress a smile.

Reese laid the uniform across the table and unbuttoned the front of the shirt.

When he flipped it open, Sable flinched back.

The entire interior was lined with a gaudy, shimmery fabric of fiery orange. Garishly colored figures were embroidered across it, dancing and leaping in a long, joyous line.

Figures of a blue kobold with wild, curly hair.

Sable clapped her hand over her mouth to stifle a laugh and stepped closer to touch the skillful needlework. "Purn!" she said, laughter sneaking out around the word. "This is…impressive."

Each embroidered kobold was distinct. Each dress had its own style and gleeful fusion of color. Each figure posed uniquely as the line leapt and spun across the entire inside of the shirt. Each blue face held its own jubilant expression that was perfectly Purn-ish.

Thulan leaned closer, grinning and pointing to one of the kobolds who was cartwheeling upside down. "This one is my favorite."

Reese just stood and stared at it.

"I assume you're not planning on taking your shirt off during the ceremony," Purn said smugly, "so you can have no objection to this."

His eyes traced the line of kobolds, and his mouth moved, but no sound came out.

"Well, try it on. I know I made it right, but you're picky. If you need anything adjusted, I'll fix it." Purn turned to Sable. "I had something more interesting in mind for him, of course, but seeing as the day the Northern Lords submit themselves to a southern woman is also your wedding day, I kept it boring."

"I appreciate that, Purn," Sable said.

"More interesting than this?" Reese asked faintly.

"Put on your dress too," the kobold said to Sable. "That tailor knows nothing. I'll get it sorted out for you."

There was a knock on the door. "Are you dressed yet, Sable?" Leonis's voice called from the hall. "What does Reese think of the shirt?"

"We'll let you in when we're ready," Thulan called back. "Have some patience."

"I need to make sure you pick good jewelry, Sable." Leonis knocked on the door again. "Whatever I told the elves, you're not actually good at accessorizing, and Thulan will do it all wrong." He waited, but when no one answered, he continued, "Sable, I know you're still wearing that horrible sword necklace from Reese, and it has got to come off. You're going to be queen! For the love of Thulan's beard, take that ugly thing off for just one day!"

Reese dragged his eyes away from the embroidered kobolds long enough to smile at Sable. "I say leave it on." He grabbed the grey uniform and headed to a small room off to the side to change, holding the shirt open and shaking his head.

Thulan began undoing the line of buttons down the back of Sable's dress, while Sable pulled off the one she was wearing, showing the sword necklace to Thulan with a wide smile.

"She *is* wearing the sword necklace," the dwarf said loudly, "and I think it's going to look good. It'll go nicely with the stitching on the bodice."

"Thulan," Leonis said with a dangerous edge to his voice. "That's not funny. Hurry up and let me in."

Thulan grinned and held the dress for Sable to step into it. The fabric was light and fit perfectly. Thulan buttoned up the back while Purnicious puttered around with the hem and the sleeves, making adjustments so small Sable could barely see them.

When she turned to face Thulan, the dwarf nodded approvingly. "It looks good. Regal even." She walked over to the door, then looked back at Sable. "Take the necklace out," she whispered.

Sable pulled on the leather cord, drawing the crooked sword necklace out and laying it on the front of the dress.

Thulan grinned at her and opened the door.

THE QUEEN AND THE KEEPERS

Chapter 6 of *What I Remember*
-Written by Flibbet the Peddler
in the 357th year of Queensland

(For a more thorough and official account of Queen Issable's coronation day, see *The Crowning of the First Queen* by Keeper Serene. For a version that brings the past back to life like magic, see the play *The Phoenix Rising* by Atticus the Playwright.)

Three distinct things stick out to me, all these many, many years later, from that very first coronation and the first official declaration of the Keepers. So much of history blends together in my mind, but that day is somehow easy to remember.

It held the seeds that would grow a nation and an order of storytellers, historians, and magic wielders who would help shape it.

Yes, there was an official wedding between Sable and Reese. Yes, a crown was placed upon Sable's head. Yes, the words were pretty. (Atticus had a hand in them—of course they were pretty. I have thought of him fondly as they have been repeated at every coronation since.) Yes, there was a feast later inside the fortress and enormous tables set out along the main avenue of the newly dubbed Queenstown, filled with bread and cheese the way Narine used to feed people at festivals.

But that was all rather to be expected and a bit dull, if I'm being honest. It may have been the first crowning I'd ever seen, but even set dramatically at the top of the barrow, it lived up to the stuffy, formal expectations anyone would have imagined.

It was the small things, as it always is, that were actually memorable.

First were the reactions to the news.

That was the evening we heard of the riots in Immusmala. How crowds had broken into the Sanctuary, how someone had set explosions that had toppled all three of the great priories.

My own reaction was embarrassingly common (as the cart has pointed out more than once since). I immediately thought that Eugessa and Vivaine had brought this on with their betrayal of the people.

Sable's thought though—despite everything Eugessa and Vivaine had done—was of Narine.

I was close enough to her to hear her whisper to Innov, "It would have broken her heart."

She was right, and I'm ashamed I hadn't had the same thought.

Even more memorable, though, was the sharp spark of interest in Serene's eyes at the news. I remember it because it was the same spark she always showed when she was about to try something nefarious with my cart.

I wouldn't be surprised if Serene had set her plans in motion before the crown even descended onto Sable's head later that night.

The second memorable thing was that Innov grew restless.

The crowning of Queen Issable was the only coronation in the history of Queensland (at least over the last three hundred and fifty years) with a phoenix in attendance. Innov was glorious, as usual. Glittering and shimmering and making the entire world better by her presence. She perched on Sable's arm at the front of that barrow, drawing every eye to the new queen and looking pleased with herself.

At first, I thought I was imagining the other thing, but Sable noticed it as well. I know she did. While Sam held the crown aloft and recited the words that would become tradition, I saw Innov shift, and I saw the sorrow creep into Sable's face.

The phoenix stayed on Sable's arm, showering flames and sparks and glorious hope over the new queen…but Innov was restless.

Finally, as the woman who'd once been a thief trapped in a hopeless situation stood on the front edge of the great barrow with the people of the north below her and the newly smithed crown settled onto her head, I felt something I've never felt on such a large scale in any of the long years since.

It could have been Innov or Sable or Atticus's words, but I think those things just added to it, because it felt like it came from the people themselves. They'd come so close to losing everything but had survived—not just survived but drawn together and grown stronger.

For a few minutes, the whole world felt…hopeful.

Centuries have passed since that day, and yet I can still feel it. And it still loosens something inside me when the world grows too tight.

Narine told me once that fear is the great disease that sickens and kills us all, but hope is the cure.

In this, as in so many other things, she was right.

EPILOGUE

ONE YEAR LATER

"WE'RE ON THE RIGHT PATH," Sable said. "There's something on the trees."

She cast out again, and both she and Reese flared up like torches. The horses beneath them blazed.

Inside Sable's slowly growing belly, the baby burned like a tiny sun.

She set a hand on her stomach, then refocused on the trunks of the pines around them. In addition to the gentle flow of *vitalle*, the trees closest to the narrow trail had knots of heat sitting under their bark.

Reese pulled his horse up next to one. "Something's carved into it. With very thin lines."

The tree alongside Sable had one, and she set her hand on it and pressed some *vitalle* into the tree. The carving glowed with heat, revealing a complicated design of lines and arcs. For the briefest moment, she had the impression that the marking reached toward her.

A pressure closed in. The choking scent of old fish dragged her back into the tightness of the walls in Kiva's office long ago in Dockside, smothering her under the weight of the debt she couldn't claw her way out of.

She yanked her hand off the tree just as the memory shifted to the cold, sterile stones of the Dragon Priory, stretching above her, around her, caging her in.

Purnicious popped into view on Sable's lap, cowering against her.

The sensation faded.

"Whatever you just did, please don't do it again." Reese sat warily on his horse, one of his knives gripped tightly in his hand.

"Ever," Purn agreed.

Sable wrapped an arm around the kobold and cast out at the rune, but its heat was already dimming.

"Was that some kind of warning?" Reese asked.

Sable rubbed the back of her neck, trying to drive away the lingering sense of heaviness. "I don't think so. What did you feel?"

He looked off through the trees, still holding his knife. "The moment when I froze in the battle at Immusmala. When the sword was coming, and I stopped fighting." He blinked and turned to her. "The fear that I'd been fighting for the wrong thing all this time."

"I was back in those woods," Purn said in a small voice, "watching that horrible Tien Sark stab you, mistress." She rubbed the palm of her hand on her pants as though trying to clean it. "And my hand was in his neck." She shuddered.

"I was trapped again under Kiva and Vivaine." Sable shifted her shoulders. "Very vividly trapped."

Reese slid his knife back into his sheath. "Not a warning, then. Just memories."

"Bad memories," Purn said.

Sable urged her horse down the trail.

What had been a warm afternoon on the road outside the forest where they'd left their escort of guards had cooled to a comfortable evening in the shadow of the forest. The normal chatter of birds and squirrels wafted through the trees, as though this were a perfectly natural stretch of forest and the trees weren't waiting to fill their minds with horrors.

The markings continued to line the small trail, but she didn't push *vitalle* into any, and aside from the general feeling of watchfulness they put off, nothing else bothered her or Reese.

It didn't take long before Sable caught the first glimpse of the Marsham Cliffs through the trees. They grew taller as the path drew near, the brightness of the sunlit rocks glinting through the dark boughs. Before long, the trail wound out of the trees into a grassy swath that ran along the cliffs.

Sable rode out into it and stopped while Reese pulled his horse up next to her. Set right against the cliff face in front of them was a section of wall made of squared grey stone. It was more than twice as tall as Sable but only stretched a dozen paces in either direction before ending abruptly.

Purn popped off Sable's lap and reappeared on top of the wall, peering down between it and the cliff. "There's no gap here. The stones are set right into the rock face."

Reese scanned the wall. "What now?"

"A good question, since the instructions were written by Serene." Sable climbed down from her horse and walked toward the wall. "She said I should 'Activate the rune to access the tunnel.'"

"The rune?"

Sable shrugged and cast out. A little to her left, something warmed on one of the rocks. She moved closer to it and saw a set of complicated markings etched into the surface. "I suppose she means this." She ran a finger over the chiseled marks.

She heard Reese climb off his horse as she traced out the shape. It wasn't words. It was too complex for that. Even more complex than the markings on the trees had been. She pushed a little *vitalle* into it. The rune drew in the energy like a sponge absorbing water, but nothing happened.

"There's something here." Reese pulled a piece of paper out from under a small rock. "From Jae." He handed it to her, and Sable saw the Keeper's quick, flowing handwriting.

Sable,

If I know my wife, the instructions she sent you were…succinct.

If you need a little more to go on, the rune is a pocket of sorts inside the rock. It holds the potential to…well, the actual working is rather complex, and Serene is very proud of it. I'll let you read her description when you get here. Suffice it to say, it can open the tunnel.

Technically, it only requires vitalle *to activate, but our minds (if we are not Serene) prefer more focused motivations. Since she undoubtedly did not supply a word to help direct you, I would suggest* aperi. *It means to open, reveal, expose. Some focused* vitalle *into the rune with that intent should do the trick.*

Once you're inside, cludo *will close it again. It means to shut, to end, to bar.*

If you do not arrive by sunset, I'll come check on you.

Sable set her hand on the rune. She pushed *vitalle* into the word and out through her palm, opening a channel between herself and the cliff face. "*Aperi.*" She infused the word with the idea of opening.

Just to her right, the stones let off a small, dry hiss as they rubbed against each other, shifting, turning, and sliding apart until an archway yawned open into a shadowy tunnel.

"That was…impressive," Reese said, stepping closer to the arch. "It goes straight through the cliff. You can see the valley on the far side."

Sable moved next to him. The tunnel was long and dark, the little light from the ends showing roughly chiseled walls of stone.

"Oooh!" Purn blinked away, and her tiny form appeared at the far end. "It's beautiful!" she called back, her voice echoing down the tunnel.

Sable and Reese brought the horses in, and Sable cast out again. She could sense the rune at the edge of the arch. She pressed her hand as close to it as she could on the rocks and funneled *vitalle* into it. "*Cludo*."

The stones whispered against each other again as they shifted and cut off the view of the forest and the evening light, leaving Sable and Reese in shadows.

Sable's horse nickered, and she patted his neck. "If you don't like this tunnel, you should never visit the dwarves."

They started toward the green grass visible at the far end, which now showed no sign of Purn. They plodded slowly over the flat smoothness of the tunnel floor, but the reins bit into Sable's palms, and she realized she was gripping them as though trying to crush them. She forced her hands to loosen.

She hadn't seen the valley since the day they'd rested at the top of it after fleeing the dwarven tunnels, but she'd been updated by Serene when the stone had arrived from the south last fall and when the dwarves had finished the tunnel six months ago. Though Sable had chosen queen instead of Keeper, and though Serene had assured her she was welcome at any time, finally coming to the valley felt like having to see again some treasure she'd given up.

Along the side of the tunnel, they found bedrolls and packs neatly stacked. Cook pots and lanterns and all the trappings of a campsite. They reached the end, and Sable stopped.

Ahead of them, the rolling land was vibrantly green with grass. A huge oak, the one she'd seen long ago from the top of the cliff, stood nearly straight in front of them. Just to the left of it, the beginnings of a white tower rose about two stories. The building was so bright white that even though the valley walls were too high to let in the evening sun, the tower still glowed slightly, as though gathering the little light there and reflecting it to the rest of the valley.

For a brief moment, it reminded her of Vivaine. Except whatever this tower was doing, it was utterly unlike what the High Prioress had always done. Vivaine had captured light and kept it for herself. This tower seemed to draw it in for the express purpose of sharing it.

Reese stood next to her. "We need to come here far more often."

The tunnel entered at the widest part of the valley, which was filled with low rolling hills. As it narrowed at both ends, it filled with trees. Not just pines. Amidst the evergreens were glimpses of brighter green leaves, many edged with the reds and yellows of fall.

Above one colorful patch of trees, the glittering form of Innov soared.

The sound of a chisel on rock dragged Sable's attention back to the wall beside the mouth of the tunnel. A wagon sat next to them, filled with white blocks of stone. Past it was another. Sable moved forward a few steps to see dozens of wagons lined up.

"Did Serene get the stones from all three priories?" Reese asked.

The chiseling stopped, and Thulan's head leaned out from between two of the wagons. "Just the Phoenix Priory." The dwarf set her chisel and hammer on the nearest rock and dusted off her hands. She strode toward them, giving them a wide smile and pointing at Sable. "Serene said you'd say the other two priories were tainted, but the Phoenix stones were still good."

Sable walked over to the nearest wagon and slid her fingers over the coarse face of a stone. When she'd heard Serene had taken stone from the Sanctuary, using dwarves to demolish the broken priories and dismantle them, managing to get the city to pay her in stones for the quick work, the thought of the Stronghold being built out of the stifling rocks that Vivaine and Eugessa had ruled had felt…invasive. As though Serene was dragging the corruption of the past into her new creation.

But stones from the Phoenix Priory felt right. Almost like a blessing from Narine.

"I agree," Sable said to Thulan. She looked back at the tower, which was decidedly brighter than the stones sitting in the wagon. "I don't remember the priory being that bright, though."

"That's some addition Serene is making. Something about pathways in the stone letting her do something or other."

Sable gave Thulan a quick hug.

"I just saw you a few weeks ago," the dwarf grunted, stepping back.

A greeting called out from the tower, and Jae strode out holding a curly-haired boy in his arms. "What do you think of our Stronghold?"

Reese went forward to meet them, reaching his hands out to take the boy. "It's shorter than I expected," he said with a grin. "Are they making it only big enough for you, little Henry?" The boy squealed with delight as Reese lifted him in the air.

"Careful when you put him down," Jae said, motioning for them to follow him toward the tower. He wore a long black robe, just like Serene usually wore, and like both Gwen and Terrane had worn in Queenstown for the past half-year. "Henry's figured out how to crawl. You wouldn't believe how quickly he can get himself into trouble."

"I didn't realize you all were wearing the black robes," Reese said. "Gwen says she wears hers for the pockets."

Sable shook her head. "I think she wears hers because it's the opposite of white, and Terrane says it makes her look imposing." Truthfully, Gwen's robe was…perfect. It *was* imposing and somehow weighty, and when she wore it, she seemed to be a part of something. Something Sable was not a part of. Gwen's help had been invaluable over the past year, but the black robe always gave Sable a small ache. Not full-blown regret, but something headed in that direction.

Jae grinned. "The pockets are a big part. We call them Keeper's Robes, and they're fantastic. Purn sent the fabric and helped with some of the design. I like that they're black. Very dramatic for storytelling."

He led them through the arched entry into a short hallway where some pegs were mounted on the wall. Another black robe hung off one of them. He pulled it down and held it out to Sable. "Purn assures us this will fit you perfectly."

Sable's fingers twitched toward it before she stopped them. "But…I'm not…"

"We all agree you're a Keeper in spirit." Jae said easily. "So if you want it, it's yours."

Sable reached out slowly and took it. "I can't wear this at court. People would definitely not believe the Keepers were actually autonomous."

"Then leave it here and wear it whenever you visit," he answered easily. "We just wanted you to have one."

The fabric was a thin wool, soft but sturdy. Light enough to easily wear over her clothes. The perfectly detailed stitching along the open front, which occasionally detoured from its straight line into a spray of embroidered starbursts, declared Purnicious's handiwork.

She slipped her arms in and settled it on her shoulders. "Thank you," she breathed.

Jae nodded approvingly. "Purn was right. Fits perfectly."

"I like it," Reese said.

Sable slipped her hands into the deep pockets at the side and followed Jae as he headed a dozen paces down the hallway into the round, open center of the tower. Several doorways led off in different directions, and a ramp spiraled up the wall, rising until it ended at the open sky above them. "The dwarves assure us there is enough stone for six stories plus a seventh that will be a covered, roof-top balcony."

"How long will it take?" Sable asked.

"They say the tower will be finished in four months." Jae crossed the tiled floor to a wide archway. "The library may take a little longer."

He led them through another short hall to the outside of the tower, stopping at the edge of a very deep hole.

It was round and easily the same width as the tower. The walls were dug straight down, and a half-dozen dwarves stood in the bottom, pick-axes resting on their shoulders. Another dwarf knelt along the bottom corner, rubbing some dirt through his hands.

"This is the deepest we should go," he was saying to Serene and Atticus, who stood next to him. "Any lower and we'll keep finding more water."

"No water can get in," Serene said firmly, dressed in her own Keeper's robe. "I don't even want the air damp."

The dwarf glanced up at her. "We'll make sure the water drains around the outside, but you can't use the white rock in here—it's too porous. Water will seep through like a sponge in the rainy season. There are some more impermeable stones in the cliff face, especially up in the northwest corner of your valley. We'll use a Jrovskich double-walled gravity channel with a sluice drain, and it'll be as watertight as possible."

"I have no idea what all that means," Serene said, "but I like the water-tight part."

"You're building your library underground?" Sable called down.

Serene and Atticus looked up.

"Only the bottom floors," Serene said, starting toward a ladder. "The top few will be above ground. It should keep the books a good temperature."

"The top few?" Reese asked. "How many are you making?"

"As many as I can." Serene climbed out the top of the hole and set her hand on Sable's shoulder. "The robe looks good. How are you? And the baby? You look tired."

"I feel tired," Sable said. "Growing a person might be more exhausting than driving off an army and a dragon. I have no idea how you did both at once."

"With extreme grumpiness, if I recall correctly," Leonis said cheerfully from the tower doorway. "And it's about time you got here. Talia, Ryah, and Evay arrived yesterday. I was beginning to think you two weren't going to make it." He waved everyone toward the far side of the tower. "Let's eat!"

"What were those things on the trees outside the wall?" Sable asked Serene as they followed the half-elf.

Serene's eyes lit. "Did you activate them? They're meant to bring to mind your deepest fears."

"That's basically what happened," Reese said. He poked Henry in the stomach. "Your mother tried to scare us to death." The little boy giggled.

"When they're finished," Serene said, "they'll activate on their own by drawing a tiny bit of *vitalle* out of anyone who comes within sight of the path." She looked at Sable. "I got the idea from Narine, who always said the things that control us the most are our own fears. I figured why should I try to create a deterrent when everyone who comes will bring their own with them?"

"Your mother," Reese said in a cheerful voice to Henry, "might be a monster."

"Every time we come, we'll have to navigate a path guarded by our own deepest fears?" Sable asked. "That is sort of monstrous."

"I take it back when I said we should visit her often," Reese said.

Serene shrugged. "It's not a bad thing, facing your fears."

"Well, it will certainly keep people away," Sable said.

"It's good for something else," Jae added from next to Serene. "If each Keeper needs to face their greatest fear to come back home, we'll all constantly be reminded of our shared humanity."

Sable nodded slowly. "Narine told me once that as soon as you see everyone around you as creatures trapped in their own fears, it's easy to have compassion on them."

"Hopefully that will prove true," Jae said.

The dwarves climbed out of the hole, and Sable watched curiously as they all headed toward the tunnel under the cliff.

"They prefer sleeping there rather than under the sky," Serene said. "And they say their food is better than ours, so we just let them have their space." She motioned to a long, low building next to the tower. "This is where we spend most of our time. A few bedrooms are finished in the base of the tower, but we eat here."

They walked inside to find a handful of bedrooms, a kitchen, and a dining table barely big enough for everyone. Sable sat between Reese and Atticus.

"How's life as a royal consort?" Leonis asked Reese, climbing onto the bench next to him. "Does she drag you to councils all the time?"

"Yes," Reese said. "Unless I can drag her away to our cottage instead."

Sable leaned forward. "I bring Reese because he's indispensable in keeping people on topic."

"They talk in circles," Reese said, "and it drives me crazy."

Sable smiled. "If I had a copper for every time Reese says, 'Just answer the queen's question. A simple yes or no will suffice,' I'd be able to fund every project idea anyone brings me."

"Maybe you should start charging anyone he has to say that to," Leonis suggested.

"How are the schools going?" Ryah asked Serene as she and Purn came in from the kitchen. She set a bottle of leeswine down next to Leonis and a pitcher of spiced apple cider beside it.

"They're moving along well."

"She's being modest," Jae said. "We just started the fifth school, this one in Ravenwick. That means there are now over a hundred students learning to read and write. From the one in Queenstown we'll be sending out our first scribes in a matter of months to copy every book they can find. Twice. Once for Sable's library in Queenstown, and once for us here. Within three years, we should have well over a hundred scribes working."

"Speaking of books," Talia said, setting a plate of meat down and sitting at the far end, "that tanner you and I both liked is willing to help us, Serene. He's happy to begin work as a bookbinder as soon as you're ready for him."

"Really?" Serene raised her eyebrows. "He seemed very set on only belts and coats."

"Talia fixed that," Ryah said. "She made it known at one of her dinner parties that he made her two favorite belts, and his shop has been overwhelmed with orders for them. His business tripled over night."

Talia shrugged but looked pleased. "He warmed to my suggestions from that point."

"His belts aren't bad," Purn said from the stool where she perched between Ryah and Talia. "They take barely any bellishing at all to be pretty."

Sable shook her head. "I swear you get more accomplished at a single dinner party in your pretty house, Talia, than I do in a week of councils."

"That reminds me," Talia said, "the Duke of Marshwell agrees to the roads and way stations that you wanted."

Sable stared at her. "How'd you manage that? He's been fighting me for months."

Talia gave a little smirk, and Purn's purple eyes crinkled at the edges as she gave Ryah a sidelong glance.

"I didn't." Talia answered. "Someone has wooed the duke's cousin."

Sable's mouth dropped open as she took in Ryah's blushing cheeks. "Little Loren?"

Ryah grimaced. "Please don't call him that. He's not a child anymore, and his uncle Loren isn't even still alive. Besides, he's taller than any of you."

"I like Loren," Reese said. "He's a lot like his uncle."

"And," Thulan said, "since the health of his cousin, the young Duke of Marshwell, is sadly growing more fragile, Loren's no more than a year from inheriting the dukedom." She glanced at Ryah. "Who thinks Duchess Ryah has a nice ring to it?"

Ryah flushed again.

Sable smiled at her. "He'll make an excellent duke, and you'd make an excellent duchess."

"Marshwell might be an interesting dukedom soon," Reese added. "Did you all hear they found gold in the hills southwest of Marshwell? It's a couple day's ride outside of Queensland, but one of the merchants from Immusmala declared himself lord of the area, and there's no one in the south strong enough to oppose him. He's calling it Gulfind, and already sending emissaries to Sable to discuss trade. The mountains there are so barren he has gold, but nothing else."

Sable nodded. "I wonder what Vivaine would have done if she'd known there really was gold in those hills? She just didn't look far enough in."

"Let's all be glad she didn't," Thulan said. "Her fake gold was bad enough."

Terrane, in his own Keeper's robe, stretched his arm in between Evay and Gwen as they shifted dishes so he could fit one more platter of roasted chicken.

"The table is going to break if you add any more food," Leonis said.

"We should eat it all quickly, then," Thulan said. "For the good of the table."

"First," Atticus said, standing and holding up a glass, "a toast."

Reese poured a cup of cider for Sable, then one for himself as the rest of the table sorted out their own drinks.

"To the first anniversary of the founding of the Keepers," Atticus said when they were all ready. He motioned with his glass to Serene. "To their fearless leader, who is already bettering the entire land by her efforts to teach reading and spread knowledge of the stories and histories that will, hopefully, shield us from repeating the greatest mistakes of the past."

"To the one who shields us!" Jae proclaimed, raising his cup and kissing Serene on the cheek.

"Our shield!" Terrane agreed.

"And to the other Keepers," Atticus said, "whether they are at court or abroad gathering and sharing stories." He nodded to Gwen and Terrane. "Or whether they are Keepers in spirit only," he said fondly to Sable, "because they chose a different path. May Queensland and the world beyond it be strengthened and guided by you for many, many years."

Shouts of agreements accompanied the clanking together of cups.

When everyone had drunk, Atticus looked down at Sable again. "And to our queen."

"She's not the Keepers' queen," Gwen said loudly with a broad smile.

Sable laughed. "As Gwen reminds me at least once a week."

Atticus chuckled. "To *my* queen, then, who officially celebrates one year of—"

"Queenliness!" Leonis interrupted.

"Tyranny!" Thulan yelled.

"Bossiness," Reese offered, grinning at the others.

"I'm going to have you all arrested as soon as we're back in my land," Sable told them.

Atticus held up his hand for silence. "To a year of successfully guiding a very young, very fragile country." He waved his cup to encompass the table. "And to this entire mismatched family. Tales could never truly capture how epic our journey has been. Entire nations are in your debt, and I dearly hope each of you has found a place to settle where you are content."

"To us!" Leonis shouted.

"Saviors of the world!" Thulan added with a grin.

"And if it falls apart now, after we just put it together," Leonis said, "we can blame Sable and Serene."

Sable awoke to a golden glow perched in the window, the light warming the white stones around it. Reese was still asleep next to her in one of the finished rooms at the base of the tower, and Innov sat quietly on the windowsill, looking out at the night.

Sable slipped out of bed, wrapping the black Keeper's robe around herself against the chill. She moved quietly over next to Innov and ran a finger down the phoenix's neck.

"You're leaving, aren't you?" she whispered.

Innov gave no answer. The phoenix had come to Sable less often lately, and every time she did, the restlessness Sable had begun to notice at the coronation seemed more pronounced. Something was different tonight, though, and Sable felt a chill on her arm where Innov often perched.

"I don't want you to go," she said quietly, "but honestly, I'm not sure why you came to me in the first place or why you stayed so long. Did you know the Sanctuary would fall? That there would never be another Phoenix Prioress?"

Innov hopped onto Sable's arm, and an image flooded her mind.

Narine's room in the priory as seen from Innov's perch by the fire.

Narine herself lay on her couch, weak and thin and tired. Sable saw herself enter the room, and Narine's face lit in a smile. The picture shifted to Sable making Narine tea, adjusting the old woman's blanket, stoking the ever-running fire.

It changed to the house on Tutella Island, the image dimmer as Innov and Narine both weakened. Innov perched on Narine's arm, and the prioress's face was drawn, each wrinkle and line of weariness clearly visible.

"They'll try to hurt her when I'm gone," Narine said. "I wish I had a way to keep her safe. I wish she'd really run away, but I fear she'll keep standing up to Vivaine and Argyros until…" Her eyes closed. "I'm tired, my flame, but I find, here at the end, that it's harder than I imagined to let go of…" She opened her eyes and focused on Innov's chest where her fingers were drawing out weak flames. "Living."

Images continued. Vivaine and Argyros at the trial. On the barrow.

Sable saw the memory of Argyros flying away from Barrowford, his scales fading into the night, and felt the sense of finality at the sight. The sense of completion.

And then a burgeoning restlessness. A yearning for trees, storm clouds. A glimpse of Cernus among the elven trees.

Sable leaned against the window frame. "I always did figure you stayed for Narine, but thank you for staying so long. I don't know if I could have done any of this, especially the early days, without your hope." She drew her finger down Innov's neck, trying to store the feeling of the soft flickering flames against her skin. Trying to memorize the way the sparks burst out in sprays, as though they'd been waiting to rush into the world and spend themselves in one fierce, joyful plunge, content to burn with beauty and hope for a single breath.

Sable watched an ember wink out on the windowsill. "We're naming the baby Narine," she whispered. "I would love it if one day she could meet you."

Innov pushed against Sable's finger, and a fondness washed over Sable. A sense of agreement.

Though the sky above them was clear, thunder rumbled somewhere far outside the valley, and Innov shifted. A bright, sharp longing flared up in the phoenix. An idea of the wide sky, piled with clouds. Wind fanning her flames into a wild trail of fire. Countless raindrops pelting against her, tumbling along her blazing feathers, throwing off hissing bursts of steam.

Sable's fingers twitched, as though she could grab hold of the phoenix, but she pulled away from Innov and clasped her hands together to keep from reaching out again. "Go find your storm, Innov," she murmured.

The phoenix paused for a heartbeat. Then another, and Sable's fingers loosened.

But Innov's talons squeezed one last time around Sable's arm before she spread her wings and launched out of the window, spiraling up into the clear night air with a thrust that flung a thousand sparks of light behind her. She swirled higher, and the trail of fire lingered in the still air.

When she reached the height of the valley walls, she soared up in a broad arc and disappeared over the cliff.

Sable stared after her as the embers fell, winking out one by one until there was nothing but the valley. She looked out into the darkness, feeling as empty and hollow as the night sky.

Except it wasn't really dark. The valley was lit by a half-moon, and the stones of the Stronghold gathered in the light and reflected it out again.

Sable cast out into the stones and found thin traces of *vitalle* running through them. The sleeping form of Reese warmed behind her, then the impressions of others, tucked in beds in nearby rooms. She was turning back toward her own when she caught the heat of someone up at the top of the tower.

Without knowing exactly how, she knew who it was.

She slipped out onto the ramp that spiraled up the inside of the tower and climbed up until she reached the open top.

Atticus leaned his elbows against the unfinished outer wall, his hands folded together, as though looking over a parapet.

"I'm going to miss her," he said quietly, not turning.

Sable moved to the wall next to him. "How did you know she was really leaving?"

The ghost of a smile crossed his lips. "That was a grand exit if I ever saw one." He shook his head ruefully. "Every time I begin to think well of my skill, I'm upstaged by that bird." He was quiet a moment. "Do you know where she's going?"

"I think to Cernus. In the Greenwood."

"A good place."

Below them, the hole for the library was an inky black void. Sable's gaze traveled through the valley. She drew in the quiet of it, letting the peace soak into her.

"You look well," he said finally.

"I am." She ran her finger over a seam in the white stones of the wall. "I finally did it." She gave him a sidelong glance, unable to keep a smile off her face. "You know that gang that was operating in Queenstown near the river gate? The Blades? They're completely disassembled."

Atticus raised an eyebrow. "For good?"

"At least for the foreseeable future. Rabbit finally infiltrated them enough to map out their power structure. The leaders were arrested and put on trial. Most were imprisoned." Her smile faded. "A few, whose actions made Kiva look saintly, were executed. But I met a little girl, Cala, who lived by the docks and has never known a life aside from pickpocketing for the boss. Now her mother owns the new net mending shop, and Cala informs me she ties the best knots of anyone, because adults' fingers are too fat and clumsy."

"A new shop? Funded by you?"

"A shop funded by an anonymous donor who felt that a place that could easily be called 'Dockside' should be filled with honest businesses instead of crime."

"Ah," he said, the sound approving.

Sable looked out over the Stronghold valley. "I thought this valley was what I wanted, Atticus, and part of me would love to stay here, but Cala's mother isn't afraid of every man who walks into her shop these days, and she doesn't fear for her daughter." She ran a pebble from the wall between her thumb and first finger. "I helped that happen, and that feels better than any life I've ever imagined for myself."

Atticus kept his gaze out into the valley. "I know the years under Kiva and Vivaine were painful, but they formed you into someone perfectly suited to this. Queensland never needs to fear that you'll turn into...one of them."

"I would rather die," Sable said honestly.

Atticus's face had a shadow of sorrow over it.

"Are you well?" she asked. "You never did accept my offer to be named Royal Playwright."

He didn't answer immediately but instead unfolded his hands to show a small, flat object, one side of which glittered in the moonlight. Sable leaned closer to see it.

A scale.

"Is that one of Argyros's?" she asked. "Please don't tell me you paid whatever ridiculous price people were charging for those when they found them in the damaged city wall."

"I did not," he said quietly. "I found it the night Vivaine died." He swallowed. "I was walking along the broken wall and saw it flash."

"Why do you keep it?" Sable asked, not because she didn't know the answer, but because she wanted to hear how he said it.

"To remember," he said simply. "I don't touch it often, though."

"Why not?"

He held the scale out to her, and she picked it up with two fingers. It was shaped like a flat seashell, fanning out on one side and coming nearly to a point at the root where it must have been anchored to the dragon. The surface was ridged with lines as thin as those in fingerprints that shimmered along the fan edge with silver and were lost in blackness near the root.

But beyond the surface, Sable felt a hunger. A greed. A gnawing sort of desire.

She dropped it on the white stones and rubbed her fingers. The feeling passed. "Are they all like that?"

"I would imagine they are."

"Well, that would explain why people went so crazy for them."

Atticus didn't pick it back up. "It's fading, that feeling. But I pick it up sometimes just to remember what she must have felt every time she touched him."

Sable shifted, watching the moonlight dance across the ridges, imagining that feeling seeping into Vivaine every time she'd set her fingers on Argyros's head.

"So much greed and grasping must have bled into her," Atticus said. "For decades."

Sable rubbed her arm where Innov had liked to perch. "Innov was only with me for less than two years and not even continually during that time. But the hope she trickled into me changed me. I know it did. It gave me a habit of trusting in goodness. Seeking out the goodness that's easily overlooked." The blackness of the scale was so dark it was like a hole in the night. "I can't imagine if I'd had Argyros's greed instead."

"Do you think you rubbed off on Innov, too?" Atticus asked.

"No, but she wasn't close to me the way she would have been to a prioress. If you're really asking whether I think Vivaine rubbed off on Argyros, I think she probably did. Narine affected Innov, at least. The phoenix was...gentler when Narine was alive. Less wild. Maybe Vivaine kept some of Argyros's greed in check, at least for a while."

He nudged the scale with his finger but didn't pick it up. "Vivaine's offer was tempting, you know." He drew his hand back from the scale. "Go to a stage as large as the Empire with someone as influential as Zenivah. You built up an armor against wanting to use power for your own gain, thanks to Kiva and Vivaine. I have no such armor, so her offer was as dangerous as it was tempting." He finally glanced up at Sable. "I'm afraid if I take your offer of being your Royal Playwright, I'll grow too used to the influence and power I could wield." He dropped his gaze to the scale again. "If Vivaine was ever good, this hungering for power corrupted her. And it did so fully." The edge of his mouth twitched up in a smile. "I'm already too impressed with myself to think I'm immune from such things."

The scale sparkled with an icy white light.

"Even if you're not a royal playwright," she said, "you'll come to Queenstown often, right?"

"You couldn't keep me away."

"Good." She leaned on the wall. "Because I expect a play by you in the new Great Hall in Queenstown at the Midwinter Festival."

"Another thing you couldn't keep me away from."

She reached over and set her hand on his. "I hope you know how thankful I am. If you ever need anything…"

He shrugged. "You're Queen Issable, not Queen Sable. You've already given me a great victory."

"I considered insisting that it be Sable," she answered with a smile, "but this way I can know who knows me formally and who is a real friend." She paused. "Speaking of names, your newest one for me isn't going to work anymore." She gestured to where Innov had disappeared.

He gave her an innocent look, and she turned to face him fully, crossing her arms. "Atticus, I was introduced as the Phoenix Queen last week at a gathering in Steepdale. Sam's last letter to me was addressed the same way. I know you don't expect me to believe that name came from anyone but you."

His eyes crinkled at the edges. "You were the Flame of the North. This is the obvious evolution of the name. Besides, it could be argued that you started the name when you leapt off a cliff into a fire—and lived."

"No. This was you, and only you. But what are people going to think now that I've lost my phoenix?"

He waved her objection away. "It was never about Innov. It was always about you. It's a metaphorical phoenix."

"Somehow I doubt the people are going to pick up on your nuance."

He tapped his fingers on the wall, struggling to hide a smile, but it broke through, splitting his face into a grin like a child bursting with a secret. "Not after they see my play at Midwinter!"

Sable laughed. "Is that what you're doing up here all alone? Composing?"

He looked out over the valley, still smiling. "Possibly."

"Do you want peace?"

"Not yet."

Sable settled against the wall again. Stars glittered in the sky overhead, and a few fingers of clouds reached out, turning the moon to a hazy smudge of light. "I've known for a long time that Innov was leaving. I thought it would feel like an end, but it doesn't. It feels like the start of something new."

He nodded. "I've always thought the most satisfying endings felt like that, like the beginning of a story you don't know yet."

Sable took a deep breath of the night air. It smelled like grass and the crispness of the coming fall. "I hope the next one doesn't have a dragon."

"What good is a story without a dragon?"

She pushed herself off the wall. "Well, if I have to live it, I hope the next dragon is as metaphorical as my phoenix." The clouds shifted, and moonlight traced silver lines through the waves of Atticus's hair and beard. "I'll leave you to your composing, and I breathlessly await your next masterpiece." She placed her hand on his shoulder. "Goodnight, Atticus."

He patted her hand fondly. "Goodnight, Sable."

She pulled the black robe close around her as she headed back down the ramp. Back into the growing Stronghold and everything it represented. Back past the room where her sisters, Purnicious, and Evay slept safely, past the room the troupe had claimed as their own, and past the room where Jae and Serene and baby Henry were fast asleep.

Back down into a place that already felt like another home.

As she moved back toward her warm bed, she glanced up at the sky and smiled. Another sunrise couldn't be far off.

THE END

FROM THE AUTHOR

Well, there you go.

I believe I promised you a happy ending for Sable and company, and I hope you feel satisfied with where they ended up.

There are, of course, thousands of more pages that could be written about the troubles and victories in their future, books written about side characters, whole trilogies about a certain peddler…but for now, we'll leave Sable and most of her friends sleeping comfortably in the Stronghold.

Instead, let's talk about feelings.

Your feelings.

How *are* you feeling?

Do you wish there was more story? (Aside from being exhausted from writing this much, I do.)

Do you wonder what elven vows look like compared to dwarven hearth vows? (So do I.)

Do you have *thoughts* you'd love to share? (You look like you do.)

Well, I'm here to offer suggestions that will help you.

SUGGESTION #1) LEAVE A REVIEW!

A review is worth more to an author than a swiped bit of sparkly fabric is to Purnicious.

So, if you enjoyed ***Phoenix Rising*** and would like to reward the author by leaving a review, you can do so on Amazon.

She'll be forever grateful.

SUGGESTION #2) READ THE KEEPER CHRONICLES!

We just saw the creation of the country of Queensland and the very first Keepers.

What will the Keepers become? I'm glad you asked. I wrote a whole trilogy to tell you. It's called **The Keeper Chronicles**, and it takes place hundreds of years after Sable's adventures.

It can be read at any time compared to **Keeper Origins**, and you may find some friends from this series being spoken about even that far in the future.

You can find **The Keeper Chronicles** on Amazon.

There's also a short story about dear old Flibbet, called "The Deal is Struck," in which Flibbet gets in a fight with his cart.

You can find out where to buy it and all the rest of my books on my website at www.jaandrews.com.

Happy Reading!

Janice

BLOOPERS

Reese stood on the boat and peered down at the ugly yellow ruffle on his shirt, damp from Purn's river-logged fingers. "Perfect, Purn. Every time you see that ruffle, remember that your strangle move won't work on someone who really wants to hurt Sable." He reached out and patted her soaking wet shoulder as he stood.

The kobold shook water droplets out of her hair and glared at him.

His attention caught downstream on Barrowford. "Look! All five lords are here." He leaned on the railing and pointed to the city. "Maybe they're actually taking this serious—"

The railing disappeared and Reese pitched over the side of the boat.

"Reese!" Sable yelled as he plunged into the river and came up sputtering. She tossed one end of a rope down to him and he grabbed it.

Purn pulled her hand off the edge of the suddenly missing railing, giggling. "Thought you were supposed to always be prepared, wastrel."

Reese slipped a hand around Sable's back, and he leaned close to her. "That is the sound," he whispered, "of you and I. Finally alone."

His words rolled out warmly, and Sable let out a laugh.

There was a small pop and Reese scowled toward it.

No Purnicious appeared.

"I know you're here, little monster," he said.

A giggle came from the air.

"Okay," Purn said. "I'm really leaving."

A very fake popping sound came from the same area, as though she'd just popped her lips.

"You don't expect us to believe that?" Reese asked.

She giggled again, and a real pop sounded.

Reese stood listening for a moment, but there was no more noise from the kobold. "There, *now* we're finally alone, right?"

Sable cast out, but found nothing around them but trees. "Right."

Reese relaxed and smiled down at her. "What should we—"

Pop.

"Purnicious!" he yelled.

"Atticus," Vivaine said gently. "Come use your skill on a stage worthy of it. Imagine what we could accomplish together. Come with me."

"Don't waste your breath, Vivaine," Sable said. "Atticus doesn't want—"

Atticus pushed past Sable, an eager smile on his face. "I do want! Let's go! Can we ride the dragon?"

"Perfect," Sable said. "My second condition is—"

"Wait," Reese interrupted. "I have one." He gave Sable a smile that held a little bit of a grimace. "If you're queen of the north, I don't want to be king."

Sable stared at him for a moment before realizing her mouth was hanging open. "I didn't even ask you! I'm so sorry!" She set her hand on his arm. "It all happened so fast, I didn't even think..."

Reese raised his eyebrows. "Fast? We first heard the title *Queen of the North* two hundred thousand words ago."

"Two hundred thousand?" Sable blinked at the number. "I..." she let her eyes run over the group. "What on earth did the author need that many words for? If she'd been less wordy, we all could have gotten to this point a lot faster."

"Which parts would you cut out?" Atticus asked curiously.

"The being stabbed in the neck part," Sable answered immediately.

"Hey," Leonis said, dropping his foot to the ground and sitting up straighter in the throne. "She could have left the dragon out all together. She could have just erased him from the story. Who put her in charge anyway? We should rebel! Can you imagine how much easier all of this would have been without the dra—"

The throne was suddenly empty.

"Where did Leonis go?" Thulan asked.

Sable glanced around. "Who's Leonis?"

The Black Horn short story.
Available free!

It's astonishing how often love and magic are mistaken for each other.

The enemy hordes are approaching, and there's nothing to protect Stone Gap except a black rams horn with powers more legend than reality, and a young woman desperate to save those she loves.

Get a free copy of The Black Horn at www.jaandrews.com!

ACKNOWLEDGMENTS

First, thank you for reading. It's a great privilege to earn a living by telling stories, and the fact that you picked up this book and spent some time in my world makes that possible. I appreciate it more than you know.

Thank you to Cheryl Schuetze and Karyne Norton for your critiques of the messy, plodding first half of this book. Yes, this is the exact same thing I put in my acknowledgments last book. Beginnings are the absolute worst.

Thank you Laura Josephsen for your amazing edits. I'm sorry about all the misplaced commas. Again. Will I learn before the next book comes to you? History says I will not.

Thank you to Constance Lopez for your support and encouragement, your help with the Stronghold on Facebook, and your excellent reading and reviewing skills. I am so grateful!

And most of all, thank you to my husband. You're practically a coauthor of this. Thank you for the brainstorming and critique and listening to me talk about these characters for three years. I love you.

ABOUT THE AUTHOR

JA Andrews lives deep in the Rocky Mountains of Montana with her husband and three children.

She is eternally grateful to CS Lewis for showing her the luminous world of Narnia.

She wishes Jane Austen had lived 200 years later so they could be pen pals.

She is furious at JK Rowling for introducing her to house elves, then not providing her a way to actually employ one.

And she is constantly jealous of her future-self who, she is sure, has everything figured out.

For more information:
www.jaandrews.com
jaandrews@jaandrews.com

facebook.com/JAAndrewsAuthor
twitter.com/JAAndrewsWriter
instagram.com/jaandrewsbooks

www.ingramcontent.com/pod-product-compliance
Lightning Source LLC
Chambersburg PA
CBHW020347310726
48979CB00015B/2538/J
* 9 7 8 1 7 3 6 2 3 2 6 1 3 *